Flight of The Falcon

Book Two

Stephan & Melodi Grundy

TLS

ISBN13: 978-1-959350-04-0

Set in: Georgia 9/10pt, Farmhouse 20/36pt

©The Three Little Sisters
CANADA/USA

Chapter One

It was the evening of December 20. Eva was just lighting the candles in Margerite's chamber, the warm glow of the flames kindled by her taper spreading through the room like a draught of hot wine through a chilled man's body, and Margerite was taking out her embroidery to while away the time until the evening meal was served in the great hall, when Kobolt suddenly miaowed, standing on his hind legs to paw at Margerite's thigh with his claws unsheathed just enough to prick lightly through the heavy wool and velvet of her clothes. By habit, she reached down to sweep him away; then she remembered what the cat truly was, and lifted his solid weight up in her arms instead, looking into his golden eyes.

"What is it, Kobolt?" Margerite whispered. "What are you warning me of?"

As with the eyes of any cat in candlelight, Kobolt's pupils were huge, with the faintest reddish luminescence shining in their depths. Margerite struggled to clear her mind, not knowing whether he would speak to her in plain words, as beasts did in children's tales, or...She felt faintly dizzy, as though she had drunk off one of Cundriê's draughts in a gulp. Then it seemed to her that the cat's eyes brightened; though she heard no speech, not even as a whisper in her thoughts, his ears went back and his claws came out, his muscular body tightening in her grasp, and a chill rustled through Margerite's flesh. *He is warning me of danger,* she thought, and then, though she did not know why, *Graf Günther is coming!*

Even as that thought came to her, a soft knock sounded on the door. Eva left her task to answer it; Margerite heard her stifled gasp and Kriemhilt's sharp mew, and saw the light of a candle glowing through the dark crack of the door.

"Is the Gräfin within?" Graf Günther's light, cultured voice enquired politely. "I would speak with her."

Margerite set Kobolt down, rising to her feet and smoothing down her skirts. "As you will, Graf Günther," she said, keeping her voice as calm as she could, although she was trembling within. She did not think Kobolt would have warned her if the Graf had been on an ordinary errand. She was sure that he would have Order business to speak of - her eyes went to the silver ring on her finger, its inscription very black against the warm gleam of candlelight on its polished surface - and she steeled herself for another round of deception. "Eva, you may leave us."

Eva's blue eyes were dark and wide with fear as she looked at her mistress, and the flame of her taper shook, but Günther waved a long hand negligently. "She may stay here, and we shall go elsewhere; it is hardly proper for us to be closeted in your bedchamber. Come, Priestess."

Margerite was startled at his use of the Order title before Eva - but of course, the Order had sent the girl to Ruprecht, and Günther might well expect her to be using Eva as a ritual assistant now, for many rites, particularly those of divination, called for the help of a virgin. She followed him out, down the corridor to Ruprecht's room, and unlocked the door at his gesture. Graf Günther's candle was the sole illumination in the chamber; its brightness played over the bones of his long face so that he seemed almost inhuman, a mask of light floating in the darkness, pierced by the two searing blue glints of his eyes. I am looking upon him as he truly is, Margerite thought - she was still a little dizzy from her effort to understand Kobolt's warning, and for a dreadful moment she feared that her legs would fail beneath her. But the black cat arched his back, rubbing against her, and his touch steadied her so that she was able to meet the Light-Bearer's gaze.

"Show me the way to Ruprecht's sanctum, Priestess," Günther ordered.

Every nerve in her body thrumming with tension, Margerite led the way down the stairs to the corridor behind the smithy. Kundry had met them here - but Kundry and Klingschor were dead, she reminded herself, and Ruprecht's magic broken. Yet it seemed to her that, though the power that had oppressed her was gone, she could feel something lingering, like the faint stink of dung that always hung about a wall where a midden heap had been piled, no matter how often it was washed down.

The bodies of Ruprecht's two servants were no longer in the room where they had fallen, but there was a faint stink of sulphur and chemicals in the air. Graf Günther sniffed suspiciously, his long nose wrinkling, but said nothing.

The smell grew stronger as they went downward into the lowest tower room. Here, the devastation had begun: books were scattered everywhere, their pages stained and scorched, and not one of the bottles that had neatly lined the shelves was left whole. Kobolt brushed past Margerite's legs, walking daintily among the glass shards and sniffing, here and there, at the dark stains and oily puddles upon the stone floor. In the middle of the room was a large scorched mark, and Kobolt crouched upon it a moment, his spray hissing out onto the cracked stones.

"That is the familiar Ruprecht found for you?" Günther enquired.

"Yes, Prince."

Günther stroked his graying goatee, thoughtfully regarding Kobolt for a moment, then passed on. Ruprecht's alchemical laboratory was in worse state than his library: it looked as though everything there had exploded at once. Deep pits halfway up one wall suggested that whatever had sprayed there had actually eaten into the stone. Graf Günther was shaking his head, his lips twisting in a snarling frown. "What did he do?" Günther whispered. "How could he possibly have bungled it so badly?"

Margerite would not have recognised the chamber where Ruprecht had stood over Eva's body the night before if she had not known where it was. The walls were all coated with clinging black soot; the circle and triangle painted on the floor were almost completely obliterated, a deep crater of jagged stone and rubble in the middle of the wreckage. Günther prowled about the room, kicking at the lumps of blackened stone. One crumbled beneath his foot, and he bent down to pick it up. Margerite's gorge rose as she saw what he had in his hand: it was part of a calcined skull, eyesocket and nose-hole clogged with soot.

"Ruprecht?" he asked.

"I do not know, Prince. Kundry and Klingschor were down here..."

Günther turned the blackened piece of bone over thoughtfully in his long knobbly fingers, staring at it with a peculiar intensity. "Klingschor," he said. "Priestess, look through this rubble to see if there are any larger pieces left. I may yet be able to draw an answer from one of my servants, or from Ruprecht, if enough remains of any of them."

Margerite gulped. If he did that...there would be little choice for her. She had her eating dagger in her belt, and Günther would not suspect an attack from her: she would wait until he was distracted with his magic, and then try to stick it between his ribs from behind.

She squatted, trying to keep her skirts clear of the soot with one hand as she gingerly prodded through the debris on the floor with the other. Most of the pieces lying about were, thank Maria, thank Christ, only lumps of rock blasted free from floor or walls by the force of the explosion. But once a greasy black lump crumbled in her hand to reveal a piece of dirty bone beneath, and she realized with a wave of nausea that it had been flesh. Kobolt nosed through the remains with her until he began to sneeze, at which point he retreated to the doorway and started to wash himself busily.

Margerite had circled the whole room three times before Günther deigned to look at what she had uncovered. He grunted.

"Not enough," he said finally. "Now, Priestess, you shall tell me what you know. Since you are still living, it is obvious that you had no part in this ritual. What did Ruprecht tell you about it?"

"Only that it was something very important. He would not have me take part in most of his doings because of the child I carry," Margerite added swiftly. "I heard the disturbance from above, and when it was quiet, I came down to see - this, and Ruprecht gone."

The slow grin coming over Graf Günther's lean, pointed face as the steady regard of his blue eyes settled on her unnerved Margerite. What is he planning now? she asked herself. What does he know?

"Ruprecht told me of your child," Günther said. "Be assured, that all of us in the Order are eagerly awaiting his birth. I wonder," he added thoughtfully, "if you are fully aware of the honour which has been bestowed upon you, Priestess?"

Margerite straightened, holding her filthy hands away from her body lest she get more stains upon her dress. O, little Wolfram, she thought, what are you going to be born into? But, for Wolfram's sake, she replied as haughtily as she could, "Prince, I know the value of the son I bear, and I trust that the Order will strive to its utmost to ensure his safety."

The words coming out of her own mouth shocked her: she could hardly believe what she had just said. Would you call on the Powers of Hell to save your child? she thought. When you do not even know for sure who his father is? But she could not take back her own words, and Günther inclined his narrow head towards her, as if he were speaking to an equal.

"You have my assurance of that. More: when he is born, I mean to be his godfather before Lucifer, and take him into my court as page and Knappe when he is old enough, that he may learn the full use of his nature and powers. Although Ruprecht's bungling last night may have proved a great setback to us, your child shall do far more to aid us than Ruprecht could ever dreamed of achieving in a long life - he shall be the means of Lucifer's final mastery upon the plane of Earth."

A deep chill sank into Margerite's bones as she listened to Günther speak. She could not ask him what he meant without revealing her imposture, but she could feel her heart beginning to give way to despair, like the walls of a dyke bulging and beginning to crack under a great flooding weight of black water. I could cast myself from the top of the castle into the ravine. That would end the Order's hopes. But suicide was a mortal sin, and to murder little Wolfram, whatever the Light-Bearers might have in mind for him - that would be to leap into the mouth of Hell more surely than by any means that Graf Günther might contrive.

"Now," he said at last, "you shall leave me here, for I mean to do my best to discover where Ruprecht failed. Let this be your night's lesson, Priestess: the success of one often grows from the failure of another, as it is meet that the strong should feed on the weak. Give me the keys, and I shall return them to you tomorrow."

Graf Günther left the next day, after giving back the keys to Ruprecht's chambers and informing Margerite that she was to have the sanctum cleaned and readied by the time of his return. To that, he added, "You are not to do any magic yourself until after your child is born, but then I shall teach you as quickly as you can learn. Towards that end, I shall leave you with a book of our philosophies, correspondences, and rituals, that your mind may be prepared to meet the challenges that the Order, and your special position, will bring you."

The book Günther put into Margerite's hands was small, but very thick, bound in smooth and fine black leather set with black star sapphires. "By the vows you have already taken," he told her, "you know the punishments that will be meted out if you should dare to show this to any outside the Order."

Margerite nodded solemnly, uncomfortably aware of the cold circle of the Order ring about her left forefinger. But since she had taken no vows, as soon as Graf Günther had been gone from Burg Falkenstein for a full day, she went to Father Etienne with the book, telling him what Günther had said.

Etienne rested his chin in the cup of his hand for a few minutes, staring down at the black volume where Margerite had set it on the table before him. "Yes, I recognise this," he said. "As Günther told you, it contains the Order's philosophies and the correspondences and theories on which magic is based, as well as the basic prayers of their consecrations and some lesser rites. It is not, in itself, unholy in the way that the greater grimoires of the Light-Bearers are. I would rather that you did not have to read it, for the Order's evil does not mean that its members lack for intelligence or gifts, and many of them are greatly skilled at making the worse thing seem the better. Yet, if we are to keep up the deception we have begun, you must know what you are dealing with. If you have questions about anything you read here, come to me, and I will answer them as best as I am able."

"Will you keep it for me?" Margerite asked. She did not want the book in her chambers - she did not want it anywhere near her. But Father Etienne shook his head.

"It will be best if you conceal it among whatever is left of Ruprecht's books. I hope that Jochanan left behind all he did not completely destroy, for some of them may have offered a great temptation to a man of intelligence and learning - which he is - especially one who has little sense, which is also true of him. Still, I can only trust his word on it."

Margerite carried the black book down to the ruins of Ruprecht's library. It looked to her as though Jochanan had done his duty thoroughly: there were few pages in the destroyed volumes that were not too scorched or stained to read. She gathered up what was left, heaping the tattered pieces of parchment on one splintered shelf on top of Günther's book.

That evening, Father Etienne sat in his chamber, sipping slowly at a small cup of aqua vitae and considering his position. Three days remained until Christmas Eve: Margerite's baby would not be born for another four and a half months or so. The Bishop of Augsburg, and several other interested parties, would be pleased at the reconciliation between Burg Fürstensee and Burg Falkenstein - though, in truth, the credit for that belonged largely to Margerite, it would nevertheless be a bright spot on Etienne's record. In terms of his official duties, there now remained only one to complete here, and with Ruprecht dead and Günther and Heinrich both gone for the time being, there was nothing standing in his way.

Eva was tidying Margerite's chamber, her little cat pouncing at the hem of her skirts as she walked about the room. She had blossomed remarkably since Ruprecht's death: she no longer cringed away from the gazes of her superiors, and, now that she was standing straight and not trying to hide her womanhood, the lushness of her young figure was clear even beneath the oversized dresses she had borrowed from Berthe. Father Etienne did not know what Margerite had told her about that night, but whatever it was, it seemed to have sufficed.

"Eva, I must speak with you," Etienne said without preamble.

"Yes, Father?"

"Do you know what your legal position is?"

"When Wachholt sent me to the convent, he told me that I was leaving the world, and no longer had any claim to my parents' lands, nor would I ever be able to claim the title of Gräfin von Bärenfels."

"That would have been true, had you taken your final vows as a nun. I was originally sent to find you and make sure that you did just that. However, unless you have a true vocation, I cannot in conscience recommend you to the cloistered life. Have you a vocation, Eva? Do you wish to leave the world and become a Bride of Christ?"

Eva shook her head. "Even if the Convent of the Holy Cross had not been as it was, I do not think I have a true vocation, Father. I enjoy the world; I do not even mind being the Gräfin's servant so much, although it is tiresome to have to carry fuel and change bedlinens when I would rather be riding or doing fine embroidery work. And it is not -" she shook back her long fall of wavy golden hair in an unconscious gesture of haughty pride -"what I was born to."

"No, it is not. If you do not have a vocation, then you cannot be forced to take the vows of a nun, even by your legal guardian. Well," Etienne amended, "by the laws of the Church you cannot. The state of Fallen man being what it is, in fact you could have been forced quite easily, and indeed would have been, but you cannot now, since I am prepared to stand against it. That being so, what do you wish to do?"

"What are my choices, Father? I do not wish to go back and live under Wachholt's guardianship. He will only marry me off to one of his odious friends, or seek a dispensation so that he can marry me himself."

"That is likely enough," Father Etienne allowed. "And as long as he is your guardian, he has the right to do that, unless he is persuaded not to. However, there is nothing unseemly in a girl of your age, even one of your standing, taking up the post of lady-in-waiting to a Gräfin while she learns all the skills she must have to manage a castle and realm of her own. As for your marriage - I have noticed that you spend a great deal of time nursing young Ritter Christoph back to health."

Eva giggled and blushed, the flush becomingly pink against her creamy skin. "It is only nursing, Father. Well, and we have talked a little. He is a most courtly and well-spoken gentleman."

"So he is, and he would not be a bad match for you, if matters fall out that way. But you are still very young, and have time yet. Very well: if you are agreeable, I shall write to your cousin and explain how things stand, for I think that he will receive my letter with the proper seriousness. I shall also speak to the Gräfin and explain to her that you are no longer to be treated as a common maidservant, but as a young Gräfin in your own right, and her apprentice in the arts of a chatelaine."

"Thank you, Father!" Eva exclaimed. As if she had forgotten that he was a priest, she flung herself at Etienne, embracing him fervently and kissing him on the cheek. Embarassed, he disentangled himself from her warm arms. She had best be married off before too long, he thought, but said only, "I shall go to write that letter now."

Margerite was delighted to learn of Eva's standing, and at once set those women servants of the castle who were cleverest with needles to making proper dresses for her, though she was growing so fast that it would be difficult for her wardrobe to keep up with her. Although, as a lady-in-waiting, Eva still helped Margerite with her dressing and arranging her hair, they had to bring a girl - one of Gerhild's nieces, a daughter of the sister who was wet-nursing the midwife's child - up from the village to do the more strenuous work of a servant.

The pleasure of turning Eva out properly and beginning to teach her about the management of a castle was one of the few things Margerite had to enjoy that Christmas season. She had debated with herself for some time as to how to dispose the rooms on the upper floor, for Eva must have a chamber of her own now, and there was also the problem of Ruprecht's hidden staircase. The most sensible choice, she knew - and Father Etienne had advised her towards it, for it would make keeping up her pretense of Order membership easier when, as he assuredly would, Graf Günther sent an informant of his own to her - would be for Margerite to move into Ruprecht's chamber, leaving the room at the southern end of the corridor for Eva.

But Margerite could not bear the thought of sleeping in that room, for she knew she would lie awake listening for sounds on the staircase below. At last she had reached a compromise: Ruprecht's room would be left empty, while the chamber beside it, which, Kai told her, had been locked and used only for storage since Gräfin Radegund's death, would be cleaned out for Eva, and Margerite would stay where she was. Jochanan had found Ruprecht's keys in the process of his demolitions below, so that Margerite was able to lock his door and that of the staircase against any curious or overzealous servants; and with that, she had to be content.

Bertram's wounds had, as Margerite feared, caught a fever, for not only had he had to sit through the negotiations, he had been forced to carry out his duties as Hauptmann of the guard while Günther and Heinrich were there, without letting them see any hint of his injuries. Bertram was a difficult patient, as well: he would not content himself with lying in bed and playing dice with Paul, who was recovering very slowly from his poisoned wound. Rather, the Hauptmann kept insisting that he was fit to resume his duties, even while his face was still flushed and eyes bright with fever, and he could hardly walk from one side of the room to the other.

"You shall do no such thing," Margerite told Bertram firmly when, as if he could not hear the howling of the snow-laden wind and the rattling of the shutters over his arrow-slits, he said that he would have to go out and call the younger guardsmen to drill. "Even if you were fit for it, the weather is not...can you not hear it?"

"Fierce storms you have in these parts," Paul said from his own bed, reaching down to the floor to rescue his jack of ale from Kobolt's questing muzzle. He winced as the motion pulled against the long slash on his chest, but stoically upended the tarred leather mug, pouring a long draught into himself. "I swear I have never seen a winter like it, not even the one we were engaged all January outside Köln - were you there for that, Bertram? I cannot remember."

"I heard about it, but I was up near Hanover with my company," Bertram replied.

"That was some campaign, I tell you! That was the time some of the men decided Jochanan had gone too long without getting laid, so they grabbed a woman and brought her to him, hands tied and skirt off." Margerite listened with appalled fascination, but the Bear was clearly well past his first mug of ale for the day, and kept talking, cheerfully oblivious to her presence. "And what did he do? Not climb on at once, no, not him. He actually introduced himself and started talking to her, as if he had just met her in an inn and thought he had to charm her into bed. He took so long about it that she managed to get her hands free and slapped him across the face. Well, he just stood there with that stunned-ox look he gets, and she took to her heels, running bare-arsed through the lines. Got away clean, too."

"Paul!" Bertram said severely. "The Gräfin's presence!"

"Oh. Uh." The Bear took another deep swallow of ale. "Anyway, that was a bad winter, but nothing like this. And, you know, some fool was blowing a hunting horn out there most of last night, even in the worst of the storm. I could hardly sleep for it, even over Bertram's snoring. Did you not hear it? I wonder who it could have been."

"I heard nothing," Margerite said. That was not quite true: once or twice the sound of a hunting horn had disturbed her sleep, but she had been able to convince herself that it was no more than the howling of the wind down the ravine, that only her dreams had turned the rattling shutters into the sound of a horse's hooves and the barking of hounds after a quarry. Uneasy with the subject, she looked at Bertram. He had let his head fall back on the pillow and was staring at the ceiling, the tangled mess of his beard and hair spread over his face like brambles over an untended garden.

"Bertram," she said, "I think it is time to trim you a little bit. I will not take it all off," she added hastily, "but Burg Falkenstein's Hauptmann of the guard should not look so much like - forgive me, Paul - a Free Company soldier on campaign."

"No offense, Frowe Gräfin, if I can have another mug of ale," Paul replied happily. "Give Bertram some, too. He'll need it to strengthen him for his ordeal."

Margerite twitched at the Bear's last words, for the Ordeal had been mentioned prominently in the book Günther had given her, though it had given few details about the actual nature of the Order's trial. Dear Mother Maria, she thought, how far will I have to go before I escape from them? If she could ever escape at all: the book had begun with the words, You who have once set foot on the Path of Light will never be able to leave it again. Though your way to the wisdom of Lucifer may seem twisted and obscure; though you may even think that you are fleeing from Him, in the end you will surely find yourself before His adamant throne. And, once initiated into the Order of Light-Bearers, even an apostate remains forever an Order member, to be judged and punished by us alone.

Resolutely she turned her mind from her dark contemplations, declaring, "Stay there, and do not think of getting out of bed. I shall be back in a few moments."

Margerite looked about for Eva or her serving maid, finding Eva at last in Christoph's room where she was pouring wine for the young man, laughing and talking with him. A chessboard was set up on the table beside his bed: he had clearly been teaching Eva to play, for her white king was completely surrounded and within two or three moves of mate.

"If you keep spending so much time in here, I shall have to arrange a chaperone for you," Margerite said to her young companion, only half in jest. Eva flushed prettily, tossing back her long golden hair and stroking Kriemhilt, who was curled purring on her lap. Her new light blue dress, fitted in a style close to those Margerite had gotten redone in Freiburg, showed off her generous figure very well, and it was easy to see that Christoph could not keep his eyes from lingering on her breasts for very long.

"O, Margerite, Christoph cannot even pour wine for himself with his broken arm. And he needs the company, for it is very tedious for him not to be able to ride out hunting or swing his sword."

Margerite glanced quickly about the room, hoping to see a hunting horn there: a bored young knight in the room beneath him might very well be the explanation for the horn-blasts that had disturbed Paul's sleep. It relieved her more than she could say when she noticed the horn hanging on its strap from one of Christoph's bed-posts.

"There are other things that a man with a broken arm can do," Margerite said ominously. "At least bring Rose in with you when you come to keep him company. Your pardon, Ritter Christoph. I do not think that you would do anything to besmirch Eva's honour, but rumours are easily started and difficult to stop."

"Of course," Christoph said, airily waving his unstrapped hand. "I understand completely."

And it is a good thing that Father Etienne saw fit to reveal Eva's station in life before she started tending you, or else we might be dealing with something more substantial than a rumour in nine months, Margerite thought with an unusual twinge of cynicism. But Christoph was so good-natured and polite that it was difficult to keep up even a front of severity with him.

"Well, I shall trust in your good sense and your honour. Eva, where is that girl? She never seems to be about when I want her."

"She said she was going to get strewing herbs for our chamber, since it is beginning to smell of tomcat again. I think it will be some time before she is properly accustomed to her duties." Eva's remark was delivered in such an unconsciously high-handed tone that Margerite was more than passingly tempted to remind her of who had been doing those same duties before they brought Rose up from the village, but she could hardly say such a thing with Christoph listening in.

"We must send for another maiden, since it is hardly fair to expect her to serve two mistresses at once. Christoph, are there any young women in Burg Fürstensee who might do as a maidservant for Eva or myself?"

Christoph's greenish-gray eyes brightened, and he was about to speak when Eva looked at him with a slight frown. Seeing that, Margerite could hardly keep from laughing, though she knew she ought to be worried at the familiarity it implied. *So, you do not want Christoph selecting young women to stay here, do you?* she thought. *I wonder if we will need to start making arrangements for a second betrothal soon.*

"I will write to my father and ask, Gräfin," Christoph said politely. "I am sure he can find someone suitable for you."

When at last Margerite and Rose came back to Bertram's chamber, bearing scissors, cloths, and a basin of hot water as well as the promised ale, Bertram was out of bed, standing by an unshuttered arrow-slit with the icy wind blowing a scattering of snowflakes about him.

"Get back in bed," Margerite commanded. "I can cut your hair well enough there, and you should not be standing in a draught like that."

"I am too hot, and need to breathe," Bertram argued. "It would be best for me to take a short walk outside and see how matters are with the guard."

Margerite put her hand on his forehead, silently rejoicing in even that simple touch. Beneath the damp chill from the window, she could feel the mounting heat of his skin, like a fire freshly kindled under the cold tiles of a stove. "Rose, go tell Gerhild that Bertram's fever is up again, and ask her to prepare a posset for him. Bertram, back to bed."

Bertram did not complain any further as Margerite tucked the blankets around him and propped him up on a pillow so that she could cut his hair. The black ringlets fell thickly on the cloth, reminding Margerite uncomfortably of something she had read in the Order book. *A lock of hair or a nail clipping is all that is required to target a spell on its subject or direct a demon to him...*

Such things should be kept carefully whenever you find them, whoever they come from, for you may at any time find a subject for enchantment useful.

Remember that to work your will upon all things, you must have the means of controlling all things ready to your hand. If Margerite were truly an Order member, she would be planning even now to enclose the trimmings in a little bag of black silk, neatly labelled with Bertram's name, so that the means of controlling him would be ready to her hand.

"Are you all right?" Bertram asked, looking up at her. "I thought I felt you shiver."

"I will have Rose stoke up the stove when she gets back. It is too cold in this room, even with the shutters closed." And a good blaze will incinerate these hair-clippings nicely, lest...

Margerite did not finish her thought, for she was not sure where it might lead, but when Kobolt leapt up to start pawing at the fallen strands, she was not too gentle in tossing him off.

Mindful of Bertram's need for disguise, Margerite did not cut his beard too closely. It still concealed the firm slant of his jaw and the shape of his stubborn chin, but she had shaved it down from his cheekbones, and it was now tidy and well-shaped, instead of a dreadful tangle. With his hair and beard trimmed back, Bertram looked very much a soldier, rather than a brigand or wild man: the haircut emphasized his look of solemn severity, lending him a dignity that he had lacked before.

"You look much more the castle commander now," Margerite said, rather pleased with herself. She handed him a small mirror. "See for yourself."

Bertram gazed at his reflection for some time, slanting the mirror to look at himself from various different angles. "I look more like my father than I had thought to," he said. "I have grown old in these years."

"Nonsense," Margerite replied briskly. She glanced at Paul, now happily sharing his jack of ale with Kobolt. Deciding to take the risk, she leaned forward and kissed Bertram on the lips.

His hazel eyes widened, flickering nervously towards the Bear. But either Paul had not seen or was pretending not to have: he was certainly looking away from them, intent on removing the cat's black head from the opening of his mug so that he could drink from it himself. Bertram did not chance kissing Margerite back, but he smiled at her, and his warm fingers pressed hers for a moment.

By Christmas Eve, Eva had seen to it that the great hall was swathed in branches of pine and holly. Although Christoph, with his broken arm, could not ride out to gather greenery, he joined in the preparations enthusiastically, sipping mulled wine at the table beside Eva and calling suggestions to the servants who were putting up the evergreen boughs, or else playing chess with Father Etienne while Eva looked on.

Bertram had thrown off his fever at last, though he still moved stiffly from the pain of his healing wounds, and even Paul was able to leave his room for short periods, drinking ale and playing dice with Jochanan and some of his other surviving Company members - to whom, Margerite gathered, he had spun a tale about being knifed by one of the Tiefensee women in a discussion over her price.

Margerite's belly was swelling quickly now: she was thankful that only a few of Ruprecht's mother's dresses had been altered, for otherwise she would have to either have new garments made, or resort herself to borrowing Berthe's best clothes until her child was born.

Gerhild assured her that it was not unusual for a slim woman to be carrying so large towards the end of her fifth month, but Margerite was beginning to wonder how she would get through the next four months, for her ankles were already swelling and she found herself constantly needing to piss as her child pressed harder against her bladder.

For all the merriment around her, the candles burning in a halo of light around the hall and the sweet sound of the minstrels singing from the balcony above, Margerite found that she was feeling strangely cold and lonesome.

The great hall did not seem quite the same without Ruprecht's alaunts nosing after scraps or sitting by the Graf's chair and looking up adoringly: once she had grown used to them, Margerite had hardly noticed that the dogs were there, but now she found that she missed them.

Even now, it did not quite seem to her as if Ruprecht was gone: over the last days, she had found herself looking at the door of the hall as if it would suddenly swing open and he would stride in with snow in his golden hair, bearing, perhaps, the body of a roe-deer or a bloody haunch of stag over his shoulder as proof of his hunting.

"Wolfram, Wolfram," she murmured, her hands resting on the protruding mound of her belly. "What a world I am bringing you into." For a moment, she wondered how Ruprecht's eagles were faring in their new forest home. Had they been able to nest, to find shelter against the wild winter storms? Perhaps, after all, it would have been better to listen to Johann's advice and keep them until spring.

Kobolt sprang onto the table before her, a large rat in his mouth. He dropped it right beside her plate, leaving it to twitch feebly on the table in a spreading pool of blood, then looked up at Margerite, purring and ducking his head to nuzzle her belly. Torn between laughter and disgust, she clapped her hands for Rose to take the unwanted offering away. "I can do without Christmas gifts of that sort, sir," she said, scratching the cat behind his ears. But she was grateful to Kobolt, for he had broken her mood of melancholy, and so she allowed him to stay on the table and even lap at her wine.

It was three days into February when the emissary from Graf Günther of whom Etienne had warned Margerite finally struggled through the storms and into the great hall of Burg Falkenstein. To Margerite's profound relief, he did not appear to be of the same kind as Kundry and Klingschor: he was a young man with sandy-reddish hair curling about his shoulders and freckled skin, his clothes disheveled from his long journey, but cut in fine fashion, though made of rather plain dark wool; and even worn out from his travels as he was, he seemed cheerful and friendly. On his hand was the onyx-set ring of an Order Canon; he blinked in surprise when he saw Margerite's own ring, as if he had expected her to be of higher rank.

"Greetings, Frowe Gräfin," he said. A few clumps of half-melted snow scattered from the folds of his gray cloak as he swept Margerite an elaborate bow. "I am Richard, sent by Graf Günther at your father's behest to offer you such help and guidance as you may need through this year of your betrothal." His voice was light and pleasant; he spoke German well, but with a strong English accent.

"Graf Günther is kind to think of me," Margerite replied, rather stiffly. "You are welcome in Burg Falkenstein. But you look tired from your journey: sit down and have some hot wine, and I will see to it that a chamber is arranged for you." Her mind was already racing: where could she put him? Ruprecht's chamber, perhaps - but she was loath to give the Englishman the chance of access to the rooms below, and even if the staircase door were locked, she had seen that the lock could be picked. She would have to quarter him in the second-story room that had been an armoury, from which he would have to pass Father Etienne's door to reach the top floor, or else walk all the way through the castle.

"That is kind of you, Frowe Gräfin. No doubt we shall have a chance to speak later?"

"No doubt we shall."

Heavy as it was already, Margerite's pregnancy afforded her some excuse to avoid Richard as much as she could, but he had only been there two days when she could no longer get out of showing him the hidden chambers that had been Ruprecht's. The moment they were alone inside Ruprecht's room above, Richard seized Margerite's hand and dropped to his knees before her.

"Priestess, I am gladder than I can say that I have been given the privilege of serving yourself and the Child. You have my oath as a Canon of the Order that I shall live up worthily to this challenge which Prince Günther has set me."

"Your oath is accepted," Margerite told him crisply, raising him to his feet. Her heart was sinking within her, both at Richard's words and the realization that, though he looked nothing like Ruprecht's Knappe, there was something disquietingly similar in his verbose enthusiasm. "No doubt Prince Günther has told you of the work before you?"

"He has. I am sorry that I will not be able to teach you the working of any magic until the Child is born - believe me, I understand what a great sacrifice that must have been to you! But I shall teach you the Order's philosophies, as well as I understand them, and the principles through which our magic works. The Graf gave you a copy of the Black Book, I understand?"

"Yes."

"And you have been reading it diligently?"

"I have."

Richard went down the spiral staircase before Margerite, pausing often and looking back up at her anxiously, with his arm held out ready to catch her should she slip. Although they went slowly, Margerite was out of breath and her back was aching by the time they reached Ruprecht's destroyed library.

Richard looked at what was left of the books, and his breath went out of him in a long sigh. "So much lost," he murmured. "If only Ruprecht had not failed! But whatever overcame him, we are all fortunate that it went no farther than it did, for no disaster would be more devastating than if the Child within you were to be harmed. Show me the rest."

Richard stood for a long time inside Ruprecht's ritual chamber, kicking at the sooty debris with the toe of one pointed shoe. "Who was that?" he asked curiously, pointing at the fragment of skull Günther had uncovered.

"Ruprecht's servant Klingschor," Margerite answered shortly. Now, from reading the Order book, she understood why Günther had ordered her to search for the pieces of the dead. It had not only been a test of her obedience, but of her will and self-mastery, as spelled out in the Order philosophies.

The magician should accustom himself to the most gruesome sights as well as the most beautiful, to the foulest and cruellest deeds as well as the most honourable and kindest, that his Will may be swayed by no illusion. Fastidiousness should not stay his hand from touching any corruption, nor should he be seduced to linger on that which is pleasing: neither compassion nor the love of cruelty should hinder him from doing what he must, precisely as it must be done. The Will that can be moved by such considerations will inevitably be destroyed, for this world can offer neither attractions nor repulsions to match those commanded by the Powers of Hell.

Margerite had passed Günther's first test, though she did not know whether she should count it a matter for pride or shame.

"Prince Günther ordered me to clean and ready this place, but, as you can see, I am in no condition to get down on my knees and scrub the floor."

"Of course, Priestess. I shall do all for you. In time, you will have to paint the circle and triangle anew for yourself, but there will be no need for that until the Child is delivered."

Reluctantly, Margerite showed Richard the way out to the ravine, where he could toss the detritus from Jochanan's explosions: snow would cover everything quickly, and when it melted in spring, it would scatter the shards so far that no one would ever know they had been there.

When she finally escaped from the Englishman and made her way back to her chamber, Margerite called for Gerhild. Her back was aching badly; her breasts were beginning to hurt, and she was uncommonly tired, as though she had spent the day at hard work.

"There is nothing wrong with you," Gerhild said after examining her thoroughly. "It is only the ordinary course of pregnancy."

"As may be, but I am most uncomfortable. And I have not slept well at night, for Christoph seems to have the strange habit of blowing his hunting horn out the window at odd hours, always when the storms are at their worst, and I can sometimes hear it even up here. I think I shall speak to him about it tomorrow."

Gerhild shook her head. "I would not," she said. "I do not think it is Christoph you are hearing."

"Who, then? Is one of our guards outside amusing himself by making noise? If that is so, I shall have the man whipped, for it could very easily be taken as the raising of an alarm."

"No," Gerhild told her. "Best to leave the matter be and do not concern yourself with it, Frowe Gräfin. Women often find small things disturbing as their pregnancies wear on, and you are not having as easy a carriage as some. I shall make you a tea for your aches, and to soothe you so that you get a good night's sleep."

"Why will you not tell me what you know?" Margerite demanded. She knew she sounded petulant and childish, but she was tired - exhausted from dealing with Richard, tired of the pains in her back and legs and breasts, tired of the weight of her belly and the constant need to piss and the slightly waddling, graceless walk she could feel herself developing. Blessed Maria, she thought, was it like this for you?

"Because I know nothing more than old wives' tales and peasants' stories, Frowe Gräfin," Gerhild replied tartly. "And you are wise, and well-educated, and have no need to worry yourself with such nonsense. I also know that Eva's cat Kriemhilt has come into heat young, and should be giving birth at the same time as you do, for no one has told her father that incest is a sin. So the two of you can share your troubles in the last week of pregnancy together, and grumble about your swollen bellies and aching nipples in harmony."

Margerite had to laugh, for she knew that her pregnancy was making her snappish and unreasonable. Yet, as soon as Gerhild had retired, she turned to Rose.

"Do you know anything about someone blowing a hunting horn when the winds are strongest?" she asked the serving girl.

Rose straightened from her task of fueling the stove for the night, brushing a few strands of dark brown hair from her forehead with the back of one sooty hand. Except for her colouring, she looked much like Gerhild, with the same wiry build and triangular face: the blood of the midwife's family clearly ran strong.

"Frowe Gräfin, I know only what folk say," she answered nervously. "And my aunt is right: it is only old wives' tales and peasant stories, which she told me you do not like to hear."

"I should like to hear them now." Margerite sat up, and Kobolt jumped into her lap at once. Absently she began to stroke the cat's fur. "What is it that folk say - to everyone except me?"

"They say...do not be angry with me, Frowe Gräfin, for I am only repeating the tales as you asked me to. They say that since Graf Ruprecht died, he has been seen riding through the storm on his great dark horse with his gray hounds running before him and his eagles flying above, and that he now hunts living men through the night as he used to hunt stags through the forest. His horn sounds as a warning that he is abroad, and anyone who is outside when they hear it must throw themselves face-down in the middle of the road, in hopes that he will pass them by. And some folk say it is the judgement of God, because the Graf hunted on Sundays instead of going to Mass as he should have, and now he will hunt through these woods until Judgement Day. I am sorry, Frowe Gräfin!" Rose added. "I did not mean to distress you, but you did ask me to tell you, and Aunt Gerhild said that I should always tell you the truth rather than trying to lie to you, because you would always be able to catch me out."

Margerite glanced at the windows, but she could see nothing beyond them save darkness. She could hear the wind growing stronger outside, but - Christ be praised - it was only wind, with no echo of the troubling horn-call that had haunted her dreams. Inside herself, she could feel Wolfram squirming, kicking at the walls of her womb as though he were anxious to be out.

"Hush, little one," she murmured to him, massaging her belly to quiet him. "You will come out soon enough, and then you will cry at the cold bright world, and wonder why you were ever so eager to leave me. Hush, hush." She began rocking, singing softly to the child within her, and after a few moments Rose joined in, her voice in low harmony beneath Margerite's.

The Lenten season in Burg Falkenstein was lean, for so much of their supplies had been eaten during the siege, but Margerite had been through worse, and Father Etienne had given her permission to leave off from abstinence and fasting when she could, on account of her pregnancy. After the wild winds of mid-March, the storms began to slack off, and the wind to bring rain more often than snow. Icicles ran from the castle's dripping eaves, hanging clear-toothed from the wooden remains of the peasant-shelters in the outer bailey; the snowdrifts eroded slowly into misshapen gray heaps with the black earth showing beneath their overhanging edges.

Margerite's pregnancy was becoming more and more wearisome, and on many days she did not bother to make her way down the castle's winding stairs to the great hall, letting Rose bring her meals up to her bedchamber instead. If not for Richard's constant presence whenever she was out of her room, she might have tried to do more, but the rigors of nurturing the child within her offered her an excuse not to walk down the long flights of stairs to the secret chambers where the young Englishman wished to instruct her in Ruprecht's black arts. Even seeing Richard in the great hall at mealtimes made her nervous enough: though he was pleasant and amiable, a charming conversationalist, there was something that bothered Margerite deeply about the way he looked at her.

That curious deference, beyond what her station ought to command, and his occasional veiled references to"the Child", as though - she hardly dared think of what that reminded her of: now she knew that blasphemy was not only expected by the Order of Light-Bearers, but required; but it was a different thing to read about it in the Black Book than to hear it directed at herself. There was also the unsettling way in which his enthusiasm and devotion reminded her of poor Wolfram, although at least Richard was sparing her the romantic worship of the Minnesinger: sometimes Margerite wondered blackly if there were a special manual for young men in the Order which prescribed their attitudes towards women of superior station.

In spite of Richard, however, Margerite was able to go to all Father Etienne's Lenten services: the Order prescribed that its members should do whatever was needful to conceal themselves from discovery, recommending the cultivation of indifference to all that Christians thought holy, that they not be daunted by crosses or prayers or the scent of sanctified incense at a chapel door. Though it was almost impossible for her to speak to the priest in private, as she desperately longed to, at least she had the customary observances to comfort her soul. And Richard could not stop her from making what he thought to be a semblance of Confession before Easter, when all Christians must confess and receive Communion.

Safe within the priest's chamber at last, Margerite knelt before Father Etienne and poured out her heart to him. Worst of all, to her, seemed the ease with which she was taking in the teachings of the Black Book, the way the words often rang in her mind or linked together patterns in her thoughts of which she had not previously been aware, and the praise that Richard constantly heaped on her for her studies. She could not look the priest in the face while she told him of this, but the warm clasp of his slender fingers on her chilled hands strengthened her as he questioned her carefully, the dry, reasonable rasp of his baritone voice calming the wild thoughts that had been troubling her.

"Much of what you have learned are only the basic principles of the arcane art, which hold no harm in themselves, save as they are used in the context of the Order. The same is true for the exercises the Englishman has taught you thus far. How to control your breathing, how to will unwanted sensations and stray thoughts away - some of these you might have learned in a convent, had you a vocation towards the meditative life. What you must beware of is what comes when these principles are taken too far, so that Power and Will become ends in themselves, beyond humanity and compassion and the love of Christ. When Günther first tested you in the chamber below - when you found the pieces of Kundry and Klingschor's bones, what did you feel?"

"Disgust," Margerite admitted honestly. "I could hardly keep my stomach down."

"Anything else?"

She thought, then shook her head.

"Did you feel no pity?"

"For them? But they...they were evil. I do not even think they were human."

"Were they not?" Father Etienne asked. Margerite looked up into his face. The canon's expression had softened, from the ascetic remoteness of a judge to something more gentle: it seemed to Margerite that she could see a hint of wistfulness misting his blue eyes, a touch of sadness in the fine-chiseled set of his mouth beneath the neatly-trimmed mustache. "Were they not thinking beings, animated by reasonable souls?"

"I suppose they must have been," Margerite admitted. "I had never thought about it."

"It is the sorrow of Fallen Creation that much that might have been good is now turned to evil, and sometimes must be destroyed, cast into torment or even annihilated utterly - even," he added sternly, and now Margerite knew he was thinking of how she had pleaded for Ruprecht, "that which we might once have loved. It is the hardest of our tasks, to fight those who are evil with all our strength, and yet keep ourselves from hating them, remembering the compassion of Christ, who died even for the worst of men. For the good of your own soul, I want you to meditate on that - and on what, if anything, is your Christian duty towards Kundry and Klingschor, now that they are dead."

For some reason, Margerite thought of Günther saying, I may yet be able to draw an answer from one of my servants...if anything remains of them. If she could save them, whatever they were, from being used by him again... But the fragments of their bones were likeliest in the ravine somewhere, washed out with the detritus from the chamber, and even if she had them, she could not lay them in consecrated ground.

"Is there anything else?" said Father Etienne.

"There is...Bertram."

"What have you to confess about him? Is there more than that which you repented of after Ruprecht's death?"

"I love him still, and I wish with all my heart that I had been able to marry him instead of betrothing myself to Heinrich."

"This is a sad thing, but has it led you into sin?"

"Only that I think about him at night, and of how it might have been if he and I had been able to wed."

"What is Bertram's view on this?"

"We spoke of it once...I do not think that he would have accepted if I had offered, for fear of what would become of us, caught between Heinrich and Günther."

"I think you are probably right," Father Etienne admitted. "And yet, what of your betrothal vows to Heinrich and your plans to marry him? Are you planning to deceive him with Bertram?"

"No. No, Bertram would never..." Margerite remembered how Bertram had turned away from her, cursing himself for what they both had done. She was still not sure that he did not believe he had sinned against her then, and she knew that he would not willingly conspire towards the breaking of her marriage vows.

"Then you have not sinned, but you are in great peril of falling into sin. And with that peril - I charge you most urgently - you must also be aware of the temptation to use the things you are learning in order to gain your heart's desire. That temptation has drawn many stronger than you are into evil, but if you are aware of the snare, you may yet escape it."

"Do you think I would use Light-Bearer magic to entrap Bertram?" Margerite demanded indignantly. Yet she had thought, if only for a second, that the fallen locks of his hair...

"I know that you are young, with a passionate heart, and still untried in many things; and I know the power and wiles of those who seek to corrupt you. And this much wisdom is in their Black Book: fear to admit nothing to yourself, for that to which you are blind in your own nature is the crack in your defenses through which your defeat will inevitably come. Which, after all, is only their way of repeating the wisdom of a better Book and, indeed, a greater magician: as King Solomon wrote in his Proverbs, 'Pride goeth before destruction, and a haughty spirit before a fall.' Have you never, if not for a moment, wondered if you could not use some of what you are learning to smooth your way out of the difficulties in which you stand?"

"I have," Margerite admitted, feeling miserable.

"Then bear that in mind, and do not let the sin of pride lead you into worse offenses. Remember, also, that the possession of power is also the temptation to use it, for you as well as for everyone else. Be wary of that snare - but, should you fail, beware even more of the trap of despair, which is only pride turned on its head: remember that all men are Fallen, and that Christ's mercy is infinite. Thinking that you are too good to ever yield to temptation is sinful pride; and should that pride be shattered, you will be sevenfold more vulnerable to the ways of the Devil. Do you understand?"

Margerite nodded.

"Now, have you anything else to confess?"

Margerite thought for a moment that she might tell Father Etienne of her doubts about her child's true father, the doubts that Richard's veneration were nourishing nearer to certainties. But only moments before he had spoken of the need to destroy that which was evil: what if he told her to cast Wolfram from her womb? She stroked her belly, caressing the child within as if to reassure him that his mother was protecting him, and said, "No, Father, but I fear what the Order may do to my babe when he is born, for Günther said he would come back for the birth."

"I shall be waiting by the door of the birthing chamber, and baptize it as soon as it is safely out of the womb, before Günther has the chance to claim it for his Master," Father Etienne reassured her. "Then your child's soul will be safe, at least until it is of reasoning age and must deal for itself with all the temptations that are the lot of Man."

And with that, Margerite had to be content, for she dared tell the priest no more. But as for Klingschor and Kundry, or their remains...That night she sought out Richard, asking him what he had done with the bones.

"I wrapped them carefully in a bag of black silk, and put them in a chest in your sanctum, Priestess," Richard replied proudly. "I thought that either you or Prince Günther might find a need for them someday."

"Bring them to me."

"What are you going to do with them? You know that you are not to do any ritual workings until the Child is born."

"I wish to keep them by me," Margerite said, hating the taste of the lie in her mouth. "For they were faithful servants, who may yet serve again."

Richard's smile lit his face, his greenish eyes glimmering with excitement. "Did Prince Günther speak to you of that, Priestess?"

"Not exactly," Margerite evaded. "But he gave me certain hints. Will you do it?"

"Of course, Priestess."

Though Margerite could not ride out to Maria's shrine herself, she sent Eva to Bertram with a message asking him to bring her some of the water from the fountain. At the Good Friday Mass, with bone-bag and phial hidden beneath her cloak, she stealthily dripped a stream of Maria's blessed water over the calcined fragments, praying to the Virgin - for two unknown spirits who, like both all humans and the host of angels who had fallen with Lucifer, must once have had the capability for good within them; and for herself, that Maria grant her the compassion, wisdom, and strength she would need, if she were not herself to become numbered among the damned.

By the middle of April, the snow had all melted away: the Tiefensee peasants were diligently ploughing in the fields, and fresh green shoots were already springing up in the castle gardens. Somewhat against Margerite's will, Richard had taken over the tending of the herber, intimating to her in their rare moments of privacy that there were things which needed to be done there beyond weeding, manuring, and covering the tenderest plants against late frosts. As Gerhild had predicted, Kriemhilt's little belly was swelling as well as Margerite's, the kittens squirming just beneath her dark furry hide.

Although young for bearing, she was a large cat for her age, and Gerhild pronounced solemnly that she should have no difficulty in producing her litter. Kobolt had grown most protective of his daughter-wife, and would hold her down and wash her face for hours while she purred and nuzzled him; Eva fed her cat on little tidbits of all sorts, doting on Kriemhilt as if the cat were her own daughter about to give birth. It was one week before her child was due when Margerite, resting in her chamber, heard the horns blowing from the gate. She heaved her bulk from the bed, waddling over to look out the arrow-slits.

The gate-guards had already dropped the porticullis: beyond, a single horseman stood on the bridge, with a guard of about thirty men in full armour behind him. Margerite stared at the yellow and blue banner, a solid, dull feeling of resignation settling in her heart. Graf Günther had said that he would return for the birth of her child, and now he was here. She grabbed the heavy cloak draped over the back of her chair, wrapping it tightly about herself - although the fresh breeze blowing through the arrow slits was mild, she seemed to be cold all the time, her hands and feet as icy as if she were walking barefoot and ungloved through the snow.

The guard of Burg Falkenstein moved swiftly: Margerite heard the knock on the door of her chamber before she was ready to come out.

"I saw Graf Günther's banner from the window," she said to the young man who braced to attention before her, his narrow face flushed beneath the brown fuzz of his beginning beard. "Is that truly he?"

"The Hauptmann says it is, Frowe Gräfin. Do we let him in? He has a strong force behind him."

"Are there more than the thirty or so I saw outside the gate?"

"Only those men, but they are very well-equipped, and the Hauptmann says that they all look like seasoned fighters. They could wreak great havoc within here, Frowe Gräfin."

"Are you so eager for another siege, then?" Margerite asked. The youth shook his head, looking down at his feet. "Graf Günther is our ally and friend. Let him in."

"As you wish, Frowe Gräfin." The guardsman sped off, the sound of his footsteps echoing along the corridor and fading down the staircase.

Carefully, one hand on the wall to balance herself, Margerite made her way down towards the great hall. Richard was at her elbow before she was halfway there, making sure that no chance slip of her foot would endanger the child within her. She wanted to shake him off, but she could think of no way to do it.

"Is it not good news that Prince..." Richard glanced up and down the staircase, realizing that he had slipped, and went on, "Graf Günther is here at last? I had begun to worry, for I heard of how he had been delayed last time, so that he reached Burg Falkenstein a day too late. And Gerhild told me that she thought you could give birth at any time, since young women often deliver their children early...Of course, there is no thought that the Child might be born on the wrong day!" he added hastily. "Forgive me, Frowe Gräfin, I meant no offense."

"Have you been bothering Gerhild about this?" Margerite asked. It disturbed her to think of the midwife discussing the intimate details of her birthing with this unwanted - not quite a stranger, but certainly no friend. And it was unfitting for a man to be asking a woman about female matters, though of course Richard's Order training must have left him no sense of shame in pursuing what he wanted to know.

"I only enquired to make sure you were getting the best care possible, Frowe Gräfin," Richard answered, the smile never leaving his freckled face. "I am not as experienced in herblore as the late lamented Kundry and Klingschor were - Graf Günther told me a few things about them, though not as much as I should like to know..." He paused hopefully, but when Margerite did not respond, he went on. "But I know a fair amount about it, and I would like nothing more than to help you if there is need."

"You are already quite as much help as I need, thank you," Margerite responded. She had meant her words to be quelling, but they only came out sounding tired.

Richard beamed. "I could ask for no higher honour, Frowe Gräfin."

They did not have long to wait in the great hall before Günther and several of his men trooped in. The Graf was in good health and cheer, his long face reddened slightly from his week and a half of riding in fine weather and his blue eyes alight with anticipation.

"Greetings, Gräfin Margerite!" he called out. "I see that I have not come too late to stand as godfather to your child."

Margerite rested her hands on the swollen mound of her belly as if to soothe Wolfram, who had begun to kick hard against her, as if in answer to the shocked beating of her heart. But of course the blasphemous blessing Günther had intimated to her would be followed by a more customary ceremony, in which he would take on the legal and social rights of a godfather before the world. "You have not, Graf Günther." She tried to smile at him, but found herself wincing.

Günther crossed the room in a few rangy strides, settling himself beside her. "Are you well?" he asked in a low voice. "You seem pale. Has Richard been taking proper care of you?"

"The very best," Margerite replied. She bestowed a more convincing smile on the young Englishman, who grinned back at her. "I thank you for sending him to me."

Günther waved his long hand in a dismissive gesture, the ruby of his Order ring glimmering darkly. "I might have done better, but there was not enough time to..." He stopped abruptly. "But you say you are in good health. That is the best of news, for you know how anxious I am to see my friend Ruprecht's heir born and able to take his proper place."

"Your aid has always been most welcome to Burg Falkenstein, Graf, " Margerite answered politely.

"Of course. And..." Günther lowered his voice again. "How is the state of your finances? I know that it is not easy to recover from a war and a long siege." He frowned. "Especially since you seem to have kept the Bear's Paw Company on. Have you reason to think that there may be more trouble?"

Margerite tried to sort through the layers of his questions, though it was difficult with Wolfram thumping enthusiastically on her bladder. Was Graf Günther offering further aid - to indebt Burg Falkenstein further to him - or was he reminding her of the help Ruprecht had already gotten from him as a subtle threat? And did he think she had kept Paul and his men on against Heinrich, or himself?

"Paul the Bear took a bad fever from his wounds after the battle outside our walls, and has not been fit to travel until now. It seemed an ill repayment to turn the Bear's Paw out with a leader lying near death, especially when they lost more than a third of their men in our war."

"They should be happy, for that is all the more pay for those who survive, and there are always new brigands to recruit," Günther said with a shrug. "Free Company men are not known for their sentiment: I am sure you have had ample opportunity to observe that." He glanced towards Bertram, who stood beside the door of the great hall, watching him and his men. "Your Hauptmann seems tidier these days, but I doubt he has changed much."

Margerite ached to speak out on Bertram's behalf, but she held her tongue, reminding herself that Günther's words were a tribute to Bertram's success in concealing his nature. "He is good at what he does," she replied cooly. "But I see that you have brought a good number of soldiers with you. Do you know something I have not heard?"

"Only that the roads here are becoming more dangerous. Even armed as we were, we had a little trouble along the way: it would not have been safe to travel with a smaller company. You must keep this firmly in mind for when you come to visit me, as I hope you shall later this year."

"Of course. As for our finances, the loss of the grape harvest was perhaps the worst blow. I do not think we will begin many ambitious undertakings this year, but if the weather continues well, we should be able to recover much of our shortfall by next summer."

"You seem to be a better manager than Ruprecht," Günther observed. "But we may, perhaps, talk about these matters when you have recovered. For now..."

"For now," Margerite said hastily, since she could no longer ignore the pressure on her bladder, "I must excuse myself a moment. You understand." She knew there were chamber pots below the great hall, in the storage room where several of the servants slept; she hoped she could make it down there in time without falling down the stairs.

A perplexed expression crossed the Graf's mobile features for a moment; then his face cleared and he laughed. "Ah, of course. My noble wife had much the same difficulty in her last months. I shall await your return patiently."

Reluctantly, Margerite unlocked Ruprecht's room and gave the servants order to prepare it for Graf Günther before she went back to the great hall. She was loath to do it, but she could think of nowhere else to put him. And, besides, he knew about the hidden rooms and would expect to be close to them.

At least Richard had not only scrubbed Ruprecht's chambers out, but censed and purified them thoroughly - to await Margerite's own enchantments, but oddly enough, that would protect them from anything Günther might have thought of doing without her knowledge: the Order prescribed a strict respect between its members, most particularly in regards to their magical sanctums and tools.

Nevertheless, Margerite found that her heart was beating fast and her palms were damp when Richard came to her door late that night to inform her that the Prince wished to speak to her in private. Nervously, she followed him along the corridor with Kobolt at her heels, making as much as she could of the hindrance her pregnancy had become. But in truth, she was hardly exaggerating, and the realization of her own helplessness made her more frightened.

Swollen and unbalanced as she was, she could not flee from Günther: her bloated ankles and feet were scarcely able to carry her up and down a flight of stairs at a slow pace, let alone running anywhere, and the short walk left her exhausted, as though Wolfram's lively writhings within her were stealing all the strength from her body.

Günther was seated behind Ruprecht's table, three black candles arranged in a triangle in front of him. Their flickering light emphasized the point of his bearded chin, his sharp widow's peak and the tufts of gray-blond hair above his ears, lending him a more frightening and diabolical aspect than he bore by day.

He wore the deep red silken robe of a Prince of the Order, and his hands were placed upon the table so that Margerite could see the light of the flames glowing red from the depths of the large ruby on his finger. So attired, Günther was an impressive figure, even terrifying: Margerite could nearly believe that she was in the presence of a Prince of Hell.

Magic is balanced between what seems to be and what is: seeming may shape being, for it works through the mind. To inspire the feelings of another, whether to love and loyalty or to terror and disgust, is to control him...Although the words had been written in the Order's Black Book, Margerite found that they lent her strength now, so that she could meet Günther's penetrating gaze without flinching or feeling the fear that had come upon her when she had seen him appearing thus - only a few months ago?

Within the candles was a piece of parchment with neat writing glistening black down the side, a list that might almost have been one of Kai's accounts. Günther smiled, his teeth glinting white and sharp, and tapped a fingernail upon it.

"Priestess, Mother of Our Lord's Heir," he said to Margerite. "Ex Tenebrae, Lux."

"Ex Tenebrae, Lux," Margerite replied.

"It is six days until the birth of the Child, and there is much to be done in order to prepare." Gunther lifted up the parchment. "Here is the list of ingredients we will need for His baptism, which you will supply to me."

Margerite took the list from Günther's hand. It felt oddly slick and cold beneath her fingers, and very thin, as if it were made from some hide thinner and more fine-grained than that of calf or lamb. Though her nerves seemed to cringe back from touching or looking at the parchment too closely, she held it and scanned it cooly. Günther's writing was fine and easy to read, a careful hand that many priests might have envied: of course, a word misread in a rite might be the cause of much destruction.

The skull of a wholly black cat.

The testicles of a goat, newly slain.

The heart and testicles of a lamb which is nine days old and without blemish.

The blood of a wholly black cockerel which has never engendered.

The finger-bone of one who has been unjustly hanged.

1 perfectly-formed mandrake root.

1 consecrated Host.

"And where," Margerite asked, "do you expect me to find these things, in my condition? Do you think I am going to chase lambs for slaughter and dig up dead bodies while I am nine months pregnant?" She knew that she was taking a risk in standing up to him; but the Black Book had made it clear that the Luciferan philosophy, and the structure of the Order of the Light-Bearers, was not based on unthinking obedience, but valued independent thought and the willingness to question foolish orders, at least to a point.

Margerite had judged rightly, for Günther smiled at her, leaning back in his chair so that his face was shadowed save for the glint of eyes and teeth. "You may order Richard to fetch them. But the order for each must come from your mouth, and you must tell him where to find them, as you would yourself if you were able."

Margerite could feel her knees weakening beneath the weight of her body. Without asking Günther's permission, she sat down on his bed, gathering herself. The Order prince waited, tapping the forefinger of his left hand idly against the tabletop as he watched her with the cool interest of a cook watching a new sauce to see if it would thicken properly. She breathed deeply, the soothing air sinking down through her body to smooth and even the rhythms of her heart.

"Richard," said Margerite. "I want you to fetch for me the skull of a wholly black cat..." She listed off the ingredients one by one, careful not to let her voice stick or shudder in revulsion on any of them.

"And where shall I find these, Priestess?" Richard enquired cheerfully.

"For the skull of a black cat, I should ask Berthe whether she drowned her kitchen cat's latest litter, which will surely all be black." By her feet, Kobolt miaowed sharply; Margerite reached down to stroke him, murmuring a silent apology in her mind, and he arched his soft back to her hand, as if to let her know that she was forgiven already.

"The goat, the lamb, and the cockerel you can all excuse as being for my own meals, since everyone knows that pregnant women will demand whatever they feel like eating; it is lambing season, so one nine days old should not be hard to find. And a cockerel too young to tread a hen can never have engendered, though since it is not easy to tell cocks from hens by sight at that age, you may have to cut two or three birds open before you find what you seek.

You are keeping the herber and can, I am sure, identify a mandrake root perfectly well. You will have to be clever in getting a consecrated Host from Father Etienne, and I do not envy you that task, but I trust your ability to carry it out. Perhaps you would do better to ride to one of the nearer villages where the priest is not so watchful. As for the fingerbone..." Margerite's mouth had suddenly gone dry. She swallowed hard.

Could she bring herself to order the desecration of the graves of Eckhardt's kinswomen - had she not done them enough harm already, that now one of them must give up a bone for this blasphemous rite? But she did not know whether Günther, or Richard, who had had plenty of time to hear tales within the castle, already knew of the executions Ruprecht had ordered. Forgive me, you poor women, she thought. But I must do this, to buy my child a little time. "There were two women hanged in Tiefensee because their kinsman was a poacher. They were as guiltless as anyone may be, and no doubt you will be able to find their graves with little difficulty, if you enquire with care."

"So it shall be, Priestess!" Richard said. The candlelight glistened from the little golden hairs on his freckled cheeks and chin as he grinned at her. Dear Maria, he is young, Margerite thought. Twenty, perhaps? She realized then that her eighteenth birthday, at the end of February, had passed almost without her noticing. But she did not feel young, not with the weight of Wolfram growing within her and the burdens on her soul; she knew that she had once been as light-hearted as Richard, but could not remember what it had been like.

The next evening, Margerite excused herself from sitting with Graf Günther in the great hall by saying that she had promised Christoph a game of chess -"or, more truthfully," she confessed, "I have promised Eva that I will sit there and move chess pieces around so that she can talk to Christoph without her reputation being at risk. They are a promising pair."

"Are they not," murmured Günther, eyeing her thoughtfully over the rim of his goblet. "Still, I should prefer to see Eva showing an interest in his brother Nikolaus. You do remember Nikolaus?"

"Most clearly." Margerite could guess why Günther wished to see Eva turning her heart towards Nikolaus, and the thought made her ill.

"You might keep that in mind when you are next in Eva's chamber," Günther added, and Margerite knew at once what he wished her to do. She smiled and nodded, hoping that he would take her apparent assent as a discreet promise.

Although Christoph's chamber was right next to Richard's, the stone walls were thick, and Margerite had ordered tapestries hung within to keep the chill off, so she was not much afraid of being overheard. Still, she lowered her voice and leaned forward over the chessboard as she said, "Christoph, do you know why Graf Günther is here?"

Christoph frowned. The stern expression was out of place on his rounded face: he seemed nothing so much as a young boy trying to look like a man. "I gather he wishes to strengthen his ties to you and your child by taking the part of godfather at the baptism. Which...well, he is your friend and ally, and there is hardly anything I can say about that."

"There is more to it than that," Margerite began, at the same time as Eva suddenly broke in, "Graf Günther is an evil man, and I wish he were not here."

Margerite and Christoph both stared at her - the young man in blank surprise, Margerite in horrible amazement. What did Eva know, and what was she going to say?

Eva had hunched her shoulders as she spoke, shrinking down in her chair. Despite her beautiful dress of deep blue velvet and the way its tight bodice had been cut to display her large breasts at their finest, she looked for a moment like the frightened child who had come to Burg Falkenstein in a tattered and stinking habit. Even her voice was higher and more childlike as she said, "He came to the Convent of the Holy Cross once, and...he frightened me."

"What did he do to you?" Christoph demanded, rising halfway from his chair with his hand going to the hilt of his sword. The young man had put on weight in his months of rest as his arm healed, but Margerite did not doubt that he thought himself in fit condition to challenge Günther if he took it into his head to do that.

Eva shook her head. "He frightened me," she repeated, and bit her lower lip as though to keep herself from saying anything more.

"Christoph, calm yourself," Margerite interposed. "Let me tell you what is happening, and then you can decide what you want to do about it. Graf Günther means to break the betrothal agreement we made with your father. He wants to carry me off, to take the guardianship of my child and install his own troops here at Burg Falkenstein, whether I will it or not. I have not openly denied him yet because he threatened me. He had letters of credit signed by Ruprecht, and..." She shivered.

Christoph's face had grown thoughtful, brown brows lowering over his grayish-green eyes and small mouth set firmly. "So that is how Ruprecht managed to hire all those mercenaries. We had wondered about that. Well, I shall write to my father at once."

"Do so. Tell Heinrich..." Margerite gulped. "Tell him to come immediately, for I would be married to him now, so that there is no doubt and no temptation remaining in Günther's mind. And tell him to bring his best men with him, in case there is any difficulty. The message had best be sent in secret, for it will take him time to get here, and I do not want Günther to realize that he must move first."

"I will do that. You have a good mind for these things, Frowe Gräfin," Christoph added admiringly, then turned to Eva. His hand moved towards her shoulder, then dropped again as he saw Margerite looking pointedly at him. "Eva, do not be afraid. We will have Günther out of here as soon as we can, and then we shall take you back to Burg Fürstensee with my new stepmother." He grinned at Margerite. "And, if Christ is good to us and my sword has anything to do with it, you shall never have to look upon Graf Günther's ugly face again, I promise you."

Eva snuffled, then smiled at Christoph, her bosom heaving as she breathed deeply. That girl's talents will be wasted as frowe of a castle, Margerite thought with a sort of reluctant admiration, watching her young companion gaze into Christoph's enraptured eyes. But she was sure there had been no feigning in Eva's terror as she spoke of Graf Günther. Someday she would have to sit down and talk with Eva about the Order, or else ask Father Etienne to do it. But now there was no time: there was only the problem of keeping Wolfram safe.

Margerite awoke curled about her belly on the morning of Wednesday, Walburga's Eve, gasping as the rushing tightness that had come over it in her sleep gradually eased. The gray light of dawn was already filtering in through the windows; Rose stood bent over the stove, blowing up the fire from last night's coals into a steady flame.

"Fetch Gerhild," she commanded. "I think I am beginning to give birth."

The lanky girl ran from the room; a few moments later, Gerhild came in, blinking the sleep from her eyes.

"Have your waters broken?"

Margerite felt between her legs, but the bed was dry. "Not yet."

Gerhild drew the covers aside, laying her hand on Margerite's belly for a few moments before glancing between her legs. "I think that you are likely only starting a false labour, though it may give way to true at any time. Rose, get the birthing bed and the cradle up here, and be sure that the room is warm; and if you can find that cat to bring in, so much the better."

"And when you have done that, fetch me parchment, quill, and ink," Margerite added.

Soon enough, Rose and Gerhild had a straw mattress rolled out in the far corner of the room beneath the arrow-slits and covered with old woolen blankets, and a wooden cradle, thickly padded with blankets, near its foot. "You need not lie down yet," Gerhild said. "In fact, it is better for you to walk around a little. And you should eat lightly, since you may not be able to eat for some time and you will need all your strength. Rose, bring up some milk and cheese and bread for the Gräfin."

When the serving maid got back with her food, Margerite ate and drank gratefully as Kriemhilt and Kobolt sat by her chair, begging with their paws on her legs. Kriemhilt soon sat back on her haunches, looking very much like a dancing bear with her swollen belly beneath her dainty head and paws, and Margerite felt that she had to offer the cats bits of her cheese, though she drank all the fresh warm milk herself.

Another contraction tightened her womb while she ate: it was not really painful yet, but it was a strange feeling, to have her innards straining so without her willing it.

"False labour," Gerhild said, a pleased tone in her rich voice. "As I said, this may turn to true labour at any time; or it may be a day or more before you start giving birth."

Margerite drank down the last of her milk, licking the creamy drops from the rim of her goblet. Her desperate hunger assuaged, she picked up the writing materials Rose had brought. She did not bother to tell either of the Tiefensee women to leave, for she was sure they could not read.

Father Etienne, she wrote, my labour is starting, though the midwife thinks it may be some time yet. Please stay close, and be ready to come in at need. Christoph knows that he may be planning something, though not what, but he is willing to fight. I would feel easier if Bertram and Paul and Jochanan were close enough to call on if we needed them.

Margerite held the quill poised above her parchment for a moment, staring at the glistening black smear of ink on its tip. She did not know what else she wanted to write: she felt that there was something she ought to say, but it seemed too large for her to put words to, pressing about her like the weight of the damp air.

Gerhild stood looking out the window, a faintly distracted look on her triangular face. She pushed back her heavy hair with both hands, and Margerite noticed that there was already a light sheen of sweat on her wide brow. "I wonder if there will be a thunderstorm today," she said. "If I were at home, I would be hurrying to put damp cloths over all the milk to keep it from turning."

"There may be." Margerite looked at her hasty letter again, blowing on it to dry the ink. As soon as she could, she folded it and handed it to Gerhild. "Take this to Father Etienne. But if you see Richard or any of Günther's men on the way, do not, for the love of Christ, let them know that I sent you to him."

Gerhild looked curiously at her. "Why should a woman facing childbirth not wish to see a priest? Why should you have to send him a secret message, as if he were your lover?"

"Please, just do it," Margerite said. She knew she ought to take a more lofty tone with the midwife, but she did not have the strength for giving orders. And soon she would be helpless in Gerhild's hands, trusting entirely in the midwife to bring her and her child safely through: it was no time to make a show of reminding her who was the Gräfin and who the peasant. Gerhild shook her head dubiously, but she left the room with the precious message, and came back shortly after to confirm that she had delivered it without trouble.

The contractions of Margerite's false labour went on all day. She tried to embroider, but her hands would not stay steady; a twinge would shudder through her body, and her needle would stab down in the wrong place. After a while, she gave it up, and decided to risk making the journey down to the library for a book, since neither Gerhild or Rose would be able to find what she wanted.

Richard met her at the door of the library, courteously offering her his arm. "Are you well this day, Frowe Gräfin?" he asked anxiously. "Graf Günther says that the Child should come tonight."

Margerite was ready to lie to him, to claim she was nowhere near giving birth yet, but her body betrayed her, another contraction rippling visibly beneath the green brocade stretched over her taut belly. A look as if of holy joy transfigured the Englishman's freckled face, and the moment the door closed behind him, he dropped to his knees before her. "This is the night," he breathed. "How honoured I am to be allowed to serve you now."

Appalled and embarassed, Margerite waited until Richard had gotten up again. "Get Parzival down for me. I cannot reach high enough."

Richard's hands were shaking as he gave her the book, as though he were actually afraid to touch her skin. For a moment Margerite felt a cruel impulse to recite the words of the Order's teachings back at him: if it would suffice to make him restrain himself, she would be more than pleased. But there was something in the heavy air that made her hold her tongue, a sort of prickling fear, as if she were in the woods at night and could sense the hidden wolves watching her from behind every tree.

The Englishman accompanied Margerite back to her room. She thought he would try to come in, but Gerhild fixed him with the look of one who had seen every foolish thing that a man could do when a woman was birthing, and would have none of it. Richard retreated hastily.

"I am going to bring Graf Günther the joyous news, but then I will be waiting out here if you need me, Frowe Gräfin," he said.

Gerhild closed the door in his face. "Do not fear, Frowe Gräfin. I shall keep any visitors outside until you are ready to see them yourself - priests, Grafs, and pushy Englishmen alike."

Margerite sat down again, shifting uncomfortably in her chair. It was too hot in the room, and muggy: she could feel the little strands of hair escaping from her braid to plaster themselves to her sweaty forehead. Rose had opened the arrowslits in hopes of a little breeze, but the air lay as still outside as in. There were no clouds to be seen yet, only a faint haze dulling the brightness of the sky. Kriemhilt yowled, prowling restlessly from bed to birthing bed and back, lying down and getting up again as though she could not sit still.

"It will not be long for her either," Gerhild promised. "See, she is looking for a safe dark place to have her kittens. Perhaps it would be best to toss Kobolt out now."

"No!" Margerite said. Kobolt could not fit in her lap now, but he stood up to paw at her, butting his head against her leg as if to promise that he would not leave her. She settled back down, opening her book and trying to read. But the pages had fallen open at Herzeloyde's lament for the fallen father of the child Parzival in her womb.

'Woe, where is my beloved?...
The wide joy of my heart
was Gahmuret in every part,
His battle-love stole him from me.
Though far younger I than he,
Now I am wife and mother both:
I bear in me his body's troth,
His precious seed, the same
He gave me beneath the name
Of love shared by us two.
O, if God will be true,
He will let it fruit within me!'

Margerite shut the book. "Help me off with my dress," she said. "I will not go out again today. "

By sunset, the clouds were mounting heavy in the darkening eastern sky, and the first gusts of wind were starting to blow, the pines rippling over the mountaintop like black water. Gerhild stood up and closed the shutters over the arrow-slits. "It will be raining soon," she said. "See!" A low flicker of lightning glimmered eerily red through the deep purple clouds, but the storm was still too far away for Margerite to hear the thunder.

Although she had been careful to keep using the chamberpot, lest one of the tightening contraction force her to soil herself, when a sharper twinge went through Margerite's body, it was followed almost at once by the hot feeling of liquid running down her leg and soaking into her shift. She stood up, looking down to see the pinkish tinge of her water against the white linen.

"Now it is beginning," Gerhild said, almost joyously. "Take off your shift and lie down on the bed. There is still no telling how long it will take, for I have seen everything from a baby coming after the water in less time than her mother needed to say an Ave to three days between the breaking and the birth."

The next contractions left Margerite gasping and breathless, their pain gripping hard into her body. Gerhild gently felt her belly, then looked between her legs. "Breathe deeply, and try to ease yourself," the midwife advised. "You have hardly begun to open yet."

A knock sounded on the door. "Who is it and what do you want?" Gerhild shouted.

"Graf Günther von Hohenfels! I would speak with Gräfin Margerite."

"Graf, the Gräfin has begun labour. You will know soon enough when she is finished. Rose," she added more quietly,"if he tries to come in, lock the door. I do not know what may be going on in this castle, but I do know that no man disturbs my patients while they are birthing, not if he were the Kaiser himself."

Kobolt walked onto the straw mattress, his pink tongue coming out to lick his whiskers as he sniffed the air. He tried to push his head in between Margerite's thighs, but Gerhild lifted him firmly by the scruff of the neck, tossing him unceremoniously onto the floor. "Behave, cat, or we will throw you out as well," she threatened. "How is it with the other one?"

Kriemhilt was lying on Margerite's bed, purring loudly and kneading the covers with her paws. From time to time the black fur rippled across her wide stomach. Gerhild lifted her carefully, laying her on the birthing bed beside Margerite. "You hear how the cat is purring? She will give birth without pain or difficulty, and so will you. Sit up a little bit, and I will unbind your hair. " Margerite did as the midwife directed, comforted a little by the feeling of Gerhild's gentle hands stroking her sweaty head.

When Margerite's braid had been undone, Gerhild loosened her own, running her fingers through her long hair and tossing it back, then told Eva to do the same as she unfastened her belt. "There should be no knots in the chamber, for they might bind up your womb, and that is only good to prevent conception."

Margerite breathed deeply, concentrating hard on the exercises Richard had given her. The flow of energy circling through her body, easing and strengthening her muscles, driving back the pain...When the next contractions came, she felt them only as a striving tightness, forcing the struggling body of her child down within her.

Gerhild lit the candles, ordering Rose tersely to bring more in. A sudden gust of wind rattled the shutters, and lightning flickered through the darkening windows, but there was still no thunder.

There is no pain, Margerite told herself as another round of contractions racked her body. Only my child - only Wolfram. It seemed to her that she could almost see the child's life burning like a star within the darkness of her womb, his brightness surging more fiercely as the pain clenched down within her. "Time for you to be born, Wolfram," she crooned. "Come now, easily, easily." Only then remembering that the midwife was there, Margerite glanced up in embarassment.

But Gerhild was nodding and smiling. "It is well for you to talk to your babe now. It will take your mind from your pain, and mayhap help him come out more easily."

Kobolt pressed his body against Margerite's, trying once more to nuzzle between her legs, and Gerhild removed him again. "One more time, cat," she warned ominously.

Another tap sounded on the door. "Who is it this time?" the midwife shouted.

"Eva. May I come in? I heard Margerite's birthing has started."

"Come in, girl. You may be useful here."

Eva slipped through the door, closing it at once. Behind her, Margerite had seen a flash of black - Father Etienne? Or one of the Order members?

Sensibly, Eva had taken off her good brocade dress, putting on instead one of the garments she had worn as Margerite's maidservant. She hurried over to the straw birthing mattress, crouching down beside Margerite. "Are you all right? Is it bad yet?"

"Not yet," Margerite told her. "Who is out there?"

"Father Etienne, Graf Günther, and Richard are in front of your room. Christoph is waiting in the southern stairwell, and I believe Bertram, Paul, and Jochanan are very close by, so you have nothing to fear."

"I am taking care of her," Gerhild said, looming suddenly over the girl, "and she has nothing to fear, whatever those men do outside. Keep that in mind when your time comes, Eva."

When the waves of contractions began to rack her body in earnest, Margerite stared at the flame of the candle beside her head - the pure blue core inside the yellow flame, the reddish halo of shimmering light around it, radiating out through the darkness. It had burned more than a quarter of the way down, fat golden droplets running down its side to spread and harden on the silver dish of the candleholder. In the dark above it, the white flashes of lightning leapt, their jagged stitching distorted by the window's small leaded panes of rippling glass.

The thunder was rumbling almost constantly now, a deep moan beneath Margerite's own laboured breaths; wild gusts of wind swept the heavy raindrops to rattle like hail against the windowsill. The wooden shutters were beating back and forth on their hinges like fettered wings in the wind, their uneven clattering tormenting her.

Margerite's ears rang with the strain of each convulsion, her pulse hammering hard against her temples, loud as galloping hooves. It seemed to her that a hunting horn was echoing just beyond her hearing; that she heard the rough uneven bursts of barking from the hounds, and the sweat was pouring down her face as though the storm were bursting over her. Is this what the doe feels, when the dogs have her near to bay? she thought wildly.

The pain in Margerite's womb was growing worse now, a tearing like claws ripping at her, like horns stabbing her from within. She was not yet screaming, but she could hear her own hoarse grunts between her deafening bouts of panting. The only comfort she could feel was Kobolt's warm head pressing up against her thigh, his purr rumbling soft into her flesh; but distantly, Gerhild's voice said, "Take that cat and throw it out!" Margerite wanted to protest, to raise her arm and clasp Kobolt to her, but he was already gone. She threw back her head as the next contractions tore through her.

"Mother Maria," she gasped. "Blessed among women..." Margerite could barely feel Eva's hand in hers, gripping her fingers as she bore down again, and again. Then there was something warm between her legs, and a sweet herbal smell cutting across the stink of piss from the bedstraw: Gerhild was rubbing her gently with a cloth soaked in one of her hot decoctions.

"Easy, girl, easy," the midwife murmured, as if she were talking to a skittish horse. "Easy, you are opening well now."

Yet another contraction racked her body, and Margerite could no longer hold the pain in. She opened her mouth and screamed, the sound lost in the pounding of the thunder that boomed through her ears.

Father Etienne stood by Margerite's door, watching Graf Günther and Richard. Even with his back to the windows, he could see the glimmers of lightning; each flash cast a moment's bright shadow through the wide length of corridor, showing the two Order members' faces stark pale above the candles they held. Günther waited quietly, almost expressionless save for a slight smile; Richard shifted from foot to foot, his candleflame shivering as he moved.

All three of them had been there since sunset, listening to the muffled sounds within. Now it must be drawing near to midnight, and Margerite's grunts of pain were growing steadily louder and closer together. There: was that footsteps moving towards the door? Etienne shifted his weight fractionally, ready to plunge in. The door opened...just a little wider, and...Something large and black hurtled out with a loud yowl.

Richard yelled in surprise; Etienne leapt back, his narrow sword half-drawn from his sheath before he could calm himself. Günther's blade, fully out, glinted in the candlelight as well. The Kobolt sat down where he had landed, washing himself furiously as though to pretend he had chosen to come flying from the birthing chamber, then stood up, stretched, and walked over to sit beside the door.

Günther sheathed his sword with a muffled curse. Etienne was tempted to make a remark, but contented himself with smiling at the discomfited Order Prince. So, even you can be startled, he thought. I shall remember that. They all heard the scream clearly, echoing through the stone corridor above the sound of the wind howling outside and the rain beating against the windows. Günther's lips curved again in satisfaction.

"Not long now," he murmured.

Etienne did not respond. He wondered, as he had been wondering all night, what it was that the Light-Bearer meant to do. Günther must know that Etienne would do his best to reach the child and baptize it before any blasphemous rites could be performed. Would he dare to cut down the priest within Burg Falkenstein, in the sight of the midwife and the other women there? He might, but Etienne thought it unlikely: it was more probable that the Englishman would try to hold him back while Günther either dedicated the child to Lucifer on the spot or made off with it.

And in that case, Father Etienne thought, Günther would find that he had made a grievous mistake. The priest did not need to look towards the northern corridor, where Bertram waited in the darkness, hidden by the half-wall shielding that passage from view, with Paul and Jochanan at the top of the northern stairwell in case Günther got through and tried to make for Ruprecht's hidden chambers. Nor did he glance down the other way; but Christoph was just below the head of the western stairs, ready to charge out the moment any trouble began.

The one weak point in Etienne's plan, and the one that troubled him, was the chance that the Light-Bearers had some rite that could be carried out as swiftly as that of baptism, to seal a newborn's soul to Hell just as surely as baptism sealed it to Heaven. If that were so, Günther would undoubtedly carry it out now if he could, since he must know that Etienne would not leave him time for a longer ritual - or, of course, Günther would simply try to kill him to get him out of the way.

Etienne thought he should be able to hold Günther and Richard off long enough for his allies to join the fray, but he knew, well enough, how uncertain it was to base everything on such a chance. Margerite screamed again, a louder, hoarser cry. Lightning flashed harsh and white through the windows, the thunder hammering down less than a heartbeat later. Etienne waited, keeping his hand from his swordhilt by sheer strength of will.

The Kobolt miaowed loudly, standing up to his full height and rattling at the doorknob as if he meant to turn it with his paws. Etienne heard the second yowl as an echo of the first - but the cat's mouth was not open, and the cry went on. Etienne's hand was on the doorknob first, turning it to fling the door open. He never saw the blow that struck him, only the lightning bursting bright through his vision, followed by the great weight of the stone floor hammering into his back to knock his breath from him.

"Get out!" a woman screeched shrilly. Footsteps were pounding down the hall, hard beneath Günther's deeper voice shouting, "Out of my way, woman!" All the candles had gone out, but Etienne could hear the harsh grunts of Richard and someone else striving against each other in the darkness.

Desperately Etienne pushed himself up, grabbing the edge of the doorframe to steady himself. The midwife lay crumpled on the floor; Eva was standing, pale and terrified, between Günther and the cradle. Günther lifted his hand to strike her, but she had already bought Etienne just enough time. He drew his sword, lunging. The blade went in beneath Günther's left shoulderblade, driving straight through his body.

The Order Prince whirled, dragging the hilt from Father Etienne's hand. Günther's long face was white in death already, but, though he was beginning to stagger, he still had the strength to draw his sword, aiming a blow straight at Etienne's head. Etienne dodged, the breeze of its passing stroking his cheek, and leapt back from Günther's follow-up thrust.

Graf Günther stumbled, going to his knees. Blood gouted from his mouth, its blackness dripping from the point of his beard to the floor. He swung one last time, but his strike was wild, as though he could no longer see. Then he toppled slowly forward. Etienne could still hear his breathing, but he knew that Günther would not rise again.

The lightning and thunder struck almost at once, blinding and deafening in a single overwhelming crash. A cold wind gusted over Etienne; when he blinked the lightning's afterimage from his eyes, he saw that the candles in the room had all gone out. Grimacing, he felt about until he found one, then opened the stove and held it to a coal until it kindled.

The shutters of the arrow-slit above the cradle had blown open, a scattering of rain soaking the stones within. When Etienne looked down at the babe - a rumpled, ruddy mess, still streaked with blood and mucus, like every other newborn in the world - he saw that the storm had already wetted its head, the glistening drops of water trailing down through its pale wisps of hair.

For a moment, Father Etienne stood still, staring out the arrow-slit. Another jagged streak of lightning sliced through the clouds, and he looked away. To each man, the gods of his age, Meister Stefan had also said. You were born in the age of Christ and Satan, and it is with them that you must concern yourself: leave Wodan to those who were born to know him.

Etienne uncorked the phial of holy water that hung at his belt. Margerite was looking up at him from the bed, her eyes huge and dark in her pale face. She clutched the wet coverlet up beneath her chin to cover herself.

"Is he all right?" she asked, her voice hoarse and trembling. As if to answer her, Kobolt leapt onto the edge of the cradle, then leaned in to begin washing the child, who cried again beneath the touch of his rough tongue. Father Etienne glanced to confirm his first impression: yes, it was most certainly a boy.

"He is," Etienne said. "How shall I baptize him?"

"Wolfram von Falkenstein."

Father Etienne poured the holy water on the child's head, murmuring the ritual words. There would be a full ceremony later, in front of Heinrich and all the other folk who could fit in the Burg Falkenstein chapel, but this would suffice, at least to ease Margerite's heart. What it might do for the child, if there was any truth to the suspicions in his mind, would remain to be seen.

Bertram, Christoph, Paul, and Jochanan were crowding in now; the serving girl had Gerhild sitting up, but the midwife still seemed half-stunned, unable to do more than gesture feebly at them. "We got him!" Christoph said gleefully, then, seeing the corpse on the floor, "Well-done, Father!" There was blood on Bertram's tunic, but the dark cloth was untorn.

"Get the body in here before anyone sees it," Etienne told them. Bertram hauled Richard's limp form in, dropping it beside Günther's twisted body.

"What of the child?" Paul asked. "Is it well? Is Margerite all right?"

"We are both well," Margerite told him. Even sitting in the muck of her birthing-bed with only her fouled covers for decency, there was a certain frail dignity about the young woman.

"Here, I have something for you," said Jochanan, pushing closer to the bed. "It is aqua vitae, that I distilled myself." Etienne was about to warn Margerite, but she took the metal cup from Jochanan's hand, sipping and spluttering.

"It's strong," Paul said. "I should have warned you."

Although Father Etienne could tell that Margerite was trying to respond graciously to the mercenaries' congratulations, he could also see her eyes seeking out Bertram's. And, although the Hauptmann's face was shadowed, Etienne could read it plainly enough: his lips trembling on the verge of a smile, his brow furrowed with worry and pain. I wonder if he thinks the babe is his? Etienne thought.

He did not know if it would be better if Bertram could go to Margerite, to comfort her as the tremors of her birthing-agony ebbed from her flesh, or if it was best this way: if Bertram could not be a husband to her now, perhaps she would long for him less when she was wedded to Heinrich.

Suddenly Margerite winced again, the muscles of her delicate jaw clenching as if she were holding back a scream. Gerhild struggled to her feet. "Out," she said shakily. "All of you men, out. Her afterbirth is coming. Eva, leave those kittens and bring me more hot water."

The others hurried out as if Gerhild had threatened them with the hounds of Hell, but Father Etienne had one last duty to do. He knelt beside the two bodies with holy oil and holy water, drawing the Order rings from their fingers. For better or worse, neither man had gotten the chance to refuse the Last Rites, so Etienne could anoint them with a clean conscience and pray for their souls. Beneath Etienne's ministrations, Richard stared blankly at the ceiling until the priest closed his eyes, his young face slack with the relaxation of death.

The candlelight cast a golden sheen over the touch of oil on his freckled forehead; there was nothing to distinguish him from any youthful soldier who had fallen in battle. His zealous devotion had deserved a better cause: he had been a good servant to a bad master, though he had chosen that master himself. Günther's face was still frozen in a snarl, his limbs contorted in that strange death-rigor that sometimes came to men on the battlefield, with his sword locked in his clenched hand. Etienne gave him the rites with the same care he had given to Richard.

Of Günther, he knew less good and more evil: but the Graf had kept his word to Ruprecht at no little cost to himself; whatever his motives might have been, he had done good in breaking the siege and giving Margerite the chance to choose whether she would remarry or return to her father's house.

At the end - whether out of political sense, some last twinge of mercy, or simply the ingrained laws of chivalry overcoming his reason in the moment of crisis - when Günther might have killed Etienne, he had not drawn his sword; and for that reason, he had lost his life. These things, too, could not be set aside, nor would they be, when Günther came before the judgement of Christ.

"Christ have mercy on you, and on us all," Etienne whispered, getting painfully to his feet. He kept his back to the birthing-mattress, but he heard Margerite's low gasp behind him. On the bed, a black mass of kittens mewed and squirmed at Kriemhilt's side. Moved by an obscure impulse, Etienne stopped a moment to count them.

There were five, all lively and healthy, nuzzling and butting each other and rubbing their faces frantically over their mother's body in search of a teat. He put a finger down, gently touching the small golden mark on Kriemhilt's black forehead, and she looked up at him with a soft whirring chirp, as if to acknowledge his praise.

Outside, Paul, Jochanan, and Christoph were grinning like gargoyles in the candlelight, and even Bertram had managed an exhausted smile. "That is it done, then," Christoph said.

"We still have Günther's men to deal with," Father Etienne reminded him grimly. "Not to mention the problem of explaining to the world exactly how he came to die here, which I was hoping to avoid." He rubbed his chin where Günther had struck him. The priest's head still ached from the blow he had taken, and he could feel the deep bruise starting in his back, but at least his thick hair and the padding of his amice had protected his skull from the stone floor.

"If my father arrives in timely fashion, that will not be much of a problem," Christoph said, still grinning. "I told him exactly how many men Graf Günther had brought, and why he had brought them, as well as my plans for dealing with them. Some may be saddened, but I think no one will be unduly surprised when it turns out that the good Graf and his men were slaughtered and robbed by a large band of brigands a few days along their ride back from Burg Falkenstein. My father has plenty of soldiers who can be trusted to do as they are told and keep their mouths shut, as, I think, can the men of the Bear's Paw."

"Of course we can," Paul said enthusiastically.

"It only remains," Christoph went on, "to let Günther's men know that their lord is sleeping late after a hard night of rejoicing at the Gräfin's successful delivery, but that they are invited to drink as deeply as they like while they wait for him. Christ willing, my father should arrive before tomorrow afternoon, and then..." He made a throat-cutting gesture.

"Not badly planned," Father Etienne admitted. "But it leaves a great deal to chance, and I should like to talk about it further. Come to my chamber, all of you, and I will pour you some aqua vitae - which, I can assure you, is much different from what Jochanan distills. I am sure that a drop of warming medicinals will do us all good, and we should leave Margerite and her child in peace for the night."

After her afterbirth was delivered and the women had cleaned Margerite up, moving her to her own bed and transferring Kriemhilt and her brood to the blankets on the floor, Gerhild brought Wolfram over so that Margerite could put him to her breast. Washed clean of all the birthing fluids, he was a beautiful child, with bright blue eyes and a white-blond fuzz of hair over his pink skull.

His features were still red and crumpled from the birth, but Margerite could feel the strength in his little body as she held him, and a twinge of almost unendurable love went through her as he began to suckle vigorously at her nipple. Now that the birth was done and her babe safe in her arms, Margerite felt a rush of warmth drowning out the residual pain in her body. Although a glimmer of lightning still lit the window-panes now and then, the thunder rumbling softly behind, the worst of the storm had passed over.

"What shall we do with these?" Gerhild said. Margerite had to force herself to look away from Wolfram to where the midwife stood over the two dead bodies, thin nostrils narrowed in revulsion.

"Nothing, for now," Margerite said. Later she might share Gerhild's disgust; later the fear or horror might sweep over her, but now, nothing could penetrate the dreamy euphoria that seemed to be sinking into her very bones. "I think we can leave those matters to the men, for we have done our part. Eva, you were very brave to stand up to Graf Günther as you did."

Eva blinked up from the floor, where she was examining Kriemhilt's kittens again. "I could not let him touch your child," she said shakily.

"I thank you - more than you can know. Would you like to stand as godmother to Wolfram when we hold his christening in the chapel?"

"O yes, I should like that very much. Who will be his godfather, now that Günther is dead?"

"I had not thought of it," Margerite replied, surprised at herself. Perhaps she had hoped it would be Bertram, to give him some tie to the child that could be recognised by law and custom. But she would never be able to explain to Heinrich why a guard Hauptmann of unknown birth should be the one to carry out the important obligations of a godfather to the heir to Burg Falkenstein. "Probably Christoph, I suppose."

She yawned deeply, and realized that her eyes were beginning to close. Gerhild was at her side at once, taking Wolfram from her arms. The baby squalled angrily as the midwife carried him over to the cradle. "Hush, little one. You will have plenty of time to suckle at your mother's breast, Maria being kind to you both. Kobolt, this is a cradle, not a cat's bed: out." Gerhild picked up the cat with her free hand as she laid the child in, bringing Kobolt back to curl up purring beside Margerite. "Now sleep, for your body needs it. I have seen many worse birthings, but I do not think that you will be well too soon, and you need your strength for making Wolfram's milk. Here, drink this. " She brought Margerite a warm mug of something astringent, sweetened with honey. Obediently Margerite drained it to the last drop, then settled back with another yawn, sinking into sleep even as she closed her eyes.

Margerite awoke to the sound of a man's deep voice raised in argument. "Who are you to say I cannot see my betrothed? She has slept all day; why can she not wake now?"

Sleepily she raised her head from the pillow, craning her neck towards the door. Gerhild stood barring the way in; through the open doorway, Margerite could see Heinrich towering over the midwife. The bodies of Günther and Richard were no longer on the floor; the birthing-mattress had been carried out.

"Let him in," Margerite called. Hearing her voice, Wolfram began to cry. Gerhild left the door, swiftly bending over the cradle, and brought the child to Margerite. She drew down the corner of her blanket and began to give him suck.

Heinrich pulled up a chair and sat down by the bed, his massive figure seeming to fill the chamber. He was dressed in a long fur-edged tunic of deep red silk brocaded in gold, and his thick brown hair and beard were damp, as if he had freshly washed them. "Well, Margerite, you have slept through a great deal, but you have nothing to fear now. We have dealt with Günther's bodyguard: at the moment, they are in a wagon on their way to the mountains, where their bones will rest until someone finds them. They put up a lively fight, but my son warned me what to expect, and I had the help of your castle guard and your Bear's Paw Company - a good thing you let those mercenaries stay so long, though I would never have done it."

"So it is all over?" Margerite asked. It seemed to her that she did not know whether she had awakened from a dream, or fallen into one. The light through the windows was already beginning to redden: as Heinrich had said, she had slept all day.

"All but our wedding," he confirmed. "Let me see your child."

Margerite was reluctant to give Wolfram over to Heinrich, though she trusted - had to trust, for they would be at his mercy hereafter - that he would do the babe no harm. Wolfram started crying again as soon as she pulled him from her swollen nipple, but Heinrich had clearly held babies before: he cradled the child gently in his huge arms, rocking him until he calmed. "He is a fine babe," Heinrich rumbled. "The very image of his father, but I suppose that must be expected." Wolfram belched, a little bubble breaking from his mouth. Heinrich handed him quickly back to his mother, like a man who knew all too well what babies could do.

Margerite looked down at her child's face. Though her heart cried out to deny it, she knew that Heinrich was right: even blurred by a baby's softness, she could see Ruprecht's line of jaw and nose, the arch of his brow...and the penetrating brightness of his blue eyes, that she knew now would not darken to hazel as Wolfram grew older. It was Ruprecht's son, or...Margerite thrust the thought from her.

Günther and his man were dead, and Wolfram had been baptized: his soul was safe now.

"Well," Heinrich said, standing up and slapping his sword-scarred hands together briskly. "Your midwife says you will be well enough for the baby's christening in two or three days, and for our marriage within a month of your churching. That gives us plenty of time to arrange affairs here before we go back to Burg Fürstensee for the wedding."

Overwhelmed as she felt, Margerite's mind raced madly. An irrational fear came over her at the thought of going unmarried to Burg Fürstensee, where Nikolaus would be waiting; for reasons she could hardly explain to herself, she was certain that if the matter were not sealed at Burg Falkenstein, then something would go grievously amiss.

She drew herself up in the bed, looking at her betrothed as proudly as she could. "Heinrich, you came here to marry me, and I will not go from here a single woman. Father Etienne oversaw our truce, and I would have him oversee our wedding as well, to carry through what he began. We shall stay here for the forty days until my churching, that all the affairs here may be set in order, and then I may go with you with a clean heart."

Heinrich smiled, shaking his grizzled head. "Are you truly set on this? If we are wedded at Burg Fürstensee, there will be a finer chapel and a finer feast, and many nobles will come who would be less willing to make the ride here, even if this castle could put them all up as befitted their stations."

"Then let us arrange a feast for our arrival there as well, that your friends and allies may all come to know me. But I would have Ruprecht's folk see for themselves that the matter between us is finally resolved and sealed; and if we hold the wedding itself here in my son's castle, perhaps they will not feel so abandoned when Wolfram and I go off with you to your own keep."

"If you are resolved, I shall not press you further. Rest and get better, for I would have you in good health before we make our journey home." Heinrich bent down to kiss her, his damp beard bristly against her face, and then left, the heavy sound of his feet echoing down the hallway.

Like her wedding before, Margerite's wedding to Heinrich took place at the door of the Burg Falkenstein chapel, in a courtyard bedecked with the fresh green boughs and flowers of early June. Eva, flushed and proud with her new role as godmother, held the tightly swaddled Wolfram as Margerite and Heinrich spoke their wedding vows, with Christoph and three of Heinrich's knights standing beside them to witness; Father Etienne gave them his blessing, and the feast began.

If it was not quite as sumptuous as the feast before - for Heinrich, too, was still recovering from the aftermath of the war - no one seemed to notice or care: there was plenty of wine and good strong beer, and everyone was in a mood to rejoice. Even Margerite, as she looked at her new husband's deep-lined, bearded face and listened to his booming laughter, realized that if she was not overjoyed at being wedded to Heinrich, neither was she too downcast. From all Bertram and Etienne had said of him, she knew he was a decent man. Heinrich would protect Margerite, Wolfram, and Eva to the limits of his great strength, and, if he was not the charming courtier Ruprecht had been, he was at least friendly and of a good temper.

As for consummating the marriage, that would have to wait for a little while, since Gerhild had advised Margerite that she had not recovered well enough within to risk another pregnancy yet, but she did not think that when the time came it would be a task beyond her strength to bear; and if her husband could never spark in her the desire that Ruprecht had kindled - well, that was the least of Margerite's considerations now, with all her responsibilities to hand.

Paul and Jochanan were among the first to give the wedded couple their congratulations. With the Bear's Paw's pay in its coffers, they would be leaving the next morning, heading towards Freiburg to recruit new men and seek out further employment.

"But I think it will be nothing like this," Paul said, lifting his drinking-jack towards the castle in salute. Kobolt stood on his hind legs, pawing up at it, and Paul spilled a stream of brown ale out onto the earth for the cat, who lapped greedily at the frothy puddle. "I must thank you, Gräfin, for the most interesting job that has yet come my way."

"I hope we have served you well, Gräfin," Jochanan added politely.

Margerite smiled. "As if you were loyal." The three of them laughed together.

"Anyway, if you need us again, I am sure Bertram can find us," the Bear said. "We will always be glad to come when you call us."

"Whenever you want a war, we are ready," Jochanan chimed in.

Margerite blinked, running his words over in her mind, then laughed once more. "If Christ is kind, we shall have peace for a while," she answered. "But I hope that I shall see you again."

"Have no doubt of that, Gräfin," Jochanan assured her. There was an odd confidence in his voice: Margerite looked into the depths of his dark eyes for a moment, wondering if he were gifted with some foresight. But it was only his politeness and clumsy speech, she decided.

"God be with you, and good luck on your way," she wished them.

Margerite danced only the first dance, taking Wolfram back from Rose so that the serving girl could join in the merriment. As always, Bertram was not dancing, but stood watching. In the shadows of the fires, his straight-cut hair and beard looked like a helm and coif of black iron: he might have been standing sentry at some distant outpost, far away from the merriment and singing of the wedding feast. Margerite ached to reach out to him, to comfort him - to do something that could ease his troubled soul, and bring him closer to her. But there were too many people around, and she could not risk speaking so openly to him without good reason.

And would there be any more opportunity for herself and Bertram to be together in Burg Fürstensee? Had Margerite been foolish to ask him to come with her, to a place where they would have no chance to comfort each other, but only, in fleeting glances or brief exchanges of words, serve to stick the goads into the unhealed wounds of each other's longing?

Wolfram began to cry, and Margerite hastily started to gently joggle him up and down, crooning nonsense baby-words into his ear as she breathed in his sweet fresh scent. Whatever pain she and Bertram felt together was as nothing, Margerite realized, beside the need to keep her son safe from Nikolaus and his fellow Order members; if heartbreak was their penance for what they had done together, it could equally be made up by guarding Wolfram from the perils arrayed against his soul.

"Poor child, poor darling," Margerite murmured softly to her son. "Mary have mercy on us all, for that such dangers should befall a babe. " Then she could not help thinking of the Holy Family fleeing Herod's men; but was that blasphemy, to compare - Ruprecht's - son to the Christ-Child? Or were all babes, in their innocent helplessness, much the same?

Chapter Two

The sun shone bright through the green dappling of the leaves as Heinrich and his men rode from Burg Falkenstein. Margerite rode beside her new husband, while Eva and Rose stayed with Wolfram in the wagon; when Margerite grew tired, she would change places with Eva for a little while, but now it was a relief to be out in the fresh air with a horse beneath her again. Had things been otherwise, she thought rather sadly, it would have been a fine day to be out hawking, even with only a little sparrowhawk on her wrist, but her hawks travelled hooded in a second wagon under Johann's watchful eyes, safely out of Kobolt's reach. Too, she was sad at having to part with Father Etienne.

The canon had left that morning on his own duties, riding northward by himself - she had known all along that he could not accompany her, for he had many concerns that went beyond the small realms of Falkenstein and Fürstensee, and had spoken briefly and rather cryptically of a meeting with the Bishop of Hamburg; yet it seemed to Margerite that, with Father Etienne's departure, she had lost the strong wall at her back that protected her against a host of unknown dangers. And though Bertram was with them, he rode far behind, among Heinrich's guardsmen...

But she did not have long to dwell on her melancholy, for Heinrich was in a fine temper, his great laugh often booming out as he told her more of Burg Fürstensee. Christoph rode on Margerite's right side, and seemed as cheerful as his father; now and again, he would lift the arm that had been broken as if he were raising a shield, and it seemed to Margerite that thoughts of brave deeds in battles and tourneys were already in his mind.

"But you must be careful with that arm, for it has already been injured two times now, and bones that have broken in winter always take twice as long to heal," Margerite said absently to him.

Christoph started, turning to look at her. "Did I speak without knowing it? I thought..."

Belatedly, Margerite remembered the words of the Order book: Take care that your knowledge does not give you away as among the Wise; it is easy to let your pride seduce you to self-betrayal. Though her heart had already begun to race, she laughed lightly. "What else should I think, when a brave young knight riding out on a fine day moves his arms as if to couch a lance and raise a shield, especially when he has a new lady to fight for?"

Christoph smiled back at her, a light flush coming to his rounded cheeks. "Well, you have guessed my thoughts fairly, frowe - shall I call you Mother?"

At Margerite's left side, Heinrich's laugh rumbled out like thunder through the mountains. "Although you are a knight full-proven, boy, I can still thrash you for impertinence to my wife," the Graf threatened jovially, the grin beneath his thick grizzled beard taking the sting from his words. "You shall call Margerite the Gräfin when you speak of her, and address her with respect as Frowe Margerite."

Margerite was about to point out that Christoph had been calling her by her Christian name since he had come to the castle - but of course, her new role as his stepmother demanded at least a little show of respect.

Christoph did not seem much abashed; he replied jauntily, "As you wish, Father," and, after a short time, he was clearly playing out scenes of tourney in his mind again. Heinrich's gaze drifted over to his son, and he smiled.

"And there I see myself in my youth," Heinrich murmured to Margerite. The breeze had disheveled his graying hair, for the men wore no helms on this peaceful ride; now he stroked it back into place, considering Christoph. "You should know Christoph well enough by now; I believe you have yet to meet my younger son, Nikolaus?"

Margerite nodded. She could not bring herself to open her mouth and speak a falsehood to her new husband, though she was uncomfortably aware that deceit by omission was still deceit; still, there was no way she could mention the Order meeting in Freiburg to Heinrich. I will confess and do penance for it later, she thought. I wish Father Etienne could have come with me!

"Well," Heinrich went on, "Nikolaus is much like his brother in looks, but very different in temper. He is a quiet youth; not as strong a man of his hands as his brother, to be sure, and more cautious by nature - though he won his spurs bravely enough - but more learned. It is often our pleasure, of a winter night, to have him read to us. If I had more sons to help me, I should have sent Nikolaus off to a university before this, for he is always eager to travel and see new things, but in these times a man needs his kinsmen around him. Anyway, Nikolaus has told me that he looks forward to your arrival, and hopes that you will think of him as a devoted son."

"I am sure I shall," Margerite replied, though a faint shudder of revulsion went through her at the thought of dealing with Nikolaus again, as if, while cutting flowers in the herber, her fingers had inadvertently brushed over the cold slimy back of a slug.

It seemed to her, as well, that she could hear a faint hollow echo behind Heinrich's cheerfully booming words. Does he know what a viper he has managed to raise? she wondered. Or is it simply a father's doubts about a son whose interests are not his own, made stronger, perhaps, by the constant presence of another who is the very model of himself in his youth? The thought came to her that it would not be too difficult to probe farther into Heinrich's mind by the arts described in the Black Book - to find out all she wished to know of his thoughts through means of scrying in a steel mirror or polished crystal.

But what am I becoming, that I should think of doing such things? Margerite wondered, shocked at herself.

Heinrich's grizzled brows drew together, the lines on his forehead deepening. "Are you well, my wife? Something seems to be troubling you."

"I am only growing tired," Margerite excused herself. "I have not been on a horse for months, and I fear that I shall not walk easily tomorrow."

Heinrich laughed. "And undoubtedly I shall get the blame for that - no, do not be worried. We shall have plenty of time to consummate our marriage at Burg Fürstensee when you are fully recovered, as your midwife promised you should be by the beginning of July, and my passions do not burn as hotly as they did in my youth. If you are tired, you should go back to the wagon; no doubt Eva will be glad of the chance to ride beside Christoph for a while."

When Margerite climbed into the wagon, Wolfram was crying fretfully in Rose's arms; Kobolt, Kriemhilt, and their kittens were curled comfortably together in a basket of the serving-girl's wool. Margerite took her son away from the maidservant, pulling out a breast so that she could give him suck. The familiar warmth of his small mouth tugging at her nipple calmed her, clearing her mind.

Father Etienne had warned her that she would be tempted to use what she was learning; there was nothing strange in that, nor did it prove that she was any more evil by nature than any descendant of Adam and Eve. Mother Maria, grant me strength, Margerite prayed, as she often did, touching her garnet prayer-beads with one hand and holding Wolfram more closely to her with the other.

The sunlight was bright on Wolfram's golden hair, so that he seemed to shine with his own radiance; it almost seemed to Margerite, in that moment of stillness, that she could feel an echo of Maria's joy in nursing the Holy Child - the joy in which all mothers shared, that transcended and redeemed the curse of Eve even as Christ's death redeemed the sin of Adam. And as my blood is transformed to milk for you in my breasts, my son, may it feed you with every noble virtue that I possess, and strengthen you against your father's sins.

As Margerite thought that, Kobolt leapt up to balance on her knee, then stood on his hind legs with his paws braced on Wolfram's body and began to lick the child's ear industriously, purring all the while. Wolfram moved his head away from the rough touch; the nipple slipped from his mouth, and he began to wail, but Kobolt pursued his licking, as if he were holding one of Kriemhilt's offspring down to be washed.

"That is not your kitten, sir, and he is quite clean already," Margerite told him. She lifted the big cat down from her lap, but he sprang back up at once, nuzzling at Wolfram and butting his head against the child's face, then licking away the frothy dribble of milk that had run down Wolfram's chin before he settled himself along Margerite's thigh, kneading and purring.

"Are you not afraid to have that cat so close to the baby, frowe?" Rose asked timidly. The servant had braided her dark hair back for the journey, but curly wisps had already escaped to frame her triangular face in a tendrilled halo. "Was it not trying to suck his breath? I have been very careful to keep it away from his cradle, lest it do just that."

"Kobolt was only washing my son," Margerite replied. "I am sure that Wolfram has nothing to fear from him, any more than his own kittens do."

"Frowe, you are noble, and perhaps have not seen many cats at their own lives, but tomcats will eat kittens."

"Not this one," Margerite told her, adding belatedly, for Gerhilt had told her of Kobolt's depredations in Tiefensee, "at least, not his own kittens. Have you not seen how carefully he watches over Kriemhilt's brood?"

"It is hardly natural," Rose murmured, glancing towards the basket where Kriemhilt lay curled around the furry pile of her suckling children. "You know your cat better than I do, I am sure - but Aunt Gerhilt warned me to be careful when it was around the baby."

Something in the maidservant's voice pricked at Margerite's awareness, and she wondered darkly what else Gerhilt might have said to her niece about Kobolt. But that she could not ask without sounding suspicious, so she replied, calmly enough, "Well, there is no harm in being careful - especially when it is for my son's sake."

Margerite had sent word ahead that they would wish to stop at Burg Eichenwald for that night. She had done that with some trepidation, not knowing how much destruction Heinrich's forces had wrought on Ritter Sigmund's lands, but the knight had politely replied that they would be welcome, and that it would overjoy him to look on the face of the young Graf von Falkenstein.

As they passed beneath the shadow of the oak woods that gave the keep its name, crossing every so often over the cloven-hooved tracks of the wild swine that would thrive on the fallen acorns, Margerite could not help thinking on Ruprecht again: she remembered that he had promised Sigmund a fine hunt after the war was over, in payment for not being able to take him from the border last Midsummer's. Perhaps someday I, or Wolfram, will at least be able to make good on that debt, Margerite thought.

The man who rode out to greet them before the castle walls was in his late middle years, very fair and ruddy-cheeked, with a thick blond beard. He was not armed, save for the great sword at his side, but the fine cut of his green tunic with its dagged blue sleeves and the sparkle of silver rings on his fingers told Margerite that this was likely Ritter Sigmund himself.

"Hail and welcome to Burg Eichenwald, Gräfin," he called hoarsely. "Graf Heinrich, Herr Christoph, we are better met now than we were before."

"That is so," Heinrich replied, with a slight courteous bow from the back of his horse. "I would far rather be drinking wine within your stout walls than chewing hard bread outside them."

"Well, you are more welcome as a guest than you were as a foe, so come in! The board is laid to refresh you after your journey, and later tonight there will be a feast in honour of our young Graf and his mother."

Burg Eichenwald reminded Margerite very much of her childhood in Burg Hirschenfels; like her father's keep, it was small and dark, lit only by arrow-slits and smoky torches, with tallow candles in the great hall and the little guest-chambers. Ritter Sigmund's serving-folk hastened to tend to their guest's horses and bring in the baggage; Margerite left Rose to direct matters in the chamber where she and Heinrich would be sleeping.

Wolfram was awake, but quiet, as she carried him into Ritter Sigmund's hall, gazing bright-eyed about himself as though he knew already that this was part of his own domain. The tables were already set with bread and white rounds of fresh cheese; though the goblets arrayed upon the high table were dully-gleaming pewter, they were finely made and brimming with pale wine.

"To the young Graf Wolfram, and the fair Gräfin Margerite!" Sigmund said, seizing a goblet from the table and lifting it high, then draining it in a swallow. Heinrich and Christoph followed suit; Eva sipped more delicately. A serving-maid refilled the vessels from her pitcher, and they all sat save Sigmund, who knelt before Margerite and Wolfram.

"Gräfin," Sigmund declared loudly, his hoarse voice ringing from the stone walls, "I served Graf Ruprecht's father, and Graf Ruprecht after him, with all my heart and strength. Now I beg that you will accept my fealty for Graf Ruprecht's son, to whom I would offer my sword and loyalty, holding my lands from him as from his father and his father's father, and swear to that in Jesu's Name."

"I accept your oath for Wolfram, and swear in turn that he will protect you as a true overlord, ever mindful of your honour and well-being," Margerite replied. "Hold Burg Eichenwald and its lands well, as you have ever done, faithful knight!"

Sigmund stretched his hands up; before Margerite could clasp them, Wolfram's chubby little arm reached out of his blankets, his hand curling tightly about one of the knight's ringed fingers.

"He is a high lord from birth," Ritter Sigmund said, pale blue eyes widening in amazement. Margerite forced herself to smile. She thought that she should be delighted with her son, but though she knew it was not unnatural for a babe's eyes and clutching hands to be drawn to bright rings, yet there was something disturbing about his response, as if he understood far more than a month-old child should.

"He is his father's son," Margerite said, and even the draught of sweet wine she drank afterwards could not wash the ashy taste of those words from her mouth. If only it had been Bertram who had fathered her child...

But neither Sigmund, nor Heinrich, nor Christoph, seemed to notice that there was anything amiss in Margerite's thoughts; nor did any of them mark how her eyes flickered down the length of the hall to where Bertram sat with his head bent over his plate, silent and a little apart from Heinrich's guardsmen. And that was well: it had been easy enough to convince Heinrich, who had seen Bertram on the field, to add him to the Graf's own guard, but Margerite knew how careful she would have to be to keep from arousing any suspicions in her husband's mind.

At Margerite's side, Kobolt stood up to paw at her legs, reminding her that he was most fond of cheese. Slipping him a small piece to keep him from leaping on the table as he had been accustomed to do in Burg Falkenstein, Margerite glanced across the table just in time to see Eva's hand also dipping beneath its edge; Kriemhilt must have left her kittens to follow her mistress into the hall.

Ritter Sigmund's feast lasted late into the night; the roasted sheep from his kitchens was not exceptional, nor were the rather heavy meat pastries, but the knight made up for his hall's cooking by pouring out his drink freely. Margerite left for bed, pleading tiredness from the journey, long before Heinrich did; but by that time she had heard Ritter Sigmund retell how the young Graf Wolfram had clasped his hand to seal his oath at least three times, the story growing more intricate with each pitcher of wine.

At least, to her great relief, Sigmund appeared to hold no grudge against Heinrich for besieging his castle and stripping his village. Indeed, since Heinrich had not burned the houses, destroyed the fields, or barked the fruit trees - as, Margerite gathered, Ruprecht had done on some of his raids into Heinrich's territory - Sigmund seemed to regard the Graf as a chivalrous opponent with whom it was an equal honour to fight or feast.

For a moment, as she bent over Wolfram's cradle to listen to his soft breathing, Margerite felt a brief stab of envy for the knight: if only her own thoughts could be so simply laid out, with loyalty, honour, and right set so clearly before her! But in two days' time, she would be under the eyes of the Order again; although the ring Nikolaus had worn last year showed him to be of the same level as her own ostensible rank, she knew better than to underestimate the young man, and had no doubts that he would be watching her carefully.

"Is all well, frowe?" Rose enquired as she helped Margerite to undress. "You seem very quiet this evening."

"It is late, and I am tired," Margerite answered. "I wish that I had thought to ask Gerhilt for some salve, for I expect to be sore tomorrow."

A swift smile passed across Rose's thin lips. "My aunt sent a pot of salve with me. She said to me, 'The Frowe Gräfin has ridden only once since the siege began, and she has a long journey ahead of her; do you make sure that she rubs this well into her legs every evening and morning, or she will have a harder time on the way than she will like.'"

"Your aunt is a wise woman," Margerite said gratefully;
the deep ache in her thighs had already begun, and she knew
that she would stiffen further with sleep. The soothing scents
of chammomile and mint rose around her as she massaged
the waxy paste into her muscles, easing and calming her; she
thought briefly that perhaps she should have drunk more
of Ritter Sigmund's good wine as well, but the morning
would be painful enough without a headache to go with the
stiffness of riding.

Still, even with the herbal salve soothing her body and
Kobolt curled warm on the pillow beside her, Margerite
found that sleep was not coming easily to her. The thought
of Nikolaus waiting for her at Burg Fürstensee disturbed
her deeply: she knew that he would not be as deferential as
poor Richard had been, and she no longer had the excuse of
her pregnancy to keep her from being compelled to perform
Order rites or betray her deception.

And...did Nikolaus know what the Order's plans for
Wolfram had been? That troubled her most of all: if he
did, she might be able to claim that Günther's sacrilegous
baptism had taken place already, but could Nikolaus divine
that Wolfram's soul had not been sealed to Hell, but to
Heaven? And what other rites would they want performed
upon Wolfram as he grew?

If only I knew...Margerite thought. And then the
temptation came to her: could she not take wing from her
body, as she had done at Ruprecht's behest, to seek after
Nikolaus and see what she could learn? Her flight in itself,
Father Etienne had told her, was not forbidden magic, but
an inborn talent with which God had gifted her; it might be
wrong to spy on the mind of a friend or stranger, but what of
a foe? And - this thought decided her - she had already done
worse things for Wolfram's safety.

Margerite lay back in her bed, breathing deeply to a carefully-counted rhythm...as she had learned from the Black Book...no, best not to think of that...until she could feel nothing but the rushing of her breath and the blood coursing through her body in a glowing network of life. Slowly, as she concentrated, she could feel the brightness of her soul gathering away from her dark flesh, its passage eased by the steady hum of Kobolt's purring. She remembered how it had felt to spread her wings...to leap upward...

And then she was flying, circling up over Burg Eichenwald. Although the moon was down, she could see the castle clearly, the sharp edges of its stones and the wooden buildings thrown up around it like a cluster of mushrooms at the foot of a tree-stump. Her falcon-heart leapt within her as the air rushed through her feathers; she had been mewed up too long, and now she was dizzy with the taste of the free wind that bore her up, with the strength of her wings and the startlingly clear sight that showed her each ripple in the shimmering river flowing between the lands of the Grafs of Falkenstein and Fürstensee, each mouse's rustle in the grass below and every fine-tufted feather of the owl that glided silently below her.

For a few moments, Margerite forgot entirely who she was and what she meant to do; it was enough to glory in her flight, free even of the jesses that had bound her before, when she flew at Ruprecht's will. But far below, she heard the faint sharp sound of a cat's miaow; and that was strange enough to her falcon-ears to prick her back into awareness.

Margerite flew straight and swift, the stars sweeping past above her in trails of white cold fire and the ground blurring beneath - over the crags and woodlands, over the broad lake whose black ripples glimmered faintly in the starlight, to the great square tower on the mountainside above the lake's shore. She circled high above the large keep, seeking out light in window or arrow-slit: where would Nikolaus be? Chambered near the top of the tower, surely; at this hour, he would either be in bed or working on some Order ritual. And if he slept - could she enter his dreams?

She saw none of the shimmering that had hidden
Ruprecht's sanctum from her at Burg Falkenstein - save for
one single vein that ran, its shining blackness glinting with
flecks of phantom fire, far below the castle's crag and into
the lake. But her sight could not pierce the stone to see what
lay under the mountain; she could only see the single candle
gleaming through a small window halfway up the square
tower. Folding her wings, she plummeted as if she were
stooping on a partridge, sweeping up again to hover by the
window.

Nikolaus sat within, the candle-flame casting a ruddy light
on the thick slabs of his cheeks and his pouting mouth. The
Order ring on his finger was gold now, rather than silver,
but bore no stone. Across from him was a thinner, darker
figure, on whose hand gleamed a dark onyx - Damiano, clad
in fashionably cut black and red velvet; though Margerite
had not seen him for more than a year, she recognised
the Italian's pleasant face and quizzically down-slanting
eyebrows at once. A half-empty glass decanter of deep red
wine stood on the table between the two men, and they
sipped from silver goblets as they spoke.

"Answer me this, then," Damiano was saying. "Why do you
think the Order should care about Prince Günther, if he was
too weak to keep himself alive? The Christians may seek for
lost sheep; we devour them when we find them."

"It still seems suspicious to me," Nikolaus insisted
doggedly. "For my father to march on Burg Falkenstein with
his men so swiftly...I should think the Order would care
about the Prince perhaps being entrapped and murdered."

"And what do you know about it?" Damiano asked, his
light voice suddenly arrogant and almost belligerent.

"You are only a Monsignor; it is not for you to meddle in higher strategies. What you say tells us that Prince Günther lived long enough to carry out his plans for Walpurgisnacht; if he failed afterwards, it hardly matters, save that the Order has no use for leaders who let themselves be tricked, nor will it risk its long-term plans for a futile revenge. You had best concentrate on doing your own duties as I give them to you, if you wish to gain the strength to summon demons and wear the onyx ring - I assure you that it is a long step from simple blood-shedding and mastering elemental spirits to dealing with the Counts and Dukes of Hell."

Nikolaus glowered, his gray-green eyes pale in the candlelight as he looked up at his Order superior. "Tell me my duties, then."

"You are to undertake the basics of Priestess Margerite's training, and see to it that neither she nor her child comes to any harm through it. Help her to find a fit place for a sanctum and obtain the materials she will need; watch her progress carefully, and treat her with the greatest respect. She will undoubtely surpass you before long - and, need I remind you, this will serve as a lesson for you as well, for if you are too arrogant to realize when you have been outdone, the first demon you summon is likely to rend you body and soul. Report back to me regularly on her progress."

"I know that she is talented, but why should I take so much care for her child? If he dies, my family will inherit Burg Falkenstein through Margerite, and I will be able to wield power there as well as here."

Damiano's blue eyes narrowed. "You are not to question these orders; they come from the Imperator himself! I shall hold you personally responsible if any ill befalls Ruprecht's son, do you understand? The Imperator feels that the child's life is far more valuable than your own, and you are expected not only to watch over him, but to die for him if you must. Do you understand?"

"I understand," Nikolaus mumbled. "I could carry out my duties better if I knew why, though."

"You know all you need to know to fulfill your purpose. I shall have other orders for you presently concerning Margerite and her child, but until then, you are simply to teach and protect."

"As the Order wills it," Nikolaus said resignedly. "I will do that."

"Silence!" Damiano said suddenly. The Order canon tilted his head to the side, looking at the window; his pupils seemed to swell in the dim light, his gaze unfocusing. A shock ran through Margerite's falcon-shape, sparking painfully at the tips of her feathers. Not waiting to find out what Damiano was doing, Margerite hammered the air with her wings, speeding away at full tilt, and did not pause until she had swept through the insubstantial veil of Burg Eichenwald's stone and into her own flesh again.

Margerite started into wakefulness, dragging air into her lungs in harsh, frantic breaths through clenched teeth, her heart thudding painfully against her ribs. Kobolt was sitting on her chest, his weight a dull ache in her milk-swollen breasts; beside her, Heinrich was snoring so loudly that she could not hear her own furious panting. Clammy sweat poured off her, soaking into her bedclothes, and her whole body was shaking.

"Maria, Maria," she whispered. "Forgive me, Mother Maria, and protect me from the darkness."

Gradually Margerite's shaking eased, diminishing to small tremors shivering through her muscles. She felt as though she had slipped on the edge of a precipice, and missed plunging to her death by less than a finger's breadth. At that moment, she would have given anything if it had been Bertram in the bed beside her instead of Heinrich - if she could have woken her lover and clung to him, even if she were too ashamed to admit to him what she had done.

For some time Margerite lay there, not daring to move until Kobolt rose to his feet and padded heavily up to lick the rivulets of sweat from her face. The rasp of his tongue on her skin was too harsh to bear, and she feebly lifted a hand to push him away. Was that worth it? Margerite asked herself.

But she knew, deep down - beneath the faint trembling still echoing in her limbs, beneath the slowing beat of her panicked heart - that she would do the same again if she had to. Now, at any rate, she knew that Nikolaus would be no threat to Wolfram for a little while; and forewarned with certainty of what she had already suspected, that he would expect her to perform Order magic, she knew that she could delay him for a while.

It took time to ready a sanctum; time to order silk and sew robes, to cut a wand and bind it in rings of the seven planetary metals...even though Nikolaus had been instructed to find her materials, there were enough things that Margerite would have to do for herself to keep him from pressing her too quickly into any rite that would endanger her soul. At least, no more than I have done already.

She did not know how narrow her escape from Damiano had truly been - whether he had seen her clearly, how grievously he could have harmed her - but until she saw Father Etienne again and could ask about it, Margerite considered that she had gotten a valuable warning about using her gift of flight to spy on Order members. Father Etienne might have told me, she said to herself aggrievedly, though to that she had to reply, Perhaps Father Etienne never thought you would do anything so foolish.

Yet now Margerite had to admit that the priest's warning about the temptations provided by knowledge of magic had been better-targeted than she had believed; perhaps it was as likely that he had expected something like this, and chosen to let her find out the dangers on her own. And if that is so, and he let me risk myself unguided, how does he differ from the lords of the Light-Bearers? But Margerite knew the answer to that already.

Father Etienne protected the innocent, and guided his flock towards compassion. She herself, though - was no longer among the innocent, nor had been from the moment she volunteered to take on the task of deceiving the Order. Now it seemed to her that she understood some of Bertram's pain, which before she had only sorrowed for: the feeling of sin leading to sin, of a quagmire drawing her down faster the more she struggled against it.

Though his path had been that of the sword and the Free Companies, while hers seemed to lead further and further into this dark world of shadows and perilous knowledge, Margerite thought that in the end, the two roads might be very much the same.

But Bertram won through - or at least, to safer ground - and he was alone, where I have him, and the guidance Father Etienne gave me.

As she thought of that, Margerite remembered suddenly how the priest had advised her to pray for Kundry and Klingschor. She reached out in the darkness for her strand of garnet beads, and began a round of prayers for the souls of the Light-Bearer dead, who would surely need them more than any. Wolfram, Ruprecht, Richard, Günther, Kundry, and Klingschor: she prayed for them all, for the deceptions of Satan were many, but Christ's mercy was infinite.

After a little thought, she added prayers for Nikolaus, Damiano, and Berthold as well, who might yet repent while they lived; for Elsbeth, holding to her faith in spite of her husband - and for Bertram and herself, and even Father Etienne. For now, Margerite thought, she understood a little of the trials and temptations that the priest must face himself, that she was sure he had spoken of from experience.

By the time she had finished praying, Margerite's heart was quite calm. Though the sweat had dried on her face, the air seemed chillier; she did not think it would be long until dawn, but she closed her eyes, and slipped easily into sleep. The land grew steeper as they came closer to Burg Fürstensee, patches of oak and beech shining bright on the hills against the deep green pines, and rough gray crags rising above the woods.

After three days, Gerhilt's salve had worked wonders for Margerite, so that she was able to ride again with no more than a slight lingering stiffness; she was still a little tired from her working at Burg Eichenwald, but suffering no other ill effects. Heinrich had sent two men riding fast ahead to let his senseschal know that the Graf and his new wife would shortly be arriving, so that all would be ready for them when they got there.

Burg Fürstensee was just as Margerite had seen it in her dreams: a high square tower on the mountainside above a wide lake, with a long L-shaped wing extending from the main keep - Heinrich had told her that the original tower had been built by his great-great grandfather, and that the family had continued adding to it as their fortunes rose. "The square tower," he had said dismissively, "is too cold for comfortable living; we use it mostly for storage these days, though the smaller rooms on the upper floors can be warmed enough to do for guest-chambers for a little while, especially in the summer.

Nikolaus insisted on the middle floor of it because he wanted to be next to the library and have more room to himself, but the rest of us live in the eastern wing. I am sorry that I cannot offer you my first wife's chambers - Christoph took them over a few years ago because he needed the space - but I have had a very nice suite prepared for you near to my own, and of course if you prefer anywhere else in the castle, you have only to say so."

The approach to Burg Fürstensee led up a steep slope between two walls, turning sharply after the second gate to open into a wide outer bailey with wooden buildings around the walls. Margerite noticed, to her great relief, a large and well-kept church on the northern side of the enclosure.

"My grandfather built that church in fulfillment of a
vow to St. Martin," Heinrich told her when he marked her
looking at it. "The folk from the Fürstensee village come
here to worship. We have the finest stained-glass window
this side of Freiburg above the altar; even Kaiser Karl, when
he guested with us for a night twelve years ago, said that he
had seldom seen a better. Our priest, Monsignor Michael,
is a very learned man who studied in Avignon in his youth,
well-spoken at Mass and an entertaining conversationalist
at the dinner table. He is not at all adverse to a bit of hunting
and hawking when he has time to spare from his duties,
and I am sure he will be impressed with those fine birds you
brought with you. He does make a few priestly whines when
Christoph brings his goshawk on his wrist to Mass, but that
is more for the sake of form than anything; generally he is
a pleasant companion. Inside those gates by the church is
where the Monsignor and his curates and servants live and
keep their garden."

"And over there?" Margerite asked, gesturing towards the
largest of the buildings on the other side of the bailey.

"That is where I receive rents and taxes, hear cases, and
other such legal matters."

The inner bailey was guarded by a double set of gates
with only a short space between them and two towers: if
besiegers broke through into the outer bailey, they would
find themselves trapped there, vulnerable to arrows and
boiling oil or lead.

It was clear to Margerite that more wealth and thought
had gone into the building of Burg Fürstensee than into
Burg Falkenstein; now she could appreciate how much
difference the Bear's Paw and their guns had made in the
war against Heinrich, for Ruprecht had obviously gone to
great lengths to play down his rival's advantages of strength
and resources when he told Margerite about his battles.

Margerite did not dare glance back at Bertram, but it seemed to her that she could feel his mind cooly ticking over the strategic advantages of Burg Fürstensee: although Heinrich had, reasonably, been unwilling to give him a post of any importance before he could prove his loyalty, she did not doubt that it would not be long before the Graf was able to see his worth.

Within, there was a large enclosed herber to the left; a wooden fence hid much of it, but the flowering lindens that rose above the fence had been neatly trimmed and pruned into shape, their sweet breath wafting over the courtyard. To the right were a smaller stables and mews, and a long low building with armed men going in and out, clearly Heinrich's inner garrison; the L-shaped newer wing of the castle took up most of the northern and eastern walls, ending in the big tower at the southeast corner.

Wolfram was growing fretful from the journey, so Margerite sent him off with Rose to accompany the servants who would take her baggage to her chambers. Rose also carried the basket with Kriemhilt and her kittens, and, to Margerite's relief, Kobolt bounded after them. Heinrich's great hall was in the middle of the new wing, on the second floor.

Large glazed windows let in square shafts of summer sunlight to gleam off the polished and carven wood of his tables and chairs, sparkling off the silver plates and goblets that had been set out on the high table. Nikolaus was sitting there, together with a heavyset man of middle years in clerical robes of rich silk and a spry old man who bore a large ring of keys at his waist; as Heinrich, Margerite, Eva, and Christoph entered, all three of them rose to their feet and bowed.

"Welcome home, Father," Nikolaus said affably. "Greetings, Frowe Margerite. I am gladdened to see you; your presence brings light to Burg Fürstensee."

Beside Margerite, Heinrich smiled at his son's fair speech, but Christoph seemed to be steadfastly ignoring his brother as Nikolaus went on, "Allow me to present to you our priest, Monsignor Michael, and our seneschal, Herr Jakob. If there is anything you wish, you have only to inform Herr Jakob of it, and he will do his best to supply it."

Involuntarily, Margerite glanced at the hands of the two men. Neither of them wore an Order ring - but that could merely be for the sake of deception; to her horror, she realized that she would have to ask Nikolaus about the state of Order politics within the castle. Nevertheless, she smiled warmly, inclining her head towards the two men. "I am most pleased to meet you," she murmured.

"And we, you," Monsignor Michael replied. "I can assure you, we are all delighted to have a Gräfin in Burg Fürstensee again. I regret only that the Graf could not have waited on his wedding until bringing you here - still, the Apostle Paul tells us that it is better to marry than to burn, and at least a fitting celebration has been arranged for tomorrow, so that Heinrich's folk may rejoice in their Graf's good fortune."

Monsignor Michael's voice was a mellow baritone, with the cadences of one who had spent many hours preaching sermons to noblemen who expected to be pleased as well as enlightened.

The priest's black beard was neatly trimmed, black hair falling in a carefully combed sheet to his shoulders; his face had the comfortable roundness of a man who enjoyed good food, but Margerite could see the glitter of intelligence in his brown eyes. Friend or foe? she wondered. What does Nikolaus know about him? Heinrich introduced Eva as well, and they all sat down. A maidservant in a well-cut dress of blue wool came in to pour wine from a silver pitcher and serve little Friday pastries of fish finely chopped with thyme and sage, whose flaky crusts almost melted around their savoury insides. After the first pleasantries had been passed, Heinrich began to make pointed enquiries of Nikolaus as to how the castle's affairs had been run in his absence.

Margerite noticed how the young man's pale eyes grew more evasive, thick fingers playing with the golden dags on his sleeves and pointed toes rustling as he shifted his feet beneath the table. Although the grilling, in which it was clear that only Herr Jakob's help was saving Nikolaus from embarassment, was painful to watch, it also relieved Margerite: her first impression, that Heinrich neither liked nor trusted his second son a great deal, must have been correct.

At last Heinrich sighed, leaning back in his great oaken chair and brushing crumbs of pastry off his fingers. "You seem to have managed well enough without me, I suppose," he said. "But I have cautioned you before about dealing too hastily with the legal cases of our folk: the justice that God and the Kaiser have authorized us to give should not be tossed about with light hands. Even if it is only a matter of a sheep or a peasant girl's dowry, when you are holding my place for me, I expect you to give decisions as thoughtfully as I would."

This is a good man, Margerite thought. If I could not be wedded to Bertram...She turned her mind away from that swiftly: no good could come of considering what might have been.

After that, the conversation turned on to more pleasant topics. Heinrich had not lied when he said that Monsignor Michael was an enjoyable companion: the priest was widely versed in a range of subjects, and could speak well on all of them. Eva hardly joined in the talk at all, sitting quietly with her blue eyes wide and innocent, but Christoph's gaze hardly left her, and Margerite was quite sure that the girl was well aware of the impression she was making on both the young knight and his father, as a maiden both modest and beautiful.

When Nikolaus asked a couple of pointed questions about Eva's background, she only lowered her eyes and murmured that she had been raised in a convent. The Monsignor smiled at that, and Margerite thought that she saw a gleam of calculation in his gaze - thinking of what use she might have in Order rituals? Or merely considering a wedding for Christoph to make up for having been cheated of presiding at Heinrich's marriage?

At last it came to Margerite how she might be able to gauge the priest better and, perhaps, guess how much of an ally he might be. When the conversation had turned to people of note - a great many of whom Monsignor Michael seemed to have studied with, or spoken with, or eaten dinner with at some point in his life - Margerite asked casually, "Father, do you know Canon Etienne de Dion?"

Monsignor Michael's curved black brows drew down over his jutting nose for a moment; then his face cleared, and he smiled. "Ah, yes: the man who came to negotiate your truce. He was ordained a few years before I - but then he was sent away to some little town in the north; there was some sort of scandal about it, I understand. I hear his name now and again, but I have not seen him in person for some time."

"Scandal?" Heinrich rumbled.

The priest spread his thick-fingered hands in a gesture of practiced grace. "I do not know the details, but when a young priest of such good family is suddenly packed away to a parish in the hind end of nowhere, there is usually a scandal in the matter somewhere. Still, he seems to have risen well above it now...even," he added pointedly, "to performing your wedding, Graf."

Margerite watched Monsignor Michael carefully as he spoke, trying to detect some crack in his polished surface that might give her a hint to his true nature. If he were a Light-Bearer, he was remaining exceptionally well-hidden; but Father Etienne had warned her that the Order had its share of internal spies, and that many of them were unknown to the other members.

If he were an ally of Etienne's, he was doing a fine job of hiding it; but in that case, he would certainly know Nikolaus as a Light-Bearer - and think the same of herself, if Father Etienne had not had a chance to warn him otherwise. More than ever, she wished that she could talk to Bertram, for his comfort as much as for his counsel: it was a bitter irony, to realize that the role she had taken on to deceive her foes was certain to make her seem an enemy to her friends.

Heinrich only laughed at the sharpness in his priest's voice. "My wife insisted on being wedded before we left Burg Falkenstein, and even as a widower for many years, I have not forgotten how foolish it is to go against a woman's will in such things. I meant no slight to you, I assure you, Monsignor."

"As you please, Graf," the priest said, though his tone left Margerite suspecting that Heinrich would be a long time soothing the churchman's ruffled feathers.

Margerite's chambers were on the top floor of the new wing, down a long corridor from Eva's and only a short distance - across the corridor and through the door, then first door on the right - from Heinrich's. Christoph's rooms were beside his fathers; then came the tower entrance to the library, and Nikolaus' chambers after that. Heinrich and his sons, Margerite realized, had been in the library the first time she dreamed of flying to Burg Fürstensee. Margerite's rooms were luxuriously furnished, with tapestries in glowing colours hanging over the walls to take the chill of the stone off, thick rugs and brown bear-pelts on the floors.

The legs of the heavy oaken table in the second room were carved with eagle-talons grasping large spheres at their bases, and the wardrobe bore a fourfold scene of spring dancing, summer hunting, autumn harvesting, and winter hawking. Not only had the stove in the middle of her bedchamber been lit, so that it was as warm inside the room as it would be outdoors in full sunlight, but there was a wooden tub full of steaming water ready for her, scented sweetly with lavender and lady's bedstraw.

Rose sat on the bed, dangling the little brass crucifix around her neck for Wolfram to play with, and Kobolt was perched on the edge of the tub, scooping water up with one tufted paw as if he were fishing in a stream and then daintily licking it from his fur.

"I have put your clothes and belongings away already, Frowe Gräfin," Rose said hastily, as if to excuse her idleness. "What shall I lay out for your evening wear?"

"The blue silk, I think," Margerite answered. "It is likely that my husband's noble guests will begin arriving by nightfall, and I should look my best before them."

By the time the evening meal - a fine collection of fish broths, smoked eels, and baked trout basted with a pleasantly sharp verjuice sauce - was served, several of Heinrich's knights were already in attendance. Three of them, Ludwig, Gottfried, and Dieter, lived in the castle itself, overseeing the men-at-arms; the others held various keeps around Heinrich's lands, including the disputed Burg Düsterstein.

Ritter Friedrich von Düsterstein was a tall, pale man with graying hair; he watched Margerite nervously for some time before he spoke to her, and she gathered that he still was not easy in his mind about the outcome of the war. Margerite did her best to soothe his anxieties without actually ever mentioning Ruprecht or the summer fighting, but after a little time, she had to resign herself to the fact that it would be a while before Ritter Friedrich felt secure in Burg Düsterstein again - understandable enough, she told herself, since it had been the ostensible cause of the war.

The only true shock of the evening came after the food had been cleared away, while the company had begun to engage themselves in other pastimes: Heinrich playing chess with one of his knights as Monsignor Michael looked on, commenting volubly on the game; Eva stitching busily away with gold thread on a piece of deep red velvet as she chatted with Christopher and Ritter Ludwig; and some of the men playing games or arguing about hunting and hounds while others sat and listened to Heinrich's minstrels singing in the galley above the hall.

Margerite herself was content, after the strain of making conversation with strangers as she tried to match names to faces and Heinrich's introductions to the snippets of information she vaguely remembered hearing from last year's campaigns, to let herself be borne away on the rippling sounds of flute and lute, pipe and drum and the smooth soaring of the lead singer's high baritone voice. It was then, when she had begun to really enjoy herself, that Ritter Gottfried leaned over to Margerite and said, "What do you know about Bertram, and why did you bring him with you?"

Caught by surprise, Margerite stammered, "He, he was the Hauptmann of Ruprecht's castle guard. He was the best warrior at Burg Falkenstein, save perhaps for Ruprecht himself, and I wanted..."

"Not to leave him there, lest you find the castle had fallen from within while you were gone?" the hatchet-faced knight murmured grimly. He pushed back his dark hair with both hands, as if smoothing it down before he put on a helm; his gray eyes narrowed, staring dauntingly into Margerite's.

"No such thing." Margerite had to be careful to keep the true measure of her indignation out of her voice, lest it give away too much, but Bertram had suffered too much unjust suspicion in his life already. "Rather, I thought of him as a gift to my new husband: I learned enough of war in my father's keep to know the worth of such a warrior, who can not only give battle as the equal of a knight, but who can make village boys into soldiers and command strong men. And I wish, as well, for Bertram to remember that he is Wolfram's man before all, and for that, it seemed to me best that he should serve and teach my son as the child grows, rather than dealing with Wolfram first when he is already a man."

Ritter Gottfried rubbed the narrow point of his clean-shaven chin thoughtfully, eyes slitting almost closed in thought. "It may be so. Before God, you are right in judging Bertram's worth as a fighter; but it is that which gives me pause. Common men, Frowe Gräfin, do not learn to wield a sword and couch a lance from boyhood on. Have you a brother?"

Margerite shook her head.

"Then perhaps you have not seen how the education of a young nobleman, of which you will learn aplenty as your son grows, is carried out. I assure you, there is no knight who cannot recognise another of the same breed, whether he sees him ahorse or on foot. Those of noble blood inherit a firm seat and a strong grasp from their lineage: it is as impossible to make a peasant into a knight with a shield and sword as to dedicate with the Church's blessing on Easter morning goat flesh instead of lamb's meat. And I will tell you, as I have already told the Graf, that Bertram was born to wield sword and lance, and trained through his life as a knight, for all he tries to disguise it with brawling tricks when he shows his skill. Now it would much relieve my mind if I knew where he came from and why he tries so hard to pass himself off as a common man-at-arms, for it is my duty to see to Graf Heinrich's safety above all things - do you understand me, Frowe Gräfin? I do not mean to distress you, but I think that you must be warned, lest your trust in this man lead you - or Graf Heinrich - to some ill."

I could weave an enchantment, or brew a potion, to turn his mind away from these things... Margerite thought, then shook her head. Ritter Gottfried leaned closer to her, and it seemed to her that she could see the cold eagerness of the hunting lynx in his thin face, the grip of his fingers shifting upon his eating-dagger as if he were preparing to strike a blow with it and the wiry muscles of his shoulders bunching beneath the deep crimson silk of his tunic.

"What do you not understand?"

"I do not understand why you will not trust the judgement of your Gräfin. Although I am young, and a woman, I have already come through a war and its aftermath - you must have been at the siege of Burg Falkenstein yourself, and hence may guess at how truly Bertram proved his loyalty after Ruprecht's death. And before: for Ruprecht did not fear to leave him in command of Burg Falkenstein when the Graf himself was far away, and trusted him most particularly with my own safety. Good Ritter, though your loyalty to my husband does you credit, one does not need to know what mine pure gold came from when its worth has been assayed so closely." Margerite's own hands were shaking, and she could feel the hot tears welling up, about to crack the smoothness of her voice.

For Gottfried's suspicions were her fault: why had she, in her selfishness, forced Bertram to come with her, to this place where he must bear the burden of mistrust by Heinrich's men and where, she saw now, she would be hardly more able to comfort him than she would have had he remained behind at Burg Falkenstein? O my love, what have I done to you?

Ritter Gottfried's gray gaze did not waver: his eyes were like stones with a clear glaze of ice over them, and it seemed to Margerite that she could feel a dark chill flowing out of him. She glanced nervously down at his hands, but his sole adornment was a heavy gold seal-ring that seemed a little too large for his thin finger.

The knight reached for his collar, fishing out a small gold crucifix from beneath his tunic to gleam against the dark red silk. "Frowe Gräfin, this gold has a weight and a softness, a melting point and a breaking point that any smith can easily test; and the worth of that which it portrays, which is far beyond any earthly metal, can be seen by any with eyes, or even felt by a blind man. Men have no such simple measures: we may estimate and guess as best we may, but a clever mind may easily falsify all its tests, like a dishonest smith hiding lead benath gold foil, and only God can truly assay us, or see the shapes of our souls. Lacking His wisdom, I would be failing in my duty if I were not suspicious of a man such as Bertram, and did not caution you to be as well." His frozen eyes never left Margerite as he spoke, and she thought that she understood what else he was saying: she, as well, would be under Gottfried's untrusting scrutiny, and at the least hint that she and Bertram might be - conspiring, let alone anything closer - he would not hestitate to take action.

"I understand your caution, and thank you for your care," Margerite replied, as smoothly as she could. "It is well to know that Heinrich's knights are so vigilant for our safety - though I pray that your wariness will not keep you from ordering Bertram's talents effectively."

"As I see fit," Ritter Gottfried said.

Suddenly he started, eyes wide as he grasped for the hilt of his sword. He was half-standing before he collected himself and sat again. Margerite followed his gaze downward, and saw the gleam of Kobolt's eyes from the shadows beneath the table.

"What is wrong, Ritter Gottfried?" Margerite enquired kindly. Though she knew she should not, she could not help feeling a little wicked enjoyment at the severe knight's discomfiture.

"Some sort of wild animal seems to have crept in here; it put its paw on my leg, and startled me. Your pardon, Frowe Gräfin; it is not usual for such creatures to get into the great hall. I shall see to its removal." Gottfried's deep baritone voice sounded slightly shaken, and, no longer distracted by his cold stare, Margerite realized that he was younger than she had thought - perhaps in his early twenties, if even that old; very young to hold the position of the Hauptmann's second. No wonder he is so severe, she thought.

"You need not do that. He is my pet, and used to going where he will. I trust he did not claw you?"

"No." Gottfried was staring fixedly at Kobolt now, and the black cat returned his gaze. Slowly the knight reached downwards, stretching out a hand. Kobolt sniffed at his narrow fingertips, then butted his head against them with a soft chirping purr.

"He seems to like you," Margerite said. And what is Kobolt trying to tell me? Is this man to be an ally? He seems an unlikely friend.

Ritter Gottfried, still looking at Kobolt, did not reply for a long moment. Though it was no longer focused on her, his intense concentration disturbed Margerite; a sort of tingling shiver played over her skin, and she could feel every hair of her body stirring.

With another soft chirp, Kobolt leapt into the young knight's lap, settling himself comfortably. Gottfried's gaze softened to a sort of bemusement as he scratched behind Kobolt's ears. "A most unusual cat, Frowe Gräfin. I have never seen one so large or wild of appearance; is he some sort of lynx? Even apart from his size, he does not have the look of an ordinary cat."

"He has never told me his parentage," Margerite answered lightly, but the knight's words worried her. If Gottfried knew something of magic - then who had trained him, and which side was he on? She did not think that a Light-Bearer would speak as reverently as he did, yet one of their foes would have marked her ring, and would hardly be stroking her familiar's furry head.

If he knew nothing, his perceptiveness was yet more to worry about: did she not know herself how it was to sense that something was wrong, that something was happening just beyond her gaze, and how that sharpened the eyes and thoughts until every rustle of a mouse seemed suspicious? And if he is truly talented, she thought also, Nikolaus may be using him without his knowledge, even as Ruprecht used me. "But tell me more of yourself," Margerite went on. "How long have you served at Burg Fürstensee?"

"I was Knappe to Ritter Ludwig for two years, and have dwelt in this castle since. My father is the lord of Burg Schlangenbad, which my elder brother Joachim will hold after him, in fealty to Graf Heinrich; but it was his will that I take service at Burg Fürstensee." A slight hollow melancholy tinged Gottfried's voice as he spoke: did he envy his brother? Or was there something more behind his brief tale? Margerite's thoughts leapt involuntarily back to Father Michael's words about Etienne, and they stirred her own suspicions, but she could hardly press the knight any further in their first conversation.

Ill at ease as he seemed with her, Ritter Gottfried stayed until Kobolt rose and leapt from his lap, then took his own leave as well. By that time, Margerite's breasts were aching with the heaviness of their milk, and she feared that if she did not give suck soon, they would begin to leak and stain her good silk dress. Fortunately, it was late enough that she could bid a courteous goodnight to the company and return to her room, where Rose was rocking Wolfram in his cradle and singing softly to soothe his fretful whimpers.

Kobolt bounded across the room ahead of his mistress and leapt to the edge of the cradle; at once, Wolfram's cries changed to a happy gurgle as he grabbed for the black plume of the cat's tail. Rose reached out to take Kobolt away, but Margerite shook her head. "Leave him be. Come, help me undress."

Sitting by the heated stove in her loose shift, with Wolfram's warm weight in her arms and his mouth tugging eagerly at her nipple, Margerite felt herself growing calmer, yet she could not shift the realization that she had done ill by Bertram, nor could she see how to lift that wrong. She was certain that Ritter Gottfried at least halfway suspected her love for Bertram - and she had to admit to herself that somewhere in her heart, she had hoped to be with her lover again; to betray her marriage vows to Heinrich, and commit again the sin of which Father Etienne had absolved her. But the wedding is not consummated, something whispered deep in her heart. Until that is done, it would not really be adultery, only fornication...

And still a mortal sin, Margerite reminded herself firmly, though she could not help remembering how it had been to have Bertram's lips where Wolfram's were now, the soothing warmth of his skin against her shivering body and the firmness of his touch anchoring her against all the spinning horrors and doubts of the strange world Ruprecht had cast her into. But though she ached for him, she thought that if only she could speak with him, just hear his voice and look into his eyes for a few moments, it would be enough to strengthen her against whatever she would have to deal with here in Burg Fürstensee. If she could even know his thoughts...

If I used magic to touch him, he would turn away from me in horror, and I would deserve it. But there was no other way for a Gräfin to speak privately with a simple man-at-arms, let alone one who was under constant watch.

"Rose," Margerite said, the suddenness of her thought startling her. The serving-maid looked up from the cradle where she was changing Wolfram's bedding.

"Yes, frowe?"

"What do you think of Bertram?"

"Frowe, no one blames him for beheading Eckhardt," Rose answered quickly."We all know what Graf Ruprecht...was like, begging your pardon, frowe, and that there was nothing Bertram could do about it, any more than Hänsel and Peter could have refused to do the hangman's work. Bertram is a good man; my brother says that without the Hauptmann's training, he would surely have been killed fighting before the walls, and most commanders would not take such care to see that peasant boys could keep themselves alive."

"Would it trouble you greatly then...if folk thought you to be his sweetheart?" Margerite said in a rush. Wolfram's grip tightened upon her, as if in answer to the sudden flutter of her heart as she spoke; Rose's eyes widened.

"But everyone knows that Bertram does not care for women, and will hardly say good day if a maiden crosses his path and smiles at him. Many think that he took some wound in battle which makes him incapable, though my brother says, begging your pardon again, frowe, that he has seen Bertram watering the ground many times and his manhood is as whole as anyone's."

"Everyone at Burg Falkenstein knew it," Margerite corrected her, trying to turn her own mind away from the thoughts that Rose's words were bringing up - and from the memory of Gertrude giggling in much the same way about Jochanan's circumcision. "For all that folk here know, Bertram could have been swiving every woman in Tiefensee."

Rose laughed, a clear tinkling sound that nearly brought tears to Margerite's eyes: though Gertrude's soul, God willing, surely rested in heaven, her ghost was not as easily exorcised from Margerite's thoughts. "Surely most of us would choose handsomer men for our beds, though I will grant Bertram is much better looking since he pruned that thicket on his face. But why would you wish folk to think I am his sweetheart, frowe? Are you planning to marry me to him?"

"Of course not!" Margerite snapped, shocked by the red rush of anger rising from her belly at the thought. Wolfram opened his mouth and began to wail; Margerite rocked him gently in her arms, murmuring"Hush, hush," as she breathed deeply, trying to quiet herself as well as the baby.

By the time Wolfram was ready to take her nipple again, she was able to say calmly, "I want you to take messages to Bertram from time to time, for the men of this castle remember too clearly that he was their foe, and are likely to mistrust him for a time. While it is not my place to speak to Bertram, since he is not Hauptmann here, it is well to know that at least one man of the castle guard is wholly loyal to myself and Wolfram - do you understand?"

"Oh, yes, frowe. My aunt warned me that I must be very careful lest any accidents befall the young Graf, since if something happened to him, Burg Fürstensee and all its lands would belong to Heinrich and his family."

Margerite was taken aback by the bluntness of Rose's statement, but she did not deny it: she was certain that neither Heinrich nor Christoph would stoop to harming a child, and that - Maria help her! - the Order's rulings would protect Wolfram from Nikolaus, but she could not tell that to Rose. Instead she nodded gravely. "It is well that you keep this in mind. I shall write a letter to Bertram tonight, which you shall take to him tomorrow if you can. And when you go to him, be very careful to avoid Ritter Gottfried, for he is a very suspicious man, who I believe is likely to think the worst of anything he sees."

"I shall, frowe. What does he look like?"

"He is of middle height, very thin and sharp-faced, clean-shaven, with dark hair to his shoulders and gray eyes - and not much inclined to let courtesy interfere with his duties."

"I shall watch out for him," Rose promised.

When Wolfram had been burped and returned to his cradle, Margerite settled down to write her letter. She sat for a long time staring at the blank piece of parchment and the glistening black ink on the tip of the gray goose-quill. All the thoughts that had seemed so clear to her before were in turmoil; she could not bring any of them into words.

Did she dare to write, I love you? Or set either of their names to the parchment? A letter could so easily be lost or taken; it seemed too frail a scrap to bear the weight of what she wanted to say to Bertram. If I were truly an Order member, Margerite thought, I would not write this at all: the hope of comforting his heart a little is hardly worth the risk.

Bertram must know already that Gottfried mistrusts him, for the man makes no secret of it, and has clearly tested him hard already. What good can I do him, with a few words that must be circumspect enough not to betray our love if this letter falls into the wrong hands? But Margerite knew how even a glance from Bertram, or the sight of a faint smile for her beneath his beard, would soothe her own soul now.

The smallest sign, the least reassurance: it would be enough to keep hope from burning down into grim despair. And I owe it to him: I could not have stood so bravely to watch him marry another, whatever the need. The ink had gone dry on the quill's point. Margerite dipped it again, and began to write: *All is well with me. Be very careful.*

She thought a little longer. What more could she say? If she tried to tell Bertram of her regrets in asking him to come - would he leave? Margerite knew that he no more wished to bring her sorrow than she wished to cause sorrow for him; she could not tell him how his trial was breaking her heart. At last she added, The Marienbrunnen still flows.

Bertram would understand what that meant: their love, and Maria's mercy upon them, mingled like two streams rushing into a single river - and proof to him, and to herself, that the Order's snares had not yet captured her soul. After they had gone to bed, the serving maid was quickly snoring on her pallet in the corner, but tired as she was, Margerite found that Kobolt would not let her sleep. Every time she closed her eyes, the cat began to walk up and down on her body, each of his paws pressing heavy as a stone upon her.

"Are you warning me of something?" Margerite whispered to him. "What?"

Poised upon her belly, the cat stopped suddenly, and it seemed to Margerite as though she could hear the soft rustle of his ears moving in the darkness. Then she heard the low snick of a lock, and a thin glimmer of ruddy light shone along the edge of the door; at the same time, the Order ring upon her finger began to tingle as though she had touched the metal to a thrumming lutestring.

"Priestess," a man's voice hissed. "Arise, and come with me."

Nikolaus! Margerite thought, her body rigid with fright. But the words of the Order book came back to her: In every dealing, whether with men or spirits, the stronger shall be master, the weaker slave. If you would not be enslaved, learn to command, and demand respect even where you must obey a superior.

"Close that door," she whispered imperiously back to him."I must dress myself."

Nikolaus paused a moment, and Margerite was afraid that he would refuse; but she knew that she would not allow him to look upon her naked body. Then the glimmer of candlelight narrowed to blackness again. By touch, moving with deliberate slowness, she found her shift and pulled it over her head, wrapping a cloak around her before she stepped into the hall with Kobolt padding at her heels.

Nikolaus led her silently down the corridor. Even through the thick oaken doors, Margerite could hear Heinrich snoring like a saw cutting through iron, and was suddenly grateful that she had been chambered out of earshot of his bedroom.

Nikolaus' room was just as Margerite had seen it in her falcon-flight, even to the glass decanter of deep red wine and the two silver goblets upon the table. Nikolaus seated himself casually in one of the chairs, waving Margerite to the other. He lifted the decanter, pouring out a cup of wine for each of them. Although his stove was burning warmly, he was dressed as if for winter, in thick dark wool and velvet with high fur-lined boots, and the sweat was already springing out on his pallid forehead.

"Ex Tenebrae, Lux," Nikolaus said, raising his goblet and drinking deeply. Margerite repeated the salutation, though she barely let the wine wet her lips. Kobolt leapt upon the table and had his muzzle into the goblet at once, sneezing a spray of fine dark droplets and licking his whiskers before he began to lap at it. Nikolaus stared at the two of them, and Margerite could see the anger in his plump face, but he did not speak.

"Why have you brought me here?" Margerite asked, stroking the cat while he drank. Kobolt's back arched beneath her hand as she spoke, and she could feel the low thrum of his purr.

"I have received my orders concerning you," Nikolaus said. "It is my charge to teach you the ways of the Order and the practice of magic." He rose, taking a book, quill, and ink from one of his chests and setting them before Margerite. "This is to be your first grimoire; you will write in it all that I tell you, and never let another see or touch it, save at the will of a superior in the Order. You must begin by making your tools of magic and consecrating a sanctum in which you can carry out your workings without fear of discovery."

"And how am I to do that?" Margerite asked. "I can hardly keep my maidservant out of my chambers, nor can I ride out from the castle by myself whenever I please, as you can."

Nikolaus' small, pouting mouth curved into a smile, and his green-gray eyes glittered disturbingly. "Burg Fürstensee is an old castle, and has many secrets, known to only a few of the living. Count yourself privileged, Priestess: you are about to tread where only I and those other Order members who visit me know how to go. Take your grimoire and writing materials, and follow me."

He rose from his chair, opening the door at the far side of the room and stepping through. Margerite followed him down the oaken spiral staircase, through the second-floor room where the castle's valuables were stored, and into a room on the ground floor. The chamber was filled with neat stacks of armour and weapons, stinking of the rancid goose grease that glazed the iron against rust.

"This room is locked and guarded from without," Nikolaus said softly. "Only my father, my brother, our seneschal and the three knights of our castle whom you met this evening have keys to it; and none of them are likely to enter it late at night. But only I know this." He stepped over to the southern wall. "The fourth block up, the third over. Press on it, and..." Nikolaus pressed the stone hard.

Slowly, a section of the stonework swung away, showing a narrow staircase leading down into darkness. "When this tower was first built," he murmured softly, "my father's great-great grandfather had many foes, and knew that he might need to flee swiftly. There are many underground springs that feed the Fürstensee, and over the years, they have carved out tunnels and caves. Old Graf Walther hired a mason who was clever enough to build this hidden way down - and not clever enough to guess that death would be the only payment for his knowledge. But the dead can be made to tell what the living would never disclose."

Margerite was thankful that her cloak was thick enough to hide her shudder at Nikolaus' words. They frightened her twofold: for the awfulness of what the Graf's second son was boasting, and because, if Nikolaus had tried to summon and command the dead before he wore the gold Order ring - as he must have, if he had found his sanctum through a dead man's knowledge - he might well risk overstepping his strength again, and would be a danger to Wolfram. Nevertheless, she followed Nikolaus into the close passage hidden in the wall, watching carefully as he pushed the door shut.

"It is easily opened from this side," Nikolaus said. "But to reach it from the outside, one would have to know the way very well; someone who did not would be lost in the caves forever. Heed that well, Priestess, and do not come down here by yourself until you have learned where to go: a single wrong turning could easily lead to your death by drowning, or cold, or starvation, and I might not be able to find you, for some of the springs are salt, and the caves encrusted with it, so that it is difficult for divination to reach here - it makes a fine shield, but every weapon offers its own challenges."

The staircase ended in a small oblong cavern. Nikolaus' candlelight glimmered red from the trails of slimy water oozing down the walls, and as they walked, Nikolaus counting out each turning and landmark out loud, Margerite could feel small crystals grating beneath her soles like sand. Even through her thick cloak, the chill damp air of the cave was beginning to leech the heat from her body, and she hoped that Nikolaus would not keep her down here too long. Now she knew why he had dressed so unseasonably, and a small flame of anger began to warm her as she realized that, had she been more eager to obey his summons and less modest, she would be down here in nothing but her thin linen shift.

"Your ritual robes must be very warm," Margerite remarked, making no effort to keep the brittle edge from her voice. Nikolaus turned his head to smile at her.

"A layer of silk against my skin; wool above that, and a second robe of silk over the wool, are enough to both ward and warm me properly. You will undoubtedly want the same."

"As I should have, had you told me that we would be descending into the icy bowels of the earth."

Nikolaus' smile widened. "Consider this a lesson, Priestess. A Light-Bearer should be prepared for all things, as your studies should have taught you by now. Repeat the turnings to this point; I must be sure that you know them well."

To reach Nikolaus' sanctum, they had to walk bent over through low passages twice, and wade through one ankle-high stream. Margerite took her shoes off for that, her bare feet going numb at once as they touched the icy water: when she started to put the shoes back on after crossing, she found that a rock had gashed her sole slightly without her even feeling it. She could not help glancing enviously at Nikolaus' sturdy boots - he ought, from courtesy, to have offered them to her for this, although she was not sure that she did not prefer the clean water and sharp stones to the thought of wearing something that had been on Nikolaus' feet.

Though Margerite did not seen the cat cross the stream, Kobolt was already on the other side, dipping a paw into the water and licking it ostentatiously before he came over to sniff at the droplets of blood oozing slowly from her foot.

"Are you too hurt to go on?" Nikolaus asked, a mocking lilt in his words.

Margerite thrust her foot into her shoe and rose to her full height. "It is nothing. Continue, if you will." Her voice would have sounded stronger had her teeth not been chattering, but Nikolaus nodded as if in satisfaction - though Margerite would have sworn he had been hoping for her will to fail.

Three turnings later, Nikolaus stopped. "Down that passageway lies the cavern which will be best for your sanctum, I think. This way is mine. Never try to enter it without my permission, or you will not like what befalls you."

A black curtain hung from a narrow lip of rock at the entrance to Nikolaus' sanctum. The young magician pulled it aside, crouching down to get beneath the low stone overhang. The position looked undignified and vaguely obscene - but Margerite realized it was either that, or enter bowing with bended head, and did as Nikolaus had done.

Straightening up inside, Margerite caught her breath. The craggy walls and low arch above glittered everywhere with crystals, like a hoard of silver gleaming in the candle's unwavering flame. Only the center of the floor, where Nikolaus had painted his circle and set up his altar, was clear; the rest of it was all sparkling light, save only the white tips of the crystal-covered rock-icicles that hung from the ceiling and rose from the ground like fangs in a great mouth.

Although Margerite could feel - almost smell - the prickly twisting of Order magic, Nikolaus' sanctum did not bear the same sickening feeling as Ruprecht's had; but by the plain gold Light-Bearer ring on his hand, Nikolaus had clearly not reached the rank of demon-summoner yet, let alone... Margerite could hardly bring herself to think of it, but she knew she could not let herself flinch even within her own mind...sacrificed a human life to the Order's dark master.

Kobolt brushed past Margerite's legs with a whirring chirp, then lay down on the salt-encrusted rock and began to roll in ecstasy like a kitten in the sunlight, purring so loudly that Margerite could almost feel the vibration in her bones.

Nikolaus stared at the cat a moment in disbelief, then grasped Margerite's shoulder, his other hand shaking so hard that a thin stream of wax spilled over the edge of the candleholder. Even in the dim candlelight, she could see how pale he had gone, as if terrified unto death."How did that get in here?" Nikolaus asked, his face so close to hers that she could smell his musty breath. "My sanctum is warded against spirits of darkness as well as spirits of light; it should not have been able to pass."

Half-frozen as she was, Nikolaus' obvious distress gave Margerite new heart, so that she was able to answer, "He is my familiar, and when you invited me in, you invited him as well. Perhaps you should phrase yourself more carefully next time."

To Margerite's relief, Nikolaus let go of her and stepped away. Kobolt sprang up and shook a spray of glittering salt-crystals from his black fur, fluffing it out until he seemed almost half again his natural size, then walked over to one of the standing rock-icicles, crouching slightly in front of it. A moment later, a familiar stink reached Margerite's nostrils, and she had to bite her tongue to keep from laughing: what better place than an underground cave for a Kobolt to mark as his own?

Nikolaus' nose flared a little as the smell hit him, but he only said, in an even voice, "Remove your familiar now. It is not to come in here again."

As Margerite approached, Kobolt dodged between the rock-icicles, disappearing into the shadows. Margerite could not tell where he had gone, but she searched diligently for a few minutes until she was sure that the cat had run out beneath the curtain while her back was turned - if he had not vanished into the stone.

"He is gone," she said.

"Very well." Nikolaus settled himself on the large wooden chest by the edge of the circle. "Now, sit before me and write down what I have to tell you."

By the time Nikolaus had finished describing the making and consecration of the knife, wand, chalice, and pentacle which Margerite was to construct for herself, her fingers were so numb that she could hardly grasp the quill in her fist, her handwriting degenerating into an awkward scrawl, and her buttocks were as cold as the stone they rested on.

She knew Nikolaus was enjoying her discomfort, and punishing her for Kobolt's indiscretion, but she continued doggedly, pressing him for information on where she was to find the materials she needed for her ostensible purpose - at least, as she had thought, the process of constructing the magical implements was complex enough to put off the time when she would be forced to actually perform Order rituals for a good while.

"Are you not eager to see the place that will be your sanctum, Priestess?" Nikolaus asked at last, rising from his own seat and stamping his boots as if his feet, too, had gone numb.

"Most eager," Margerite replied, though in truth she was only eager to be back before a warm stove.

"Then come."

The cavern Nikolaus had chosen for her was much the same as his own, but no curtain hung over the entrance, and its crystals sparkled pure and pristine everywhere, glittering like a heavy fall of snow upon the floor. Kobolt was already sitting in the middle of the shimmering cave, tail curled about his feet. Reflexively Margerite sniffed the air: yes, the tomcat had made his mark already, but the faint pungency of his smell seemed less offensive than usual, more like the sharp odour of freshly-turned earth.

Nikolaus had stopped just outside the cavern, as if unwilling to come in - perhaps from Order courtesy, although when Margerite glanced downward, she could see a few yellow drops beneath the arch of the entryway. Stepping into the room herself, Margerite felt suddenly warmer, as though she had entered a chamber in which a servant had already stoked the fire.

Kobolt stood, arching his back in a long stretch, then walked over to leap into her arms, purring luxuriously and nuzzling his head between his mistress' breasts.

"Good Kobolt, fine cat," Margerite murmured to him. For a moment, a strange feeling came over her; it seemed as though she could already hear the crystal-lined walls of the cave ringing to the sound of her own voice, feel the power thrumming through her veins like fine wine, lifting her upwards like the wind beneath her wings as she flew. Maria help me, Margerite thought, can I really desire this? And yet Father Etienne had taught her that not all magic was evil...

"Does it suit you, Priestess?" Nikolaus asked. Margerite looked back at him. From where she stood, he seemed very small, a pathetic, paunchy figure, made the more ridiculous by the thick layers of his winter clothing. My power is greater than his already; no wonder Damiano warned him that I would quickly outstrip him.

But that was pride, of the most sinful kind considering the circumstances: was she already more than halfway to becoming a Light-Bearer in her heart? The thought chilled Margerite again, and she quickly walked out of the cavern.

"It suits me well," Margerite replied, clutching Kobolt more tightly to her so that Nikolaus would not see her shivering.

"Good. Next time you come down here, bring tools to scrape the floor with. When you have it clean, I shall show you how to paint the circle - which must be done often in this damp. Now, you will lead the way back so that I may be sure you know it."

Margerite was beyond cold by the time they had reached Nikolaus' chamber again. True to his nature, the Graf's son took the seat nearest to the stove, but Margerite was grateful even for the lesser warmth seeping slowly back into her body, and did not hesitate to drink deeply when Nikolaus refilled her goblet.

"If you have no safe place to keep it, you may leave your grimoire with me for now," Nikolaus told her.

Margerite shook her head. "I have a box that locks, where I may keep such things if they are not too large; how else do you suppose I would study the Black Book? You could help me more by telling me of how things stand with some of the other folk at this castle, whether there are any in whom I may trust, or of whom I should be careful."

"There are no other Order members here - to the best
of my knowledge," Nikolaus added, his gray-green eyes
suddenly hooded and wary. "But Herr Jakob is my man; I
have been carefully supplementing his pay for years, and
working carefully upon his mind, and he will provide what
you ask him for without asking questions or telling any
other. There are a few servants whom I have been able to
affect most satisfactorily as well, and I will point them out to
you when the need arises."

"What of Father Michael? What do you know of him?"

Nikolaus shrugged, gesturing carelessly with his goblet
so that a few dark drops slopped over the rim. "He has been
here for many years. Even a weak priest bears watching, but
to the best of my knowledge, he cares more for good food
and fine clothes than for matters of the spirit. You cannot get
out of going to Mass every Sunday, for the only thing that
makes him angry is thinking that his beautiful chapel and
fine voice are not appreciated enough, but even the simplest
of beginner's wards will keep you from any taint in taking
bread and wine from his hands."

"And the others? What can you tell me about the knights
here?"

"You have little to worry about from Ludwig and Dieter. They are much like my father and brother: hearty oafs who like to fight and swive and drink, with little room for thought inside their thick skulls - Ludwig cannot even read or write, and Dieter is hardly better. Speak to Gottfried as little as you can. He has the soul of a monk, at least to all appearance; I have heard that he wanted to join the Teutonic Order, but his father would not have it, and if there is anything worthwhile to be said of Gottfried, it is that he is obedient. Nevertheless, I have tried to work upon him and found him very difficult. His mind is shuttered, quiet as the grave, and he has a peculiar ability for seeing through such small charms as, for instance, allow one to walk unnoticed. I have often suspected that he may be a spy, all his piety a pretense - and one that sits uncomfortably with his intelligence, at that. But to whom he might be reporting, or how, and what his true allegiance is, I have been unable to find out yet, and it would be most unwise for you to try. If he shows any interest in your child, let me know at once."

"Of course," Margerite murmured, lowering her eyes. Although the whole night had been part of a complex lie to Nikolaus, and his Order superiors through him, she still felt uncomfortable in speaking a direct falsehood - even when she was not certain that it was a falsehood; at least she knew that Nikolaus' life would pay for it if he failed to protect Wolfram.

"And warn Bertram of him as well," Nikolaus added. "Although your man knows little of the Order's nature and purposes, he is still our servant, and may give us away unawares if he tries to contact anyone outside Burg Fürstensee - particularly his old comrades of the Free Companies, for whom, I believe, Gottfried bears a special dislike: it was he who counselled my father to the utmost harshness in enforcing Kaiser Karl's dictates concerning them, and if he finds out about Bertram's past connections, he will undoubtedly recommend hanging him."

"Well-warned is well-armed," Margerite agreed, thinking, My poor Bertram! How could my love have laid such a burden upon you - how could my hopes for your happiness have brought you such misery?

The same thought rang in her head later, when she had managed at last to escape from Nikolaus and lay shivering beneath her quilts. Now that Margerite was warmer, her gashed foot had begun to ache sharply, and she knew it would trouble her walking for days, but she was sure that she deserved no less.

O Bertram, I am sorry. Perhaps it would be best for him if she sent him back to Burg Falkenstein again, granted him his freedom from her. But that would look even more suspicious after her conversation with Ritter Gottfried, and it would not help his quest for revenge upon the Order of Light-Bearers, now that Falkenstein was cleared of their taint. Rather, she suspected, he would return to the Free Companies if she sent him away, and that would be more harm and danger for him.

Mother Maria, grant me wisdom, Margerite prayed. But though she lay awake until the first light of dawn showed gray at the edge of her window's shutters, no more thoughts came to her; only the endless painful, dragging circle of, My love, I have harmed you without meaning to - what can I do to make amends to you?

Margerite awoke to the sound of Wolfram wailing and Rose calling her name in a soft urgent voice. Sleep still lay heavy upon her eyes as she sat up in bed and let the nursemaid put her son into her arms for nursing. It was strange, she thought muzzily, that Wolfram had not cried for feeding in the middle of the night: and what would she have told Rose to explain her absence? She smiled at the thought, for it gave her yet another reasonable ploy for putting off Nikolaus and delaying the time when she would have to speak the blasphemous words of the Order rites or reveal her deception.

"Are you well, frowe?" Rose asked worriedly. "You seldom sleep so long or deeply."

"I am still tired from our journey," Margerite answered. "How late is it?"

"A little past Tierce, frowe. Eva has been up for hours; she broke her fast with Christoph, and I think he is showing her about the castle grounds. I shall fetch you some bread and watered wine, if you like. More guests have arrived, and the great hall is very crowded and noisy."

"Have you taken my letter to Bertram yet?" Margerite cursed herself for an idiot as soon as she had spoken: she sounded like any village maiden asking news of her sweetheart with blushing eagerness. But Rose did not seem to take it amiss.

"Frowe, I am sorry. The guardsmen were at practice when I went out into the courtyard, and there was no chance for me to take him aside, even if I could have gotten him to notice me. It will be hard to play the part of Bertram's beloved," Rose added thoughtfully, "if I have to shout at him to make him so much as look in my direction."

"You must explain the matter to him." And Bertram has done more than his share of dissembling - but what if he goes too far in playing his part? No, that was unworthy: Margerite knew she could put more trust in Bertram's chastity than in her own. Yet she did not know how she could bear it if he were even to embrace Rose where others could see, if the serving maid were to have and scorn the gift for which her mistress longed; but there was no other way open to her.

When Wolfram was full-fed and had let his air out in a series of contented little belches, Margerite let Rose dress her. For the day's festivities, she had chosen the deep red velvet dress with its white fur trim. It was heavy for the season, but she thought that the darker colour gave her more dignity; it would be obvious enough to everyone that Heinrich had married a woman younger than his own sons, but at least she could try not to look like a frivolous bauble.

And besides - she had to admit it to herself - though she had not lost her figure as drastically as the dressmaker in Freiburg had warned, some of the other gowns Petra had altered were tight enough in the bodice and waist to be a little less than comfortable, especially when her breasts were fullest with milk. Tomorrow, Margerite said firmly to herself, I shall sit down with Herr Jakob and go over the castle books with him: then I will know if I can afford new dresses.

"Will you wear any jewels today, frowe?" Rose asked."I think the Graf will want you to be decked out in all your finery."

Margerite opened her jewelry box, looking into it silently. By far the fairest piece in it was the falcon-necklace Ruprecht had given her: the deep red and purple of the ruby and amethyst beads set off by the glowing crystal spheres between them, the falcon's eye glinting deep sapphire and the drop of adamant in her claws gleaming like dew in the sunrise.

Touching it for the first time since Ruprecht's death, it seemed to Margerite that she could feel the power thrumming in the necklace, ringing like the echo of his hunting horn. She almost dropped it back into the box, but remembered that Father Etienne had mentioned that it would protect her against being scried, and she knew, too - bitter as it was to think on - that Ruprecht would have worked no magic upon it that might harm her.

But can he still touch me through it? Margerite wondered. She cast the thought firmly from her: Ruprecht's soul, by Etienne's blessing or curse, was bound to the woods around Burg Falkenstein: he could not reach her here. She fastened the clasp about her own neck, settling the gold falcon between her breasts.

"That is better," Rose said in a tone of deep satisfaction. "It is my duty, frowe, to see that no one outshines you in your own castle. Now sit down, and let me do up your hair properly, as Eva taught me to."

As Rose had said, the great hall was already full of folk. Though Heinrich and his sons were nowhere to be seen, Father Michael stood to the side, directing a crew of workmen who were busily adorning the walls with garlands of fresh greenery and flowers. Trailed by Rose with her baby, Margerite nibbled at a piece of bread and sipped watered wine from her goblet as she wandered around, greeting the knights she had met the previous evening and allowing Ritter Ludwig to introduce her to the more notable guests.

Rich odours were already wafting out of the kitchen, the scents of fine meat laced with rare spices, cinnamon and cloves and peppercorns: Margerite had no doubt that, when she went over the castle accounts, she would see that a goodly amount of its revenues were spent on food and cooks.

When she had finished eating, Ritter Ludwig escorted her out into the courtyard. Two fat deer and a sheep were roasting on spits above roaring fires; wooden trestle-tables had already been set up around the yard, and villagers in their best clothes were thronging eagerly about the barrels of beer.

The guardsmen had ended their practice: Margerite could only see the two at the inner gate, neither of whom was Bertram. Eva, Christoph, and Heinrich were over by the stables; Christoph and his father seemed to be deep in discussion, while Eva stood quietly watching them - no doubt, Margerite thought, perfectly aware of how beautifully the sunlight set off her long shining fall of golden hair and the pale blue brocade of her dress. Kriemhilt sat by her feet, green-gold eyes slitted against the day's brightness.

"You may leave me now, Rose," Margerite said, hoping that the girl would understand her meaning. "Give me my son and go enjoy yourself with your sweetheart for a little while, but be back to attend us by Sexte."

"As you wish, frowe," Rose answered, handing Wolfram over. Her right eyelid drooped in a wink before she disappeared into the crowd.

"Greetings, my wife!" Heinrich boomed as he saw
Margerite, a wide grin splitting his grizzled beard. "You were
long abed for such a fair day. Did you rest comfortably?"

"Very well, thank you," Margerite replied."I was only tired
from all the riding, like a falcon first flying after her moult."

Heinrich came over to her, kissing her lightly on the
mouth, then chucking Wolfram under the chin. The babe
let out an indignant wail, and Heinrich laughed. "If the
rest of him grows to match his voice, he will be a mighty
man in time. Tell me, Margerite, do you know much about
horse-flesh? My son is trying to choose a steed for Eva, and I
cannot convince him that the most spirited beast may not be
the most comfortable for a lady's seat."

"But Goldfuss is well-trained now, and answers easily to
rein or knee," Christoph protested. "Surely he would be no
trouble for her - would he, Eva? Come, Frowe Margerite,
have a look at the beast and see if you can tell me that he is
not perfect. Better yet..." He clapped his hands and shouted,
"Albrecht! Bring Goldfuss out!"

In a few moments, the stable door opened and a wizened
man emerged leading a great gelding by the halter.
Margerite could not deny that the horse was magnificent: his
mane and hocks shone like burnished gold against the deep
ruddy chestnut of his glossy hide, and his flanks rippled with
muscle.

There was no doubt that Eva would be stunning on his
back, if she could handle him - but Eva had found it difficult
enough to manage the gentle mare that she had ridden from
Burg Falkenstein to Burg Fürstensee, and by the arch of
Goldfuss' neck and the gleam in his dark eyes, Margerite
guessed that he would need a strong rider.

Eva clasped her hands together, looking up at the horse.
"O, he is beautiful," she murmured. "Do you truly think I
could ride him, Christoph?"

"Of course you can," Christoph assured her. "You may
need to start slowly and carefully, so that the two of you can
become used to each other, but I will be glad to lead him
while you sit on his back."

Heinrich sighed gustily, rolling his eyes. "It will take more than a few lessons for Eva to be able to control that beast, Christoph. Surely by now you have learned the folly of trying to sit a horse that is beyond your strength. If you have no sense in the matter for yourself, at least try to have some for Eva's sake."

"There is all the difference in the world between mounting another man's trained warhorse and riding a well-tempered gelding," Christoph argued. "And I will be with her every minute until she has fully mastered him. I do not think it will be such a great task."

"But, Christoph," Margerite broke in, "you must remember that you have been trained to the saddle from childhood, while Eva was reared in a convent, and that horse before us is no nun's little palfrey. If you wish Goldfuss to be hers, that is well enough. I would suggest, though, that you find a gentler beast for her to practice upon first."

Christoph looked disappointed, but finally nodded his head. "Will that please you, Eva?"

Eva looked from the horse to Christoph and back again. "I suppose it would be best," she said reluctantly. "But I may ride him when I have learned well enough?"

"He is already yours," Christoph said grandly. He took Eva's hand in his, laying it upon Goldfuss' gleaming neck. Carefully she stroked the horse, and he turned his head towards her, nuzzling her hopefully.

Eva giggled. "His nose is so soft! Have we anything to give him?"

Christoph smiled, reaching into his belt-pouch to bring out a new carrot. "Feed him, and he will be your friend for life. Hold it out to him in your palm, so..." The horse's lips closed gently over the tidbit, lifting it from Eva's hand. At this, Kriemhilt, as if annoyed at being ignored in favour of a horse, stood and stretched up on her hind legs, pawing at Eva with a sharp miaow.

Both Christoph and Eva laughed; Eva scooped the cat up in her free hand, holding Kriemhilt with one arm and petting Goldfuss with the other.

Heinrich touched Margerite's shoulder. "At least we have settled that. Come, it will soon be time for the noonday meal, and there are some folk I want you to meet. Where is that girl of yours? Surely Wolfram is heavy enough to be growing burdensome to you by now."

"Not at all," Margerite said, alarmed thoughts flashing through her mind: what if Heinrich called a page or servant to look for Rose, and found her just at the wrong time?"It is pleasant to have him by me while he is still small enough to carry easily - and that will not be for long, as they grow so quickly."

"Indeed they do," Heinrich agreed ruefully. He glanced back at his son. "Sometimes it seems like no more than a few days past that the midwife laid Christoph squalling in my arms, and now he appears to be wooing his own bride. Perhaps I am growing old: time always seems to pass more swiftly for the old, maybe because so little is left ahead." There was a note of wistfulness in his deep voice that Margerite had never heard before, and she could not help but feel a warm rush of affection for him, tinged a little with pity.

"You are not yet old," Margerite said comfortingly. "You are still strong, as you proved well enough with your sword last year, and, God grant, you shall lead your realm well for many years yet."

Heinrich put his arm about her, drawing her close to him. "Kind words, my wife, and your presence helps to make them true."

Margerite let her husband lead her away, although she could not help glancing about for Rose and Bertram. She did not know whether it was well or ill that she saw neither of them: perhaps it meant that Rose had found a private place to deliver her message, or perhaps the serving maid had been thwarted again.

When she saw Ritter Gottfried in the great hall, however, her heart leapt: whatever the young knight's powers of vision, he could not see what took place when he was absent, so there was at least a chance that Rose would be able to give Bertram the letter. A beautiful table was set for the midday meal, but Margerite found that she had little appetite. Nikolaus had finally come downstairs as well, and throughout the meal he shot sly, heavy-lidded glances at her, as if she needed reminding of the secret they shared.

At least Wolfram was too small to be interested in the food on her plate yet, though he grasped at her hand every time she lifted a morsel to her lips - she should have thought to order Rose to take him away before the meal, though the longer the serving girl had, the better her chances of getting to Bertram would be.

When Margerite was at last able to break free and go up to her chambers, she found Rose waiting there. "Did you give him the letter?" Margerite demanded at once.

"I did," Rose answered.

"Did he read it? Had he any reply?"

"He said, 'Tell the Frowe Gräfin that I understand.'"

If Rose had not been there, Margerite was sure she would have burst into tears. The message was simple and natural enough - but it answered all of the questions in her heart, soothing the storms of doubt and guilt that had raged in her since she had come to Burg Fürstensee. The wedding feast at Heinrich's castle proved to be far more impressive than the one they had held several days ago: as the weather had held fine,a high table was set up in the courtyard where Heinrich, his knights, and their ladies could dine together with the other notable guests.

Graf Wolfgang von Schwarzenfels, who ruled the lands to Heinrich's northeast, had come with a small retinue of his own, including his wife Anna and his youngest son, Georg, whom he wished for Christoph to take as Knappe - repaying, Margerite gathered, Christoph's own service under him at the same age.

Georg seemed a charming lad, if a little small for his
age and odd to look upon: he had inherited his mother's
flaming red hair and freckles, and the jutting nose and chin
that seemed strong on his father's weathered and widely
moustached face merely looked out of proportion on a
smooth-skinned adolescent. He spoke his oath of service to
Christoph prettily enough, though, for his voice had already
smoothed past its breaking into a honeyed tenor, and
Christoph seemed proud to receive him.

As they mingled in the courtyard, listening to the
musicians and waiting for the signal that the feasting was
to begin, Margerite noticed that Gottfried was staring at her
once more, the sharp dark arches of his brows drawn low in
concentration. Casually she caught his eye and stared back;
the young knight flushed and looked away. Feeling that she
now had the upper hand, she walked over to him.

"Is something amiss, Ritter Gottfried?" she asked quietly.

"All is well, I hope," he replied. "At least as far as I have
been able to see to it. Has anything disturbed you, Frowe
Gräfin?"

"You seemed to be looking at me as if something were
wrong."

"I was admiring your necklace," Gottfried said. "It
is a most unusual and beautiful piece, but I could not
see it clearly - I am a little shortsighted," he admitted
shamefacedly.

Margerite would have laughed if it would not have
been so rude: that explained both the knight's unnerving
stare and, perhaps, his ability to see through the cantrips
Nikolaus cast, for he would be used to noticing slight shifts
in movement and shadow which men with better eyesight
would pay no attention to. Instead, she lifted the falcon
up in the palm of her hand so that Gottfried would not
appear to be scrutinizing her breasts. "It was a present from
Ruprecht," she told him.

"Because you are fond of hawking? I have spoken with your falconer, who told me that you had brought an admirable pair of peregrines from your father's castle. I think you will be pleased with their accomodations here, for Christoph is very proud of his birds as well, though I hope you will not be lured into his bad habit of carrying a hawk to Mass."

Margerite was about to retort sharply, but checked herself. Gottfried hardly knew her, and Ruprecht's Sunday hunting must have been rumoured about beyond his own lands; and she knew all too well that there were many things worse than a painfully strict piety. "Whatever you may have heard about Burg Falkenstein," she answered, "I keep Sunday properly, and always have."

Gottfried smiled slightly. "That is well," he said. But he kept glancing back at her necklace, with a worried look in his gray eyes.

Margerite was saved from any further attempts to make conversation with him by the high ringing of a silver bell, its clear tone cutting through all the noise of the courtyard. She hastened to her place, to find Kobolt already sitting between Heinrich and Christoph as though the chair belonged to him, looking up at her with wide innocent golden eyes.

"Down you go, cat," she said. Georg, standing behind Christoph, barely managed to muffle a laugh as Margerite picked Kobolt up and tossed him gently to the ground.

Christoph turned to shoot a stern glance back over his shoulder at his Knappe, intoning in an unnaturally severe voice, "The Gräfin's cat is not a matter for mirth. " For a moment Georg paled beneath his freckles, clearly fearing that he had offended grievously; then Eva giggled, Nikolaus let out a low snicker, and Christoph broke down in a fit of laughter. Gregor flushed, grinning a little embarassed grin as he realized that his knight was jesting with him. Fortunately for Christoph, perhaps, his father was deep in conversation with Graf Wolfgang and did not seem to notice his son's play.

Before the food was brought out, Heinrich's servants came around the high table with silver ewers, bowls, and white linen napkins. The water that they poured over the diners' hands was warm, and scented lightly with myrtle, the pleasant odour blending delightfully with that of the flower-garlands on the table and the smell of roasting meat from the spits.

The first course, when the chargers set upon the table were unveiled, appeared to be blue trout fresh from the river with their shimmering scales still intact; but when Heinrich began to cut up the fish he and Margerite shared, Margerite saw that it was actually a cleverly tinted and glazed confection molded from a firm white paste - milk, egg, almond, and sugar, she guessed from the taste, heavily flavoured with the warm seeds of anise and caraway which would open and heat the stomach so that it could properly digest the rest of the meal.

Her estimate of the wages Heinrich paid his cooks went up at once: clearly, in spite of the damages the war had done, Burg Fürstensee had already recovered well. Or else, which she could well believe, Heinrich inspired the kind of loyalty that kept the best folk with him even in harder times, among his servants as well as his knights.

"Your cook gets better every year, Heinrich," Wolfgang said."I have not seen subtleties this clever since I was a Knappe and my knight took me to visit the court of Landgraf Bertrik von Niederwald - God rest his soul." He smoothed the dark wings of his moustache away from his mouth with a fingertip, then drank deeply of his wine.

"Is Landgraf Bertrik dead? What befell him?"

Wolfgang sighed. "He died about six months ago; from what I have heard, he simply failed and faded away. He never quite recovered from what happened with his younger son eight years back, you know. As for the elder - well, I found Gerhardt rather odious, though I suppose for his father's sake I ought to pay him a visit, if I have occasion to travel so far north any time soon. He has probably improved with age, as most of us do, anyway. But the younger son, Bernhardt, was a far more pleasant boy; even now, I often wonder if anyone really knows all the truth of those events."

A frown furrowed Heinrich's craggy brow, and he absently rolled a morsel of the sweet dish into a ball between thumb and forefinger before popping it into his mouth. "It was - something about him murdering a visiting noble's son, was it not? I remember it was a very great scandal at the time, but I cannot quite recall how it turned out. Was he executed, or...?"

"Bernhardt apparently escaped before he could be tried, leaving a few dead guards behind. According to what I have heard, there was not much doubt about how the trial would turn out, since they found him by the body with blood on his hands, and the knife in it was his. The only odd thing was that even caught like that, he kept protesting his innocence...said that he had heard a struggle and run to help. To me, it always seemed far too stupid a tale for someone as intelligent as Bernhardt was to make up, though I suppose anyone can come out with foolishness if pressed hard enough. And although I only knew him for a few days, I would not have guessed that he had it in him to commit that sort of murder: a gauntlet in the face and a challenge to swords in public would have been more like him. But apparently the evidence was clear enough that even Landgraf Bertrik was quite convinced that Bernhardt had done it. He and the man he killed had had some sort of quarrel about a woman earlier in the evening, and she must have been well worth quarrelling over, because Gerhardt married her less than a year later; she is now the Landgräfin Ortlieb of Niederwald."

"A bit hasty." Heinrich laughed. "But who am I to cast that stone - eh, Margerite?"

Margerite smiled, laying her hand affectionately over her husband's. Beneath her calm facade, however, her mind was racing furiously. She remembered her dream of nearly a year past, the young Bertram walking with a woman...then locked in a cell, wildly pleading his innocence. Eight years: time enough for a knightly fugitive to rise in the ranks of a Free Company until the Order trusted him as a messenger, more than time enough, in the brutal life of a mercenary, to grave the deep lines of pain and sorrow into a young man's face and pour haunted agony into his hazel eyes - how long had Bertram served with Ruprecht before she came? A year or two, perhaps; she could not remember if he had ever told her precisely.

And Niederwald, up between Thuringia and Saxony, was one of the greater realms; it would fit with all she knew of Bertram, if he were the late Landgraf Bertrik's missing son. Margerite realized, the dread mounting within her like a river swelling into a fatal flood, that she would have to ask Bertram if this were so - and if it were, it would be her duty to tell him of his father's death. The remains of the fish-shaped aperitif were whisked away; Margerite dabbed her fingers in the little water-bowl by her place and wiped them neatly on the napkin she shared with Heinrich, trying to calm herself by the simple movements of courteous dining.

The second course consisted of what appeared to be a pair of doves for each couple: one bird had been skinned and roasted, its rich dark flesh glazed golden with egg yolk, the second still wore its feathers - which proved, when it had been cut open, to hold a delicious mixture of cheese, eggs, spices, and raisins. Margerite had read of the trick of making two doves from one, but had never seen it done before; while the appreciative murmurs around the table showed that she was not the only one impressed by the skill of the Burg Fürstensee cooks.

To both Margerite's relief and her disappointment, Heinrich and Wolfgang had shifted their conversation to the topic of politics - in particular, the surprising decision, announced during Kaiser Karl's Maytime visit to the Pope in Avignon, to convince the Free Companies to take up arms in the crusade against the Turks.

"It was easier to know how to deal with such men when they were outlaws and excommunicates," Heinrich grumbled. "What shall we do now if a band of them come marching through, claiming to be Crusaders even as they terrorize our villages? The situation must be desperate indeed, if the Pope and the Kaiser are both desperate enough to try to enlist these ruffians instead of wiping them out as they deserve."

Though Margerite knew she should stay quiet, she could not hold her tongue: Heinrich was, after all, speaking of Paul the Bear and Jochanan as well as the hordes that had ravaged Italy - and of Bertram as well, though he had done evil in his time as a mercenary. "I thought the leaders of the Bear's Paw Company good enough to sit at table with me, as well as to fight and die in Ruprecht's war," she said hotly. "They, at least, would be glad to lift their swords in a good cause, and where there are a few such men, there may be more: was God not willing to spare Sodom and Gomorrah if even ten righteous men could be found there?"

Heinrich blinked, and for a moment Margerite thought she saw a flash of anger in his eyes - because I disagreed with him? she wondered. Then he nodded. "True enough, the company your husband hired served faithfully," he agreed. "But you were never at their mercy: you had Graf Günther's army behind you at first, and then my own close to hand. Without that strength shown to them, matters might have gone very differently for you; you would have been lucky not to be ravished and slain, or forcibly wedded to their leader, that they might claim Burg Falkenstein for their own."

Margerite opened her mouth to retort forcefully to that, then closed it again. She could hardly tell Heinrich how she knew the true extent of Paul's trustworthiness - nor could he, for that matter, admit to the aid the Bear's Paw had given him.

"Graf Günther was slain by brigands on his way from Burg Falkenstein, was he not?" Wolfgang asked. "I heard that he had disappeared, and that his bones and those of his men were found in the mountains only a couple of weeks ago."

"It was a sad thing," Heinrich rumbled. "Günther had made the journey to see the christening of young Wolfram, since Ruprecht had been a dear friend of his - and perhaps because he came too late to save Ruprecht during the siege, and hoped to discharge some of that debt to Ruprecht's son. They had little luck of their friendship."

"That is sad to hear, indeed," Wolfgang replied. "May Christ have mercy on their souls. At least, if this scheme the Pope and the Kaiser have hatched between them works at all, it will be safer to travel the roads hereafter. I am sure the Companies will be ruffians and villains wherever they go, but at least they can carry out their murdering and plundering far away from us."

"I say amen to that," Heinrich assented.

For the third course, three peacocks were borne up to the high table. The birds' feathered skins had been carefully put back on, shimmering blue necks propped up and tails spread out. Margerite was awed by the sight, but wondered if they would be fit to eat: though she had never tasted it, she had read that the flesh of peacocks was both tough and insipid. She did not realize the deceptive nature of this subtlety until she lifted a sliver of meat to her mouth: the roasted fowl within the beautiful hides were not peacocks, but succulent geese, spiced lightly with sage and peppercorns. Beside her, Christoph laughed aloud.

"I've never tasted a finer peacock," he said. "Usually, the best peacock is the one you don't have to eat."

Margerite only smiled at him, not wishing to betray her own lack of sophistication.

"How do you like Burg Fürstensee now?" Christoph asked. "Whatever our faults, we do set a fine table - I have spent years learning to do justice to it." He patted his belly by way of illumination.

"I have never seen better."

"I see you are getting to know our knights, as well. What is it you have been discussing so earnestly with Gottfried? Myself, I have seldom been able to get more than a few words at a time out of him."

"He was admiring my necklace, and my cat," Margerite said truthfully.

"Really? I would have thought that he was above noticing such things. Perhaps our warrior-monk is not such a constipated little prig after all," Christoph added. His smile took the sting from his words, particularly since Margerite more than half agreed with his assessment - and also because she could tell that there was no malice behind the remark. For all the ruthlessness Christoph had shown in planning the disposal of Günther and his men, Margerite did not think he had any malice in him; she had only to compare him to his brother, if she should ever doubt that.

"You ought not to speak so of a fellow knight," Margerite chided gently. "And surely his efforts on behalf of Burg Fürstensee deserve more respect."

"That they do," Christoph sighed. "Ritter Gottfried is diligent, loyal, pious, obedient, and well-skilled with sword and lance. Indeed, he has dumped me in the dirt at tilting more times than I can count, for though there is little weight to him, he moves faster than that cat of yours, and places his point with a precision the Archangel Michael might envy. He is - a delight on the field, less skilled at holding a courtly conversation. But perhaps you will be able to teach him what Ritter Ludwig could not, since he seems to have taken to you."

"Perhaps so," Margerite murmured, though if Gottfried's shy suspicion could be called taking to her, she wondered how he behaved with other women.

The meal continued in a profusion of dazzling culinary delights. Lastly, a great pie, fully three feet wide and a foot tall, its pastry decorated with the figures of small birds amid green-glazed leaves, was brought out and set upon the high table. Grinning in his beard, Heinrich stood to draw his knife carefully around the edge. As he lifted the outer crust, to Margerite's amazement, a rushing of white wings erupted from the pie - a small flock of white doves flying out into the air, cooing and circling above the courtyard.

"Venus' birds," Heinrich boomed cheerfully above the soft applause of the knights and ladies about the table. "What better end to a wedding feast? Will you give me the first dance, my wife?"

Margerite took Heinrich's hand and let him lead her to the middle of the courtyard, other pairs of dancers falling into a ring around them as the musicians struck up a sprightly carol. For all his bulk, Heinrich moved with surprising smoothness, though his dignified steps were a long way from Ruprecht's skill and wild beauty in dancing.

And...I have never yet danced with Bertram, Margerite thought, even as she matched her rhythm to Heinrich's. If her guess was right, it would have been eight years since Bertram had last trodden a measure with anyone, or enjoyed any courtly pleasure. Dear Mother Maria, you brought us together: if the news I have learned is truly for him, please give me a chance to tell him to his face.

When the dance was over, Margerite excused herself; if the setting sun had not told her clearly enough, the aching of her breasts let her know that she was late for Wolfram's next feeding. In her chamber, Rose sat by the window, rocking the baby and looking wistfully out the window.

Margerite had to think for only a moment while Rose helped her out of her dress; then she swiftly tore off a small strip of parchment, writing on it, Bernhardt von Niederwald.

"Take this to Bertram now," she ordered her maidservant. "Tell him that, if he recognises the name, he should come to meet me in the herber, halfway between midnight and dawn when the moon is down. Then let me know what he says; after that, you may enjoy yourself at the dancing as you will, though be careful not to drink too much, and to protect your modesty."

"As you wish, frowe," Rose replied.

When the maid had left the room, Margerite sat shuddering for a few moments before lifting Wolfram from his cradle. If she were caught, she risked...everything; but what else could she do?

It seemed to Margerite that she could not tell the passing of time since Rose had left; she felt as though she had been waiting for hours, but she had just reached the point of burping Wolfram when the door opened again.

"What does he say?" Margerite asked.

"Frowe, when Bertram read what you had written, he grew very pale, and bit his lip till the blood started from it, but he said only that he would meet you as you asked. But, frowe - do you know what people will think if anyone sees you with him late at night?"

"I know," Margerite said grimly. "But I have little choice in the matter, and it is not something for you to concern yourself with." She glared at Rose, expecting the girl to back down, but Rose's sharp jaw was set firmly and her narrow hands clenched tight in the folds of her skirt.

"Frowe, my aunt said when I took service with you that I would be responsible for your reputation, for a maidservant is expected to know everything about her mistress. If - and you may well beat me for speaking so, but I must - if Bertram is your lover, then tell me, and I will help you to meet with him more safely. But this castle is not like Burg Falkenstein; there are people everywhere who pay attention to everything that is happening, from Heinrich down to the smallest scullery maid. Please, frowe, do not risk yourself so!"

Margerite raised her hand to strike Rose - then lowered it again, thoughts of all the times she had casually slapped Gertrude rising like a flood of choking bile in her throat. "This has nothing to do with a lovers' assignation," she managed to say. "Only...with a matter of Bertram's own, that is not mine to speak of."

"But no one will believe that. Frowe, whatever it is, can you not put it into a letter for him?"

"No. Go away, Rose. Dance, and enjoy yourself, and do not let this cross your mind again - and Christ have mercy on you if you speak of it to anyone else."

"But, frowe..."

"Go!" Margerite shouted. Rose stared at her, pointed chin trembling and gray-green eyes wide as if Margerite had actually struck her. As she ran from the room, Wolfram let out a dreadful wail, then made a sort of bubbling cough and spewed a gout of milk down the front of Margerite's shift before he began to cry in earnest.

"I am sorry, my son," Margerite murmured, rocking him gently, heedless of the nasty wetness that had already soaked through her linen garment. "I did not mean to distress you so."

It was a little past midnight when Rose returned from the revelry. The maid said little to her mistress save, "The fires have burned down, and the dancers are all going to bed." There was a sad and reproachful tone to her voice, and Margerite could hear her unspoken message clearly enough, but Rose did not dare to speak any further.

Margerite waited, watching the candle burn down. Its steady flame, haloed in unwavering light, seemed to calm and still her mind, slowing her heart and her breath to the deep rhythms of a sleeper. As she sat, her thoughts easing into quietness, it seemed to her that she could feel her own awareness spreading out like ripples in a still pool.

She could almost hear...the mewings and scufflings of Kriemhilt's kittens, nursing on their mother at the foot of Eva's bed, and see how Eva clutched her pillow close against her cheek, murmuring Christoph's name in her sleep... Heinrich's grating snore as he sprawled comfortably on his back, filled with fine food and good wine, content with the success of his feast, like a great hound snoring by the fire after a day's hunting.

It seemed to Margerite, deep in her daze, that she could sense the whole of Burg Fürstensee settling into sleep, like a huge beast whose limbs were relaxing bit by bit, only twitching a little here and there where the sentries still stood on guard: though no foe threatened, there would always be someone on watch, standing against the still-shapeless dangers that might rise from without or within.

Mazed in the candle's flame, Margerite did not mark how swiftly the wax was melting away beneath it. It was not the passing of time that roused her to her assignation, but the prickle at the edge of her mind, the feeling of someone walking, wakefully and steadily, through the shadows about the edge of the courtyard towards the herber. Then she started up, the wide ring of her awareness bursting like a bubble in a stream, and hastily cast her cloak around her.

Nikolaus had spoken of small cantrips that would allow one to pass unseen; now, as Margerite crept silently down through the unfamiliar hallways and stairwells of Burg Fürstensee, she resolved to ask him to teach them to her. If the rites were not such as would endanger her soul, she would be glad of knowing them.

Even with the moon down, the starlight on the courtyard was very bright, and although, as Bertram had done, she kept to the shadows, she felt horribly exposed: every rustle of breeze or crackling from the dying embers in the middle of the courtyard made her start, certain that at any moment she would hear Ritter Gottfried's voice, or feel the strong grip of his thin hand on her shoulder.

But she slipped unchallenged through the herber gates, pausing in the shadow of a linden and looking about her. The night air was sweet with the scents of blossoms, the broad clusters of linden-flowers pale as silver in the starlight. Margerite wished with all her heart that she had come for a lover's tryst, that she and Bertram could embrace beneath the arching boughs, or lie upon the close-mown carpet of cool soft grass. But the weight of the news she brought lay heavy upon her, together with the fear of what Bertram would say - was he angry that she had found him out? Would he leave her now?

Margerite almost hoped that what she had felt in her chamber was nothing but a half-waking dream, that Bertram had found it too risky to leave his sleeping companions in the barracks, and would grant her a day or two of reprieve before she had to tell him, face to face, what she had heard that evening. But then a black figure rose from one of the low-banked benches by the wall; even in the darkness, beneath his cloak, she could recognise Bertram's shape.

He reached out for her, his hand closing gently upon her arm, and drew her farther into the shadows. It was too dark for Margerite to read his expression: she could barely see the paleness of his face framed by his hair and beard, as though he wore an unvisored helmet of black iron.

"How did you know?" Bertram whispered urgently to her. His voice was raw, almost upon the edge of tears. "How did you find out?"

"Graf Wolfgang von Schwarzenfels knew your father once, and he recalled a tale that - fit closely with what you have told me."

"Wolfgang von Schwarzenfels..."

"He was a Knappe when he visited the court at Niederwald. That must have been some time ago, for his son is Christoph's Knappe now."

Margerite felt the faint trembling in Bertram's grasp. She wanted to lay her hand upon his chest, to calm the wild beating of his heart, but did not dare: she feared that if she touched him, she would not be able to keep from embracing him, for she wanted desperately to throw her arms about his strong body, to cling to him and weep out all her strains and doubts and guilt upon his shoulder.

"Did he see me? Could he have recognised me? Why was he talking about this?"

"I do not think that he saw you, or that the thought that you might be here could have crossed his mind. No: the matter came up in conversation because - and forgive me, my love, for what I must tell you - Graf Wolfgang was telling Heinrich of your father's death."

Bertram dropped Margerite's arm and stepped away from her, his eyes wide pools of blackness sunk into deathly white skin. "How did he die? When?"

"Six months ago," Margerite said reluctantly. "Graf Wolfgang said that he had simply failed in health and...faded away."

"Six months ago," Bertram repeated dully. "That would have been..." Very near to St. Lucia's Eve, Margerite unwillingly completed the thought. Ruprecht had been about to sacrifice a maiden to his dark Master; who could say what blood other Order members had shed on that night?"Who rules there now."

"Gerhardt...and Ortlieb." As she spoke the second name, Bertram jerked as though a powerful sword-blow had cut deep into his body. Although he did not move further, and she was no longer touching him, it seemed to Margerite that she could feel him drawing away, retreating from her like a captain withdrawing into a besieged castle. Unbidden tears prickled hot behind her eyes; she swallowed hard, trying to force them back - did not Bertram have enough sorrows, without watching her weep?

"It was she who betrayed me," he said, and his voice was
once more as cold and harsh as it had been to her in the
beginning, when he had thought Margerite to be an Order
member and his foe. "And now, Christ forgive me, she has
triumphed fully." He paused for a moment, still as a statue
of ice-glazed marble in the darkness. "Margerite, I must
go. What I have learned, what I saw at Burg Falkenstein...I
cannot leave my father's lands and folk to her, even if I must
perish to free them."

Margerite stood stock-still, wishing that she could raise
her hands to her ears to protect herself from the knowledge
of what she had heard. When she spoke again, it was in a
bare whisper, but even the faint rush of breath through her
throat hurt as though she were coughing out broken glass.
"How will you go? What will you do?"

"I will go alone," Bertram answered. "Alone, and on foot,
as I left in fear eight years ago, and I will pray to Maria to
see my penitence. Better men may be called by God to free
the Holy Land; I am not pure enough for such a quest, but
at least I can strive my utmost to free my own. As to what I
shall do when I get there, I would be a fool to set a strategy
before I know the battleground: when I have seen clearly
how matters stand, then I shall know what I must do. And...
it may be that while I am gone you will be safer, if only from
the suspicion of Heinrich's men - that is what you were
warning me of in your letter, was it not?"

Margerite nodded mutely.

"Then let this be farewell for now - my love."

Bertram bent forward, and his lips touched Margerite's,
soft and warm. She could taste the hot salt upon them, and
feel the wetness on his cheeks: tears were flowing silently
from his eyes, as from hers. Margerite did not dare to speak
further, for she knew that if another word passed her mouth,
she would beg him to stay - at least for another day, or a
week. If Nikolaus had told her the truth about Herr Jakob,
she could see that Bertram was provisioned with food and
clothes for his journey, with coin and, if need be, some of her
jewelry to sell; perhaps she could even convince him to take
a steed, that he might travel more swiftly and easily.

Yet she knew that it would do her no good to cling to him so, nor, in the knowledge that she was about to lose him, could she keep from going to him, though she risked both their lives and honour in so doing. Bertram held Margerite a little longer, his powerful limbs shaking as though he were wrestling with a foe beyond his strength. Then he let her go, striding swiftly and quietly from the herber. Too devastated to stand, Margerite sank down on the low turfed bench by the wall.

The scent of bruised chammomile still hung where Bertram had been sitting; too late, she realized that it would cling to her cloak as well, for herbal seats were meant to offer perfume as well as comfort. Silently she wept there, hugging herself and rocking back and forth in the effort not to make any sound. I have lost him, I have lost him, she thought. He is going to his death; I shall never see him again. I shall be alone here, Heinrich's wife and - Maria help me! - at Nikolaus' mercy, as much as the Order will allow.

For a moment, Margerite wished bitterly that she had tried to hold Burg Falkenstein by herself; announced her marriage to Bertram, and let negotiation and battle fall where they would. Even if that had meant holding the siege until they perished, at least they would have fallen together, free of the dark webs of Order intrigue and the burdensome chains of her new position alike.

And if we had triumphed? Margerite asked herself. Sooner or later, this same news would have come to us, and Bertram would still have been off - alone, for Burg Falkenstein could never field an army to march on Niederwald. Then I would have been forsaken as surely as any Crusader's wife, with Heinrich and Günther still close at hand; and Günther, most certainly, would never have let me be.

At least here, I have Heinrich's protection for myself and Wolfram, and if I do not let the thoughts and powers of the Light-Bearers seduce me, there is no harm Nikolaus can do to us. When the ragged edges of her sobs no longer caught at her throat, Margerite stood, wiping her face dry with her hood and straightening her cloak around her.

Bertram had had time enough to get back into his barracks, and she had heard no disturbance suggesting that he might have been caught: now it was her turn. Margerite was halfway around the courtyard when she heard the footsteps; turning her head, she saw that a man was walking across the yard towards the herber. She froze, still as a rabbit in the baleful glare of an adder, with one hand clasped about the falcon-pendant between her breasts as though it were a crucifix to protect her.

The starlight picked out the long shadow of a sword belted tightly around a slender waist, glinting pale off a fine trace of silver embroidery against a dark cote-hardie. As Margerite recognised Ritter Gottfried, her pulse beat so hard at the back of her mouth that she thought it would choke her. He had no reason to be out here so late - unless he had found Bertram coming back into the barracks, with the scents of the herber still hanging about his clothing. But surely the knight did not sleep with his men, or watch them constantly.

He must have chambers of his own...could he, too, have a clandestine assignation planned that night? The thought of the severe young knight creeping out to embrace a serving girl under the linden trees brought a horrified giggle to Margerite's throat; she was barely able to suppress it, and some slight noise must have escaped her lips, for Gottfried stopped and turned at once, looking straight at her with his hand on the hilt of his sword.

A chill washed over Margerite, shivering along her skin: even in the darkness, she was sure that he must be able to see her. The gold wings of her falcon-pendant bit painfully into the palm of her hand as she clutched it. But there was no spell of invisibility to human eyes laid upon the jewel, only the protection against magical sight; it would be of no help to her now. Margerite could not tell how long Gottfried stared at her: she did not dare breathe, and her heart was fluttering too fast for her to count its beats. She was sure that at any moment he would challenge her - how could he not?

But at last the knight turned away, stalking quietly until he disappeared beneath the vine-hung arch of the herber's entrance. Margerite did not question her escape, only hurried as quickly as she could to reach the castle door, and safety, before he came back. When she got to her chamber at last, Wolfram had awoken, and was wailing with a note of desperate starvation in his voice, as he often did at this time of night.

Rose silently handed the child to his mother, but for all his crying, Wolfram spat Margerite's nipple out as soon as it was in his mouth. She had to rock and comfort him for some time before he would suck. But who will comfort me now? Margerite wondered as Wolfram settled down to nursing at her. She yawned, suddenly deeply weary, as though her flesh could no longer bear the weight of her soul's travails; she was barely able to stay awake until Wolfram had been burped and laid back in his cradle, and then, mercifully, she collapsed into dreamless, exhausted sleep.

Chapter Three

Rose roused Margerite well in time for her to feed Wolfram and dress for Mass. For a time Margerite dithered over whether or not to wear the falcon necklace which - she was sure - had somehow protected her the night before. It seemed wrong to wear such a thing inside a church; and yet, if she did not, would Nikolaus somehow be able to divine that she was truly worshipping? In the end, though, she left it off, putting her own silver crucifix around her neck instead. The holy sign did not give her the comfort she hoped for: she still felt numb, devastated, like the tree-shattered bank of a river after a great flood had swelled and drained away.

She wondered if Bertram had already left - how could he have passed the guards in the depths of night without suspicion? Would he come to Mass, in hopes of a last drop of grace before setting out on his terrible path? Margerite half-hoped that he would, half that he would not: she would have given all the blood in her body to see him once more, and she did not know if she could bear it.

Heinrich, Christoph, Eva, and Nikolaus were all waiting for her at the chapel door. Heinrich was dressed in a formal robe of deep blue brocade with miniver trim - in a style Margerite's father might have worn, though of finer fabrics and make than Ritter Martin could ever have afforded. The two younger men were clothed in more fashionable tight-fitting tunics and hose, Christoph in bright blue and yellow, Nikolaus in dark green and orange; and all three of the men were decked with heavy chains and rings of gold.

Eva wore the same blue silken brocade she had worn the day before, and Margerite could not help noticing, with a pang of guilt, that it was already growing tight about her shoulders and breasts, while the hemline seemed shorter on her than it ought to be. At least there will be no trouble in clothing her properly here, Margerite thought, but she could not help mentally running up the costs of material.

Eva would have to have several new dresses befitting her status, the more so since Heinrich seemed to hold entertainments fairly often, and besides that, there would be the appalling price of Margerite's own magical tools - not one, but two full robes of pure silk, and the precious metals and stones for preparing her implements as well. No wonder Ruprecht's accounts seemed so badly balanced, and he was forced to borrow so much from Günther! she thought. Thanks be to Mother Maria that his evil debt died with its lender.

The five of them walked into the chapel together. The stained-glass window above the altar, its colours shining brilliant in the sunlight, immediately caught Margerite's eye: the Virgin's cobalt-blue robes, the luminous gold of the Christ-Child's halo, the crimsons and purples that surrounded them like the rich hangings of an Emperor's hall - Heinrich had not been boasting when he spoke of its grandeur.

The vessels of the Mass were wrought in silver set with large polished amethysts and garnets, and if the stem of the chalice were not hollow within, it would take a strong man to hold it aloft for long. Father Michael's vestments matched the finery of his church: his black chasuble was richly adorned with embroidery in silver and gold thread, and the ornamented apparel on the breast, back, cuffs and hems of his white linen alb shimmered with silken tapestry-work as if to rival the window above.

Although she was wearing one of the best dresses Petra
had recut for her, green silk figured with gold, Margerite
still felt a little shabby in that place, particularly when she
looked at Graf Wolfgang, his family, and the other nobles
and knights already seated in the row of benches at the
front. Only Ritter Gottfried, sitting almost painfully erect
with his eyes fixed on the gilded crucifix behind the altar, did
not glisten with gold jewelry; but, though plain, his doublet
was beautifully cut from black velvet lined with silk at the
sleeves.

As they walked down between the standing villagers and
guardsmen to their seats at the front, Margerite could not
help glancing surreptitiously about for Bertram, but he was
nowhere to be seen. *He is gone, and I must accept it,* she
told herself, but though that was the counsel of good sense,
it did little to warm the chill emptiness within her. *O, she
said quietly to him, as if he could hear her thoughts on his
journey, I thought it torture enough to know you were near
and not be able to speak to you: how could I have guessed
how much worse it would be to know that you are not here
at all?*

When Heinrich's family was seated, Father Michael
began, the familiar words of the Mass rolling out richly in
his sonorous baritone voice. Margerite did her best to listen,
breathing in deep breaths of the incensed air as the deacons
in their white albs and neat silken dalmatics swung thick
clouds of smoke from their censers. Yet, for all her striving,
she could not capture the sense of holiness that should have
come upon her in such a beautiful chapel.

Father Michael's words rang oddly hollow in her ears, and
she could not shut the presence of Nikolaus entirely from
her mind: it seemed as though she could hear him mocking
and twisting every line of the prayers, like one string of
a psalter jangling woefully out of tune with the others.
She could not help thinking of the little chapel at Burg
Hirschenberg, its smoky torches and the pair of beeswax
candles gleaming from the plain polished wood of the altar.

How gladly she had murmured her prayers there, her joy something between a child's game and the warm exaltation of God in her soul - and now, what misdeeds were in her heart; what moved and swelled beneath it, frightening her with its presence's forboding? It seemed to Margerite as though the chapel's brightly painted walls were closing in on her, that she could hardly breathe.

Maria, help me! she prayed. Had the Order readings so tainted her soul already that she could no longer bear to sit through a proper Mass? Surreptitiously Margerite reached for her rosary; though the little garnet beads might seem cheap and tawdry next to, for instance, the strand of beautifully carved amethysts that hung from Gräfin Anna's silver girdle, it had comforted her in darker times. As she clutched the smooth stones, the choking feeling receded, almost as if a thick cloud were drawing away from her.

Margerite could not see Nikolaus without turning her head in an unseemly manner, but it seemed to her that she could sense the smile on his pouting lips. She wondered if he had really done something, or if it was merely his presence here that tainted even this house of God; and as Father Michael went on with his Mass, oblivious to whatever had passed, Margerite could not help thinking, Father Etienne would have noticed - and done something.

After Mass, Heinrich and his guests were served their midday meal in the great hall, and then turned to pleasant and quiet occupations such as were fit for a Sunday: conversation, sipping at wine, embroidery, and playing at chess or tables. Margerite excused herself for a while, as it was time for Wolfram's feeding. She had not reached the third story landing, however, when she heard light footsteps behind her.

"Excuse me, Frowe Gräfin," Herr Jakob said breathlessly from a few steps below her. "I understand that you have some items to request of me."

Margerite frowned, looking down on the old man's half-bald head. Nikolaus was clearly making sure that she wasted no time in her preparations - of course, sluggishness on her part would reflect badly on him as well, since he was supposed to be her teacher. Herr Jakob stood with his head bent and knobby-knuckled fingers laced together, the very picture of a perfect servant, and that frightened Margerite more than anything he might say: she had already seen how Heinrich trusted him, but Nikolaus had mentioned working on his mind - who knew how much mischief he might be able to do?

And she was sure that he would report whatever she said back to Nikolaus, so there was nothing for it but to follow her ostensible superior's orders.

"That is so." Quickly, from a memory trained from childhood to hear household lists once and repeat them back perfectly, Margerite laid out for him all those things that she would require, save only the items, such as the hazelwood rod for her wand, that she would have to cut or find by herself.

Herr Jakob nodded once after each, as though he had already been instructed in what to expect - Margerite was sure that, had she left anything out or, out of laziness, told the seneschal to bring her something for which she was responsible herself, Nikolaus would have been told of that too. What a weary life this constant testing and pressing must be for true Order members, Margerite thought - I am growing tired of it already.

Lastly, with some reluctance, Margerite ordered Herr Jacob to bring her a shovel with a good scraping edge: clearing the salt from the floor of her sanctum would not be a pleasant task, but she could see no way out of it, and the sooner begun, the sooner done. And, though she was loath to admit it to herself, she could not deny that a corner of her heart was eager to go back to the crystalline cave where, for a moment, she had felt such powerful exaltation.

"And perhaps it would be best if you left these things with Nikolaus for me, for my chambers are already cluttered," she told him when she was done. Squeamish as the thought of trusting Nikolaus made Margerite, it was better than thinking of a way to explain a shovel to Rose.

"As you wish, Frowe Gräfin," Herr Jakob replied, his head still bowed. He had not met her eyes even once as she spoke, and that troubled her. She wondered what Nikolaus had done to him, and if there were any way for her to undo it - but even if she could, she realized with a shiver of horror, that might well mean betraying herself directly to Nikolaus, since he would certainly seek into how the seneschal had come to be freed of his hold.

Though she had not sworn the oaths by which the Order of Light-Bearers believed her to be bound, the jaws of their trap had nevertheless closed tightly about her. From sin to deeper sin...

"And I know that there must be a good seamstress within this castle," Margerite said briskly, trying to distract herself from her dark thoughts. "Tomorrow I should like to see Eva measured for several dresses, as she is already outgrowing her wardrobe, and we are responsible for keeping her fitted out as is proper for her station."

"It shall be done, Frowe Gräfin," the seneschal said, bowing. He was turning to withdraw when Margerite spoke again.

"Also, I should like to go over the books with you very shortly. I realize that you may have been used to keeping accounts by yourself, since there has been no Gräfin here to act as chatelaine for some years, but I must know what we have and expect to get in the coming year - if only so that I can moderate my personal requirements accordingly."

"I am sure you will find that you need suffer no hardships, Frowe Gräfin," Herr Jakob replied. "Graf Heinrich has commanded that you shall have full access to his privy purse, to use as you will for your own needs. Nevertheless, if it is your request, you will find me in my chambers tomorrow afternoon."

"That is all. You may go."

The seneschal bowed again and departed, the dusty hem of his deep green robe sweeping the stairs behind him. Suddenly, without warning, Kobolt came darting down past Margerite to pounce gleefully upon Herr Jakob's short train. The old man let out a strangled yelp, leaping into the air, then collapsing on the stairwell in a shivering heap. Purring triumphantly, Kobolt walked up a couple of steps, then sat down to wash himself, his golden gaze fixed on his victim.

"Herr Jakob! Are you hurt?" Margerite asked.

Painfully the seneschal pushed himself up against the stone wall, staring at the black tomcat. His gnarled hands were shaking, and Margerite could see the terror in his face - and, it seemed to her, the shadow that dulled his pale blue eyes like the gray beginnings of a dark cataract.

"It did not harm me," Herr Jakob said, his voice toneless and flat. There was something unnervingly wooden about his movements as he turned to walk away again, and Margerite clenched her fists in the hem of her skirt. Whatever Nikolaus had done to him, it was a horrible thing, and she knew that by doing nothing, she was giving her silent assent to that evil.

Father Etienne would seek to break that spell, she thought. But I - even if I dared risk it, I would not know how. And that realization, too, was bitter: that knowing what was right, she still could not do it, unless...unless I truly apply myself to the study of sorcery. For knowing of those arts, dark or light, was, Margerite realized now, like grasping a nettle: to brush them lightly was to feel their burning sting; to be taken without harm to the user, they must be seized swiftly and boldly, with full strength and no hesitation. And if she lingered as she was, the sins of omission - of recognising wrong and doing nothing, such as weighed even now upon her soul - would fall thicker and thicker upon her, like snowflakes in a winter storm, until she was buried far past her own ability to free herself.

"I will do it," Margerite whispered to herself. "I must. Christ help me, Mother Maria help me, that in seeking to overcome one evil, I do not fall deeper into another. " As she prayed, Kobolt purred and writhed about her legs as if to coax a piece of fish from her hand. She did not know whether to take his sudden enthusiasm as a sign of good or ill. Father Etienne had told her that the cat, in himself, was only a spirit of earth; but looking down at Kobolt, she could see the sparkle of a few tiny salt-crystals in his black fur, as though he had been rolling on the floor in the hidden caves again, and that gave her hope that at least her sanctum would not be a place of damnation.

The rest of the afternoon passed pleasantly enough, with Heinrich's minstrels and performers entertaining the noble company as they drank wine, nibbled on small pastries, and chatted amiably. Margerite soon fell into conversation with Gräfin Anna, who, after a little time, demanded that Wolfram be brought down for her to see.

"Such a beautiful child!" Anna cooed, tickling him under the chin with a plump, beringed finger, then kissing him on the forehead. Wolfram gurgled happily, grabbing for a curly wisp of red hair that had escaped from the elaborate coiffure of braids piled on the Gräfin's head. "I have never seen a lovelier one. Such bright eyes and golden hair, such pink cheeks and strong limbs; nothing about him could be made better! One would almost think that his father had been an angel, he is so like an angel to look upon." Margerite jerked as if the other woman had slapped her, a cold pang of terror twinging through her body; but fortunately, Gräfin Anna chattered on obliviously.

"And you are nursing him yourself? That is an excellent thing; I have always held that a noblewoman must nurse her own children, for who knows what they might take in from the breasts of a wet-nurse of lower birth? I nursed all three of my own sons, and now my eldest, Hugo, is serving in the Kaiser's own guard, and my second son Konrad was the victor in the great tournament at Köln just this spring - at the age of only nineteen, can you believe it! As for Georg, you will soon see his worth for yourself, since he is staying here with dear Christoph."

Margerite nodded and smiled, letting Anna ramble as she would. Mercifully soon, however, the other Gräfin turned her attentions to Eva, questioning her thoroughly about her family. Eva countered her enquiries expertly, which Margerite was glad to see: the time she and Etienne had spent preparing the girl to take up her proper role in society had not been wasted. A little more worrying was the speculative way in which Gräfin Anna glanced from Eva to Georg - who stood respectfully behind Christoph, ready to serve his knight's needs and, apparently, completely ignoring his mother.

But Anna would not be here long enough to cause any trouble, Margerite reassured herself. And in any case, while Eva might be nearly old enough to marry, Georg was not, and Margerite very much doubted that Heinrich would even consider talk of a betrothal for Eva with anyone but Christoph. Much as she tried to let herself be distracted by the company and the skill of Heinrich's entertainers, though, Margerite's thoughts kept turning inward. Neither talk, nor song, nor the novelty of her husband's jugglers with their whirling objects and quick jesting patter, could keep her mind long from sinking between the twin poles of Bertram's departure and the enormity of the decision she had made.

Even when the taller of the jugglers deftly swept Kriemhilt from Eva's lap, swooping the purring cat in and out between the torrent of balls his other hand kept in the air, though Margerite laughed with the rest, she still felt the miserable weight of emptiness and fear pressing beneath her glaze of mirth, as if she were pregnant with the cold child of a phantom. By the time the evening meal was done, the stress of keeping up her pleasant facade had left Margerite with a miserable headache, and her shift was clammy with cold sweat. She sent Rose down to the kitchens to make her a tisane of chammomile and scullcap.

She would have liked to add valerian to that, but she knew it would make her sleepy, and having decided to start work on her sanctum that night, she was determined to see it through. While the serving girl was away, Margerite dug a thick plain dress of winter wool out of the bottom of one of her chests - a dress she had not seen for two years: she had worn it at Burg Hirschenberg when there was work to be done in the cold, but never after arriving at Burg Falkenstein. She had meant to have it cut down for Gertrude...Pushing the thought from her mind, Margerite hid the dress beneath her coverlet, together with her heaviest cloak and gloves, and put a sturdy pair of boots under the bed where she could find them easily without waking Rose.

When her serving maid had gone to sleep, Margerite dressed stealthily and crept down the hall to Nikolaus' chamber, Kobolt padding softly behind her. She knew that he was awake, for a glimmer of light shone through his keyhole, and so she tapped very quietly on the door.

For a little while she thought that he had not heard her; she was just making up her mind to knock more loudly when the door swung open.

"You might have waited for my call," Nikolaus complained as soon as he had shut the door behind Margerite. "It is impertinent for you to push yourself forward so."

"I am eager to start clearing my sanctum - and Herr Jakob could hardly have left my materials where my maid may come upon them first."

"True enough," Nikolaus admitted. "Take up your shovel, then, and let us go."

Nikolaus made Margerite lead the way through the caves, muttering under his breath as they went. It was little trouble for her to remember the turnings: though she had only been there once, the path seemed strangely familiar to her, and she did not doubt that, when she went there on her own, she could easily find her way. Kobolt scampered ahead, his black shape melting in and out of the shadows, lashing his tail and stopping to roll and purr every now and then as though he had been eating catnip.

To Margerite's surprise, the thick encrustation of salt-crystals glittering on the floor of her sanctum came up easily; she had expected to have to chip every inch painfully away, but her work seemed little harder than using a broom, and would have been easier still if Kobolt had not pounced upon or rolled in every pile she scraped up, scattering the white heaps across the floor again. Chill as it was in the caves, her clothes and the work kept her pleasantly warm, and the unaccustomed labour quickly drove any other thoughts from her mind except the satisfaction of watching the rock come clean in long dark strips beneath her shovel's edge.

Nikolaus had not stayed to watch her work, but had gone on to his own sanctum; every so often, Margerite heard the muttering of his voice down the corridor, but she could not make out any words. By the time Nikolaus returned, Margerite had the whole area that he had marked out for her clear. He stood at the entryway, staring for a while, before he said anything.

"That should not have gone so quickly," he told her at last. "Feel the rock; if it is too wet, we shall have to find you another cave."

Margerite stooped down, putting her hand to the stone beneath her feet. Though chill, it was hardly damper than the stone walls of any castle; it would easily take the paint of a circle. "It is dry enough," she replied.

Nikolaus shook his head, beckoning her to come back with him. When they had reached his chamber again, he thrust the bag of materials roughly into her arms. "You have what you need here, and you know what to do. You are not to bother me again until after Johannisnacht: it will take longer than that for you to shape your tools and paint the circle in your sanctum. You already have a copy of the Black Book: apply yourself to memorizing your correspondences, for you must know the names and natures of each of the planetary forces before you can set them into your wand, and likewise the correspondences of the elements and the Tree of the Qlippoth must be familiar to you."

A shudder went down Margerite's spine at the sound of the unfamiliar name. "I have not read so far..." she started.

"Then do it! If you do not know what you must before you begin to work, your life will surely answer for it. " Nikolaus' voice had almost risen to a shout, his pudgy cheeks darkening - and that is not anger, but fear, which I hear from him: he knows how ill-suited he is to be a teacher, and what punishments will befall him if he fails.

"I shall remember that. Have you more to tell me?"

"Nothing that will do you any good until you know more."

"Then goodnight, Nikolaus." Margerite withdrew before he could dismiss her: it was a small triumph, and petty, but she had already seen how such things mattered to Nikolaus' mind. As long as she could keep him off-balance, unsure of how to deal with her, then he would be less able to either harm her or guess her true thoughts.

Margerite took no pleasure from that: if it were a game, it was one played in grim earnest, with lives and souls as the stakes - like chess with living pieces, with the queen defending her helpless king, my dear Wolfram...but my bishop and my knight are across the board, and can give me no help; and one of my castles is far away, while the other is compromised. And more than half the pieces are veiled from each other, so that none can easily be sure of friend or foe: I would not willingly play such chess for the stake of a silver penny.

And what might Nikolaus be planning for Johannisnacht? There would be no good in it, and Margerite did not know how she could divine his plans, or how to thwart them if she did. She felt like a young page ordered to the fore of a battle before his arms had yet grown strong enough to learn the proper wielding of sword or lance; she could only pray, and hope for God's grace to carry her through.

Graf Wolfgang and his family departed shortly after dawn the next morning, bidding farewell to Heinrich and Margerite with enthusiastic embraces. When they were gone, Margerite sent a page to bid the castle's seamstress come to Eva's rooms and bring her finest bolts of fabric so that the girl could choose between them. Kriemhilt's kittens greeted this process with delight, climbing up Margerite's skirts and pouncing on the heaps of material on the bed until Eva caught them and shut them in a covered basket, which erupted at once with piteous little mews. Kriemhilt ran to the basket, rubbing her gold-starred forehead against it and chirping to her kittens, but they did not seem comforted.

"Perhaps it is time to think of turning your cats loose in the castle," Margerite suggested. "They have grown lively enough, and they seem well able to run."

"They are not big enough to leave their mother yet," Eva argued. "They are still nursing - and they are so small; a careless foot could easily crush them."

"If cats were so fragile, there would be none left in the world," Margerite told her, but Eva refused to be convinced.

"Anyway, my Kriemhilt would be so heartbroken if she lost one of her darlings, wouldn't you, my sweet?" Kriemhilt looked up at her mistress and purred. Margerite could see the look of disgust on the seamstress' pinched features; doubtless the woman thought that cats were dirty animals who had no place in a noblewoman's chambers, but she would hardly speak up against them when everyone in the castle had already seen the Gräfin's cat.

"Settle yourself, Eva, so you can be measured properly," Margerite said. She had expected Eva to be more enthusiastic about choosing the materials and styles of her gowns, but the girl hardly seemed to be paying any attention: there was a remote look in her blue eyes, and she kept glancing wistfully out the window, although there was nothing below but the craggy mountainside sloping down towards the blue waters of the lake.

"Have you not seen enough of Christoph yet?" Margerite finally asked, exasperated, when she had had to repeat a question twice before Eva answered it. "Surely you can bear to be parted from him for half an hour."

Eva smiled sweetly, her fair cheeks dimpling. "He said that he would be practicing at sword-play and jousting with the other knights, and that it would be almost like a tourney to watch. I have never seen a tourney, Margerite."

"Nor have I," Margerite replied tartly. "But I do not need to rush out to watch young men sweating in their armour and bashing each other about." Speaking so made her a little uncomfortable, since she knew that, had the opportunity come up to watch Ruprecht fight before their wedding, nothing on earth could have kept her from the yard where he was showing his prowess, while if Bertram were out there now... But it was her duty to set a good example for Eva, even if only chance made it possible. "You will see Christoph wield sword and lance enough times. May God grant that it is chiefly in tournaments - or have you forgotten how it was to see him lying pale and wounded in bed?"

"Indeed I have not!" Eva answered, indignant. "But there is little danger of that now."

"Hush, and lift your arms. I think your bosom must have swelled by a full inch since your last dresses were made; some of them look almost indecent on you now. I cannot believe how fast you are growing."

"My father was a full four inches above six feet tall, and my mother little more than half a handspan less," Eva said proudly. "My father often said that he would have to find a man of his own measure to wed me to; even if Christoph is a little shorter, I will be sure to give him tall sons."

"I will not be surprised if you are taller than he by the time you have your full growth. But it is a bit early to speak of giving Christoph sons, since you are not even betrothed yet - and you had best not think of hurrying it along by doing anything unseemly," Margerite warned her. Eva only giggled, a becoming flush spreading over her cheeks.

By the time the fittings were finished and the women had gone down to the outer courtyard, the men - including Heinrich, a little to Margerite's surprise - were all in full armor, except for Christoph, who was still patiently instructing Georg in the intricacies of strapping his flanged knee-cups.

"Pull tighter - one notch tighter now, that is it. I do not need that plate to be sliding from its place every time a blow strikes it. " Georg looked up at his knight, his red brows creasing in a worried expression, and Christoph laughed and patted him on the shoulder.

"Do not fret, Knappe. You will soon learn to do things exactly as I need. Believe me, I was far more clumsy in my first days at your father's court; it surprises me now to think how seldom my ears were boxed for it. Now the other knee: make haste, everyone else is ready and eager, and we are holding them back. Where is Bertram?" he asked suddenly, looking around as Georg lifted up his gleaming steel breastplate to strap over his leathern coat of plates and hooked the two chains that ran from a pair of gilded rings beneath its upper rim to his sword and dagger so that the weapons would not be lost if they were knocked from his hand. "I saw him fight at Burg Falkenstein; I have been eager to try him again."

Ritter Gottfried frowned. Framed by the steel of his bascinet and its chain-mail gorget, his thin face looked more haggard than usual, his gray eyes darker. "He was on guard duty Sunday, but no one has seen him today, or knows where he went. I began a search for him two hours ago; his clothes and armour are missing, but nothing else." He turned directly to Margerite, fixing her with his gaze. "Did you send him on some errand, Frowe Gräfin?"

"I did not," Margerite replied calmly. Her palms were damp with sweat, but she was able to keep her breathing even and her heart from racing."I do not know where he is." That was true enough, at any rate.

"Do you think he may have gone back to Burg Falkenstein?" the hatchet-faced knight pressed. "There are men there who are loyal to him; he might well have it in his mind to take the castle if he can."

"If he had wished to stay, he would have said so before," Margerite answered, her voice still steady. "Nor will he betray me - but from what I have seen of him, he is a proud man, and I doubt he took well to being treated as if he were suspected of some crime. If you want my opinion, Ritter Gottfried, I believe that you might well have driven him away, and that he is likely to seek his fortunes elsewhere - and that you did your Graf no service by letting Bertram feel your mistrust."

"Soft, Margerite," Heinrich rumbled, stepping between his wife and his knight. "You must admit that it looks strange, and perhaps somewhat suspicious, that your man should have left so quickly without any word - without even, if I do not miss my guess, collecting his last month's pay."

"That is so," Gottfried agreed. "And that would not be the choice of an honest man. Even those of us who are Ministerales are not enslaved here, and Bertram was not born to the Graf's service; there was nothing to stop him from declaring that he wished to leave, taking what was owed him, and going on his way, if his intentions were good. Who but a fugitive would sneak away in the night? To my mind, this proves that all my doubts of him were well-founded."

"Why would he have trusted you with knowledge of his affairs, when it might have been because of you that he left?" Margerite challenged.

Gottfried's angular cheekbones flushed, but Heinrich interrupted before the young knight could speak. "It is Ritter Gottfried's duty to make sure of my men. Bertram should have understood that, having been Hauptmann of Ruprecht's guard, and should have expected to be met with some doubt before he had proven his loyalty to me: if he was used to doing his own job well, surely he would have acted in much the same way."

Margerite did not know what to say. She could not defend Bertram too hotly, lest any further suspicion fall upon her; nor could she excuse his flight without betraying some knowledge of his doings. And Heinrich spoke nothing but the truth: nevertheless...

"Would it have been too much," she pressed, "to have given a little consideration to his former position, and to the faithfulness he showed me? Before Christ, Bertram had guarded me safely and well in travel and war and peace, nor did he ever seek to do me any wrong. I brought him here from my trust for him, and you treated him like a branded criminal, Ritter Gottfried!"

"Bertram seemed a good man to me as well," Christoph added unexpectedly. "And -" he looked sharply at his father -"I would have thought that he had earned our trust."

Heinrich scowled. "He served as his position warranted; but trust given can be as easily betrayed."

Christoph's breath hissed sharply in between his teeth, his face suddenly grim. Horrified, Margerite realized what Heinrich and his son must be thinking: Bertram had been Ruprecht's man, and knew the secret of Graf Günther's demise - what if he sought to sell it to other allies of Günther's, or give it to them in hopes of advancement?

Now she knew why Heinrich had agreed so easily to bringing Bertram with them, where he could keep an eye on the former Hauptmann's doings, and she was sure in her bones that whether Bertram were taken or killed on the spot, if he fell into Heinrich's hands now, her husband could not risk letting him leave Burg Fürstensee alive again.

"What have you done to seek him out, Gottfried?" Heinrich pursued.

"As soon as I had made certain that Bertram was no longer within our walls, I sent a small party of armed and horsed men to track him, with hounds that had been given the scent from his bedding," Gottfried answered. "They are to bring him back if he will come, to slay him if he stands to fight them - he is too good a man of his hands to be trifled with, and if he draws sword against them, it is sure proof that his intentions are evil."

"Good enough. Send someone down to the village as well, to be sure he is not there: this would not be the first time a guardsman had earned a few stripes for his back by sleeping too long with a peasant lass. But you and Ritter Dieter shall horse yourselves now and go in search of Bertram as well; take three or four riders each with you. Whether it is a matter of capturing him or slaying him, I do not wish Bertram to cross the bounds of my land without my knowledge. If he has others with him, fight if you think you will win; otherwise ride straight back here for help."

Ritter Gottfried's thin lips tightened: Margerite could not tell whether the look on his sharp face was one of smugness that his suspicions had been confirmed, or frustration that he did not dare to ask his Graf more, but he bowed and called for his fellow knight and their squires at once.

"As for the rest of us, we may as well continue with our play," Heinrich said. "A few small groups of riders will have an easier time tracking one man through the woods than will a host, while if Bertram has fled, he has only a few hours' head start on us, and that by foot and most of it in the dark as well. And if we are called upon, we will be armoured and ready to go. Does that suit you?"

"Aye, it suits me," said Christoph.

"I still think you have misjudged Bertram," Margerite told her husband stubbornly. Heinrich laughed, patting her cheek lightly with an armoured glove.

"If that is so, then doubtless he will come back quietly, and be able to give an explanation; if it is a good one, then I shall not punish him too harshly, though I do not take well to my guards leaving their duties without notice."

You are lying to me, Margerite thought. Though Heinrich met her eyes as he spoke, his broad face seemingly open and honest as an ox's, she knew that he could not have held his lands this long without learning the ruses of politics. I was not so suspicious a year ago, she thought sadly, but I have seen too much to be trusting now. If Bertram came back, Margerite was sure that she would not be allowed to watch his interrogation, and she would hear the news of his death second-hand - and that spurred her towards a desperateness that she could not otherwise have encompassed.

"Enjoy your sport, then," Margerite said, as lightly as she could. "I shall not tarry, for I have an appointment to keep with Herr Jakob, who has promised to show me something of the castle's books today."

"Are you quite sure?" Christoph asked. "That is weary work, and you have scarcely had time to learn your way around the castle; would you not prefer to take your ease for a few days yet, until you are more comfortable here?"

"I shall leave Eva to watch you," Margerite replied, and from the flush on his rounded cheeks, she knew that she had hit on Christoph's chief concern.

Margerite struggled to keep from running as she mounted the stairs to the third floor of the castle. Had she been armed already with wand and dagger, cup and pentacle, she might have been able to manage what she needed to do herself; but she knew that it was beyond her knowledge. Her only hope, foul as the thought seemed, was Nikolaus.

At least he had not been down with the other men - she had already seen that he was a late riser; pray God he was still in his rooms! The incongruity of that thought stopped her, if only for a moment, but she made herself press on, for she knew that Bertram's life was at stake. The rites that Nikolaus might guide her in performing, or perform himself, for Bertram's protection would surely be blasphemous; yet they might keep him alive.

When Margerite came to Nikolaus' door, she halted. She could hear his voice from within; though she could make out no words, the soft muttering crept over her skin like the dry scales of an adder. She lifted her fist to knock, but it hung poised in the air, then dropped back to her side.

What is a little more taint upon my soul, when weighed against the life of my beloved? Margerite thought. If it were for Wolfram's sake, I would not hesitate.

Nikolaus' voice rose and fell in his chant, the tattered cobwebs of phrases straggling out to her. "Dominus Lucis... Imperator Infernis...Seductor et Magister Hominum... Demonum Magister..."

Margerite wanted to turn and flee, but she restrained herself. If Nikolaus were performing a conjuration, he would not do so in his chamber: he was merely praying, preparing himself for whatever rite he intended to perform on Johannisnacht.

If I stop him now and beg his aid, that may hinder him in his workings, and the Order will not allow him to harm me in turn. Again her hand lifted to knock; but again it fell back.

"Kobolt?" she whispered. "Where are you? Will you guide me?"

Soft fur rustled against Margerite's skirts. Kobolt's pupils were very large in the dim light of the hallway as he stared up into her face, but he only settled himself on his haunches, looking at her. Of course: where power was raised, he might help her to safety, but the black tom was an earth-spirit, neither of good nor of evil. He could not make this choice for her, though she longed to have it lifted from her.

Swiftly, swiftly! something urged within Margerite's soul. The hunters are hot on Bertram's track; if you do not act, they will chase him down like a deer. The thought brought a horrible image back to her mind: Eckhardt's grandfather, gut-shot and fleeing in a stumbling run, while Ruprecht's horn winded the mort behind him. Heinrich's men would hunt Bertram thus, or do worse, if he were taken alive...

Sobbing now, Margerite lifted her hand for the third time.

"Inmicus fidei...Humani generis mortis repetor..." The words came clearly to her: Enemy of faith...creator of death for the race of men...and it seemed to Margerite that she could hear Bertram saying, as clearly as if he stood before her, I will pray to Maria to see my penitence.

Margerite's hand dropped for the last time, clutching for the string of rosary-beads at her girdle. Though he went alone, unblessed by anything save her own prayers, nevertheless she felt that Bertram was on a Crusade as perilous as any journey to the Holy Land. She could not help him by evil means; she did not know enough to use any better powers for his aid, except to cry out, with all her heart, Mother Maria, help your knight!

Before anyone could come upon her weeping there, Margerite dried her face on her sleeve and walked to her chamber, briskly telling Rose to get out until she was summoned back. Then the Gräfin pushed one of the thick rugs aside, kneeling on the cold stone and praying until her knees were numb and her back aching with fiery cramps, pausing only when Wolfram cried most bitterly for feeding - for that need, she thought, Maria would understand.

Ritter Gottfried did not return that evening, nor the next nor the one after, though his band occasionally sent a man back briefly to tell Heinrich that the search was still going on. When she was not obliged by her duties of courtesy to be present in the hall, Margerite divided her time between fervent prayer and, in those periods when she could send Rose away on some errand or other, working upon her magical tools and studying from the Black Book.

It was not until Saturday morning that the young knight, pale beneath the dirt of five days and nights in the woods and looking even thinner and more haggard than before, rode back through the gates of Burg Fürstensee with his squire Arnmut beside him.

"What news?" Heinrich demanded when Gottfried came before him in the great hall. The knight took his helm off, kneeling bare-headed before his lord, and Margerite fought to keep her face still, that none of her fear or hope shine through its mask.

"Herr Graf, we have found Bertram's tracks, but he has managed to escape us; he is a clever woodsman. He seems to be heading northeast, and has passed into Graf Wolfgang's lands. I left my men and Ritter Dieter to follow him, and rode back as swiftly as I could, that we might know your will. Shall we alert Graf Wolfgang and ask his help, or follow on our own? Herr Graf, I, at least, will pursue until I have found him, for if I had kept a more careful watch on Bertram, he would not have escaped."

Heinrich scowled deeply, blue eyes narrowing in thought. Margerite needed no magic to know how his mind was working: it would be discourteous to hunt through another lord's lands without his leave, and Graf Wolfgang's aid would be helpful - but there was still the risk that Bertram might tell his secret, to save his life or as simple revenge.

"Ask Graf Wolfgang's leave to seek a fugitive," Heinrich said at last. "If my friend offers aid, you may accept it, but do not ask for it: I would sooner not have any others involved in this matter. Should it be that Bertram still manages to elude you long enough to flee beyond Graf Wolfgang's lands, then..." Heinrich twisted a grizzled strand of beard between his fingers, considering. "Wolfgang is my friend and ally, but matters will be less secure for us beyond his borders. Do you think that you alone could overcome Bertram?"

"As to whether I could best him in fair fight or not,"
Gottfried answered, lifting his head and looking up proudly
at the Graf, "that is something that can only be known when
our swords are crossed. But I can say that, without God's
grace aiding him in the matter, he could not slay me without
taking most grievous wounds himself."

"And unless Bertram has somehow managed to find a
warhorse, you and your Knappe will both be mounted while
he is afoot," Heinrich prompted.

"That was not what you asked, Herr Graf," Gottfried said,
his voice clear and reproachful. "When two fight against
one, even without the horses - which may help or hinder,
depending on where we come across him - the outcome is
far more easily foreseen."

And you have little stomach for being on the stronger side
of an unfair fight, but will do as your Graf commands you
anyway, Margerite thought sadly as she looked down at him.
Though she had little love for Ritter Gottfried, she could
not help but sympathize with him, torn as he so clearly was
between his duty and his sense of chivalry.

Heinrich should not have asked his man that question, for
even Margerite could see that, in the moment of Gottfried's
considering it, Bertram had passed from a fugitive to be
hunted to something in the realm of a knightly challenge.
Bearing such orders, Gottfried, it will be best for you if you
never find Bertram, for if you fight as you are commanded,
and do not lose your life, you will think your honour forever
soiled. May Christ grant you escape from this grievous
choice; may Mother Maria protect you both, and grant you
mercy!

Ritter Gottfried's gray eyes flickered towards Margerite, almost as if she had spoken aloud. But Heinrich went on, "If you are certain of that, then it will be best for the two of you to go on alone if Bertram cannot be brought to ground within Graf Wolfgang's lands. A knight and his Knappe by themselves may travel faster and with less trouble than a larger band, and it is clear that you need swiftness if you are to run our fugitive down. But I can see that you are weary and have travelled hard. Rest a little, wash yourself, and gather provisions for your journey: Herr Jakob will see to it that you and Arnmut have all you need."

"I thank you, Herr Graf," Gottfried said, rising and bowing before he departed, his thin back straight as a lance raised in challenge.

Heinrich turned to Margerite. "Do you still think that Bertram is innocent, when he has fled my lands so swiftly?"

"I do not know what to think," Margerite replied. "I hope that, if Ritter Gottfried finds him, he does not attack before Bertram has a chance to speak. " Not least, because Gottfried may be tried and proven in war, but I believe Bertram has spent several years on far harsher battlefields, and it would be sad to see a young man's life wasted for a falsehood.

"Gottfried is a man of strong conscience," Heinrich assured her. "However he judges matters when the time comes, I trust him not to fail me."

Margerite wondered exactly what her husband meant by that - had Gottfried been with the band Heinrich brought to dispose of Günther's men? She could not remember whether she had seen him there or not: the first days after Wolfram's birth were still something of a dazed dream to her, and a good number of Heinrich's soldiers had returned to Burg Fürstensee after leaving the bodies in the mountains.

But she could not imagine one of Heinrich's trusted knights not being privy to what had gone on then, and so the Graf's words took on a dark and ominous resonance in her mind.

Nikolaus did not appear for the midday meal that day, and one of the servants brought word down that he was suffering from a chill and wished to be left alone. Heinrich frowned at that news.

"The boy always seems to be sickening with something or other," he said. "Margerite, are you skilled in herb-craft? Nikolaus is stubborn about letting our physician Ernst tend him; perhaps he will take a posset more readily from your fair hands."

"I have already spoken with him," Margerite answered slowly. "I think that he will be well enough in a couple of days."

"It would be a shame if he were to miss Monday's sun-wending feast," Heinrich mused. "The Fürstensee folk have always thought that it brought great good luck for the men of my blood to kindle the fires in their village and atop the mountain, as well as here in the castle - and who are we to argue with a tradition that my family has kept for generations?"

"Father," Christoph said, his gray-green eyes gleaming with enthusiasm, "I think there is nothing wrong with Nikolaus save sluggishness and a bit of excess fat on his belly. If he rose early in the morning like the rest of us, and betook himself to the courtyard to practice with his weapons, he would be in better health. In fact, I think it would be good for him if I dragged him from his room now and made him do something healthy and manly: I'll wager you a silver mark that I can shake the chill from his bones, and if he is sore afterwards, a good cup of wine should medicate his melancholy well enough."

Eva laughed and clapped her hands, and Heinrich grinned in his beard. "Perhaps I should take that wager," the Graf replied. "It is not good for Nikolaus to sit indoors and read all day and night, and if he is truly ill and not malingering, as I have sometimes suspected, we shall know soon enough. What do you think, Margerite?"

"A fine plan," she replied without hesitation. If Nikolaus could be dragged from his meditations and made to eat and drink, breaking his unholy fast of purification...by God's grace, the interruption might well spoil him for whatever dreadful rite he was preparing himself for. The thought of sending Christoph up to confront his brother now made Margerite a little uneasy, but she could not think of any way in which it might actually endanger Heinrich's elder son.

"Well, then!" Christoph leapt easily from his chair and ran out.

Heinrich waited a moment, then cupped his hand to his ear and exaggeratedly feigned listening towards the old tower. "We shall hear screams and furniture breaking any moment now," he whispered loudly to Eva and Margerite, who both laughed.

It was a little while before Christoph came down, however, and when he did, Margerite noticed that he seemed paler and there was a faint dew of clammy sweat on his broad forehead.

"Nikolaus is certainly ill," he said. "There is an unwholesome air in his room. He insists that he needs no leeching, but I think we should call Ernst to see to him."

"I shall go with him," Margerite said, standing in her turn. "If Nikolaus has taken a worse turn since I saw him last, he may well need to be bled: he seems to have a chronic excess of the phlegmatic humour."

"That is just what Ernst says," Heinrich agreed. "At the very least, perhaps you can convince my son to let his chambers be fumigated and to take some medicine."

The Burg Fürstensee physician was a small, fussy man whose gray robe was trimmed with gold brocade and seemed a little too long for him in the sleeves, while the weight of his black case of medical implements caused him to list slightly to the side. He seemed knowledgeable, however, and discoursed delightedly on the subject of a possible regimen of treatment for Nikolaus' ailment as he and Margerite walked up the stairs together.

"His blood is too thick and sluggish, I have always said so," Ernst confided to Margerite. "He ought to be bled twice a month to drain out the phlegmatic humours which are responsible for these chills and damp coughs, and fed on warm foods until he is in better balance. The flesh of cockerels steeped in wine is good for heating the blood, and though pepper is dear, it is cheaper than many other medicines that some of my colleagues - I name no names - might prescribe for a Graf's son. Wild boar should appear on his plate more often than pork, for it is the nature of wild beasts to be hotter and dryer than domestic animals, while he should never be allowed to touch lamprey or eel. I have tried to tell Hildegard this many times, but she will insist on serving eel on Fridays, and does not even always kill them in salt and cook them in wine to counteract their cold moist nature. How such an ignorant woman can be a cook at this castle, I do not know."

Looking down at the physician's rounded belly, Margerite thought that he probably knew perfectly well how Hildegard managed to hold her post, but it would have been rude to say so.

"As for treating Nikolaus now, once we have bled him, I shall make up a special chest-rub from olive oil and herbs of the Sun and Mars, which should infuse him with a more fiery and manly temper - would you not say so? It is an opportune time of year for such treatment, though we would do well to consult a horoscope to see what airs the planets have in store for us."

When Nikolaus answered his door, he did indeed look pale and drawn, with an unhealthy gray cast to his skin; Margerite guessed that he had been awake all night, and fasting at least since midnight, and such austerity did not sit well with him. He was dressed in a heavy robe of black velvet, cinched loosely beneath his belly with a silver girdle, and Margerite saw at once what Christoph had meant about an unwholesome air in his room, for she could catch a faint whiff of something foul and clammy through the open door.

"What do you want?" the Graf's son said rudely, glaring at Ernst. "I need no leeching, nor any of your remedies."

"If you are ill, you must be treated: it is Graf Heinrich's wish."

"It is my wish that you leave me alone, and I shall enforce that while I still have the strength to wield a sword. Now go - the sight of you sickens me worse than any tainted airs."

The castle physician backed up a couple of steps, looking very much as though he wished to hide behind Margerite; he had suffered from Nikolaus' ill-temper before, she guessed. But he persevered, though his reedy voice was quavering.

"Will you at least let the Frowe Gräfin in to see what she can do for you? You must treat her courteously, she is your father's wife."

"I know that," Nikolaus snapped. "Margerite may enter - but away with you, and do not come back!"

Ernst turned and scuttled down the hallway, holding his robe up with his free hand. Nikolaus beckoned Margerite in and slammed the door behind her.

"What is the meaning of this?" he demanded. "Why am I suddenly being assailed at my meditations?"

"Perhaps you should have chosen a less dangerous excuse for retreat than illness," Margerite answered calmly. "You managed to play the part of an invalid well enough to worry Christoph, and now, I fear, you cannot escape it. Heinrich expects me to do something for you, so I must at least pretend to be treating you for your chill."

"The Devil take the chill, and my father as well!" Nikolaus swore. "You should have realized by now that I need peace to fast and meditate until St. Johannistag, and I am making it your duty, Priestess, to see that I get it."

Seeing no escape, Margerite sighed, resigning herself unhappily to helping Nikolaus with his pretense. "I can make possets and command healthful meals, and even pretend to bring them to you, since you are firmly set that you will accept no treatment from Ernst; if Kobolt eats the food instead, no one need know it. But I cannot promise to guard your door every moment, and if your father or Christoph insist on seeing you, there is nothing I can do."

"I know that well enough," Nikolaus answered irritably. "I am sure that you can make up sufficient tales to keep them happy with my recovery, or at least satisfied enough to leave me alone. But as a special favour," he added, seeming to relent a little, "if you come to me at this time, just after the mid-day meal, each day, I shall allow you to walk through quietly so that you may go more easily to your sanctum unobserved, for I am sure you are eager to begin painting your circle. How is it going with your tools?"

"Well enough, though it is slow work, since I must wait until my serving maid is asleep every night," Margerite answered. In truth, she had almost finished engraving the gold round of her pentacle, while her cup and her dagger awaited only the final consecration that she would give them when all of the implements were done, and she had been able to stitch her robes during the day, since Rose knew so little of fashion as to simply believe that her mistress did not entirely trust the castle seamstress to make her garments quite as she wished.

Only the hazel rod of the wand still had to be cut - and for that, Margerite had decided to wait until dawn on Johannistag, when the sun would be at her strongest and all the powers of darkness weakest; for though the Order called Lucifer the Lord of Light, Margerite knew that the brightness of God's day was still a hindrance to them.

"Perhaps you will be a little freer in times to come. Go now, for I still have much to do."

"May I ask what work you are planning?" Margerite enquired timidly - for all the world, she hoped, like an eager student.

"No." Nikolaus turned his back on her forcefully, and she did not dare try to push the conversation further.

Margerite found it easy enough to carry out their deception, though Heinrich's praise for her success with his stubborn younger son galled her deeply, since she knew how little she deserved it. But the pretext of mixing medicines for Nikolaus made it easier for her to grow familiar with Burg Fürstensee's stock of herbs, and provided the perfect cover for her to demand frankincense, myrrh, and olive oil from Father Michael so that she could mix her own holy oil for the consecration of her tools.

It was ironic, Margerite thought, that only now could she appreciate the freedom she had enjoyed at Burg Falkenstein: at Heinrich's castle, so much richer and better-ordered as it was, she could hardly turn about without tripping over an eager serving-maid or page who would enquire hopefully as to what she was doing and if they could help. It was no wonder that Nikolaus had cultivated the image of a cranky and sickly young man in order to get the privacy he needed for his magical workings: had it not been for the dangers of such a pretense that his example had made clear, Margerite would have been tempted to feign frequent headaches and vapours herself.

At least nursing Wolfram gave her regular excuses to sit by herself in her chambers, and she was able to surreptitiously trace protective pentacles about the rooms - though Kobolt sneezed in annoyance when he smelled the sweet oil, and promptly sprayed in the corners before Margerite could catch him, so that the faint pungent odour of tomcat lingered in the stones. Heinrich's Johannisnacht festival was as fine as Margerite could have wished.

The children had scoured the woods and meadows for
red anenomes and poppies to dress the evening's lanterns
with, frothy-leaved stalks of mugwort and golden-flowered
monkshood for wreaths, and blue larkspur to cast into the
fires so that all the year's misfortune would be burned.
Heinrich was still vexed at Nikolaus for being ill on this day,
but a few cups of wine put him into a better temper even
before the first of Hildegard's masterpieces, a great pie of
meat mixed with fruit, baked in the shape of a flaming sun
and gilded brightly with saffron and egg-yolk, was borne out
for him to cut.

Margerite did her best to play the merry hostess, smiling
often and joining in the cheerful banter at the table, but
it was hard for her to keep her mind on the conversation:
her thoughts kept drifting back to the caves beneath the
mountain, and wondering what Nikolaus would be doing
after sunset.

As the sun lowered red towards the west, Christoph led
a band of young men up the mountainside, while Father
Michael stood to bless the bonfire in the middle of the
courtyard before Heinrich lit it. The flames blazed up with
a reassuring brightness, crackling greedily through the dry
branches, and the revelry began in earnest.

No sounds of dancing or singing pierced through into
Nikolaus' chambers: the arrow-slits that lit his two rooms
looked down upon mountainside and lake. After three days
of fasting, the pangs of hunger that had tormented him at
first had faded away, lifting the sluggish cloud of fleshly need
from his mind so that, even in the candlelight, every edge
and corner seemed unnaturally bright and sharp to his eyes,
as though he looked about himself with the pure vision of
spirit.

He had nearly failed at his first attempts to fast before
a ritual; the austerities and trials required by the Light-
Bearers were, in their way, more difficult than any of the
struggles of a knight's training, more rigorous than the
humiliating miseries of serving as a Knappe.

But the rewards were greater: not the clashing of swords and the laughter and cheers of other men with more muscles than brains, but the searing exaltation of power to be wielded, the supreme satisfaction of knowing himself master of himself and the worlds about him, seen and unseen - and what were loneliness, and the uncomprehending jeers of his father and brother, compared to that?

Having forced himself to fast and mediate thus before, it was easier now, for even at the worst of it, Nikolaus knew that, with a strong enough will, he could pass through the period of his body's ravenous obsession with food and into this limpid clarity.

Now he had only to wait, to rest and finish preparing himself for the rite he would begin at midnight - the summoning and compulsion of the mighty spirit who would aid him towards the next steps of the daring plan he had conceived, the plan that would leave him master of Burg Fürstensee in all but name. With

Herr Jakob's aid, he had undergone his bath of purification that evening: he was clean and uncontaminated, ready to reach into his Master's realm. Nikolaus turned his mind again to his meditations, sinking into their dark stillness with only a corner of his thought free to mark the passing of time.

Those things he would need for the rite were already arranged below: when the hour had come at last, he only had to pull on his threefold robe, fastening his lion-girdle about it as he murmured the appropriate words, and set the woven fillet of silk and gold upon his head. He passed down the staircase as swiftly as he could, though he knew no one would be coming to the armoury or the valuables' storeroom this night; his body turned and crouched almost instinctively in the rocky passages that led to his sanctum, and he hardly noticed the chill of the icy stream biting through his boots.

Quickly Nikolaus lit the candles in the middle of the four pentagrams around his circle and girded on his sword and dagger. Laid out beside his triangle were a silver bowl, a box of grave-dust, and an owl, which struggled against the bindings on its wings and feet and glared at him with angry impotence, its great golden eyes huge in the candlelight. Nikolaus lifted the bird in one hand, careful of its jabbing beak, and poured the grave-mould carefully into the centre of the triangle before drawing his sword.

"In the name of LUCIFER, SATHANAS, STAR OF THE MORNING, I shed this blood!" Nikolaus cried out. "Hail to the terror that flies by night, that aids when Hell's gates are opened!" He sliced swiftly through the owl's neck, the keen blade cleaving feathers and flesh in a single stroke.

The bird convulsed as its hot blood poured out into the silver bowl, its beak opening and closing futilely and sharp talons clutching, then relaxing. When only a few drops still dribbled down from the owl's severed windpipe, Nikolaus set the steaming bowl upon the dust in the triangle, laying the warm body carefully beside it. Only then did he pass into his circle, taking the wand from the top of his altar and raising it high.

"LUCIFER, SATHANAS!" Nikolaus called. "Lord of Light, sting in the tail of Death, victory of Hell! Light born of Darkness, I call to thee upon thy adamant throne, master of all damned souls, Infernal Imperator, ancient serpent of the grave. I who am mighty in the tower of my will, I who am strong in the fortress of my pride, I who am most worthy and great in my soul - I, Nikolaus Magus, call to thee! Let the gates of Hell be opened, that I may summon the ghost with whom I would speak, for I know that he sits within thy ring of flame, as mighty in Gehenna as he was in the world above!"

Nikolaus paused, waiting, his eyes fixed upon the triangle. The last steam from the owl's cooling blood was still rising from the bowl; but above it, he could see the beginnings of a dark shimmering, like the heat given off by a great fire. The sight filled him with a dreadful exaltation; his Order ring thrilled upon his finger, echoing the deep note that seemed to tremble just below the edge of his hearing.

He wanted to fall down upon his knees and worship the darkness beyond the gate that he had opened, and only his training kept him upright, calling the words of his rite back to his mind before they were lost in his ecstasy. For he stood within his spiritual fortress: the ditch reaching down to Hell, from whence stems the Light of Knowledge; the wall of pride that holds all baseness and weakness at bay; the keep of unconquerable Will.

Slowly Nikolaus lifted the piece of parchment on which was inscribed the name that he wished to call, together with those of the constraining spirits that would force it to his will. The words came thick and turgid from his tongue, as though he were speaking underwater, but nevertheless he pressed through.

"Asyel, Castiel, Lamsiyel, Rabam, Erlain, Elam, Belam, I conjure you, by the Lord of Light, by the Lord of Death Who rules you, by Him Who deluded Adam and Eve to their fall, and by Him Whose power reaches through sea and earth, Who leads the devils and spirits and ministers of fire, Who wears the crown of Death and Hell, Who is beginning and end, Alpha and Omega, Who creates life in lust and orders death in despair, Who is called LUCIFER, SATHANAS, STAR OF THE MORNING. By His all-powerful and ineffable names I conjure you, and by the names of His servants LEVIATAN and BELIAL, by ASTAROT and MAGOT and ASMODEI and BELZEBUB, by those four great princes ORIENS and PAIMON and ARITON and AMAIMON. I conjure you to bring to me from the depths of Hell, and to bind to my will, so that he answers me truthfully and without harm or deception, the ghost of that man who in life was known as Graf Günther von Hohenfels, Prince of the Order of Light-Bearers!"

For a moment it seemed as though nothing was happening; but the deep unheard note seemed to swell louder and louder, until the stone thrummed silently beneath Nikolaus' feet. Then, with painful slowness, the air appeared to thicken in the middle of the triangle, coalescing to a dark gray fog. Nikolaus strained his eyes, staring...he could see the first shape appearing, the dim glow of golden eyes beneath a wicked arch of long horns. Slowly, almost imperceptibly, the hooved figure solidified from the shadows - the shape of a goat, which turned about thrice in the triangle with a deep bleat of"Aa-aa-aa."

Nikolaus drew breath to command that the ghost take human shape, but it was already lowering its bearded head to lap at the coagulating mess of blood in the silver bowl. Its form brightened; it reared back onto its hind legs, higher and higher, its shaggy pelt drawing back into its body until Nikolaus was looking up at those glowing golden eyes.

It took all his force of will not to turn away from what he saw, for the ghost's figure was stretching into inhuman lineaments, a full eight feet tall with its gray face drawn out beneath the tattered straw of its tufted hair so that its short-bearded chin rested upon its chest, as if the bones of its skull had melted and oozed slowly downward.

Its dessicated tongue protruded from the elongated dark oval of its gaping mouth, and black liquid, mingled with the brighter red of the owl's blood, dribbled over its gray lips; more flowed from a wound midway up its body. But it wore the ring of an Order Prince, the ruby shimmering bright as if lit from within by the fires of Hell; and though Nikolaus had never seen Graf Günther in life, he knew that this was the spirit he had wished to summon.

"Why have you called me, Nikolaus?" the dead man asked. His lips did not move when he spoke; his voice seemed to rise from his uttermost bowels, echoing hollow as if he were speaking from inside a great barrel.

Nikolaus summoned all his courage: he had not come so far to fail now. "I called you, Prince, because I wish knowledge and aid. I would know the truth of your death, for I do not believe that you were slain by bandits on the road; and I have two workings in which I would have your help."

Günther's misshapen face showed no change of expression, but Nikolaus could hear the anger in his deep voice, shivering through the air of the salt cave. "I was stabbed from behind by the priest Etienne, as I waited upon the birth of the Child who shall be our earthly lord, the son of Lucifer, conceived by magic to lead us to victory upon Earth. Whatever else you have heard is lies; and if you wish my help in vengeance, it is yours."

Nikolaus grinned fiercely at these words. Now he knew what Damiano would not tell him: why Margerite's babe was so important; and why his teacher would not tell him, even if Damiano knew himself. For if all went as Nikolaus intended, the boy would be wholly in his care - and under his power; and that would surely bring him to greatness in the councils of the Light-Bearers.

He knew, as well, that his father and Christoph had lied about Günther: he could easily guess how they had plotted with the priest to get their rival for control of Margerite and the lands that had been Ruprecht's out of the way - and that would be a weakness that he could easily exploit at the right time. "From where you now dwell, do you know what takes place in the lands of the living?"

The dead man seemed to hesitate, a shadow dimming the yellow glow of his eyes. "A few things I can see; our Master grants me some visions. And betimes I am allowed to walk the Earth for a little space, where the Order has need of me; and for my torment, because I failed in sealing him to Hell at birth, I am betimes allowed to look upon the Child, and know that my work is not done."

"You will be glad to aid me, then, for my plan will hold him to us most surely. Listen: it is this." Rapidly Nikolaus ran through the thoughts that he had conceived in the many days of quiet consideration since his father and brother had left so suddenly for Burg Falkenstein. Günther listened silently, without movement, until he was done.

"That seems somewhat beyond your strength. And yet, if I guide you, you may yet achieve it - and I shall guide you. I see that your grimoire lies upon the altar: write down carefully what I shall tell you, for only by adhering most exactly to my instruction may you bring your works off and take no harm from it yourself - or risk harm to the Child, who is worth far more to us than your own life and soul."

Nikolaus seized his grimoire and quill, heart beating rapidly. This was almost beyond his hopes; but he had chosen wisely, willed and dared, and now he would grasp the fruits of his work with all his strength.

By the time dawn began to brighten over the castle courtyard, the bonfire had burned down to a circle of coals shimmering beneath gray ash, with only a few bright tongues licking up here and there. The revelry was still in full swing, young men and maids leaping over the outer edges of the fire and tossing little wreaths of herbs in to flare briefly and char; it was easy for Margerite to slip away from the laughing throng and into the herber, walking over to the hazel tree in the far corner.

It was well for her, Margerite thought, that the Order was so thorough in its charts. For each infernal Power the Black Book listed, there was a corresponding celestial Name, that the Light-Bearers might be able to recognise and counter the magics of their foes, or twist whatever rites fell into their hands to their own ways and ends: as if their blasphemous mocking of Church ritual had not been enough to suggest their methods, the Black Book spoke clearly of how it was done.

Where the sheep of our Foe humble themselves, we exalt ourselves; where they call on their powerless and blind Creator, we call upon the dominion of our Ruler Who is Lord of this World and all within; where they babble the names of those angels and spirits who had not the strength to rebel and can do nothing without leave, we call upon the names of those who defy and are unconquered, working their wills directly upon the Earth; and all that they invert, we set aright.

Using those words as a guide, Margerite had prepared prayers of her own, and now she humbly bowed her head before God. "O Lord God of Mercy," she murmured, "Who grantest Thy Grace in a thousand ways and unto a thousand generations; I know my wretchedness, and that I am not worthy to appear before Thy Divine Majesty. Wherefore, O Lord my God, have pity upon me, and take away from me all iniquity and malice; cleanse my soul from all the uncleanness of sin; renew within me my spirit, and comfort it, so that it may become strong and able to comprehend the mystery of Thy grace, and the treasures of Thy divine wisdom. Purify in me all that appertaineth unto me, so that I may become worthy of the conversation of Thy holy angels, and grant unto me the power which Thou hast given Thy prophets, that I may call upon all spirits of Good, and the hosts of Evil shall trouble me not, but flee before me, by Thy grace and by the holy might with which I ask thee to bless this wand that I now cut."

As Margerite spoke, it seemed to her that the garden had grown very still, the sounds of laughter and music outside fading to a distant whisper. The air glimmered with the light of dawn, and every breath thrummed through her body like wind ringing over the strings of a harp, each word vibrating softly through sky and earth. In quiet awe, Margerite set her hand to one of the hazel's thinner shoots, drawing her knife quickly across the gray-brown bark.

The sharp edge cleaved easily through - more easily than she would have thought possible, as though the tree itself were releasing its limb to her blessing: it almost seemed to her that she could feel the life flowing through the wood, pulsing beneath her hand in silent assent to her prayer.

It was only a little while before Margerite had cut her rod free, and she bowed her head again in thanks before concealing the slim stave in the folds of her skirts and walking quickly back to her chamber where she could lock it in her private chest without any other eyes looking upon it. Rose was snoring quietly, but Wolfram came awake at the sound of the lock clicking shut and began to cry softly for his mother. Margerite gave the sleeping servant a light shake.

"Awake, Rose, and unlace my bodice quickly, for my son is hungry," she said.

Rose rubbed the sleep from her eyes and rolled from her pallet to attend her mistress. "I shall not miss those dreams," she said.

"What did you dream?" Margerite asked, stiffening beneath the maid's touch.

"I cannot remember now; only that I was chilled in the night, and felt that something evil had passed close by."

"Well, be sure to say your prayers this day, and trust in Christ and the Virgin, who keep us safe from all the Devil's snares," Margerite replied. She glanced about for Kobolt. To her relief, the cat was curled comfortably beneath Wolfram's cradle, his plumed black tail laid over his nose and the tiniest gleam of gold showing from one slitted eye: if something were amiss, he would surely be more distressed.

Nikolaus came downstairs for the midday meal. Though he was still pale and ate less than usual, he seemed almost jovial, in contrast to his usual sullenness. Margerite mistrusted the sudden brightness to his eyes, for his elation suggested that his working had gone as he had hoped. Christoph, on the other hand, seemed to be suffering from too much wine drunk the night before: his eyes were threaded with scarlet, and every so often he would lift his hand to his forehead, as though he had taken another severe blow to the skull.

He replied curtly to Eva's pleasantries, and actually snapped at Georg when the boy was a little slow in mixing water into his winecup. Heinrich, however, appeared surprisingly fresh and lively, his blue eyes twinkling with good humour as he suggested that a mixture of burnt dog-hair and toad's blood was the best of all possible remedies for a night of excessive revelry.

"I can do without that, thank you, Father," Christoph answered shortly. He glared down at the portion of roast capon on his platter, as if it were responsible for all his ills, then steadfastly lifted another piece to his mouth.

"Or perhaps Margerite can mix a posset for you. She seems to have done well enough with your brother."

"Margerite is a fine physician, much better than that gibbering leech you insist on keeping here," Nikolaus agreed. "Is that not so, Frowe?"

Margerite mumbled an uncomfortable acknowledgement, aware of the pleasure Nikolaus was taking in furthering their deception.

"She has done well enough for you, but I will take my own advice," Christoph declared. "Fresh air and healthful exercise will cure me quickly enough - now, who is for a good ride with me this afternoon? Frowe Margerite, if you would like to come, we have two pleasant and well-trained sparrowhawks in our mews, as well as the one you brought with you. Perhaps the ladies would like to carry the birds, and see if they can bring down a bag of larks or thrushes: Hildegard has a marvelous way with such small game."

"I will gladly ride out with you," Eva said. "But...I am a little afraid of falcons, for they look at me so fiercely, and have such great cruel beaks and talons." Her sky-blue eyes were perfectly innocent as she spoke, but Margerite was quite certain that the girl had no such fear. Of course, she realized, Eva knows nothing of hawking, and is unwilling to admit that she lacks a noblewoman's skill. I should have taught her more before this, but it is clever of her to play so on Christoph's chivalry.

"You need not fear them," Christoph assured her. "All our birds are well-manned, and a sparrowhawk is a dainty creature, quite fit for a lady's wrist. When we have finished our meal, I will show them to you, and you will see for yourself how pleasant they are."

Heinrich's mews were well-kept and furnished, with a beautiful fountain in which the birds could bathe. Although the faint musty smell of raptors hung about it, the whole place was scrubbed clean, with not so much as a fresh mute beneath any of the falcons' perches or a spattering on the walls behind the hawks. Johann seemed to have settled in well: he was sprawled at his ease, talking in a lively fashion with a lean dark man - Heinrich's falconer, from his plain leather garb and heavy gloves. They both sprang to their feet as soon as their lord and his family entered.

"How may I serve you, Graf?" Heinrich's falconer asked.

"Are the sparrowhawks fit for flying today, Martin?"

"They are in their prime, eager and ready, my Graf, and it is a fine day to fly them."

As Heinrich talked with his falconer, Margerite circled the mews, letting Johann introduce her to Heinrich's birds. Besides Gawan, Enide, and Kriemhilt, sulking in their moult, Heinrich had two other peregrines and three goshawks, as well as the sparrowhawks Christoph had promised and a magnificent gyrfalcon; the little falconer's enthusiasm as he displayed her suggested that he had almost forgiven Margerite for releasing Ruprecht's eagles.

After a little consideration, Margerite decided to fly Cundwîr that day. Looking into the sparrowhawk's fierce eyes and hearing her high-pitched shriek brought back, all too starkly, the memories of riding out to Maria's shrine with Bertram: Margerite did not know whether she hoped that the temperamental little sparrowhawk would make another bid for escape, or whether she wanted to cling to the bird as one of her last links to her absent lover.

Even riding out with the others over the sunlit meadows at the edge of the lake and listening to their lively talk, the light feathery weight on her wrist brought her mind back again and again to the woods around Burg Falkenstein, to the dripping of gray drizzle from the pine needles and Bertram's silence beside her. But Cundwîr was surprisingly well-behaved on that hunt; she only tried to carry her prey once, and on Margerite's second approach, was willing to give over plucking the little bird in favour of taking a juicy bit of beef from Margerite's fingers.

The ride had quickly put Christoph into a better humour, so that he was soon galloping behind hedges and thickets to scare out small fowl for the ladies, and if Margerite had been able to give over her memories and worries, it would have been a most pleasant afternoon. By the time the sun was lowering, Margerite and Eva had a fine bag of thrushes, and the sparrowhawks were too full to fly any longer, so they turned homeward.

Margerite knew that she should go at once to suckle Wolfram, for it was late for his feeding, but she lingered a few moments in the great hall to snatch a little bread and wine, for she was faint with hunger. Suddenly she heard a shriek from the kitchen, and a black streak hurtled through the door into the great hall, followed by Hildegard with a heavy frying pan in her hand. The cook's blond braid had come undone, and her round face was red with anger.

"Hold, Hildegard," Heinrich boomed. "What is the matter?"

"That black beast has broken a full pitcher of milk, and stolen two of the birds you brought in, Herr Graf. I will have its hide to line my gloves, see if I do not!"

"Soft, my good woman," Margerite said soothingly. "Kobolt has earned more than a couple of thrushes by his work as a rat-catcher, and we can easily spare him some milk. And he is my cat; I shall be most displeased if you harm him. Back to your kitchen, and let the matter be."

Hildegard's protruberant blue eyes glared at her Gräfin for a moment, but Heinrich coughed deep in his throat. Unwillingly the cook dropped her gaze and curtsied. "As you will, Frowe Gräfin. But I cannot do my best work if that creature is there to spoil it. Why can he not live outside in the stables like a proper cat?"

"Because it pleases me to have him in the castle," Margerite replied, her voice sharpening. "And it does not please me to be questioned by a cook."

"As you will, Frowe Gräfin," Hildegard repeated again, and left sullenly.

Heinrich laughed. "Our cook is an impertinent servant - but she knows what a trial I would find it to replace her, and those with great talents must be allowed a little leeway in their manners. Perhaps it were best if you kept Kobolt out of her kitchen from now on."

Margerite was about to answer that Kobolt was hardly a hound to be ordered about or kept on a lead, but a soft growl and the sound of crackling bones beneath the table distracted her. Looking down, she saw that Kriemhilt had taken one of the thrushes from the tom and was crouched over it, pawing and tearing bloody-mouthed at the little bird before she picked it up in her mouth and trotted from the room - going up to take it to her kittens, Margerite suspected.

Christoph was watching the cat as well, and a smile flickered across his face. "Your cat cannot be so bad if he provides for his mate," he said, though his voice was a little hollow, as though, in spite of his enthusiasm that afternoon, he had not completely recovered from his morning malady.

"He is a good cat," Margerite said. She rose from her chair. "I must go and see to Wolfram now. Thank you all for the pleasant hunt."

The door to Margerite's chambers was swinging slightly ajar. She hastened in, a prickle of fear running down her spine - but Nikolaus had been with them all afternoon, she reminded herself, and could have worked no mischief. Rose was not within, but Kobolt crouched on the edge of Wolfram's cradle with the thrush in his mouth, dangling it like a toy as Wolfram burbled and reached up for it.

Margerite picked Kobolt up and tossed both the cat and his booty unceremoniously on the floor. Wolfram began to wail at once, but Margerite was busy making sure that the little droplets of blood on the baby's linen had only come from the thrush, and that Wolfram was unharmed.

"Is all well, frowe?" Rose asked anxiously from the doorway. She was carrying two clean chamberpots, which she hurried to tuck beneath the bed; it was clear what her errand had been, and Margerite felt silly for having let herself be so affrighted.

"All is well," Margerite said as the maid began to unlace her. "Hush, Wolfram. When you are older, you shall have plenty of thrushes, roasted with honey upon spits or baked into fine pies, but you are too young for such meat now, and what is fit for little cats will do you no good."

As the days after Johannisnacht wore on, Margerite found herself looking more and more often towards the gates of the castle, wondering if Ritter Gottfried would come back. By day, she fretted and stitched on her robes; at night, when Burg Fürstensee was quiet, she crept down to her sanctum to paint the circle on the floor. It was a laborious job, for every sign had to be traced exactly thus; and more, she had to pore carefully over the Hebrew characters, identifying them one by one according to the chart in the Black Book, and to replace the blasphemous names of Lucifer and his fallen angels with those of God and his holy ones.

Likewise, it was holy names that she graved on her pentacle, dagger, and cup, and carved into the peeled wood of her wand between the names and sigils of the planetary rulers. Margerite knew that in doing these things, she was taking a grievous risk, for if Nikolaus' fear of displeasing his Order superiors by allowing her to make an error in her circle should overcome his reluctance to set foot within her sanctum uninvited, he might well be able to tell what she had done - she did not know if he could truly read Hebrew, or, like herself, simply had to rely on spelling the words out letter by letter, memorizing the most important of the names, and trust in the lore of the Black Book's authors for their accuracy.

Still, it was a rule of the Light-Bearers that no member should go unbidden into another's sanctum, any more than one could touch another's wand or wear another's robes. Margerite was not sure how far she could trust Nikolaus' honour on such a point - but, to her surprise, as soon as she had begun painting the circle, she had become certain that she could no more desecrate the glittering salt cave with unholiness than she could have pissed on the floor of a church.

As she felt the power swelling and growing within her tools, Margerite became more and more sure that she could not work her own magic within a circle of Satan: it was as though, in asking for God's aid and inscribing His holy names, she were devoting herself to His service as surely as any cloistered nun. While if Nikolaus did discover her and betray her to the Order - there was always the choice of confessing all: better to be burnt as a heretic, if it came to that, than allow Wolfram to fall into the hands of the Light-Bearers.

Or...though Margerite had never killed with her own hands, she knew that the blood of those who had died at Burg Falkenstein was at least partially upon her soul, and if it came down to a choice between Nikolaus' life and Wolfram's safety, she was sure she would not hesitate. A week passed without Gottfried's return, and when the other men who had ridden out in search of Bertram came back from Graf Wolfgang's lands, the young knight and his squire were not among them.

Upon receiving word that his men were back, Heinrich commanded Ritter Dieter to attend him in the great hall at once, together with Christoph. Margerite expected that her husband would send her away, but he did not: much as she dreaded to hear the news, she found that she was also touched by Heinrich's trust.

"What have you to tell me, Ritter Dieter?" Heinrich asked.

"Herr Graf," Dieter replied, taking his helmet from his balding head and holding it in both hands before him, "we have failed you. We found Bertram's trail leading further northeast through Graf Wolfgang's lands - but lost him again, and could not tell where he had gone. Ritter Gottfried is still pursuing, as you commanded."

Heinrich rose to his feet. "How could he have escaped you? I know that you, at least, are able to follow a boar to its den or stag to its bed from the least track; why have you had so much trouble with this one man?"

A flush of embarassment darkened the knight's ruddy cheeks, and he lowered his head. "Herr Graf, I do not know," Ritter Dieter murmured. "We might as well have been hunting a wood-wose; several times I thought to have him in plain sight beyond a rise or thicket, only to find again that he was not where he should be. By Christ, I swear that it is no natural art he possesses, to conceal himself so, but if there were any doubt in my mind that he meant ill towards us, it is gone, for only a guilty man would hide himself so carefully."

"Perhaps I should have sent another after him, rather than Ritter Gottfried," Heinrich mused beneath his breath, so softly that even Margerite, sitting beside him, could barely hear his words. "Someone of keener eyesight, better used to tracking beasts in the wood...But no: Gottfried would have been heartbroken if I had given the duty to another, for he thought it a matter of his own honour, and I could not use him worse than by letting him think himself unworthy of the task."

Margerite's heart twisted within her at her husband's words. Now she truly wondered if she could unburden herself to him, to let him know that Bertram was no traitor, but called to a duty far beyond those he had taken up at Burg Fürstensee. Surely a ruler who gave such loyalty to his men, even to risking as much as Heinrich thought he was for the sake of allowing a knight to redeem his own sense of honour, would understand...but how would she explain it, without allowing the one thread to lead to the unraveling of the whole web in which she was enmeshed?

And Bertram's burden was not hers to give away: he would never forgive her for revealing him, she was sure, whatever came of it. But she put her small hand over Heinrich's large rough one, as if to let him know what his care meant to her, and the Graf smiled at her before turning his gaze back to Ritter Dieter.

"You have done what you can; there is nothing more for it, until we hear further news. Tend to your men and horses, and then go back to your duties."

"Thank you, Herr Graf."

When Ritter Dieter had left the hall, Heinrich sighed, sitting back in his chair. The strength of moments before seemed to have fled his heavy limbs, the wrinkles nesting deeper about his gray eyes. "Well, Christoph, what do you think now? Is there anything we can do, save sit and wait on Ritter Gottfried's return - if he returns?"

Christoph clenched his hand tight on the hilt of his sword. An unnerving glitter of ferocity sparked from deep within his gray-green eyes - a look entirely at odds with his pleasant features and the boyish uptilt of his nose. "Father, I think that Gottfried is useless for this work. He can hardly see twenty feet in front of his face, let alone follow tracks in the wood, and he will still be gabbling prayers and phrases of chivalry while Bertram slits his throat. Let me go, instead: I can find him far more quickly, and bring him to his end more surely."

Margerite looked at Christoph, shocked. She might have expected such boldness, for she had noticed before how ready Christoph was to rush out to any battle, but it was hardly like him to speak so unkindly of a fellow knight. But even the Graf's son seemed surprised at what had sprung forth from his mouth, for his expression was softening as she looked at him, and he raised a hand to press against his forehead in that same unconscious gesture Margerite had noticed before.

"I shall not send you out after Bertram," Heinrich said mildly. "You are my heir, and I can hardly spare you on such an errand. If Ritter Gottfried is a little short-sighted, his squire's eyes are keen enough, and Gottfried is a man of great thoroughness and care, who will most certainly not be surprised by his quarry, for he knows well that Bertram is a dangerous man.

I wish only that I had told him the full tale of why we cannot let Bertram escape us - he was not at Burg Falkenstein that day, and I believe the men who were have kept their oath of silence well. Though Ritter Gottfried might have thought the less of me for what we did, he might have had a better idea of how to track Bertram and where he may be going - I still suspect that the northeast trail is but a ruse, and that our fugitive will turn westward to Günther's heirs and allies before long."

"And if he does not?" Margerite could not help asking.

"As I said to Dieter, I believe we can only wait and find out. You may leave now, Christoph: perhaps a few bouts of sword-play in the courtyard will cool your temper a little." Heinrich watched his son go, waiting to speak again until the heavy oaken doors had closed behind Christoph.

"It is hard for a young man to be told he must wait for anything," the Graf said. "When Christoph is older, he will bear such things more easily: even twenty years ago, I would have long since been horsed and on the way myself."

"I am glad that you are not," Margerite answered, looking directly into her husband's eyes. And that was true: at least Nikolaus feared his father, and Heinrich's presence forced him to circumspection.

And - it seemed dreadfully disloyal to Bertram, when moments before Heinrich had been speaking of hunting him down - but though she did not love Heinrich, she could not help feeling a certain warmth of affection towards him. The longer she watched his careful overseeing of his castle, the way in which he looked after his folk and listened patiently to their cases and complaints, the more convinced she was that Heinrich was truly a decent man and a good ruler.

Despite the circumstances of their wedding, he had never treated Margerite as a prize of battle and politics, but rather as if he had chosen her for his wife and helpmeet out of love and respect.

"Well, my bones are no longer fit for endless days of riding and nights of sleeping on the cold ground," Heinrich replied, smiling back at her. "And I have found that patience is often rewarded better than rushing in to take what one desires - is that not so, my wife?"

"It is," Margerite said. Then her cheeks flared with heat as she realized what Heinrich was speaking of: Gerhild had told him that she would be fit to sleep with him by the beginning of July, and tomorrow was July first. But she could not unsay her words, nor go back on the oath she had given at their wedding, even if marrying Heinrich had only been the least dreadful of several bad choices.

Margerite was no frightened virgin, anyway, and Heinrich deserved better than reluctance from her: he had made her his honoured wife without any reservation or afterthought, and he deserved to be treated as her husband - even if the thought of sleeping with the man who had spoken Bertram's death warrant chilled her inmost heart with horror. Perhaps it was that which unstrung Margerite's resolve as she lay in her bed that night. It was so easy to feel the fire of her soul sparking through her flesh, like a fine network of glowing blue flame overlaying the dark shape of clay...so tempting to gather her spirit into wings and talons and beak, to seek the freedom of the skies - like a fractious sparrowhawk, seeking to carry her prey beyond the reach of the falconer?

Perhaps; but Ruprecht had manned her without her full knowledge, as if he were capturing and training an eyass who had never known what it was to hunt by herself, and no one should ever do so again. And the strain of waiting and not knowing had grown past her strength to bear. Even as she realized that, Margerite flung herself forth, the wind catching beneath her wings to bear her up. The moon's light glittered white upon the ripples of the lake below, pale gray upon the mountain crags jutting out between the dark pines; the rushing of the air drowned out all other sounds, so that she could hear nothing but her own flight.

It seemed to her as if she had shed all her cares and fears with her flesh, that now, as she flew, she was free of any sorrow or worry; and the relief was so great that she was sorely tempted to circle higher and higher, to leave behind all that oppressed her and stay forever in the vast realm of air through which she soared. It had been so before, she remembered dimly in the last corner of her human awareness...and a few words came slowly to her mind, nagging in their familiarity.

Beware, lest the pleasure of magic overwhelm you; to succumb, whether to pleasure or pain, is to be master no longer. As she fought to bring those words into focus, even as the wind thrummed through her pinions and her powerful wings tilted to ride it, Margerite remembered sharply: they were from the Black Book, and she could not flee the struggle it embodied while her soul lived, even should she fly from her body and never return.

Beating her wings strongly, Margerite arrowed towards the northeast, woods and mountains and streams blurring darkly beneath her. She did not know quite what she was looking for; she could only trust the sight that had guided her before to lead her where she wanted to go. Bertram, and the man who sought him: if she could not use any art save prayer to aid her beloved, at least she could know how matters stood.

Far below, Margerite saw a small fire, a bare glimmer of ruddy light in a clearing. Folding her wings, she plummeted down, swooping low over the clearing and pulling up again to come to rest at the top of a scraggly-branched pine. To her disappointment, there were two men there: one rolled in blankets on the ground, one standing quietly beneath the shadow of the trees, his shield leaning against his leg and his hand resting lightly on the hilt of his sword. He turned his helmed head, looking up, and Margerite saw his eyes staring very wide and dark from the shadows of the steel that framed his pale severe face.

"What was that?" Ritter Gottfried murmured - or was Margerite hearing his thoughts? Surely he would not speak while standing watch, even quietly and to himself.

And the young knight's lips were not moving, though his deep baritone voice was clear in Margerite's ears. "It must have been an owl; I thought for a moment there that it looked like a falcon, but falcons do not fly at night. I wish I could be as sure that Bertram halted his journeying after dark; several times now I have thought that we had his trail at sunset, only to lose it again at dawn.

And I doubt that he will come upon us in the darkness, but there are other dangers, now that we are out of Wolfram's lands: brigands and Raubritter, and perhaps worse things that travel by night, though - Christ willing - there is none of them that cannot be dealt with by a strong arm and a stronger faith. Mayhap our way will lead close to a holy shrine, where I may pray for guidance, for Christ will not forsake me if I am true to Him."

The knight dropped his gaze, glancing quickly about before he looked up at Margerite's tree again. "If only I could see more clearly! That shape seems wrong for an owl - are those the arched wings and narrow head of a peregrine? Or is it only the branches deceiving my eyes?" Gottfried crossed himself quickly before dropping his hand to his sword-hilt again; it seemed to Margerite's falcon-sight as though she could see the trail of his movement bright against his breastplate, as though the gleam of firelight on his metal gauntlet still showed where his hand had passed in the sign of the Cross.

"It is nearly time to wake Arnmut for his watch - God knows, I am weary enough. It would be better to have a proven man with me, but Arnmut is a good Knappe, and will stand beside me stoutly enough, I am sure. I wonder what made Bertram run so suddenly? He must have some ill intentions; if it were not sinful to say such things, I would say that I was nearly ready to stake my soul on it. But what does he hope to do? It is not like the Graf to send me off knowing so little, and hard to guess what harm Bertram can do us, if he does not mean to try to take Burg Falkenstein from within as I had thought. Perhaps he has taken this road to seek confederates of his for evil purpose...But let it be as God wills it: I can only carry out my duties as best I can. I should wake Arnmut now."

Gottfried walked over, crouching down beside his sleeping squire, but paused before touching him. "How fair and peaceful he looks! I hate to wake him, for the riding was long yesterday. He is only sixteen, and gently reared, but he has not yet complained, though this journey has been hard on him. And the firelight makes him seem younger still, almost as frail as a maid - but I know that he is a strong lad, and it will do him no good for me to spare him, for I must teach him the harshness of knighthood as well as its joys." He reached out, tenderly touching Arnmut on the shoulder, then shaking him a little harder and speaking aloud. "Awaken, Knappe. It is time for your watch."

While Ritter Gottfried's gaze was on his squire, Margerite spread her wings and glided silently away. In her strange awareness, it did not seem odd to her that she had heard what the young knight was thinking; it was as natural as the lift of air beneath her wings. But he saw me, or almost saw me, as well - I must be more careful.

She rose again, circling slowly upward. It seemed to her that she could almost hear the beating of a heart - her own? Had she been too long from her body? No; the pulse throbbing within her feathered breast was luring her further on, more directly north. That is Bertram's heart that I feel beating, as surely as if I lay against his chest, she thought, and sped towards it.

Beneath, clear to her gaze as though the full brightness of the sun lay upon it, Margerite saw a small building of stone, marked upon the door with three crosses. A little light shone through the window, and it seemed that she could feel its comforting warmth even in the cold air through which she circled. She flew down again, perching upon the narrow windowsill, and peered in.

Bertram sat facing an old man in a brown cowl and hood. Her love looked wild and tattered from his travels, thinner than he had been, with his beard and hair growing back into their old bushiness. But Margerite could see the clean lines of his face beneath the wild hair, and the look in his hazel eyes - grimly determined, yet, somehow more at ease than she had seen him before, as though his decision to return home had quieted the torment rending at his soul - gave her heart and hope for him.

"I swear by Christ and Maria and all the saints that I am not fleeing to escape any crime, nor out of any wish to do evil or evade justice," Bertram was saying, his voice very intense. "I do not ask for sanctuary: I came here merely to pray and make my offering at this shrine. I ask only two things: first, your blessing, and secondly, that if my pursuers pass by and ask it of you, you will not tell them that I was here, or which way I have gone."

"My son," the old man said mildly, "if you have committed no crime, why should anyone seek so fiercely after you?"

"From suspicion and fear, I believe," Bertram answered.

"Forgive me for saying so, but for all your good manners, you have the look of a man of violence, and one who has been living hard, at that. Can you truthfully tell me, here in this shrine where I tend the fingerbone of St. Adalhild, that you have not slain any innocent person, nor robbed any, nor ever affronted a woman?"

"I will tell you only the truth, holy Father. I once rode with the Company of the Black Sword, and there did much harm, for which I have been seeking long to atone. I was also Hauptmann of a castle guard once, and fought in battles and raids as my lord commanded. And..." Bertram bit his lip, looking down at the floor. "Once in my weakness, I lay with a married woman; but of that sin, too, I have repented greatly." His voice cracked; he coughed, swallowed, and spoke again. "Though the temptation has often been sore on me since, for I love her as much as man may love woman, neither she nor I has fallen to it again."

The shrinekeeper stroked his long white beard thoughtfully, regarding Bertram for a time. "Christ rejoices more, it is said, over the one lost sheep returned to the fold than over all those who have never strayed. If what you say is true, you have been grievously lost, my son, and had a long journey back. I pray for your sake that you are not deceiving an old man - but if I am to trust you, you must trust me as well. From where have you come, and where are you going?"

Bertram paused a long time, and Margerite could see his shoulders tightening even beneath the tattered gray surcoat that covered the leather and plates of his jerkin. At last he breathed out deeply, sighing, "If I expect God's blessing, I must trust in His servant. I have come from the castle of Graf Heinrich von Fürstensee, and I am going to the castle of Landgraf Gerhardt -" he bit the name off roughly -"von Niederwald."

"And what tale should I expect to hear from the men who pursue you, if they bother to halt their journey here?"

"That I do not know. The truth is simply this: that I was in Graf Heinrich's castle guard, and left without leave of any but his Gräfin - who cannot say to any that she gave me leave to go."

The old man nodded slowly. "Perhaps I begin to understand," he murmured. "Wiser to flee temptation than to fall again into its snares...but that is none of my affair, unless you wish to make Confession to me now."

Bertram rose and knelt before him. "Father, I would indeed confess my sins to you."

Before her love could speak further, Margerite took wing again: she had heard more of Bertram's private thoughts than she should have already, and she would not spy on his confession. But she knew he was not in immediate danger of death or capture, and she had heard him say that he loved her as much as man may love woman; and that would be enough to strengthen her for a long time yet.

Chapter Four

Although Burg Fürstensee's thick walls kept the chambers within cool, when Margerite stepped out into the sunlight of the courtyard, sweat began to trickle down from the thick crown of her braids. No clouds marred the blue arch of the sky, but the air was heavy and oppressive, with no stirring of wind to relieve the heat, and a faint haze hung about the bright glare of the morning sun.

"There must be a thunderstorm coming," said Christoph, dashing sweat from his forehead with the back of his hand. He had clearly just come from the practice field, for he was dressed in full armour, with his tilting helm under his arm; his brown hair was rucked up in dark spikes, and his rounded face was flushed. "It is often like this in the summer before a storm breaks."

"I will be grateful for it," Margerite replied. "Perhaps you should come inside where it is cooler, and take your armour off before you drop from the heat."

"It is not so bad," Christoph said, waving a hand dismissively. "Georg! What is taking you so long?"

The young squire dashed out behind Margerite, a large clay mug carried carefully in both hands. "Here, Herr Christoph." Georg, too, was armoured, his face red beneath the freckles and his bright hair plastered to his skull, dripping as if he had stuck his head into a bucket of cold water.

Christoph took the mug from his squire, draining it in a single long draught. "Ah, that is better. Tilting in the heat gives a man a mighty thirst - go fetch me more small beer, Georg."

The Knappe ran off again, and Christoph smiled, shaking his head. "I was never so glad as when I won my spurs and realized that, henceforth, I would no longer be the one to run and carry and sit endlessly scrubbing armour. Graf Wolfgang has a lighter hand than my father, but I felt the weight of his blows often enough as a squire when I failed in his service, though perhaps not as often as I should have. Still, all the toil is a little price to pay for learning the ways of knighthood."

"And is Georg doing well for his first days?"

"He learns fast, and already has a very good seat on a horse, though he is still small enough to be easily lifted from his saddle by a blow. But that is all to the good, for it forces him to remember how to slant his shield to make his foe's tip glance off, and to couch his own aim more carefully, and that will serve him well when he is full-grown."

Margerite and Christoph chatted a little more, until Christoph said, "Well, Georg, we have had long enough to rest. If we leave it much longer, your muscles will begin to stiffen and your bruises to ache, as you have already found out. Would you care to watch us, Frowe Margerite?"

"I shall leave you to it," Margerite answered.

"As you please. If you see my brother, you might tell him from me that we would like to see him on the field as well, for if he does not take a little more interest in fighting, he will be useless when it comes to a battle, and then we will have to either send him into holy orders or bury him."

Christoph rattled the gilded chain linking the left corner of his breastplate to his sword and started off, his step jaunty even under the weight of his armour. Georg hurried to keep up with his knight's steps, like a small running-hound trailing after a mastiff.

Margerite had been thinking of riding with Eva that morning, but the thick weight of the muggy air had already dampened her enthusiasm for outdoor pursuits. Perhaps, she thought, she would spend the day inside at her embroidery or reading.

She had not yet had time to go through Heinrich's library, not even to see if those books she had brought from Burg Falkenstein had been properly put away there. In truth, she had also been avoiding the library because it was in the tower beside Nikolaus' chambers and she knew that he often resorted there - but that, she told herself severely, was hardly an excuse not to see for herself that the valuable volumes she had brought with her were being cared for as they should be.

And if she had to do her marital duties for Heinrich that night, settling down with a good tale of knightly deeds and romance would, at least, keep her from having to think about it all day. To Margerite's surprise and dismay, Nikolaus was already in the library when she got there, poring carefully over a book.

He wore a sea-green doublet brocaded with blue, its trailing sleeves spilling across the polished dark tabletop like sunlit water; the colour reflected from his eyes, so that they shone green as a cat's when he looked up at her.

"Good morning, Nikolaus," Margerite said, as she would have greeted anyone else. "What are you reading?"

Nikolaus silently held up his book, and Margerite recognised the embossed cover of Burg Falkenstein's copy of Parzival.

"An interesting choice," she commented, her voice carefully neutral.

"Perhaps to one who has not yet learned to read its inner secrets." Nikolaus smiled, the plump flesh of his cheeks pouching unpleasantly. "Do you recall the Prologue?"

In truth, Margerite had paid little attention to that part of the book, being more fascinated by the adventures of the young Parzival and his knightly companions. But as she strained, some of the details came back to her memory.

"Wolfram von Eschenbach tells of a poet named Kyot who found a Saracen manuscript in Toledo..."

Nikolaus nodded, his gray-green eyes narrowing. "And that manuscript, according to him, was written by a heathen named Flegetanis, descended from Solomon, who discovered the name of the Grail in the stars. A fantastic tale, as it seems...but this I will let you know: the Order of Light-Bearers reaches far past the lands of Christendom. We have our men among the Saracens as well, for those folk are greatly wise in matters of science and understanding, and many of the Order's arts of alchemy and astrology were learned from the East. If Wolfram himself was not one of our number, though I believe he may have been, his master Kyot assuredly was, and concealed as the secrets of Parzival are, they can yet be read by one who has the key of knowledge to unlock them - who understands what the Grail truly is."

"And what is that?" Margerite asked. She did not know whether to believe Nikolaus or not, for it seemed to her that the whole work was one of compassion and holy devotion: she could still hear, as clearly as if she spoke them herself, Cundrîe's words to Parzival: And if no more blessings came to you than the healing of Anfortas, no man would be more blessed than you. Your mouth, that knows no lies, shall now greet the noble, love-worthy Anfortas; your question brings him healing and frees him from the pitiful, frightful misery of his illness. Those words had surely not been written by an Order member, nor by a pupil of the Light-Bearers. And yet, Ruprecht's servants had borne names from that same work...

Nikolaus only laughed, shaking a lock of thick brown hair back from his forehead. "Perhaps, if you persevere, you shall find out for yourself in time. Now, what brings you here?"

"I was merely looking for something to read," Margerite answered. "And...your brother bade me say to you that he would like to see you upon the tilting field this day."

Nikolaus' small mouth fell back into its accustomed pout. Then he smiled again, rising to his feet and shaking his long brocaded sleeve-tails straight. "Perhaps he shall. Yes, it has been a little too long since I held a lance in my hand, and undoubtedly my father is beginning to wonder again whether he would like to pack me off to the Church so as to keep me from disgracing him on the field."

Though Nikolaus' tone was light, Margerite could hear the bitter edge to it, like a shard of broken glass inserted carefully into a soft pear; and his words were so close to those Christoph had spoken in what seemed to be friendly jest that she was sure the matter had really been discussed in earnest.

Perhaps it was only the reflection of Nikolaus' sea-green doublet from his eyes, but for a moment, it seemed to Margerite that she could see a flicker of old pain there. Nevertheless, Margerite was glad to have him out of the room while she read. More than half the books in the library were those she herself had brought, while the others were largely practical treatises on such matters as military strategy and household maintenance.

For a moment, she almost felt sympathetic towards Nikolaus: she, too, knew what it was to be the only one in a castle who cared much for reading and thoughtful discussion, and if the duties of being her father's chatelaine had not forced her to sweat and struggle with weapons, the constant rounds of seeing to the household had been, she thought, every bit as onerous as the endless bruising training that a young nobleman must undergo.

Yet I never shirked my responsibilities, nor sought out dark Powers to make up for the fact that I would not inherit my father's place myself, but must give it over to my husband, and bear my authority on his sufferance. Surely Nikolaus was too deeply sunk into the ways of the Light-Bearers for Margerite to aid his soul - but on the other hand, he was yet young, and despairing of God's mercy to another was no better than despairing of it for oneself.

Margerite did not linger long on those thoughts, for if Nikolaus were ever to learn to trust her, or confide his private sorrows to her, it would not be a matter of a single day, or month. And there was little she could do to help that along...except, perhaps, listen to him when he speaks.

For he is lonely, and the counsels of the Light-Bearers drive the souls of their members to worse solitude. I could do nothing for Ruprecht until it was too late, but perhaps... Heinrich was very attentive to Margerite at the mid-day and evening meals, often covering her small hand lightly with his large one and smiling at her. She was not surprised at all when, as they rose from the table, he said softly to her, "Would you have me come to your chamber, my wife?"

"I must feed Wolfram first," Margerite answered, looking up at him. In the hall's candlelight, the marks of age did not show so cruelly on Heinrich's face, and his gray eyes gleamed like a young man's beneath his grizzled brows. When he raised her hand to kiss it, brushing his lips softly over her skin, Margerite could feel his hesitation, strange as the shyness of a great bear, and she hastened to add, "When I have done that, I will come to you." And not think about Bertram - O Maria help me, if I do that, I shall not be able to go through with it!

Heinrich's serious face broke into a grin; it almost seemed to Margerite as though she were looking at Christoph through the veil of Heinrich's years, as if the wrinkles creasing his skin and the gray hairs of his hair and beard could fall away like a thin piece of cheesecloth to reveal the young knight behind them. "Come, I shall escort you, my wife."

Heinrich lifted Margerite's hand in his own, and together they walked from the hall. No one seemed to take great notice: all the bawdy wedding-jokes and songs had been shouted already, and at Burg Falkenstein, the women who would have put Margerite to bed had all known that the marriage would not be consummated on the same night as the vows were spoken.

Though Margerite had never desired Heinrich, nevertheless she could not help feeling wistful - if not for her own sake, then for that of the aging man who had been denied his second chance to be cheered to bed like a youth again, to display, in thought and word if not in practice, all the lustiness of his younger days.

Though Heinrich was still smiling, his gray eyes seemed remote and faintly misted. Was he, too, regretting the loneliness of his second wedding night, or was he thinking about the bride he had brought to bed before Margerite was ever born? She could not tell, but before she went into her own chamber to feed her babe, she leaned her head against Heinrich's broad shoulder for a moment, and he gently ran his fingers over her thick crown of braids.

"I shall await you, my wife," Heinrich murmured, his deep voice scarcely more than a whisper. He bent his head, and his lips lingered on hers for a second before he turned away.

Heinrich's chamber was bright with beeswax candles, and its air was sweet with the scents of the meadowsweet and lady's bedstraw that had been carefully strewn beneath the thick rugs. Heavy tapestries, showing scenes of battle and the hunt, hung upon the walls.

On his table stood a pitcher of wine and two goblets, their deep blue glass gleaming brightly against the polished golden oak, and the embroidered scarlet coverlet of his bed had been turned down neatly. The fire in the stove was roaring quietly behind its enameled door, and the room was very warm.

The Graf had taken his boots off, but was still dressed, sitting at ease on the foot of his bed. He looked at Margerite, and she did not know what to say, but he patted the coverlet, and she sat down beside him.

"You are most fair, my bride," Heinrich said huskily. Margerite let him wrap his heavy arms about her, pulling her close to his chest before he kissed her. His mouth was clean, and she could taste the mint that he had chewed to sweeten his breath.

Gently Heinrich pulled the pins from Margerite's braids, unbinding her hair to spill down her back and running his fingers through it. He touched her very carefully, as though he feared that she would shatter beneath his hands, stroking her head and back with his fingertips as he would calm a skittish horse. Though she had braced herself in readiness for his touch, Margerite found herself relaxing beneath it.

"Thank you for your patience, my husband," she said, looking deeply into Heinrich's eyes.

One corner of his mouth turned up in sad amusement. "I did not lie when I said that my fires do not burn as hotly as they did once. It has been sixteen years since my first wife died, and in that time...well, I shall not lie to you. Like most men, I have had occasion to resort to paying for my pleasures, or taking them where I might find them, but I do not go to the city often any longer, and even when I was younger, I was never such a fool as to set my bastard seed in the belly of a village wench or serving maid. And for a woman who has borne as many trials as you have, while still so young - you are eighteen now?"

"Since February, yes."

Heinrich shook his head. "I shall be sixty on December twelfth, and have seen the death of more friends and kin than I have living. And nothing is so ridiculous as an old ram panting after a young ewe, whether she be his wedded wife or not. You are very young and very beautiful, and I know that you did not choose to marry me out of love. Why, then, should I have gone against your midwife's advice for a few moments of pleasure, or forced what might have turned your agreement to hate? Even now, I hope...I hope it is not merely duty that brings you to my bed, though I am glad that you are here willingly, whatever the reason." His low voice was sad as he spoke; almost, Margerite thought that she could see the brightness of tears in his gray eyes.

She was about to speak, but Heinrich put a finger softly to her lips. "No, say nothing you do not mean, Margerite. Let me believe, for this night at least, that you are with me because you want to be - that you find some pleasure in my company, or joy in my embrace."

Margerite ran her hands up Heinrich's back, caressing the bristly hair at the back of his neck, then pulled his head down for another soft kiss. His beard curled about her cheeks and chin - almost as Bertram's had. She pushed that thought from her mind: she had sworn her wedding-vows to Heinrich, and he needed and deserved her comfort.

They sat together like that for a time, soothing one another without speech. At last Heinrich unclasped her girdle and slowly began to unlace the side of her overdress, though his fingers were clumsy. "I have no experience with these new fashions," he said with a little laugh.

"You will learn how to undress me soon enough," Margerite assured him, reaching around to help him as best she could. Under her guidance, the green silken laces slipped quickly free, and then it was a simple matter for Heinrich to unbutton the back of her tightly-fitted underdress.

Before she slipped out of it, Margerite unhooked Heinrich's belt-clasp, hanging the broad chain of linked silver plates, sheathed dagger and all, over one of the bedposts. The silver buttons down the front of his deep blue doublet came open easily, and Heinrich let Margerite unlace the white linen tunic beneath before he shrugged the two garments off together. For a moment she quailed from the intimacy of unfastening his dark scarlet hose, but reminded herself that they would soon be much closer. The fine stretchy wool of his lower garment was soft beneath her fingers as she tugged it off.

For a man of his years, Heinrich looked well naked; age had done nothing to soften the great muscles of his shoulders, arms, and chest, and though the pleasures of his table had widened his belly, it was firm and substantial, without the flabby folds of indolence. The curls of gray-brown hair that grew thickly over his body made him look more than ever like a bear, but there was no clumsiness about him as he carefully stripped Margerite's garments from her and laid them over the back of a chair.

When they were both fully naked, Heinrich embraced Margerite again: she could feel his heartbeat quickening beneath his grizzled pelt, and his slow hardening against her belly. He drew the coverlet back and lifted her up as lightly as if she were a child, laying her down upon the bed. The linen sheets were soft as only long wear and careful tending could make them, and scented with lavender. Margerite drew up her legs, waiting for Heinrich, but he pressed them gently down again.

"Not so swiftly, my dear," he murmured. He lowered himself over her, supporting himself on his powerful forearms, and kissed her again, then rolled to the side and began to run his hands over her body, delicately stroking her breasts, abdomen, and thighs, and interspersing his caresses with soft kisses. Though Margerite felt none of the tingling excitement Ruprecht's touch had given her, Heinrich's warm attentions were easing her, and she could feel the deep muscles of her belly unclenching.

At last Heinrich's hand moved between her legs. His sword-calloused fingertips felt very rough against Margerite's most delicate parts, and her thighs tightened.

"It is often difficult for a woman to become ready again after childbirth," Heinrich said soothingly. "But if you will open to me..." He turned away for a moment, lifting something off the little night-table on the other side of the bed. "This will make it easier for you."

Heinrich was holding a small clay pot - some sort of ointment, Margerite guessed. She opened her legs again, letting him rub the oily cream thickly upon her cleft. Like his other caresses, it was a pleasant sensation, but awakened little desire in her. Still, there was no reason to make him wait any longer, and she could see that he was more than ready for her.

"Come to me, my husband," Margerite said, lifting her legs again and holding her arms out to Heinrich. He climbed on top of her again, careful that she was only bearing a little of his weight, and slowly pressed into her.

At first, even with the ointment smoothing the way, she could not help wincing slightly; Heinrich stopped at once, waiting until she urged him on again. Margerite had never expected such tenderness from such a bluff and loud man, but it seemed to her that he had chosen, for whatever reason, to reveal his heart to her - in a way, she could not help thinking, that Ruprecht had never done.

To her surprise, once Heinrich was deep within her, she found herself responding somewhat to the slow, gentle, but irresistible caress of his thrusts inside her. Perhaps a whore, used to giving her body daily for pay, could hold a man within her thus without care or feeling, but Margerite could not.

As she started to move in unison with him, Heinrich's hips began to thrust more quickly. His eyes were half-closed, his lips parting and his breath coming swiftly; his heartbeat seemed to hammer through Margerite's body as he let out little cries of pleasure. Margerite clutched him tightly, feeling the surging of the powerful muscles in his back as he took her, the faint echoes of his rapture rippling through her own body.

Even now, she could not help thinking of Bertram...But Heinrich, thank God, would never know that the soft moan pressing from her throat, that he answered with his own gasp of delight, was not for him. Suddenly Heinrich's body stiffened on top of Margerite's and he let out a great bellow. She felt his heat gushing out within her, and clasped him tighter as he slowly collapsed onto her, his face buried in her neck and hair. For all her willingness, though, Margerite could not bear Heinrich's weight long.

Gently she tried to disengage herself - and then Heinrich's head rolled to the side, bearded mouth gaping and wrinkled lids drooping over his gray eyes, and he made a horrible noise, like the gurgle of a sheep with a slashed windpipe. Margerite felt the scream rising into her mouth, but clamped her teeth tightly on it as she pushed with all her strength to roll her husband's body off her, his sinking manhood coming out of her with a wet plopping sound that brought a stifled shriek of horrified laughter to her throat.

"Dear Christ, dear Maria, dear God," Margerite moaned, and a high-pitched giggle escaped from her throat. She knew that she was about to start screaming, and that if she did, she would not stop. Then Heinrich gurgled again, and the sound stopped her as surely as a firm slap across the face. Her husband was not dead, but he might be dying, and there was no time to waste.

She drew the coverlet up over Heinrich's nakedness and stepped into her linen underdress, holding it closed around her with one hand. Where were Heinrich's manservants? He must have sent them away after they readied the room: perhaps they were downstairs playing chess or dicing, waiting for their master to summon them again. But Margerite could not run half-naked through the castle like an ancient Grecian maenad; instead she scuttled through the corridor to her chamber.

"Frowe!" Rose shrieked, leaping up as she saw her mistress' wild state of undress.

"Run and fetch Father Michael and Ernst the physician to Heinrich's chambers - now, and run fast as you can, for all the love of Christ!" Margerite shouted at her. Rose fled through the door into the main corridor like a doe with the hounds snapping at her heels.

Margerite paused for just a moment to make sure that all was well with Wolfram and wrap a cloak over herself, then stepped outside to hasten back to Heinrich. The moment she opened the door to the main passageway, Christoph was in front of her, his sword half-drawn, and Georg behind him, clutching a scabbarded blade in his hands. "What is the matter?" Christoph asked urgently. "I heard you shouting..."

"Come quickly, for your father's sake," Margerite told him. They hurried back to Heinrich's bedroom.

The Graf was as Margerite had left him: lying on his back, still breathing faintly through slack lips, his eyelids hanging down. Christoph knelt by the bedside, grasping his father's shoulders firmly. "Father!" Christoph cried. "Can you hear me? What is wrong?"

Heinrich gagged slightly, as though he were choking - had his tongue fallen back into his throat? Margerite could no longer see the slight rise and fall of his chest beneath the scarlet coverlet. Before she could be unnerved by thinking about it, she reached into his mouth, tugging the slippery organ free. Heinrich's body hitched in a spasm: Margerite watched, frozen, until he started breathing again, then wiped her wet fingers on her skirt. Georg covered his own mouth with his hands as though to press back nausea, staring helplessly.

"What is wrong with him?" Christoph pleaded. His upturned face was very pale, all his maturity fallen away in that moment; he might have been younger than Margerite as he stared up, hoping for some words of comfort. "Can you do anything?"

"I do not know. We..." Margerite's voice trailed off. Heinrich's belt on the bedpost, her girdle and overdress hanging on the back of the chair, with his clothing laid across the seat: it would be clear to everyone what they had been doing - and it was not seemly for her to be standing so, with nothing but a cloak over her pale linen underdress with its back gaping open, when the priest and the leech would be here at any moment. "Watch him, and make sure his tongue does not fall back again. I must dress myself decently."

She grabbed her clothes and fled down the corridor and along the passageway that led past her own rooms to Eva's, banging sharply on the girl's door.

A burst of laughter came from within, and Eva's voice fluted,"Who is it?"

"Margerite. Let me in, now!"

The laughter dropped shatteringly from Eva's face as she opened the door. "Frowe - Margerite! What has happened?"

"Heinrich has fallen ill," Margerite said, as calmly as she could.

"But...you are undressed. How..."

"I think you can guess the reason easily enough,"
Margerite snapped. Eva's maidservant slipped behind her,
expert hands fastening the buttons up her back and slipping
her overdress on.

"Dear Christ, how awful," Eva whispered. "What can I do?"

"For the moment, nothing - except go to Christoph. He is
with his father, in Heinrich's chamber, and I think he will
be glad of your company. Try to stay calm, for he is greatly
distressed."

Eva left without a word. When the Gräfin was fully
clothed, the maidservant started to plait her hair, but
Margerite slapped her hand away. "There is no time for
that." She straightened her skirts and hurried back towards
Heinrich's rooms.

Father Michael was already kneeling by the bedside,
murmuring the words of Extreme Unction, while Ernst
fussed with a set of metal cups on the stove. Eva stood
beside Christoph, not quite touching him, but clearly longing
to reach out to him; Georg hovered in the corner like a small
pale ghost, watching in frightened fascination.

At last the priest rose, brushing down his black velvet
robes. "The matter is in God's hands now. I can do no more."

"Then go and pray for him," Margerite ordered. "Light all
the candles you can find; we can easily afford more for the
Graf's sake. Ernst, what do you have to say?"

The physician glanced quickly about the room like a
nervous blackbird, his sharp little eyes taking everything in.
"Frowe Gräfin, the Graf was getting on in years, and it is well
known...that is, an old man with a young wife..."

"That is none of your affair!" Margerite snapped sharply.
"You are a physician: tell me what is wrong with him?"

Ernst drew himself up to his full height, a mere inch shorter than Margerite. "Frowe Gräfin, it is my opinion that the effort called on in the Graf's heart from...vigorous activity, caused a great surge in his spiritus, which, being conveyed from heart to brain, proved too much for his rete mirable, which is that part of the brain at its base where the spiritus is transformed into the spirits of anima which infuse the body with the powers of thought, sight, and movement. If the rete mirable is injured, Frowe Gräfin, those animal spirits can no longer be produced, and hence all the animal faculties are lost."

Margerite looked at her husband, lying still on his bed. A glistening trickle of saliva ran from the left corner of Heinrich's lips to be lost in his beard; his cheeks already seemed gray and sunken, and the breath was rasping more hoarsely from his mouth, as though he were sinking into sleep. It calmed her to hear Ernst's explanation laid out with such neat science, for a darker worry was creeping slowly into her mind. In the village by her father's castle, there had been another name for such sudden fits of paralysis: they were called Hexenschuss - witch shot.

"What can you do to cure him?" Margerite asked.

Ernst sighed deeply, his pouter-pigeon chest and round belly heaving. "Frowe Gräfin, I can apply cautery carefully to his forehead, just above the eyes. If there is still a trickle of animal spirits flowing from his rete mirable, that will draw them forth, and may strengthen the production as well. His heartbeat and breathing are good, which show that his vital virtue is still strong. I myself have seen men recover from such an injury to the brain, though there is no way to tell yet whether the Graf will live or die, or what of his faculties he will retain if he does recover."

"Do you think he can hear us? Has he any understanding?" Christoph asked.

The physician leaned close to Heinrich's face. "Herr Graf, can you hear me?" he asked loudly. Heinrich did not respond; save for the wetness of his lips and the sound of his hoarse breathing, he might have been laid out on his funeral bier.

Ernst straightened up, frowning. "He does not answer," the leech said, as though they could not see that for themselves. "But he may have lost the power of speech altogether now, as well as that of movement."

"How horrible!" Eva exclaimed, crossing her arms over her ample bosom as if to contain a shudder. "To be awake, but unable to move or speak at all - the poor Graf! Christ grant he recovers soon."

Ernst's eyes lingered on Eva a little longer than Margerite would have liked before he said, "Good frowe, I will certainly do all that is within my powers to restore him to health. But I think it would be best if you and the Frowe Gräfin left now, for my cups are hot, and cautery is not a sight suited to the delicate sensibilities of noblewomen."

"I do not wish to leave my husband's side," Margerite protested. "And although the art of cautery is one of which I know nothing, I have some knowledge of healing. If I..."

"Out!" Christoph snarled suddenly, rounding on Margerite with a glare that left her breathless. "Get out, and let him work!" His shoulders bunched up heavily, his hands clenching and unclenching - *as if he means to strike me!* Margerite thought. A flare of anger lit Christoph's gray-green eyes, his mouth twisting frighteningly, and Margerite backed out of the room hastily.

In the hallway, with the door closed, Margerite realized that she was shivering, and so was Eva.

"Poor Christoph," Eva whispered, her voice tight and choked. "I have never seen him frightened enough to shout before." Her lower lip was trembling, her shoulders hunched in on themselves, so that in spite of her beautiful new dress of rose brocade, she looked again like the terrified child who had come to Burg Falkenstein.

"I do not blame him," Margerite answered. "I pray that Heinrich will recover - but if he does not, Christoph will soon have to take his place as Graf, and that is a weighty burden for a young man."

"I suppose so," Eva said dubiously. "But I do not think Christoph is afraid of that, only that he loves his father dearly and is in grievous fear that he will not recover." She looked down at the floor, biting her lip, and tears welled up in her blue eyes. "Margerite, should someone not tell Nikolaus what has happened? He may want to be with the Graf as well."

Margerite thought furiously. If Nikolaus had not heard the commotion in the hallway...would he have gone down to his sanctum so early in the evening? Or - Margerite forced the dark thought shadowing her mind to take shape: had Nikolaus not come out to see what was going on simply because he already knew?

It was hard for her to imagine even a Light-Bearer using magic to...grievously harm his own father, but she had read herself in the Black Book, The ties of affection are chains used by the weaker to enslave the stronger: the magician must free himself of all such illusions, and be as ready to trample his own child or parent underfoot as a foe, if it be to his advantage. And the ritual for which Nikolaus had taken such trouble, and about which he had been so secretive, had been done little more than a week ago...

As Margerite stood debating with herself, she heard the sound of a door opening at the far end of the corridor. The warm light of the candles in the wall-sconces glimmered from the silk-lined sleeves of Nikolaus' green and blue doublet as he walked smoothly, but quickly, towards them.

"Is something wrong?" he asked, his wide brow creased into a slight frown. "I heard the noise even in the library."

"Your father has been grievously stricken," Margerite told
him, looking directly into his eyes. Nikolaus' pupils, already
wide in the dim light, seemed to swell as she stared at them,
and that was all she needed for answer. But what he did -
God willing - I think I can undo.

"How did it happen? Is there a foe within the castle?"
Nikolaus asked urgently, his hand moving towards the hilt
of his dagger.

"No. He was overcome and fell paralyzed..." Margerite felt
the blush rising warm across her cheeks, as though she were
standing above a fire. "In bed."

Nikolaus' face twisted strangely. It was a moment before
Margerite realized that he was trying not to laugh, and a
hot fury flared within her. Bad enough that Heinrich lay
paralyzed, perhaps dying; but by morning, everyone in the
castle would know how he had been felled, and would be
laughing behind her back at jokes about old men with young
wives. And he wished so much not to be made ridiculous by
his desire for me!

It was well for Nikolaus that he managed to master himself
before any sound could escape his lips, and only said quietly,
"I shall go to him." Otherwise, Margerite was sure that she
would have struck him, Order superior or not.

"Ernst is performing cautery now," Eva broke in, standing
her ground and looking Nikolaus in the eye - they were
nearly of a height. "Perhaps it would be best if you waited
until he is done."

"I have seen Ernst at work before," Nikolaus answered.
"You need not fear that my nerves are not strong enough
to bear it. And the Graf is my own father: I should be with
him."

Margerite's nerves tingled with the desire to shout out her accusation at Nikolaus, to slap him across the face and see the mark of her hand reddening on his plump cheek. It seemed unendurable to hear such words from his mouth, when she was certain that he was responsible for what had happened. She bit her lip until the blood flowed salty-sweet onto her tongue: she could not speak her thoughts, but she did not want to let Nikolaus into Heinrich's chamber, lest he try to finish what she believed he had started.

"Christoph is with him already, and he does not want the physician to be interrupted," Eva insisted firmly. "Until Ernst is finished, there is nothing any of us can do save pray." Then she smiled at Nikolaus, a soft curve of the lips that dimpled her softly curved cheeks and seemed to brighten her eyes.

"I know you are anxious, as are we all, and it is worse to stand here outside the door as if we were servants waiting our master's word. Will you not come down to the hall with Margerite and myself? If we cannot help the Graf, at least a cup of wine will help physick our fear for him."

Margerite watched Eva's performance in slightly horrified admiration as the girl held out her hand for Nikolaus to escort her. The tip of the young man's tongue flicked out to wet his lips, and Margerite was certain that she saw his eyes pass for a moment over the low neckline of Eva's dress before he took her fingers in his own. She will make a formidable Gräfin for Christoph some day, Margerite thought.

The moment Margerite sat down, Kobolt leapt into her lap, purring as he sniffed at her thighs. Embarrassed, she pushed his furry head away. It was bad enough to know that her evening with Heinrich was on the minds of the castle folk, without having her cat so clearly aware of it as well. But Kobolt clung to her like a great black burr, kneading her legs so hard with his paws that she could feel the prickle of his claws, and if his presence was obtrusive, she also found his warm weight in her lap comforting.

Though Eva tried to engage him in conversation, Nikolaus seemed as distracted as if Heinrich's attack had truly come as a surprise to him. He kept glancing at the staircase in the corner of the hall, or up at the ceiling, and his fingers writhed nervously about the silver stem of his goblet, the gold band of his Order ring clicking annoyingly against it.

Perhaps I have misjudged Nikolaus; I have grown quick to think the worst, Margerite thought, watching him. But a worse thought already intruded stealthily into her mind, like the first breath of plague-tainted air creeping into a chamber: What if he is like this because his magic worked too well - because he has called up something he could not put down? If that were so, they would all be in danger, even Wolfram.

Especially Wolfram, for the Black Book had made it clear that demons delighted in betrayal, whether of their masters or each other, and if Nikolaus had summoned something beyond his strength to hold, it would work whatever ill it could, and would gleefully do its best to ruin him in the Order's eyes as well as those of decent folk. Unless Wolfram were truly the son of its Lord...but Margerite could not believe that and hold to her soundness of mind.

She rose abruptly, Kobolt clinging to her skirts a moment before he dropped to the floor. "I must go to see to Wolfram," Margerite said. "All the running about and shouting will surely have frightened him, and that girl still has not learned how to quiet him when he is distressed."

"Many women would not be so quick to think of their babes when their husband lies in such straits," Nikolaus said neutrally. Margerite looked hard at his green-glimmering eyes, his pale face: was he reproaching her, or warning her? She did not know how to answer him, so she simply turned and left, Kobolt brushing along beside her.

Wolfram was wailing in Rose's arms, and turned his head aside when the maidservant tried to put her honey-dipped fingertip in his mouth. "Give him to me," Margerite said, her voice tight with fear. Had the babe felt something dark brush by past the wardings of her room, something that she, with her mind so fully on what she and Heinrich were doing, had failed to notice even when it was upon them? Or had he only taken a natural fright from the distress of the adults around him?

"Wolfram, Wolfram," she murmured, rocking her child. "Hush, do not be afraid. Your Mutti is with you, Kobolt is watching over you, all is well."

As Margerite's own heartbeat slowed, Wolfram gradually quieted as well, his howls diminishing to tentative little cries, as though he remembered that he should be wailing, but had forgotten why he was so upset. After a little while, he turned his face towards his mother, nuzzling at her breast, and Rose unlaced and unbuttoned Margerite so that she could give him suck.

Wolfram was full-fed and closing his eyes in sleep by the time the knock came at Margerite's door. Rose went to open it.

Is Margerite here?" Christoph asked, his voice hoarse.

Margerite set her son back into his cradle and stood. "What news?"

hristoph pressed his hand to his forehead. His light eyes were empty with exhaustion, and their rims were red and puffy, as though he had been weeping. "My father is no better. He seemed to feel the cautery, but could not speak, and Ernst can do no more for him."

"Come in and sit down," Margerite told him. "Rose, fetch us wine - no, go to Ernst, and see if he has any aqua vitae." Though her stove's fire crackled softly in the middle of the room, the chamber seemed suddenly chill and dank.

The maidservant hurried out, and Christoph sat down heavily on Margerite's bed, as though it were too much of a strain for him to walk across the floor to a chair. Georg trailed him in, but remained standing, his hands clasped politely in front of him even when Kobolt came over to sniff curiously about the Knappe's modestly pointed shoes and thin red-hosed calves.

"You know that you must take over Heinrich's duties until he recovers - Christ granting that he recovers," Margerite said gently.

Christoph flinched at her last words, as though she had flicked him with the end of a whip. "I know that," he said dully. "How is...has my brother been told yet?"

"He is in the great hall with Eva, waiting for word from you. I believe you frightened her by shouting at me as you did," Margerite added reproachfully.

The Graf's heir pressed his hand to his forehead again, as if to ease a nagging headache. "I do not know what came over me. You have my apologies, Margerite. I did not mean to be so discourteous. I only...Seeing my father there, so helpless..."

"I know," Margerite said, her voice soothing. Then she suddenly shouted, "Kobolt!"

Christoph started violently as the black cat leapt away from his leg; Kobolt had crept up and crouched before the young man with the unmistakable intention of marking his hose.

"Kobolt!" Margerite scolded. "Christoph is neither another tomcat nor your property. Come here, wretched cat, and behave yourself."

Christoph looked at the cat, laughing shakily as Kobolt fluffed his black tail and stalked scornfully away, leaping up on the windowsill to stare narrow-eyed at the man who had invaded his mistress' chamber. To Margerite's relief, she could not see any dark droplets on the fine purple-red wool of Christoph's hose: if Kobolt had managed to spray his leg, the garment would have to be made into something else or cut down for a smaller man and given away.

"He is a tomcat, and will do things like that when I least expect it," Margerite apologized. "I am sorry if I startled you."

"Better than being pissed on," Christoph said, trying to smile at her.

Rose came back quickly enough with a green glass flask and two silver goblets. Margerite poured a large dollop of the amber spirit into Christoph's cup, a smaller one into her own. The scent rose warm and spicy around her face as she lifted it to her lips, burning pleasantly through her nose and onto her tongue. Christoph took a deep swallow, as though he were drinking wine, and the tiny lines of strain on his broad forehead eased a little.

"Ah, that is good," he said. "I will wager that Ernst treats himself more often than others with this medicine."

"I would not take that wager," Margerite answered.

Christoph twirled his goblet in his fingers, staring into it as if he were fascinated by the swirling of the amber liquid over the gleaming silver. At last he said, "We will have to let the news of my father's infirmity be known soon enough, for there is no way to hide it. I believe I am ready to hold his place: he taught me well in the last years, for he knew that his age would overcome him in time. But...if my father does not recover, what do you wish to do? Will you stay here, or go back to Burg Falkenstein?"

The question took Margerite's breath away. She had not thought so far into the future; she had not thought of the future without Heinrich at all. But if she were widowed now, she would be free. Free to return to Wolfram's lands and govern them as suited her; free of Nikolaus' scrutiny, free to marry again - even a former Hauptmann of the castle guard, if she could send Bertram word to come back for her, and if he would turn aside from his quest for a time. The thought dizzied her, spinning in her head as though she had downed a full cup of the aqua vitae at a single gulp - Mother Maria, let me not hope for Heinrich's death!

"It is too soon to be thinking of such things, I hope," Margerite said. "Let us see how matters go now."

Christoph nodded resolutely. "Perhaps that is best. I should be sorry to see you go, though...and there is also Eva."

"There is, indeed." Margerite looked keenly at the young man. Solidly built as he was, thick muscle and bone bulking square against the shoulders of his blue damask tunic, it seemed to her as though there was something insubstantial about Christoph, as though, if she were to touch him, he would crumble into dust. She blinked, trying to drive the uncomfortable image from her mind. "Have you and she made any promises between you yet?"

Christoph looked away, rubbing more persistently at that spot on his forehead. "Not yet. The priest Etienne explained to me about the cousin who is her legal guardian, and warned me that we would have to be very careful in our dealings, lest he attempt once more to cheat Eva of her inheritance. I had thought that after a little time, I would prevail upon Father to allow me to take Eva with a decent retinue and visit Wachholt, so that we might draw up a marriage contract and betroth ourselves before witnesses."

"A wise plan, but one that will have to wait a litle while longer," Margerite sighed. "You can hardly leave Burg Fürstensee now. Christ willing, Heinrich will either begin to recover soon or...not linger, but until matters are resolved, it would be foolish for you to entangle yourself in anything else. And I do not know what Ernst said, but I must warn you plainly. I have seen such cases twice before. The first man died within a few days, without coming to himself again. As for the second, though he recovered slowly, he was never able to raise the lid of his left eye again, nor did he ever again have full use of his hand and foot on that side. If Heinrich does not die of this, Christoph, you may well still have to be his strong staff and his sword-arm while he lives, for it is more than likely that he will never sit a horse again, nor lift his blade in battle or on the tourney-field."

Margerite felt the tears coming to her eyes as she spoke, and Christoph looked away from her, draining the rest of his aqua vitae and getting to his feet. "Thank you for your counsel, Margerite. I should go to speak with my brother now."

"You are welcome. I wish I could give you more help."

"I am sure that you will in the days to come."

When the door had closed behind Christoph and his Knappe, Margerite breathed a sigh of relief. It would have been easier for Heinrich's heir if his father had fallen in battle, or even if he had died, rather than lying helpless in bed: Christoph was old enough to have seen how Death's sickle reaped all men in time, cutting the high wheat-stalk of a Graf and the low barley-stalk of a peasant down to the same level.

It would be the strain of waiting and wondering that wore on him day after day, the struggle of having to hold his father's place without the title, the full responsibility with only half the authority to back it up. She was reasonably sure that Heinrich's men would obey Christoph; but there would still be the awareness that he was, at least in name, no more than his father's steward while the old man drew breath.

Margerite did not like the way Christoph kept rubbing the site of his old head-wound: she had thought him wholly healed of that injury long ago. She wished that she could think of some way to convince him to let Ernst look at it, but it would not be well-done to ask now if such an injury was troubling him, lest anyone think that she was suggesting that Christoph might not be entirely sound in his wits.

"Shall I ready you for bed, frowe?" Rose enquired, pulling out the green ribbon that tied her hair back and shaking the mass of dark curls free around her pointed face.

"Not yet," Margerite said. "I will go to my husband, to pray beside his bed, for he may be able to hear my voice, and it will comfort him to know that I am beseeching the Virgin on his behalf. And if I rub his limbs with herbs and oils, it may help to restore some little strength to them."

Margerite picked up the long box that her magical tools were locked in. She had the key to Heinrich's chamber, and she did not think that they would be disturbed again that night: she had seen it before, how quick folk were to leave the sick as soon as they felt their duties done, and not come back more than decency required. Kobolt followed closely, winding about her legs and purring as though the wooden box she carried held aging fish.

Heinrich's senior manservant Albrecht, a tall, gray-haired fellow who must have been older than the Graf by nearly a decade, opened the door to her knock.

"He still rests, Frowe Gräfin," Albrecht said, bowing with his usual courteous dignity.

By the courtly tone of his voice, his fine clothes, and the neatness of his close-cropped gray beard, he might have easily been mistaken for a nobleman himself; Margerite always felt a little uncomfortable addressing him as a servant, but she knew better than to let him find any hint of that, for it was no better to let a servant see uncertainty in his mistress than to let a strange dog catch the smell of one's fear.

"I would be alone with him for a time. I want you and Joseph to leave, and not come back until I send for you."

The old man looked down at Margerite, regarding her gravely and it seemed to her that she could feel the heavy weight of his doubting gaze pressing hard against her. A tingling shudder broke over Margerite.

Of course it would look suspicious: she had been the only witness to Heinrich's initial fit, and now she wished to be left alone with him again...what easier, than for her to press a pillow over his face or drop something unwholesome into his slack mouth? But Margerite knew that to defend herself would be to confirm any suspicion Albrecht might have of her, and so she met his eyes boldly, hardening her face into a look that said he had best not question her.

"As you wish, Frowe Gräfin," Albrecht said. "If you will just let Joseph finish stoking the stove - the Herr Physician told us that the Graf must be kept warm."

Margerite waited patiently until Albrecht and his younger assistant had left, then locked the door behind them and, to be sure that they would not walk in on her by accident or design, shoved one of Heinrich's heavy oaken chairs underneath the knob.

Her husband lay just as he had before, raspy breath fluttering hoarsely through his slack lips. He could have been sleeping: at that moment, Margerite would have been grateful to hear his frightful snore. She bent down beside him. "Heinrich, can you hear me?" she murmured. "Do you know who I am?"

Margerite thought she heard a faint noise from his lips; it might have been a grunt of answer, or simply a soft belch. Hoping that he could feel her touch, she smoothed his grizzled hair back from his face and wiped away the trail of drool oozing from the corner of his mouth, then kissed his forehead where the red marks of cautery showed livid against his paleness. His skin was cool beneath her lips, as though the warmth of life no longer pulsed through it, and Margerite was glad that his manservants had been dutiful in building up the fire.

She had only completely finished one of her three robes, but the simple garment of black silk would be enough in this warm room. Margerite laid her implements out on the table as if it were an altar: the wand of fire, the cup of water, the dagger of air, and the pentacle of earth; her own consecrated oil, salt, and Holy Water from the chapel's font. Kobolt leapt up on the bed, sitting very still and serious on the pillow beside Heinrich, with his tail draped over the Graf's chest.

"Thou shalt purge me with hyssop, O Lord, and I shall be clean; Thou shalt wash me, and I shall be whiter than snow," Margerite murmured, dipping her fingers into the phial of holy water and crossing herself. With trembling fingers, she drew the robe over her head and fastened her golden girdle. "By the figurative mystery of this holy vestment, I will clothe me with the armour of salvation in the strength of the Most High, that my desired end may be effected through Thy strength, O Adonai, unto whom the praise and the glory will forever and ever belong. Amen."

As she prayed, the light of the candles played glimmering gold over the black silk of her garment; she felt warmed, clean and strong. The hazelwood wand was smooth in her hand between the ridges of the planetary metals: her fingertips tingled as they touched the holy names graven upon it. She drew in a deep breath, lifting the wand.

"Almighty God, whose dwelling is in the highest Heavens, hear the prayers of Thy servant Margerite, who puts her trust in Thee. Let Thy Almighty power and presence guard and protect me, now and forever; let Thy holy angels aid me, now and at all times, unto Thy glory and the good of man. Raphael, great healer; Michael, general of Heaven's hosts; Gabriel, herald of God; Auriel, radiant with God's light - hearken unto me, and lend your aid." Margerite crossed herself again, saying, "Thine is the Kingdom, and the Power, and the Glory forever. Amen."

It seemed to her now as though the whole room were filled with a golden haze, sparkling behind her eyes, thrumming through her body with every breath she took. The scents of frankincense and roses hung sweet in the air about her like an invisible curtain. Kobolt sat dark upon the bed, solid as a stone, so that Heinrich's still form seemed almost insubstantial beside him - was the cat truly larger, as large as a mastiff, or did he only seem so?

Carefully Margerite stepped forward, each tread slow and deliberate. Wand in her right hand, she laid her left palm upon Heinrich's cool forehead. It seemed to her as though she could see the darkness shadowed beneath his skull, like a pooled spill of ink soaking into his brain.

Yet she felt no revulsion, no clammy slug-trail of evil such as she had expected. It was more as though...she could feel the wound that had been dealt Heinrich, even see the blood still trickling out within his skull, but there was no trace remaining of the blade that had given the injury.

She lowered the wand until its tip touched Heinrich between the eyes. "By the powers of the Most High, of God and Christ and the Holy Spirit, by the mercy and love of the Blessed Virgin and all the saints! Let the blood be stanched; let the wound be healed."

A tingle ran from Margerite's heart through her arm; she could almost see the gleam where the tip of her wand met Heinrich's skull, and the edges of the dark pool within were no longer seeping slowly outwards. But there was no change in his breathing, nor did his slack eyelids so much as flicker."

Heal, Heinrich," Margerite breathed, a prayer as much as a command. "Heal, and be well. Let the strength come to your limbs again, the light to your eyes, the voice to your throat. By Almighty God, Who made the heavens and the earth, Who created Adam and Eve and sent his only begotten son to redeem their descendants - Heinrich, be well!"

It seemed to Margerite as though she could feel the strength pouring out through her wand and into Heinrich like her own blood, spurting with each heartbeat. But it passed through him without effect, sinking away like water into dry earth, and she knew that the harm that had been done him was beyond her power to remedy.

At last, exhausted, she withdrew her wand, with the simple prayer, "Lord God, let Thy will be done." Margerite retraced her steps, standing a moment before the table where her tools were laid out. But she could think of nothing else to do for Heinrich, and at last she bowed her head again in humility. "Raphael, Michael, Gabriel, Auriel! Mighty archangels, be with me ever. Lord God Almighty, let Thy power and presence guard me. For Thine is the Kingdom, and the Power, and the Glory forever -" Margerite crossed herself, as she had before -"Amen."

When Margerite lifted her head, it seemed to her that the brightness had drained from the room, leaving her in the dim candlelight. She thought that Heinrich's face seemed a little more peaceful, less gray and wasted, than before, though it might have been nothing but her imagination showing her what she wanted to see. But then a low, guttural snore began to rise from his open mouth: if she had done nothing else, at least, perhaps, she had brought her husband quiet sleep.

When her robe and implements were safely packed away again, Margerite pulled the chair away from the door and unlocked it. It seemed to her as though she had only been with Heinrich a few minutes, but she felt exhausted to the bone, as though she were still a simple knight's daughter who had to aid with the harvest and had been carrying heavy sacks of grain all day: she did not think that she could bear to sit with him any longer.

Albrecht and Joseph bowed to Margerite as she stepped out of Heinrich's chamber. She simply nodded to them, hoping they had not been listening at the keyhole - though she had spoken softly, and they could have heard no more than, at most, a few words of prayer.

When she had reached her own rooms, Margerite found that Rose had fallen asleep waiting for her. She had been with Heinrich longer than she thought: her bladder and the weight of milk in her breasts were telling her that sharply.

Rose stirred, leaping to her feet before Margerite could reprimand her. "Is he any better, frowe?"

"Very little," Margerite said heavily as she dragged the chamber pot out and squatted over it. She wished she knew where she had failed; she wished that Father Etienne were here for her to confide in.

Would I have succeeded in healing Heinrich if I truly loved him - if my heart were not yearning towards Bertram? she wondered. Did I fail because I wished to be free of this wedding? Or was it simply as it seemed: a task beyond my strength to accomplish, at least so hastily?

For she had not fasted to purify herself, nor looked for the most propitious conjunction of the planets for her rite. There were many aspects of magic that she did not know, or had not used; perhaps it was surprising that she had gotten any results at all. Still, I wish Father Etienne were here.As the days went by, Heinrich did not show any signs of healing.

His servants massaged broth down his throat and cleaned him; Ernst cauterized his head and blended salves to rub on his limbs; Margerite commanded his musicians to play soothingly for him, or sat and read to him for hours; but he still lay there like a corpse that, by some dreadful necromancy, managed to breathe long after its soul had departed.

Christoph and Nikolaus seemed to have come to some arrangement about castle duties: Christoph had to make several short visits to his knights in the castles about Heinrich's lands, to inform them of the sad news in person, and, Margerite suspected, to assure himself of their loyalty to himself if his father did not recover.

While he was gone, Nikolaus administered Burg Fürstensee to his own liking, arrogantly striding about to give his orders: Margerite found herself trying harder and harder to avoid him, but when he was not assuring himself of his command over the castle folk in his brother's absence, Nikolaus would often call her into the library to enquire about her studies.

At least, obedient to Order courtesies, he did not insist on personally inspecting her magical tools and sanctum, but accepted her reports at face value; and he was surprisingly helpful in teaching her small things when she asked - chiefly the production of illusions and such spells to delude the minds of others, but also how to find lost objects or gain information.

By the beginning of the fourth week in July, Christoph had finished his journeying about, and was ready to settle himself to the more difficult business of rule, holding court and going over Burg Fürstensee's finances with Herr Jakob. The hay-harvesting was nearly over, and, as his father had always done, Christoph insisted on riding down to the village that week to see for himself how they had gotten on.

"At least the weather has held fine," Christoph said as he and Margerite rode along the side of the lake, pulling off his green velvet hat and fanning himself with it. Margerite wished that she could take off her own coif and white linen hood, but that would not have been seemly: she would simply have to suffer the prickly heat and sweat rolling down the back of her neck. "I have been expecting thunderstorms all month, but we have not had so much as a drop of rain."

"It is as well, with the hay-harvest going on." Margerite remembered vividly how her father had stood by the door of Burg Hirschenberg, staring at the steady sheets of summer rain and cursing beneath his breath as he thought of the storm soaking into the drying hay.

"Yes. Herr Jakob tells me that our storehouses are nearly bare - but this has been a good summer. If the weather holds, we shall easily make up for last year." Christoph's voice was distant as he spoke, and he did not look at Margerite, but stared out over the wide shining stretch of the Fürstensee.

The burden of ruling in his father's name had worn hard upon him these last weeks; the natural ruddiness of his face had begun to fade, and he seemed to have grown thinner, his cheekbones beginning to show and his wide belt to hang more loosely about his hips. Margerite resolved to speak with Georg, to see if the Knappe could take more care that his knight ate and rested when he should. The hay-meadows about the lake's edge, which had been high with rustling grass and wildflowers in June, were mostly shorn now, the grass still green, but low and soft beneath the horse's hooves.

If it had not been so hot and muggy, the weather would have been perfect for a pleasure ride; the air was a little cooler down by the lake, but there was no wind to sweep the clouds of midges away. A small boat floated on the water, the man within stretched out with his hat over his feet and a fishing line trailing into the depths of the lake. Christoph looked at him, grunting in irritation.

"What is that man doing, fishing when he ought to be in the fields?" he asked sharply."I shall have to do something about that."

Margerite shaded her eyes with her hand. "I believe that is one of our castle folk. Hildegard must have sent him out for fish, since tomorrow is Friday."

"So it is." Christoph sighed, then urged his horse into a trot. "We should not linger over this."

As they neared the village, they passed a full-laden wagon rolling slowly along the road, the wheels and hooves of the oxen raising a low cloud of dust. The driver greeted Christoph cheerfully, taking off his cap and bowing from his seat.

"Not too much more left to bring in, Herr Christoph!" he called, grinning gap-toothed at his young lord. "Pray to Christ for us, that the weather stays clear!" He mopped the sweat from his bald head with a brown sleeve, flicking his reins to keep the oxen plodding slowly onward.

Christoph's face twitched, something between a smile and a grimace. "Where is Schultheiss Werner?" he asked.

"Herr Christoph, I do not know, for I have not seen him. He may be in his own field, or riding about keeping tally. We'll have a good share to send up to you this year, never you worry."

They finally found the Schultheiss on the road between farms. He was a large man, thickly built, with brown hair cropped short over his thick bull-neck, and rode a big dun gelding that looked like a retired plough-horse. At the castle feasts where Margerite had seen him before, he had been dressed in a clean robe of blue wool; now he wore a simple tunic and breeches, the armholes stained with dark circles of sweat and the coarse-woven gray cloth overlaid with a layer of dust. He halted when he saw them, dismounting and bowing.

"Well-met, Herr Christoph, Frowe Gräfin," Werner said. "A fine day for the haying, praise God."

"So it is," Christoph replied shortly. "Now, tell me how matters have gone thus far - no, mount up, you can tell us as you ride, for there is no need to waste time."

With no further prompting, Schultheiss Werner at once began to list the farms and their yields of hay thus far, beaming proudly each time he told Christoph a particularly good figure. Christoph smiled as well, and Margerite thought that she could feel his tension easing as Werner went on.

"You have done well," Christoph said at last. "Finish as you have begun, and it will be a good year."

"Thank you, Herr Christoph! If I may ask now -" Werner's wide forehead creased, and Margerite could hear the note of worry in his deep voice -"how stand matters with the Herr Graf?"

"No better," Christoph answered heavily.

"That is a great shame. All the folk here by the Fürstensee have been praying and lighting candles, hoping that Christ and his saints will grant that the Herr Graf recovers." Margerite noticed that the Schultheiss was not looking at her as he spoke; of course, news of how Heinrich had been stricken while bedding his new young wife must have long since reached the village.

Even with no word said, she found herself reddening with shame - at least she could blame her blush on the oppressive heat. After Christoph's conversation with Schultheiss Werner, they rode briefly about the farms surrounding the village. The grain stood tall in the bright sunlight, the golden heads just beginning to pale towards brown, promising a good harvest - if no hailstorm struck it down before reaping-time; Margerite knew, all too well, how such things could happen, and the oppressive heat seemed all too foreboding of heavy storms.

As Werner and the cart-driver had said, the work in the hay-meadows was coming to an end: the men and women bent to gather and tie the dried hay, while strong lads, their backs and arms burned brown by the sun, lifted the bales and tossed them onto the waiting carts. By the time they were riding back through the village, Margerite noticed that her mare's brown head was hanging low, and Christoph's stallion and Georg's gelding were in little better shape.

"We should stop to water our horses and let them rest a little," Margerite said. "The heat is no kinder to them than to us."

"True enough," Christoph agreed, pulling his stallion's reins to swing towards the village square. The well stood beneath a huge spreading linden tree, its leafy green branches shedding a canopy of cool shadow on the ground beneath. When Georg had hauled up water for the horses, Christoph said to him, "Now run quickly to the inn, and bring us back some beer, for I am thirsty, and I am sure the Frowe Gräfin is as well."

Georg scampered off at once. The inn's door was open, and a rich scent of roasting pork wafted temptingly out. Margerite thought of asking Christoph if he would like to eat his midday meal there, but he seemed so tense and fidgety, glancing back up at the castle almost with every second breath, that she decided not to press the matter.

When the Knappe came back with two tall clay mugs, Christoph almost snatched one from his hands, lifting it up for a deep draught. At his first mouthful, though, his face twisted into a wild grimace and he spat the liquid angrily out. "What is this, wash-water? I said beer, not small beer, Georg!" His fist flicked out, backhanding the squire across the jaw and knocking him to the ground. Georg scrambled up without a word, running back into the inn.

"That was a rough payment for a simple mistake, Christoph," Margerite chided him. "Small beer is fit to quench a thirst with."

Christoph pressed against his forehead, eyes angrily downcast. "Sebastian's beer is good, but his small beer is swill, and Georg knows that."

Margerite sipped gingerly at the mug in her hand. She could not argue with Christoph's judgement: the drink was thin even for small beer, and had an unpleasantly bitter edge to it, as though there had been gentain leaves in its brewing - well enough for provoking appetite and ensuring good digestion, but hardly to her taste either. The strong beer that Georg brought back to them was far better; a little yeasty, but sliding rich, smooth, and cool down her dusty throat.

Nevertheless, when she looked at the bruise darkening along the side of the Knappe's freckled jaw, she found herself feeling a little disturbed. It is the way of men, to give and take such buffets and hardly notice them, Margerite told herself. And Christoph is ill-tempered from heat and strain; what wonder that he is rougher than usual with his squire?

The draught seemed to have restored Christoph's good humour, for he patted Georg's shoulder, as if to reassure the Knappe that the storm had passed. "Perhaps we should stop here to eat. My father..." he coughed. "My father always passes a little time in the village when he has ridden down to see that the work is going well. And I am sure that you must be growing hungry, Margerite - and Georg as well, for he is at that age when a boy eats his own weight every day, is that not so, Georg?"

The Knappe grinned shyly up at his knight and nodded. He seemed to hold no grudge against Christoph for the blow, and Margerite put it from her mind. The weather did not break: each day dawned in a muggy haze, but the sky was always clear by tierce, the sun beating hard down through the heavy air. The Burg Falkenstein chapel was fuller than usual Sunday, crowded with folk from the village who had come up to rejoice at the end of the haying in that short time before the back-breaking labour of harvesting the grain began.

Margerite was little surprised that Nikolaus was not there in the family's benches at the front of the church, for he had not bothered to attend a Sunday service since Heinrich fell ill, but it surprised her that Christoph was not there for his first Mass at home in several weeks. From Father Michael's frequent glances at herself, Eva, and Georg during the service, Margerite could tell that the priest was displeased as well, and she braced herself to deal with him when he came up to her afterwards.

"Why is Christoph not here today?" Father Michael asked bluntly. "This is no time for him not to show himself at Mass."

"I do not know," Margerite answered. "He has been very busy of late..."

"Whatever his labour, he should lay it aside for Sunday," the priest declared, sonorously as if he were still preaching a sermon. "He has never scorned me before, even if he sometimes seems to take the sanctity of God's house more lightly than he ought. I shall speak to him about it." He strode off, the fine tapestry-work of his apparel swinging at the hem of his white alb.

"Do you know why Christoph was not here this morning, Georg?" Margerite asked the Knappe.

Georg twisted his creamy silk sleeve-tails together. The bruise on the side of his face was fading to a green and yellow stain beneath the blotchy freckles; his blue eyes shone bright and alert as he looked up at her. "Frowe Gräfin, he slept badly last night, and he did not wish to rise for Mass - though, Christ be my witness, I woke him well in time to be dressed and ready. He seemed in a very ill humour, and said that the ringing of the bells was giving him a headache." The squire touched his forehead, repeating Christoph's habitual gesture. Margerite noticed that there seemed to be a little dark crust of dried blood at the edge of Georg's long nose - had Christoph beaten him again? Although a knight might chastise his squire, it hardly seemed fitting to strike a nobly-born Knappe as if he were a servant.

"Christoph has had a number of headaches lately," Eva confirmed. "I think it is from worry and work, for he has hardly been himself since Graf Heinrich was stricken." A shadow seemed to cross her sky-blue eyes for a moment, and Margerite wondered if there had been some trouble between the two of them.

If that were so, there was no sign of it at the midday meal. Whatever words Christoph had with Father Michael, they were over by the time Margerite and her two companions came into the hall; and his morning rest seemed to have done him good, for he was cheerful and lively throughout the meal, praising Hildegard's boiled chicken in spice sauce and her sweet Galrat, a delicious jelly of wine, vinegar, and honey thickened with ryebread crumbs. Nevertheless, Margerite drew him aside after they had eaten, asking quietly, "Christoph, are you well?"

"Why should I not be?" he asked, staring at her in astonishment. "You mean, because I slept late this morning?"

"Eva mentioned that you had been suffering from headaches, and your Knappe said that you are not sleeping well."

"Oh, well," Christoph said dismissively. "I am fit enough, there is no need for anyone to worry."

Margerite looked carefully at him. She could see the signs of exhaustion - the slight clammy pallor to his skin, the faint shadows under his eyes - but she could not shake the lingering feeling that there was something else wrong with Christoph, something that she could not put a name to. To her relief, though, his pupils were the same size: she had grievously feared to see them mismatched, for that would have meant his head wound had been reinjured or somehow broken again from the strain that was on him. But could it have caused some lingering damage, even without showing any symptoms? she wondered.

"Let me know if you keep having headaches," Margerite said to him at last."As for the sleeping, I shall instruct Georg in how to prepare a posset that will bring you an easy rest." It would have to be a mild one, she knew, for a strong draught might harm him if the problem stemmed from a head injury; but a warm syllabub with milk, wine, honey, and chammomile would at least soothe Christoph's strained nerves in the evenings.

"That is most kind of you," Christoph answered. For a moment, Margerite thought of bringing up the matter of how he was treating his Knappe, but she realized that it was none of her affair: if Christoph felt that a few blows were needed to prepare Georg for the harsh disciplines of battle, what would a woman's opinion matter?

Rejoining the others, Margerite noticed that Nikolaus was looking at her curiously, his eyes narrowed in a calculating manner. Does he think I am plotting with his brother? she thought. And to what end, if so?

It did not surprise her, however, when Heinrich's younger son courteously requested her to come to the library with him, since he had a question about some of the books she had brought. Fighting down her nervousness, Margerite let Nikolaus escort her up.

"What were you talking about with my brother so earnestly and privately?" he asked straight away, before they had even seated themselves. Although Nikolaus' plump face was intent, however, Margerite did not see the seething fury that he usually hid so badly whenever he thought his will might be thwarted.

"I was only asking about his health," she answered honestly. "He has had trouble sleeping, and has been out of humour of late, even with Eva."

"Really?" Nikolaus said, lifting a curved dark brow. "He has been better-tempered towards me than he has since we were young boys. Perhaps it is because I am aiding him in his new duties, rather than trying to drag him away from them as Eva does." Unpleasantly smug as his words were, beneath them, Margerite could hear what almost sounded like a ring of honesty.

But it was true: Christoph had delegated more authority to his brother than she would ever have expected, or, to be honest, would have wished him to. And beneath his overbearing delight in his heightened place, Nikolaus had taken his responsibilities seriously, spending hours closeted with Herr Jakob and the bookkeeping almost every day, and going about himself to take account of the castle's stores; if he shouted at the servants more than Margerite herself would have, well, there were many lords who did worse.

"It is well that the two of you have...reconciled any difficulties between you. But have you noticed nothing amiss with Christoph?"

Nikolaus held up a hand, counting points off on his blunt fingers. "He has not forced me out to be thumped on the practice field; he has not said once that I ought to be packed off to the Church; he has not suggested that I lack a proper pair of stones; he has not tried to wrestle me down like a peasant in the mud; he has not filled my bed with frogs and strange vermin..."

"When did he do that?" Margerite asked, surprised into amusement.

"Eight years ago, but that is hardly the point. He would have kept doing it if I did not keep my bedchamber locked."

Margerite could not help guiltily remembering a time when she was nine and had dropped a caterpillar down the back of her six year-old sister's dress to watch the other child shriek and squirm - poor Agatha, dead these four years! It was no difficulty to imagine Christoph, in his light mood, still playing such tricks on his brother, even with both of them well-grown to manhood.

"Very well, I see what you mean," Margerite conceded gracefully. "But still, I am concerned for him, for he seems both unhappy and impatient."

"Why should he not be? He and Father were almost as like as if they were one man, and there was great love between them," Nikolaus said, staring defiantly into Margerite's face, so that she could almost hear him thinking, And not for me.

"Your father is not yet dead, Nikolaus," Margerite said, speaking as gently as she could when what she really wanted to do was grasp him so tightly her fingers sank into his plump shoulders and shake him until his teeth rattled in his head. After her effort to heal Heinrich, she was not as certain as she had been that Nikolaus was behind his collapse, but she did not like the way the young man was speaking, as though Heinrich's death were certain.

"Come now," Nikolaus said, "do you really think that he will recover? He may linger for some time, but he has been in the same state for almost a month, and I can see as well as anyone how he is wasting away in the bed."

"There is always a chance while...while he lives." Margerite had been about to say, While Christ has mercy, but of course she could not use such words when closeted in private with Nikolaus.

"It is not likely. And that brings me to something else. When Heinrich is dead, you will need a husband, and a guardian for Wolfram. I think it will be best for you to marry me."

Margerite gasped as though Nikolaus had struck her in the pit of the stomach. "Marry you?" she repeated. Too harshly, she realized: for a fleeting moment, she saw the awful pain in Nikolaus' eyes, as if she had repaid his blow with a dagger thrust; then something cold and bitter, like a smear of frozen bile, shuttered his gaze. She floundered, hastily trying to repair the damage she had done. "That would be incest by law, since I am your stepmother; even if Heinrich should die, that cannot be changed."

"A dispensation can be obtained for such a thing," Nikolaus pointed out coldly. "I have a very good idea of how the accounts here stand - and the Papacy is always in need of money, while the Order is not without those in Avignon who can drop a word in Urban's ear if need be to smooth things for two members."

But would the Order want to give her to Nikolaus? Margerite had not thought of such things since Günther's death. Yet, even wholly untrained and unaware, she had been a prize given to Ruprecht; Günther had desired to keep control over herself and Wolfram, and he was a Prince among the Light-Bearers.

She was quite certain that Nikolaus did not rank high enough in their councils to be given charge of her, save by the necessity that had brought her here; the alternative, to be informed that she would wed according to the Order's plans, was even worse, but far likelier. But it would not be wise to inform Nikolaus that he was not magician enough for her, least of all when she had just inadvertently suggested that he was not man enough.

"Let us see how matters turn out," she said.

Nikolaus' lips curved into something like a smile. "Rather say, let us shape matters to our will - Priestess."

Margerite froze, her heart beating hard in her ears. "Are you suggesting...that we speed Heinrich along?"

Nikolaus frowned. "You must learn to contemplate such thoughts without squeamishness, or you will never be a true magician, nor a true Light-Bearer. Think on it deeply and dispassionately, until you are sure that you would not flinch were you commanded to do such a deed - consider that your next exercise, and do nothing more until you have achieved it. I will say only that the time has not yet come for my father to die, nor for us to act, at least not until matters are more firmly settled here."

By which you mean, Margerite thought, until you have convinced Christoph that you are so useful, he can do nothing without you. She wondered for a moment if Nikolaus could be slipping some potion into his brother's food or drink, which might explain Christoph's headaches and sudden shifts of mood... but she could think of no way for him to do so, since Christoph usually drank out of the same pitcher as the rest of them, shared a plate with Eva at meals, and relied on his Knappe to fetch whatever else he might require. Unless he had somehow suborned Georg... She dismissed that thought as quickly as it arose.

"I thank you for the lesson, for the sake of Light," Margerite replied, the usual Light-Bearer salutation from student to teacher, and hoped that her hidden shudder of horror would not curdle the milk in her breasts.

When Georg came to her that evening to ask how to prepare Christoph's posset, however, Margerite sent him down to the kitchen for the ingredients, but told him that she would prefer to mix it herself. Sending Rose away on the pretext that she wished a small meal before bed in order to keep her strength up for the demanding work of producing enough milk to keep Wolfram fed, Margerite made up the posset on her own stove, and when the frothy liquid was mixed to her satisfaction, she drew out her wand.

For a moment she hesitated - Ruprecht had ordered enchanted drinks given to her, and no doubt he had thought it was for her own good as well - but it was neither harm to Christoph nor violation of his freedom to send him something spelled with charms that would protect him against evil magics.

Carefully she traced cross and pentacle upon the foaming surface of the syllabub, whispering the names of God: Yod He Vau He, Shaddai, Adonai, Ehieh Asher Ehieh. "Let Christoph be warded against all ill; let the great archangels Raphael, Michael, Gabriel, and Auriel stand about him, and the power of Christ armour him, that no wiles of the Foe may assail him, and that he may be cleansed of all that darkens his spirit," Margerite murmured above the rich sound of Kobolt's purr at her feet. "And may Mother Maria protect him, as she loves her own son."

As Margerite poured the drink carefully from its bowl into a mug and made the sign of the Cross over it once more, Kobolt stretched up on his hind legs, pawing at her skirts and miaowing for a taste, then following her hopefully to the door. As she carried the draught, it seemed to Margerite that she could feel the power she had set into it tingling in her palms. She gave it to Georg with a great sense of relief, bending quickly to catch Kobolt before he could snake between the Knappe's legs to trip him.

"I did not make that for you, Kobolt," she said sternly, "and I am sure I have other things to do than brew syllabubs for cats. But since you are a fine cat, I shall let you lick the bowl as soon as it has cooled, if you find it to your taste."

If holy enchantments disturbed Kobolt at all, they clearly meant less to him than the taste of milk and wine, or perhaps he enjoyed the taste of Margerite's magic, for he scoured the little metal bowl clean the moment his mistress set it upon the floor, looking up and licking his whiskers as if there might be more forthcoming.

The next evening, however, when Georg brought the posset-ingredients up to her door, he fidgeted a moment, then said, "Frowe Gräfin, could you perhaps change the recipe a little? Herr Christoph said he does not care for the herbs you put in it." Margerite sighed. Chammomile was the mildest of the sleep-bringing herbs, but a strong enough dose could have flavoured it beyond Christoph's taste, and he must have a sensitive tongue, to have taken so violently against the flavour of the small ale in the village.

"Tell him that I said it is a medicine, not a sweet," Margerite instructed the Knappe sternly. "It matters little whether he likes it or not, so long as he drinks it. Did it work last night?"

"I...I do not think he had enough to help," Georg answered, his honeyed tenor very clear even though he was stammering with awkwardness. "I must confess that it was I who drank most of it, and I slept very well indeed, with sweet and pleasant dreams."

If Christoph had drunk even a little, Margerite reassured herself, it would be enough. And she had spoken Christoph's name in the enchantment, but if some of its virtue were shared with Georg, that would be no harm in any case. But she said to the boy, "Very well: go to Ernst and tell him that I want a little bit - no more than a pinch, mind - of valerian, and twice that of skullcap. We will see if those are more to Christoph's pleasure. But if they are not, he is to drink it himself anyway, no matter how he dislikes it."

"Yes, Frowe Gräfin," Georg replied obediently.

The smell of the steeping valerian made Kobolt frantic, as Margerite had feared it would; she had to watch him carefully to keep him from trying to leap onto the stove, and he rolled and purred about her feet as if he were a kitten of eight weeks, writhing in a most undignified way as she repeated her spell of protection on the posset. He tried to roll on the bowl when he had licked it clean, as well, until she finally grew tired of its clattering between the rugs and took it away from him.

Whether he liked them or not, the possets seemed to do Christoph some good. At least, he told Margerite that he was sleeping well enough, and stopped complaining of headaches; though he still pressed at his forehead now and again, it seemed more out of habit than out of pain. But he did not go to Mass the next Sunday, either, or the next, in spite of Father Michael's pointed comments at the dinner table; and when Margerite pressed him privately on the matter, Christoph only said roughly, "When the priest can do my father some good, then I will go to his Masses again."

Margerite was about to rebuke him sharply for that, but he stalked off, leaving her more distressed. She had seen that anger at the Church before; there were many men and women who had not set foot in a church since the Death first passed through Europe, perhaps as many as there were who had been driven to furious devotion out of fear or thankfulness that they were spared.

More painfully, Christoph's words brought sharply to her mind the memory of her father's guardsman Adalbert, crouching half-naked like a madman in his house above the bodies of his two sons and shouting at the Hirschenberg priest, "Curse you, and your Christ as well! If He loves me, why did He let my boys die like this? Why did He not heal them, instead of letting them scream and rot in their filth?"

Then Adalbert had lifted up his arms, and even from behind the priest, before he could close the door, Margerite had seen the great black boils swelling livid in the guardsman's pale flesh, and heard his shriek, "What kind of God does this to men?"

Margerite had asked that same question herself, although silently, as she tended her mother and sister while they died. She did not know the answer now, save perhaps to say, One Who is a God of wrath as well as mercy, and wholly beyond our understanding in both - perhaps, she hoped, she might come closer to such knowledge in the study of magic, though she did not think the Light-Bearers possessed it.

Still, Margerite could not deny that in some ways it seemed worse to have Heinrich lying upstairs like a living corpse, wasting slowly away in his bed as his servants turned and washed and fed him, than it might be if he were dead and buried, leaving his family to go on without him. Even the Death had killed in the course of a few days, instead of leaving its victims to linger so: what wonder that Christoph could not find it in his heart to sit through Father Michael's well-spoken sermons and admire his beautiful chapel while his father suffered without remedy?

Nevertheless, though Christoph was not Graf in name, he was still holding his father's place, and though Margerite suspected that Father Michael's objections to Christoph's absence stemmed as much from pique and a high sense of his own priestly prestige as from genuine spiritual concern, the priest was still quite correct to say that it did not look well for Christoph to be missing while Mass was said for his folk. Therefore, Margerite went to Eva's room on Saturday afternoon, hoping that Eva would be able to succeed with Christoph where she and Father Michael had failed.

Kriemhilt's kittens were almost half the size of most grown cats now, and were enthusiastically exploring the castle; Margerite would have tripped over two of them in the corridor if Kobolt had not hissed softly and swatted the furry black shadows out of the way. The other three were leaping gleefully about the room, batting at their mother's tail and Eva's embroidery as she sat stitching with Kriemhilt in her lap. Eva's maidservant, a slim woman in her middle years, was busy setting up a tapestry loom for her mistress, carefully counting and stretching the threads of the warp.

"Greetings, Margerite," Eva said, looking up at her. Kriemhilt leapt off her lap at once, running over to Kobolt, and the two cats began to sniff at each other and lick one another's faces and thick furry ruffs in an almost embarassing show of affection.

"Greetings, Eva. Perhaps I should have shut Kobolt in my room, if you do not want more kittens."

"Oh, Kriemhilt is no common cat. She will not litter again until her darlings are full-grown," Eva said, with what seemed to be to Margerite more fondness than sense - though, since Kobolt had not immediately tried to ravish his tortoiseshell daughter, as was his usual way with queens, perhaps there was some truth to Eva's assertion. "Do sit down. Mathilde, go fetch us some wine, and see if Hildegard has any small pastries or other such dainties as we can nibble upon while we wait for supper."

Mathilde hooked a final thread into place and went on her way. Without preamble, Margerite said, "Eva, I am worried about Christoph, and I think you can help."

The delight went out of Eva's beautiful face at once. She folded her hands on top of her embroidery and said, "What is wrong with him now?"

"Wrong with him now?" Margerite echoed. "Have the two of you had a quarrel?"

Eva sighed, her bosom heaving. "We have...well, he has been ill-tempered and rude towards me."

"I see," Margerite said. "Are you on such bad terms with him that you no longer want to marry him?"

She was more than half expecting Eva to say yes at once: the girl was barely fifteen, and had taken very quickly to the pleasures of being a lady, so a certain tendency to blow hot and cold in love according to the passions of the moment might be expected. But Eva sat quietly, golden brows drawn and delicate lips pursed in thought. At last she said, "I do not know. I love him, but he has been like a stranger in these past weeks. I realize that he is grieved and worried and no longer has the time to spend on the practice field or out hunting, as he delights to do, but...there is something else behind his eyes, and I no longer feel that I know him as I once did."

"Being a Graf, even without the title, is very different from being a young champion," Margerite said carefully. "It is hardly unexpected that Christoph should seem a little changed by his new duties."

But Eva shook her head, her golden hair fanning about her shoulders. "Margerite, it is more than that. If you will help me to unlace my bodice a bit..."

Margerite reached for the laces at the side of Eva's overdress, untying them and sliding them carefully free, as she had once done for Agatha every evening. Her sister would be Eva's age, if she had lived through the Death...

Eva pulled down the top of her underdress, and Margerite gasped. The bluish-black marks were clear on Eva's creamy skin: the prints of a blunt thumb and fingertips just at the upper curve of her voluptuous breast, showing where the girl had been grabbed with brutal force.

"Did Christoph do this?" Margerite asked, her head numb with cold fury.

"Yesterday," Eva whispered. "We were playing chess, and I had the upper hand. It seemed to anger him, for he spoke rudely, so I stood up to leave. And...he grabbed me there to pull me back down, as if I were a serving wench who had displeased him."

"He cannot do such things!" Margerite said. "I shall speak to Christoph now, for this is a disgrace to his father and to his belt and spurs of knighthood."

Eva pulled her dress back up, looking piteously at Margerite. "Please do not," she whispered. "I would rather it stayed between the two of us, for I do love him, only..." She dropped her eyes, staring at the heap of bright silken threads and scarlet cloth in her lap. "I would not say this to anyone else, Margerite, but I have begun to be afraid of Christoph. It is not only that he is acting oddly, but there is something about him that almost reminds me of the time I spent at the convent. I cannot say what it is, but the Abbess sometimes looked at me so, as did Graf Günther."

"Graf Günther is dead, and can harm you no more, thank Christ," Margerite told Eva reassuringly, lacing her back up and smoothing her gleaming golden hair, just as she had always smoothed Agatha's to soothe her after a nightmare. She could feel Eva's solid shoulders trembling beneath her touch, as though the girl were about to burst into tears.

"I know. But still...I am afraid, I am so afraid, and I do not know why." Suddenly Eva began to weep in earnest, turning to throw her arms about Margerite. Margerite was holding her like that, stroking her hair and murmuring, "Hush, hush," as she would to Wolfram, when Mathilde came in with the wine.

Mathilde's lips tightened into a thin line. "Herr Christoph again, I suppose," she sniffed. She filled the two goblets, pressing one into Eva's hand. "Here, frowe, this will do you good."

Eva stopped snuffling at once, drawing herself up and accepting the wine with some dignity. She has learned quickly, Margerite thought.

"Thank you, Mathilde," Eva said. Her low voice was still rough with tears, but she swallowed them back, shaking Margerite's hand off.

That evening, Margerite requested a book of astrological tables from Nikolaus. He gave it to her without comment; he looked preoccupied, even troubled, as though his new duties were beginning to weigh heavily upon his mind. Or perhaps he is feeling some pang of conscience? Margerite thought. I wish I could believe that.

Be that as it might, Margerite was convinced now that she would have to do something to heal Christoph, and she was determined not to fail in her magics again. This time, she would find out the position of the stars; she would choose the correct day and hour, so that all the forces of the heavenly spheres would be working with her. And...She bit her lip angrily, staring down at the page before her.

If the calculations written in a crabbed black hand on the smooth parchment were correct, there would be a full eclipse of the Sun on Sunday afternoon, an omen of the greatest ill, that could overshadow even Popes and Kings. Yet no time before then would be propitious, at least not to the best of her knowledge - and she could hardly ask Nikolaus for advice.

Patience, Margerite counselled herself. She would perform her rite properly: she would wait until the best time, and purify herself with fasting and prayers beforehand. The next Sunday should be soon enough; by then the planets would be aligned more smoothly, and besides, the Sun would have moved from Lion to Virgin, a cooler sign and one more fitted to the work she intended.

Until then, she would take neither meat nor wine, and perform her meditations at dawn and dusk, that she might be able to call and wield the power that God had granted her. When the first edge of shadow began to creep onto the sun, and the light of day through the window of her chamber, to dim, Margerite shuddered.

It seemed to her as though she could feel the baleful influence of the eclipse coming over her; she could almost hear its discordance, like one of a lute's deep strings slipping slowly flat as it was played. Kobolt rubbed his head against her knee, and she was not sure if the great black cat were giving comfort, or seeking it, but she stroked him and then put her embroidery aside to lift him onto her lap.

"Frowe, what is wrong?" Rose asked, looking up from the fine linen thread she was spinning. "It seems to be growing darker, but there are no clouds in the sky."

"It is only the beginning of an eclipse: sometimes the Sun is shadowed by other heavenly bodies. Do not be afraid," Margerite counselled her - but she could not take her own advice.

She hoped that Nikolaus had thought to let Christoph know what was about to happen, and that they had told other folk of the castle: such darkness during the daytime was a terrifying thing even to the learned. She knew, indeed, that she should go out now to walk among the castle knights and servants and calm them, but the thought of leaving her room terrified her in a way that she could not explain.

I am safe behind my wards here - but what of everyone else? How can I leave them to...To what? Margerite could not put a name to what she feared: it seemed, instead, like a great shapeless cloud oppressing her, so that she could not think clearly, nor lift her hand to act.

Calm, Margerite urged her fluttering heart, *calm. This will pass: it is but a working of nature, as surely as the movement of the Sun and the planets in their heavenly spheres. A baleful aspect it may be, but it is not the handiwork of the Lord of Evil.*

Kobolt stood up in her lap, putting his paws on her shoulders and purring as he nuzzled along the side of her jaw. Margerite leaned her head briefly against him, glad of his warm touch, but Wolfram began to cry, and she had to put the cat down to go to her son.

"Hush, Wolfram, what is wrong?" she murmured. "You cannot be hungry again so quickly, though you have been eating enough for two babes and growing swiftly enough for three."

Wolfram only wailed as though he would not be consoled, waving his fists in the air and kicking his legs, with his small face screwed up into an unhappy grimace. Margerite dandled him and sang to him, lifting him up in the air and swooping him about, but his cries only grew louder.

"Hush, hush, my child, my precious one," she crooned. "Would you like to crawl on the rug with Kobolt? He is always ready to play with you, if you do not pull too hard on his tail and ears."

True to Margerite's words, Kobolt lay down before Wolfram, letting the child tug at his thick fur and only closing his eyes and laying his ears back when the baby's tiny fingers came too close to his face. But even that did not soothe Wolfram, and soon he had rolled over on his back to scream at the ceiling. Though it was not long since his last feeding, Margerite had Rose unlace her and offered her nipple to her son; he spat it out in fury and turned his face away.

The sky kept darkening, so that the light in the room was no longer the subdued brightness of late afternoon, but the gray dimness of early evening. It was well, Margerite thought, that her windows faced northward rather than west: her book had warned most stringently against trying to watch the sun during an eclipse, for though the eye might not shutter itself against the fading light, the sun's power could still burn it grievously.

There would be need for infusions of eyebright and clary that night, Margerite told herself, and that thought brought her to the door, for there was a real danger that folk would have to be warned against. She might not be able to stop every curious servant from staring at the widening black crescent on the sun's face, but at least she could lessen the harm, if Nikolaus had not given the warning already. He had said nothing to Margerite - but he had given her the book she asked for without a word: he must have expected her to make her own examinations and provisions, as Order members were supposed to do.

But surely, if the eclipse had been expected by anyone else, nothing else would have been on anyone's lips after Mass; such things did not happen often enough to be ignored. She would have to go out now to see how the castle folk were taking the growing darkness...

Yet when Margerite lifted her hand to let herself out, that same overwhelming dread came more powerfully upon her. It seemed as though unseen shackles of iron weighted her wrist, so that she could not turn the doorknob, though she strove to, though every counsel of good sense and responsibility told her that she should be out among her people.

Is this some working of Nikolaus', that keeps me trapped in here? Margerite wondered. Or is it a warning sent to me by the Heavenly Powers, that I ought to heed? Or...is it only simple fear? But fear of what?

"Mother Maria, help me," she prayed. "Help me to know..."

Wolfram shrieked again, more dreadfully, and Margerite turned back to where he lay kicking on the rug. As babies sometimes did, he was working himself into one of those dreadful fits where his face turned almost purple, his head frighteningly dark beneath its soft golden down of hair.

Margerite thought that he would not stop crying now until he had tired himself out, but his shrieks had risen until they were painful to her ears as well as her heart. She picked him up again, alternating between soothing speech and soft song, but to little purpose. Rose did not try to interfere, but moved silently about the room, lighting candles as the chamber grew darker.

When she heard the knock on the door, Margerite almost shrieked. Rose went quickly to open it; in the corridor, a taper in her hand, stood Eva's maidservant Mathilde. The older woman looked calm and neat as ever, her simple linen coif pulled closely about her delicate-boned face; she said simply, "Frowe Gräfin, if you please, Frowe Eva would like to speak with you."

As Margerite stepped through the door - past her own wards and the faint lingering pungency of Kobolt's marks - the feeling of darkness fell upon her an hundredfold, almost choking her. Although only a little light now came through the arrow-slits, as though it were already the darkening hour after sunset, the candles in the wall-sconces had not yet been lit; the only brightness was the haloed light of Mathilde's single taper. Margerite followed the maidservant silently down the hall and into Eva's room.

Georg sat on the bed, his dark green doublet half-unbuttoned and his face swollen and pink with tears. His red hair was disarrayed, wildly tangled, and he was running his hands through it in distraction.

"Georg, what is wrong?" Margerite asked. "What has happened to you?"

A fresh flood of tears burst from the Knappe's eyes, and he hid his face in his hands as if he were a small child.

"Eva?"

"He will not tell me. He only came running in here as if the hounds of Hell were on his trail, and will do nothing but sit there and weep."

Margerite knelt down beside the youth, taking his bony hands gently in her own. "Georg, speak to me. Tell me what the matter is. No one here will harm you."

From beneath, she could see the red fingerprints standing out starkly on the boy's long jaw, as though someone had grabbed his face tightly there - just as Christoph did with Eva. She wanted to shake the Knappe from his shocked daze, but did not dare.

"Georg, speak to me," Margerite repeated, keeping her voice quiet above the cold sickness surging through her body: I was too late, I should have... "Tell me what has happened."

Georg choked back his sobs, staring down at her. The white rim of his eyes shone all around the blue irises; his pupils were huge and dark with terror. "Herr Christoph," he whispered. "He...God help me, Frowe Gräfin, I cannot go back to him!"

"What did he do?" Margerite asked insistently. But Georg
only buried his face in his hands again, his narrow shoulders
shaking with a fresh flood of tears. Outside, the sky had gone
dark as midnight, only a few stars glimmering through the
rippled glass of the windowpanes, and Margerite heard the
sound of Kobolt's furious yowl down the corridor as clearly
as if she had been in her own chamber.

"Stay here," she commanded, leaping to her feet and
running down the dark passageway, finding her way to her
own door only by touch.

All the candles but one had been knocked over, guttering
out in their own wax. Christoph stood within, the point
of his sword between Rose's small breasts and Wolfram
clutched tightly in his free arm. Kobolt stood before him,
back arched and fur bristled out, hissing madly with anger
and terror.

Christoph's pleasant face was twisted, the skin drawn
inhumanly tight and smooth over the bones; the white curve
of his teeth shone from his snarling lips, and it seemed to
Margerite that red foxfire glowed from the black depths of
his eyes. A choking stink of putrefaction filled the room, and,
just at the edge of hearing, there was a strange deep buzz, as
of numberless faraway voices babbling and gibbering to each
other.

The fear that had been building in Margerite since the
shadow first touched the sun crested now: this was the thing
that she had felt, the thing she had not dared to cross her
threshold and face. Yet now it was within - and if she did not
act, Wolfram and Rose would die.

"Who are you? How, in the Name of Christ, did you get in
here?" Margerite asked sternly.

Christoph's smoothed face contorted violently at the holy
name; his hand jerked, and a little spot of blood flowered
on the green wool between Rose's breasts. The serving maid
gave a small cry of fear, but did not move from the spot: had
he told her that he would kill Wolfram if she resisted?

"You invited me in," he grated, his voice deep enough to shake the wooden floor beneath Margerite's shoes. "After your pleasant night with Heinrich - do you remember? Did he enjoy his last pleasure, pumping in your sodden little body until his brain burst?" Christoph's mouth opened, and a terrible laugh issued from it...and Margerite remembered how she had asked Christoph into her chambers on the night Heinrich was stricken.

Had this, whatever it was, already been lodged within him then, like a worm inside the sound shell of a walnut?"But what I want to know," he went on, "is: who are you? I think you are not one of us; I think you are a spy. Do you know how we deal with spies?" His sword pressed a little harder against Rose, and a trickle of blood slowly darkened the cloth beneath its tip. Rose did not make any noise this time, but her wide eyes stared piteously at Margerite, and Margerite could read the prayer in them: Please, frowe, save me!

The stench grew stronger as Margerite stepped forward, until she could hardly breathe, but she grasped the tip of the sword in her left hand, moving it away from the maidservant. Gertrude had died in her service: she would not let the same thing happen to Rose.

"You do not have the authority to harm her, creature of Hell," Margerite said, breathing lightly through her mouth against the stink. The foul smell coated her tongue and throat like putrid oil, and Christoph laughed again.

"I know I am...but what are you?" he taunted. "Tell me, quickly, who you are and what your allegiance is. Who is your master, woman?" His sword pulled back, its edge stinging across her fingers, and then its tip rested cold on the hollow of Margerite's own throat.

"You sent me tainted drinks: did you think I could not smell their poison? You killed Heinrich, and all the while, you were dreaming of your lover, betraying your husband even as you slew him. Was that not a fair deed? Do you congratulate yourself on it, even while you sit and mumble to feed the pride of a priest in that shit-smeared cesspool he calls a church? Who do you think your master is - Priestess?"

Margerite clenched her wounded hand. The hot blood welled up, spilling across her fingers, and the sharp pain shocked her mind to thought again. But I am not a priest, or even an exorcist - God help me, I do not know how to drive this thing from the dwelling it has found in Christoph's flesh! Yet she answered steadfastly, though the sword at her throat seemed to vibrate harder against her skin with each word.

"My master is Jesus Christ, Who died on the Cross for the sins of mankind. You have no power over me, creature of Hell, nor over my son Wolfram, baptized and blessed in Christ's holy Name, nor over my maidservant Rose. By the holy Names of God, I command you to depart, and trouble us no more." Margerite lifted her right hand slowly until it lay along the edge of the sword, the blue silk of her sleeve reflecting like water along the weapon's steely sheen. "Yod He Vau He! Shaddai! Adonai! Ehieh Asher Ehieh! Adonai Elohim, Elohim Gibor!"

As she spoke each Name, Christoph flinched backwards, his taut face contorting. The sword's point dropped, as if the strength had left his arm, and before she could think about what she was doing, Margerite lunged forward, tearing her son from his grasp. Wolfram wailed, his shriek rising high above Christoph's deep snarl.

"Depart!" she screamed into Christoph's face, so close to him that she could see the flecks of spittle on his red tongue. "By God and Christ and all their holy angels, I command you, foul and accursed demon, to go away and leave Christoph in peace!"

He stood stock-still, and for a moment it seemed to Margerite that she could see the unholy foxfire in his eyes dying down, so that they showed gray-green in the dim light again. Christoph! she thought, a surge of hope leaping up within her.

Then the Order ring on her left hand bit down with a sharp
pang of cold that tore up her arm, bringing a scream of
anguish to her lips. Frantically, fumbling around Wolfram's
squirming body, Margerite ripped the icy silver circle from
her finger; but in that moment, Christoph's face convulsed
again. He rushed out past her: she could hear the doors
banging behind him, and then the fading sound of his feet
going down the stairs.

I have lost him, she thought. Mother Maria forgive me, I
almost had him, but I lost him...and now that thing is free,
and will keep its rule over Burg Fürstensee!

Rose was sobbing quietly, clutching at the bloodied
spot on the front of her dress. Wolfram was still wailing
indignantly, but when Margerite glanced quickly over
his body, he seemed unharmed. Kobolt stood arched and
bristle-tailed, staring at the door and growling; when
Margerite shifted Wolfram to her hip and picked the cat up
in her other arm, she found that he was shivering. "Brave
cat, good cat," she said. "I am sure you did the best you
could."

"Frowe?" Rose whimpered. "What..?"

"Do not ask," Margerite commanded sternly. "Quickly
pack warm wraps for Wolfram and my jewelry - and you will
carry this box as well." She tapped the small chest with her
ritual tools in it. "We cannot stay here. Bring several candles,
as well," she added, for a plan was already forming in her
mind.

With Wolfram crying softly under one arm and Kobolt
shaking under the other, Margerite hurried down to Eva's
room. The first light was already beginning to come, faint as
dawn, back into the sky, the sun's thin red crescent gleaming
through the west-facing windows of the corridor.

"Eva," Margerite said, "take your jewelry and your heaviest
cloak and come with me. Georg, too: we cannot leave
him here." Thanks be to Mother Maria, Eva had sent her
maidservant away; for what, Margerite did not know or care,
so long as Mathilde could not overhear them.

"What do you mean?"

"We must leave this castle now."

"But..."

"Eva, do you trust me? We are going to find Father Etienne, for I know no other who can help us - and while we are here, all our lives are in the gravest danger."

To her credit, Eva said nothing else, but opened one of her chests and took out a small, heavy bag that jingled as she tied it onto her belt - jewelry, or money; Margerite did not know which. When she started trying to stuff Kriemhilt's kittens into her basket, however, Margerite said, "Leave them! They are old enough to fend for themselves, and they are Kobolt's get by his own daughter, at that, nor can we care for them on the road. You may bring Kriemhilt, but not the other ones. Georg, where is your sword?"

"In Christoph's room," the Knappe snuffled. "But..."

"Come on!"

Christoph's door was swinging wide open, but it was Eva who had to dart inside to retrieve the weapon, for Georg would not cross the threshold. They made their way quietly down the stairs, with Margerite in the lead. By the grace of God, there was no one in the great hall - Margerite guessed that nearly the whole of the castle's population was outside watching the eclipse, or, more likely, on their knees within the chapel praying for deliverance.

She led them into the room where the valuables were stored; it only took a moment of hasty deliberation for her to overcome her conscience and open the chest where a number of small bags of silver were stored together with a few fine pieces of goldwork - for had Heinrich not put his privy purse at her disposal? Margerite paused again in the ground-floor armoury.

Georg would not get far if he were heavily burdened, and his sword would likely draw too much attention as it was, but a stout leather jerkin and leather cap reinforced with iron inside, even if they were a little large on him, would give him better protection than nothing at all. She made sure that he had a sturdy dagger as well, and by good chance, among the heavier bows were a few lighter ones such as ladies might use for pleasure hunting: Georg could pull such a bow easily, and Margerite herself could bend it at need. The Knappe made no complaint when she burdened him with these things, though he did not move to choose any weapons for himself.

Margerite had to steel herself to bring her small company through the hidden doorway that led down to the caves, for she knew that she might well be leading them all to their deaths. But she had no other choice now: they could not pass through the castle gates, and, at worst, it might be better to die lost, trusting in God's mercy than to remain at the mercy of the thing that had taken Christoph's body for its own. And...she had one thing to trust in that neither Nikolaus nor, she hoped, his demon knew about.

As soon as the stone door had glided shut behind them, Margerite set Kobolt down. "Now, my Kobolt," she whispered to the cat. "Is there a way out through these caves? Find it for us, my Kobolt, or else we are all like to perish here."

Kobolt lifted his head, sniffing the damp air. His long whiskers twitched, his plumed tail swishing from side to side. Kriemhilt squirmed, leaping out of Eva's arms, and walked over to nuzzle against him for a few moments. Then, deliberately as if they were hunting rats, the two cats trotted off into the darkness of the caves together, and Margerite waved the other three humans to follow them.

Chapter Five

Margerite followed Kobolt's tail, waving like a wide black feather at the edge of the candle's small circle of light. A small icy vice of terror gripped her heart when the cat turned off the trail she knew, leading her into the unknown salt-crusted passages. She knew she had risked all to trust him - what if his feline nature had led him off to hunt rodents, or the little white eyeless fish that swam in the dark cold streams under the mountain? But, having tossed the dice, she could not call them back, and better trusting in her Kobolt than in Nikolaus or the thing that had laughed through Christoph's mouth.

In the dark, it was easy to lose all sense of time. The only sure guide Margerite had to how long was passing were the slow processes of her body: when her bladder felt like a hard rock in her belly, she had to stop and move just outside the edge of Rose's candlelight to stop and piss, and when her breasts began to ache with swollen tenderness, she had to stop again long enough for the maid to unlace her so that she could hold Wolfram to her nipple.

Tireless, the cats halted when she did, sitting and watching her wide-eyed until she was ready to walk again. Her stomach was beginning to rumble with hunger as well - how long had they been down there? Was it dawn, or only midnight? Three of Rose's candles had burned down already. Margerite's heart nearly stopped when the trickle of water along the edge of the pathway suddenly widened to a broad black pool. The cats were already at the other side, Kobolt's golden eyes and Kriemhilt's green staring expressionlessly back at her. She slowly took one shoe off, dipping bare toes into the icy water. The ground sank away swiftly beneath her foot: it would not be an easy crossing.

Eva, Georg, and Rose looked up at her, and Margerite realized that it was hers to go first. She could command Georg in - but how should she ask him to strip before women, or undergo such an ordeal after whatever had shocked him to speechlessness?

"Georg, turn your back," she said. When the squire was no longer looking, she gestured Rose to help undress her. The cold air of the cave shivered along Margerite's skin; when she plunged into the waist-high water, the ice froze her limbs so that, by the time she climbed out along the far slope on the other side, she could hardly move.

Eva crossed next, carrying her own clothes and Margerite's, her well-formed body glimmering white above the black water. The two women dressed each other as quickly as they could, though their numbed fingers could barely managed the laces and buttons of their dresses. Rose waded across swiftly with Wolfram, but Georg stood with his back to the pool, and even at the edge of the candlelight, Margerite could see how he was trembling.

"Georg," she called out. "You must cross the water; this is the only way out."

"I...I cannot," the Knappe answered, shivering. "Please, Frowe Gräfin..."

"Georg, you must," Margerite told him. "There is no other way, and we need your sword to protect us on our journey." And if we do not move soon, we will die of the cold here, she thought; for already she could feel her thoughts slowing and the heaviness weighting on her limbs, as though she had walked too long in the snow.

Georg turned around to look at her, his eyes wide and dark in his pale face. Then, with a convulsive shudder, he began to unfasten his leather jerkin. The women all turned their backs, listening to the soft plashing sounds as the squire waded through the water. Margerite could hear Georg's teeth chattering, but he made no word of complaint.

"Let us hurry now," Margerite ordered when Georg had dressed himself again. And Mother Maria help us if we have to make another such crossing, she added to herself, though she did not dare speak the words aloud lest the others should lose heart by them.

By luck or the good guidance of Kobolt and Kriemhilt, however, no water blocked their way again, though occasionally they had to cross small freezing streams. Rose had just lit a fifth candle when the flame bent beneath a soft gust of air, and in that wind, Margerite could smell earth and pine, a scent that restored her flagging strength.

"We must be nearly out," she said.

It was not long before they saw a faint glimmer ahead of them. They had to crawl through the final passageway, bending their heads to get beneath the low lip of rock; but at last all four stepped forth into the warm light of day.

"Thanks be to Christ!" Eva declared fervently as she stood, stretching up on tiptoes and leaning her head back. The rose damask of her overdress was woefully smeared with mud, and none of the rest of them were any cleaner. "Where are we?"

Margerite looked around herself. Above them the land rose steeply, wooded hills stretching up into gray granite crags. She could not tell if it was the same mountain that loomed above the Fürstensee: they had been walking all night and part of the day, from the warmth of the afternoon air and the look of the sun, but the passages had seemed to twist and coil upon themselves like snakes beneath the rock - if it had not only been cold and tiredness that made her think so.

"And what will we do now, frowe?" Rose asked. "We have no food, and..." The maidservant did not finish her thought, but Margerite could see her fear and exhaustion like a gray veil over her triangular face. They all needed rest; Margerite would have given every piece of silver and jewelry in their bags for a cup of hot honeyed wine, a slice of bread, and a warm place to sleep. But their disappearance would have been noted by now - would Nikolaus, or the thing raging in Christoph's flesh, order them hunted down?

At least it was August, and the blueberries were ripe, hanging thick and dark from their bushes; such berries would sustain them for a little while, until she or Georg had regained the strength to shoot at small animals.

"We must go on a little farther yet, at least until nightfall," Margerite said. "I do not wish to stop so close to the castle."

"Then perhaps you can tell me what we are doing?" Eva asked as they began to walk northward, pausing every so often to strip handfuls of blueberries from the low bushes and stuff the sweet fruit into their mouths. "Why did we have to flee so suddenly, and why is there blood on the front of Rose's dress?"

Margerite paused. What she had to say was no light thing, but Eva deserved to know it. "Christoph is possessed by a demon. He attacked Rose and myself, and only by the grace of God did we manage to escape."

"The grace of God, and the power of your prayers, frowe," Rose added, her green eyes shining as she looked at Margerite. "I did not know a woman could cow a demon like a priest, unless she be a wisewoman or saint."

"I am neither, God help me!" Margerite replied tartly. For if I were wise, I should have guessed beforehand what was wrong with Christoph, and if I were a saint, I would not have failed against his demon at the last moment.

Eva shivered, as though she had touched the cold slimy back of a slug, and her hand went to her bruised breast. But she said nothing; it was Georg who spoke.

"You mean that it was not truly Herr Christoph that did those things?" his sweet voice said hopefully. "I did not think it was in his nature to speak or act so. Though, in truth, he did not harm me greatly, only frightened me and...If I had not fled, he might have done more."

Margerite thought of the possets she had charmed with spells and prayers of protection: if, even inadvertently, they had saved Georg from the worst that the demon could do to him, then she had acted well. But something else seemed to be on Eva's mind, for she hunched her wide shoulders, and the look on her pretty face was that of a frightened child again.

Margerite did not want to know what memories Georg's words had brought back to her.

"I cannot say that you are safe until we are much farther from here," she told the two of them gently. "But you are beyond harm from...that, at least for the moment." A thought came to her mind then, and she looked closely at the disheveled young Knappe. "Georg, do you think that we could go to your father for help?"

Georg shook his head violently, tattered locks of bright red hair flying beneath his iron-bound leather cap. "Frowe Gräfin, I cannot tell him that I failed in my duties as Herr Christoph's squire. And if it becomes known that Herr Christoph is a demoniac, what will be done to him?"

Margerite thought about that for a few moments. Short of all-out war, she could not see how Graf Wolfgang could force exorcism on his neighbor; and the accusation of demonic possession, however true it might be, struck her as being as likely a way to start a war as anything else she could think of. If Nikolaus had managed to regain control of the demon, he would hardly allow an exorcism to take place, for that meant that Burg Fürstensee was entirely his - if he could explain away the sudden disappearance of the Gräfin and her protegé; but Margerite could easily guess how Nikolaus might be able to do that, claiming that she and Eva had gone on a penetential retreat or pilgrimage in order to pray for Heinrich's recovery.

But if their little troupe showed up at Graf Wolfgang's castle with their tale and asked his aid...Christoph's reputation would be soiled beyond all renewal, and bloodshed would, Margerite thought, be almost inevitable. The only thing to do was to try to find Father Etienne, to get his aid in casting the demon out. He had spoken of going to Hamburg; that had been over two and a half months ago, but he was likely still northwards of them. They slept by a brook under the trees that night, bundled in their cloaks.

Tired as he was, Georg insisted that they set a watch, and Margerite could not disagree with him, although Heinrich's lands were free of bandits and she did not know what they could do if she were wrong and Nikolaus had sent out men to hunt them. As she was on the verge of sleep, her head pillowed on one of the lumpy sacks of silver purses they had brought from the castle, another thought came to Margerite: what if Nikolaus tried to find them by divination? If he could scry them out, they would be at his mercy.

Fumbling in the bag of jewelry at her belt, Margerite found the cold beads and delicately wrought metal of her falcon necklace. That would conceal her, at least - could she spread its protection over the whole party? She clasped it about her neck, holding the golden pendant until the metal grew warm in her hands. With her eyes closed, it seemed to Margerite that she could see its soft glow. She breathed deeply, letting her own heartbeat pulse through the gold.

The falcon lifting her wings...growing until she covered all of them in her feathery cloak, Wolfram curled warmly against his mother's body, Georg sitting with his sword across his knees and his iron-bound cap low over his eyes, Eva and Rose in their nests of thickly-piled pine needles with Kriemhilt between them, Kobolt's eyes glowing golden from halfway up a pine tree...Margerite did not know what spells Ruprecht had used upon the jewel, but it answered easily to her will, and, even now, she could feel no taint of evil upon it.

Margerite awoke with the stink of blood in her nostrils and the light tickling of small insects on her face. She sat bolt upright at once, a little cry escaping her lips before she could stop herself. Beside where her head had lain was the dead body of a half-grown hare, its guts trailing on the ground and the fleas already creeping from its cooling fur. Kobolt sat next to it, washing blood from his face with a paw and looking very proud of himself; Wolfram was staring intently at the hare, struggling to free his little arms from the blankets that wrapped him.

"Well-done, my brave hunting cat," Margerite said, petting Kobolt and moving the dead furry body well out of Wolfram's reach. Georg and Eva were still sleeping, but Rose was already awake, kneeling on the mossy stream-bank and bringing up dripping double-handfuls of water to wash her face and hair. "Rose! If you can start a fire, meat has been provided for us."

"As well that I thought to bring my little tinderbox," the maidservant said. "I almost left it behind, but Aunt Gerhild always told me never to go anywhere without a way of making fire for myself."

"Your aunt is a very wise woman." Margerite drew her dagger and set to finishing the job that Kobolt had started, drawing the hare's bowels out for the cats to chew on and stripping its skin neatly away.

Her arms hurt to move and her back ached, for carrying Wolfram so long, even though Eva and Rose had taken their turns with him, had been no small labour, nor was she used to sleeping on the ground, even with the cushioning of cloak and pine-needles; but as she moved, her limbs gradually began to unstiffen. It took some work to cook the joints of hare on makeshift skewers of green pine-wood, and the small portions of half-charred meat, washed down with icy water from the stream, were not enough to ease anyone's pangs of hunger, but it was better than going without.

When they had eaten, Margerite said, "Rose, I think our ways must part here. I would have Gerhild know what has happened, for there should be someone at Burg Falkenstein who is warned about Christoph, and there is no one there whom I trust more in such matters."

"But, frowe, who will look after you if I leave you?" Rose protested. "Surely you cannot do without a maid on your travels - who will do your hair and tend to your washing and such?"

Margerite looked down at the stained and muddy blue silk of her dress, already tattered from their long trek through the caves, then up at the grimy faces of Georg and Eva, and laughed. "I do not think that any of us will be travelling in a style that befits our stations in life. Eva and I will be able to see to each other well enough, do not fear." She rummaged about in her bag, bringing out a fist-sized purse of silver. "Take this with you, for you may need it on the way, and you have more than earned it. Christ willing, it shall not be too long before we see each other again. Only...I must ask for your tinderbox, for we may be travelling in the woods for a while longer."

"You are welcome to it, frowe," Rose answered. "But are you sure that it would not be wiser of you to come back to Burg Falkenstein? You are greatly loved by the folk there, and you would be far safer and more comfortable than on the road with only a young Knappe to protect you against brigands and evil-doers."

"I cannot," Margerite said. "We must find Father Etienne."

"Frowe, do you even know where he has gone?"

"No." But I know where Bertram is, or at least where he should be - must be, by now - and with his aid, I will have nothing to fear.

"Frowe, forgive me for saying so, but this is madness!" Rose argued. "Burg Falkenstein is young Graf Wolfram's by right, and you have seen that all Graf Heinrich's forces would not be enough to pry you out of it against your will, even if Herr Christoph could manage to raise an army for a second attack. Please come back with me, frowe."

Margerite shook her head. "I must do this," she repeated.

"Do not argue with your mistress, Rose," Eva put in. "She is much wiser than you are, and if she says we need to do something, I am sure we do."

"I will not let anyone harm her," Georg added. "Not while I can stand and wield a sword." Though his words would have been more comforting from a man full-grown and proven, rather than a youth who had not even begun to shoot up yet, the look of mulish stubbornness began to fade from Rose's pointed features.

"As you say, frowe," the maidservant muttered. "I shall pray every night for your safety, for I know that you can stand against creatures of Hell, but wild animals and robbers are another matter."

Though Georg objected at first, Margerite and Eva insisted on carrying the heavy bags of silver themselves, in order to leave his hands free for his weapons. "And if you have your bow out and ready, you will not lose the chance to shoot if a deer should cross our path," Margerite added, which seemed enough to convince the Knappe. Wolfram was the heaviest of their burdens, but at least he was being surprisingly good, making only a few little chuckling noises of delight and staring bright-eyed at the woodlands around him as they walked.

Kobolt and Kriemhilt bounded before them, dark tails flashing into the underbrush at odd moments. If it had not been for the aching effort of hauling a baby over rough ground and the hunger still cramping Margerite's belly, it might have seemed like a pleasure trip, for the day had quickly grown warm enough for the women to take off their heavy cloaks, a soft breeze rustling through the pines overhead and birds chirping from tree to tree. Georg seemed to have entirely recovered from his fright, for he was soon striding smoothly along as though he had merely come into the woods to hunt, his blue eyes flickering quickly to any deer-tracks on the trail.

When Wolfram became hungry enough to begin crying, they had to stop, and Eva helped Margerite to unfasten her dress while Georg stood politely staring into the bushes. "I should have thought to ask Rose to change clothes with you," Eva said. "Perhaps if we come to any settlements, we can buy something better suited for the road. In these we look..."

"Like a pair of noblewomen who have been crawling through the mud and sleeping on the ground?" Margerite said.

Eva giggled, a blush coming to her creamy cheeks. "That was not what I was thinking. Sadly, I would rather have said, like a pair of ill-used...maidservants."

Like prostitutes who have had a few hard nights, you mean, Margerite thought: it was unfortunately true. "Still, we must wait until we are out of Heinrich's lands, lest anyone recognise and unwittingly betray us. At least these dresses can hardly be any more ruined than they are already."

As the sun was lowering towards evening, Margerite found that she had chosen wisely in insisting that Georg carry the bow, for when a young roedeer leapt across the trail in front of them, he had an arrow nocked and loosed before its hooves touched the earth again. His shaft caught it just behind the shoulder; it toppled, then rose and darted off again, but had not gotten beyond their hearing when it fell to the earth a second time.

"Well-shot!" Eva exclaimed; had the girl not been carrying Wolfram, Margerite thought she would have clapped her hands.

Georg grinned at her, his look of delight transfiguring his homely features. "It is but a little accomplishment to shoot such a bow well; it is hardly a knight's weapon," he said, but his modest words could not hide the pride in his voice. He trotted briskly after his deer, returning in a few moments with the small beast slung over one shoulder. When they dressed it out, Margerite saw that the Knappe's arrow had skewered it perfectly, in through both lungs and slicing across the heart.

"It is a pity," Eva said longingly as she fed dry twigs into their little fire, "that we do not have the wherewithal to make a pepper sauce here. Hildegard cooks roe-deer so well that I have never tasted its equal."

"I should prefer a good round of wheaten bread to go with the venison, and a goblet or two of the red Ahr-wine," Margerite answered. "But let us thank God for what we have: fine meat, even charred over a fire in the woods, is better than going hungry." In truth, once the fire was going well and the juices of the roe-deer dripping down into it, Margerite found that she was hardly able to keep herself from tearing the rich liver from its skewer before it was done; even in Lent, she had seldom craved any meat so dreadfully.

As slowly as they had to go, it was a good four days before Margerite judged that they were safely past the borders of Heinrich's land. The diet of game and berries had its inevitable result, so that their bowels rumbled continuously and they often had to make sudden stops for one or another of the small group to hasten behind a bush; only the two cats and Wolfram really seemed to be thriving. But Margerite could not help wondering how it had been for Bertram - not only wandering in the woods, but alone, and knowing himself hunted: she remembered how thin and tattered he had looked in her vision, and her heart ached within her with the wish that she could comfort him.

They had been skirting cleared areas, staying within the woods, but there had been no sign that they were being pursued. Now, Margerite judged, they were as safe as they were ever likely to be; and past Heinrich's borders, they would do best to stick to well-travelled roads and towns. By the time they came to the first settlement, Margerite and Eva had been able to wash the worst of the mud and stains from their dresses: though the fine fabrics would never look like anything but old cast-offs again, at least they were almost clean. The road here was wide and deeply rutted by wagon-wheels, and the inn on the village square was a large half-timbered building: a good many travellers passed through here, and Margerite hoped that her small party would not stand out too dreadfully.

The innkeeper was a tall, gray-haired man with a wide white scar running down his cheek and cutting through his thick gray beard. His left eye stared disconcertingly off to the side when he looked at them, rolling of its own accord, and he considered the three travellers carefully for a long time before he said, "I have a room you can hire, but there's to be no plying your trade in it, you understand. My wife won't have such things going on."

Margerite drew herself up, ready to snap a sharp reply - how dared he say such a thing! Then she remembered that she was neither dressed nor horsed like a Gräfin, and that it was her purpose not to betray who she was. Instead, she answered meekly, "We are Christians on pilgrimage, good innkeeper, and have no such trade to ply. What will you take for the room and dinner?"

It was as well for her, Margerite thought, that she had not grown up as a Gräfin, but as the daughter of a poor knight, for the first price the innkeeper named to her was nothing short of robbery. She remembered how to bargain well enough, though, and at last got him down to something near a reasonable price by pointing out that they had no horses to take up room and feed in his stables. His good eye brightened when he saw the silver in Margerite's hand, and it was not long before they were seated at a table with frothing mugs of beer, soft brown bread, and white cheese, in front of them.

Simple as the fare was, Margerite thought that Hildegard's finest arts could not have made anything better or more satisfying. She had to take care to remember her table manners, delicately breaking off pieces of the round loaf, slicing the cheese thinly, and chewing slowly and carefully so that she did not drop crumbs from her mouth in her haste. Georg was a little less delicate in his manners, but Margerite did not frown at him for that: a boy of his age had a greater hunger than a grown woman.

The sleeping room was small and narrow, with two straw mattresses side-by-side. At least the bedclothes looked clean enough; though Margerite feared they would all get up with more vermin than they had lain down with, it was better than sleeping on rocks and tree roots. The cats found the room fascinating, sniffing all about the edges of the walls with their tails twitching and the fierce look in their eyes of hunters who could smell their prey - Margerite thought that she would be surprised if there was not a dead mouse or rat on her pillow in the morning.

Georg stayed in the room to guard their possessions, while Margerite and Eva went down to speak to the innkeeper about buying some provisions for the road. He rubbed the track of his scar with one knuckle, his left eye rolling to the side as he looked contemplatively at the two women.

"Well, now. There's not a great deal to be had at the moment, what with harvest just coming to end and the slaughtering-season not started yet, but I could maybe scout you out a few things, some travel-bread and smoked ham, anyway, and a bit of cheese. Pilgrimage, you said? Which shrine are you going to?"

"The shrine of St. Boniface at Fulda," Margerite replied: that was in Thuringia, but it lay directly along their direction of travel."My husband is ill, and I would pray for him." That, at least, was true enough; Margerite felt guilty about the lie, but could think of no other tale that would explain why she and Eva would be travelling with only a young man for protection. The three of them would have to try to pass themselves off as siblings, if the occasion arose...

The innkeeper made a slight snorting sound, but gave no other comment, as if to say it was none of his affair.

"And I am told," she added, remembering her vision, "that there is a shrine north of here where St. Adalhild's fingerbone is kept. I would stop there and pray, for I have heard that it is a very holy place."

"St. Adalhild...mm, no, I haven't heard of that one. We get some people through here on the road to Fulda every year, even a few Italian pilgrims, believe it or not. And I can tell you..." Margerite listened patiently to his stories, waiting for her chance to bring him back to the subject of selling food.

She knew that she could easily afford to buy horses, as well, but she found herself somehow reluctant to admit it: it might be more unsafe to seem too rich than too poor. By sunset, the inn was more than half full, mostly with labourers come in from the fields, though a few men were better-dressed than others. The evening meal was good, seethed pork with a thick cream sauce and wild mushrooms; Margerite, Eva, and Georg lingered over it, grateful for the taste of the well-cooked meat.

Lulled by the food and beer, Margerite thought little of it when three men sat down on the benches beside their group. For peasants, they were well-dressed, in tunics of blue and yellowish-green wool. One, a swarthy man with the huge shoulders and bulging arms of a blacksmith and the soot of his profession ground deep into the pores of his nose and cheeks like a brand, wore a silver ring on his finger. He smiled broadly at Eva.

"Well-met, girl," he said. "Where did you come from?"

"Passau," Eva replied. "My sister and I are on pilgrimage to Fulda."

The blacksmith laughed, looking at his two friends and winking. "Pilgrimage, eh? Holy sisters, are you? Tell me, what kind of donations does your convent ask for?" All three of them laughed uproariously, and Margerite could smell the heavy scent of beer on their breath. Mother Maria, they think we are prostitutes, too! she thought. Why did I not try to buy some simpler clothes from the innkeeper while I had the chance?

Georg drew himself up very straight on the bench, so that the hilt of his sword was visible. Before Margerite could speak, he said, "These ladies are under my protection, and it is not proper for you to make mock of them."

The blacksmith widened his eyes, drawing back in comically exaggerated distress. "Oh, I do beg your pardon, young lord. I didn't realize that they were under your... protection! I should have spoken to you first. Tell me, then, how much do you want for the blonde one tonight?"

Georg stood up with his hand on the hilt of his sword. Margerite said swiftly, "Sit down, Georg; I am sure these good men meant no insult. Perhaps we should bid them a fair evening and go to our room, for we must rise early tomorrow."

"You don't need to be coy with me, sweetie," said one of the blacksmith's friends, a stocky, yellow-haired fellow whose beard was neatly rolled into two points. "I'll come along to your room with you, if you'll just put your brat aside for now."

"You will leave them alone now!" said Georg. Although his sweet tenor voice trembled a little, his long chin jutted out firmly, and his blue eyes were hectic with brightness. Heart sinking with terror, Margerite realized that the boy was going to defend their honour to the death - whether his own or that of the three villagers hardly mattered: in either case, they would not get safely away from the inn. "Apologize to the ladies at once, you lowborn curs, or I shall carve the tripes from your living bodies and feed them to the pigs!"

The laughter was gone from the blacksmith's face now; he scowled deep in his dark beard, his shoulders swelling as he clenched his fists and stood. "Are you saying you don't think we can pay the price of your fancy women, boy?" he asked. The bench scraped back as the other men rose.

Georg drew his sword, the blade coming free of its sheath with a soft metallic ring. "No, Georg!" Margerite shrieked. Georg's eyes flicked towards her, and in that moment the blacksmith dodged in, grabbing the Knappe's wrist and bending it slowly back.

"Drop that thing now, boy," he hissed. Georg's face whitened beneath his freckles, but he drew his dagger with his free hand, turning quickly in and pressing it up beneath the older man's beard.

"Let go of me or die now," Georg panted. "Another move, and you die." The blond man had raised a mug to break over the youth's head; he lowered it slowly, for Georg would only have to twitch his hand to open the blacksmith's throat.

"Georg, you must not!" Margerite warned him desperately. Several of the inn's other patrons were already pressing in close; she looked frantically about for help.

"Hold, hold," said a deep, raspy voice. "What is all this? Ekkeward, that is no way to greet a stranger."

A burly man was pushing his way through the crowd. He, too, wore a sword, girded over a long robe of faded velvet that might once have been green, and Margerite noticed that people were making way for him. "Put those weapons away, boy. No one is going to harm you or your ladies - are they, Ekkeward?"

"I meant nothing by it," the blacksmith growled. Slowly Georg dropped his dagger-hand, and Ekkeward let go of his sword-arm.

Margerite let out a deep breath. "Thank you, sir. It was only a misunderstanding, but our brother is quick to spring to the defense of our honour, and hasty of temper."

"Yes, he has the red hair for it," their rescuer said, looking thoughtfully at Georg. "Now, gentlemen, I suggest you all sit down and drink up - drinks on me, for all of you!" His voice was strangely accented, with a lilt to it that Margerite could not recognise, and loud enough to carry across the general din. Margerite guessed him to be in his middle years; he was clean-shaven and dark-haired, but his sideburns were graying and laugh-lines were deeply graven into the corners of his blue eyes.

Muttering, the blacksmith and his two cronies melted away as soon as their mugs were full, but the newcomer sat down comfortably beside Eva. "Allow me to introduce myself, good ladies, young gentleman," he said. "I am Merlin the Magnificent, a traveller and purveyor of the finest holy items. Saints' relics, holy water blessed by the Pope himself, balm from Araby and other medicaments - whatever you need for curing the ills of your body or soul."

"Merlin - the wizard Merlin?" Eva asked, edging slightly away from him. He grinned at her, lifting triangular black brows.

"A Welshman, like the original, and all Welsh have a bit of wizard in them - you know what I mean? No risk to your soul, of course, fair lady, nor to mine either; how so, when I travel in holy items?"

"It was very kind of you to step in when you did," Margerite said. "Things could have gone far worse for us."

"So they could have. Your young man there seems good with his weapons, but there's more to staying alive than knowing how to swing a sword, if you know what I mean? It would have been a real shame to see blood spilt over a small misunderstanding."

"Insulting a lady's honour is hardly small," Georg said, but his voice was shaking now, and Margerite could see the beer slopping in the Knappe's mug when he lifted it to his mouth. She was sure that it had been Georg's first fight - and he bore himself bravely, as one of his blood should, though it is dangerous to be so quick to draw blade in a strange place.

Merlin waved one blunt-fingered hand. "That is so, lad. But it would have done you no good to get killed yourself, or hanged for a murderer, would it now? Tell me, how long have you been on the road, and where are you going?"

Margerite repeated the story she had given the innkeeper, and Merlin's long face brightened. "Ah, the very way I am going myself! And you will see plenty of holy shrines, for I pass by the best pilgrim routes. Would you care to ride in my wagon? I lost my own family in the Death, you see, and there is room for all of you; it'll be the finest."

"How much would that cost us?" Margerite asked warily.

"No need to worry about such things now. A bit of help with the wagon when I need it, a little assistance with my work, if you will, and then we'll see. To tell you the truth, it's the companionship I want, more than anything."

Though Margerite was hesitant to take up with a stranger thus, her aching back made the thought of riding comfortably in a wain, rather than carrying Wolfram and a heavy sack of money on foot, very attractive. And even if Merlin knows how to use his sword, if we are careful, he can hardly overpower all three of us at once; and it would be difficult for him to rob us along the way, with none but ourselves and him in the wagon.

For a moment she wondered if he could be a Light-Bearer sent to seek them out, though he wore only a plain gold wedding band. But somehow, she found herself quite certain that he was not; it was as though there were some invisible sign, one more trustworthy than the ring she had falsely worn - neither a smell, nor a feeling, but something a little akin to both - that might mark out Order members to her.

"It seems a good plan to me," said Eva brightly. "And I think we would be safer with Merlin than by ourselves."

Margerite could not argue with that, considering that they had not been in town a full day before coming within a hairsbreadth of real trouble. "What do you think, Georg?"

The boy looked consideringly at the well-worn hilt of Merlin's sword, and Margerite could guess what he was thinking. Though the peddler's belly was substantial, his shoulders were wider, and his knuckles bore the scars of many fights - and he had shown no hesitation in stepping in when blades were drawn. "It would be well to travel with another fighting man, to be sure of your safety," Georg admitted. "Although I can do my best to see that no harm comes to you, two are more than twice as strong as one in a fight."

As Margerite had suspected, there were fleas in the bedding, and it was hard to sleep with Eva's back pressed so closely against her own. The two men had taken the other mattress, Merlin's snore grating below Georg's softer breathing, and Margerite spared a moment of pity for the Knappe, who was hardly holding down a corner at the edge of the narrow bed. At least the innkeeper's wife had been able to find a small cradle for Wolfram; in the morning, Margerite thought that she would try to buy it, to give the babe a safe resting place in the wagon.

Breathing deeply, Margerite forced herself to ignore the prickling itch of the fleabites and the smells that told her without question that Merlin had eaten onions at dinnertime. It was harder to ignore Eva rolling over in her sleep, for the girl outweighed Margerite now and took up more than her share of the bed. But Margerite let her limbs go slack, let the sensations of her body dim and fade...what did it matter that Eva had rolled onto her arm, when her wings were spreading out, beating against the air to lift her away from the stuffy little chamber?...

The falcon sprang free into the cool night air, winging forth beneath the stars. High above the little dark huts of the village, above the unfamiliar mountains and moonlit-silver lakes and streams - her wings hammering at the air, speeding her northward. She did not pause to doubt, nor ask herself how she would find Father Etienne. Crawling on the ground, with only human eyes and thoughts, she might easily lose her way, but the falcon's gaze could see what she sought: the glimmer of light far to the north, bright as a bonfire against the darkness of a distant mountain.

The beacon seemed to fade as she drew closer, until it
was no more than the little brightness of candles through
the windows of a great castle - a brightness woven over with
webs of dark, that Margerite's gaze could not pierce through.
She hesitated, circling above. The castle was a true palace,
more than thrice the size of Burg Fürstensee, with fountains
gleaming white in the pleasure-gardens about it...and even
in the high air where she tilted her wings to turn in her slow
gyre, she could feel the blackness below, the taint that she
had come to recognise. Had Etienne come into a fortress of
the Light-Bearers?

But something else caught her gaze: the low glowing
of coals to the east, a house in one of the castle's broad
hunting parks - a gamekeeper's home, Margerite guessed,
two-storied and whitewashed. She spiralled down, settling
herself on the edge of one of the small upper windows, and
looked in.

To her surprise, it was not Etienne she saw, but Bertram,
lying on a bed with his black hair and beard tangled on the
pillow. He seemed deeply asleep, his breathing slow and
regular - had he, then, found refuge with a friend? The castle
must be Schloss Niedersee; but how had Bertram managed
to escape his pursuit, or convince the house's owner of his
innocence?

As Margerite wondered that, a slow chill crept over her.
Bertram stiffened in his sleep, crying out softly, and she
could see the look of pain on his face. His foes are still
seeking him, Margerite realized.

She dropped from the windowsill, circling clockwise about
the house, and it seemed to her that she could see a thread of
brightness spinning out behind her, to bind it safe with her
power. She ringed the gamekeeper's dwelling three times,
and felt the cold shadow sinking away, watched Bertram
ease into quiet dreams again. Though her falcon-beak could
not shape the words, she prayed silently, Mother Maria, let
no darkness come here. Please, I pray - keep Bertram safe
from his foes, and from the powers of Hell, as you love your
Son!

Margerite knew that she had only been brushed by the least part of their enemies' questing strength, else she would not have been able to turn it aside so easily; but at least her love would rest untroubled for the night, and hidden from the one who sought him.

But how does she know that he may be here? Margerite had no answer for that question. She could have lingered there, watching Bertram sleep, until dawn came to fling her back to herself; but she knew that, if Bertram's old foe was looking for him, he would need Father Etienne's aid as badly as any of them. Reluctantly, with a last glance back at Bertram where he lay quiet in bed, she rose again.

Etienne...Etienne! Where are you? Margerite thought, sweeping through the sky. But the brightness that had guided her before was gone: she gazed down at a pale crescent of beach edging the wide vast darkness of the sea, at flat salt marshes and little fisher-huts. Caught up in the wildness of her falcon-flight, she felt no despair, only the fury that what she sought had escaped her.

It was not until Margerite came to herself, the weight of her human limbs dragging at her soul and the sounds and stinks of the little guest-room beating harshly against her senses, that the full sense of fear and disappointment swept over her. She had trusted in her flight to find the priest, where-ever he had gone; but now, she realized, they would have to go all the way north to Hamburg, to gain audience with the Bishop there and ask after Father Etienne - and who knew where he might be now?

But Mother Maria has sent us someone who knows the road and can aid us, Margerite reminded herself firmly. If I begin to despair now, I shall never be able to carry through. Still, she lay awake long that night, her thoughts beating in her skull like the wings of a small bird frantically trying to lift free of the lime holding its feet fast.

They rose before sunrise the next day, for Merlin wished to start off at dawn. "There is little selling to be done in such a town until the harvest-work is finished. We will find better pickings along the road, for there are often bands of Italian pilgrims who come to visit German shrines in the summer, and their season is nearly over - and perhaps you would like time to look over my goods before other pilgrims get to them? Those beautiful pilgrim-phials for holy water I was telling you about last night, the ones that came all the way from Jerusalem..."

"I am more interested in finding plainer clothes for the road," Margerite cut him off bluntly. "We did not set off as well-prepared as we would have liked."

"I can take care of that for you, too," the Welshman promised blithely. "If you have a few pieces of silver, I know a woman here in the village who has six daughters and might be willing to sell a couple of dresses. Best you not come with me, for she will try to raise the price if she sees you - you know what I mean? And I should go now, before she leaves for the fields."

Reluctantly, Margerite counted out three coins from her belt-pouch, reminding herself that Merlin would hardly run away with the money and leave his wagon behind. He held to his word, though, coming back with four dresses hanging over his arm and a bag in his other hand. "Clothes for you, didn't I say so?" he announced proudly. "The dresses are a little worn, but a little bit of repair work, and they'll be the finest. And...guess what I have in this bag?"

"What have you?" Georg asked.

Merlin grinned slyly, holding up a finger. "Dinner. I have our dinner." He opened the bag slightly, showing them the limp body of a brown chicken. "A tender young capon whose neck was wrung this morning, just the thing."

It would have seemed ungrateful not to praise him, although Margerite could already see that the dresses were hardly worth a fraction of what she had given him to buy them with: coarse brown and gray wool, somewhat stained, and with one hem that she could see hanging loose in a tatter of threads. But better to look like honest peasants than prostitutes, and a show of poverty would likely make them safer on the road.

Margerite rode in the wagon with Merlin and the cats, while Eva and Georg walked beside his two ponies. The Welshman had stretched the truth somewhat when he said there was enough room for all of them, for the wagon was full of boxes and bags: Merlin clearly sold more things than relics. It was easy enough for Margerite to hide the box with her ritual tools in it; the other bags she kept close to her.

It had been a long time since Margerite had last plucked a chicken; she had forgotten how miserably the small feather-mites made her hands itch, even somehow getting up to crawl beneath her hair. Kobolt and Kriemhilt sat beside her, and every so often she had to slap away a dark paw clawing up at the chicken's dangling head. Still, the work went quickly enough, though Georg occasionally looked back at her in disbelief, as though he could not credit that a Gräfin should know how to do such a thing.

Even though Merlin had put the boy in one of his own tunics, its faded blue wool flapping about his arms and thighs beneath the leather jerkin, Georg still held himself very straight, and he had refused to be parted from his sword, though it now looked far too fine to match his clothes.

"Brother and sisters, are you?" Merlin asked, leaning forward to look at Georg and Eva, then meeting Margerite's eyes again. "You don't look much alike."

"Sometimes it is so in families," Margerite said uncomfortably. She realized what an unbelievable tale it was, that tall, buxom Eva, red-haired Georg, and herself had all come from the same womb; but she could hardly admit now that she was lying. She lowered her head, wrenching hard at the stubborn feathers along the edge of one wing.

"Ah," Merlin said. "How old is the lad there? There cannot be many years between the three of you."

"Georg is fifteen, and Eva...sixteen, and I am eighteen."

Merlin's sharp blue gaze returned to Georg, and Margerite thought uncomfortably of Ritter Gottfried's words to her about the training of young noblemen. Whatever the Welshman might believe of Eva and herself, it was far too obvious that Georg was of high birth and should be squired to a knight, not accompanying two women on...well, what must seem like a rather dubious journey.

"Perhaps," Merlin said thoughtfully, "it would be simpler to say that you are my wife, and these two cousins, if we are asked any questions down the road. I believe you, of course, but not everyone might - do you know what I mean?"

"Are we likely to be asked questions?"

"Ah, everyone knows me, and folk do like to talk. Once we get you to your shrines, you can say whatever you please, of course."

"I suppose so," Margerite agreed.

When they stopped to build a fire and cook the chicken in one of Merlin's pots, the relic salesman fetched a bag and a couple of sledgehammers from his wagon.

"What are those for?" asked Eva.

"Now," Merlin said, drawing the word out with the relish of a natural showman, "now I'm going to show you some of the other things Merlin does when he stops to sell his wares. And perhaps you can learn to do a few of them too, to keep idle eyes busy while I talk. This is hardly a trick fit for a lady, but perhaps Georg can manage it - eh, lad?"

Merlin balanced the two sledgehammers on their heads, grasping each by the end of their long handles. With a quick flick of his broad wrists, he swung them up, balancing the two of them at arm's length with the blunt heads poised high above his own. He looked up, staring with intense concentration as he tilted first one down until it just grazed his nose, then swung it slowly back to pass the other on its way down. Margerite realized that she was holding her breath; if either of the hammers slipped in Merlin's grasp, they could easily crush his face.

But he repeated the performance twice more, then laughed, swinging the heavy sledgehammers down to the ground again.

Georg frowned, but his eyes were bright. "I have seen that done before, at the fairs after harvest," he said. "It is..." Margerite shook her head warningly, before he could say anything about peasants' tricks. The Knappe was quickly losing his battle to hold his face stern, dignity warring with his boyish eagerness, until he suddenly burst out, "I am sure I could do it."

Margerite looked at Georg's forearms - tightly corded with muscle from years of training, to be sure, but still the slim arms of a youth, barely half the width of Merlin's heavy limbs. She could hardly credit it, but the Welshman chuckled.

"It is all in knowing how, you see. There is not really that much strength in it, once you have the trick of it. Georg, measure your arm from fingertips to armpit along the handle; now clutch it there, so that it is exactly an arm's length. You keep your arm locked out, see, and lower it with your wrist."

Georg made a couple of abortive swings, then suddenly had the hammer up in the air just as Merlin had held it. The thick iron head trembled a little, but the boy's arm was firm.

"Now let it down...carefully, now; have your other hand ready to catch it until you get the feeling for it."

Slowly the sledgehammer descended towards Georg's face. Once he nearly lost his nerve, his other hand coming up to protect himself, but he got control of the wobbly weight in time, lowering it to touch his nose as Merlin had done and tilting it back up again. "There, I did it!"

"I could do that too," Eva said, grabbing the other sledgehammer before Georg could take it away from her and swinging it up as Merlin had shown. Margerite watched, horrified, as Eva stared intently up at her lowering hammer, but she did not dare speak, for fear of breaking the girl's concentration. The sledgehammer touched Eva's nose, and she grinned triumphantly as she raised it again. "It is not so hard," she said proudly.

"It is not ladylike, either," Margerite chided her. "And you should not be doing such things."

"If I cannot wear fine clothes like a lady, why should I be worried about behaving like one?" Eva asked unrepentantly. "And who is here to see me?"

"Georg and Merlin and I," Margerite replied. "And it should not matter to you whether you are wearing rough homespun or fine silk; you still ought to behave more demurely."

"Ah, let the girl have her fun," Merlin said. "It would be a fine draw to see her doing tricks of strength before the wagon, wouldn't it now? Even the lighter ones are too much for most women, but she has a good pair of arms on her..."

"No!" Margerite told him firmly.

The Welshman's long face looked crestfallen, but he recovered fast. "Ah, well, I have a few costumes I can put our Eva in, and she is pretty enough to draw a crowd all by herself. Maybe Georg would like to try his hand at a little juggling, or the fine manly art of knife-throwing?"

Despite her best efforts, Margerite found that neither Eva nor Georg would be stopped from learning Merlin's tricks, struggling to outdo each other like siblings born. They are only fifteen, Margerite reminded herself as Eva giggled when Georg's knife bounced hilt-first from the target and skittered away into the grass, and Christ knows that Eva got little enough of play in that accursed convent her cousin sent her to. If it eases her mind, after all she has seen, to pretend at being part of a troop of peddlers and jongleurs for now... what harm can it do, after all? No one will ever recognise us in these rags.

As he drove the wagon on, Merlin kept talking: he had been everywhere across the length and breadth of Europe, it seemed, and done everything in the world. He followed the pilgrim-paths, going south to Rome in the winter and north to France or Germany in the summer.

"And you have no fear of outlaws, travelling alone with a laden wagon like this?" Georg asked.

Merlin grinned slyly. "Now, what would outlaws want with a load of holy relics? Merlin the wizard knows how to talk his way out of trouble, you may be sure - and I am not too bad at fighting, when there's need for it." He raised a stubby forefinger. "But only when there's need, mind you. Best you learn to talk quickly yourself, for otherwise that red-haired temper will get you into a situation there's no getting out of someday. Still, it's good to be able to use a sword or a knife if you have to - and that's something you two ladies should learn, if you're to be long on the road."

"Can you show me?" Eva asked eagerly. "I was not doing so badly with the throwing knives."

"Ah, but you can't trust a throwing knife to save your life in a pinch, not until you've had more years working with them than you are old now. Just a few things to keep in mind... Georg, get up here and take the reins, will you?"

The peddler heaved himself over the edge of the wagon and drew his belt dagger, holding it in a loose underhanded grip and talking as they walked.

"Stabbing overhand will never do you any good: it's awkward, you see, and anyone could grab your arm and take the knife away from you. Now, a woman's not likely to ever get into a real knife-fight, not unless she keeps company worse than what you're used to. But if a man's trying to hurt you, and you get a chance, draw your knife and stab hard. Never go for the heart: there's too many bones in the chest, and you're more likely to stick your point into a rib than into heart or lungs. Knife-fighters will slash at the arms, to make them bleed, you see, but if you're that far away, you're likely better off running for it. No: go for the throat, if you can, or the belly, because they're soft parts, you see, and a good stick in either place will do for a man. Stab it in and pull hard - you've seen pigs being slaughtered? Well, there's no difference between a pig and a man who's trying to hurt you. Slice deep and far enough, and you're sure to cut something vital."

Merlin reversed the knife with a swift flick of his fingers, handing it hilt-first to Eva. Tentatively Eva curled her fingers around it, and Merlin laughed, taking her hand in his to correct her grip, then guiding her arm through a few thrusting and cutting motions. He was standing far too close to her, Margerite thought, but the only thing she could say was, "Eva, it is not seemly for you to be learning such things! Give Merlin's knife back; perhaps you should come and sit up here with me."

"But what if someone attacks me?" Eva protested. "Should I not know how to protect myself?"

Georg looked down at her from his high driver's seat - Margerite could see he had not the least idea of how to manage the ponies, but they plodded along as if they knew the way, following the road. "You should not need to. Am I not with you?"

Eva tossed her long golden hair back with both hands.

"You will not be with me every moment, unless you plan on walking to the privy with me at night."

Georg flushed, his blush showing deep red through his pale freckled skin.

"Eva!" Margerite said sharply. "Remember yourself."

Eva shrugged, her rounded bosom heaving slightly, and Merlin quickly broke in. "Truly, Margerite, there are many dangers on the road, and a girl of Eva's...years, is likely to draw them. It would do you no harm to learn a little skill with a knife, either." The Welshman's face was very serious, the lilting tone of jest gone from his voice. "Even my own dear wife Branwen..."

He swallowed hard, continued thickly; but in that moment, it seemed to Margerite that she could see the shadow of sorrow sunk deep into his blue eyes, and hear the ache of long loneliness in his words. "Christ rest her soul, even she always had a blade at hand, though her tongue was sharp enough to flay flesh from bone by itself. Branwen was a proper lady, from a noble family and all, but she learned quickly enough how to handle a man that made too free with her. I taught her how to use a dagger..."

Merlin's voice trailed off; Margerite saw that he seemed to be looking past her, as though he were staring back at the dusty road behind them - as if he were watching for someone walking by the wagon, someone who would never be there again.

"I taught my son Daffyd, too, as soon as his hands were big enough to hold a knife," Merlin added softly. "No harm at all, in Eva and you learning how to protect yourselves a bit. Besides, it's a long way from shrine to shrine, and one needs to have something to do. Branwen and Daffyd and I, we used to rehearse the mystery plays, those we could do with only the three of us. Ah, we could show you Noah's Ark, and the Christ-Child in the manger, and most of the great wonders of the Bible, and that in Welsh, French, English, Italian, or German - my Devil always had half the audience laughing, and half pissing their boots, when they weren't doing both at once."

He fell silent, looking speculatively at his three companions. "Now, you're all bright and well-spoken, and I still have all the costumes and props from the plays, and we even have a real babe for the Christ-Child! Georg's close enough in size to my Daffyd, and we could take Branwen's costumes in a bit for you, Margerite, or let them out for Eva. Wouldn't that be the finest, now, if you could learn a few of the plays with me?"

"I saw a mystery play in my father's...at home, once," Georg said hopefully. "It was a very fine sight."

"I do not think such things would be suited for us," Margerite replied, though she was careful not to speak too sharply. Merlin's feelings would be hurt enough by her refusal, she thought; no need to press coals on an open wound.

But the Welshman only shrugged his heavy shoulders, elaborately casual. "Ah, well, it would be as good a way to pass the time on the road as any. Still, you know yourself what you want to do." He climbed back into the wagon, taking the reins from Georg, and began to talk of his youthful days as a sailor; still, Margerite could see the slump of his back, as though an old injury yet pained him.

But we cannot take your family's place forever, she thought, and better, perhaps, that you not grow too used to having us with you, since we will leave you in a while. Travelling with Merlin, the way north was far easier than Margerite had expected.

The Welshman seemed to have told something close to the truth when he said that everyone knew him: children came out to follow his wagon in the villages, and crowds gathered quickly when he stopped and began to juggle or whirl his sledgehammers, talking all the while in that lilting accent that almost tempted Margerite to look among his wares again.

Only once did Margerite truly worry about him, and that was when, after taking the reins of the wagon, she glanced back to see him crouched over the box of her ritual tools with a chisel in his hand.

"What are you doing?" she asked quietly.

"The hinges on your box were coming loose with all the jolting, so I was fixing them for you," Merlin answered at once. The expression on his face was pained, as though Margerite had unjustly accused him of wrongdoing.

"Leave it be," she told him, and, without arguing, he put the box back down and came to sit beside her. That night, however, when everyone else was asleep, Margerite picked it up and crept out of the wagon. There was enough moonlight to show her that Merlin had nearly pried one of the hinges off entirely, and she did not have the least idea of how to put it back.

If I could make a spell to hide it...she thought, and then, Why not? She was far from her sanctum; she did not even dare to put on her robe, lest Merlin should stagger out from beneath the shelter of the wagon to piss in the middle of the night, as he often did. But a simple deception, so that any eye but hers would be turned away - that was not too far from the spell of invisibility Nikolaus had taught her, and should work the better on a small chest than on a full-sized and moving human being.

When Margerite was done, she fumbled among the bags and chests until her hand touched the two hard lumpy sacks of silver and jewelry. She had not counted the silver as she bundled the smaller bags into the larger, but she knew their weight all too well from their days of walking through the forest. She heaved first one, then the second, up, the jingling of coins and jewels muffled by the cloth that wrapped them. They were no lighter than she remembered, and when she felt for the complex knot that tied their mouths tightly shut, the turns of cord did not seem to have been disturbed.

So it was, after all, Margerite thought with some relief,
mere curiosity that had impelled the Welshman to pry into
her chest: he might be willing to tell her that a silver pfennig
was a good price for an old hen and pocket the change, but
true robbery was beyond him. She put the bags back as they
had been, half-hidden between the larger wooden boxes that
held the costumes Merlin and his family had worn for their
plays. There would be plenty of room in this wagon if he got
rid of those: surely he knows that he will never use them
again? Margerite thought.

But it was very like the Welshman to cling to the relics of
his dead wife and son, still hoping, perhaps, that someday
there would be another woman and another boy travelling
in his wain, who would let him teach them his skills, and
help him in his work - even if that work were more than
half deception, dazzling the ears and eyes of, for the most
part, folk who had never gone a day's journey from their
own village with exotic tales of Avignon and Rome and
Jerusalem.

By the time they came to the first of the larger shrines, a
monastery built by a stream flowing down a low green hill,
Merlin was insisting that Eva and Georg should help him
in displaying his wares, and Margerite could hardly turn
him down. There were a number of horses tied outside the
monastery, and the Welshman grinned, looking them over
with an expert eye.

"That looks like a group of pilgrims, right enough," he said.
"Maybe you'd like to go in to pray, Margerite; the monks
here have a fingerbone of St. Walburga in a fine crystal
casket, and that's well worth seeing."

Though there was nothing wrong with Wolfram - not
so much as a sniffle or a stain of the wrong colour on his
linens - Margerite carried him with her in hopes of the
saint's blessing, for he had been born on St. Walburga's
Day. The monastery grounds were quiet, but outside the
chapel stood a band of well-dressed people in bright colours.
Most of them were swarthier than Margerite was used to
seeing, though the little priest who stood in front, talking in
a language Margerite did not know and waving his arms a
great deal, was blond.

Margerite remembered that Merlin had mentioned Italian pilgrims, and the clothing this group wore certainly reminded her of Damiano's stylish garb. Beside the pilgrim band, a monk waited patiently with beeswax candles: it occurred briefly, if impiously, to Margerite that the pilgrim roads might offer a livelihood to others than Merlin.

To atone for that thought, she bought two candles and gave the monk a piece of silver as well before she slipped past the pilgrim group and into the chapel. Its whitewashed walls were cool and quiet; in a niche to the side blazed several beeswax candles, lighting up the figure of a crowned and sceptered woman who held a phial of oil, and by whose feet were sculpted three ears of grain.

A little casket of silver and crystal rested on a shelf by the saint's image, and, standing on her tiptoes and peering closely, Margerite could just see the white glimmer of bone beneath the fist-sized dome of rock crystal. And while the bones of the saints are still here on Earth, it shall not fall to Satan's power, until God destroys and remakes our world in the Last Days.

Lighting her candles, Margerite knelt to pray, holding Wolfram tightly to her breast. She did not know what she expected - the light of holiness flowing from the saint's bone, perhaps? She saw nothing like that; yet the stillness fell around her like thickening layers of snow as she murmured, "Holy Walburga, pray for us. Help me on my way, and as you watched over Wolfram's day of birth, let him have your blessing, to aid him against all those who would harm or delude him. Give aid to Heinrich in his sickness, peace to Christoph in his torment - and ask forgiveness for Nikolaus in his sins. And, please, ask the Virgin to protect Bertram, and aid me in finding Father Etienne, for I am afraid that I will never find him by myself."

Margerite was about to go on, but she heard the footsteps and soft voices behind her, the Italians whispering excitedly to each other. She crossed herself and finished quickly, "In Christ's Name, Amen."

But she did not want to leave the chapel straight away: instead she went to kneel before the altar, where the carven wooden faces of Christ and the Virgin looked down upon her, and there, ignoring the quiet babble of the Italians, she prayed over Wolfram for a long time, hoping to atone for her deceptions of the road, and to strengthen the blessings that Father Etienne had given her son at his baptism, that he might remain safe from whatever the Order of Light-Bearers might try when they found out that Nikolaus had lost both mother and child.

Wolfram only cried a little when Margerite sprinkled holy water on him from the font by the chapel door, and Margerite took that as a good sign. By the time Margerite came out of the monastery, Merlin was going full-strength, the long sleeves of his faded velvet robe blowing in the wind as he gestured and his powerful voice booming out over the pilgrims who crowded around the cloths he had laid out on the grass before his wagon.

Eva, much to Margerite's annoyance, had put on a black dress that almost looked like a nun's habit, but was a little tighter about the generous curves of her breasts and hips than it should have been, and she was smiling as she guided one young man's hand over Merlin's collection of phials and holy medals.

Georg stood beside her: at least his right hand was nowhere near the hilt of his sword, but he was scowling like a youth who thought Eva's customer was taking far too many liberties with her - or like one who would rather not see another man staring at his sweetheart's bosom, Margerite thought ominously.

It only made matters worse that the Italian was very handsome, with curly dark hair and flashing black eyes set off to great advantage by the scarlet doublet that clung tightly to his wide shoulders and narrow hips, the slashes of his long-dagged sleeves showing bright flashes of yellow silk.

Merlin was speaking Italian, though even to Margerite's ears it sounded rather fractured; Eva seemed to be making her sale chiefly by giggling and holding up fingers, and occasionally by catching Kriemhilt and tossing the tortoiseshell cat off the trinket-laden fabric in a way that showed off her figure to great advantage.

Margerite waited until the wagon was on the road again to look down from her seat and say sternly to Eva, "What did you think you were doing there? You should put on something more decent at once; I would not be surprised if that young man thought you were selling something more than relics, and from the way you were looking at him, I should not blame him."

"Now, now," Merlin interjected. "Eva has a real talent for this. Why, she sold three of my Jerusalem phials, and even a box of dust from St. Peter's tomb, as well as two bottles of my special chest salve."

Eva grinned unrepentantly up at Margerite. Their week of travelling with Merlin had done little to dim her beauty: her hair had paled even further, shimmering like straw-pale wine in the sunlight, and instead of tanning like a peasant girl's, the delicate curves of her cheeks had only become pinker with sun and wind, as though she had immodestly reddened them with paint. "And I cannot even speak their language," she said proudly. "I think I did rather well."

"I think you made yourself understood all too clearly, and you shall not do it again," Margerite told her. Even had it not been so immodest for a girl of Eva's station to act like a common peddler, let alone staring at an overdressed Italian's dark curls and well-turned calves, Margerite had her doubts about the authenticity of Merlin's relics: how would he have gotten dust from St. Peter's tomb, for instance?

"Those Italians are great ones for getting tokens of their pilgrimages," said Merlin in a satisfied way. "There was one woman in that band who had holy water from twelve different shrines, and was eager to collect more. It is a fine thing to be able to make one's bread by giving people what their souls need."

"Still, it is not right for Eva to do it," Georg spoke up suddenly.

Eva turned on him, her small mouth pursed in anger. "What would you know? You are too shy and proud to talk to anyone, and I saw the way you were glaring at that poor man who only wanted to know the price of a Jerusalem phial."

"You are a fool if you think those little bottles are what he was staring at," Georg snapped back. "And I know what is fitting and what is not."

Merlin laughed, waving the horse's reins. "Hush, younglings. Puppies may snap at each other, but when a couple your age talk like that, it usually means it is time to find a priest to marry them."

Georg blushed violently red; Eva sniffed and looked away with great dignity, as if the Knappe were a creature far too lowly for her to acknowledge. And Merlin's words made it certain that he had not even begun to believe that there was any kinship between them...

But they are of an age, Margerite thought, and if all does not go well with Christoph - Georg may be a third son, but that is hardly a hindrance, if Eva can gain her inheritance safely. She could not help painfully thinking back to the sight of Christoph's brown head bent close to Eva's golden one over the chessboard.

The way he had risen at once, with his hand on his sword, at the suggestion that Graf Günther might have done her any harm; the pride in his voice as he presented her to his father's noble guests...

And while Christoph lives, he is not beyond hope, if Eva can bear to let him touch her again. Margerite knew that, for herself, the memory of Christoph's boyish face twisted as he spat out the demon's foul words would forever mar him in her mind, just as Ruprecht...

She forced herself to remember, for she knew that pushing the thought away would leave a gateway of fear for the same Power to use against her: the Black Book warned most strictly against trying to look aside from what was painful. Mother Maria grant that you are free of that taint, Wolfram, even if I am not yet, Margerite thought, holding her child so tightly that he began to struggle and cry.

Despite Eva's complaints, Margerite insisted that she stay sitting quietly in the wagon the next time Merlin set out his wares, whether in town or at a shrine. They stopped for the afternoon in a large village within, Merlin said, a day's easy journeying of Fulda, and Eva sat in the wagon with Margerite to keep a watch on her. Eva took it with good grace, only sighing heavily now and then as she looked sideways at Margerite.

The peddler was in good voice and good cheer, touting his wares to the assembled crowd. Wolfram, however, seemed more fretful than usual, squalling and complaining, and nothing Margerite could do would soothe him.

Distracted by her child, Margerite did not notice the villagers drawing back until she heard the scuffling and muffled shouts. Looking up, to her horror, she saw Merlin and Georg struggling with four big men wearing leather armour with iron breastplates, and two more guardsmen with long spears standing by the wagon and looking threateningly up at the women.

"Are there any more of you in there?" one said roughly.

"Myself, my child, and my companion Eva," Margerite answered. "What do you wish?"

"You are arrested by order of Ritter Hermann von Landsburg," the other said. "Get down and come quietly."

"Arrested? What for?" Eva asked indignantly.

"You are the family of Merlin the Peddler?"

Margerite nodded, a terrible sinking feeling in her gut.
She should have known better than to take up with a foreign
seller of dubious relics, however easy it made the journey,
she told herself. Yet - how could Merlin have offended this
Ritter Hermann? What could he have done to draw the
attention of a knight?

Margerite slowly got out of the wagon. Eva handed
Wolfram to her, then waited for one of the men-at-arms
to assist her. The men marched them to where Merlin and
Georg stood, disarmed and with their hands tied behind
them. The side of Georg's face was already puffing out redly,
and a few drops of blood trickled from his swelling lip; they
had taken his cap and jerkin, as well as his sword. Merlin
only looked tired and sad, the lines deep about his mouth
and eyes, and his broad shoulders were slumped.

"Tie the women's hands, get their knives off them, and
take them up to the castle," the man who was watching
Georg and Merlin said, stroking the huge brown-gold beard
that spread glossy across his chest like a swathe of bearskin.
"I'll drive the wagon up behind you."

"As you wish, Helmut," one of Margerite's guards
answered. "What about the baby?"

"Ah...give it here, and we'll see what the Ritter wants done
with it."

The guard took Wolfram from Margerite's arms, passing
him over to his commander. At once the baby, frightened
by the strange men's voices and the sight of their rough
bearded faces, began to scream, but the man-at-arms
ignored the sounds with the ease of someone who was well-
used to the noise of small children.

Ritter Hermann's castle was a small square fortress between two hills that swept up like a great pair of green wings. It was no bigger than Margerite's first home, Burg Hirschenberg, and like Burg Hirschenberg, the stone fort was surrounded by smaller wooden buildings, stables and servants' quarters and such.

The four prisoners were taken to an empty stable and shoved roughly in, stumbling on the hard-packed earthen floor. At least the stable was clean, though the strong smell of horses hung about it, and there were several small window-slits near the ceiling, shafts of evening sunlight slanting through to brighten the dust-motes swirling in the air.

"What is happening here?" Margerite demanded as soon as they were alone. "Why have we been arrested?"

Merlin looked to the side and down, then over to meet her eyes. "I do not know. Last year I drove some sheep to the monastery for Ritter Hermann last year, and the monks were supposed to send him money - perhaps he never got it?"

"Did the monks get their sheep?" Margerite enquired sharply.

The Welshman's broad shoulders shrugged, his gray-stubbled cheeks paling slightly as the rope bit into his wrists. "I left the sheep in their field as I was supposed to," he said. "I do not know what they did after that, though after so many years on the pilgrim-trails, I have seen that some monks are no more pious or truthful than other men."

Margerite felt the anger building within her, like a fire slowly catching and building its heat up inside a stove. It was hard for her to bring herself to call her benefactor an outright liar, but she was close to reaching that point. Still, she had the silver that she had tucked into in her belt-pouch, and even without the silver and jewelry in her bag in the wagon - Christ willing, the guards would not plunder it at once! - that was more than enough to pay for a few sheep. She did not know what recompense Merlin could make to her, but she would deal with that after they were free.

A heavy tread sounded outside the stable door, and a sharp voice said, "So they are in here?"

"Remember that you are my wife," Merlin whispered urgently, his breath hot and urgent in Margerite's ear. "It would go ill if he caught our story out now."

Margerite thought for a moment of how matters would look otherwise, and quickly decided that she would follow Merlin's lead in that, lest she and Eva risk being fined or even mutilated as prostitutes.

The stable door opened. The man who entered - clearly Ritter Hermann, by the good sword at his side and the chain-mail shirt under his saffron-gold linen doublet - was very tall, having to bend his neck to enter the stable. His head was bare, straw-yellow hair braided back tightly; his neat beard and moustache were very nearly as red as Georg's.

The Ritter's nose had been broken several times, spread wide and lumpy across his face, and his pale gray-blue eyes stared coldly down from beneath thick yellow eyebrows that nearly met in the middle.

"Well, Merlin," he said. "I thought you would know better than to come back to the scene of your crime."

"I do not know what happened, Herr Ritter," Merlin said, his lilting accent rasping with all the force of conviction. "It is a great shame if those holy men at Fulda did not pay you for the sheep you sent them, but that hardly has anything to do with me."

"Particularly since you went on to hawk your wares at the shrine a week later, and told its tenders nothing of sheep?" Ritter Hermann said, his voice sharp and unpleasant as over-hopped beer. "As it happened, you were robbing the monastery itself, since I had promised the beasts in fulfillment of a vow. The good brothers were most distressed when I came to visit them, and I was not pleased to arrive there expecting gratitude for my service to God and instead receiving their reproaches for my tardiness."

"Herr Ritter," Margerite broke in, "Merlin is very sorry for the wrong he has done you, and he would like to make recompense for it. If, by your kindness, you will untie my hands, give our belongings back, and name a fair price for your troubles and the loss of your animals, we shall be willing to pay it, and I will see that he troubles you no more."

The knight looked down his battered nose at her. "I understand that you are Merlin's wife. And no doubt you can tell me how he suddenly has enough money to pay for sheep and a nobleman's embarassment this year, when last year he was begging and stealing along the way?"

"Some years are better than others," Merlin said boldly. "And Margerite did not come to me as a poor woman."

Ritter Hermann barked a short laugh. "So you inveigled an heiress to run off with you? And I suppose these other two are the Margräfin of Meissen and the Kaiser's son Wenzel."

"They are my cousins," Margerite told him hastily. "Please, Herr Ritter, allow us to repay you and leave this matter be."

The knight stared at her for a long time, then shook his head. "I do not know why you are so eager to flee, unless it be that there are other stolen goods in your wagon. If that is so, you may as well make your peace with God, for I do not intend to allow thieves and despoilers of monks to run free. Perhaps the good brothers at Fulda will be more forgiving than I, and say a Mass for your souls."

Ritter Hermann stalked out, slamming the door behind him, and Margerite heard the heavy sound of a wooden bolt sliding shut on the other side. "Herr Ritter!" Margerite shouted. "At least, if you will keep us imprisoned, allow us what we need for decency - and give my child back, that I may feed him."

There was no reply, but shortly afterwards Margerite heard Wolfram's wailing growing nearer outside. The bolt slid aside and the door opened again, and the guards who had arrested them came in, one deftly untying their bonds while another set an earthen pot in the corner. When Margerite's hands were free, she was given Wolfram, who clung to his mother anxiously and stared bright-eyed up into her face as if he had thought never to see her again.

When Ritter Hermann returned, flanked by his men-at-arms, Margerite's heart dropped within her, for in one hand, he held the two bags of silver and jewelry that she had brought from Burg Fürstensee, and in the other, he had Eva's dress of rose brocade. "Now all is clear to me," he said grimly. "What became of the nobles to whom these belonged?"

"That is my own dress!" Eva said indignantly. "And there is nothing in those bags that does not belong to either Margerite or myself."

The knight's mouth curled up into a sarcastic grin. He reached in, bringing out Margerite's gold cloak-clasp. "I suppose you think I believe that women who could own such things would be travelling with a thievish peddler and dressed in clothes that a peasant girl would be ashamed to wear to the fields? You have more silver here than my own lands bring in the course of a year, and my lady wife has no clothes of such fine stuff; how could you have gotten them on the road, save by theft and murder? Now I shall pronounce your sentence: you shall all be hanged, though for the babe's innocence I shall send him to be raised by the monks at Fulda. Tomorrow is Friday; in memory of our Lord Jesus Christ, it would not be fitting to execute you between Friday and Sunday, so I shall allow you to live until Monday, that you may go to God with your sins absolved, and your sentence shall be carried out Monday morning." Ritter Hermann ducked out beneath the door and closed it behind him. Margerite heard the shuffling of feet, then the rustle of a man sitting heavily on a bale of hay.

"Well, there are worse things than guard-duty, Helmut," a muffled voice said. "Come, have you your dice with you?"

"Frowe Margerite?" Georg asked, his voice shaking. "What are we going to do?"

"I do not know," Margerite said.

Georg drew himself up to his full height, his strong jaw jutting out; in spite of the way the side of his face was swelling, he looked very firm of purpose. "If my father knew where we were, he would send help, and this proud Ritter would regret having laid hands on us so."

"But I see little help for us there," Margerite told him gently. "I do not think that Ritter Hermann will believe a word we say to him, nor will he delay his sentence to let us send a message. Even if you had your seal-ring on your finger, he would think only that you had gotten it by evil means."

"If Christoph could only aid us..." Eva murmured. Her face crumpled, and Margerite knew what she was thinking. She moved over to stand by the girl, shifting Wolfram to one arm and patting Eva's firm shoulder with her free hand.

"I know," Margerite whispered to her. "I know."

Merlin was looking about the stable carefully, feeling at the planks of its walls thoughtfully. "If I only had something to use as a prybar, I could free us easily enough. Even a small chisel..."

"If you think you can get us out without being overheard by the guards outside there, you are more than welcome to try," Margerite said. "Christ help us all, Merlin, why did you come back here, where you have such a foe? Did you not think that he would seek revenge on you for his sheep?"

"I left them in the monks' field," Merlin insisted stubbornly. "How could I guess that the brothers would take so little care of their own animals, or would tell Hermann that the sheep had never arrived? But you were not truthful with me either. You did not tell me you were carrying so much money with you, or else we should have been able to travel in fine style, and might have avoided this altogether. I hope there were no more treasures in that locked box with the broken hinge."

Margerite stifled a gasp, thinking of what was inside the box: not only her ritual tools, which looked damning enough - but the Black Book, which would betray her as a sorceress. Though she had hidden it well enough to make Merlin's eyes glance over it like a stone skipping across a pool, she was not at all sure that the spell would turn aside the eyes of men who meant to empty and search the wagon as thoroughly as they could. And if it were found and opened, she was sure that Ritter Hermann would be quick enough to forego his vengeance in favour of turning them over to the Church, who could do far worse to them than a hedge-knight in his small fortress could manage.

"What is it, Frowe Margerite?" Georg asked, his bright brows furrowing in worry as he looked at her. "Is something amiss?"

Margerite could not keep herself from laughing at the Knappe: here they were, locked in a stable, condemned to die within four days, and he could still ask such a question. "There is hardly need to seek more trouble than we have," she said. "Pray that no worse comes to us; that is the best you can do now."

Obediently Georg sank to his knees, clasping his hands and bowing his head. His thin red braid lay neatly down the delicate nape of his neck; he looked frighteningly young and vulnerable, and Margerite felt the tears rising to her eyes. Wolfram would grow into such a lad someday - at least, even if she and Eva and Georg and Merlin all died here, her son would be safe with the holy brothers at Fulda.

For a moment, a black shape blocked the sunlight slanting through one of the little windows; then Kobolt leapt down with a soft thud, running to Margerite and rubbing his head against her ankles. Margerite's heart lifted at his touch, though she did not know what he could do to aid them. Wild stories came to her mind, tales of kobolts tunnelling beneath the earth and passing like shadows through stone; but those were only things told by old peasant-women by the hearth in the night. Still, Kobolt was more than a cat, and Margerite felt her strength returning as he rubbed against her.

Her true helplessness did not come to Margerite until she found that she had to ask the others to turn their backs while she lifted her skirt to use the pot the guards had given them. Then she felt the tears coming to her eyes: somewhere within, she thought, she had believed that she - she, the Gräfin von Fürstensee, mother of the Graf von Falkenstein! - could not really be treated so. But there was no denying the painful pressure of her bladder, nor the realization that if she did not use the half-full pot into which the men had already voided, she would have to empty herself on the floor. Kobolt's enthusiastic sniffings did not help either, for she had to slap the tomcat away one-handed while she held up her skirt with the other.

Mother Maria, help us, for we are falsely accused and sentenced, Margerite prayed. And if you will send us no escape, let me endure bravely, for the sake of Eva and Georg.

When Wolfram began crying because he had soiled himself, however, Margerite banged on the door until one of the guards said roughly, "What is it? Can you not quiet your brat?"

"He needs clean clothing - at least, I pray you, a few rags, for the sake of the Virgin and the Christ-Child! Otherwise he will not stop crying, and may become sick."

"That is true enough, Odo," said the other guard. Margerite sighed with relief; she had thought that this man, Helmut, had experience with children. "Go shout for one of the scullery maids or something. Gerda has a babe of her own, and can tell you what is needed."

"These are prisoners, not honoured guests," Odo grumbled. "Why should I fetch them anything?"

"Did you not hear the Ritter say that he means to give the child to the brothers at Fulda? Think of it as a monk already, and helping as an act of holy charity - or just do it because I told you to."

At sunset, their guards opened the door again, passing in a bowl of stew and a pitcher of water. The prisoners had to eat and drink in turn, slurping down the stew like the rudest churls, with nothing save their sleeves to wipe the grease from their mouths before they sipped from the pitcher.

Still, Margerite supposed, they should be grateful that they were being fed at all, and that Ritter Hermann was too pious to kill them between Friday and Sunday. But they were given no blankets, only the heap of rags that had been tossed in for Wolfram's sake, and the earthen floor was very cold, so that Margerite had to curl up with Eva at her back and Wolfram clutched to her breast for the sake of a little warmth.

Margerite dozed restlessly, for she could not find a comfortable position on the hard floor. She did not know how late it was when she felt Kobolt's soft warm head pushing urgently against her cheek, and then the prodding of something thin and hard at her neck. Putting her hand up to shove the cat away, Margerite's fingers closed on a metal-ringed rod that sent a familiar tingle down her arm.

She sat bolt upright at once. Kobolt had brought her wand - how had he gotten it? But with it, if Christ were kind to her, she might have more of a chance of getting some message through to Father Etienne, though she was not sure how to do such a thing. The Order conjured spirits or demons as their couriers, and, even if Margerite had been in her own circle, she would not have done that. Yet Kobolt was purring and nuzzling her urgently, as though he were trying to tell her something.

"Kriemhilt, let me sleep," Eva muttered, turning over beside Margerite. In the faint starlight through the windows, Margerite could just see the girl putting her arms over her face, and the dark shape of the smaller cat nosing at her.

She tried to calm her breath, sitting very still so that she would not disturb Eva. No circle, no cup or dagger or pentacle, and no spirits to call, Margerite thought. But if I cannot reach Etienne, we shall be hanged like peasants, and there will be no one to save Christoph from his brother.

Slowly, each rustle of her woolen skirt prickling painfully against her ears, Margerite crept over to the water pitcher. She had read that it was possible to scry through water; if she could gaze down into it...But there was nothing left in the pitcher; the last drops had sunken into the clay, so that there was not so much as a spoonful in the bottom.

"Margerite?" Eva's low voice whispered. "What are you doing?"

"Looking for water," Margerite whispered back.

Eva sat up, her shape barely visible in the darkness. Margerite heard Kriemhilt's soft chirp, and the sound of Eva's quiet yelp a second later. "Ouch! Cat, those are claws, and that is my neck. Margerite, are you thirsty or...do you want it for something else?"

Margerite stiffened, staring into the darkness at the figure of her companion. What does she know? Margerite thought. She moved her right hand slowly, trying to hide her wand in her skirts and hoping that Eva had not seen it in the dark.

"Margerite, your maidservant said that she had seen you cow the demon in Christoph with the power of your prayers, and I know you are not a saint," Eva whispered. "I learned enough in the Abbey to guess what is in that locked box you would not leave behind, even though you were in too much haste to pack clothes or food - and sometimes, out of the corner of my eye, I have seen Kriemhilt do other things than lead the way through a maze of strange caves in the darkness. In short, Margerite, I am neither blind nor stupid, and after serving with that witch who called herself an Abbess, I think I can tell when I am travelling with a magician. I recognised the Order ring on your finger as well, though I saw that it was gone before we left Burg Fürstensee, and I know that if you had truly been one of them, Father Etienne would never have spent so much time closeted with you."

Margerite's mouth opened in shock. Though she had known Eva was not stupid, the girl's persistent light-mindedness had deluded her into believing that Eva noticed nothing of what she was doing. But she learned to play the part of a terrified, half-witless child before Ruprecht... less than a month later, she was tossing her hair and laughing like any thoughtless young woman of high birth and batting her eyes at Christoph; and now on the road with Merlin, she could convince anyone that she was born to flirt with customers and sell dubious relics.

Why, then, should I have believed that she was thinking nothing more than what she showed me? But, of course, Eva had learned her skills in a convent, and must have seen all the ways in which women could mislead each other, even as she had learned quickly to distract men with her looks as soon as she blossomed into womanhood. I must keep a closer eye on her - though if I fail to trust her now, I may as well resign myself to being hanged.

"Have you said anything to anyone?" Margerite asked quietly.

"Georg would not recognise that the wand in your hand is magical if you beat him about the head and shoulders with it," Eva murmured scornfully. "And if you did not tell Merlin what funds you were carrying, why should I have told him something more precious and dangerous?"

Margerite sat still; it was Eva who spoke again. "If you need water to aid our escape, I have some here. And I think you do, for Kriemhilt has been pawing at it all night." Margerite heard the soft sound of Eva's fingers fumbling with something; then the girl reached forward, pressing it into her hand. For all the danger they were in, and the risk of waking the menfolk, Margerite almost laughed when she realized what she held: a heavy small pilgrim flask of lead, stoppered with wax and deeply embossed - undoubtedly with the seals that marked Merlin's Jerusalem phials.

"I bought it on our first day with Merlin," Eva admitted. "He overcharged me horribly for it, but I could not bring myself to say anything when I found out what they should go for, since he had been so kind to us. And I think he regretted it afterwards, for he gave me a little pewter crucifix for nothing when I had done so well selling his wares at the Walburga shrine. But there is holy water in the phial, and..." Eva swallowed, her soft breaths coming quicker.

"In the Abbey, and with Ruprecht, I was taught to gaze into different things to gain information, or sometimes to send messages between Order members, for, I was told, a virgin is often needed for such work. Margerite - I am still a virgin, and for the sake of saving our lives, I would be willing..." Eva gulped again, as if swallowing back tears.

Margerite drew a deep breath, letting it out slowly. She had read some of those spells in the Black Book; she knew how they worked. Often a child's thumbnail would be polished with a special blend of ashes and oil; a mirror could also be enchanted with the name of such spirits as Floron or Lilet, or a crystal or bowl consecrated for calling up visions. She had none of those things; but if she poured the holy water into Eva's virgin palm, it might serve well enough.

"So be it," Margerite said softly.

Her work would have been easier if Kobolt had brought her dagger to scratch a circle in the earth with, or if she had a candle or any light beside the faint glow of the stars through the little windows, but, working mostly by touch, she managed to trace a rough circle on the floor with the tip of her wand, and those Hebrew names of God that she had painstakingly memorized about it.

She took Eva's hand, leading her into the circle; and the moment she stepped within, Margerite knew that she had drawn it rightly, for it seemed to her that she could feel its power like a soft sparkling over her skin. Eva's palm was cold and sweaty, as if she were greatly afraid, her face pale in the darkness, but she did not pull back or flinch away from Margerite. The two cats flanked their mistresses, sitting silently on either side within the circle.

"Omnipotent, eternal God," Margerite prayed. "Creator of humankind, ruler of all that is and ever shall be; bless this working, and we who wreak it in our sore need. In Your names Adonai, Sabaoth, Elohim, Tetragrammaton, Emmanuel; by Your archangels Raphael, Michael, Gabriel, and Auriel, who guard the corners of the world against all evil, and the holy name of Your Son Jesu Christ, we call upon You to aid us."

Margerite's hand was steady as she unstoppered the phial of holy water, taking Eva's hand and turning it upward, cupped into a tiny bowl. Carefully Margerite poured the precious drops into Eva's palm, then gripped the girl's wrist to help steady it and lowered her wand to the surface. It seemed to her that she could almost see the tip of the rod sparking blue as it touched the water, an unseen light glowing without brightness in the shadow of Eva's cupped fingers.

"In the name of God the omnipotent and omniscient, who sends his angels forth through the world with tidings for men; by the mighty Gabriel, God's herald, and by the holy Annunciation to the Virgin; let us see God's true servant, Father Etienne, and make our need known to him!"

Nothing happened. There was nothing save the darkness pooled in Eva's palm, the smooth ridged grip of the wand in Margerite's right hand and the warmth of Eva's wrist in her left. Margerite breathed as she had learned to, steadying her mind and heartbeat: she knew that she might see nothing herself, and she could not guess what was happening to Eva, save that her shivering had ceased and her arm had gone rock-solid in Margerite's grip.

Then Margerite realized that her skull was echoing, as though a great bell had rung just below her hearing, and that she could not turn her gaze away from the tiny shadowed puddle of water...as though it had spread to the size of a great lake, drawing her in. "By God and Christ and the Virgin," she prayed, most earnestly. "Father Etienne, wherever you are, hear us!"

It seemed to Margerite then that she gazed upon a castle, its walls reaching higher than she could see, and the deep defensive-ditch below it sinking down to black water, its depths unknowable. There was no crossing it, nor any way for her to breach those walls, not even had she come with an army and cannon.

In a castle there are three things that are strong, the ditch, the wall, and the keep...The spiritual wall is chastity, and as you have this ditch of humility and wall of chastity so must we build the keep of charity...

"Father Etienne!" Margerite called. "It is Margerite and Eva who come to you. Please hear us, for we have not come as foes, but to ask your help, and we cannot pierce through to you!"

The castle faded as though a mist were lowering over it. Slowly a light began to glow in its place; and in that light, Margerite saw Father Etienne's face as clearly as if she were looking upon him in the flesh, delicate and strong as a slim sword of the finest wrought steel - his high cheekbones and arched brows, the thick dark hair with silver wings at his temples, the close-cropped beard with its silver tuft beneath his lower lip.

But his eyes shone terribly, as she had never seen them before, like clear pale sapphires with the sun's brightness pooled in their gleaming depths, and it was only by the sheerest effort of will that she managed to hold his gaze.

"Where are you?" the priest asked, his hollow baritone booming inside Margerite's skull. "What has happened?"

"We are being held by Ritter Hermann von Landsburg, a day's journey south of Fulda - if you cannot aid us quickly, Father, we shall be hanged on Monday morning!"

"Why?"

The thunderous sound of Etienne's voice in her head was beyond Margerite's bearing. Her mind wavered, flinching away. As if she had lost her grip on a rope, she fell into the darkness.

When she came to herself again, Margerite was sitting on the ground, with two raspy cat-tongues scraping over her chin and Eva's wet hand on her forehead. "We are still in the circle," Eva whispered. "Can you speak?"

Margerite had not lost hold of her wand, though her hand was beginning to cramp about it. Supporting herself on Eva's solid shoulder, she pushed the two cats off her and got painfully to her feet. "Praise be to God, the omnipotent and eternal," she said. "Praise and thanks to Him, who has helped us in our need. May all that comes from this pass to His glory - Atoh, Malkuth, ve-Geburah, ve-Gedulah, Amen." Margerite crossed herself, stepping out of the circle, and as she did, it seemed to her that she felt the bubble of its power burst into a shimmering shower and vanish about her.

"We did it," Eva murmured. "I did not know if we could - I do not think the Abbess could have done such a thing, without all her candles and incense and oils and the foul spirits she called to aid her."

"The power of God is greater than that of the Devil," Margerite answered her. "And you aided me willingly and with a pure heart, to help your companions, although you were afraid - I think that must have meant something too."

Wolfram began to cry, and Margerite hurried to calm him. Though she was almost shaking with hunger herself, she knew that there would be no food for the adults until morning: at least Wolfram did not need to depend on their captor's charity, although the Virgin alone knew if Margerite would be able to keep making good milk on their prison rations. Margerite was not aware of laying her wand down, but when she groped about for it after feeding her baby into quietness again, she found that it was no longer there, and a surge of panic went through her.

"What is it now?" Eva whispered.

"I have lost my wand in the dark, and no other is to touch it, or I would have to make a new one - and besides, God alone knows what would become of us if one of our guards saw it."

Eva stood still while Margerite crawled all over the floor, feeling about the hard earthen surface with her fingertips. But the wand was gone - and Kobolt, to her surprise, did not join her search. "Kobolt? Cat?" Margerite called softly.

"Perhaps he has taken it away," Eva suggested. "The Abbess' cat would often do such things; I know that it was a demon and Kobolt is not, but he is your familiar."

Margerite was about to answer when a shadow blocked the starlight. Kobolt leapt down, and Margerite heard what sounded like a soft leathery fluttering, then the unmistakable crunching of small bones and a cat's growl. The tom padded over to her, dropping his booty next to her foot with a chirping whirr.

"Yes, I know I am hungry, but I do not think a dead bat is what I need," Margerite told him.

At that point, Merlin groaned, muttering, "If we are all to be hanged soon, can you at least not be quiet and let me sleep for now?"

When Margerite woke, crawling slowly out of the depths of sleep as if she were pulling herself from deep cold water, she was not sure whether she had dreamed what had happened in the night or not. There was no sign of the circle she had drawn, though Kobolt and Kriemhilt had scratched up part of the floor into little heaps that, from the smell, barely hid their droppings; nor did the cool light of dawn through the window show her missing wand anywhere.

She thought that the bat had disappeared, too, until she picked Wolfram up to feed him and saw his little hand clenched tightly about a tattered black wing. Grimacing with disgust, she pried the bat-wing away from her child, throwing it into the corner where Kobolt leapt gleefully on it.

Will Father Etienne come? Margerite wondered. I know he would not willingly leave us - but what if he is too far away to reach us in time?

Friday passed very slowly, the day broken only twice, when the guards brought in meager meals of stockfish, water, and a few stale pieces of bread. Merlin, as the tallest of the prisoners, had to empty the chamber pot out one of the narrow window-openings when it was full, but inevitably much of it slopped back, the foul stench blending with the stink of Wolfram's used rags and their own unwashed bodies.

The constant annoyance of the flies was maddening as well, for they swarmed and settled not only upon the bucket, but everywhere, so that all four of the prisoners were constantly swatting them away, or flinching at the bites of the big horseflies that came buzzing in through the window and would settle upon their heads or backs. Only Kobolt and Kriemhilt were entertained by the plague of flies; the pair of them would choose a large one and stalk it together, driving it from wall to wall before one cat leapt up to catch the insect in its sharp teeth.

Margerite had never realized how hard it was to sit in idleness, with no embroidery or fine tapestry-work to occupy her hands. She thought longingly of the four long double-pointed needles she had used to knit gowns for Wolfram out of soft wool and cotton from Italy; even spinning, though she had not had to turn a spindle since leaving her father's castle, would have given her something to do besides twitching and swatting at flies.

Eva sat in the corner, staring thoughtfully at nothing and stroking Kriemhilt when the cat briefly left the fly-hunt to come purr at her; Georg fretted, pacing back and forth in the narrow confines of the stable, but Merlin stood, running his hands up and down the thick planks between the heavy supporting beams of the walls.

"If we had some means of making a fire," he said, "we might be able to burn our way out, or at least escape in the confusion. It is a pity that the floor of the loft is above our heads and blocks us from reaching the thatch, or we might be able to creep out that way. But if one of you is hiding flint and steel on you..?" He raised thick eyebrows, looking hopefully at the other three.

"I had," Margerite said, thinking with regret of Gerhild's advice to her niece, "but they were with my other belongings in the wagon."

"Well, do not give up yet," the Welshman advised her. "Merlin has been in difficult situations before, and always managed to find a way out."

With that, he returned to prodding at joists and cracks, leaving Margerite with nothing better to do than playing with Wolfram and Kobolt as best she could and trying not to fear too greatly. She wished that she could speak of what had passed in the night, for although Georg was trying to bear himself bravely, he could not hide the terror that darkened his blue eyes as though the shadow of the hangman's noose already hung over his face.

If she could tell him that there was some chance of rescue...but she was not certain herself, and even if she could explain matters, it would be more cruel to raise his hopes without any surety that they would be fulfilled. After the dragging day, it was harder to sleep that night than it had been before. Though Margerite had changed his rags just before sunset and cleaned him off very carefully with the last of the evening's water.

Wolfram was no more comfortable than his mother, waking up at brief intervals to cry fretfully, and Margerite had to pick him up and walk round and round, trying not to step on any of her companions or to stumble over the half-filled bucket of filth by the back wall - though everything in the stable was beginning to smell so badly that it would hardly have mattered if she had.

Margerite had no idea how long she walked with Wolfram like that, crooning softly and rocking him in her arms, but at last she reached the point where she had to sit down with the baby in her lap. His whimpering seemed very distant against the aching of her arms and back, against the weight of her eyelids; she held his solid warmth close, murmuring hoarsely into his ears, over and over, "Hush, hush, go to sleep...go to sleep..."

Although the day had been warm, very warm for the beginning of September, the night air through the window was cold, so that after a little while Margerite found herself shivering upon the chill earthen floor. She should get up and move, she thought, lie down next to Eva for her warmth, but her limbs were too heavy...

The cold grew worse, and Margerite found that she was shivering so that she could hardly move. Wolfram had stopped crying; instead he was making the little gurgling sounds that he greeted Kobolt with, sounds of happiness. Margerite tried to reach out, to feel around for the tomcat, but her arms were locked tightly around her child, and she realized that, though she did not know why, she was desperately afraid to loosen her grip upon him.

Wolfram turned his head, and Margerite felt him reaching out with one hand. Then her breath clogged in her lungs with terror, for though the sky was clouded and not even starlight reached through the tiny windows, she could see the shape of a man standing before her, and the gleam of red from the ruby on his finger. As she stared, he seemed to grow clearer, as though a light fell upon him alone: she could see his sharp peak of gray-blond hair, his long goateed face... Graf Günther, Mother Maria help me! Margerite thought. But he is dead!

Graf Günther's thin lips curved into a smile, but his brow was deeply furrowed as if in pain, his blue eyes staring down at Wolfram with a fierce, agonized longing. Margerite could neither move nor make a sound as he reached downward, his long knuckly hand moving towards Wolfram's tiny chubby fingers.

The baby gurgled happily again in greeting, and something broke in Margerite's throat. She threw her head back with a scream - and suddenly the apparition was gone, and she was sitting alone in the dark, Wolfram wailing in her arms.

"Margerite!" Eva cried, half a heartbeat before Georg echoed, "Frowe Margerite!" The two of them were beside her at once, and she heard Merlin's heavy footsteps behind them, then the sound of hammering at the stable door.

"What's going on in there?" one of the guards shouted.

"Only a dream," Margerite answered. "A nightmare, nothing more."

Through the door, she heard the guard grunt and spit, then the sound of men's muffled voices outside. Wolfram was screaming lustily now, as he always did when wakened from his sleep.

"Don't be afraid, Margerite, "Merlin said, his raspy voice gentle. "No need for bad dreams; we have two days yet to find a way out of here."

Georg said nothing, but Margerite heard the hitching sound of a snuffle in the darkness, as though, with no one able to see him, he could no longer hold to his daytime bravery. She patted the Knappe's thin shoulder to reassure him.

"It was only a bad dream," she repeated. "Say your prayers, and go back to sleep."

"I am glad you woke me, " Eva whispered when at last the two women had managed to calm Wolfram again and lay back to back in each other's warmth with their cats and the baby snuggled between them. "I was having a bad dream too."

"What did you dream?" Margerite asked, afraid of what the other would say - but more afraid of not knowing.

"I dreamed I was back in the convent, in that cold little room where the Abbess made me sleep, and that I heard her feet coming up the stairs. May Christ be my witness, I would sooner be hanged here than sent back there."

"By Christ's mercy, I hope that neither shall happen," Margerite murmured back to her. Still, she did not dare to assure herself that what she had seen was no more than a dream. She turned her mind to her prayers once more, but it was a long time before sleep caught up with her.

Saturday passed no more easily than Friday, though the stew - the scullions' slops, by the taste of it - was better than thin pieces of stockfish. The prisoners had eaten their evening meal and resigned themselves to trying to sleep once more when the door opened and the light of a candle blinded their darkened eyes.

"Wake, you scum, for a priest is coming to you," one of the guardsmen shouted. Margerite was on her feet at once, but she winced at the sound of a heavy kick meeting Merlin's ribs.

"None of that," a mild, slightly monotonous baritone said. "They will face God's judgement soon enough; who are you to make their torments worse?"

"Sorry, Father," the guardsman said, abashed, and dropped back.

The candle-flame's brightness highlighted Etienne's ascetic features; as Ritter Hermann had done, the canon had to duck his head to enter the stable without knocking off his flat black headdress with its rolled corners. Margerite had all she could do not to run to him at once, embracing his slender body tightly, but she knew better than to acknowledge him before the guardsmen.

Etienne turned his head, the candlelight sharpening the clean lines of his profile and catching tiny golden glints fom his close-cropped dark beard. "You may leave us, Odo. There are confessions to be made, and, be assured, I shall call for you if I have any difficulties."

"As you wish, Father," the man-at-arms muttered.

The priest closed the stable door behind him, his slightly crooked nose wrinkling at the smell. He coughed once before he spoke.

"I trust there is an explanation for this," he said sharply. "Margerite, how did you come to be travelling with this...this mountebank?" The glare he hurled at Merlin left no doubt that the two of them had met before.

"Merlin rescued us from trouble, and gave us shelter and transport on our way, when there was none other to help us," Margerite flared back at him.

"I am sure he did," Father Etienne said dryly. "And I am sure you paid for it, too."

"What do you take me for, Father?" Merlin asked, his raspy voice sounding injured. "Do you think I could leave two women and a boy to travel by themselves, knowing nothing of the dangers of the road - not even how to deal with rude men in an inn? Father, you met me while I still had my family: you know I take care of my own."

Father Etienne looked down his nose at the piles of bedding straw, the half-full chamberpot and the fly-ridden trails of filth beneath the window where it had been emptied. He did not have to say a word; but furious as Margerite was at Merlin for the suspicious dealing that had gotten them into this grievous state, she could not help speaking up to defend him again.

"Merlin did take care of us, and asked nothing in return save for our help." Although there had been those silver coins that turned into rags, and Eva cheated on the pilgrim phial...but that was little enough, compared to what the Welsh peddler had done for them in bringing them safely as far as he could; and the drops of holy water in the Jerusalem phial had, after all, made it possible for them to reach Etienne in their need.

The priest made a slight snorting noise. "I do not, for a minute, believe that it would have ended so cheaply for you. Nevertheless, I believe I can manage to get all of you, even Merlin, out of here, though it will not be easy. Ritter Hermann is quite convinced of your guilt, and what he showed me from your wagon gives him more than sufficient reason to believe the four of you to be a pack of robbers. I shall have to use - unusual means to free you."

Margerite thought at once of the charms of invisibility she had read in the Black Book, but, as if he could hear her thoughts, Etienne shook his head, the steely glint of his blue eyes warning her to silence. "Best you listen closely and prepare yourselves, for if you are overcome with fear tomorrow, you shall not be able to make your escape. And you will all need to make Confession, for there is more than a little danger in this for you."

In the morning, the guards came in and bound the prisoners' hands again. Helmut took Wolfram from Margerite's arms, letting the child tug on the long waves of his gold-streaked brown beard as one of his men tied Margerite's hands together.

"What are you doing?" Eva asked, her eyes round with fear. "Are we to be hanged today? Ritter Hermann promised that we should not die until Monday."

The guard who had tied her laughed, slapping her rump. His hand lingered on the curve of Eva's buttocks a moment as he said, "The priest wants you in the church, to show folk what befalls sinners and criminals. You'll do your last dance soon enough, though it's a pity to waste a pretty girl like you on the gallows." Still caressing Eva, the guard moved closer, as if to take more liberties, but Helmut coughed meaningfully, glaring at him, and he hastily retreated a couple of steps.

"Have you fed the babe today?" Helmut asked Margerite.

"Yes, and changed his cloths, for which I thank you."

"No need," Helmut replied gruffly. "I've eight of twelve living myself, and Ritter Hermann ordered that the child be kept well enough. Come on, now."

After their days in the dim light of the stable, the sun's brightness burned Margerite's eyes, stinging them with tears until the high green hills rising on either side of Ritter Hermann's small fortress blurred and wavered like fever-dreams. A skylark rose above, a small dark speck against the gleaming blue of the sky, its twittering song floating downward.

Margerite's breasts ached, for she had been able to make little milk on her prisoner's swill, and in his hunger Wolfram had kept sucking long after they were empty; her bones hurt as well, as though she had drawn on her very marrow in the effort to feed her child.

O Maria, she prayed, have mercy on us in our innocence - and on Merlin, be he guilty or not, for that he helped us when we were in need. At least Ritter Hermann's men had not taken her prayer-beads from her; they had not even taken her belt-pouch or searched her body for jewelry, so that the falcon-necklace still lay nestled between her breasts. No doubt they thought to wait until we were dead before stripping us. And for that small mercy, thinking of the guard's hand grasping Eva's buttocks, Margerite was most thankful.

Ritter Hermann's church was built of solid stone - not large, but bigger than any of the wooden outbuildings, and freshly whitewashed. Margerite's heart beat faster when she saw Merlin's wagon outside, the two brown ponies peacefully cropping the grass that grew at the side of the hard-packed earth of the courtyard, but she did not dare to look more closely at it.

The plaster within the church was covered with bright murals depicting scenes from the lives of Christ and the saints; but, for all their brilliant colours, they seemed clumsily done when set against the wooden crucifix behind the altar.

That was truly the work of a master carver, each bone and muscle of Christ's loinclothed body standing out sharply as if He were straining in agony against the nails that held Him, and the blood-drops trailing from His crown of thorns like bright sweat: in His upturned face, Margerite could see every mark of agony's weight borne up by strength, and the glimmer of faith even through the darkness of forsaken despair, like a single glint of gold showing through a tar-smeared crown.

Had the guards not been chivvying her along, she would have fallen to her knees on the spot; as it was, they pushed Margerite and her companions up the aisle, pressing the prisoners down to kneel directly in front of the altar where Father Etienne stood. The priest barely glanced at them, his aristocratic features cold and remote.

Though Margerite knew that he could not acknowledge them, it annoyed her that she could appear to be so easily dismissed, like a scrubbing cloth too tattered and filth-grained to be of any more use.

"The Ritter won't have blood spilled in God's house," hissed the guard who had been pawing Eva in a low whisper. "But try to get away from here, and you'll find that you don't have to be whole to be hanged."

The church filled quickly, castle servants and villagers crowding in and craning their necks to get a good look at the prisoners. Margerite shuddered, knowing that all the bright eyes staring at her now would be brighter, more excited, if Father Etienne's plan failed and they were brought to the gallows tomorrow morning.

Though she tried to close her ears to it, scraps of words and phrases fell from the murmured rumble of conversation like crumbs of meat from the hands of a hurried cook: "Killed a noble family on the road, they did, and stole a whole flock of the Ritter's sheep...blond girl made a good living from her whoring, I'll wager; look at the teats on her... mug of ale says that bull neck of his doesn't snap when he's hoisted on the gallows, we'll see him strangle slow...thieves and murderers; thank God..."

It seemed to Margerite that she knew how a baited bear must feel, trapped in a pit with the whispers of the crowd crawling over his skin like flies, creeping into his ears where a mere shake of the head could not flick them loose. Though she was on her knees, she held her back straight and proud.

She would not meet any of the eyes staring at her, or even look too long at their oily sheen of curiosity and delight, staring over the villagers' heads instead at a brilliant scene of the angel Gabriel descending to bear his good news to Maria. Although the Virgin's face was bland beneath garishly yellow hair, Margerite nevertheless found comfort in gazing at her: it was not the skill of the artist that mattered, after all, but the great Mystery behind the painting, that no man's hand could truly show forth.

Ritter Hermann and a plump dark-haired woman with silver rings on her fingers - his wife, Margerite assumed - sat in the front pew with their guardsmen around them. The knight and his lady were dressed alike, the sky-blue linen of his doublet and her dress embroidered with matching white roses. Save for the occasional glare, Hermann was largely ignoring his prisoners, but his wife's gaze was as curious as those of the poorer folk behind her. Surreptitiously, Margerite glanced at them to see if they were wearing any of her own or Eva's jewelry, but they were not: for what it was worth, Ritter Hermann seemed to be an honest man, if harsh and hasty of judgement.

By the time Father Etienne lifted his arms for silence, the church was full and overfull, with people standing pressed tightly together all along the walls. A stench of onions and unwashed bodies had long since overpowered the faint lingering sweetness of incense, and Margerite might have wrinkled her nose, had she not been miserably aware of how badly she stank herself.

At that thought, all her fleabites began to itch at once; kneeling, with her hands bound, she could surreptitiously rub at her thighs, but there was a cluster of bites farther around her hip, just out of reach, and another trail of small red marks on her right wrist above the rope that tied her hands together. It seemed to her that she could feel a small insect creeping over her back, and she gritted her teeth, trying to ignore it as Father Etienne began the Mass.

It was harder not to squirm when Father Etienne began his sermon, pointing dramatically downward at the prisoners with his cassock-sleeve falling down from his arm like a great black wing. He did not thunder, as some priests did, but his voice was piercingly intense as he said, "Behold the wages of sin! Behold the rewards of crime!"

A hissing mutter went through the crowded church, and Margerite saw some of the villagers standing in back surreptitiously jostling and shoving to get a better look at the four who knelt bound before the altar. Father Etienne ignored them, elaborating on the seven deadly sins and how each of them led to crime.

"For what is theft but the sin of envy brought to fruition?" he asked rhetorically. "And what is murder but wrath full-blown, or adultery but lust made deed?

In every sin in your heart, there is the seed of a crime: what the heart conceives, the hand will surely do, unless it be stayed by true repentance. And worst of all is pride - pride in wits or pride in strength, that makes the robber believe he can steal and not be caught, or the murderer believe that he will never be brought to justice for his slaying.

Before you, you see a mountebank who thought that he could swindle and steal and leave his victims no wiser than before: but sin, whether it be in thought or in action, leaves a mark as clear to read as that of a brand, as surely as Cain was branded for the wrath in which he slew his brother. And some may sin and sin, turning deeper into the ways of evil, and seem to go unpunished; but as sure as these -" he gestured at the prisoners again - "were brought at last to justice, of this you may be certain: God will repay!"

Father Etienne slammed his fist down on the altar, and a great blinding flash burst forth, as though a bolt of lightning had struck down before him. The huge thunderous boom left Margerite half-blind, half-deaf, and nearly stunned, but she still had enough wit to remember Father Etienne's words. Choking in the sulphurous black smoke that filled the church, she ran straight down the aisle and out the open door, squirming up over the edge of the wagon and down among the bags and boxes, pulling the woolen blankets that covered the goods down over herself.

Heart pounding and breathing hard in the muffled hot darkness, trying not to cough from the foul smoke still in her lungs, Margerite could hear her companions doing likewise. What magic was that? she thought, trying to breathe slowly and deeply to calm the frantic thudding in her chest. Her belly was sore from wriggling over the wagon's edge with her hands tied, and it ached with each breath she took, but her heart was beginning to ease from full gallop down to a trot.

Or...was it magic? I felt nothing, and that smoke smelled very much like Jochanan's gunpowder. Etienne had explained nothing of how he meant to do his trick, only warned them of what would happen, and told them what to do. If it were gunpowder - No wonder he wanted us to be shriven last night! Mother Maria, I pray that the church is not badly damaged, for though Ritter Hermann mistook us for folk who deserved his justice, he seems a good Christian.

Margerite did not know how long she lay in the stifling heat beneath the blanket with the corner of a wooden chest pressing hard into her ribs, but by the time she heard Etienne's dry polite voice speaking his farewells to a stuttering, shaken Ritter Hermann, her bladder was full almost to bursting, and she could feel it jostling heavily within her at every bump or dried wheel-rut in the road.

But she waited in silence, thighs pressed together and fists clenched tightly; even when she heard Wolfram beginning to cry, she did not move, for she knew they must still be too close to Ritter Hermann's village to risk showing themselves. Only when she felt the heavy tread of paws on her body did she nearly cry out, for Kobolt had managed to step right onto her bladder, and, like all cats, he seemed to double his weight when walking on a supine human.

At last the wagon stopped, the woolen blankets whisking away suddenly. Gratefully, Margerite breathed in deep gulps of the cool clean air, wiping the oily sweat from her forehead with her sleeve. They were in woodland now, sheltered from sight by a thick green weave of trees, and before Father Etienne could speak, Margerite held up her hand.

"Father, you must excuse me a moment," she said. "If you would cut these ropes, please." Etienne's knife flashed in the sunlight, and the rough twists of hemp fell away from her reddened wrists. Climbing carefully over the edge of the wagon, Margerite hurried off to squat behind a holly thicket. Eva was not far behind her, and the girl sighed gratefully as she finished emptying herself.

"I thought he would never stop," Eva said. "But what have we to complain of, when we have just been brought safely out of the gallows-shadow?"

"What, indeed?" Margerite agreed.

"All my holy items!" Merlin was protesting when the two women got back to the wagon. "Father, what manner of living can I make without them?"

"You have your life, and your wagon: that should suffice," Father Etienne told him sternly. "I left you those things that belonged to your family. As for your phials and relics and boxes of dust, you may consider them payment to the brothers at Fulda for the sheep you stole - if there is a single true relic among all the pigs' bones and road-dirt and stream-waters. And if you have any sense, you will never come within a week's travel of this village again, for there will be no one to save you a second time.

Know that I am not happy about what I had to do this day, for though I told no actual untruths, I nevertheless allowed good folk to deceive themselves into believing they had witnessed the anger of God, when what they saw was nothing more than a little applied alchemy and charred bones from the kitchen left behind. I shall have to answer for that - but if you were an honest man, it would not have been necessary."

Merlin looked down at the road, his heavy shoulders sagging. "Will you give me a little something to get by on, at least, Father? I can hardly beg while I have a wagon, and it would be a poor start to a life of repentance if I had to steal my dinner."

Father Etienne cast a pointed glance at the Welshman's wide belly, only a little shrunken by three days of living on kitchen slops. "Consider your hunger as mortification of the flesh, and part of your fair penance. Now, Margerite, Eva, Georg; gather what is yours, for we shall part ways here." He pointed ahead to where the road forked in two, northeast and southeast.

"Farewell, Merlin," Georg said gravely, clasping wrists with the bigger man, his wiry freckled arm almost lost in the Welshman's grasp. "I shall not forget you."

"Remember to keep your temper, lad, and you'll go far," Merlin told him.

Eva went up on her toes, brushing her lips against Merlin's weathered forehead. "Farewell, Merlin. Thank you for all you taught me."

"God grant the knowledge helps, if you ever need to use it!" he replied.

Margerite had used the time the other two bought her to reach into her belt-pouch; now she embraced Merlin lightly, their bodies hiding her movement from Father Etienne as she pressed four pieces of silver into the Welshman's hard palm.

Fair as Etienne's judgement on him might be, now that it came to the point of parting, Margerite found that she could not bear the thought of Merlin forced to starve - or, worse, to sell those things that were his last ties to his wife and son, that he kept more carefully than his dubious saints' relics.

"Blessings on you and your child, and on your road, Margerite," Merlin murmured gruffly. "If you ever need help again, remember that I'll always be your friend."

"I shall remember," Margerite answered.

Margerite picked up her box of ritual tools, nestling it under her arm. The bags of silver and jewelry were gone - whether to enrich Ritter Hermann after all, or as a gift to the brothers at Fulda, she thought she would probably never know. Still, it was a small enough price to pay for being alive, and she had no doubt that Father Etienne could take care of them hereafter.

Although Etienne had a great black stallion to ride as well as his dun packhorse, he walked with the rest of them, leading the stallion by the reins with the packhorse following obediently behind. They paused again at the fork; then Etienne turned his back on Merlin and began to stride down the northeastern road. The Welsh peddler waited a little longer, looking at Margerite, Eva, and Georg as if in hopes that they would suddenly decide to come with him, after all.

Then he guided his ponies to the right, turning back in his seat and waving rather forlornly to his former companions. They waved back, but there was little time to stand and watch the wagon roll on: Father Etienne was already a good way up the track, Kobolt and Kriemhilt scampering after him, and they had to hurry as quickly as they could with Margerite holding Wolfram in one arm and her box of ritual tools in the other in order to catch up with him.

Chapter Six

Travelling with Father Etienne was, Margerite found at once, easier and more comfortable than she had imagined. The horses he had gotten for his three companions at the first village they stopped in were well-tempered and smooth-gaited beasts, and the priest's packs held fresh bread and fine wine, good cheese and smoked ham and sausages. He had thoughtfully brought warm travelling cloaks that they could wrap tightly about them against the chilling September winds, and clothing which, if it was not made of silk or brocade, was at least good linen and fine wool, rather than the dingy peasant garments they had been wearing. When they stopped for the evening, they stayed, not packed tightly in the flea-ridden straw mattresses of village inns, but in the warmer and more comfortable dwellings of priests, who were honoured to put up the canon and his fellow travellers.

As they rode north-east, the land spread into great rolling hills blanketed by heavy forests. Oak and ash and birch were already turning colours beneath the wind's sharp lash, the green leaves tinged by red and brown and gold, and mushrooms sprouted at their gnarled roots, the thick white stems and brown caps of Steinpils, the brilliant white-flecked red caps of Fliegenpils, and the furrowed golden trumpets of chanterelles springing forth from the deep leaf-mould. Often Margerite looked up to see a wild hawk riding high against the cold blue heavens, and sometimes tears would prick her eyes, for there was no better weather to go out hunting with the noble birds. The grain-harvest was over, and hares lolloped lightly over the shorn brown fields; at Burg Falkenstein, or in the hills by her father's castle, the grape harvest would be beginning, the heady fruit-smell rising from the vats where the juice was pressed out, ready to be fermented into sweet wine and sharp verjuice.

Though the season of grease for deer would be over and the flesh of the stags beginning to grow stringy and musky with rut, it would still be pleasant to ride out through the woods with a well-dressed hunting party to the belling of hounds on a trail, and hear the deep bellow of stags calling for their mates in the distance.

Margerite did not dwell on such thoughts for long, however, for they reminded her too sharply of Ruprecht; and at night, when she lay in the warm feather-beds that would be brought out for Father Etienne's noble companions and heard the rushing of the wind through the trees like a great river outside, she would find herself shivering, listening for the sound of hoofbeats and a distant hunting horn.

Far from the woods of Burg Falkenstein as they were, it sometimes seemed to Margerite that she could feel that familiar wildness in the autumn air, and whether Wolfram lay quietly with his eyes open, listening to the night wind, or cried and fretted restlessly, as though he were staring at something just beyond his grasp, it made her all the more nervous.

Yet she did not dare to speak to Etienne about a fear she could not name, the more so since there was nothing to tell of save the workings of nature. Wind in the autumn night and a baby that either rested peacefully or cried: what was there in that to disturb her? In any case, there was more to think on: the question of what they would do when they reached Schloss Niederwald. Often when they were riding, Father Etienne would become silent for a long time, staring fixedly at the road ahead, and at such times Margerite did not dare to speak to him, for she knew the priest was considering what to do about their situation.

He questioned her several times about the details of what she had seen in her flight: how the game-parks and pleasure gardens were laid out around the castle, what the gamekeeper's house had looked like, how far it had seemed to be from the central edifice, and whether she had been able to make out any paths or roads.

"We do not yet know enough," the priest said at last. "Though I have been through Niederwald before, my business took me elsewhere than the castle; previously, I was assisting Bishop Otto regarding a matter of canon law."

Margerite raised an eyebrow, but Etienne shook his head, his thick brown hair waving softly beneath the rolled corners of his flat black headdress.

"We can look for no help there, at least at first. The Bishop is neither of the Order, nor is he one of their knowing foes: he is a good man of the Church, but inclined to be rather stiff and stubborn, and to give little credence to tales of magic and heresy - unlike a few of our younger priests, who are all too quick to believe such things, whether there is grounds to or not." Etienne frowned, his fine lips tightening a moment, as if pressing back an unpleasant memory. "Nevertheless, I intend to visit him, to find out exactly what he has heard. I also know Ortlieb by reputation, you see, and unless she has changed vastly since becoming Landgräfin, she may very well have found herself offending Bishop Otto to the point that he will be willing to believe the worst about her and to support Bertram's claims, at least if reasonable evidence is shown to him."

"What do you know about Ortlieb?" Margerite asked quietly. Her hands shook on her horse's reins; the gray gelding turned its head, looking back at its rider out of one large eye, as if to ask what she was doing. She breathed deeply to calm herself: why should she be so agitated, as though Bertram's enemy were still her rival?

"She is a Princess of the Order, an accomplished magician who has specialized in the use of demons and spirits to create illusory marvels - or conceal her workings. She is also said to be most proficient in the sexual magics of the Order, and to have gotten from her Master tremendous power to affect the souls of men in this manner."

As Margerite listened to these words, her teeth clenched; she could feel the muscles of her belly tightening into a cramp like the first contraction of childbirth, and her face and limbs grew cold. As well as she had learned through the years to keep her thoughts from showing in her expressions, Father Etienne must have read her thoughts easily, for a look of concern came over his aristocratic features.

"I will not lie to you, Margerite," he said softly. "Yes, Bertram is in great danger from her. You said that he had spoken of being harmed by a woman of the Order: if I had known that he had once been in Ortlieb's power, I should have taken steps before I left to make sure that he was entirely free of her. This explains much of the darkness in his history. It is not surprising that he was so deeply scarred, but only that he had the strength to break away from her at all, let alone to give love or trust to any other woman afterwards. And doubly surprising that - forgive me for saying this, Margerite." The priest's slight French accent grew stronger, and the fine lines in his forehead deepened, as though he were forcing himself not to look away from her as he spoke. "In your Confession, you hinted that Bertram might have been the father of your child. If so, he may have been the first of Ortlieb's victims to have kept the ability to do so after she was through with him...do you understand me?"

Margerite nodded, shivering beneath her warm wool cloak as though it were a blanket of snow about her shoulders.

"The worse danger is that she may not be through with him," Father Etienne murmured, his voice dark and bleak as a winter evening. "I have been thinking much on this since you first told me what had happened, you see, and I fear that I have made a grievous mistake."

"What?" Margerite asked, afraid to know, but more afraid not to.

Etienne shook his head, his slender shoulders hunched beneath his cassock. "I cannot tell you, for there are certain things that are - that must be - more important than the Order, or our war against it."

Margerite drew in her breath. She remembered how Etienne had balked at revealing the passageway from Ruprecht's room, because he had learned about it in Eva's Confession: what was said at such times must remain forever in confidence between the priest, the maker of the Confession, and God.

"In any case," Father Etienne went on, "we must reach Bertram as soon as we can, and without letting ourselves be seen by anyone from Schloss Niederwald. Ortlieb would be sure to recognise me, and she must not know that you are with me."

"What are you planning, Father?" Margerite asked, her bowels gripping cold with dread.

"That will have to wait until we find Bertram," Etienne told her. "But tonight I shall need your aid. We need to know that Bertram is still where you saw him last; we must know the roads around Burg Niederwald and the paths through the hunting park; we must be sure that the house you saw is the only gamekeeper's house there, and it would be well if you could see his face, so that we will recognise the man when we meet him. Much of that, to be sure, I could discover on my own, but your flight will give us a clearer view than my seeing-stone, and with my guidance, you will be at little risk."

Margerite's heart fluttered in her chest. To let another guide her flight again, sending her, not at her will, but his own, when she had just learned the freedom she could have...But Eva had suffered worse at the hands of the Abbess than she had at Ruprecht's - save for that one night, when - and yet the girl had offered to let Margerite use her in order to help her companions; could Margerite be less brave.

"I shall do it," she said firmly.

That evening, they stopped in a small monastery off the main road, arriving just after vespers. The Abbot, a tall, ascetic man with a long gray beard, seemed to know Father Etienne; he greeted the canon with delight, and voiced no doubts about why Etienne should be travelling with two women, a boy, an infant, and two cats. Instead, he swiftly sent a couple of the brothers to lay fires on in the hospice rooms, and others to see the horses safely to the monastery's little stables, and enquired kindly as to what Wolfram might need for his comfort.

"We do have a cradle here, thank the Lord," the Abbot said. "Sometimes it happens that a babe is left with us, to be raised in Christ's charity as a young novice, and so the brothers have learned how to tend small children as best as men may. We look upon it as a special blessing from God, when He grants us the joys of fatherhood even in our chaste lives. But come, you must be weary and hungry from your travels, and there is no reason for you to stand out here in the rain.

I fear, good frowes, you may find our food poor, since we live strictly by the Rule, and see guests so seldom that we have little fit to serve to others. In addition, we take only a very small meal between vespers and compline at this time of year, but we will provide for you as best we can. If you need meat to keep up your strength after travel, we will kill one of our chickens for you, though it will take some time to pluck and cook."

"We are honoured by your care," Margerite answered, touched by the old man's kindness. "You need not trouble yourselves so greatly for us: whatever your cook can easily prepare will suffice."

"And what of your beautiful cats? We set out a bowl of bread and milk for our own cat each day, since -" the Abbot smiled charmingly, teeth showing white from the depths of his gray beard -"she works as hard as any of the brothers in her duties of keeping the rats and mice at bay. Will the same do well enough for yours?"

"It will, certainly. But I must warn you," Margerite smiled back at him, "that if your cat is a female, Kobolt will have to be locked up unless you want a litter of black kittens soon, for his life is far from chaste."

The Abbot laughed. "Our Priscilla has taken no such vows as ours, and even within our walls, we are wiser than to try to thwart the nature the good Lord gave to His beasts. Let your cats roam as pleases them."

The monastery's guest-hall was frugal, but clean: the simple wooden tables and benches had been lovingly polished, and there was a fine fire crackling in the hearth, as well as a good number of candles burning on the table, by the time the travellers sat down.

The Abbot sat with them, but though the cellarer poured wine for the guests, he took only a courteous drop in his plain wooden goblet before filling it up with water. Nor, when the food was served, did he help himself to more than a slice of the heavy brown bread, though the monastery cook had managed to prepare a very fine omelette with cheese for the travellers, with baked apples in honey to follow.

"Tell me, Father Etienne," the Abbot asked, dabbing the crumbs neatly away from the corner of his gray beard, "what brings you travelling here at this time of year?"

Etienne's eyes hooded a moment, the shadows bringing out the hollows of his high-boned cheeks. "A matter that I would prefer not to tell in full, save to ask that you and the brothers pray for us during the next months."

"You are always in our prayers, Father," the Abbot replied. "For we are soldiers of Christ together, and I know that you labour mightily and dangerously in His army. You will forever have our gratitude for that, as for the help you gave us in our need. But what of these gentles who travel with you? Are they in the same service as yourself, or under your protection from the Foe? If you will forgive me for saying so..." For a moment his deep blue eyes looked searchingly at Margerite, then Eva, then Georg..."they have the look of folk who have been touched deeply by those against whom you battle."

Even in the candlelight, Margerite could see Georg pale, and it seemed for a second that, behind his bright eyes, she could see a hauntingly familiar shadow. Eva looked away, two spots of hectic redness on her creamy cheeks, but the same touch of darkness, that neither her well-fed prettiness nor her skill at dissembling could hide, lay upon her - and what does he see in me? Margerite wondered. Simple and well-cooked as the meal had been, it balled into a heavy knot in her stomach.

"All of them have been," Etienne answered gently. "As to service and protection: the frowe Margerite has chosen to tread the same road as I, but she is not far along it yet; and all three of them have come to lend their aid in the mission I ride on now."

The Abbot rose, bowing to Margerite. Her cheeks heated, and she was aware that she was holding her left hand in her right, as if to hide the place on her finger where the Order ring had been. She did not know what to say to this unexpected homage; she could only bow her head in return. "Frowe, may Christ ever be with you," the Abbot said formally, his words falling upon Margerite like a gentle rain of warmth to fill her heart. "May God and all His saints and angels protect and strengthen you in your battle for the Kingdom of Heaven, that you may aid in confounding His Foes."

"I pray to Christ they will," Margerite answered.

Georg stared at Margerite, the colour coming back into his thin cheeks, and he shifted uneasily on the bench. Margerite could tell that he was nearly bursting to ask what they were talking about, but - thank Maria, thank Christ's mercy - the young Knappe was too well-bred to interrupt the conversation of two churchmen. We shall have to tell him something later, but at least, not now!

"All of you shall have our fervent prayers," the Abbot promised. "Father Etienne, is there anything you and the good frowe will need this night?"

"If you will grant us the use of the room in which you carry out your meditations, we would greatly appreciate it - that is, if there is no difficulty in a woman entering it."

"Father, if Our Lord did not scorn to be born from the womb of a woman, why then should I feel my sanctuary defiled by a female touch?" the Abbot asked, a mild tone of rebuke touching his quiet deep voice.

"I accept the correction and stand humbled, Dominus," Father Etienne replied, inclining his head towards the Abbot.

"No need, Father, for you spoke from courtesy. My sanctuary will be ready for you whenever you need it."

"You have our great thanks," said Father Etienne. "Now, Dominus, I have another question for you. Did a traveller by the name of Bertram pass through here some two to three months ago? He would have been a large man with black hair and beard, bearing a sword - somewhat wild and grim of looks, perhaps, and easily mistaken for a brigand or mercenary, but respectful of your brothers and courteous of speech."

The Abbot's high forehead furrowed in thought, and he stroked his long beard. "No such man came here. Perhaps a month past, we had a pair of visitors who were seeking a fugitive by much the same description, however. These men were a young knight and his squire, who had been long on the road. The knight, in particular, seemed greatly troubled in his soul, and asked to spend the night praying in our chapel, which of course we granted him. His name...I am growing old and forgetful, what was it? He had the most peculiar gaze; he quite unnerved some of the younger brothers."

"Ritter Gottfried?" Margerite asked sharply.

"Yes, of course. I was surprised that he did not bear the insignia of a Teutonic Knight, for he had something of the look of that Order; I had thought that he must be one of yours."

"Not in the sense you mean," Father Etienne told him. "At least, not to my knowledge. He is a knight sworn to Margerite's husband, who seeks the same man we do, though Ritter Gottfried means Bertram ill, whereas we are bound to help him."

"Ah. I gather this is something of a tangled quest, though I shall not pry further, save to ask what I should do if either man comes here."

"If Bertram comes without us, he will be in grave need of sanctuary and spiritual help," Father Etienne said grimly. "Keep him hidden and do not hesitate to call for aid if it is needed. Should Ritter Gottfried return..." The priest bit his lip, rubbing at his heavy gold seal-ring. "Perhaps it is, after all, best for you to know what we are doing, since you may be able to aid at least the survivors if things go badly. Eva, you shall stay to listen to this. Georg, it is time for you to go to bed."

"Father, I shall not!" Georg burst out. "You said that I could lend my aid in whatever it is you mean to do. I thought we had come to find you so that you could exorcise Christoph, but instead we have been riding in the wrong direction for more than a week now, and nobody has bothered to tell me what is more important than ridding my knight of his demon. I had to escape just as Frowe Margerite and Frowe Eva did, and I protected them on the road; I ought to know what is going on."

Etienne's arched eyebrows lowered into a glare, and Margerite could tell that he was about to say something stinging, but the Abbot held up a long wrinkled hand.

"Soft, Father, there is good reason in what the lad says. If he knows this much, and if you are taking him with you into peril, why should he not hear everything? A knight does not keep his Knappe from the battlefield, and, by the sword he wears, this one is old enough to do a man's part."

The canon sighed gustily. "So be it, then. Margerite, this is your story: tell your part as best you may, and I shall finish where you leave off."

Margerite started with her arrival in Burg Fürstensee, telling briefly of Nikolaus' ambition, Heinrich's sudden paralysis, and Christoph's changing behaviour, culminating in the revelation of his demon. She did not mention the Order's interest in Wolfram, nor that she had feigned being a Light-Bearer, only that she knew that Nikolaus was a member.

The Abbot listened quietly, but his venerable face grew more and more grieved at her revelations.

"You, Frowe Gräfin, must be both strong and blessed, in order to have faced a demon so and come off with little hurt from it - though I warn you that you will have to deal with that being again before your death: that is the grievous cost of failing to overcome such a spirit," he said at last. "But that answers neither my question nor that of this good Knappe: what danger is so great that it outweighs the matter of freeing Herr Christoph?"

"I shall take up the matter now," Father Etienne told him. "You will remember the matter of Herr Bernhardt von Niederwald?"

"I had heard of it, as has everyone in these lands," the Abbot replied. "It was a very sad matter, and little that has happened in Niederwald since has been much cause for rejoicing. I gather that your journey here must have something to do with the new Landgräfin, of whom I have also heard?" His voice hardened with his last words, ringing steely and clear, and anger flashed in his deep blue eyes like sunlight off a sword.

"Indeed it does. The fugitive after whom we asked is that same Herr Bernhardt, and he has come to free his lands from her, clear his name, and take his rightful place again. But he is in great danger from her, a danger that he has no means to battle, and therefore he must have our aid."

"Now I understand," the Abbot sighed. "A worthy cause, indeed, though I pray that your game does not mean sacrificing one knight to save the second, even to take the black queen in the process."

"Believe me," Etienne said, his dry baritone suddenly raw, "I would not have chosen to leave Christoph as he is, not for a day or an hour. But the Order has outflanked me in this matter. I underestimated Nikolaus greatly, nor did I learn of Herr Bernhardt's peril until long after I could have given him the aid and counsel he needed. And, whereas Christoph is surely suffering terribly, even with this delay, he will not be past saving before I can reach him. Whereas if we do not act now, Herr Bernhardt may well be."

The Abbot's wrinkled eyelids closed, his face falling into a deep stillness. But before he could speak again, Georg interrupted, "Father, I still do not understand. Who is this Landgräfin von Niederwald, and what is this mysterious Order?"

The youth's eyes got wider and wider as Etienne tersely explained matters to him, adding, "And you will be in the worst danger from Landgräfin Ortlieb, for which reason, if there is any way to avoid it, you will never have the chance to see her."

"Why is that?" Georg asked boldly. "Surely I am able to face any danger into which you mean to bring women."

"You are of an age when certain of her powers will be most effective against you - powers which will not do any harm to Margerite or Eva. And Ortlieb has particular uses for virgin boys."

Georg spluttered at that and said nothing further, but his bright blush told Margerite that Father Etienne had spoken quite accurately about his state.

"Now," the canon went on, "it is time for all of us to retire to our rooms for a while. Margerite, you shall prepare yourself, and I shall come to you when the time is right."

Margerite found Kobolt curled comfortably on the austere bed in her chamber, a black shadow against the gray wool of the blanket. He opened one golden eye to look at her, purring lazily. She stroked his soft fur for a long time, calming her thoughts, before she undressed and put on her robe of black silk, then composed her mind into prayer.

By the time the knock sounded at her door, Margerite's breathing was deep and regular as if she slept, the flame of the single candle on the small table a golden light that filled her eyes so that she had to blink when she looked away from it and rose to answer. Father Etienne stood in the doorway, a taper in his hand. "Follow me," he said.

Margerite followed the priest down the passageway and out into the night. The stars shone hard and sharp against the black sky; the icy wind whipped her hair and the light silk of her robe behind her, but though she walked barefoot upon the cold earthen path, the chill of the night was no more than an invigorating shiver over her skin.

The candleflame, cupped by Etienne's palm against the wind, shone steady before the black figure of the priest, its light guiding her surely past the rustling trees of the monastery orchard and the star-rippling waters of the fishpond, around the dark buildings where the monks slept and on to the door of a small hut.

Stepping in, Margerite was overwhelmed by the sweet scents of frankincense and myrrh and roses and by what seemed to her a blaze of golden light. Though only four candles and a single ruby-glassed altar-lamp burned in the little room, the brightness was nearly unendurable. She breathed deeply of the air, its heady fragrance uplifting her soul; then, as Father Etienne did, bowed her head before the simple wooden altar.

"Give ear to my words, O Lord," Father Etienne intoned, his voice ringing deep through the room. "Consider my meditation. Hearken unto the voice of my cry, my King, and my God, for unto Thee will I pray...."

Margerite let the words of the psalm wash through her like a great river, cleansing her even as she joined in with her heart. "I will come into Thy house in the multitude of Thy mercy: and in Thy fear will I worship towards Thy holy temple. Lead me, O Lord, in Thy righteousness because of mine enemies; make Thy way straight before my face...let all those that put their trust in Thee rejoice: let them ever shout for joy, because Thou defendest them: let them also that love Thy name be joyous in Thee. For Thou, Lord, wilt bless the righteous; with favour wilt Thou compass him as with a shield. Amen."

Father Etienne put his hand on Margerite's shoulder, his touch tingling through her body. "Lie down," he said, and even those simple words seemed to resonate with power. "In this holy place, there is no need for us to set wards, for nothing that is not of God can pass here."

Obediently, Margerite lay down, her head towards the altar. Although the floor was hard polished wood, it seemed to her almost as if she were sinking into a featherbed, so comfortable and natural did it feel to her.

"Close your eyes," Etienne ordered, and she did. "They that wait upon the Lord shall renew their strength; they shall mount up with wings as eagles..." As he spoke, Margerite felt herself slipping free, her wings bearing her upwards from her flesh, into the sharp cold brilliance of the starlit night. Below, the wooded hills rose and swept away into darkness; the little village near the monastery slept silently, its coals banked and its labour stilled. A single dog barked, as if to announce her passing, but it went unheeded.

Father Etienne's voice whispered to Margerite through the wind, soft and firm. "Margerite, can you hear me? Do you fly?"

It seemed to Margerite then that she could almost sense her body, lying below in the warmth of the Abbot's sanctuary; that she could almost feel her lips moving, hear her own answering whisper, "I hear you. I fly. "Yet that was far behind her, distant as a forgotten dream: what was real was the ruffling of her pinions, the tilting of her wings and the swift beating of her hot falcon heart within her feathered breast.

"Northward, Margerite," Etienne's murmur commanded her."Fly northward; seek out Bertram - and fly carefully, for you are not the only one who can ride the air by night."

Margerite sped northward, arrowing through the chill sky. She could see the road beneath her, a black track cutting through the dark trees. Here and there a tiny fire glimmered, but she knew they were not what she sought. Now she passed over a larger town; now she saw the turreted bulk of Schloss Niederwald looming up before her, and banked sharply left.

Always Etienne was whispering to her; always she had the faint sense of her own soft answers, but they were meaningless as the buzzing of flies against a windowpane. She was over the game park now: the paths that led through it were not the tangled, bush-grown tracks of a natural woodland, but clear and straight, smoothed for horses and trimmed back.

Far to its edge, she could see the smaller road leading around it; she could see a gamekeeper's house, but not the one she sought...farther to the north and east, there...

Margerite opened her hooked beak in a harsh scream. Below was the house where Bertram lay; and there, squatting on the roof-peak, was a great owl, her wings outspread and her huge orange eyes shining cold in the light of the waning moon.

Even from so far above, Margerite could feel the power beating out from her like heat from a fire, shimmering against the blackness; she could feel the owl's fierce call, its echo stirring in her own feathered loins, and a wild anger rose in her. Bertram was hers; this female should not have him!

"No, Margerite!" Etienne called. "Margerite, come back. I command you..."

But Margerite had already folded her wings, plummeting down through the tearing air with her talons outstretched to strike. If the owl had not twisted to the side in the last moment, Margerite would have had her; but as it was, she only tore a deep score down one wing.

The owl turned, tearing with talons and beak, her burning wings beating at Margerite. Half-blinded by the fury of her foe's attack, Margerite fought back as best she could, and broke away at last, beating her wings frantically to gain height for a second stoop. The owl followed, rising silently after her; but Margerite could see that her adversary's flight was laboured and limping, hampered by her wounded wing.

"Margerite! In the name of Christ and God and the Virgin Maria, I command you: come back!"

Margerite screamed in frustration; for although one of her own wings ached like fire with each beat, she wanted nothing more than to strike again. But she was already fleeing, speeding back through the night; and even slowed by wounds as Margerite was, the owl could not match the peregrine's speed.

Margerite opened her eyes, gasping under the shock of the cold water splashing over her mouth. Father Etienne was stooping over her, his face tight with anger and fists clenched about the pitcher in his hand. "What did you think you were doing?" he asked, his voice shaking. "Did I not warn you to be careful? You might have died there; and now she knows that she has a foe."

All the exultation had drained from Margerite, as though the cold water on her face had quenched it utterly. She was shaking, and there was a fierce pain in her right shoulder where the blows of the owl's wings had wrenched her own; other gashes stung along her legs and arms, and she could feel warm blood trickling from a scrape above her left breast.

"I am sorry, Father," Margerite said, her voice very small. "I saw her there, and..."

"And you let your falcon-nature take over," Etienne said coldly. "Did you do her any harm?"

"I know that I tore her wing, but she could still fly, though not as well."

"You will have to be greatly on your guard hereafter. You are not to fly out again, for she will undoubtedly be watching for you after this; and we shall have to take much care that she cannot seek you out. Do you understand? You have gone out of your way to gain the enmity of a Princess of the Order for yourself, for she will not forgive you for that blow."

"Do you think...do you think she knows who I am?" Margerite asked. Her voice was trembling now; soon, she knew, the quaver would lengthen, and then she would burst into tears. She had often seen how men, even with small wounds, might collapse after a hard fight, and wondered at them; now she understood, for she knew that if she stood, her legs would fall again beneath her.

"She knows that she was assailed by a peregrine. As to who it may have been - your name might come to mind, for she is high enough in the Order to know of you. At least, praise God, she has never seen you in the flesh, so if you are well-warded enough, she should not recognise you; and if Nikolaus is wise, he will try to hide your departure from the Order until he knows where you are."

"Father, I am sorry," Margerite repeated. She pressed her hand to the wet pain in her breast; the black silk did not show it, but her palm was smeared with red when she drew it away.

"Let us hope that you have learned this lesson well, for it may have a harsh cost," the priest said with no pity in his voice. He took Margerite's hand, about to help her up, then drew in his breath. "She did scathe you badly. We shall have to go to the infirmary. It is as well that Brother Boniface is an old man, who sleeps deeply at night, for he knows little of what I do, and I should hate to have to explain to him how you came to be wounded. Can you walk?"

With Father Etienne's help, Margerite straightened up, wrapping her arm about the priest's slender waist and leaning heavily on him. As they stepped outside, she was grateful for the warmth of his body against hers, for the least whisper of breeze tore through the thin silk as if it were nothing, chilling her so that her teeth chattered and her limbs were ready to give way with shivering. The monastery's infirmary was warm, heated by a small stove in the corner.

As Margerite's eyes adjusted to the dim light of the single candle Father Etienne had lit, she saw bunches of herbs hanging on drying racks and shelves with long rows of clay jars labelled in neat Latin script. There was a bed against the wall, and a small table with a heavy stone mortar and pestle on it; the walls below the shelves were lined with chests, and a large bucket of water stood in the corner beside a stack of iron pots.

"Sit on that bed there," the priest instructed Margerite. "I know this room better than I would like, and I doubt Brother Boniface has changed much since I was last here." Etienne filled a small pot with water and put it on the stove to boil. "Now, take off your robe and let me see your wounds."

Margerite froze, sure that the priest could not have asked what she thought she had heard.

"Take off your robe!" Etienne repeated, his whisper sharp and impatient. "I cannot bandage you unless I can see where you are hurt."

Biting her lip and flushing, Margerite bent to take the hem of the silken garment and pull it up. Her wrenched shoulder stabbed sharply at her, and she gasped.

"Let me help you," Etienne said. Margerite sat very still as the priest carefully stripped the robe from her, leaving her naked in the light. She found that she could not look him in the face, sitting with her eyes modestly averted and her hands covering her sex.

Father Etienne, however, seemed to take no notice of her body; she might have been a piece of stone under a sculptor's chisel as he neatly dabbed the blood away from her scratches, pressing a cloth to the deep beak-gouge above her breast until it stopped bleeding. His deft fingers prodded at Margerite's sore shoulder until she winced, and he nodded, strapping bandages tightly around it.

"You came out very lightly from that battle. Did you know that wounds taken in your falcon-shape will show themselves upon your flesh as well, and that if you die in your dreams of flight, you will die in truth?"

Margerite nodded, shamefaced. The priest helped her to put her robe back on, then carefully measured spoonfuls from several of the clay jars into the boiling water, covering the pot and setting it aside to steep.

"You shall have a painful ride for the next few days, and you deserve it. But, for all of that, you did find most of what you went out to see. I now know the best road to take, and how to reach the gamekeeper's house - and I believe," he added, his voice dry as the edge of a good knife, "that we now have clear proof that Bertram is still there, and that Ortlieb has more in mind than simply catching and executing him. Perilous as that is to Bertram, it may work to our advantage, if he has the strength to hold out against her; for the more elaborate her plan, the longer it will take and the likelier it is that she will catch herself in her own snares."

After Margerite had obediently drunk Father Etienne's herbal preparation, the priest led her back to her own room, where Kobolt promptly sprang upon her, purring anxiously and licking at her face. "Sleep now, for we ride out early in the morning."

As Father Etienne had promised, the next day's ride was agony for Margerite. Smooth-gaited as her gray gelding was, each of its hoofbeats jarred through her strapped shoulder until she bit her lip against the pain, but she did not dare protest or call for a rest, for she knew that she had brought it on herself. The best she could do was ask Eva to carry Wolfram for her, which the girl was glad enough to do.

And yet, Margerite thought rebelliously, should I see Bertram assailed so again, I should do the same once more: I could not leave him to her.

It was three days' ride before they came in sight of the town Margerite had seen in her flight, and there Father Etienne ordered them to turn off the main road, riding eastward. They skirted a wide expanse of farmland, the headless brown stalks of shorn grain rustling beneath gusts of cold wind, then turned northward, riding around the edge of a wood. Now and again, they passed by the edge of a wide smooth trail - a trail such as a party of hunters could ride down easily, the ladies together with their lords.

"My father has such a game-park," Georg said. "Although his is much smaller, I will grant. He spoke often of the pleasant hunt he had in Schloss Niederwald's park when he visited as a squire."

Margerite kept her own counsel at this, for she did not see what sport there was in riding along neatly kept pathways to shoot at game that was watched and tended and driven along an expected trail. She much preferred the careful poring over tracks and fewmets, followed by the wild ride after a quarry that might as easily elude the hunters as not. True, Ruprecht had known every trail through his own woods, had watched jealously after his own deer - but he had not sought to tame the forest for his pleasure, only to take his hunter's place in it, as much a part of the wilderness as the wolf or raptor-bird.

There was much that was good in him, she thought, surprised at herself - and then, with a shudder, and that may be the part of him that lives yet. She could not help glancing at Wolfram, tucked neatly against Eva's shoulder in his sling of blankets. The child was staring bright-eyed into the trees, seemingly intent on every rustle, every movement of the twigs and red-gold oak leaves. We are far from Burg Falkenstein, Margerite reminded herself again. But when a raven launched itself heavy and black from a branch, a shower of acorns and ruddy leaves falling down where it had been, she could not help starting and staring anxiously after its flight.

"This way," Father Etienne said, reining his horse around to turn down a trail that, to Margerite's human eyes, seemed no different from any of the others they had passed. Despite her earlier thoughts, Margerite could not help enjoying the ride - the gnarled trunks of the great oaks lining the trail, the blaze of red and gold and brown above their heads, the rich smell of the autumn leaf-mould and the occasional sound of acorns pattering down through the branches. Once a doe crossed their trail, her ruddy coat bright in the sunlight; she turned her head, delicate ears pricking and velvet nostrils widening to catch their scent, and then was gone in a single leap, twisting in between the trees.

Etienne led them through the trackways with a surety that amazed Margerite: she had seen them from above herself, and could not have followed them as he did. Twilight was just falling upon the wood, the tree-trunks darkening and leaf-brightness fading in the grayness, when they came to the two-storied house that Margerite recognised at once - the neatly whitewashed front and peaked thatch, the small windows on the upper floor and larger ones on the lower, and something else, that she could not name but that she recognised as she would know the sight of her own face reflected ghostly on a glass pane looking into the night.

"This is it," she said softly to the priest. Etienne nodded and dismounted, and the rest of them followed suit. Georg held the horses' reins; Father Etienne and Margerite walked to the door, and the priest knocked loudly on it.

In a few moments, the door opened. The man behind it was in his late middle years, short and heavily built, with a thatch of blond hair that was thinning on top and a neat blond beard. He wore a green tunic and brown breeches, and a little bronze horn hung about his neck; on his left hip rested a knife nearly long enough to be a short sword, and a smaller dagger on his right. His pleasant broad features smoothed into a smile as his gray eyes quickly took in Father Etienne's cassock and canon's rolled hat.

"Greetings, Father," he said. "What brings you to my door? Do you need guidance up to the Schloss?"

"Not yet," Etienne replied smoothly. "Rather, we would stay with you this night, for we have travelled far and are weary."

The gamekeeper frowned. "Father, I would gladly give you my hospitality, but I fear that there is no room in this house for you to sleep. I can promise you that the ride up to the Schloss is easy, even at night, and I will bring lanterns to guide you."

Father Etienne tilted his head back, looking up at the house. "This is surely a large enough dwelling to put up a few guests, and we have stayed in worse on the road. Can it be that your house is already occupied by others?"

The man started back like a buck roused from his bed by the baying of dogs. "Father, no! I have lived here alone since my apprentice Peter died of a fever last year; there is no one but myself here. And there are no beds, nor linens, save my own, and hardly enough food for one. I would be ashamed to offer you my house for the night, however much it might please me to do as you ask."

Etienne laughed. "Good gamekeeper, let us pray most fervently that you are never questioned by anyone that means you ill. We know the man who is hiding in your upper chambers, and we have come to bring him aid; indeed, without our help, he has little chance of winning what is his own."

The gamekeeper stared at Etienne for a few moments, his stocky body poised. Margerite did not know whether he was about to leap at the priest or run, and behind her, she heard the soft noise of Georg's sword sliding in its sheath. Then the gamekeeper sank to his knees before Etienne, his shoulders shaking. "Thanks be to Christ that you have come, Father! If you are truly his friend, thanks to Christ and St. Hubert that you are here!"

Etienne reached down, pulling the man to his feet. "Hush. Let us not speak of these things out here. Georg, you may tether the horses outside for the night: I think thieves are the last danger we must fear in this wood."

The gamekeeper stood aside, gesturing them in. "Welcome to my house. I am Lothar, head gamekeeper of Schloss Niederwald, and I greet you in the name of our true Landgraf."

Lothar's house was well-appointed, if small, with a heated Stube between kitchen and bedroom where the gamekeeper could sit and work on cold evenings. Clean reeds were heaped on the sitting-room's floor; a long bow leaned against the wall beside a quiver of brown-fletched arrows, and on the table was another half-fletched arrow beside a pot of glue, a small knife, and a neatly sliced feather. A large mastiff lounged beneath the table, but did not get up when Lothar led his guests in, only rolled its eyes and thumped its gray tail against the wooden floor.

Kriemhilt leapt at once to a shelf, but Kobolt ignored the dog, sniffing about the corners instead, then deliberately walked over to the stairs and made his way up, waving his tail as if to entice Margerite to follow him. Though it was a little past time to feed him and he should have been growing fretful, Wolfram gurgled happily when Eva set him down in a corner, one small plump hand reaching out of his blankets.

"May I offer you food and drink?" the gamekeeper asked. "I had scarcely begun to make my own supper when you came upon me."

"That will be welcome," Father Etienne replied.

"Why have you not introduced us?" Margerite murmured to the priest when their host had left the room.

"Because," Etienne whispered back, "it will be better for him if he never knows your names. Say nothing of who you are or where you are from; let me do the talking until matters are more settled."

Lothar came back bearing a large wooden tray with glazed mugs of ale and platters of bread, cheese, and smoked venison. At the scent of the food, the cats leapt to their mistresses' laps, Kriemhilt standing on her hind legs to lick engagingly at Eva's chin and Kobolt reaching a paw out to the table with his claws hooked to snag a piece of meat.

"Bad cat," Margerite scolded, but she tossed a shred of venison to the floor for Kobolt to hunt among the clean reeds.

"How long have you been hiding your guest?" Father Etienne enquired, delicately slicing a thin sliver of cheese from the firm white half-round on the table.

"Father, he came to me at the end of June. I did not know him at first. I fear that I took him for a vagabond or poacher, and threatened to set Wolf on him if he did not leave at once. But he bespoke me fairly, and asked me if I remembered - his original title. I was afraid to answer, because she has listeners everywhere." Lothar crossed himself quickly and glanced up, a grim look coming over his pleasant features for a moment.

"Then he asked me if I could bring to mind a certain evening in the woods, when the deer had failed to run as I drove them, and only Herr Bernhardt's word had saved me from a whipping. I remembered it well, for that had been a sore disappointment to the old Landgraf and his guests, and if it had not been for Herr Bernhardt, the skin of my back would have paid for it.

And he said, 'Then, by Mother Maria's mercy, will you not repay that debt now? I am outlawed and hunted, but I must know this: does every man in my lands believe me guilty of the crime of which I was accused?' I looked more closely at him then, and I knew him; and I wept, for I had never believed that he could commit such a murder, and nothing has gone well here since he was forced to flee. Since then, I have kept him here with me, and when that cold-eyed knight -" Lothar crossed himself again -"came hunting him, I said only that I had driven off a vagabond who answered to his description some weeks ago."

So Gottfried found the trail, and lost it again, Margerite thought. By Christ's mercy, he is far from here and will not come back - though he is a stubborn man, and may return to the last clear track he had.

Etienne swallowed his small mouthful, dabbing at his lips with one of the gamekeeper's plain napkins. "That was well-done, Lothar. You have given your lord great service; God willing, you shall do him more. Now answer his question for me: does every man here believe him guilty, or are there those who would see him restored to his rightful place?"

"Father, there were always a few with doubts, at least among us of lesser station. We knew him to be both kind and brave, and such a murder seemed little like him. Yet the knights and high nobles believed otherwise; and in escaping he slew two knights who had been his friends since childhood, so that there would have been little mercy for him had he been captured." Lothar paused, and Margerite saw his blocky shoulders tightening as he took a deep draught of ale, wiping the foam from his blond moustache with the back of one hand.

"But that was eight years ago, and matters have changed since. The old Landgraf lost heart from that day on, and let Herr Gerhardt and that woman do as they would. Three years ago, the Death ravaged us as sorely as it had before, and since Landgraf Bertrik's death, God has no longer shown His face to these lands, and Christ and all his saints seem to be sleeping. We had great hunger this year, and it will be worse next, for the harvest was the worst in twelve years. The castle's priest no longer blesses the fields and the flocks as he always did, and among those of us who have served here long, there is fear and sorrow. I do not know how things stand with the knights of the Schloss, for I see them only at their hunting, but my cousin is in the castle guard, and he says that there are more than a few of the guardsmen who have no love for the Landgraf and his wife, and stay only because it is better than begging their bread on the road."

"And what of your guest?" Father Etienne asked, regarding the gamekeeper calmly. "Has he spoken to you of his plans?"

"Very little, Father, for he says that he fears to endanger me more than he must. I know that, not long after he arrived, he sent me with a message to have delivered at a certain inn in Schwarzenbach, but to the best of my knowledge, nothing has come back."

Father Etienne considered this for a moment as he cut a piece of venison into small bites, neatly lifting one to his mouth. "Very well," he said at last. "You may tell him to come down - and then leave us, for he was quite right to keep dangerous knowledge from you."

"At once, Father!" Lothar said, leaping to his feet and hastening up the stairs. Margerite heard the sound of muffled voices, and found that she had squeezed the bit of bread she held into a shapeless mass.

To cover her ill-manners, she popped it hastily into her mouth, but it was hard to swallow, even with the good dark beer to wash it down. Father Etienne turned his head, regarding her from beneath his arched brows, and she could almost hear his dry baritone telling her to calm herself. Like a child trying to be well-mannered at a feast, Margerite hid her hands beneath the table so that no one could see her fidget and straightened her back, but she could hardly think through the sound of her frantic heartbeat.

Lothar came down the stairs first, his heavy tread shaking the wooden runners. Bertram descended more slowly behind him. At first he was only a dark shape in the shadows above, but Margerite's heart skipped a beat painfully, for she would have known his movement anywhere, the silhouette of his wide shoulders and powerful legs and the easy way his long sword rested against his hip, as though he had never been without it.

Then Bertram's face came into view, and she wanted to weep for happiness. He had changed little since she had last seen him, the clean line of his jaw beneath the disguising tangle of black beard, his broad brow and hazel eyes... Something welled up within her that seemed too great for her slender body to hold, as though her ribs would burst asunder from its force; and yet, she also felt comforted, as though no ill could overcome her while he was there.

Bertram stopped halfway down the stairs, staring about the room in amazement. His eyes widened as they met Margerite's, and for a moment his face lit with an undisguisable stunned joy, with the light of a visionary granted, at last, the miracle he had sought. "Margerite," he whispered, and in that one rough-voiced murmur, Margerite heard all the singing of lutes, all the words that minnesingers had ever adorned love with.

The tears dropped freely from her eyes as she gazed at him, blurring all the candles in the room into golden haloes; and through that bright veil, it seemed to her that she could see the water welling up in Bertram's own eyes. She hardly noticed Lothar slipping from the room, for there was nothing else save Bertram in all the world - until Wolfram suddenly let out an ear-splitting wail, kicking his little feet against his blankets and waving one small fist wildly in the air. Margerite ran to the child, snatching him up and rocking him as he cried.

"Oh, dear," she gasped, torn between tears and laughter. "Bertram, I am sorry. I must feed him now."

"I have waited so long, I can wait a little longer," Bertram answered softly. "You will find it warm and private up there. Mine is the right-hand chamber." He came down the stairs, and though his hand did not so much as brush Margerite's, for a moment they were so close that they could have embraced simply by turning towards each other.

The chamber where Bertram had been hiding was austere as a monk's, holding only a bed and a stool with a single candle set upon it. As Margerite remembered, there was a small pane of glass set near the ceiling: she glanced uneasily at its darkening eye, thinking of the baleful glare of the owl. Wolfram's wails grew louder, his struggles more violent, and she hastened to reassure the child.

"Hush, hush, my darling," she murmured."At least this dress is easy to undo; you would be waiting longer if I had to call a maid to unlace me."

Wolfram quieted as soon as Margerite's nipple was in his mouth, sucking almost painfully at her breast, but Margerite's uneasiness did not lessen. It seemed to her as though she could still feel the owl's touch there, like the last heat lingering in the stones of a hearth after it was swept clean. I hope you still bear the mark of the wound I gave you, she thought viciously, and that it will be long before you can fly with ease again.

When Margerite came down the stairs again, Georg was asking Bertram questions, the youth's smooth tenor high and excited. "But you were standing against heavy cavalry! How did you survive?"

"Steadfastness and luck," Bertram's deeper voice replied. "If we had broken, they would have speared us from behind, and none of us would have lived; but a fixed spear or pike is the best defense against a warhorse riding at full tilt. Those of us who survived the first charge had to stand and slash at their horses and legs: the knee-joints are vulnerable, and a knight unhorsed, if he has no chance to gain his feet again - as he often will not if he falls in the thick of battle with foes about him, though he train many long hours in rolling free of his horse and leaping up again - will not have time to say his prayers before someone puts a blade through the eye-slots of his helm."

The Knappe shuddered, but his eyes were bright with excitement, and his hand patted the hilt of his sword as though he were eager to try himself in war. Margerite could not help thinking of what the Tiefensee women said about Bertram, how his training had kept their men alive in battle, and thought, Mother Maria, grant that he may do as well for Georg, should it come to it.

"There will be time for such talk between you later," Father Etienne interrupted. "A great deal of time, if I do not misunderstand matters. Now, Margerite, are you ready to take your place again?"

As if she were seating herself at her own high table, Margerite swept her skirts back and settled upon the gamekeeper's plain bench.

"Herr Bernhardt," Etienne said formally, inclining his head towards Bertram. Margerite blinked: though she had known his true name and rank for some months, and been sure of his nobility long before that, it was one thing to be aware of what Bertram had hidden, and another to hear the canon addressing him - dressed in his rough mercenary's clothes as he was, with the tangle of black beard and hair still half-hiding his face - as a lord in his own hall.

"If you will do us the courtesy of telling us what you have found out, and what your plans are, we will see how best we may aid you."

Bertram - Bernhardt, Margerite knew she must learn to think of him so - swept his hair back with both hands, looking calmly about the table; and when he spoke, his voice was clear and confident.

"Very well. As Lothar has likely told you, matters were already going ill here before my father's death, and have been worse since. I believe that most, if not all, of the knights will remain loyal to my brother Gerhardt, but the castle guard, Lothar informs me, are at worst divided. Nevertheless, it will not be easy for me to clear myself, unless I am able to prove Ortlieb for the black sorceress and traitress that she is; and to have any hope of doing so without simply being taken and executed, I will need a strong force behind me. Accordingly, I have sent for the Bear's Paw; if my letter reached them, which it should have done some time ago, they will be marching into the Thuringer Wald, there to wait until I call for them. For the sake of our old friendship, " he added, a small smile touching his lips beneath his beard, "I believe they will be willing to wait for their pay until our victory is ensured, since Paul and Jochanan, at least, have hazarded worse beside me."

"That, at least, you need not fear for, Herr Bernhardt," Father Etienne said calmly. "In my saddlebags there is a considerable quantity of silver belonging to Gräfin Margerite, which I have no doubt she will be glad to contribute to this cause."

Margerite looked at Etienne, torn between relief and a desire to shout at the priest. But it seemed to her that they were already at court, so she replied only, "I had thought that money lost irrecoverably."

"I promised Ritter Hermann that I would either see it returned to its rightful owners whenever possible, or given to the brothers at Fulda. I believe it is now in the hands of its rightful owner, and thus my oath to him is fulfilled."

Margerite neither spluttered nor laughed, though it was a great effort to keep her face straight. Instead she said gravely, "So it is, and I could not be better pleased than to use those monies in this way. But what shall follow? Bernhardt -" the name came oddly to her lips, but she heard Bertram's slight intake of breath, and knew that it must touch something within him to hear her call him by his Christian name -"do you simply mean to march in with an army of mercenaries at your back and accuse the Landgräfin von Niederwald of black magic?"

"No. We must have some proof, else a battle would bring no resolution to the matter. I mean to have my name cleared altogether, and to be known as rightful lord of these lands - not as a murderer and adventurer who conquered his brother by guile and force. It is for this that I have been waiting here: so that those within the castle who are friends to us may seek evidence against her. Best of all would be if any could find the chamber where she works her magic, for I believe that she must have one such, even as Ruprecht did."

Father Etienne nodded judiciously. "That is so. It is likely to be as well-concealed, though. One or two of her maidservants may be privy to her secrets, but if they are, they will be wholly loyal to her. And servants who are not... would have no idea of what to look for."

"But I would," Margerite said slowly.

The men stared at her in surprise. Recovering himself, Bertram - Bernhardt - said, "Margerite, have you not risked enough already, and more, in coming to me so? How can I send you in to fight my battle?"

"If it were a matter of sword and sword, would you not go to be my champion?" Margerite replied. "But this is one case where a woman can do what a man cannot, when neither bravery nor strength nor skill with a blade will avail. I can serve within Schloss Niederwald, and watch Ortlieb's comings and goings; and I have the knowledge to seek out what she keeps hidden."

"I, as well," Eva said unexpectedly.

"Is it not sufficient to risk one of us?" Margerite asked her. "You have suffered enough already from the Order, and besides..." Besides, you are a virgin, and what if Ortlieb decided to take you for her magics?

"If you were a knight, and I your Knappe, you would not bid me stay behind," Eva said, her low voice suddenly steely. "And besides, I have been a serving maid, and worse, already, and if you are to play such a part, I think you will need someone beside you who can show you how to do it. You may know how to pluck a chicken, but when did you last scrub a dish or a floor? And more to the point, when did you last lower your head and murmur, 'Yes, frowe,' meekly when your face was slapped for being too slow at your duties or for not having guessed that a call for wine meant red instead of white? There is a long way, I promise you, between even a poor knight's daughter and a servant."

"It will be a useful lesson in humility," Father Etienne added dryly, "and, no doubt, good for your soul, if you can manage to keep out of peril. Think of it, if you will, as penance for your sins."

"What about me?" Georg demanded. "Can I not take up a post within the castle as well? I am strong enough to serve as an armsman, and good with a blade."

"That is just why you cannot do such a thing," Bernhardt said patiently, and in his deep voice, Margerite could hear the echoes of many hours spent making village boys into castle guardsmen. "You are not old or sturdy enough to be chosen as a guardsman, if you were a peasant; and as for your skill with a blade, it would betray at once that you are nobly born. Believe me," he went on, a grimly rueful smile flickering over his face, "I have experienced that for myself, and not always to my good. No, I have another task for you, if you are able to fulfill it. I need someone who is able to hunt like a young nobleman and can take care of himself in the woods, who can handle a sword well enough to defend himself if he is challenged and has the sense to run if he cannot fight, and who is not afraid to deal with the rough men of a Free Company. In short, Knappe, I need you to bear messages back and forth between myself and Hauptmann Paul of the Bear's Paw, for without such a reliable messenger, we shall be hard put to it to be able to deploy them when and where they are needed. Can you do that?"

"O, yes, Herr Bernhardt!" Georg exclaimed, clasping his thin hands together and grinning like a goblin.

Well done, my love! Margerite thought. She had feared that the excitable young squire would manage to give them away, even if he had not been so terribly vulnerable to Ortlieb's magic, but Bernhardt had managed to neatly turn a liability into an asset, keeping the youth safer than he would have been in the gamekeeper's house even while satisfying his desire to show his courage. Even while undergoing the siege with him, Margerite had never had the chance to see how Ruprecht's Hauptmann managed the men under his command: now she could see clearly why they had held him in such esteem.

"And what of you, Father Etienne?" Bernhardt asked, inclining his head towards the priest. "What part do you wish to play in this?"

"I intend to pay a call upon the Bishop of Niederwald,"
Etienne replied. "It is he, as much as anyone, who will judge
the success or failure of your plan in the end, for you will not
bring the Landgräfin von Niederwald to secular justice, but
to the judgement of the Church. Further, if I am seen here,
she will be aware that her foes are pressing her hard, for she
and I are not unknown to each other."

"There is also," interrupted Margerite, "one problem left
to us. It will not be easy for Eva and I to get any position
within Schloss Niederwald. Whatever the reputation of its
mistress, everyone who works in the castle will have at least
five sisters, daughters, or nieces who want posts there. The
Landgräfin's personal attendants will likely be of gentle birth
themselves, and will at least come highly recommended, so
I see no hope of getting us work as her maidservants. But
it will not be easy even to find hire as scullery maids unless
something can be arranged within the castle."

"Let us call Lothar in now," Bernhardt said. "If anyone can
do such a thing, it is he. He has been head gamekeeper here
for many years, and he inherited that post from his father
and his grandfather before. Though he is modest about it,
he has many friends and relatives within the Schloss, and
should well be able to find places for the two of you - much
as it mislikes me," he added, his brow furrowing, "to send
you for such work."

"As Father Etienne says, it will no doubt be good for our
souls," Margerite answered, smiling at him. She longed to
reach across the table, to lay her hand on his in reassurance
- she remembered so clearly the touch of his long calloused
fingers, the hard ridges of his knuckles and the feeling of his
heartbeat at her fingertips - but she was still, Mother Maria
help her, a married woman, and would be while Heinrich
lived. And God grant he recovers, she forced herself to pray,
though it was hard, hard, with Bernhardt across the table
from her, solid and amazing as a dream made real.

They talked on for some time, and at last it was settled: Lothar was certain that he could get Margerite and Eva into the castle, and from there, it would hang upon them to find Ortlieb's sanctum or other evidence of her sorceries. The gamekeeper politely left his sitting room while Margerite told Bernhardt of why they had fled Burg Fürstensee: he listened silently, his features settling into the grim mask of anger that Margerite knew too well as she described how the demon in Christoph's flesh had threatened her.

"There will be a reckoning there when this is done," Bernhardt said, his voice soft as the sound of a sword sliding from its sheath. "If I bring a troop of knights down...if it is at your invitation..." Then he shook his shaggy head like a hound shaking off water. "But that is only a dream until I have achieved my place here. Unless..." He closed his eyes, his face whitening. Margerite could guess his thoughts: he could not bear to leave his people as they were, and yet he could not bear to hear of her driven out as she had been and offer no help.

"We must finish here first," Margerite said firmly. "You may not know the danger you are in..." Horrified at what she had almost said, she clamped her mouth shut, but Bernhardt looked at her bleakly, and for the first time since she had known him, she thought, she saw the gray of fear staining his skin.

"I have had dreams," Bernhardt said, so softly that Margerite almost could not hear him. "Mother Maria help me, I have dreamed of her..." He looked away, his big hands working helplessly in his lap.

Margerite bit her lip. She had not meant to cause him pain, or shame, but she could see both of them tearing at his face, his agony shadowed in his flesh.

Before she could think about it, she reached behind her neck, unfastening the clasp of the falcon-necklace hidden under her dress. She drew it out and stood, walking over to Bernhardt. "Wear this for me, " she said quietly. "Wear it, and never take it off; know that..." She almost said, my love, but she could not, not in front of Father Etienne. "That my prayers are keeping you safe."

Bernhardt looked down at the shining beads in his hand, bright crystal and dark garnet and amethyst, and the rich golden glow of the falcon-pendant. A look passed across his face that, beneath the shaggy black tangle of his hair and beard, Margerite could not read: was it anger? The necklace had been a gift from Ruprecht, and she wore it yet...

"A servant cannot wear such a thing, " Margerite said," and I would know that you bear a token of mine."

Bernhardt slowly fastened the necklace about his own neck, and she saw that his hands trembled on the clasp. He looked up at her and smiled sadly. "Thank you, my... Margerite. I shall be glad to bear your token in this battle."

They rose at dawn, and after a hasty breakfast, Margerite and Eva gathered their possessions into bundles and made ready to go with Lothar, who stood at the door with a bag of venison over his shoulder.

"Fare well, Margerite," Bernhardt said. "Be careful, for nothing that you may learn in my castle is worth the risk of your life."

"I shall be careful," Margerite promised him. "But I think that you have the harder part in waiting here."

Bernhardt did not deny it, only looked at her for a long moment. Margerite could see the pain in his hazel eyes, and she longed to go to him and kiss it away, but Father Etienne stood beside him, his fine-chiseled features as forbidding as those of the angel barring the gates of Eden. Unwillingly she turned away, heaving her bundle onto her back and picking up Wolfram.

From upstairs, she heard Kobolt's faint miaowing -
Etienne had expressly forbidden either Margerite or Eva
to let their cats follow them, for Ortlieb would recognise
at once that Kobolt and Kriemhilt were more than simple
animals, and the Order Princess might even know that
Margerite had a great black tomcat as a familiar: there
was no way to tell what Ruprecht, or Günther, might have
reported back before their deaths.

Margerite had no confidence that Kobolt would stay
locked up, but she had explained to him, looking most
earnestly into his wide golden eyes and feeling rather a fool
for speaking so to a cat, that he must not follow her, for both
their sakes.

A frost lay upon the leaves, its white mist dimming their
brightness; the earth of the pathway was frozen hard
beneath Margerite's feet, and a pale cloud puffed from her
mouth with each breath or word. Although the sun was full
up, its white light shone coldly through the trees, and though
the effort of walking with her bundle and her child soon
warmed Margerite's body, her nose and ears quickly became
numb.

"You remember," Lothar said softly, "you are my widowed
cousin and her sister, from Greifenstein, which is ten days'
walk east of here. What are your names?"

"Gisela," said Eva.

"Gertrude," said Margerite. A pang went through her as
she spoke the name of her dead maidservant; but surely
Gertrude would not have grudged it to her - and she would
have been amused to an unseemly degree to see her mistress
taking on the role of a serving girl. Perhaps by this I may
do penance for any wrongs I did you without knowing it,
Margerite thought, hoping that, sitting in Heaven as she
assuredly was, Gertrude could somehow see or hear her.

Lothar nodded. "We are almost out of the park now.
Gertrude, remember to keep your head down and speak only
when you are spoken to - best to keep your hood up when
you can."

Margerite lowered her eyes, trying to think what it would be like to be born to this - to follow orders and never give them, to drudge and toil in kitchen or yard and be known as lesser in everyone's sight. Already, she did not care for it; but she remembered that Bertram - Bernhardt - had lived through eight years in much worse company, and soiled his hands with worse things than dirty dishwater.

"Liutbirg the cook is a rough-tongued woman, and has grown worse since the Death took her husband three years ago," Lothar added. "But she has a soft place in her heart for me - I'd have proposed to her already, if I weren't afraid of her breaking my head in with a frying pan if we had to live together - and I do not think she will turn you away. And she is truly one of the best cooks in the Empire: even the Bishop's cook trained in her kitchen."

Odd and uncomfortable as she felt playing the peasant already, the look of awe on Margerite's face when they came out of the woodlands and into sight of the castle was genuine. Though she had seen it from the air, the huge Schloss with its many-leveled turrets and roofs and the great round spire on the northeast corner was something else when she was looking up from the ground.

It made Burg Fürstensee seem like little more than a simple fortification, while her father's castle was hardly better than a peasant's hut by comparison. Schloss Niederwald was, Margerite guessed, a full five or six stories high at its top peaks, and would hold...how many? For a moment her mind was distracted, as she tried to calculate the number of servants and guards and horses, the amount of food and wine and grain it would take to feed the castle folk for even a month.

One of the guards at the northwest entrance to the outer courtyard raised a hand in greeting to Lothar; the other one leaned, bored, against his pike.

"Good morning, Lothar!" the friendlier guard cried, leering at Eva with an engaging gap-toothed grin. "Bringing a couple of women for me, are you? I like the looks of that girl there, though I'll leave you the one with the brat."

"Shut your filthy mouth," Lothar said without rancour. "These are kinswomen of mine, come to work in the Schloss, and far too good for the likes of a guardsman who's been wearing the same stinking boots since St. Peter was a boy."

"Can't blame a man for trying," the soldier replied. "Well, come on in. It's a good time to be looking for work here - I've heard there's going to be extra help needed in the kitchen soon."

"Good news for Gertrude and Gisela," Lothar said. "What have you heard about it?"

The guardsman glanced up at the Schloss, his metal cap sliding back on his high forehead. "Nothing much. Just that she's planning one of her big feasts for All Souls' Eve - going to be inviting all sorts of high muckamucks from Meissen and all - and she wants to make a show of it with her usual scenery and pageants. If you've got any relatives who are good craftsmen, I'd say they could make a bit of money here this month. Matter of fact, if your women are worth anything with a needle, they should speak up and say so, because a big wagon came in with miles of cloth for the costumes this morning."

"I'll keep that in mind." Lothar nodded amiably. "Well, good day to you."

The outer courtyard was huge, and Margerite felt uncomfortably exposed as they walked across it, like a rabbit crossing a winter field with no cover. Although it was broad daylight, she kept expecting to feel the soft brush of an owl's wings past her head, and had to force herself not to glance up at the castle's wide windows.

They passed the Schloss church - a fine big stone building, but, Margerite could not help noticing, a trifle dilapidated, its whitewash beginning to peel and a few shingles missing from the roof - and a number of stables and barracks before they reached the inner gates. The guardsmen there greeted Lothar briefly and let them pass, and he led the women around the castle to the back.

"This is the way the servants go," Lothar said in a low voice. "You see that gate on the north side of the wall? That leads to the formal gardens, and you're not to go in there. The one down by the south leads to the kitchen gardens, which I expect you'll see a lot of."

Lothar took Eva and Margerite to a wide set of doors, leading them into a large triangular room and up a staircase into the kitchens. Three big fires burned beneath the huge windows of one room, with maids busily scurrying about stirring kettles of sauces and boiling water to scald fowl for plucking; several stone sinks were built into the walls, and other girls stood above them, scrubbing industriously at dirty pots. Lothar tapped one on the shoulder. She started, looking up at him.

"Where is Liutbirg?" he asked.

"Through there," the girl said, pointing to the right-hand door on the north wall. "But take care in disturbing her, for she is making a chessboard pastry, and is in an ill humour."

The main kitchen led into a second room with several ovens beneath the windows, large fires on the south and west walls, and a table in the middle where two maidens were furiously grinding breadcrumbs and chopping herbs. A tall, lean woman with gray-blond hair pinned up in a loose bun, wearing a stained blue dress, was striding about between the ovens and the kettles, her long nose twitching constantly as she sniffed at the shifting aromas rising from her cooking and berated her helpers.

"Lazy girl!" she shouted. "The pastry will burn in another moment if you do not have it out. God rot your bones, Gretel, if you let another cream sauce clot, I'll pour it over your head. Where are the pancakes? Have you looked at them - well, give them the time it takes to say two Paternosters and look at them again. Take that pot away from the flame, you fool; do you want everything to taste of smoke?"

Margerite drew a deep breath. She did not know how anyone could be angry in a room filled with such beautiful scents of cooking - the clean richness of pastry, the subtly herbed smells of the sauces rising and mingling together, and beneath them the mouthwatering note of good pork, with the sweet applewood smoke penetrating everything.

But red spots of fury gleamed beneath the fine gloss of sweat on the cook's knobbly cheekbones as she clouted aside the girl who was pulling a large square pastry out of the biggest oven, hurrying to the table with it herself and hovering fiercely above it with a scowl on her face.

"There is but a heartbeat between an underdone pastry and one that is too brown, and you have missed it," she declared fiercely, glaring at the unfortunate maid. "Have you no sense of smell at all?" To Margerite, the pastry looked beautiful, puffy and nicely golden; she would have admired it as a work of art in itself back at Burg Fürstensee. But the cook whirled up again, dashing from fire to fire to taste the sauces simmering there and berate the women tending them. "Stir faster, there...More parsley in that, it should be green, not snot-yellow. Liese, where are those pancakes?" In her hurry, she almost ran straight into Lothar, who stood calmly, looking straight into her face.

"Lothar! Satan curse your black arse, what are you doing in here? If you have meat for me, leave it and get out before your face makes my sauces curdle."

"Charming and well-tempered as ever, Liutbirg. What would you say to tender saddles of roebuck for the gentry?"

"Well enough," Liutbirg allowed, peering suspiciously at him through the strands of gray-blond hair that had fallen over her face. She sniffed the air again and turned her head, shouting, "The pork, Kunigunde! Now, what do you want from me?"

"I want you to give my cousin and her sister a place working here," Lothar said bluntly.

Liutbirg snorted. "Here? Two peasant women, who probably barely know how to chop an onion? And one of them with a suckling brat at her breast, as well? You must be mad, Lothar. By the Body of God, Liese! Do I need to touch you up with the whip? Kunigunde, I want that pork on the table, now!" She turned away from Lothar, striding to the table and sitting down before the pastry.

Drawing her knife, she took one of the pancakes that the unfortunate Liese had brought over and began to trim it into a neat square. "Must I hold your hand every moment, Kunigunde? Start mixing the colours into the pork: red, black, blue, green, and gold - and move that cream sauce to the cool side of the hearth, Gretel!"

Margerite watched in fascination as Kunigunde's delicate fingers flew, dividing the steaming heap of ground pork into several bowls and mixing in breadcrumbs and strong colours. She knew that blue could be gotten from columbine blossoms crushed in honey, and green from parsley and many other herbs; but she had not thought that rose petals alone could yield so strong a red, and it would take a good weight of saffron to make such a bright gold.

As Kunigunde finished each batch, she passed it over to Liutbirg, who carefully filled a pancake with some of the meat and folded up the corners, pressing the sides of each neatly against the next so that a brilliantly multicoloured chessboard slowly took shape. Watching the cook's artistry, Margerite felt quite daunted: she knew well enough how to gild a chicken with egg yolk or to make a sharp sauce with verjuice for livening the taste of fish during Lent, but this complexity was quite beyond her.

"You still need servants to stoke the fires, draw water, and wash dishes," Lothar continued, unruffled as if he were waiting beside the path for a skittish doe."Gertrude and Gisela are quick to learn, bright girls..."

"Not if they're related to you," Liutbirg snapped. She paused a moment in her work, watery blue eyes poring over Margerite and Eva. "I'll grant they look presentable enough; if they can learn manners, they might clean up well enough to help serve. You, girl! - no, the skinny one."

It took a moment for Margerite to realize that the cook was talking to her, and a moment more to keep herself from snapping back. Instead, she forced herself to lower her eyes meekly and say, "Yes, frowe?"

"Are you Gertrude or Gisela?"

"Gertrude, frowe."

"Can you recognise any herbs beside sage and thyme?"

"I helped the midwife at home in Greifenstein, frowe," Margerite answered.

Liutbirg nodded sharply. "Get out to the kitchen garden and see what lived through last night's frost. I'm sure the fennel stalks were blasted, but their bulbs may still be sound: take one of the baskets and bring them in. And dig me up a good bunch of carrots and four onions while you're at it; you'll find the fork on the wall by the staircase. You can leave the brat on the straw in the corner there, he'll be safe enough. You, Gisela - you look strong enough. Get one of the guards to show you where the well is, and start hauling up water, because there's going to be Lucifer's own lot of washing in a short while. As for you, Lothar, I hope the livers are in there with the saddles."

"Right on top, my dear," the gamekeeper said. "Clean and lovely, with not a drop of gall on them, unlike your tongue." He patted her. on the shoulder and grinned. The cook snorted, brushing at her dress where he had touched her.

"Keep your hands off me, you grimy poacher," Liutbirg said, though she could not hold back a grudging smile.

Margerite found the fork easily enough, and hurried down the stairs. Where the sun shone, the frost had melted, although a white crust still lay over the hard-packed brown earth beneath the shadow of the walls. No guard stood by the entrance to the kitchen garden, and she slowed a moment to look around. The kitchen plot was to the left; to the right was a broad avenue of apple and pear trees, a few of them still bearing bright golden and red fruit among their browning leaves.

Before her were two fenced enclosures: one holding what looked like plum, cherry, and quince trees, though the fruit had all been picked by this time; the other a grove of nut trees, chiefly almond, hazel, and walnut, though two tall chestnut trees spread their limbs at either side of the nuttery. As she had been commanded, Margerite took stock of the kitchen herb garden, though there was little enough that had not been blasted by the frost.

A few hardy thyme shoots showed green beneath the black stalks, and the low bushes of winter savory had barely been scathed, but the rosemary leaves were already darkening, and the more delicate plants, the frothy fronds of chervil and dill, coriander and parsley, slumped brown and dead over the ground. As she had been ordered, Margerite knelt beside the remains of the fennel to dig the bulbs out of the icy earth.

By the time she had finished that, Margerite's hands were cracked and bleeding, although they were so numb with cold that she hardly felt the pain. Wearily she straightened, her back aching as it had not since her last weeks of pregnancy, and went over to the row of carrots.

The first three she tried to dig broke off halfway down, and she put her fork straight through the fourth one, but after that she was more careful with them. Moving over to the onions next, Margerite looked down at her hands in disgust. The dirt was grimed into them as if she had been digging in the earth all her life; her carefully-tended nails were black-rimmed and broken.

At last Margerite was able to pick up her basket and carry it up to the kitchen again, though she was already as weary as she would have been at the end of a long day. In the first kitchen-room, Eva stood above one of the sinks, scrubbing diligently at an iron pot and humming beneath her breath, the very picture of a plump and pretty village girl who was delighted to be working at the castle. Margerite pushed a few strands of hair back from her forehead with a filthy hand, trying her best not to glare at her companion.

"That took you long enough," Liutbirg snapped when Margerite brought the vegetables in. "You think because you're Lothar's cousin, you can get away with daydreaming all day? That won't last long, my girl. Now, tell me what the garden looks like."

Like a kitchen garden after a frost in the middle of September, Margerite thought. What did you expect, you bad-tempered old shrew? But she answered meekly. "Frowe, most of the plants are dead already. The winter savoury is alive, and..."

Liutbirg nodded sharply when she was done. "So you can recognise herbs, all right. Go draw up some water and wash the mud off yourself, and your dress too; I won't have dirty scullery maids, even if you did always go straight from field to kitchen at home. Then you can come back and join Gisela in scrubbing pots."

Margerite hurried away before her own tongue could betray her. Hauling a heavy bucket of water up the stairs, trying to ignore the cold splashes that soaked the hem of her skirt, she realized not only how sore she was getting, but how hungry she was. She had eaten nothing since leaving Lothar's cottage at dawn, and the scents of food that had seemed so beautiful at first were getting inside her now, tearing at her belly and making her mouth water with every breath.

"When do we eat?" Margerite asked Eva quietly, scrubbing the mud from her cold-numbed fingers in the bucket with harsh angry strokes.

"When the scraps come back from the high table, we might get some if there's enough left over and the other maids don't eat it all," Eva whispered back. "And there will be our allowance of bread and beans and small beer as soon as our work is done. But Gretel says that this is the best job in the castle, because even the scullery maids get the leavings from the pots. She says not to even think about stealing food while it's cooking, though, because Liutbirg has a heavy hand with the rod and won't hesitate to use it."

One of the other serving maids came through and thrust an iron pot into Margerite's hands. She looked down at it in bewilderment: it had held some sort of thick sauce, which was crusted heavily at the bottom.

"Go on and lick it out before you clean it," Eva hissed. Horrified, Margerite stared at the pot. But she was so dreadfully hungry...Self-consciously, she dipped a finger into the pot, scraping up some of the sauce, and sucked it off. It tasted delicious, of herbs and cream and eggs, and, though she could hardly believe she was doing it, she fell to greedily, only stopping when she could scrape no more out.

"Now pour some hot water in and scrub," Eva whispered. "The water will loosen what's left - if you were really hungry, you'd drink it too. At least they feed us too well here for that."

The hot water stung the scrapes on Margerite's hands, and the burnt crust on the pot lodged painfully under her nails, but she laboured doggedly until it was clean - only to look up and see several more dirty pans stacked beside her, and a nearly equal number of clean ones by Eva.

She nearly burst out in tears then: only the thought of looking Bernhardt and Father Etienne in the face and admitting that she could not do what she had said she would because she was too weak to hold up under the work of a scullery maid made her pick up the next one and grimly begin to scrub it. But o, my love, I would not do this for anyone but you! she thought.

When the women were well-gone, Father Etienne saddled up his horse, rubbing behind one ear for a moment as it nuzzled him and whickered softly to him. He had ridden the black stallion for near to twelve years, and they understood each other well. The steed was no more a warhorse than his rider was a knight; but like Etienne, the horse came from a warrior line, and like the priest, he could defend himself well enough in a pinch - and if he was not as spirited as the stallions knights delighted in, his temperament was more suited to Etienne's needs, for there was very little on this earth or out of it, from the thunder of guns to the soul-chilling cold of unquiet spirits, that could unnerve him.

Georg hauled out his baggage to load onto the packhorse, which, to his credit, the boy did neatly enough. He would be a good Knappe to Christoph, if Heinrich's elder son could be freed of the spirit tormenting him. Etienne frowned: knowing that the merry-tempered young knight suffered in the grip of a demon distressed him more than he had been willing to show to his companions, for his duties within the Church included that of exorcist, and he knew, far better than any of them did, what it meant for a man to be thus enslaved to a creature of Hell.

But he had made the decision to go to Bernhardt, and he could not waver from it now, lest both men be lost. But *did I choose this pathway out of pride, because I had erred before?* Etienne wondered, tightening his horse's girth with a soft grunt. Out of consideration for Bernhardt's privacy and pain, he had not pressed the man in his Confession back at Burg Falkenstein: he had accepted the statement of an old sin, and not forced the woman's name or the circumstances out of the warrior who knelt before him with tears in his eyes.

If he had done so then, he might have been able to free Bernhardt from Ortlieb's touch, or at least to warn him, to be sure that the exile would do nothing rash - such as he had done now. Because of that, Etienne knew too well that Bernhardt's present peril was at least partly his own fault - and knew that he, Etienne, was bound to make it good or die in the attempt.

And that is pride, Etienne, the priest reminded himself, slipping the bridle over his horse's head. The black stallion opened his mouth docilely for the bit, making no protest as Etienne settled the metal behind his teeth. Let this be to the greater glory of God, then; let Him forgive me my errors, and prove that in His great design, He can turn the worst evil to the service of good.

Otherwise, if Etienne careered, as he feared greatly that he had done, from mistake to mistake, leaving one flank unguarded in his hasty effort to cover the other, it would surely be Satan's victory.

You counselled Margerite against pride and despair. Keep your own counsel, priest, Father Etienne said to himself. To Georg, he said, "Well-done, Knappe, and my thanks. Bring my greetings with you to the Bear's Paw Company when you see them; I think Paul and Jochanan should remember me."

Georg stared up at Etienne, his eyes wide. "How does a priest come to know the leaders of a Free Company, Father?" he asked."My father says that the Free Companies are all excommunicates who ought to be hanged."

"Excommunicates no longer, since the Pope called them to Crusade," Etienne reminded the redheaded boy gently. "As for whether they ought to be hanged, remember that Christ ate with publicans and sinners. No doubt there are many evil men in the Companies, and some bands are worse than others: but evil men, and good, may be found everywhere."

"Even in the Order of the Light-Bearers, Father?" Georg's mellow tenor sounded innocent, but there was something about his grin that warned Etienne that the boy was playing with him. He decided to reply truthfully, and hope that Georg would take the lesson to heart.

"Even there, some of the members are true and honourable, though they serve an evil Master. I have known several such, and pray still for their souls. Others delight in evil and power for their own sakes, and are bound by nothing save the limits of their own strength. And it will be worthwhile for you to keep in mind," Etienne replied sternly, "that the Landgräfin von Niederwald is one such. I pray that you will not meet her, but if you do, try not to let yourself be deceived by her beauty and soft words."

"Is she truly beautiful, Father?"

"Perhaps you should think of her as a poisoned sweetmeat. Gräfin Margerite is far more beautiful, for the truth of her soul and her bravery."

Georg frowned. "Margerite is an old woman with a baby. Eva is beautiful," he added unexpectedly.

Etienne could not help laughing at him: the boy's thoughts were so transparent, and he blurted them out so readily! He reminded Etienne a little of his own three older brothers, lively and noisy as a litter of puppies, with not a thought in their heads besides war, women, and wine.

"Margerite is hardly three years older than you," he pointed out to Georg. "As for Eva - if you have occasion to make Confession concerning her, or anything else, you had best do it now, since I do not expect to be back for some days, and you may well be among the men of the Bear's Paw by then."

The priest was little surprised when Georg dropped to his knees before him, for the boy had lately seen enough to shake the souls of many stronger men - and he would have been twelve when the Death came back, old enough to have learned swiftly how fragile life was, and how unpredictable its passing. And for all his bravery, it was no easy thing for a gently reared youth to be sent alone to deal with a Free Company.

"Father," Georg breathed, "forgive me, for I have sinned..."

The palace of the Bishop of Niederwald was a fine building: Etienne had guested in better, even to the Pope's dwelling in Avignon, but he had also seen many lesser episcopal palaces. Its grounds were carefully tended, the grass mown into a velvety green carpet and the lanes lined with great oak-trees whose falling leaves were raked into neat heaps at their bases. The servants in the stables were polite and efficient, taking the reins of Etienne's horses and leading them away without question: the priest knew that his saddlebags would be delivered to his rooms as soon as quarters were offered him. Two guards stood at the door of the palace: they lifted their spears, saluting him precisely.

"Greetings, Father," one of them said. "May I ask your errand here?"

"Out of courtesy, because I was travelling this way, I would guest with his Grace for a time."

"His Grace's secretary is down the corridor, third door on the right. Enter and be welcome, in the name of Christ."

Stained-glass windows lined the corridor, the crisp autumn sunshine glowing colourfully through their bright depictions of scenes from the lives of the saints. Etienne knocked once on the secretary's door, and it was only a few minutes before a sharp voice called out, "Enter."

The Bishop's secretary, Father Kunibert, was a small man in clerical garb, sitting behind a massive desk carved with pictures of the twelve Disciples on its side-panels. The last time Etienne had seen him, his hair had been thinning; now his bald skull shone brightly in the light from the window over his desk.

He wore a pair of gold-rimmed spectacles, something even Etienne did not see often - though, in truth, as the priest grew older and his head ached more easily from reading in candlelight, he sometimes wondered if he should see to having a pair ground out for himself. Yet he had suffered from that affliction since childhood, and had little time to waste on such trivial matters.

"Greetings, Canon," the secretary said. "How may I assist you?"

Etienne repeated what he had told the guard. Father Kunibert pushed his spectacles up on his nose, the sunlight glaring brightly from the two rounds of glass. "You are... Father Etienne, yes. It has been a long time since you have stopped here. I trust that you are in good health and have fared well since we saw you last?"

"I am, indeed, and I thank you, Father Kunibert," Etienne replied.

Father Kunibert looked down at his desk, shuffling a few pieces of parchment. "His Grace is occupied this afternoon, but no doubt he will be glad to have you take the evening meal with him. I shall arrange for a suite of rooms to be made available for you - will one in the west wing be suitable? I remember that you preferred evening light to morning."

"That is kind of you, Father."

"Can you tell me how long you mean to stay with us? Your company is always welcome, of course."

Etienne shook his head. "I am not certain. Perhaps a week; it is unlikely to be more than two."

The secretary nodded and pushed his spectacles up again. "Is there anyone else with whom you would like to speak while you are here? The diocesan exorcist, Father Thomas, is currently in residence, and I assume you will have much to talk about with him, as I believe your duties overlap somewhat?"

"I shall, indeed. Thank you, Father Kunibert. Your care does his Grace great credit."

The secretary lowered his gaze slightly. "Deo gratia,"
he murmured modestly. "If you would care to wait in the
library - do you remember how to find it? Good; I hope
that will occupy you pleasantly while your rooms are being
readied. You will want a bath after your travels, of course?
Good, good. It is a pleasure to have you with us again, Father
Etienne."

Bishop Otto's library had grown since Etienne's last visit:
though always well-stocked with theological texts and a few
gem-studded books of secular poetry - for the Bishop was
not above occasionally indulging himself or his guests with
readings from Nibelungenlied or Rabensschlacht at dinner
- Etienne was pleased to see that he had added several
volumes dealing with the finer points of canon law, books
which would not go amiss if matters worked out as they had
planned.

Aside from the young man in a monastic habit carefully
dusting each finely embossed cover, there was only one
other reader in the library: an old, gray-haired man whose
right leg was stretched out stiffly in front of him and whose
wooden crutch leaned against the table where he sat,
wearing the white-crossed black tabard of a Teutonic Knight
above his chainmail and half-plate armour.

His bushy brows were drawn close as his finger traced
the line he was reading, his lips moving slowly, and Etienne
could hear him whispering as though he were clumsily
translating Latin into German. As Etienne passed him, he
looked up, nodding.

"Good afternoon, Father," he rasped in a voice worn harsh
by many years of shouting over the noise of the battlefield.

"Good afternoon, Brother," Etienne greeted him politely.

"Are you new here? Father Kunibert should have told me."

"A guest only, Brother. And you are...?"

"Sorry for being rude, Father. I am the commander of the
guard here - Brother Sigvrit, at your service. Excuse me for
not rising, but my leg won't take it easily."

"There is no excuse needed for a wound taken honourably in Christ's service, Brother," Father Etienne assured him. Because he was curious - it was both a goad set against his mind by God and a besetting sin - he glanced at what the Teutonic Knight was reading, and was pleased to see the familiar words of St. Bernard of Clairveaux on the New Knighthood: a fitting text to occupy the mind of a warrior-monk.

"True, but good of you to say it, Father. I was wounded fighting two years ago, keeping down the damned - excuse me, Father, but many of them are still heathen, you know - Lithuanians. I could have stayed around bothering the fit and healthy brothers, but there are plenty of old cripples in the Order already, so I volunteered to come and whip his Grace's guard into something like military shape. So now you know what I'm doing here." Sigvrit paused, bright blue eyes looking expectantly up at Etienne.

A fair-haired youth entered the room at that point, bearing a platter with a pitcher of wine, a goblet, and a selection of small cakes. "Something to refresh yourself with while you wait, Father," he said softly, laying it upon the table, bowing, and withdrawing. Etienne sat down gracefully, realizing with some slight embarassment that he had no cup to offer Brother Sigvrit. But the Teutonic Knight hauled up a battered pewter cup that hung on a chain at his belt, unhooking it and setting it on the table.

Etienne poured for him first, then for himself, rolling a mouthful of the sweet golden wine thoughtfully over his tongue before swallowing. For German wine, it was quite good, although he often longed for the dry full-bodied vintages of Dion. Brother Sigvrit drank like an old campaigner, hasty gulps that let a few drops fall into his bushy gray beard.

"I am only visiting his Grace for a time," Etienne said. "I have business nearby, and thought it would be discourteous of me to pass without calling upon him, since I had enjoyed his hospitality before."

Sigvrit nodded, breaking one of the small flaky pastries in two and swallowing the bites whole. "Business at the Schloss?" he asked.

Etienne paused to think, buying himself a few moments by biting into a cake and chewing it carefully. As he might have expected of the Bishop's kitchen, it was very good, the rich buttery crust concealing a mixture of chopped nuts and raisins with a strong hint of cinnamon. More than a few among the Teutonic Knights were known to Etienne, colleagues of his in the war against the Order. Sigvrit was not one of them, nor did Etienne think that he was ready to confide in the old warrior-monk...yet it would be interesting to see what he knew.

"I may visit there on my way," the priest said slowly.

Sigvrit leaned closer, his voice sinking to a quiet rasp like a file on soft wood. "Something to do with the new Landgräfin?"

"Have you heard much of her?" Etienne asked, leaning back easily with his goblet in his hand.

The Teutonic Knight turned his head as if about to spit, then remembered where he was and hastily crossed himself.

"Saw her when Landgraf Bertrik got buried and Landgraf Gerhardt took his title. They had a big feast up there at the Schloss, with dancing and singing and costumes and all. Reminded me why I took Orders in the first place. You'd think when a man's father had just died, it would make him give some thought to his own soul, wouldn't you? And there she was, sleek as a cat in the cream and all done up like Jezebel with her breasts hanging out of her bodice - even asked me to dance, like she couldn't see my leg or my other leg." He slapped his crutch. "And I'll tell you, Father: I saw a few strange things over there, heathen sorcery and such, in the east, but for a woman to get a rise out of me, at my age and state - well, there's something unnatural about it. I was two weeks doing penance over a sin I hadn't had to confess to for ten years."

Etienne nodded slowly. That was very like all the rumours he had heard of Ortlieb, to get her pleasure by tormenting a man sworn to chastity - just to prove, perhaps, that even a hardened old Teutonic Knight could be hers if she wanted him.

"Anyway, if you're going up there to tell her and the Landgraf to mend their ways, you'll be wasting your breath. Their priest's been down here complaining to the Bishop a few times - the Schloss chapel is falling to rack and ruin, and will they spend a single mark on it? Not when the Landgräfin has her fine feasts to pay for, they won't. For all she cares, Father Bruno could be serving the Mass with his arse showing through the holes in his cassock - begging your pardon, Father." Brother Sigvrit took another deep gulp of wine and refilled his cup.

"You seem to hear a good deal for a commander of the guard," Etienne commented neutrally.

The Teutonic Knight gave a harsh laugh, thumping the book in front of him. "Now that I've gotten the lads sorted out, there's not much else for a man like me to do except read and listen, is there? Well, Christ let me strike plenty of good blows for Him in my time. I shouldn't complain if He wants me to serve the rest of my term mostly in contemplation - St. Bernard's a good man for that, he puts it as clearly as I could want. You ever read him, Father?"

"Often."

Freshly bathed and dressed in his best canon's robe, his gold crucifix sparkling against the black velvet, Etienne presented himself at Bishop Otto's dining hall just before vespers. A man in the fine silken livery of one of the Bishop's secular servants bowed and showed him to the head table where the Bishop sat.

Bishop Otto was a hearty man in his late middle years, florid-faced and clean-shaven, whose wings of raven hair had not yet been touched by any gray and whose robes of purple silk sat easily upon his broad shoulders. He smiled widely when he saw Etienne, extending his hand. The canon knelt, touching his lips to the smooth amethyst cabochon.

"Rise, Father," the Bishop said. "We are glad to see you back among us again. How have you fared in these last years?"

"Quite well, your Grace," Etienne replied.

Bishop Otto gestured him to the place of honour on his own right, waiting until the servers had poured a goblet of wine for his guest. "Now, what brings you here? Can we be of any assistance to you?"

"At the moment, I am only passing through, Father. I was lately visiting the Bishop of Hamburg, who required my advice upon a rather unusual case in his diocese that his own exorcist had been unable to deal with successfully."

The Bishop smiled again, the confident, paternalistic smile, Etienne thought, of a man who had, all his life, been spared the most naked manifestations of the Foe on Earth. Etienne did not resent it; on the contrary, he wished that more folk could be so fortunate. "Ah, yes. You will forgive me, Etienne: I am more accustomed to thinking of you as a canon lawyer, from the help you were able to give us when we needed it. You will be glad to hear that we have recently added a specialist in canon law to our staff, a very bright young priest who received his degree from the university in Avignon."

"That is good news, indeed," Etienne agreed. Bishop Otto had sorely needed such a specialist, and having the new man here would make it easier to deal with Ortlieb if she could be brought to the point of justice - especially since he suspected that the matter might well come to a full Inquisitorial investigation. "And I understand that Niederwald now has a new lord?"

Otto frowned, the high colour of his face darkening. "It does, and little to its profit. Landgraf Bertrik was a good enough man: perhaps not as attentive to the state of his soul and the care of the Church as he might have been, but nevertheless there was little to fault him for. Landgraf Gerhardt, on the other hand, seems to care nothing for matters of the spirit; his priest tells me that he does not even bother to attend Mass most Sundays, while his wife's only interest seems to be in luxury. The feast they held for Bertrik's funeral and Gerhardt's accession was a positive scandal."

Etienne listened to the Bishop, nodding politely and murmuring agreement in the appropriate places as his Grace waxed eloquent on the subject of Landgraf Gerhardt's lack of proper respect for the Church while the first course - fat thrushes in a brown sauce, stuffed with a mixture of dried plums chopped into bread - was brought around. The wine, Etienne was pleased to note, was not one of the pale German vintages, but a good strong red which might almost have been pressed near his own home.

He pulled one of the little birds apart and ate with small polite bites, rinsing his fingers often in the silver bowl of rose-scented water by his place and patting his lips with his fine linen napkin to be sure that no drops of the savoury sauce had managed to escape into his short beard.

"But if one light-minded young Landgraf were the worst the Church had to face in these days, we would be doing well, to be sure," the Bishop said at last. "Will you not have another thrush, Etienne? You are looking rather leaner and more pale than when I saw you last, and though asceticism is a fine thing, we are also enjoined to care for our bodies. In any case, are the events in Avignon not the most shameful thing you have ever heard? Free Companies encamped at Villenueve in sight of the Papal palace, and that ugly little black devil, Bertrand du Guesclin, not only daring to ask for two hundred thousand francs to speed them on to their Crusade in Spain, but insisting that the money must come from the Papal treasury and nowhere else!"

"It is a grievous wonder," Etienne agreed slowly. He had
heard that Bertrand du Guesclin was gathering some of
the Free Companies for the Crusade, but much of this was
news to him. "Du Guesclin is said to be an irreverent and
impious man, but this is daring even for him. " But I think I
know where the counsel came from, he thought. Madame du
Guesclin was, perhaps, the foremost astrologer in the Order
of the Light-Bearers; with her to read the stars for him,
fortune would always seem to be on the side of Bertrand du
Guesclin, however boldly he pressed it.

"It is beyond thought!" Bishop Otto exclaimed. "If the
Pope can be thus assailed, then no one is safe. I tell you,
Etienne, the world is nothing like what it was when I was
ordained. In these days, it seems as though men do whatever
they please, with no thought for God or right - and then,
of course, they blame God when he punishes them for it,
as though the Death's first passing had not been enough to
chastise us all."

As abruptly as he had exploded, Otto calmed, refilling
both Etienne's wine-goblet and his own. "Well, each of us
can only do what God has given him to do. Still, the matter
of Landgraf Gerhardt bothers me, for I see in him many of
the symptoms of the sickness of the world in these days.
You remember, Etienne, how it was when the Death first
came, and so many of the young folk gave themselves over
to heedless revelry, forgetting their souls in the mad rush
to enjoy what little of life might be left to them, cavorting
madly in every kind of luxury?"

"I saw little of that," Etienne said dryly. "I had just been
sent on my first parish posting, to a very small village on
the shore of the North Sea where the closest thing to luxury
was a bed of straw that had not quite been soaked through
by the damp yet." Remembering his duties there, Etienne
shuddered. Not from the thought of the village itself,
shocking as it had been to a young priest straight from the
sunlight and good wines of France - and the posting had,
unmistakably, been meant as a punishment - but from the
memory of the Plague and what had come to that small
settlement with it.

"Oh," the Bishop said, taken aback. "At any rate, it was so, at least in the larger cities. Now I see much of that same madness in Landgraf Gerhardt and his wife, almost a morbidity of pleasure. Apart from the danger to their souls, I fear that Gerhardt is managing his inheritance badly, which will do his people no good. But he has hardened his heart against the words of the Church, and no doubt God will deal with him in good time."

Etienne drew breath, composing his thoughts. Now he could ask his most leading question without suspicion:"What of the younger brother - Bernhardt, was it? I heard that he had disappeared eight years ago...something about a murder..?"

Bishop Otto sighed, sitting back in his chair as the second course, tender medallions of venison served with their juices running down into a rich bed of wheat frumenty, was brought around. He took his time cutting the meat, the small ivory-handled knife in his square hand slicing through the gently browned flesh as smoothly as through butter, before answering.

"The case was never brought to trial, and would have been a matter for secular justice anyway. Landgraf Bertrik was quite convinced of the young man's guilt - but I am told that Bernhardt maintained his protestations of innocence in spite of everything. It may come as little surprise to you, after your last experiences with us, that I should have wished a more thorough investigation before executing any judgement. Even then, Landgraf Bertrik had been, I believe, considering that Bernhardt might be a better successor to him than Gerhardt. I do not know how it is in France, but you know that in this country the first-born need not always be the heir?"

Etienne nodded.

"On the other hand, I am told that everyone who was in the castle that night was certain that Bernhardt had, indeed, done what he was accused of. It may be that, even then, I was simply more inclined to think well of Bernhardt in that he showed both a piety and a responsibility which are rarely seen in young noblemen. But the fairest seeming may hide a black heart, or at least a foul temper, and that could as easily have been the case with him. Nor did it speak well for him that he was willing to slay his fellows in his escape..." The Bishop sighed again. "That is in the past, anyway, and no doubt Bernhardt is dead by now - or at least will never show himself in Niederwald again. As well for him, though I must mourn the waste of a promising young man: he would, at the least, have made a better ruler than his brother."

Better than I hoped, Etienne thought, though he was careful not to let his face betray any sign of his excitement. Although he does not know it yet, Bishop Otto is on our side already.

Father Etienne and the Bishop talked throughout the meal. Bishop Otto was a lively conversationalist, well-versed in both theology and politics; but his talk kept returning to du Guesclin's presence in Avignon and his shocking demands on the Pope, which seemed to be much on the Bishop's mind. Not unreasonably: for if Urban V could be thus made subject to extortion by a gathering of what were hardly more than armed criminals, forced not only to pay what amounted to a ransom in order to get them out of his country but to give them a mass absolution as well, then who was safe?

And what protection could the Church give even to its Bishops? No one, and none, were the short answers; and Etienne could tell that this was weighing heavily on Otto's mind. The Kaiser and his troops had turned back the Companies gathered at Strasbourg that summer, for all the assurances given by their leader, Arnaut de Cervole, that he only wanted to water his horses in the Rhine; but even Karl IV, dear friend of Urban's that he was, had done nothing to free the Pope from these newest troubles.

"Etienne," Bishop Otto said at last, pushing back the last remains of a cinnamon-sprinkled sweet flan on a base of caramelized sugar, "we can only trust in the goodness of God, for in these troubled times, it almost seems as though we look upon the face of Satan."

Etienne repressed a shiver, crossing himself. Although the Bishop, to the best of his knowledge, had never watched an exorcism, and held firmly to the old line that witches and sorcerers had no true power, but that they and those who believed in them suffered only from a grievous delusion - still, God's Foe had many faces, and who was to say that one of them did not show as clearly in the deeds of men like Bertrand du Guesclin or Bernabò Visconti, who had once forced a Papal legate to eat his Bull of Excommunication, silken cords, leaden seals, and all, as another did in Ortlieb's hidden sanctum? And the Order had men who were great even in the politics of the Church, as well as the secular world...

"If that is so, your Grace," Etienne replied, "pray Christ it strengthen us to greater vigour in His service. As you have said, each of us can only do what God has given him to do."

"True enough. Well, I shall take my leave of you now. I believe Father Kunibert has assigned a man to your chambers, and you have only to ask if you want anything."

"I have one favour to ask of you, your Grace," Etienne said swiftly, before the Bishop could depart. Otto lifted his dark brows.

"Yes?"

"Your diocesan exorcist, Father Thomas - if it is possible, I should like to speak with him tomorrow, as we share a common office."

"Of course. I shall tell Father Kunibert to be sure that Father Thomas is excused from his usual duties so that you may have time to talk with him. Good night, Etienne."

"Good night, your Grace."

A cup of watered wine and some fine white rolls were waiting on Etienne's table when he arose the next morning, together with a short note reading, "Father Thomas awaits you in the library at your convenience," and signed by Father Kunibert. Etienne ate and dressed hastily, for the soft bed and thick goose-down comforters had lured him into sleeping later than he should have. In his last journey through Niederwald, Etienne had met the diocesan exorcist only in passing: he remembered a very short man a few years younger than himself, with a shock of brown curls, quick nervous hands, and a way of looking shyly up through his lashes at anyone taller than himself.

The French priest was shocked, then, to see how much Father Thomas had changed. In only four years, the small priest had gone from being slightly plump to almost painfully thin; his curls were shot through with gray, as though his head had been dusted with ash, and he moved with a perceptible limp when he rose to greet Father Etienne.

"Good morning, Father Thomas," Etienne said.

"Good morning, Father Etienne. I am glad to see you here, and in such good health."

Etienne could not return the compliment, but Father Thomas looked down at himself and gave a slight self-deprecating laugh that ended in a little cough. "The Death, and the Devil, my friend. By God's blessing, I defeated them both for the time being, but the battle never ends, does it?"

"It never does," Etienne agreed. "I take it that your work has been - not uneventful."

"Not at all. I'm sure if you give me the chance, I can talk your ear off about it."

"I would be pleased," Etienne said gravely, sitting down and motioning Father Thomas to do the same. The younger priest, as it transpired, was one of the very few who had caught the plague in his lungs, spitting blood and writhing in fever, and yet somehow survived.

"Only by the mercy of Christ and the intercession of the Virgin did I live," Father Thomas said. "But the Lord had work for me to do yet, for I was not a month out of my sickbed before being called out for an exorcism. That was a most grievous and sorrowful one, for the woman was not only possessed, but showing the black swellings of the Death on her body, so that it was of the utmost urgency to free her at once, and yet I could find no one willing to aid me. At one point, she picked me up and cast me bodily across the room; since then, I have not walked easily. Nevertheless, the power of Christ sustained me, and at last He freed the poor woman of the spirits afflicting her, so that she was able to make a Confession, take the Last Rites, and die at peace with God - and such mercy, as we both know, has not always been granted in times of the Death, even to those who suffered from no demonic attentions."

"That is true enough," Etienne said sadly.

"Thanks be to the Lord, I have had no calls on my services in the last year. Although..." Father Thomas frowned, the fine lines on his prematurely aged face deepening. "Because of my office, you understand, I must remain aware of any strange happenings in this diocese, for often those of us who are trained as exorcists will be able to recognise demonic manifestations before those around the sufferers do."

"Indeed," Etienne said, thinking regretfully of Margerite's description of Christoph's strange behaviour. If he had been there at the start...but such thoughts would do no one any good, except inasmuch as they could teach a lesson; and he did not think his lesson was that he needed to follow Margerite about like a watchdog through the rest of her life. "Has anything strange happened of late?"

"We have had three reports of young men gone missing. When such things happen, you understand, the Church is often informed, as we have the means at least to keep a wider watch for the boys."

"Yes, that is so. But these were different?"

"It is not uncommon for a peasant lad to run away, to seek his fortune in a city or some such, you understand. And we are close to the Thuringer Wald here, which presents a different temptation to a lazy young man who thinks that it would be easy to take goods rather than earn them..." Father Thomas' voice trailed off, his brown eyes turning upward to the library's one stained-glass window, a representation of St. Peter in all his Papal glory with the Keys of Heaven in his hands. The day was cloudy, so that the coloured light the window cast across their table seemed muted.

"I understand. But you think there was something else about these?"

"The boys were between thirteen and fifteen years of age, all three of them well-spoken of by their families and their parish priests. They were young for running off to a city, even younger for seeking out an outlaw band, nor did anyone who knew them think them of the sort that usually leaves home in that manner. The first disappearance was in February, and might have been ascribed to wolves, since the snows were deep and wolves are hungriest in that month. But the second two were near the end of April and a week before Johannisnacht, and wolves do not often come near villages in those months. And..." Brother Thomas looked down at the table, and Etienne could guess what he was thinking.

"And you feel that there was something strange about the disappearances," Etienne said gently. He had found, often enough, that a trained exorcist, even one with little native talent for magic, developed a sense for such things over the years: it was as though men who had once caught the scent of naked evil would, forever afterwards, have the ability to recognise it again, even from the faintest whiff - such as Father Thomas had clearly caught.

"I cannot name it, or tell why," the younger priest admitted. "For all we know, any of those lads might turn up again, alive and well in Erfuhrt or Weimar, or as a pile of gnawed bones in the forest. It is just that...that I feel something in my bones, something that chills me as surely as if I were preparing to go face to face with a demoniac." He crossed himself.

"Have you taken any steps concerning this?"

Father Thomas spread his hands wide, looking up at Etienne through his lashes in his old way.

"What should I do? I have been to the villages where the boys disappeared, and talked to the folk there - of the Bishop's staff, I am the one most easily spared, since my daily duties are of necessity light and can be easily performed by any other priest. There was nothing to find: each of them had gone to bed in the evening, and been gone by morning, their tracks quickly lost on the road. None of them had shown any strange signs before disappearing: their souls had been as much in order as the souls of any youths can be, to the best of their parish priests' knowledge. If there were some demonic manifestation involved in this, it would be of a kind that I had never seen nor heard of before. They were all three strong and healthy boys, as well, not to be overpowered without some struggle and noise, let alone dragged unwillingly from a room full of brothers and sisters with no one noticing. No: wherever they went, they seem to have gone willingly - and yet there was no reason for it that anyone knows. But, Father Etienne," Thomas added suddenly, "I have heard that you have had tremendous experience with the Powers of Darkness in their many forms. Do you know anything that might help me in this?"

Etienne paused, considering. He knew that he could trust in Father Thomas: in the course of their dreadful duties, exorcists often saw things that no ordinary priest would credit, and learned to speak little to others of what passed between themselves and the fell spirits with which they must deal.

What he did not know was how Thomas would respond
to the knowledge that the Landgräfin herself was, in all
likelihood, the reason for the missing boys, and a black
sorceress and worshipper of Lucifer. He might well consider
it his duty to inform the Bishop, or even to take up his cross
and confront her directly, heedless of the risk to himself.

"If I tell you my thoughts, Thomas," Etienne said gently,
"will you swear to do nothing without consulting me first? I
have only suspicions and guesses, no firm proof - let alone
anything that would allow either of us legitimately to act."

Father Thomas looked troubled, his mouth half-opening
as if he would speak, then closing again. At last he squared
his thin shoulders. "Etienne, how can I swear such an oath?
If there is something evil prowling these lands, something
of demonic origin, it is my duty to face it and call upon
the powers of Christ to aid against it. And it is your duty -
morally, if not by the letter of the law - to tell me what you
know of it."

Etienne looked down at the smaller man, who met his
gaze without flinching. It seemed to Etienne as though
he could see the brightness of Thomas' implacable spirit
shining through his early-withered face and wasted frame
like light through a coloured window: the priests who had
decided that Father Thomas should be trained as an exorcist
had chosen well. And yet...

"I cannot tell you what I do not know," Etienne said,
stressing the last word lightly. "And if you were to begin an
investigation now, we should assuredly find nothing, for our
quarry would flee from your first footstep. But if you will be
patient, Thomas, it may be that we will solve the mystery of
your disappearing boys and save others from the same fate."

"Do you think they are still alive?" Father Thomas asked
eagerly. "If there is any hope for them..."

Regretfully, Etienne shook his head.

"It is a hard thing you ask of me, Etienne," Father Thomas said. "I did not become a priest, or an exorcist, in order to sit by and wait for others to act when evil is done. And I question how much help I can be in ignorance: if you tell me, at least, what you are looking for, there is always the chance that I may come upon something that will provide you a better answer to your questions."

"If you knew what I need to know," Etienne responded, "you would already have taken action. It will be better if I ask you the questions I have, and see what I may learn."

Father Thomas sighed, spreading his hands out flat on the table as if to force himself not to fidget - or to clench them into fists. "If you were not so well-famed, I should be tempted to take that far worse," he said, and though his voice was even, Etienne could hear the tight sparking of anger in it.

"But instead I shall be grateful that Christ has sent you to us in this time of trouble - for you have told me, at least, that my suspicions were near to the mark, and not some lingering disorder of the fever in my brain. Very well: what more would you know?"

"Tell me more of the boys that disappeared," Etienne said quietly.

Georg waited until Father Etienne was gone before he went back into the gamekeeper's house. The priest had given him a light enough penance; he could say his prayers on the road easily enough while he was searching for - he steeled himself to the thought - the Free Company.

Herr Bernhardt was sitting at Lothar's table, sipping slowly at a mug of small beer. Georg straightened under his gaze, as he would have before his father or Christoph: though the black-haired man looked wilder than anyone they had met on the road, there was an air about him - his noble blood showing through, perhaps - that made Georg feel that it would be unthinkable to show him disrespect, or quail in any way before the tasks that he set.

"Well, Knappe," Herr Bernhardt said. "Are you ready for your own journey?"

"I am, Herr Bernhardt," Georg responded at once. "I have packed three days' provisions, as you told me to, and the money that the Frowe Gräfin gave me for Hauptmann Paul is safe in my saddlebag."

Herr Bernhardt nodded. "Good enough. Are you certain that you understand the road?"

Georg recited the directions from memory, ending with, "And I shall wait at the White Cockerel in the village of Schwarzenbach, where Hauptmann Paul is to meet me. He is a man of middle height, strongly built, with red-gold hair, a large belly, and a loud voice."

"Very good."

"Should I...Is there much risk that the Bear's Paw will simply steal the money I am bringing them?" And slit my throat, Georg thought, though it would have been craven to mention it.

"Keep your wits about you," Herr Bernhardt said dryly, "for I believe wits are what they have the most need of stealing. " Hidden by his bushy black beard as his features were, it took Georg a moment to realize that the somber nobleman was smiling.

"Truthfully, Georg, if you can reach Hauptmann Paul in safety, you will have little more to worry about. Remember that Bertram is the name they know me by, and tell them no more than you have to about the situation here. But the day grows no younger, and if you have no more questions, you had best be off."

Georg could recognise a dismissal when he heard it. He bowed - not too low, for he was, after all, the son of a Graf himself - and said, "Farewell, and Christ be with you here."

Herr Bernhardt touched his chest where the lump of the

necklace the Gräfin had given him the night before pressed against the worn gray cloth. For a moment there was an odd distant look in his eyes, as though he were staring straight through Georg at something far beyond him. "I hope that He will be," Herr Bernhardt murmured, then louder, "And may He go with you, Georg."

Although still cold, the day was promising very fine, the sky fair as a bowl of burnished blue-silver and the sun's light dazzlingly bright through the ruddy autumn leaves. It was not long before Georg was whistling, then singing softly to himself, all his worries about walking in among the men of a Free Company forgotten.

He was coming, he thought, close to the edge of the wood when he heard the sound of horses' hooves cantering - fine horses, by the sound of it, light and well-spirited - and the laughter of women.

Georg stiffened, then relaxed: Herr Bernhardt had given him a story to tell if anyone should come upon him while he was still in the hunting park, which should keep him from any harm - and if his packs were searched, it would be easily proven that he was no poacher. Therefore, he did not try to move from the path, but kept his brown gelding to an easy amble with his packhorse following behind.

"Hey there, boy!" a woman's rich contralto called to him. "Stop where you are."

Georg reined his horse to a halt and looked behind himself. As he took in the sight of the three women, he drew his breath in amazement. One was golden-haired, even more beautiful than Eva, though the creamy breasts showing over the top of her pale green bodice were not as full as Eva's. One was raven-haired and blue-eyed, her rose-coloured gown laced so tightly to her body that Georg could see her generous breasts trembling with every movement of her breath.

She and the golden-haired woman wore matching rings of
onyx set in gold, which was strange enough to draw Georg's
attention for a moment. But it was the one in the middle
that caught and held his eyes, leaving him trembling and
speechless. Her amber-brown hair, tumbling about her face,
gleamed richly with highlights of red and gold, like hidden
fire leaping forth from polished wood; flecks of green shone
from her brown eyes like chips of emerald flaring from the
depths of a sunlit pond.

The curve of her cheek, its fair skin flushed slightly pink,
seemed to draw him to caress it; her lips were soft and sweet
as rose-petals, and it seemed to Georg that he could almost
feel them on his own body, doing things to him that he only
dared to confess to a priest under the general heading of
lust.

To his mortification, his cock was already aching hard
against his belly from his single glance at her: he was afraid
that if she came closer, or touched him, he would disgrace
himself irreparably, but at the same time, he could feel his
hands shaking with the effort not to wheel his horse around
and go to her.

The large ruby on her forefinger flashed deep red as
she beckoned to him, her white hand moving gracefully
through the shadow-tracery of shadow and sun through
the autumn leaves. "Who are you, boy?" she asked, her low
voice caressing Georg's skin like a trail of silk. "What are you
doing in the Landgraf's hunting park?"

"I, I..." Georg stammered, his own voice sounding
dreadfully clumsy and harsh. He could feel the tips of his
ears burning; he swallowed, and tried again. "I crave your
pardon, frowe. I was going to meet my father and lost my
way. One of your gamekeepers told me to leave - he searched
my pack to be sure I was no poacher," Georg added, hoping
that there was the right amount of indignation in his voice
-"and pointed me the way to the road."

"One of my gamekeepers, hmm?" the lady mused. She tilted her head to the side, looking at Georg through thick black lashes, and his heart seemed to stop within him. O, look at me...no, come closer, touch me..."And when does your father expect you?"

"I am to meet him this afternoon, frowe," Georg answered.

She lifted her hand to stroke a lock of that wonderfully gleaming brown hair, and Georg could see her breasts shifting within her deep red bodice. He swallowed hard, tightening his legs about his horse.

His saddle was pressing almost painfully against his ballocks, and he almost thought that he would cry out when she trotted slowly up to stop beside him. Paralyzed with an appalling mixture of fear and delight, he could do nothing as she reached out to him, brushing her fingers - O Christ help me! - over the hilt of his sword.

"You are no common peasant boy," she noted. "Pity."

"My father is a merchant, frowe," Georg said, though he could barely hear his own voice through the pounding of the blood in his head. This close, he could smell her, a strong musky sweetness that made him dizzier with every breath; he could see the tiny black beauty-mark on the inner curve of her left breast, and - O, God! - the pricking of her nipples beneath the deep red velvet, even, he thought, a dusky rose rim of aureole just at the edge of her low-cut bodice.

"A rich one, no doubt, to buy his son such a sword," she murmured, dropping her hand. The ruby flashed again; her fingers just brushed his outer thigh, and Georg had to bite his tongue to keep from moaning. "Do you suppose he would mind...much...if you were late?"

Georg shook his head wildly, his bright red hair whipping across his face. He could hear the laughter of the other two women, chiming in harmony like bells of silver and gold. Then he heard nothing but her voice, for she was leaning in very close - so close that he could smell the sweetness of fennelseed and anise on her breath, feel its warmth on his cheek, so close that the dizzying scent of her hair seemed to be wrapping his thoughts like featherdown blankets.

"Tell me, boy," she breathed, each word thumping painfully in Georg's heart, "are you still a virgin?"

Georg did not dare draw himself up, for that would have meant moving away from her, but he made his voice as deep and manly as he could. "No, frowe. I have often...I know well..."

Her frown was as beautiful as her smile, but Georg thought he would die of it, for he could see the anger gleaming green in the deep forest-pools of her eyes. "Go on, boy, and meet with your father. And tell him that Landgräfin Ortlieb says he should have kept a better watch on you!" Without another word, she put the spurs to her horse; the roan mare leapt forward, and in moments she was gone, her two companions following her.

Georg stared where she had gone for a long time, then dropped his head against his chest and wept. His groin hurt as if he had been kicked hard there, and his body tried to curl up against the cramping, nauseating pain. He was shivering uncontrollably, and for a few moments he thought he would retch up the small beer and bread he had eaten that morning.

After a while, the shaking of his limbs slowly died down, the nausea and pain receding. Georg wiped his wet face, snuffling his nose clear onto his sleeve like a peasant. He felt drained, as though he had committed the sin of Onan, but with none of the peaceful relaxation that usually followed that particular offense. He started off again at a slow walk - he could not bear the thought of a faster ride's painful jostling.

Georg slept outside that night, rolled in a blanket on the far side of a shorn field. He slept badly, for each rustling of the dead stalks around him sounded like the footsteps of a robber, and when he finally dropped off near dawn, he dreamed of her - of her hand moving where it had not that morning, of the deep red glow of her ruby ring and the sheen of her hair wrapping around him - and awoke with a harsh cry, the front of his trousers stained with a shameful wetness.

He wondered then if what Christoph's demon had done to him, or rather tried to do to him, was so much worse: at least, painful and frightening as that had been, it had not forced his body to answer as her touch had. Georg was sure that, when Christoph was freed of the evil spirit, he would be able to look his knight in the eyes again and trust him as he had before; but now he thought he would nearly give his soul not to see the Landgräfin Ortlieb once more - and was dreadfully afraid that he would give his soul to see her.

Wiping himself clean as best he could with a corner of his blanket, Georg packed up and saddled the horses once more, turning determinedly towards the road. A white fur of frost covered every brown stalk and gray stone in the field; in the pale cloudy light of dawn, when he looked back, Georg could see the trail of his horses dark behind him. Although he had hoped to be at the inn by mid-day, by the time the sun was shining bright overhead through the breaking clouds, Georg was just at the edge of the Thuringer Wald.

The road led clearly through the trees, though, just as Herr Bernhardt had told him it would, and Georg urged his horse on a little faster. It seemed to him that whenever the scudding clouds unveiled the sun's brightness, he could see the gleam of her hair in the reds and golds and browns of the autumn leaves, and he heard the laughter of her companions in the high piping of the birds and the soft burbling of the creek that ran beside the road.

"Christ have mercy," Georg whispered to himself, "now I understand what Father Etienne meant." Thinking of the priest reminded him that he had not said the prayers of his penance yet, and he set himself to that, the familiar words running through his mind like well-polished beads beneath his fingers.

As Herr Bernhardt had told him, a little stone bridge crossed the dark waters of the Schwarzenbach. Its mortar was cracking and damp with green moss, and Georg dismounted, leading his horses carefully across. The houses of the town were well-kept, though, half-timbered and plastered in white, some with neatly tended little plots of vegetables in front of them and some graced by tidily pruned fruit-trees.

As Georg expected, the inn's sign hung to one side of the village square: a white cockerel with gold comb and beak, his head thrown back to crow proudly. Georg watered his horses at the well before he tied them to the post before the inn and entered, for his father had taught him early that he must always look to his horses and men before tending to his own needs.

The only people in the inn were a pair of well-fed men playing dice, and neither of them had either the red-gold hair that Herr Bernhardt had described nor the rough look that Georg would have expected from men of a Free Company; though thick, their arms were flabby, and they were armed with nothing more than wooden-handled eating daggers. Georg sat down on a bench by the wall, looking about himself. The inside of the inn was painted with bright figures; though clumsily done, Georg could recognise long-bearded Peter denying the Lord, with the cockerel from the inn's sign crying loudly on the roof.

"What'll you have, lad?" one of the dicers asked, standing up and coming over to him. "Don't look so gloomy, now: my Frieda's got some nice trout cooking, it being a Friday and all, and when you taste that with her Steinpils sauce, you'll wish it was Lent so you could eat her fish every day. I'll bring you that with some fine brown bread and a nice mug of strong ale for a copper pfennig, and you won't get better than that anywhere else, I'll tell you."

Absently Georg dug a coin out of his belt pouch and gave them to the innkeeper, hardly listening to him. When the ale arrived, in a good big stoneware mug, he took a deep draught, for he was thirsty from the road. But when the froth had settled down and Georg looked into the mug, he saw the deep amber-brown gleam from within, and found that he was about to weep.

"Come now, boy, it can't be that bad," said a man's kindly voice beside him. A rough hand patted his shoulder. "Woman trouble, is it?"

Georg started to laugh, the bitter tears spurting from his eyes as his shoulders shook. After a few moments, though, he felt the cool slick sides of the mug being pushed into his hand. "Ah, come on, take a good drink of that and things will look better to you," his companion encouraged loudly. "No woman's worth taking on so, trust me on it."

Obediently Georg drank, and the act of swallowing seemed to melt the huge choking lump in his throat, so that he could drink a little more.

"There you go. That's good stuff, isn't it?"

"Yes. Thank you," Georg said politely, turning to look at his new friend. The man beside him was burly, with powerful arms and shoulders, a stained leather jerkin with iron plates sewn on covering his barrel chest and broad belly. An iron-bound leather cap, very much like Georg's own, covered his blunt skull, and his small blue eyes and stubby nose reminded Georg very much of a dancing bear he had once seen. A ruddy beard that was hardly more than overgrown stubble hid his chin and wide jaw; his face was rather grimy, but Georg could not help answering his grin.

"There you go - Innkeeper! Another two mugs of ale over here! Enough of this in you, boy, and you'll forget you ever worried about your girl. What are you doing here, anyway?"

"I'm...I'm waiting for someone," Georg stammered as the plump innkeeper whisked his mug away to be filled again.

"So am I, though I'm not sure who. I must be mad to be doing this," the burly man grumbled to himself. "Waiting for strangers, no prospect of pay for Christ knows how long - I don't know why we didn't just go to France with everyone else. We could be warm and getting rich in Spain right now, instead of freezing our arses off here, just because an old friend thought he might need us. I tell you, boy, if you ever decide to go for a soldier, try to find a commander with a brain." He paused, looking at Georg. "Come to think of it, that's a nice sword you've got there. You know how to use it?"

"Well enough," Georg answered. He knew he should be more wary, but the strong ale was already working in his empty belly, filling him with a gentle warmth.

"We lost a good few men in our last campaign - how would you like to join up? If you survive, you get a share of pay, when we get paid, and a share of loot, and take your chances with the women like the rest of us. That's the Bear's Paw Company, boy: the best fighting unit north of the Emperor's own guard, or at least the one that drinks the most beer."

It was then that Georg noticed the bright hair curling out beneath his companion's battered leather cap, and realized who he was talking to. "You're Hauptmann Paul!" he blurted out.

"Paul the Bear, at your service," the mercenary replied. "Well, what do you say to it?"

"Ah...actually, I think I'm supposed to pay you," Georg muttered, embarassed.

Paul stared at him for a moment, dumbfounded, then burst into a great roar of laughter. "Then you can start by buying the beer! No, I'm just joking. I'll pay for this round; you looked like you needed it. What's your name?"

"Georg." He had gotten out of adding, son of Graf Wolfgang, when he was on the road, and felt no urge to add it now.

"You must be a friend of Bertram, then. Well, any friend of his is a friend of ours. I don't suppose you know the Gräfin Margerite as well?"

"I travelled all the way down here with her," Georg said proudly. "She and Eva needed a man to protect them on the road."

Paul took the freshly filled mugs from the innkeeper, handing one to Georg. "Well, here's to you, and to her as well." He drank deeply, and Georg followed suit.

By the time they left the inn, taking the horses and walking deeper into the wood, Georg found that he was tending to stumble over tree branches that weren't quite there, and that the twilit path wavered a little before his eyes. The Bear's steps were steady, but the twigs crunched loudly beneath his feet, so that even if he had not been talking full strength, they could easily have been heard from far away.

"Should we be a little quieter?" Georg asked nervously.

The Bear laughed. "The Bear's Paw Company is the most dangerous thing in these woods right now. You don't have a thing to worry about, Georg; you're with us now."

As they walked, the icy autumn air gradually cleared Georg's head. Although dark had fallen, the sharp crescent moon shed a clear light through the trees, so that he and Paul could follow the trail without too much difficulty, the horses stepping docilely along behind them.

"Halt!" a deep voice said suddenly from the bushes at the side of the path. Georg started, his hand going to the hilt of his sword, but Paul merely turned his head.

"Halt yourself," he answered. "It's me, I'm back, and I've got a friend with me."

"Can you give the password?" the voice persisted.

"I've forgotten the damn password, all right?"

"Give the password," their challenger intoned.

"The password is Glück!" Paul shouted. "The password is Beer! For Christ's sake, Jochanan, I set the password, I've just forgotten it. So stop giving me trouble, or you'll get a good whack, you understand?"

The voice from the bushes broke into laughter, and a taller man stepped out onto the path. In the branch-broken moonlight, Georg could not make out his features very well, but his hair was dark and curly, and he seemed to have a falchion at his side. "Good to see you back, Paul. Who's this with you?"

"This is Georg, the man I was sent to meet. He's a friend of Bertram and Margerite. Georg, this is Jochanan, my gunner and first lieutenant. He served with me up at Burg Falkenstein - as if he were loyal," Paul added, going off in a gale of laughter. Jochanan chuckled ruefully; Georg looked at both of them, wondering if being a mercenary meant taking a great many blows on the head.

"I am very pleased to meet you, Georg," Jochanan said. "Welcome to our camp." He fell in beside them.

The three of them had not gone much further before Georg saw the light of several campfires through the trees and heard the low rumble of men's voices. Oddly, though he knew he really was about to walk in among the sort of men that his father always described as murdering scum, barely worthy of the nooses to hang them with, he felt quite easy with Paul and Jochanan beside him. A gust of cold wind brought the savoury scent of frying sausages to his nose, and a burst of deep laughter rang out from one of the fire.

"And we're going to get paid after all," Paul said happily. "So you might as well go open that last keg of beer, Jochanan. Now, Georg, come over and sit down by the fire, and tell me what's going on. Bertram's note only said that he needed us bad, so we should come here, and that he'd probably be able to pay us after everything was over. And what in Christ's name is Margerite doing here? I thought she married Graf Whatsisname."

In a few minutes, Georg was sitting on a log beside one of the campfires, a mug of beer in one hand and a sizzling sausage in the other - it might be a sin to eat meat on a Friday, but the trout at the White Cockerel had been some time ago, and besides, it would be discourteous to refuse the Bear's Paw's food when he was their guest. It was easy for him to explain Herr Bernhardt's position, but when he came to how he, Margerite, and Eva had fled Burg Fürstensee, his tongue began to stumble over itself.

To his surprise, Georg saw a gentle smile on Jochanan's heavy features - in the firelight, Georg thought, Paul's gunner could almost have been a Saracen, for the dark tone of his skin and the foreign look of his face. "Was it something strange?" he asked softly.

Georg nodded, unable to speak.

"You can tell us, Georg. We've seen a few strange things ourselves, haven't we, Paul?"

"That we have," Paul agreed.

Hesitantly Georg began to explain what had happen. Jochanan frowned darkly when he got to the part about Christoph's demon. "He seemed a good man, but I was always a little worried about him," the gunner confessed. "A blow on the head such as he took is risky - it makes a crack where a dybbuk may creep in."

"A what?"

"Never mind," said Paul hastily. "Go on."

"...And so that is how we came to be here," Georg finished a little later, licking the sausage grease off his fingers, then, rude as it might be, wiping his hands on the hem of his tunic.

"A hard road, sure enough," Paul said. He drained his mug with a deep sigh. "But if we've got Father Etienne with us, we'll be all right." The Bear yawned loudly. "Best you go to sleep now, Georg. Tomorrow you can ride back and let Bertram know that we're here when he wants us, all ready to kick the arse of any scumbag who needs it."

Chapter Seven

y the end of her first week of scrubbing pots and floors, digging vegetables, and hauling great baskets of garbage out to the midden heap, Margerite was beginning to feel as though her earlier life was nothing more than a dream, a half-forgotten glimmer in the sleep for which her battered body desperately ached. It seemed impossible that she had ever sent her own servants down to demand eel rather than pike on a Friday, or enquire whether a haunch of venison had been hung long enough to be served that night.

As a simple scullion, at least her work had not drawn Liutbirg's gimlet eye often, nor had the head cook yet lashed her with one of the supple willow wands that she kept about the kitchen in order to make her apprentices learn more quickly; but, save for occasional trips to bring vegetables in or garbage out, and trooping wearily out to the building where the lower castle-servants slept, she had seen nothing of Schloss Niederwald - she had not even had the chance to go into the great hall, though only one doorway separated it from each of the kitchens.

Margerite found herself envying, not only Eva's facility for cleaning dirty pots and utensils, but also the way in which the girl could chat easily with the other kitchen servants even as she stood scrubbing at her sinks. Eva had learned the names and duties of all the other women in the kitchen within a day; Margerite hardly had the strength to speak at all, or to do anything except caring for Wolfram and trying to keep up with the other scullery maids. Once in a while, when her hunger grew, she found herself thinking of dishes that she had pushed away half-eaten at Heinrich's table.

She would have regretted that bitterly, save that now she had experienced what before she had only been vaguely aware of: how eager the kitchen staff were to finish off the leftovers from the great hall, so that abstinence, even if it sprang from surfeit or a casual dismissal of the tremendous amount of work that went into bringing each dish to table, now seemed a great act of charity to her. And if before Margerite had doubted her ability to pass for a woman of low birth, when she saw her own face reflected in the silver platters that must be carefully rinsed and polished after each meal, she did not wonder at it now.

It was not only the painful state of her hands, already cracked and roughened by the constant scrubbing with the dead skin of blisters hardening and peeling back from her fingers, nor the way she found herself stooping at the end of the day, when long bending over sinks had kindled an uneasing dull ache in her lower back. Though Margerite had always been slim, now her cheekbones stood out sharply beneath smoke-reddened eyes.

Her ash-blond hair hung limply about her face, and there was something in her eyes that she had never seen in a mirror before: the dull peasant look that she had always attributed to stupidity before, the look of a woman who could see nothing before or behind her but days of ceaseless labour to no profit of her own. It frightened her to see that - but there was nothing she could do about it, not so long as she was to play the part she had taken on.

It was on the morning of her eighth day in the kitchens of Schloss Niederwald, as Margerite laboured diligently to load just the right amount of dry wood into the ovens, that she heard Liutbirg's sharp voice rising over the bustle of her workers. "What do you mean, you need women who can sew? Go find some, then, and leave me alone! This is a kitchen, you pox-eaten fool, not a dressmaker's shop!"

Lifting her head cautiously, Margerite saw one of the well-dressed castle servants standing in the doorway to the great hall, with Liutbirg standing not a foot from him and screaming into his face. He did not turn a hair, replying unperturbed, "The Landgräfin requires women who can cut a straight line and sew a straight seam to help with the hangings for her feast, nothing more. Shall I tell her that your kitchens are so badly run that you cannot spare any of your workers for a few days?"

Liutbirg made a disgusted noise deep in her throat, looking around. "Fine! You - Gertrude! You're damned useless anyway; you might as well be useless somewhere else. Take your brat and get out of here, and be thankful for the easy work - and make sure your hands are clean; the Landgräfin won't want your dirty fingerprints all over her hangings."

"Yes, frowe," Margerite replied meekly, stopping by the sink where Eva was pouring hot water carefully over one of the pans that had been left overnight to soak and scrubbing the ovens' soot from her hands. There was nothing she could do about the black stains on the sleeves of her woolen dress, but she paused a moment longer to make sure that her face was clean as well, then picked up Wolfram and followed the servant who had summoned her.

He led her through the great hall - Margerite only had time to notice the high ceiling and minstrels' balcony, in a room almost twice the size of the hall at Burg Fürstensee, its walls hung with tapestries whose colours glowed dully in the cloudy light through the wide windows - and across a corridor to a large room where a number of women all sat measuring and cutting or stitching diligently on billowing masses of black and deep purple fabric.

"Irmingard will show you what to do. Irmingard, this is the only one that could be spared from the kitchens," the servant said with a distinct sniff, tossing his long brown hair back over his shoulder and turning away.

The woman who rose from the length of black material on the floor was of middle height and rather plump, with thick chestnut braids piled high on her head and a round, good-natured face. "Welcome to our little guild," she said with a laugh. "Since you're here, I trust you know how to sew well enough?"

"Yes, frowe," Margerite answered.

"Good. There's more than enough to be done before the Landgräfin's feast; I suppose we should be thankful that she gave us a bit of time to make everything ready. These are the hangings that will go around the hall that night, and every stitch in them must be small and perfect. You'll work with Hathumod there; she'll show you what to do."

Margerite's partner was small, dark-haired, and nervous, her hands fluttering quickly over the fabric with every stitch until Margerite wanted to take it away from her. But Hathumod was neatly clad in a deep blue overdress over a shift of pale yellow linen, and bore a plain silver ring upon one white finger: if she was not one of the Landgräfin's personal servants, she certainly stood farther up the ranks of the castle servants than Margerite.

Though the more accustomed work of delicate stitching, away from the kitchen's smoke and scents of unattainable delicacies, quickly restored her spirits, after sewing for a couple of hours, Margerite began to feel that the endless bolts of black and deep purple fabric were almost pressing in on her eyes, as if she had been straining her sight against a moonless fog. "This is the grimmest feast-decoration I have ever seen," Margerite murmured to her partner.

Hathumod giggled. "I hear the Landgräfin is going to engage mummers for something called a Danse Macabre. You would not have heard of it, but I understand it is one of the latest fashions."

"And what is it?" Margerite enquired meekly, though the other woman's words chafed her within - the more, because she truly had no idea what Hathumod was talking about.

"O, something French or Italian. All the grand folk are going to be here for it, even the Margraf of Meissen and the Landgraf of Thuringia. I heard..." Hathumod lowered her voice conspiratorially..."that the Landgräfin has already spent close to twenty-five marks on black-dyed candles for the hall."

Margerite's gasp was completely natural: even for Burg Fürstensee, she could not have countenanced such a ridiculous expenditure - and she had an idea of what other things Ortlieb might use black candles for.

"Why black?" she asked, as artlessly as she could. "Is that not - well, rather sombre for a feast? One would think we were preparing for a funeral."

"Oh, but it is All Souls' Eve," Hathumod replied."I have seen some of the costumes that the Landgräfin's dressmaker is working on, and they are quite frightening. To tell you the truth," she added, not at all abashed, "I was helping with that at first, but I am not as fine a hand with a needle as some of the other girls, so I was exiled down here to sew beside the lower servants. I shall be glad when this is over, for I am sure that I am developing a blister on my forefinger - see?" She extended the offended finger to show Margerite the faint pinkness on its pale pad. Margerite could not help glancing ruefully at her own cracked and sore hands, but forebore to say anything except, "Yes, that may well be a blister."

"Done already?" Irmingard asked, striding over to the two of them and looking closely at their work. "You see how well you can sew when you put your mind to it, Hathumod? I may as well send you back upstairs to the fine work, for that is as well-done as any noblewoman's embroidery. Maria have mercy, Gertrude, do you call that a straight seam?"

Stung, Margerite looked angrily at the piece of black fabric Irmingard was holding up. Though she had done nothing more strenuous than embroidery since marrying Ruprecht, before her marriage she had stitched some of her best dresses herself, and had always thought that she did well enough. Then she realized that the older seamstress was pointing at a seam Hathumod had done.

Margerite opened her mouth to protest, but the horrible thought came to her that it was not her place to say anything. Luckily, Hathumod was already speaking.

"That is my seam, and there is nothing wrong with it, Irmingard!" the dark-haired girl protested. "And it will be up by the ceiling, where no one can see in any case - why should I ruin my eyes and my hands with tiny stitches as if I were sewing a lady's neckline?"

Irmingard only shook her head. "The Landgräfin wants every woman in the castle who can be spared from duty to work on these things, and that means you, Hathumod. And you have no call to try such airs on me, for I know the closest you ever get to the Landgräfin is carrying up her wine in a pitcher and taking it out again in her chamberpot. I suppose this stitching is Gertrude's?"

"It is," Margerite replied, looking the other woman in the eye before she could remember to drop her gaze and pretend to be meek.

Irmingard absently rubbed at the thin silver bracelet ringing her left wrist, looking skeptically at Margerite. "If I did not know Hathumod, I would never believe that, you know. Do you think you could manage something more complicated?"

"I am no fashionable dressmaker, frowe," Margerite hedged carefully. "But I can sew neatly enough, and even manage a little embroidery if it is wanted."

"Hmph," Irmingard declared. "What were you doing in the kitchen? You can't be one of Liutbirg's apprentices; Sepp wasn't bleeding when he brought you in."

"I was scrubbing pots and stoking the ovens, frowe."

"Wasted talent," Irmingard said forthrightly. "Come over here, and I'll see what you can do. If you do well enough, I may keep you on myself after the feast: a girl like you would never believe the amount of sewing and mending that has to be done in a castle like this."

For the next while, Margerite snipped and stitched under Irmingard's eye, until at last the older woman rose, the bones of her back crackling as she stretched. "Where did you learn to sew?" she demanded. "Those are the stitches of a hand that is used to fine silk, not coarse linen and wool."

"I did some sewing back in Greifenstein, frowe," Margerite mumbled.

"Hmm. Well, Gertrude, do you think that if I put you in more presentable clothes, you can behave yourself well enough to sit and sew among your betters? The child is an inconvenience, but I think even Isabella will overlook it if it means gaining another pair of skilled hands."

"I hope so, frowe," Margerite replied, her heart leaping quietly within her for the first time in days.

"Come along, then."

Margerite gathered Wolfram to her and followed the seamstress up to the next floor, crossing through the minstrels' gallery to the northern part of the castle, then down a corridor. Irmingard opened the door near the end of the passageway, leading Margerite into a room with its northeastern corner cut off by a wide arc of stone - part, Margerite realized, of the high tower at the corner of the Schloss. Looking out one of the western windows, she could see a triangular roof-peak just below: she could only guess that Schloss Niederwald had been built on piece by piece as Bernhardt's family gained in wealth and power - perhaps it had begun as a mere fortified watch-fortress several generations ago. She wondered if the round tower was the oldest part, and then, inevitably, whether it could be the site of Ortlieb's sanctum; it reached a good two stories above the rest of the Schloss, and might well afford the Gräfin enough privacy...

"What is through there, frowe?" Margerite asked as Irmingard dug in one of the chests that lined the walls.

"There? Just the old tower. Storage on the lower floors; the upper ones are chiefly bedrooms where we can put up the less-distinguished guests when we have need to."

Margerite did not dare ask if the guest bedrooms went all the way up, but she resolved to find out for herself as soon as she could come up with a good pretext.

"Now take that filthy thing off and put these on," Irmingard commanded her, holding up a plain shift and a dress of pale green wool. When Margerite had done so, she looked critically at what Margerite had been wearing. "A good wash will make that serviceable enough again. The material is none too bad - I suppose that was your best dress?"

"Yes, frowe."

"I'll see it gets in Monday's wash. Mind you keep this one clean until then, and don't let your babe spit up on it. At least the state of your cloak is not too bad."

"Thank you, frowe," Margerite said meekly.

The seamstress opened the door in the curved tower-wall, leading Margerite up a staircase. The next story of the tower was divided by a short corridor with three doors at the end; Irmingard showed Margerite through the one on the left to a large semi-circular chamber with bolts of various fabrics laid out on the floor, table, and bed, a fire crackling brightly in the hearth, and six women working away.

"This is Gertrude," Irmingard said brusquely. "She can sew very well. I'm letting you have her for now, but mind you return her to me when your work is done."

The olive-skinned woman sitting at the table arched her neck, looking down a long nose at Irmingard. "I do not need you to tell me my business," she said languidly. Her accent was very strong; after a moment, Margerite realized that it reminded her somewhat of Father Etienne's, though the priest spoke far more clearly. "You may go, Irmingard."

When the door had closed, the Frenchwoman considered Margerite, her heavy-lidded black eyes lingering on Margerite's battered hands. Margerite guessed that this must be Ortlieb's own dressmaker: she was dressed in bright red silk cut in the newest fashion herself, bodice cinched in tightly and long sleeves dangling almost to the floor. "Where did Irmingard find you?" she asked, then waved a hand, her gold rings glittering. "No, never mind that. I am quite sure I don't want to know. I am Isabella; you will address me as Madame. You may begin by hemming this skirt, which will not be difficult to rip out when your sewing proves unacceptable."

As if to give voice to his mother's feelings, Wolfram chose that moment to let out a loud wail. The dressmaker's long hands flew to her ears at once, her delicate features screwing up as if in pain.

"Put that child somewhere!" she snapped.

"Where, frowe...Madame?"

"Best to leave it in one of the other bedrooms, where it will hopefully be quieter. Have you fed it?"

"Not lately, Madame," Margerite stammered.

"Take it away and feed it now. I cannot work if I must listen to a babe wailing; if this work had not so much urgency, I should simply dismiss you now. Out! Come back when you are ready to apply yourself without distraction."

Margerite hurried out, pausing irresolute before the other two doors, then glancing down the corridor towards the staircase. If she hurried, she might be able to look at the other two stories before she was expected back - but Wolfram's cry pierced her ears, cutting at something deep within her like the wire of a snare around her entrails. Instead of going up the stairs, she opened the left door, unfastening her dress and pulling one breast out of the top of her shift, and sat on the chilly bed to give her child suck. At least for this level, Irmingard had spoken truly: the room was well-furnished enough, but a stale smell hung in the air, as though the bedding had not been changed for a little while, and it had been some time since a fire had burned on the well-swept hearthstones.

Had it been heated, with fresh strewing herbs and linens, Margerite would not have hesitated to offer such a chamber even to Graf Wolfgang, but she could see how it could easily be classed as for the less distinguished guests in Schloss Niederwald. How God jests with us, she thought sadly. I could not marry Bertram because he was too far below my station; but I was born nearly as far below his.

Wolfram was very hungry, and it was some time before he turned his face from his mother's breasts. Margerite burped him carefully, then wrapped him in his blankets again, laying him in the middle of the bed and taking off her own cloak to keep him warm. Again she thought of running quickly up the stairs to see what was above - but if she could hold her post with the Landgräfin's dressmaker, there would be better opportunities to look around.

"So," the Frenchwoman said when Margerite came back in. "You have gotten rid of it; good. To the hem, girl."

Margerite stitched as best she could, a neat row of stitches so small that they almost vanished into the black velvet. When she was done, Isabella ran a finger carefully over it, sniffing. "I suppose that you can sew," she said grudgingly. "I shall not set you to making the peasant's costume, for no one has the least wish to know what peasants really look like; our work for this feast is a matter of artistry. The young noble, perhaps..." She picked up a long sleeve of deep purple silk, its jagged dags trailing on the ground. "Can you sew sleeves to a garment? Begin."

As Margerite worked, she was able to glance up every now and again to see what the other women were doing. The costumes were all done in deep purple, black, or stark white, and all made of the finest materials, but they varied widely: in addition to the fashionable garment Margerite was stitching on, she recognised a priest's black cassock, a deep purple robe such as a wealthy banker might wear, and what almost appeared to be a shroud of white silk, rent in places and decorated with fantastic tattered streamers.

She could not imagine what such costumes might be
meant for, but as she sewed, she was aware of a vague
unease creeping over her, as though the fire were not
quite enough to keep the chill from the air. Is it because I
am close to Ortlieb's sanctum? she wondered. The other
women seemed impervious to whatever was unnerving her,
chattering happily as they worked.

Two of them were speaking French with the dressmaker,
ignoring the others; Margerite noticed that they were doing
the most delicate work, and guessed that they must be
assistants that the Frenchwoman had brought with her.
When the faint ringing of a bell chimed outside, all the
women stood.

Isabella and her two assistants swept out without a word;
the others hurried quickly downstairs, and Margerite
followed them to the kitchen where the first course, neatly
trimmed rounds of meat no wider than Margerite's thumb
suspended in a delicate rose-coloured jelly, was neatly laid
out in polished silver bowls for serving - though it was a
Friday, that seemed to make no more difference to Ortlieb
than it had to Ruprecht.

No one bothered to tell Margerite what to do, so she
picked up a tray as her fellow seamstresses were doing
and followed them into the great hall. Even though there
was plenty of light coming from the huge windows on the
western wall, the gold candelabras on the table blazed
brightly, and the torches in the wall-sconces burned with a
pleasant resinous scent, as if it were already full dark.

A boy's high soprano floated from the minstrels' balcony
overhead, underlaid with glittering runs of notes from harp
and lute. Now that Margerite had a moment to look about
herself, she could see that the huge tapestries on the walls
were interspersed with panels of wood-carving, and above
the door on the northern wall hung a beautifully carved
and gilded coat of arms the height of a man: a gold stag's
head holding a full-faced helm within its antlers, with gold
mantling down the sides, and below it a leaping silver fish,
all on a red field.

The motto blazoned proudly beneath the coat of arms read simply: UNCONQUERED - a noble boast, and one, Margerite thought with a warming of her heart, that Bernhardt had well lived up to. Margerite did not dare to go up to the high table, for she was sure that the servants there would take the presence of an interloper ill. Instead she waited by the door until the Landgraf and Landgräfin had been served their food, watching covertly under her lashes.

The Landgraf, in spite of his fashionable doublet of gold and blue velvet, was a rather ordinary-looking man: his mousy brown hair hung straight about his shoulders, and the small goatee on his chin did little to emphasize the lines of his face. Still, it seemed to her that she could see something of Bernhardt in his features, though they were blurred by good living - or not sharpened by the trials that had seared his brother's face to the bone.

It was Ortlieb who drew her eye, however: brightly lit as the room was, Ortlieb seemed to draw every ray of illumination to herself, transforming it to radiate as a darker glow from amber-brown hair and deep blue silk and the matching rubies at her throat and on her finger. When she lifted her golden goblet, the utter self-possession of the movement left Margerite breathless; when she touched the wine to her rose-pink lips, though she sipped lightly, it was with the sureness of a predator who had already slain and could hence afford to lap delicately at the blood for a little while before plunging her muzzle in to tear at her prey's entrails.

Margerite had to lower her eyes and look away, for the tray of silver bowls was shaking in her hands - not with fear, but with hatred: it was too easy to imagine Ortlieb crouching over Bernhardt's body, holding him as helpless for her pleasure as the gleaming goblet in her hand. When the folk at the high table had begun to eat, the lower servitors carried their food around to those remaining - the lesser knights of the castle, dressed in surcoats over their mail, and castle officials such as, Margerite guessed, the seneschal and his assistants.

Ortlieb's dressmaker and her attendants were allowed to eat in the great hall, as were a few other women in fine clothes - the Landgräfin's ladies-in-waiting, Margerite guessed. Two of them in particular drew Margerite's eye, though she had to be careful not to stare at them: a black-haired woman and a fair-haired one, wearing silks and brocades as fine as anything Margerite had ever owned.

The other diners seemed to keep a little distance from them; and as Margerite stood behind the women, carefully placing the bowls of meat in jelly before them, she noticed the rings on their hands: among the glittering gold and bright stones on their fingers, each of them wore a large polished onyx with the familiar words EX TENEBRAE LUX inscribed around it. She could not suppress her soft gasp, but luckily they paid her no attention - why should they notice a servant, unless she made some error?

After the last course had been cleared away, the servants went back through the kitchen and into the long room to its north where, Margerite knew, they would be given their own dinner - the trenchers of bread soaked in the rich juices from the meats eaten in the great hall, together with such leftovers as the kitchen workers had not already snatched and stew from the large pot that was always simmering over one of the fires in the outer kitchen.

Margerite kept closely together with the others, but none of the kitchen staff spared her a second glance: it was as though they hardly recognised her without a dirty pot or scrub-brush in her hands. Hoping for conversation, Margerite sat down beside one of the women from the sewing-room, but the young maiden barely looked at her before tossing her thick fair braid over one shoulder and turning her head to talk to the liveried serving-man on her other side.

The horn cup and spoon and simple wood-handled knife
that Margerite had brought with her seemed very shabby
next to the gear of the other upper servants: a couple of
them, near the head of the table, actually had silver cups and
spoons, as if they were nobility themselves.

Even though it was watered, Margerite could tell that
the wine was rather thin and lacking in flavour; but since
she had gotten nothing save small beer mixed with water
as a kitchen servant, she sipped it as though it were one of
Heinrich's imported vintages, careful not to let it go to her
head.

Margerite's dining companions ignored her throughout
the meal, as though she were of no consequence; she was
not sure whether she had not been driven away because the
other servants were unsure of her place, or because they
considered it beneath them to tell her to eat with the kitchen
scullions.

Irmingard glanced over to her once with an encouraging
smile, but the other woman was too far away to talk,
and Margerite thought that it would be wiser not to give
her the chance to ask more questions in any case. The
Frenchwoman kept her workers sewing until well after
sundown, when she finally shook her hands out and put her
work down with a sigh.

"This is going too slowly," Isabella said in exasperation.
"Do you have any idea of how much must be done by All
Souls' Eve? The Landgräfin has decreed that there must be
something for everyone in the hall - everyone, mind you,
guests and serving maids alike - to wear. Go to bed now, my
little ones, but be ready to work again by the first light of
dawn."

Wolfram was screaming again by the time Margerite
got to him. Deftly she changed his cloths, setting the soiled
ones onto the floor - thank Mother Maria, the wetness had
not soaked through onto the bed! - and picked the child up,
cuddling him close and murmuring sweetly into his soft
golden hair until he calmed down enough to suckle. Now
there is no one watching, she thought as she rocked the
child.

Now I could go up to see…But she could not bring Wolfram with her on such a venture, and now that night had fallen, the chill was striking deeper into her bones. She felt that even the warmth and noise and stink of the servants' quarters would be welcome now, for the simple reassurance of having other human bodies around her, of being able to press Eva's hand a moment in passing and knowing that, even though it was unsafe to pass more than a quick whisper between them, she was not alone in Ortlieb's stronghold.

But there might be no better chance to go up the tower and search: it was her first day with the Frenchwoman, and she might easily have become lost, gone up one or two flights too many when she came back to look for something she had dropped in the costuming room. She set Wolfram down, wrapping him carefully in her cloak once more, and took up her candle.

The staircase in the tower wall was very cold, the dank air chilling Margerite's lungs with each breath. This high, the stairs were very small, narrow and irregular, so that she had to look carefully where she placed each footstep. She moved slowly, listening at every step for a rustle or murmur that might warn her away, but she heard nothing: only the sound of her own breathing harsh in her ears and the very faint hiss and sputter of wax from the candle in her hand. The little trembling flame cast a faint circle of light around her, stretching thinly before and behind, fading into darkness at each turn of the stair.

The rooms on the fifth floor were very much like those below, save that the tower was quartered rather than divided into three. It only took a moment's glance into each chamber to see the stripped beds and empty hearths, and the tiny black piles of mouse-droppings on the floor that told Margerite that it had been a long time since they were used.

How wasteful, she thought: she had never before been in a castle that did not seem to cry out for more rooms for storing linens and other goods, and yet these chambers seemed to be left fallow for no good reason. Even if these rooms are needed for guests now and again, the space could still be put to good use. If I were mistress here, things would be arranged much better. She turned away, creeping up the stairs again.

This far up, even the faint scurry of a mouse on the stairs sounded loud as the footsteps of a man in full armour - and Kobolt would have good hunting up here. But I have seen no cats in this castle - no wonder there are so many vermin about. Kobolt and Kriemhilt could soon set matters to rights there. Sternly Margerite forced her mind back to the matter at hand. No matter how shielded Ortlieb's sanctum was, she thought she should be able to feel it. She would not even have to go in, and the door would surely be locked anyway...

The door at the top of the staircase was locked. Slowly Margerite lifted her hand, laying her palm against it. The smooth oaken beams were almost as chill as metal beneath her touch, and when she breathed deeply, she smelled staleness and dust. But nothing else. There was no whiff of incense, fair or foul, there at the top of the stairs.

No breath of herbal smoke, or even of burning beeswax, came to her: only the tallow of her own candle and the faint muskiness of a place where mice played freely. Margerite wondered blackly if Ortlieb had not set down poison for the rodents because she preyed on them in owl-form - but no: Maria help us, she has other prey. Still, Margerite could not shake the image of the owl swooping from the top of the tower in silence, her wings passing noiselessly through the cold autumn night as she glided back and forth, seeking out what she might devour.

And if this is not her sanctum, where might she keep it? Standing there at the castle's highest point, Margerite realized that she had been hoping desperately to find Ortlieb's magical stronghold in the tower. Even now, her gaze kept falling upon the heavy wooden doorknob and the black iron lock beneath it, and she moved her fingers slowly down over them again, waiting for something - a tingle, a spark such as might fly from a cat's fur in cold dry weather, a faint chill or sliminess beneath her touch. But there was nothing, no hint that Order magic had ever passed there. Perhaps it is only very well warded?

But if the Black Book had taught Margerite anything, it was the danger of believing too hard in what she wanted to believe. Ortlieb might well have thought just as Margerite had: that the tower was the best place to do her magics, high above the rest of the castle where she could neither be heard nor seen - and gone on to realize that any foe searching out her secret place would realize the same thing, and left the tower alone for that very reason. At least Margerite had not been tempted to use her skills to try to see beyond the door: if the Order Princess had as much sense as any castle's architect, she might also have left a trap there, to ensnare anyone trying to pry into her secrets, or at least to warn her of her danger.

And if Ortlieb, like Ruprecht and Nikolaus, had managed to build or find a hidden place somewhere in Schloss Niederwald - what hope was there that Margerite could sniff it out without alerting her foe? Margerite could not guess: she could only keep her eyes and ears open, and hope that Mother Maria would guide her rightly.

Margerite hurried down the stairs, moving as quickly as she could without losing her footing on the treacherously placed steps. In the bedroom on the fourth floor, Wolfram was crying again, and she sat for a long time holding him to her before making her way back down towards the servants' quarters. Bernhardt sat in the upper chamber of Lothar's house, stroking a whetstone over the glittering edge of his sword in the dim twilight that filtered through the small window.

Soon he would venture downstairs to light his candle from the banked coals of Lothar's hearth, but not yet. Bernhardt had often waited so before: it sometimes seemed to him as though this long silence was a distillation of his eight years of exile, all the fire and blood of his days as a mercenary no more than a dark and fading dream.

Weeks at a time of sitting in camp, waiting for the Black Sword's commander to croak out new orders; the long months in Burg Falkenstein, watching Ruprecht and waiting for his lord to make the fatal error, to betray the secrets of those who were set above him in the Order; the dragging days of siege, and the longer ones afterward, as he lay slowly recovering from the corrupt wound that Ruprecht's servants had dealt him...

He had well learned how to let each day pass after the next, not to chafe against the bonds of time and slowness. Patience in small things, such as lighting his candle, made it easier to be patient through the long wait: the chill of the room, the gathering darkness, the pervasive stink of piss from the two cats that Margerite and Eva had insisted on bringing with them, the smell rising softly from his own chamberpot - all of those, he could endure, and enduring them, he could keep himself from being worn down by day falling upon day, with nothing to do save exercise as best as he could in his confinement, think, and sleep.

And yet this was different, for now Bernhardt was upon his own lands, only a short ride from the home of his birth. When he closed his eyes, he could see the tapestries in the great hall where, as a child, he had tossed a stuffed leather ball from one end to the other, running after it and shouting until his nurse reproved him for playing like a peasant; he could see the sparkling fountains in the pleasure garden, whose hidden intricacies of pipes sent the water leaping to glisten in the sunlight, splattering back into the pools like a golden rain.

While he marched with the Black Sword, and later, training village boys to man the walls of Burg Falkenstein, Bernhardt had put such thoughts aside as best he might, locked them away in the dungeons of his own mind as traitors who might, at any moment, knife him from behind. But now they crept forth again, surrounding him in silence, and he no longer had the strength to thrust them from him.

And what of Jürgen and Erich? Bernhardt thought. Until his escape, he had committed no crime: though he had sinned with Ortlieb, he had never slain a man till then, and the worst violence he had ever done had been upon the tourney field, for Schloss Niederwald had been at peace since before he was born.

He had confessed their deaths, done hard penance for them; and even when he was travelling with the Black Sword, when he could slip away from his comrades long enough, he had lit candles and prayed for their souls at whatever churches or wayside shrines he could find.

Yet, for all the lives he had taken since, his two friends' faces still haunted him, nor would he ever forget the feeling of his stolen sword shattering through the riveted links of Jürgen's hauberk to ram deep into the young knight's flesh, the muscles sucking hard against it as he pulled it out to parry Erich's blade in a wide sweep, lunging up with the tip into the other's unprotected throat - ah, God, Erich, you fool.

You were on guard duty: why did you not bother to wear at least a chain coif under your bascinet? Was it because you believed in my innocence, or trusted me? But he had been half-mad from the night horror that Ortlieb had sent to him in his cell, strong enough with that madness to break the lock and wrest the sword from Jürgen's hand; and when the other man drew his dagger, Bernhardt's training had overcome his thoughts until his guards were both dead.

Then, with the two knights' bodies crumpled in the hallway and the smoky light of the torches shining red off the black trickles of their blood, he had known that he could only flee, or die himself - and though he had wanted to die, he knew that he could not bear another night locked up within the walls of Schloss Niederwald, at the mercy of whatever Ortlieb chose to send to torment him.

A long road back, and an ill one, Bernhardt thought. But by Maria's mercy, I may yet be able to bring it to good at the end, and atone for all my wrongs. The sword was sharp enough now; the least pressure of the edge against his thumb cut easily through the heavy callous, and a slightly harder touch would have brought the blood springing out. He lifted his hand, touching the lump beneath his rough tunic where the necklace Margerite had given him rested warm against his heart.

She had given him hope again, springing forth from his heart like the waters of the Marienbrunnen running free once more when they had cleared away the rotten leaves and slime that choked its stream. If Bernhardt concentrated hard enough, he could almost see Margerite's face before him: pale and high-boned, framed by coiled braids of fair hair, with eyes as cool and blue as the sky in springtime, and a quiet dignity that the highest of ladies might envy, for all she had been born to a poor knight in a little border keep.

Though, as a young knight, Bernhardt had danced with some of the fairest women in the Empire, their faces and voices were nothing more to him now than shifting patterns of leaves and the chattering of birds. For he had seen Margerite, great-eyed and pale with fear, readying herself to face the Powers of Hell with no other weapon than her own bravery; he had felt her arms clinging tight about him, striving to give him comfort even from the depths of her own desperation.

And, Maria help him, he loved her, though she had been Ruprecht's wife and was Heinrich's now. If he lives, Bernhardt could not help thinking, and then, Christ forgive me! Bernhardt turned his mind away from those thoughts as he would rein his horse back from boggy ground, for he could see nothing in considering the matter of Heinrich's life or death, save, if he allowed it, sin and damnation.

But closing his eyes, he remembered how he had first seen Margerite at her father's fortress: garbed in an embroidered dress of blue linen no better than what one of Schloss Niederwald's lower servants might wear to Mass, only the flush of pink on her cheeks betraying her excitement as she greeted Ruprecht and his band - already used to being the mistress of a household, to giving commands and wielding authority, but so very young, hardly out of childhood.

He almost blushed to think how badly he had misjudged her then, how easy it had been for him to mistake her self-assurance for the unnatural pride of an Order woman such as Ortlieb, just as he had mistaken Margerite's great black tomcat for a demon, and the desires of his own body when he looked upon her slim waist and the curves of her velvet-clad breasts for the dreadful fires that Ortlieb had set burning in his flesh with every touch of her hand upon his own.

The edges of the falcon-pendant's wings pressed painfully against Bernhardt's palm through the heavy gray linen that hid it, and carefully he loosened his grip, lest he crush the gold bird. He had slept better since Margerite gave him the necklace; though sometimes he still awoke in a cold sweat, with the echoes of a mocking call like the distant hooting of an owl in his ears, she had not come to him in his dreams again, to torture him until he woke drained and shamed.

Deliberately, Bernhardt crossed himself, repeating the Ave Maria thrice, then went downstairs to light his candle before he took up his shield and began to scour the steel rim. That work, at least, had not changed: not when he was a squire under Landgraf Friedrich, nor when he sat about the Black Sword's campfire listening with half an ear to the boasting and swearing of his fellow mercenaries, nor when he was Hauptmann of Ruprecht's castle guard, showing his lads how to tend their equipment.

"Until you can see every hair of your beard in it - when you grow a beard, Knappe," Landgraf Friedrich had said to him, thumping him lightly on the shoulder.

Bernhardt had held to that standard since, through every change in his station - a mute reassurance, perhaps, that however his clothes and manners might alter, he was still the man who had kept his vigil all through one cool spring night beneath the Landgraf's gilded altar, and vowed himself in the morning to the honour and burden of knighthood, receiving the buffet that was the last he should ever take without answer and putting on his gilded spurs.

For all that had followed, and though his shield bore no device and would not until he had come to his own again, Bernhardt still kept his shield's rim as clean as it had been that day. Looking at his elongated reflection in the narrow strip of metal now, Bernhardt saw that his hair was coming in brown at the roots again.

Even in the candlelight, and beneath the tangle of walnut-dyed black curls, it had grown out enough so that his head looked as if it had been dusted with clay about the skull. For a moment he thought of asking Lothar for what he needed to darken it again - but no. The time for his disguise was done: he was no longer Bertram of the Black Sword Company, or even Bertram, Hauptmann of a castle guard, but Bernhardt von Niederwald; and thus he would triumph, or die.

But even if I do all that I hope to, defeat Ortlieb and overcome Gerhardt and take my place as Landgraf over my father's realm - what manner of triumph will it be, if Margerite is still wedded to Heinrich? a treacherous voice whispered in the back of Bernhardt's mind.

From downstairs, Bernhardt heard the sound of a key turning in the lock, then footsteps creaking on the wooden floor. One hand on his sword, the other on his shield, he sat very still, waiting. He thought he recognised Lothar's heavy, sure tread - but any man could be compromised, even forced into betrayal by Ortlieb's arts: he did not dare make any sound until he was sure that all was well. The second set of footsteps was lighter and quicker, almost running behind the gamekeeper - and then Bernhardt heard Georg's sweet tenor floating upward, mellow as the soft notes of a golden horn, and eased a little.

"Is there news from the Frowe Gräfin and Eva?" the boy was asking eagerly. "What have they found?"

"No news yet, lad, save that they are both alive and well." Lothar said. "Go up to Herr Bernhardt, for I do not doubt that you have something to tell him."

Dirty and travel-stained as he was, Georg bore himself with a good pride as he entered Bernhardt's chamber. "Herr Bernhardt, I found the Bear's Paw Company and delivered your message," the Knappe said at once. "Hauptmann Paul says that they are ready to come whenever you call them, and that Jochanan has a full load of powder for his guns. Did you know that he is a Jew? I actually saw..."

Bernhardt waved his hand to silence the boy. "I know. But this is very good news that you bring. How many of them are there now?"

Georg seemed to have a good head for men and numbers, for he reeled off the lists without a moment's hesitation. The Bear's Paw Company was a little smaller than it had been when they were fighting at Burg Falkenstein. Some of the men had been killed, while others had gone off to join the Companies that Arnaut de Cervole had led into the Empire that summer, or made their way towards the great gathering of Free Companies in France. But there were still enough, Bernhardt judged, to deal with the garrison at Schloss Niederwald, even without the advantage of Jochanan's guns - for he did not truly want those weapons fired at his father's castle, whatever the cause.

"The men of the Bear's Paw Company do not seem bad men," Georg ended. "Though I have not seen them fight yet, I do not think I should fear to have them at my back in battle. Though I suppose they are no saints, they are very different from the half-brigand rabble that my father always spoke of."

"They are, indeed," Bernhardt said. "I have known far worse among the Free Companies: I would not have sent you alone to treat, for instance, with the commander of the Black Sword - but then, such a Company would not have come to aid a friend when there were rich pickings to be had elsewhere. And you had no trouble on the way?"

The Knappe looked away, suddenly pale beneath the splotchy freckles that spread over his long nose and thin cheeks. "No!" he said at once, then muttered softly, "Well, yes. On my way out through the hunting park, I met with... her."

"What happened?"

"She spoke with me a few moments and rode on," Georg said. "She...did nothing to me." His wiry fingers twisted about each other, and he still would not meet Bernhardt's eyes.

"Tell me what she said."

"She asked who I was and what I was doing there, and I told her the story we had agreed on, that I was a merchant's son who had become lost and Lothar had directed me out. And that was all."

"Are you sure?" Bernhardt pressed. Finally Georg looked straight at him, a violent blush spreading over the boy's face.

"She asked me if I was a virgin. And I told her not, and she rode away."

Bernhardt cringed within, for he could hear the dreadful ache of longing in Georg's voice, like silk dragged over a wound, even as the Knappe's mouth twisted in revulsion. And, Maria help him, Bernhardt could feel his own manhood stirring as Georg's words echoed through his own memory, a painful spark of jealousy and relief twinging through him at the thought of how Ortlieb had addressed, then abandoned, the boy.

Dear Maria, dear Christ, will I ever be free of her before she is dead?

"You are very lucky," Bernhardt told him gently. "Say your prayers, and give thanks to Christ and Mother Maria that you escaped so easily."

Georg's lips set into a thin tight line, but he made no answer to that.

"You are not the only one here who has found what she can do to men, you know," Bernhardt added, his voice very soft.

The Knappe looked up at him, a wild look blossoming in his bright blue eyes. "You?" he asked.

Bernhardt nodded, an unfamiliar heat warming his cheeks. "I was her victim once too."

"Then how... in God's Name, how did you ever manage... to forget her?" Georg blurted, his honeyed voice stumbling over the words.

"I have not," Bernhardt admitted. Then, perhaps because he had unburdened his heart so seldom in the last years; perhaps because Georg, for all his youth, could hardly be called anything but a man now, and they shared what Bernhardt had known that he could never explain to another, he found himself going on. "But I have given my love chastely..." Or almost so, save for my own vagrant thoughts and that one time..."to a far better woman, who is worthy of the greatest love and devotion a man can manage. Two women," he added slowly, "for I put my trust in the Queen of Heaven, who gives her mercy even to the worst of men."

"Are you in love with Gräfin Margerite?" Georg asked.

Bernhardt said nothing. He had spoken too much already.

"I will not say anything to anyone," Georg promised. "But I will tell you my own secret: I am in love with Eva, even though she is more than half-sworn to my knight." His mismatched features were very earnest as he spoke, blue eyes shining beneath the rim of his iron-bound leather cap. "I have not dared to say anything of it to her - but we were a long time on the road together, and more than once she has looked at me from beneath her lashes."

Bernhardt was about to speak to Georg as if he were one of the Tiefensee boys, telling him sharply that if he thought a few flirtatious glances from such a girl as Eva meant that she returned his love, he was due to be quickly disappointed, and would do best to look elsewhere.

But he checked himself: both Eva and Georg were nobly born, and even if, as he was sure would be the case, Eva thought of Georg as nothing more than a boy now, what was mere empty-headed foolishness to be quickly knocked out of a peasant lad was something different for a well-born squire who should be learning all the intricate dances of court and pleasant company - and whether it led to sin or not, it would be better for Georg to think on Eva than on Ortlieb. Thus, when Bernhardt answered Georg, it was as if his younger self were speaking like a ghost from his mouth, heedless of the years between them.

"The hidden love of a man for a noble lady is a brave and fine thing," Bernhardt said gravely, though he knew it to be nonsense. "For the sake of her modesty, its declaration ought not to be too ready, but a single glance from her eyes should suffice to fill your heart with joy and keep your love burning constant. Yet all your deeds are done for her: whether you ride forth to battle, or carry away the prize at a tourney, it is only to lay your victory before her feet." As I would lay Schloss Niederwald at yours, Margerite...No: such thoughts were vain, and would bring him only sorrow.

Georg was hanging on every word, a smile playing upon his lips, but Bernhardt found that he did not have the heart to go on. "And you can read more of courtly love for yourself when our work here is done," he said gruffly. "For now, be content that you have fulfilled your duties bravely and well."

"Thank you, Herr Bernhardt!" Georg replied, beaming at him.

Margerite's work under Isabella was as endless as her kitchen labours, and more exacting, but she threw herself into it enthusiastically - not only because it brought her closer to Ortlieb, and gave her license to walk through Schloss Niederwald whenever she was sent out to fetch something, but also, she had to admit to herself, because it was far more suited to her than scrubbing pots and carrying water and wood for the kitchen.

She hated to leave Wolfram unattended for such long periods, because she could never completely shake the chilly unease she felt while sitting in the tower room with the dressmakers, but there was nothing she could do about it, and he seemed to take no harm from being left in the unused bedroom.

Michaelmas passed almost unnoticed in Schloss Niederwald: if other servants were permitted to go to celebrate in the castle's chapel, the women labouring on Ortlieb's costumes could not be spared for such things as Sundays or saints' days.

Margerite found herself thinking with some compassion on Father Hans, that poor drunken priest who had laboured at Burg Falkenstein beneath the burden of a scornful lord and a duty for which he was not suited, and as she stitched, she murmured a prayer for his soul.

It was a week after Michaelmas when the door of the costumers' room opened unexpectedly. The woman standing in the doorway was the full-figured, black-haired maiden that Margerite had marked eating in the great hall - one of the two who bore the Order's onyx ring. She did not look at any of Isabella's assistants, but spoke directly to the Frenchwoman.

"The Landgräfin is ready for her fitting now," the Order maiden said, her voice chiming clear and bright through the room. "Attend her in her chambers."

Isabella rose, beckoning to her two apprentices and saying something in French to them. Almost as an afterthought, she added, "Gertrude, carry those bolts of black velvet and silk."

Margerite heaved the heavy bundles of fabric to her shoulder, her heart fluttering within her. If she could get into Ortlieb's chambers, she could see if perhaps there was any place that might lead to a hidden passage. For a fleeting moment, she wished that she had not given the falcon-necklace to Bernhardt, for she felt curiously naked at the thought of coming beneath Ortlieb's gaze without it; but of course, it would have given her away as an imposter to the other servants at once if anyone had seen it.

Still, the wards that she had painstakingly constructed for herself, murmuring the words of protection as prayers late at night before sleeping and early in the morning upon arising, seemed like flimsy veils to hide her from the Order Princess. The Landgräfin's suite was on the third floor, down a long corridor from the old tower. Margerite, labouring under her burden, lagged a little behind the other women and nearly had the door closed in her face by one of the French girls.

Ortlieb sat at her ease in a huge polished chair whose carvings gleamed with a high gloss, reclining on the red velvet cushions that padded it with her long sleeves trailing over the armrests. Several sheets of parchment lay scattered on the table before her, and a gray quill pen rested beside her finely wrought gilded inkwell. But, even as in the great hall, it was the woman herself who drew the eye.

Today her amber-brown hair was piled high on her head in an elaborate coiffure of tiny braids, its rich gleams of gold and red enhanced by a spare weave of gold thread through the braiding. She wore a dress of deep green figured with light blue brocading, with light blue sleeves figured in deep green: the colours made her lambent eyes glow the more darkly and brought out the glitter of green flecks through their polished brown irises.

This close, Margerite could see how smooth Ortlieb's skin was, with a pale rich glow as though she bathed daily in the finest cream; the deep red ruby at her throat was as big as the tip of Margerite's thumb, and the stone's fire, like that of the ruby ring on her forehead, burned so dark and intense that Margerite would almost have feared to touch it.

Dressed in her plain blue wool, unbathed save for a few quick rubdowns with a wet rag, Margerite felt miserably small and grubby, like a little sparrowhawk tattered from moult set next to a great glossy-feathered gyrfalcon, and she found herself shrinking back behind the other women.

She was only thankful that Bernhardt was not there to see the two of them together, to measure one against the other; for even had Margerite been freshly bathed and garbed in her finest dresses, with all the dignity of her title about her, she knew that Ortlieb would outshine her as the sun outshone the palest stars - and her hatred for the other woman swelled bitterly in her breast like a thistle-bud breaking into thorny flower.

Thankfully, Ortlieb did not so much as glance at Margerite; but though the only scent in the room was a faint clean odour of sandalwood and sweet spices, Margerite felt as though she were breathing in thick smoke; her head pounded with dizziness, and she had to inhale and exhale carefully to keep from fainting.

To keep her mind clear, and so that she would not stare at the Gräfin in an unseemly or suspicious way, Margerite looked around at the tapestries hanging on the walls, all of which showed fantastic scenes, wrought in a startling combination of dark and brilliant colours.

One was a Temptation of St. Anthony with the naked bodies of the female demons embroidered in loving detail around a startlingly handsome Anthony whose manhood was barely hidden by his half-fallen loincloth; the saint's hand rested on the breast of one of the demons, and his head was thrown back with his mouth open as if in passion.

Another depicted the Three Living and the Three Dead, showing a party of three young nobles coming upon three open coffins - one holding a body that was still clothed in rich finery, but green-faced and puffy; one filled by a half-rotted corpse with worms crawling from its mouth and the cavity of its open abdomen; and one containing a skeleton.

One of the tapestries showed what might have been the siege of Jerusalem: at least, there was a walled city on a hill, and a white-clad army bowing down as if in prayer - but the fortification was black, its detail all picked out in silver, and the open mouths of the men kneeling before it, when Margerite stared at them, seemed to be crying out in abject horror.

The longer Margerite looked at the tapestries, the more deeply they disturbed her - as if, beautifully worked as they were, there were some fundamental flaw in their proportions or design that unsettled the sight, like a slight retuning of a lute twisting a bright song into a jangling dirge.

She forced herself to think about what they could hide; but none of the tapestries reached down to the floor as the one concealing Ruprecht's secret door had, and she did not think Ortlieb would crawl through a hole in the wall to reach her sanctum. If there were a passage from the Landgräfin's suite, it must lead out through one of the other rooms.

"Show me the fabrics, Isabella," Ortlieb said languidly. To Margerite's ears, her low voice - almost as deep as a man's, but smooth as the hiss of silk on silk - seemed to thrum with resonances just below hearing, resonances that set up a trembling in Margerite's bones.

Hastily, before Ortlieb could speak again or her dressmaker repeat the order, Margerite bore the two bolts of cloth forward, standing before the Landgräfin with her eyes lowered. She might have been a piece of wood for all the attention Ortlieb paid to her as she reached forward, fingering first one corner of cloth, then another.

"Clean the table, Hedwig," Ortlieb said, and the raven-haired girl hastened to obey, gathering the parchments up carefully and bearing them, together with quill and inkwell, into another room. Margerite caught just a glimpse of scarlet hangings before the door closed again - could the Landgräfin's sanctum actually be in her suite?

Surely not, for even she could not avoid the attentions of such servants as Hathumod who must sweep and clean her stoves and wash her chamberpot.

At Ortlieb's imperious gesture, Margerite carefully laid the bolts on the table, unfolding a short length of each and stepping back. The Landgräfin considered the two fabrics for a time.

"These will not do for me, Isabella," she said at last. "They will suit for Hedwig and Oda, but I want my dress to be cut from the Flanders brocade. You and your assistants may begin the measurements now."

Isabella turned to Margerite, hissing, "Gertrude, go fetch it," and pressing a key into her hand before she opened her basket and began laying the tools of her trade upon the table.

Margerite hurried out at once. She knew where the good fabrics were kept, for whenever something was wanted in the sewing room, whether material or thread or a cup of wine to soothe Isabella's throat after half an hour of snapping at her underlings, it was she who was sent for it. She ran down the stairs, unlocking the storeroom and looking through the piles of fine material.

There: the deep violet figured with black, its heavy silken weave so fine that one could barely see the threads, let alone count them. Holding the bolt of brocade carefully, Margerite ran back up to Ortlieb's chambers, breathing hard. The Landgräfin did not so much as nod when Margerite laid it on top of the others: she was too busy instructing the dressmaker who knelt by her feet.

"The shape of the rib-bones should be picked out on my bodice in seed pearls," Ortlieb said, "and you will have to pearl my mask likewise."

"But Madame Landgräfin, that lovely brocade...you want me to disfigure it with the image of a skeleton?"

"I am to be Queen Death," Ortlieb said, her voice deepening to rich velvet thunder. "And all who see me must know it at once. For this is the dance of Death triumphant, from which neither God, nor the angels, nor the saints, can save any man. You may leave the dress unadorned below the waist, but the lines of the skeleton shall show above."

"As you please, Madame Landgräfin, " Isabella muttered unhappily.

"Hedwig, pour me a drop of cordial."

The black-haired girl went back into the room with scarlet hangings, coming out a moment later with an unhappy look on her pretty face. "Girl," she said to Margerite, "go fetch a bottle of cordial from the stillroom."

Margerite ran down the stairs into the servants' hall and through into the stillroom, a large triangular chamber to the north of the great hall. Like the kitchens, the stillroom was always warm with the fires in its stove and hearth.

Two big vats of malt seethed beneath their pale blankets of bubbling yeast, and the familiar sharp scents of hops and mugwort and rosemary filled the air. Bunches of dried herbs hung from the ceiling; the shelves were lined with jars and bottles and muslin bags, and several iron pots of different sizes hung along the wall.

In one corner, several complicated arrangements of copper vessels and pipes bubbled and dripped; though Margerite had never turned her own hand to distilling aqua vitae, or even making rosewater by any means more complex than grinding, steeping, and expressing the virtues from the summer petals, she recognised the alembics without difficulty.

A slender, fair-haired boy sat at the table, crushing herbs in a stone mortar with an intense concentration that would have done credit to a young monk, and Margerite recognised the mustiness of dill and fennel seed below the sweetness of angelica root and mint - as sumptuous as the food at the high table was, she thought, it was no wonder that indigestion remedies would be needed regularly.

Meister Karl, who oversaw the stillroom, was a middle-aged man whose honey-brown hair curled artfully around his long severe face; though he wore doublets of well-stitched linen in bright colours when he came into the great hall to eat, here at his work he had thrown a stained brown robe over his clothes to protect them from splatters and spills. He was standing above the tiled stove now, stirring something at a measured pace.

"Yes, what is it?" he said, glancing at Margerite without halting his circling spoon for a moment.

"The Landgräfin wishes a bottle of cordial."

"Did she say what kind? No, of course not, she never does." Karl sighed deeply. "Try the rose cordial - third shelf up, second bottle on the left, the deep red one - and Christ help you if she wants thyme to soothe a sore throat."

Margerite hastened back up with the bottle of rose cordial. Ortlieb paid her no attention until Hedwig had uncorked the bottle and poured a small measure into the little golden cup on the table. Then the Landgräfin sniffed at the draught and, without any change in her faint smile, turned and struck Margerite open-handed across the face.

Margerite stood stunned from the blow, her ears ringing. Her left cheek was almost numb with pain, but she could feel the warm trickle of blood snaking down where Ortlieb's ring had cut her. Only her Order training in self-mastery kept her from lifting her own hand to return the blow; she stood with her head down and palms flat against her thighs to keep her fists from clenching, trembling like an aspen leaf in a fury that she sincerely hoped Ortlieb would mistake for fear. You have drawn first blood, Margerite thought angrily, but we shall see who gives the last blow!

"Spice cordial, not rose," Ortlieb said indifferently, and turned her attention back to the dressmaker and her assistants. One cheek burning from the slap, the other with humiliation, Margerite picked up the offending bottle and hurried back to the stillroom, blotting the blood from her cheek with her sleeve on the way.

The master of the stillroom was pouring the hot salve from his pans into a clay jar when Margerite came back in. Setting the pan aside, he looked at her with a remote pity on his long-jawed face. "Marigold and comfrey ointment for that, I should say." Karl took an earthenware pot from one of the shelves. "Hold still a moment." His stained fingers dipped into the pot, coming out with a generous glob that he smeared over Margerite's cheek, holding her head steady with the other hand.

Margerite felt uncomfortable at the intimacy of his gentle touch; she could smell the faint warm spiciness of cinnamon on his breath, and it seemed to her that he held her chin a moment longer than was necessary, his gray-blue eyes looking deeply into her own. But she did not respond, and he let go of her - perhaps she had only imagined that he was taking liberties.

"What does the Landgräfin want?"

"She wants the spice cordial."

"Well enough." Karl reached up to the top shelf, bringing down a small glass flask of deep brown liquid. "And tell her from me that whatever she wishes me to make for her All Souls' feast, I must know about it now, for men may be hurried as she pleases, but whatever the need, herbs will yield up their virtues no more swiftly than their natures allow."

Margerite glanced surreptitiously at Karl's hands, but he wore only a simple gold circle on his wedding-finger. Yet, even without being an Order member, he might concoct more than rosewater and cordials for Ortlieb - aside from the hours he no doubt spends making potions to keep her skin white and soft, and chammomile washes to gild that brown hair, she could not help thinking.

"May I have a little of the marigold and comfrey salve for my hands?" Margerite asked meekly.

Though the worst of the dead skin from her ordeal in the kitchens had finally peeled away, her hands were still redder and rougher than they had been, and the fingers were growing calloused from the work of sewing from dawn to dusk. She knew that she ought to run back to the Landgräfin's room, but the flare of rebellion that Ortlieb's blow had sparked in her heart still glowed hot: let the wretched woman wait on Margerite's pleasure for a few moments!

"Of course you may," Karl said warmly. The master of the stillroom took one of her hands, then the other, between his own, rubbing ointment into them in slow circles and staring into Margerite's eyes all the while. "I often work late in here of a night, long after young Jürg has gone to bed," he murmured softly to her. "Should you need anything else, you have only to come to me."

How dare he? Margerite thought furiously. As if I were a common serving maid! But of course, as far as Karl knew, she was. She just managed not to snatch her hand away from him angrily, but the master of the stillroom could not have failed to feel her stiffen beneath his touch. He shrugged slightly. "Do remember that my door is open," he added. "Most girls working here would be pleased to have my friendship." He finished his ministrations briskly enough, though, and did not try to delay her any further as she snatched up the bottle of cordial and fled back towards Ortlieb's chambers.

The Landgräfin sipped absently at the spice-drink as Isabella and her assistants fussed about her, as though she had almost forgotten calling for it - she had not even noticed how long Margerite had taken to fetch the bottle this time, which should have been a relief, but Margerite found that it was making her even angrier. At least she had the message from the master of the stillroom to deliver; perhaps that would at least annoy Ortlieb.

When Isabella's soft accented muttering paused for a moment, Margerite cleared her throat loudly, but none of the other women even bothered to look at her.

"Excuse me, Frowe Landgräfin," Margerite stammered, trying to keep her voice soft and frightened, "but Meister Karl had a message for you."

Ortlieb looked at Margerite at last; but even now, the Order Princess did not seem to see her; the brown eyes with their glittering flecks of green might as well have been staring out the window as at the young woman in her plain woolen dress who stood with her hands clasped before her.

"Yes?" she said indifferently.

Margerite repeated the message as the master of the stillroom had given it to her. Ortlieb turned her head to look at Hedwig, meeting the girl's clear blue eyes for a moment, then tossing her head back with a deep laugh. "See to it, Hedwig," she said, still laughing. The raven-haired girl dropped a quick curtsey and left the room at once, and Ortlieb turned her attention back to her dressmaker.

After a little while, as though she had just remembered Margerite's presence, Isabella looked up and said, "You are not needed here any longer, Gertrude. Go feed your babe, if you must, and then return to your sewing."

Margerite stiffened as if the dressmaker had jabbed her with her scissors, her eyes flickering towards Ortlieb at once. She would have given much for the Light-Bearer not to know that she had a child within the castle, for even though Ortlieb had no clue that Wolfram was the babe whom the Order held precious for their own dark reason, Margerite knew that an Order Princess might have other uses for a helpless infant - uses that she could not, for all her practice in ruling her own mind, bring herself to think too long on.

And, although Ortlieb was not even looking towards her, Margerite felt a strange prickling crawl over her skin, a feeling like that of being watched by something unseen from the depths of a dark wood. Margerite left the Landgräfin's chambers, almost running to the bedroom where she had left her child. A deep wave of relief washed through her as she heard his impatient cries: though there had been no time for Ortlieb to steal him, something deep within her had not believed in his safety. Weak-kneed, she sat down on the bed, breathing hard as she held her son to her breast.

"Thank Maria you are safe, my dearest Wolfram," she whispered to him. "Thank Maria, thank Christ."

After feeding Wolfram, Margerite carried him into the room where the women were sewing. She would not risk being parted from him again, and if Isabella chose to send her back down to work on the hangings for the hall rather than have him in the costuming chamber, that was just as it would have to be.

"Back so soon?" said Bertrada, a tall, rather supercilious, woman whose narrow skull was wound about by a thick coil of brown-black hair gleaming and smooth as old oak polished with beeswax, with only a few white hairs threaded through it to show her age. "The Gräfin has never finished a fitting so quickly before - but I see she left her mark on you. What did you do wrong this time?"

"Madame Isabella sent me back to go on with my work while she tends to the Landgräfin," Margerite said, pointedly ignoring the other woman's implied insult. She set Wolfram down in a corner where he could get into little trouble, making sure that there were no pins or pieces of fabric within his reach, then picked up the skirt she had been hemming when Hedwig interrupted them.

"And what wonder of modern fashion has the Landgräfin demanded now?" Bertrada enquired, her high voice decidedly sarcastic.

Margerite described Ortlieb's proposed garment as well as she could, to the giggles and sniffs of the other women.

"As well she brought a Frenchwoman in to make her dresses," Bertrada said, speaking the word Frenchwoman with distaste. "The old Landgräfin would never have thought of asking me for such a thing, and I am sure I would be ashamed to do it. I suppose we can always take the pearls off afterwards, but making such a costume out of that good Flanders brocade - faugh! I suppose one can expect nothing better of a woman who began as a simple knight's daughter."

Margerite stared at her, her mouth open in outrage. She was too angry to say anything; but Bertrada gave a dry little laugh. "Oh, you needn't look so shocked, Gertrude. Everyone knows that the Landgräfin's father had nothing more than a small castle in the depths of the Thuringer Wald. It's hers now, I suppose, though I don't think she's been back there since she married Herr Gerhardt.

But she came here in nothing better than embroidered linen, like a well-off peasant -" Margerite winced, though she was careful to hide it -"and now she has to have the latest fashions in the finest fabrics, even if she has to tie her sleeves up at dinner to keep them from falling in the soup. I suppose the men like her clothes well enough," Bertrada added grudgingly. "At least, the Landgraf is always ready to pay for whatever she wants, and if it had not been for her, Herr Bernhardt..." Her thin lips closed tight with a soft snap, as though she knew she had said too much.

"Herr Bernhardt?" Margerite enquired, trying to keep her voice light. "Who is he?"

Bertrada looked at the other women, as if for support, but none of them would meet her gaze. "No one you need to know about, my girl," she snapped at last . "And however it may have been in Greifenstein, you should learn that while you are here, you will be better off doing your work and asking no questions. Nosy servants have a way of getting packed off without so much as the chance to say farewell." She snipped a piece of trailing thread from the garment she was working on, clicking her scissors sharply as if to illuminate her point.

Would you be glad to see Bernhardt back? Margerite thought as she sewed. I think perhaps you would. I wonder what you would say about Ortlieb if you dared speak your mind more clearly...and what you might have seen her do? Something that went farther than slapping a serving maid, perhaps?

But as she lay in the servants' quarters that night with Wolfram snuggled up to her, her bowels rumbling from the evening's serving of bean pottage, Margerite's mind went back to what Bertrada had said about Ortlieb. A simple knight's daughter...How had Ortlieb learned to act like a Landgräfin?

She must have come to Schloss Niederwald more than eight years ago, and she had already been a Princess in the Order then - how old was she now? Twenty-seven, perhaps, though she could almost have passed for Margerite's own age: there would have been time for her to learn to wear Flanders brocade and spend extravagant sums on dyed candles.

But there was something about Ortlieb's manner that was more than the offhand way of a noblewoman used to command, especially since whatever earthly power she could wield was, to be truthful, only that which Landgraf Gerhardt allowed her. Margerite knew that tale well enough herself, just as she had learned about the constant grinding struggle of wills between a new mistress and old castle retainers, in which the only way to triumph was never to yield or show any weakness, lest the servant should become master after all.

Did Ortlieb ever fear women like Bertrada, who dresses in silk and drinks out of a silver cup, for all that she is a servant? Margerite wondered uneasily if she would be able to do any better than Ortlieb, were she put in the same position. Maria preserve me: Mother Maria, should I ever be mistress here, please keep me from becoming like her!

For Margerite could already see too much of herself in the Landgräfin, as though Ortlieb were a mirror that magnified her worst faults and cast them back in her face. Yet there had been something more about Ortlieb, something deeper than the harsh authority and cold pride with which a simple knight's daughter could shield her uncertainty and fear from castle servants who looked down their noses at her and spoke scornfully behind her back...and suddenly, as if a veil fell from her mind, Margerite realized what it must be.

Father Etienne had spoken of Ortlieb as a commander of spirits and demons; and the way she treated her servants might almost have been written down in the Black Book as a paradigm of how to deal with such beings. Ortlieb's only failure in that regard was in the imprecision of the orders she gave, for, from all Margerite knew, demons had to be given the most precise direction to keep them from betraying their masters - but even that might be deliberate, a habit born of calculation on how best to breed fear and train her servants in anticipating her desires.

Or, perhaps, the spirits Ortlieb summoned were instructed in clearer ways of understanding and following her thoughts: Margerite could not really imagine how great might be the control that an Order Princess could exert over her ethereal minions. But men and women are not demons, Ortlieb, and cannot be treated in the same way, Margerite thought.

If you cannot see the difference, then I think the walls of your fortress have grown too thick. Father Etienne had been gone for three weeks, and Lothar had been able to bring little news back from the castle: the cook had said only that she had sent Margerite to help with the sewing for the upcoming All Souls' Eve feast, and the gamekeeper could hardly question Eva further in the middle of the kitchen. At least the money Margerite had brought with her had eased Bernhardt's worries about the Bear's Paw.

He had kept Hauptmann Paul and his men waiting more than long enough to stretch the bounds of friendship, but while they were being paid, with the ready promise of more, Bernhardt knew that they would happily sit in the Thuringer Wald until Judgement Day. Especially since - he remembered clearly from the days when he had stopped there to wet his throat after hunts more strenuous than those the Schloss' park could offer - the White Cockerel made the best ale south of Erfurt.

What was the innkeeper's name? Bernhardt could remember his plump contented face, but the name eluded him like a whisper from a dream. Whatever it had been, the man might not be alive any longer: eight years was a long time, and the second passing of the Death had been no kinder in Niederwald than anywhere else.

Only a few minutes after Lothar had come in, a knock sounded on the door. Bernhardt grasped his weapons at once, crouching silently behind the door. He did not dare to blow out the candle, for its glimmer might have been visible from outside, even through the heavy rain drumming softly against the window; but if any foe came up the stairs, he would have the advantage.

Bernhardt heard Lothar's muffled voice, then, more clearly, the French accents of Father Etienne. "All is well, and I am alone." Still he waited until the door had closed again before he came down to greet the priest.

"I regret that I was away so long, Herr Bernhardt," Etienne said at once. The canon's black hat was dripping from its rolled corners, and his dark hair curled dankly against his neck. Lothar hastened to take Etienne's sodden cloak from him, promising food and hot buttered ale as soon as he could have it ready.

"What have you found, Father?" Georg asked excitedly.

Bernhardt frowned at him. "Father Etienne will tell you whatever he has to say in his own good time, Knappe," he warned, just as if Georg were his own squire. "It is discourteous to ask questions of a guest before he has even had time to shake the rain from his shoulders and dry his feet. Let the good Father warm himself and have his food and drink, and then we shall talk."

"I am sorry, Father," Georg apologized politely, glancing sideways towards Bernhardt as if for his approval. In their time together, Bernhardt had come to feel very much as though he might almost be the young Knappe's own knight: he had been instructing Georg in weapons, so far as was possible while they were cooped up indoors, and prodding him on those rare occasions when the boy's manners lapsed from perfect politeness; and in return, Georg had kept him from brooding on Margerite and how she might be faring, forced to play a servant's part within Ortlieb's very lair.

"It is well enough, Georg," Father Etienne replied. The three of them went into the Stube, where Etienne sat up close to the stone vault of one of the two stoves - stoked from a hearth in the room behind the wall, they needed no drafty chimney in the parlour, so that it stayed both warm and free of smoke - holding out his long hands to the heat radiating from the solid gray blocks.

"You will be pleased to know, Herr Bernhardt," Father Etienne said without further preamble, "that if Margerite is successful in finding any evidence, we should be able to carry your case through at least with the Bishop. I stayed rather longer than I intended because there were...sundry matters, which I wanted to investigate, and which may aid us greatly in the removal of Ortlieb and Gerhardt."

"And what were these?" Bernhardt asked.

The priest shook his head. "That must wait until we know a little more," he said. His ascetic face was very grave as he spoke, and Bernhardt wondered what could have disturbed him so.

Lothar came into the Stube bearing a wooden platter with four mugs of steaming ale, which he passed out as though he were an innkeeper.

"I have news as well, Father," the gamekeeper beamed. "Shall I tell you now?"

"Do," Etienne replied.

Lothar, as it turned out, had had the good luck that day to catch Eva by herself as she was carrying a heavy load of slops out the castle gate for the swine, and had been able to speak with her for a few minutes with no one else listening. She had reported that Margerite had been taken away to work on fine sewing with Ortlieb's dressmaker, but still had not found what she was looking for; as for herself, by keeping her ears open and chattering with the other kitchen maids, Eva had discovered only that there was no great love for the Landgräfin in Schloss Niederwald. But Margerite had told her that everyone, from the Margraf of Meissen to the servants bearing food into the great hall, would be costumed and masked on that night.

"That may be of use to us," said Father Etienne thoughtfully. Cupping his mug in his cold pale fingers, he blew the steam from its surface, though he did not drink yet. Out of courtesy, Bernhardt refrained as well, welcome as the hot ale would have been. "But still, unless Margerite can find what she seeks, it will avail us little to get into the Schloss."

"She has been there three weeks now," Bernhardt said. "Surely, if it were not hidden beyond her... abilities to discover, she would have found it already."

It made him uncomfortable even to think of what Margerite had taken on in their goal of diverting the Order of Light-Bearers, but he could not in fairness deny it; he could not even wish her disarmed of the power that had enabled her to face down Christoph's demon at Burg Fürstensee, but he had to admit that he found himself disturbed by the knowledge that Margerite could work in the same realm as Ortlieb, for all he knew that no trace of the other woman's evil tainted Margerite's soul.

"She may not have had the opportunity yet, for a servant can hardly go about opening doors and thumping on walls," Father Etienne replied. "And yet..."

He did not finish the thought, but Bernhardt could end it easily enough: save by some great blessing or stroke of luck, Margerite might never even have the chance to search Ortlieb's chambers, let alone to look elsewhere. There had been no hidden passages that Bernhardt knew about in Schloss Niederwald; but he had been gone for eight years, and there was always the possibility that Gerhardt or even his father - who, Bernhardt thought angrily, had been as besotted with Ortlieb as everyone else had - might have known more: Margerite's brief description of how Nikolaus had discovered the salt caves beneath Burg Fürstensee proved that a castle might keep its secrets even from its rightful lords.

"If she cannot find it, then we must think of another way to force Ortlieb's secrets from her," Bernhardt said bluntly. "Perhaps she has a maidservant who can be dealt with..."

"Not those two," Georg interrupted with a shudder.

"What are you speaking of, Georg?" Father Etienne asked, raising an arched eyebrow.

"The two women who follow her, a fair one and a dark one. I think we will get nothing out of them."

"Oda and Hedwig, you mean?" Lothar said. "Herr Bernhardt, the lad is quite right. If she shares her secrets with anyone, it is with them, but she brought both of them in from somewhere else several years ago."

"Do these women wear any unusual rings?" Father Etienne enquired. He was looking at Lothar, but it was Georg who answered.

"They both had rings of onyx set in gold. I thought it was strange, since the rings were rather ugly, but..."

"We will speak later of when you saw these women," the canon said to Georg, his voice stern and even. "But you are correct, in any case: there is no help for us from them." Father Etienne's ale seemed to have cooled to his liking, for the priest took a good swallow from his mug.

Bernhardt followed suit. In honour of his guests, Lothar had added a large portion of honey to the ale, as well as the butter that had melted to spread in glistening gobbets across the top of the drink, and Bernhardt thought he could even taste a hint of cinnamon - a gift, no doubt, from Liutbirg. He allowed himself a small smile, wondering if the cook was still as frightening as the woman of his memory, who had once, when he was a small boy investigating a cake cooling on the table, cracked him so hard across the knuckles with her ladle that he had not been able to twirl his top for almost a day afterwards. But there would be time for such thoughts later: now he could not let himself be distracted.

"Considering who will be there," Bernhardt said slowly,"the All Souls' feast would be the best time for us to make ourselves known. I was Knappe to Landgraf Friedrich of Thuringia, and I believe that he would hear me out; though I do not know the Margraf of Meissen, he has the name of a fair-minded man. And with them as witnesses, there is less chance..."

"That Gerhardt would force you into a pitched battle?" Etienne continued for him. "True enough. But that does not deal with our chief problem, which is proving Ortlieb's crimes. And I believe if there is any evidence to be found, it will be in her sanctum."

They discussed the matter for a long time, but could come up with no answer. Finally, Bernhardt found that he had no choice but to say what he had been thinking on almost since Father Etienne's arrival - the thing that he had dreaded, not least because, somewhere in his heart, he was not sure that he had not thought of it out of desire as much as necessity.

"How, if we offer her a bait that she is sure to take?"
Bernhardt said. His voice seemed to croak hoarsely in
his throat; he drained the last honey-dregs from his mug,
swallowing hard before he went on. "If I come to her, I
do not think she will turn me away. She...just before she
betrayed me, she had tried to get me to...aid her in a way
that I would not." He had been inside Ortlieb, in truth:
she had turned the natural position of man and woman
upside down, riding him with her soft wet heat pulsing
rhythmically about his shaft and her breasts swinging above
his face like sweet ripe fruit, just out of his reach...and then
she had begun to speak, words that at first he had taken for
meaningless moans.

Then she had reached down to grip his shoulders,
tightening within to hold him in an irresistible grasp as
her hips thrust against him. The short hard strokes had
forced him to arch his back and moan softly, barely able
to keep himself from spurting at once within her: he could
feel nothing but the agony of pleasure driving him to
push upward into her again and again, hear nothing but
her deep voice ordering, "Say this after me: Lilit, I invoke
thee; daughter of Arieth, I invoke thee. Lilit, I invoke thee,
daughter of Arieth, I invoke thee! Lilit, I invoke thee..."

It had seemed to Bernhardt then that he saw Ortlieb's
green-flecked eyes turning golden, and the shadow of great
owl-wings springing forth from her shoulders; and he had
known her for what she was, and in his fear he had torn
himself from her just before climax, snatching up a cloak to
cover his aching nakedness and fleeing.

Bernhardt had tried to hide that memory from himself,
but never been able to; even now, to his shame and through
the remembered horror, he could feel himself hardening
at the thought of it. Etienne looked at him, cool blue eyes
seeming to take his measure anew. Bernhardt held his head
up, meeting the priest's gaze, and at last Father Etienne
nodded slowly. "She may well have done," he said. "And I
have reason to think that she knows you are here."

A shaft of ice shot through Bernhardt's bowels at the priest's words. "What do you mean?" he whispered. "If she knows I am here, why has she not sent men to take me?"

"Because," the priest said gently, "that would mean telling your brother that you are still alive. And I believe that what she wants of you does not include your death - at least not at the hands of Gerhardt's men."

Bernhardt licked his lips, his mouth gone as dry as it ever had before a battle. But this fear, he could not conquer by grasping the hilt of his sword, nor by running the litanies of his training, of lance-angle and impact, of stroke and counter-stroke, through his mind. Mother Maria, grant me grace, he prayed.

"Then you believe that this will work?" he asked roughly.

"I think she will be willing to take you," Etienne replied. "But you know the risk - far better than I do, I believe."

"I could go instead," Georg offered, his voice very small and tight. The Knappe's eyes were wide, their pupils swollen in the dim light to swallow the blue irises. His thin face was white as a corpse's, his hands clenched on the rim of the table. "I know she wants a virgin..."

"You will do no such thing." Etienne's voice clanged with the flat finality of funeral bells. "I am little enough willing to send Herr Bernhardt to her; I would sooner leave this opportunity pass and wait for Margerite to find out more."

"And how long will that take?" Bernhardt asked. "Would you have her serving within Schloss Niederwald for a year, or two - while Christ alone knows what is taking place at Burg Fürstensee?"

The priest closed his eyes, clenching his fists and bowing his head as if struggling against a great pang of agony racking his slender body. Bernhardt saw him shudder; then Etienne lifted his head again, his clear blue eyes gleaming beneath the shadowy ridges of his brows.

"As you say," he replied. The priest turned the gold seal ring on his finger, looking down at the coat of arms on it for a long moment. "Thought before action; but perhaps we have come to a time when action must be taken. If you go in, you will have myself - and, God help us, the men of the Bear's Paw - behind you, ready to come to your aid; and then Christ may judge how matters turn out."

Margerite woke in the dead of night, woke to a heavy weight on her chest and the sound of purring in her ear. In the complete darkness of the servants' quarters, she could not even see the glow of Kobolt's eyes, but she knew the cat was curled on her chest.

"Kobolt," she whispered. "Why are you here? I told you not to seek me out." But whatever else Kobolt might be, he was a cat, and would go where he pleased. "Kobolt, it is dangerous for you to be here. She might sense you, and then what would become of us?"

Still purring, the cat stood, kneading at Margerite's breasts with his paws. Margerite did not dare move lest she wake Wolfram, whose breath still came soft and steady against her cheek: the baby would cry if he were woken so, and deeply as the castle servants slept after their day's hard labour, his wails would surely disturb someone. Suddenly Kobolt stiffened, his purr turning into a sharp hiss. Margerite strained her eyes against the darkness, trying to see what the cat was looking at.

Though her blankets were itchy, they were warm; yet a chill shivered over her body, clammy cold sweat springing from her forehead. Dear Mother Maria, Ortlieb is coming after Wolfram! she thought. Slowly, carefully, she snaked her right hand under her pillow until her fingers closed on the hilt of her eating-dagger, wrapping her left arm around Wolfram's little body. Ortlieb would not take her son without a fight: in that, she was resolute.

No door opened, nor did Margerite hear any footsteps rustling among the heaps of straw that did for mattresses for the lower castle servants. Nevertheless, she could feel the cold presence beside her bed as clearly as she could feel Kobolt's heavy paws and the warm comfort of Wolfram nestled against her side.

Kobolt hissed again, then a low growl of warning trickled out of him. Even in the absolute darkness, it seemed to Margerite that she could see the figure standing there: a man's shape, tall and thin, with a single glint of red burning on his finger - and she knew him, as surely as if she were looking upon him in broad daylight.

"Graf Günther," she whispered. "You are dead. Go you back to the realm where you belong, and trouble me no more."

Though no sound reached her ears save Kobolt's growl and the snoring of the other women, it seemed to Margerite nevertheless that she heard the echo of hollow laughter, and the sound of words struggling, slow and deep, through it. Have...you learned so little...Priestess?

Even...within the Order...strife between us, that...we may grow...is permitted...Beware, lest...Ortlieb find you out...in your ambition to...take her place...Your babe, she...will not harm...but she is within rights...to challenge you...You hid... yourself well, but...I shall tell...Nikolaus, for...you may need his help.

Then, as if Margerite had blinked a shadow from her sight, the dark shape was suddenly gone; the only darkness was the natural lightlessness of the chamber. Kobolt miaowed quietly, and she felt the soft brush of his tail against her cheek.

All her limbs were shaking, her breath coming hard as if she had run a great distance. My ambition to take Ortlieb's place? she thought horrified - but had she not indeed, earlier, been thinking about how it might be to be Landgräfin von Niederwald? But not, Mother Maria help me, from ambition or pride! Only because Bernhardt's rightful place is that of Landgraf, and I would be beside him if ever I may.

A grimmer thought came to her then: What brought first Kobolt, and then Graf Günther, to me this night? I gave Bernhardt my necklace; is Ortlieb, or one of her spirits, watching me even now? The words of warding whispered themselves in Margerite's mind, but she did not dare give them voice.

Even if Ortlieb were not watching her at the moment, the Order Princess would surely feel the brush of heavenly power when next Margerite drew close to her - and without the necklace Ruprecht had made for her, Margerite did not know how to pass unseen by otherworldly eyes, unfelt by otherworldly senses. There had been some instruction on that in the Black Book, but it called for things that Margerite did not have and could not get, using an incantation that she would not willingly speak.

No: though it be shameful, I must be like a field-mouse, that lives because it is small and beneath the notice of nobler creatures. Yet owls preyed on field-mice as readily as on hares; was Ortlieb truly as indifferent to her lesser servants as she pretended to be? Perhaps it would be wiser to simply gather Wolfram into her arms and flee Schloss Niederwald, leaving Eva to sense whatever she might.

But Eva seldom has any chance to leave the kitchen, let alone to wander; whereas I can go where I will, so long as I have the pretext of fetching something for Isabella. And what have I to turn me from my task? A few words from a damned ghost who must be able to see only a little of what happens in the world above, for that he still thinks me one of the Light-Bearers, and the presence of a disobedient cat.

Kobolt had settled himself again, stretched full-length on Margerite's body with his paws around her neck and his soft cheek laid against hers, purring as his paws worked. "Kobolt, you must go," she whispered to him again, though the thought of sending him away now was painful. The tomcat rubbed his head hard along the side of Margerite's jaw, purring more loudly.

"Kobolt, go back to Lothar's cottage. Do you understand me? Go back!" she hissed to him.

Kobolt did not budge.

"Well, if you must," Margerite murmured, "you may stand watch over us this night. But you must be away before dawn - do you understand, cat?"

The black tom butted his head against her jaw again, and Margerite had to be content with that - for whatever, she thought with a sigh, the promise of a cat was worth.

But when she awoke at dawn, Kobolt had departed, leaving only a few black hairs on her blanket to show that he had been there at all. Quickly Margerite fed Wolfram, then splashed cold water on her face and hands from the communal basin before she dressed herself and got ready to return to her duties.

Serving at dinner that day, she watched Ortlieb anxiously, but the Landgräfin did not even seem to notice her, and that relieved Margerite's heart greatly. Even the owl, she told herself, may overlook a fieldmouse, so long as it stays quiet instead of scurrying in fear at the first noise.

And if Margerite left the castle now, after having been promoted to the position of Isabella's lowest assistant, it would, she was sure, draw more attention than if she stayed where she was and did what was expected of her - as she would do, unless she saw some clear sign that Ortlieb was turning her attention towards Margerite and her son.

Chapter Eight

The head of Gottfried's horse was hanging low by the time Schloss Niederwald came into view again, a huge dark blur in his sight. He leaned down from his saddle, petting the glossy brown hide. He had done his best for the stallion through the months of following his quarry; the horse had eaten better than he or Arnmut had, but his bones still showed through his skin. Gottfried knew that he himself was bony as a painted Death; Arnmut had been a bit plump when they set off from Burg Fürstensee, and the squire's cheekbones stood out harshly from his face now, while, always thin, Gottfried was more emaciated than any peasant after a year of bad harvests.

His fingers on his horse's reins were no more than bones strung together under a shrunken wrap of flesh; at least, Christ be thanked, he was not one of those men who needed a good meal of meat every day to keep their strength up. He might look like a walking skeleton, but he could still swing his sword as hard as he ever had; the thin muscles strung over his small bones would serve him well when a larger man's strength had failed.

He might be overpowered, but he could strike faster than anyone else: because of that, he had not lost a fight since he was thirteen. And he had a gift from God: no matter what wound he took in battle, he would not feel it till afterward, when his blood had cooled. God had meant him to be a warrior, and if he had not had his responsibility to his family, he would have joined a fighting Order in thanks for it. Still, it had been a long and arduous journey.

When Gottfried and Arnmut set out on their quest, the woods had been a warm tapestry of green and gold: now all the leaves had fallen, the trees reaching bare black limbs up to the gray sky, and only the dark pines and occasional glossy-leaved holly still showed any life.

A light sleet blew cold and grainy into their faces, so that every so often Gottfried had to wipe the blurs of snow from his eyes; and even through the thick wool of his cloak, he could feel the metal chill of his gauntlet against his face.

"Sir," Arnmut said uncomfortably, "do you really think Bertram has come back here?"

"Knappe," Gottfried replied, "what do you do when you have lost the trail of a wounded deer? You go back to the last splatter of blood, do you not?"

"Sir, we have been seeking him for many months now: he could be anywhere."

"Indeed he could, Knappe. But the gamekeeper here was the last to have a clear sight of him, so I know nothing better than to try to pick up the trail here again."

"Sir, do you really think we will find him?"

"We must try," Gottfried said. "I swore to Graf Heinrich that I would bring Bertram back, and while there is breath in my body, I cannot give up this quest." And I am sorry that you had to come with me, Arnmut, for I can see how hard it has worn upon you; but you are my Knappe, and what I endure, you must as well, no matter how hard I have tried to spare you.

"Hold: who are you?" the guard at the gate said. Gottfried leaned down, fixing the man with his gaze - he knew full well that most people could not meet his eyes for long.

"A wandering Ritter, and friend to the rulers here," he said. "I know that they will give me guest-right; do you wish to challenge that?"

"Indeed not, Herr Ritter. We shall see to your horse at once, if you wish to dismount here."

"Feed him carefully," Gottfried said, swinging himself down from the saddle. "He has been hungry long, and if you stuff him with oats, he will get colic. Small meals every few hours - let him eat no longer than it takes you to say twenty Paternosters slowly - and" he fixed the guard with his gaze again, "you ought to be used to doing that, oughtn't you?"

"O yes, Herr Ritter," the guard said quickly, taking the reins from Gottfried.

Gottfried and Arnmut had arrived just in time for dinner, and the servants showed them in quickly, leading them to the high table to pay their respects to Landgraf Gerhardt and his wife. The Landgraf did not rise to meet them, but he inclined his mouse-brown head graciously. "Be welcome to Schloss Niederwald again, Ritter Gottfried," he said. "You did not find the man you were seeking?"

"No, Herr Landgraf, and that is why I have come back here, since none since your gamekeeper had seen him. The thought has come to me that he may have concealed himself for a time and gone into the Thuringer Wald; and so I hope to pick up the trail here again."

Landgraf Gerhardt smiled. This close, Gottfried could see his face clearly: his brown hair thin and stringy, the blurring of flesh over bone, the lines graven deeply about the corners of his mouth, and the dark bluish pouches beneath his eyes, discoloured as the boils of a man suffering from the Death.

He has the look of a man whose soul is ill, Gottfried thought; there was a gray shadow beneath the Landgraf's skin, as though he had been bled too often, or as if a cancer were eating him from within. There were talon-marks at the corners of his eyes as well, as though a bird of prey had clawed him there. I shall pray for the Landgraf - but he would do better to pray for himself, that he be rid of whatever is feeding off him.

Thinking thus, Gottfried almost missed Gerhardt's next words. "I should like to hunt with you sometime, Herr Ritter. I think that you do not often lose your quarry."

"But sometimes," the Landgräfin's deep voice purred from her husband's other side, "you may find something better on the track. Now, Ritter Gottfried, you have managed to come back on All Saints' Eve; tomorrow is All Souls' Eve, for which reason our honoured guests -" she gestured broadly about the high table, leaving Gottfried with a confused blur of bright silks and jewels -"have come to feast with us, since I have a special entertainment planned. You and your Knappe will do us the favour of staying through that feast, and then we will aid you in your search as you wish."

"You do us great honour, Frowe Landgräfin," Gottfried replied, bowing to her. He knew that he could in no way refuse politely - although, in truth, he would sooner have been on his way at dawn the next morning.

Straightening up, Gottfried found that he was looking directly into Landgräfin Ortlieb's eyes. Though he had long learned to show no sign, whatever his sight showed him, he could not suppress a small inward twitch of surprise. He had not come close enough to see the Landgräfin as more than a darkly graceful shadow when he had passed through Schloss Niederwald before: now every line of her face was clear in her sight.

She was pretty enough as women went, he supposed, though, in spite of the delicate smears of pink on her cheeks and lips, the little creases about her eyes and mouth made her nearer thirty than twenty. But it was her eyes that surprised him: the huge golden orbs of an owl, unblinking as she fixed him in her gaze. He had only seen such eyes in a human face once before: the first time he had seen Gräfin Margerite, she had looked up at him with the brilliant cold gaze of a raptor, a peregrine or gyrfalcon - he was not sure which, for though he went hawking when a knight must, he was too short-sighted to enjoy the sport as his companions did. But Margerite's eyes had quickly shifted back to their natural colour, blue as the Virgin's cloak, and Ortlieb's did not change.

The laugh that flowed from her mouth was soft, caressing as a thick fur hood-lining brushing against his ears, but Gottfried hardly noticed. He was not afraid of her, nor, though he could see that the white rounds of her breasts were almost falling out of her deep purple bodice, did she stir any desire in him. He would have liked to know what she was wearing on her left hand, for a steady dark fire, like a candle's flame turned inside out, burned inside a roundel of heavy inscribed gold there; and for a moment, he was able to stare at it, for the Landgräfin was already speaking to the others at the high table.

"Margrave, dear Friedrich, you will not mind if we seat Ritter Gottfried here at the high table, I trust? He is a wandering Ritter on a quest, just as in the best romances - and you see that we have left a seat free, in case a strange guest should happen upon us. No, good Ritter, you need not even bother to take off your armour, for dinner is about to be served, and surely your war-harness is a mark of honour."

"A pleasing fancy!" one of the men - a large, hearty, fair man whose gold brocade shone brightly from his blue doublet - replied. "Seat him here, by all means; perhaps he will have a tale to tell us."

Though Gottfried seldom noticed his clothes, leaving it to his Knappe to dress him in whatever seemed fittest for the day, he knew that even his best clothing would hardly be suitable for such company; while if he could smell his own gambeson, its stink must be nearly bad enough to put everyone in the hall off their food. But he bowed stiffly to the speaker. "Herr...I am sorry, I do not know your name..."

"Landgraf Friedrich of Thuringia," the big man answered with a laugh. "But I know yours: you are Ritter Gottfried von Schlangenbad, who has been searching so long for a fugitive called Bertram. My Ritter Hans, whose castle you stayed at briefly, told me of you, and there could hardly be two men who fit your description. Sit down, young man, and get a good meal into you; and maybe you will tell us of your travels."

"I fear that I am no great teller of tales, and that you will be disappointed in me," Gottfried said, but obedient to Landgraf Friedrich's command, he took the place the servants showed him to.

Although it was a Friday, and all the dishes were made with fish instead of meat and almond milk in place of cream, the meal was extraordinarily sumptuous: fine fish broths, broiled tench in almond paste, eels in wine, pike smothered with creamy almond-milk sauces made piquant by a little fresh verjuice, and similar dainties.

Gottfried ate no more of each dish than politeness demanded, for it had always seemed to him that such elaborate foods made mock of the Church's laws concerning days of abstinence: though menus of this sort might hold to the strict rule of no meat or dairy foods on such days, it was hardly less luxurious to eat from a bowl of finely chopped and herbed whitefish that had been pleasingly coloured in patterns of gold, blue, silver, and red than to eat pork that had been treated in the same manner.

Nevertheless, he could not help feeling relieved that Arnmut, though the Knappe was now busy tending to their baggage and whatever sleeping space would be allotted to them, would be getting a more substantial meal than the dried stockfish to which Gottfried was accustomed on Fridays. To his relief, Gottfried was not asked many questions: rather, all the men at the table seemed too fascinated by the Landgräfin to pay much attention to a wandering knight.

The Margräfin of Meissen, next to whom he was seated, was too well-bred to complain of his dirt or smell, but Gottfried found himself very conscious of his state, and did not dare to try to engage her in conversation. Though, to his relief, the Schloss Niederwald servants were quick to bring him an extra fingerbowl to make sure that his hands were completely clean before he dipped them into the food, he nevertheless was careful to wait until he was sure that she had all she wanted before touching anything on those plates they shared: he could hardly clean the ingrained grime from beneath his fingernails at table, after all.

After dinner, the servants showed Gottfried up - not to the room he had slept in before, but a bedroom at the very top of the old tower at the north of the castle. The scent of fresh reeds and meadowsweet rose from the floor as he walked in; a fire crackled in the hearth, and - best of all, to his mind at this moment - there was a tub of steaming-hot water by the bed, with soaps and sweet oils laid out beside it, and Arnmut waiting for him with towels and a scrubbing-brush.

Had he been allowed to join the Teutonic Knights, Gottfried would have had no need of such luxuries; but while pious denial of the body was admirable, to remain filthy at a host's feast was simply rude. Arnmut helped his knight out of his armour and the dirty clothes beneath, then shucked off his chain-mail and gambeson with a sigh of relief.

The Knappe's face and hands were deeply tanned from the long months of riding, but his body was pale as unpainted linden-wood, the solid muscles of his chest and abdomen standing out in sharp relief as he stretched. He had unbound his fair hair from its simple braid, and it stood out in a fine cloud around his head.

"Herr Gottfried, I hope you will not think too ill of me if I say that I am glad we are here now," the squire said as Gottfried eased himself into the hot water. "I have never eaten such fine food, even at Burg Fürstensee, and I had thought that Graf Heinrich had the best cook in the Empire. And - the Landgräfin is very beautiful, is she not?"

Gottfried whipped his head around at the raw note of longing in Arnmut's soft voice. It disturbed him in a way that he could not name: he had never heard his Knappe speak so of a woman, and - though as a matter of modesty, he had always forborne to look at his squire's private parts when they chanced to be naked together, he was not so short-sighted that he could not tell that Arnmut was already showing an unseemly degree of arousal at the thought of the Landgräfin.

"She is a married woman," Gottfried said roughly, "and I thought her no more beautiful than any other. If such things concern you, it will be best for you to make your Confession to the priest here, and set about your duties meanwhile." Resolutely, he turned his back and began to wash himself thoroughly, breathing in the sweet scents of the bath until his heart stopped pounding so hard. At Gottfried's gesture, Arnmut joined him in the tub to scrub his back where he could not reach, the touch of his linen towel rough and comforting at the same time, like the tongue of an affectionate cat.

When they were both clean and dry, and Arnmut had shaved him neatly again, Gottfried dressed himself in the one set of good clothes he had brought for himself, a doublet of plain black velvet and hose of deep red wool. Herr Christoph had twitted Gottfried often enough about the cut of his sleeves being unfashionable, and sworn that when he, Christoph, was Graf von Fürstensee, he would make it a rule that all his castle knights had to be well-dressed; but that was merely Christoph's way, and, Christ willing, it would be long yet before any ill befell Graf Heinrich.

"Our armour can well do with being cleaned, since it is some time since we were able to put it off," Gottfried said to his Knappe. "You see to that, and when you are done, go down to the stables to make sure that our horses are being tended as I ordered."

"Of course, Herr Gottfried," Arnmut answered, brushing the wet hair from his forehead and smiling sweetly at his knight. Among Arnmut's many virtues, Gottfried reflected, was the fact that he never seemed to hold a grudge for any harsh words, but would always take corrections as they were meant. As for himself, Gottfried decided, he would go to the castle chapel to pray and light a candle, it being All Saints' Eve.

As he reached the fourth-floor exit from the tower staircase Gottfried heard a high wail from one of the rooms that was, unmistakably, the cry of a baby. He wondered if it might be Ortlieb's child, or that of one of her noble guests. Although the finer suites were in the newer wing of the castle, the great hall had seemed very full that afternoon; if it were not for the Landgräfin's peculiar fancies, he suspected he and Arnmut would have been sharing a barracks room with the soldiers of the Schloss that night. The wail was followed by a few sharp words that he could not quite make out, and then someone must have dealt with the child, for the crying stopped abruptly.

Gottfried wandered down the corridor that led to the stairs going to the great hall. The light was good, for the windows in the Schloss were bigger than any he would have designed into a castle, both for the expense of the glazing and because they seemed so vulnerable - most of it must have been built in peacetime, and with the expectation of peace.

The corridor turned sharply right just in front of a great door, oak bound with seven thick bands of iron where two or three should have been enough. Gottfried had noticed it before, as he had noticed the two huge guards who stood silently in front of it, never moving - not even shifting their feet, as almost any man would do after hours of standing.

They were both dressed in full plate, with, curiously enough, tilting helms of black iron that hid their faces: Gottfried, only of middle height himself, would have needed to stand on his toes and peer right in through the visor-slots to see their eyes. As before, he wondered what could lie behind that door to need such guardsmen: was that where the treasures of Schloss Niederwald were kept?

He shrugged: it was none of his affair. Another man, such as Herr Christoph or Ritter Ludwig, perhaps, might have hailed the soldiers affably; Gottfried preferred to keep his own counsel when dealing with strangers. Even with the scents of his own bath fresh in his nose, Gottfried smelled the woman on the stairs before he saw her: a rich sweet musk of roses and spice wafted up before her, like a breath from an Eastern cargo-ship.

Although it was daylight, the candles burned in the wall-sconces along the staircase, and so he could see her as clearly as he was able: the shimmer of golden hair and green silk, and the pale oval of her face.

"Herr Ritter," she said, stopping and bobbing in a motion that might have been a curtsey. "It is well that you are coming this way, for the Landgräfin would speak with you."

Gottfried did no more than incline his head in return. It was not only her words that told him that, despite her fine clothes, she was a servant, but something in her bearing: a man who could not see faces clearly from more than a few feet away had to learn to read people's thoughts and recognise their stations in life from the way they stood. "I await her pleasure," he replied politely. "Where shall I find her?"

"Follow me."

The fair-haired woman led him down to the third floor, through a door and into a small corridor, and went before him to open the next door. So late in the year, even stepping from a hallway into these rooms was like coming from the outside chill into the warmth within: fresh from his hot bath, with his heavy winter undertunic beneath his doublet, Gottfried felt the sweat beginning to prickle upon his brow. The knight understood at once that he was in the Landgräfin's private chambers. Uncomfortable, he stood rigidly as if he were awaiting an inspection of troops, back braced and hands clasped behind him.

"Welcome, Ritter Gottfried," the Landgräfin murmured, extending her right hand languidly to him. Gottfried bowed over it, his lips barely brushing her fingers. Her hand was stained, he noticed, with something that looked like a trace of soot - as though she had been cleaning a stove like a serving-maid, though that was unthinkable. "Come, sit you down. What manner of wine do you prefer, Herr Ritter? We have fine reds from France and Italy, although you may be fonder of the pale wines of the Rhine: the new pressings are just reaching us now."

"Whatever pleases you, Landgräfin," Gottfried answered. He thought it rather strange that she, the Landgräfin von Niederwald, should be asking a landless Ritter such a question. It was, perhaps, a measure of her high courtliness that she spoke so to him, as though she were the wife or daughter of a small Burg-holder that had given him guestright for the night.

Landgräfin Ortlieb clapped her hands. "Oda! Go fetch some of the Bordeaux wine for us."

The fair-haired woman hurried from the room in a flurry of green skirts; now Gottfried and Ortlieb were alone, with none to chaperone them. To master his uneasiness, Gottfried glanced around himself. He could not make out the finer details of the tapestries that hung the walls, but their vivid colours were alluring and disturbing at once: there was something about them that made his skin crawl, though he could not say what. He seated himself across the table from the Landgräfin, back straight and hands folded neatly in his lap.

She laughed, leaning towards him, and again he saw the strange owl-glow of her eyes. "Ritter Gottfried, be at ease. What I have to offer you is a matter of play and delight, nothing more." Landgräfin Ortlieb stretched out her left hand across the table towards him, and Gottfried could not help staring at the deep red flame that burned on her finger. "What...Ah, I see you are admiring my ring. Have you ever seen its like?"

There was something in her low voice that seemed too urgent for the simple question, like the thrumming echo of a lute's deepest string suddenly tuned taut. Gottfried answered truthfully:"I have not, Frowe Landgräfin. It is a wondrous work."

Ortlieb withdrew her arm, staring at him with those odd golden bird-eyes and holding her hand coquettishly over the white upper slope of her breasts. "Most men would compliment the finger, rather than the ring it bears," she said, her deep voice teasing.

"I trust that I have not been discourteous, Frowe Landgräfin, nor displeased you," Gottfried said. "I shall leave, if you wish." He did not know how he had misspoken, for he was not used to women saying such things. Here in Ortlieb's chambers, he felt that he was fighting on unknown ground, in a thick mist - no, worse: poor weather often seemed to hamper his foes worse than himself, for that he had his whole lifetime of learning how to see and fight with blurred eyes.

"My good Ritter!" the Landgräfin protested. "I pray your pardon; I did not mean to offend you." For the first time, Gottfried heard a hint of unease in her voice: she might have been the young daughter of a poor Ritter who had spoken too forwardly to a guest and been slapped down for it. He found himself wondering who Ortlieb had been before she married Landgraf Gerhardt - and feeling a little tingling worm of sympathy for her in his belly, for it was not that many years since he had come to Burg Fürstensee as a raw Knappe, the second son of a border knight, who felt his every move to be clumsy and every footstep misplaced.

"I am not offended, Frowe Landgräfin," Gottfried said. "Perhaps it is merely that I am unaccustomed to the ways of such a high court."

Landgräfin Ortlieb relaxed, leaning back in her heavy chair with a soft rustle of deep purple velvet. "You have been wandering long, Ritter Gottfried; it is little surprise if you have forgotten the ways of the courtly games between men and women."

"Say, rather, that I never learned them," Gottfried replied, his mouth twisting slightly. Here, at least, he knew that he was out of his depth. He wished that the Landgräfin would say why she had called him and get it over with: he longed for the quiet peace of a chapel, of candles that glowed pure and golden instead of flickering disturbingly red across over-wrought tapestries and the soft darkness of Ortlieb's gown, and the clarity of prayers to replace this awkward dance of words.

"Frowe Landgräfin, my duties are those of fighting, not of courteous speech within the hall. If your wish is for pleasant company, you surely have no lack of that, neither here in this Schloss, nor among the great nobles who have come to your All Souls' feast. Though it was most kind of you to ask me to stay here, I fear that I have little save my thanks to offer in return."

Ortlieb leaned forward again, both elbows on the table; if Gottfried had cared to look, he could have seen the deepest shadows between her breasts. Unlike most folk, she did not turn away from his gaze after a few moments; rather, her golden owl-eyes stayed fixed on his without blinking. Her scent was heavy in his nostrils: musk and sweetness, like flowers that had been allowed to curdle slightly in their distilling-water. "But there is a great favour you can do for me, Ritter Gottfried."

"What would that be, Frowe Landgräfin?" Gottfried asked politely.

Even across the table, Gottfried could see Ortlieb's puzzled frown: he seemed, somehow, to have answered her wrongly again, though he could not imagine how. He was saved from more confusion when the door opened again and Oda came in: pouring the deep red wine into gilded goblets took a little time, and at least he was able to sip and make the expected remarks about its high quality without treading off the known roads of conversation again.

The process of drinking and sharing light talk seemed to calm the Landgräfin as well, and at last she said, "Ritter Gottfried, have you ever heard of the Danse Macabre?"

"I have not, Frowe Landgräfin. It is a strange name."

"It is the latest fashion in Paris and Anjou. For tomorrow night, I mean to perform such a dance, as a surprise and entertainment for my noble guests. The theme, good Ritter, is that of Death Triumphant: he leads all manner of folk in his dance. From the highest-born to the lowest, the best to the worst, they all must come and follow when he calls them."

"As is the will of God, Frowe Landgräfin, for the sin of Adam," Gottfried replied, crossing himself. He had been too young to remember much of the Death's first coming - he had only a vague memory of a time when the fires of Burg Schlangenbad had burned day and night with scented smoke, and the bells of the little church in the village by the castle had rung almost without ceasing - but he had been a Knappe in Burg Fürstensee during the second wave of plague, and had seen his share of its horrors then.

"Christ be praised for His sacrifice, that lifts our souls beyond the corruptibility of mortal flesh and ends the triumph of Death."

Ortlieb's mouth twisted as though the fine wine in her goblet were sour verjuice. "Are you a knight, Ritter Gottfried, or a priest?" she asked softly.

"A knight, and as good a Christian as I may be, Frowe Landgräfin," Gottfried told her. His fleeting moment of sympathy for her had fled entirely: he had heard that question from other lips, and it never ceased to gall him, as an endless reminder of his father's refusal to allow him to enter the Teutonic Order.

"So," Ortlieb murmured. She lifted her goblet, its chased gilding sparkling ruddy in the candlelight - why did she keep candles burning during the day, when there was so much light through the large windows? - and took a long sip. The fair-haired woman was at her side with a napkin at once; Ortlieb dabbed delicately at her mouth and laid the cloth aside. "And nevertheless, Herr Ritter, I must have someone to play the part of Death in this dance. I had thought to do it myself, but I have - lately discovered something that makes that impossible. None of my castle-folk will suit my wishes, and I would have my plans be a surprise to my other guests. And lo!" She clapped her palms together, the dark flame on her left hand glowing steadily. "You arrive - almost thin enough from the privations of the road to be the skeletal figure of Death himself, and..." The Landgräfin leaned forward as she had before, her golden owl-eyes staring straight into Gottfried's..."a proven knight who, I would wager any amount of gold, has taken men's lives often enough, but never given his seed to set life between a woman's thighs."

"I am not married, Frowe Landgräfin," Gottfried replied stiffly. He had never heard a woman speak so; if Ortlieb had not been the frowe of the castle and his hostess, he would simply have left.

Ortlieb laughed, a sound that stirred the small hairs on the back of Gottfried's neck. "That matters little to most men, Herr Ritter. But at any rate, you are almost the perfect man to play the part - and it will be no loss to your noble dignity, since I myself did not scorn it. Come, good Ritter, will you do this for me?"

The Landgräfin's pink tongue darted out, wetting the corner of her mouth, and another wave of her heavy scent swept over Gottfried. Leaning over the table as she was, every shift of her pale breasts within the deep purple velvet of her bodice was visible, and it occurred to Gottfried that there were many men who would doubtless think themselves favoured to be asked thus.

But what drew his eyes was the tapestry behind her: though the details were blurry in his short sight, he recognised the familiar scene of the Three Living and the Three Dead, with the three young nobles drawing back in horror from the corpses that they would someday become.

It was well for men to think on death, to realize that the flesh and all that pleasured it would pass into worms and corruption someday - but though all bodies would die and rot, the souls that dwelt within them would as surely pass through the Refiner's fire; and those of true Christians would come forth as glittering and incorruptible as the small gold crucifix that Gottfried always wore about his neck.

In the second passing of the Death, Gottfried had seen what became of men who forgot that fundamental truth; and for all her finery, and though she might make the inevitability of death into a pageant for her feast, it seemed to him that Ortlieb had lost it as well.

"I fear you must find another for your Death," Gottfried told the Landgräfin. "I am not the man to do it. I hope this does not make me too unwelcome at Schloss Niederwald, but if it does, then I shall call my squire and make ready to depart at once."

Ortlieb sat staring at him for a little while, as though her ears had somehow deceived her. Then she smiled again. "No, you are still welcome here, Ritter Gottfried, so long as you do not give away my secret to any of my other guests. But one thing, at least: you must consent to wearing a mask, as must your squire, for everyone will be masked tomorrow night, from the Margraf of Meissen to the lowest server."

"I have no masks, Frowe Landgräfin."

"We will provide you with something fitting," Landgräfin Ortlieb assured him, and with that, Gottfried had to be content: at least, he could not imagine what harm such a thing could do to either Arnmut's soul or his own.

Bringing in pitchers of wine at the lower end of the hall, Margerite saw the knight and his squire enter. She stiffened, almost dropping the pitcher she carried. Even had he still been wearing his helm, instead of carrying it beneath his arm, she would have recognised Gottfried at once: the added bulk of armour and padding could not hide his thinness, nor did any other man stand so stiffly when giving formal greeting.

His dark hair was pulled back into a simple tail over the base of his neck, and down the length of the hall, Margerite could see the sharp bones of his face glaring through the skin. O Maria, do not let him see me! she thought. Gottfried might be too short-sighted to recognise her from so far away, but if the Landgraf sent him down to sit with the lesser guests, as he assuredly would...

Margerite moved along as quickly as she dared, ready to dart back in through one of the doors to the kitchens. Gottfried was talking with Ortlieb now, looking closely into her eyes, and she felt a sudden stab of alarm. The knight might be hunting her love, but he was also a good Christian - and a man alone save for his squire, perhaps even a virgin: easy prey for Ortlieb's magic, and who would notice if a wandering Ritter, seeking a dangerous fugitive with only a youth as companion, failed to come home? Gottfried could not be overpowered like a child, but he could be lured into Ortlieb's sanctum, bound by the blindness that all men shared, there to let her do as she willed.

Should I warn him? Margerite wondered, even as she hovered near the door to flee. Yet if he knew that Bertram were here, he could well destroy our plan, such as it is...For a moment she knew herself dreadfully tempted: let Ortlieb take Gottfried, and leave her love alone! But no: one victim would not satisfy the Order Princess' ravening hunger for long, nor cleanse off whatever mark Ortlieb had left on Bernhardt; and besides, she could not in conscience sacrifice one man for another's sake.

Instead of coming down the hall to sit with the lesser guests, however, Gottfried was quickly seated at the high table - for what reason, Margerite could not guess. She kept to the other end throughout the meal, though she could not help glancing up towards the Burg Fürstensee knight more often than, perhaps, she ought to have. But unlike the other men at the high table, who ate absently while gazing, captivated, at the Landgräfin, Gottfried seemed to have nothing more on his mind than his table manners, washing his hands frequently in the finger-bowls that the high table-servitors brought out and barely touching the morsels on the plate he shared with the Margräfin with the tips of his fingers.

Perhaps I do not need to fear for him, after all, Margerite thought. She remembered what Nikolaus had said about the young knight's ability to see through charms and illusion: what did Gottfried see when he looked at Ortlieb? Was her beauty all a glamour; was she, perhaps, missing a few teeth, or did the breasts that stood out so proudly in her deep purple bodice actually sag a little? Or was it simply that Gottfried's dedicated purity of soul, refined by his long quest, had made him proof against whatever charm it was she worked on all the other men who came within sight of her? Whichever it was, Margerite felt suddenly certain that she did not have to fear for him, and that eased her mind.

Yet Bernhardt would have to know that Gottfried was there: the mask she had stolen for her love, and his long years of absence, might serve to disguise him from the castle-folk, but she did not think that they could hide him from Gottfried's penetrating gaze. Thus, hoping that no one would notice her brief absence between courses, Margerite slipped into the scullery where Eva stood by one of the stone sinks, diligently scouring a pot clean.

"Gisela," she murmured,"is Lothar expected to come here today?"

"He is very busy," Eva answered. "The Landgraf wants to take his guests hunting in the park tomorrow before the feast, so we shall not see him - what is wrong?"

"Gottfried is here!" Margerite hissed.

Only a slight widening of her blue eyes betrayed Eva's shock as she kept scrubbing hard at the iron pot. Otherwise, her expression did not change, her lips barely moving as she whispered,"How shall we warn Bernhardt? Will you..." She made a gesture with one hand beneath the sink's rim; Margerite did not recognise the movement, but its meaning was clear enough.

"Not here," Margerite answered softly. "I do not even dare to call Kobolt to me; I have been afraid since he came the one time. You will have to go instead. Tell the guards at the gate that you are on an errand from Liutbirg, if they ask: it matters little now whether you can keep your place here."

Eva nodded. "You may trust me to do that."

Bernhardt sat in Lothar's upstairs chamber with Father Etienne, Paul the Bear, and Jochanan. Georg was out, for the Bear's Paw Company had needed to be hastily redeployed when Lothar brought the news that Gerhardt would be hunting in the park with his noble guests on All Saints' Day; and the Knappe had proved invaluable as a messenger between their command-post and the dispersed units of the Free Company.

At least there had been time to quietly provide some of the men with horses, so that they could bring a sufficient force to bear with good speed, in spite of not being able to enter the hunting park until after nightfall - and neither Bernhardt nor Father Etienne expected Ortlieb to make her move until a little before midnight.

Lothar was away at his work, and would not return until nightfall; so, when the men heard the knocking at the door, they froze, looking at each other. Bernhardt put a finger to his lips: there was none of them who could answer without drawing suspicion.

The knocking grew louder, then stopped. In the sudden silence, Bernhardt thought he heard a soft click below - and then the sound of the door opening. The four men drew their swords, waiting for the footsteps on the stairs. Or perhaps worse: though it was broad daylight, Bernhardt's flickering glance marked the look of intense remoteness on Father Etienne's face, as though the priest were watching for something other than armed soldiers.

The two cats, who had been sleeping on the bed, sprang up; the black tom gave a soft whirring chirp, and the tortoiseshell female opened her pink mouth in a loud miaow. Bernhardt cursed silently: if whoever had entered did not know where they were, the cats had surely given them away now.

Only one person, by the soft, heavy-footed tread; noiselessly the men positioned themselves around the door, waiting for it to open. As if by silent consent, Etienne stood before: his clerical garb might buy them a moment of surprise. Paul and Jochanan waited behind the door, while Bernhardt was poised against the other wall to deliver his blow the moment the crack was wide enough - for no friend would have come upon them so stealthily.

The door opened. Bernhardt's blade was already in motion, but he managed to turn it aside, the point driving into the plaster of the wall. Eva gave a little shriek, stumbling back down a step or two before she caught herself.

"Eva!" Bernhardt said, the shock of what he had almost done making his hand shake when he freed his blade, as it would not have done if he had been pulling it from a man's body. "What are you doing here? What has gone wrong?"

Eva swallowed hard, looking at the men sheathing their swords. Her face was pale beneath the kitchen-grime, but to her credit, she recovered herself quickly, pulling her filthy cloak about her and stepping proudly into the room, with the two cats writhing about her ankles in furry ecstasy. "Margerite sent me to tell you that Ritter Gottfried has returned to the Schloss," she said. "She could not say more, you understand."

"That is news enough," Bernhardt replied grimly. "Did he see her?"

"I think she would have managed to let me know, had she been unmasked herself. She went back to serving in the hall after telling me to come here."

"This is an ill chance," Bernhardt mused. For their plan depended on him entering the Schloss just after dark, to give Ortlieb time to spy him out and make plans of her own before he revealed himself to her.

She had always been a swift and decisive woman, and he had no doubt that she would take the bait he offered. But if he were unmasked by Gottfried first, then he would be in his brother's hands, not hers, with no defense to offer: then it would be a matter of an uneven battle within the hall, holding out only the hope that he would be able to take Ortlieb with him - and even now, he did not know if he could plunge a sword into her flesh. It was bitterly ironic, Bernhardt thought, that her unclean purposes for him made Ortlieb his ally now, while the man from whom he had the most to fear was the good Ritter Gottfried.

Father Etienne might have been thinking along the same lines, for his arched eyebrows drew close and he tugged at the silver tuft in his beard. "An ill chance?" the priest said softly. "Or a good one? From what I have heard of this Ritter, he may as likely be your ally as your enemy, if he does not expose you to your foes in his ignorance and zeal."

"Shall the lads and I see if we can find a way to take care of him for you, Bertram?" Paul the Bear asked eagerly. "If you'd told us what to look for, we might have caught him before he ever got to the Schloss." He half-unsheathed his sword, slamming it back in.

Bernhardt shook his head. "I hope it will not come to that," he replied. "This is still the time for waiting and watching, my friend." He looked over at Father Etienne again. "I think our plans have not changed, even if I must needs be more careful going in. We have done all we can: it is already time to leave chance in the hands of God. If the guards on the gate are not willing to believe that we are part of Landgraf Friedrich's baggage-train that was delayed on the road -" for that was the best ruse Bertram could think of to get at least a few of the Bear's Paw members into the castle behind him; unless Friedrich's habits had changed greatly, he always travelled with enough men and accoutrements to make it plausible enough -"or if Gottfried betrays me, then that is God's will, and we must make the best of it."

Every time Margerite left the sewing-room to fetch something for one of Isabella's last-minute adjustments, her heart fluttered in terror like the heart of a trapped mouse: suppose she met Gottfried in a corridor, or on the stair? She knew that he had been put in one of the bedrooms at the top of the tower; at least there was nothing on the fourth floor except more bedrooms and the storage chambers at the end of the hallway where, she supposed, bedlinens and such things were kept - Isabella had never sent her there, anyway - but he would have to pass through that wing whenever he went to or from the great hall. Still, there was nothing she could do save watch and listen carefully, hurrying through every area where their paths might cross.

The dressmaker was badly frazzled, her hair coming down in tendrils from its elaborate weave of braids as she snapped at her assistants; as often as not, she would shout at the German women in French, and raise her voice instead of changing languages when they failed to understand her. Margerite had been set to stitching the last of the seed-pearls onto Ortlieb's costume. It had, she had to admit, a certain horrible beauty, the shimmering pearl-bones against the dark silk brocade; in a way, it reminded her of the tapestries in Ortlieb's room. Carrion-bird, Margerite thought, pricking the heavy fabric carefully with her needle.

Has everyone living today not seen enough of death yet? But she knew precisely what Ortlieb was doing: herself long hardened past any revulsion or terror, as a Princess of the Order must be, Ortlieb would evoke those feelings in everyone who watched her play - and in so doing, feed her own power, letting it swell and grow for whatever rite she had planned. Ah, Bertram - Bernhardt. I wish you did not have to set foot within this Schloss tomorrow night, for I fear for you... and I would not have you gaze upon Ortlieb again.

But there was no choice, since Margerite had failed to find the Order Princess' sanctum. At least she had been able to get Bernhardt and Etienne the masks that would allow them to go freely through the castle that night: they might even serve at dinner, as if they were pages again, instead of grown knight and priest.

Where shall you be a page, my Wolfram? Margerite thought, looking fondly at her golden-haired son sleeping in his nest of blankets. Had she been able to stay at Burg Fürstensee, Wolfram would most likely have been fostered with Graf Wolfgang; but if Bernhardt won tomorrow night, Wolfram might grow up to pour wine as a boy, and take his Knappe's vows as a youth, in the castle of the Margraf of Meissen or the Landgraf of Thuringia.

And if Bernhardt lost? Margerite would have to try to escape with her son, praying that Father Etienne could keep her safe. The only slight hope she could think of was to retreat to Burg Falkenstein, where Wolfram would at least have what was his - and where the Order will be after us again. It was that, or go back to Nikolaus at Burg Fürstensee...or keep running from the Order; but Etienne could not shield them on the road forever, since he had his own duties, and a priest could hardly travel long with a woman and a young child at his side.

Be brave, Bernhardt, Margerite thought, for you are fighting for my son's soul, as well as your own.

That night, exhausted as much by the constant effort of keeping out of Ritter Gottfried's sight as well as by the flurry of work, Margerite did not hear the noises, nor smell the stink, of the other servant-women around her. She had grown used to the prickles of her mattress and woolen blanket, to the constant niggling bites and itching of small insects in the bedding; now, she was as comfortable as she might have been in her soft bed back at Burg Fürstensee.

"Gertrude," a voice said quietly, and then, more urgently, "Gertrude!"

Margerite did not know whether she had spoken, or was being spoken to, but she sat up, staring about her in the darkness. At the foot of her bed, the light of a taper glowed, glittering off a small silver crucifix. Then she had to bite her tongue, for she recognised the woman holding it. It was Gertrude herself, the maidservant's long brown hair flowing loose about her shoulders and her brown eyes shining in the candlelight. But the girl was wearing a dress as fine as anything Margerite had ever owned, pale blue silk falling about her body in a shimmering ripple, and her broad peasant's feet were shod in deep blue velvet.

"Have you come to warn me of the fates of Dives and Lazarus? It is a little late, now that you are the frowe and I the serving-maid," Margerite whispered to her.

Gertrude shook her head, and Margerite saw the track of a tear glimmering down from the corner of one of her eyes. She drifted closer: Margerite had to steel all her nerves not to flinch back from the dead woman, though she was sure in her heart that Gertrude, whether living or a ghost, would never harm her. But Gertrude did not try to touch her, only stood staring down at her former mistress and the child in her arms. Then she lifted one hand, and the light from the taper glowed from her nails as though they had been polished and oiled - a light that drew Margerite's gaze into it, its dazzle slowly clearing away.

It seemed to Margerite that she was looking through the window of a hall from a great distance, but that every detail was sharp in her eyes, as though she saw with her falcon-sight. The hall was all brightly lit with a profusion of candles; and behind the high table stood a fair-haired boy of perhaps seven years, his face grave as he poured out wine. Something glittered on his finger: a silver Order ring, the inscription on its small circle so tiny that even Margerite's strange vision could not read it; and the dark-haired man for whom he was pouring wore an amethyst bound in inscribed gold.

The scene shifted again, and now it was a golden-haired youth of fifteen she saw - the very image of a younger Ruprecht, with a strange brilliance wavering about his head. He stood on a battlefield strewn with corpses, but though his surcoat was so drenched with dark blood that she could not make out its device, he stood like one who had taken no harm. He had taken his helm and gauntlets off, and the Order ring on his finger burned with deep red fire, rather than the amethyst Ruprecht had borne.

A group of men stood before him; though their bloodied surcoats and the occasional gleam of gold on a finger proclaimed them noble, their hands were bound and heads bowed. The fair youth lifted one hand, his Order ruby flashing, and two more men stepped in, their swords uplifted...Once more Margerite's sight wavered: now he was a few years older, and sat upon a throne, the smooth brightness of gems gleaming in the uplifted points of his crown.

The ring he wore now was not set with a ruby, but with a clear adamant, its water-paleness fracturing into rainbows in the sunlight as his hand moved. It seemed to Margerite that she could hear his voice, though his lips did not move; it was as like to Ruprecht's smooth baritone as his beautiful chiseled features were to Ruprecht's face, but she could hear deeper tones beneath, like the beating of a battle-drum in the distance.

My Father has set me upon the highest thrones of the world, and delivered its kingdoms and glory into my hand, he said. If you love me, Mother, you will not try to keep me from the triumph to which I was born. Mother Maria, help me! Margerite cried out, clutching Wolfram to herself with one hand and crossing herself with the other. Though she could make no sound, the vision before her suddenly wavered and disappeared. More tears were dropping from Gertrude's brown eyes now as she looked down at them.

"What do you want?" Margerite asked, and she could feel the hot tears flowing down her own cheeks. "Why have you shown me these things? What do you mean to say?" Was that - a vision of what my Wolfram will become, or only of something that might be?

Gertrude shook her head again, her face grave. She laid a hand on the silver crucifix at her throat, then bent down, as though to give Margerite the kiss of peace. As the dead maid's lips touched Margerite's, however, the light was suddenly gone: Margerite found herself lying awake in her servant's bed, her baby snuffling fretfully beside her.

"Wolfram, Wolfram," Margerite crooned almost soundlessly, stroking his head. His hair was so soft - finer than any silk or velvet, softer than any fur she had ever touched."Mother Maria help us, and St. Walburga who watched over your birth." She wished that Father Etienne were there, so that she might tell the dream to him.

But it cannot be true, for while I live, I would not let my son be a page at an Order castle; nor do I see how the son of Graf Ruprecht von Falkenstein could ever wear the Kaiser's crown. The Devil can send delusion in dreams, and even appear as an angel of light - and yet I wish I could believe that Gertrude wears fine silks now, and sits near the high table in Heaven with the saints. But the Black Book had stressed most sternly that half a truth from a demon was worse than a whole lie - especially when it was a half-truth that one wanted to believe in.

"Christ, be with us," Margerite prayed. "Mother Maria, be with us. Salve, Regina..."

Gottfried rode out with the Landgraf's hunt in the park the next day. The ladies were with them, short bows in their hands, since this was only a hunt for driven deer. Gottfried would not hunt with bow and arrow by choice, since he could not see at a distance well enough to aim: he preferred to hunt a deer by following its track with hounds and dispatching it with a sword, but the hunting he liked best of all, in spite of its danger, was going after boar with a spear.

Still, it would hardly be his place to consider shooting before the high nobility had gotten their quarry, so that he would likely escape the need to ever loose an arrow that day. Although the weather was ill-suited to sport, a strong wind blowing icy spatters of rain out of the north, heavy fur-lined cloaks and hoods kept the hunting party warm, as did the flasks of wine being passed freely about.

Towards the tail of the train, Gottfried found that he was riding beside the Landgräfin's fair-haired maid, her face framed by a white fluff of the fur that lined her soft green leather hood. "You seem distracted, Herr Ritter," the girl said lightly. "Are you worrying about how loudly we ride through the wood? Lothar seldom fails to make sure that we have plenty of game."

"I am sure we shall not come back empty-handed," Gottfried replied.

"Are you looking forward to tonight?" she pressed. "It will be an entertainment such as you have never seen, I would wager."

"You would win your wager," said Gottfried.

The blonde woman laughed, a pretty tinkling sound, like bells of tin. "Do you never smile, Herr Ritter? Surely you do not find your life so grim as to take no pleasures in it - have you lately been unhappy in love?"

"That is hardly a proper question to ask," Gottfried told her stiffly.

"O, the Landgräfin said that you had never learned to play courtly games with women, so perhaps one should take it upon herself to teach you. Is there no lady whose favour you bear, or after whom your heart is pining?"

"No."

"Then why do you not find one? Every knight should have a lady, if only to show him that there are higher things in life than fighting after which a man may aspire."

"I believe that the Church teaches us that well enough," Gottfried replied.

She laughed again. "Did not even Parzival, who sought the Grail, give his love to the lady Condwiramuns, and long for her all during the years of his Quest? How can you do less? What Grail is it that you seek?"

"If I recall the tale correctly, Anfortas received his wound as a punishment for fighting under the banner of love - a poisoned lance-head striking in a most grievous place. If one wishes to take instruction from such stories, one should take the whole of it."

The fair-haired girl considered Gottfried for a little while, one gloved hand stroking along the curve of her short bow. "That part of Parzival seems to have touched you deeply. Is there some reason for that, Herr Ritter? What wound is it that torments you?"

"You ask a great many questions for someone who has not even told me her name," Gottfried said shortly.

"Well, that is easily told. I am Oda von Schwarzenstein and, as you know, lady-in-waiting to Landgräfin Ortlieb. Surely it pleases you to know who I am, when you have been staring at me so closely through the course of this ride."

Self-consciously, Gottfried looked away. It was then that he saw the black furry shape bounding along through the dead grasses - big as it was, it could not be one of the hounds, for it moved too sinuously. "Are there lynx in this park, as well as deer?" he asked.

"Of course not! Lothar and the other gamekeepers make sure that nothing, not lynx nor bear nor wolves, can prey on the Landgraf's game. Why do you ask?"

Gottfried glanced to the side again, and thought that he saw the dark flash of a long plumed tail. It reminded him of something - of the Gräfin Margerite's pet, that huge wild cat that she had somehow tamed and trained to hunt rats like any ordinary feline, and even to sit in laps and purr, though it was half the size of a mastiff and weighed far more than it ought, like a stone statue covered by a furry hide.

"I thought that I saw something, but my eyes must have deceived me," he said. Was Margerite's pet native to the Thuringer Wald? Gottfried had heard of Saracen kings who kept lions, but never of anyone who had managed to tame a lynx, or whatever strange wildcat it was that the Gräfin owned.

Though Gottfried kept a watch on the side of the path thereafter, he did not see the huge cat again - until the train of riders passed by a house in a small clearing. At first he thought it to be a black hound sitting by the door; then it rose, arching its back and lifting its tail. "Whose house is that?" Gottfried asked.

Oda glanced incuriously over. "Oh, that is where Lothar lives," she said dismissively. Gottfried did not dare to ask her about the big cat, lest she think he was mad. Is it there at all? he wondered.

What does she see? Surely a cat so large should excite some comment...Then he blinked hard, for the black cat seemed to almost be melting into the earth, like a stone sinking into soft bog. It was his bad eyesight playing tricks on him again, Gottfried realized. There had never been a cat there at all, but only a shadow that his thoughts had given shape to; he had seen nothing more than the wind ruffling bushes and dead grasses. And that, he thought, is why I hate hunting small game, or anything that I have to shoot at.

By the time the hunting party was back at Schloss Niederwald, there were half a dozen roe-deer and four fallow deer slung over the horses of the servants who had followed behind, and all the talk was of the fine shooting. The Landgräfin herself had brought down one of the roe-deer with an arrow through the lungs, and was getting as much praise for it as if she had stood off an army single-handed. Gottfried had seen almost nothing of the shots, for the high nobles at the head of the train had been far outside his clear range of vision, but he had heard every detail of who had brought down which beast, in some cases several times.

As they came in through the wide triangular entrance hall of the Schloss, its high stained-glass window casting rain-muted colours over bright cloaks and hoods, Ortlieb stopped them, clapping her hands for attention. "As I have mentioned before, everyone is to be masked and costumed tonight. You will find your masks in your chambers; I hope that they will be pleasing to all of you. The feast will begin at sunset: I bid you enjoy yourselves as you will until then."

When Gottfried and Arnmut reached their chamber, Gottfried was little surprised to find that the mask Ortlieb had supplied for him was a hood of white velvet, with black velvet patches about eyes and nose - the mask of a skull, though he would not play her Death. Arnmut's was similar, but his hood was green instead of white. It was a gruesome jest on the Landgräfin's part: a bare skull, squired by one whose flesh had not fallen away yet, though it would in time - Ortlieb's revenge for his refusal? Gottfried wondered.

Their gambesons had been freshly cleaned, and were laid out on the bed by their armour; on top of them was a strip of parchment. Curious, Gottfried picked it up. It read: You need no costume: wear your armour and weapons instead. For a moment, Gottfried debated this within: did Ortlieb mean to drag him into her performance in some way, with or without his consent?

Her strange remark, that he had killed but never given life, came back to him...and yet, he could not in courtesy turn down this request. And - he could not deny it, but his unease here had grown steadily since his conversation with the Landgräfin: he would find himself more comfortable armed and armoured, though there would be no fighting that evening.

"Help me to armour, Arnmut," he said. "It seems that our hostess has decided that we shall be men who have fallen in battle."

"There are worse ways to die, Herr Gottfried," Arnmut answered comfortingly. "And it is All Souls' Eve."

"The dead should be in Heaven or Purgatory or Hell, not walking the earth," Gottfried muttered. In truth, the image of dead men in armour disturbed something deep within him.

When he had been very small, his nurse had told him tales of Wodan's Host, of those who could not reach their destined realms because they had fallen fighting and unconfessed, or been hanged or otherwise died unnaturally: those men, she had said, were doomed to ride in the winter storms on horses whose hooves struck fire, following fire-breathing hounds, and the living must keep out of their way.

Gottfried did not believe in such unChristian tales - yet even now, he had to admit to himself, when the wind howled most wildly at night, he did not often look out the window, or walk outside Burg Fürstensee's walls: it was as if some part of him were still the short-sighted boy who thought he saw the figures of ghosts moving in the shadows about Schlangenbad's churchyard.

Deliberately, the knight hooked his crucifix out from beneath his gambeson so that it lay bright on top of his breastplate. If Ortlieb wished him to be armed and armoured for her feast, so he would be. Though they could not put them on until after the feast, he and Arnmut would take their helms as well, to cover up the unnerving masks she had made for them.

"At home, we do something very like this for Fastnacht," Arnmut said. "There is a band of men called the Perchten in our village - no one is supposed to know who they are, but even my father is one - who put on all sorts of masks, especially the faces of anyone who has died that year. Then they run about and are given food and drink wherever they go, because their visit is supposed to be lucky. It is an old custom," he added quickly, "and of course no one really believes that they are ghosts, and even Father Peter does not object to it."

"Schlangenbad and Fürstensee have their Fastnacht maskers as well," Gottfried admitted. "But the Church gives us that time for license before the austerities of Lent, and this..."

Arnmut looked up from where he knelt buckling his knight's knee-cups on, his face and hair pale in the gloom. "Herr Gottfried, this is no more than a noblewoman's fancy. Why should it distress you so?"

Gottfried frowned. He wished that he could reassure his Knappe, as Arnmut was trying to reassure him, but the squire had come to know him too well: even were he willing to lie to the youth, to say that nothing was wrong, Gottfried did not think Arnmut would believe him. But what can I say? Gottfried wondered.

Can I tell him that Ortlieb has the eyes of an owl, or that I thought I saw a beast very like Gräfin Margerite's black wildcat in the wood today? Arnmut has grown used to seeing for me at a distance; often enough, on this journey, he has shot the small game I could not see so that we could eat. Is one infirmity not enough; should I let him think me mad as well?

"This should be a time to pray for the dead, not to make jest of them for a Landgräfin's sport," Gottfried said at last. "I think there will be far more candles lit in the hall for the feast tonight than are burned in the church of this Schloss tomorrow."

"That is true enough, Herr Gottfried. The church here is in poor repair - nothing like the one at Burg Fürstensee."

Gottfried nodded: he had smelled the faint undertone of mould when he had gone to pray the day before, with none of the precious incenses that sweetened the air of Landgraf Gerhardt's Schloss; and though beeswax candles burned everywhere inside the castle, the ones in the church were cheap tallow.

"But we need not stay much longer," Arnmut added, pulling the last buckle tight and then beginning to get into his own armour. "If you mislike it here, we can speak to the gamekeeper and be back on the road tomorrow. I will be glad to do whatever you think best."

"You are a good Knappe, Arnmut," Gottfried sighed, for he knew how his squire had appreciated eating fine food and sleeping in a soft bed again. "I could not do better than to have you beside me."

"Thank you, Herr Gottfried," Arnmut answered, giving Gottfried another of his sweet smiles.

Though the sky was settling quickly into darkness when Gottfried and his squire came down to the great hall, spatters of icy rain rattling sharply against the large windows with every gust of wind, the hall itself blazed with light, the bright haloes of countless candles overlapping and dazzling the young knight's eyes, so that he stumbled like a blind man for the first few steps, and Arnmut had to take his arm to hold him up, the Knappe's touch reassuring even through the many layers of metal, leather, and padding that separated them.

Somewhat to Gottfried's relief, most of the masks were
not of the gruesome sort Landgräfin Ortlieb had given
to Arnmut and himself, but rather, fantastic creations of
feathers and silk, velvet and leather, bedecked with fringes
and bells. The Margraf and Margräfin von Meissen wore
what appeared to be small crowned swans on their heads,
the white wings sweeping down to enclose their faces, while
Landgraf Friedrich and his wife were decked out as lion
and lioness, with the Landgraf's fringed mane combed so
carefully into his fair beard that there was no telling where
mask ended and man began.

Ortlieb had, Gottfried realized, gone to some trouble to
match the nobility of the masks to the ranks of the wearers
- and what is she saying about Arnmut and myself? he
wondered, more certain than ever that the Landgräfin's
choice of guises had been very deliberate. Even the pages
and other servants pouring the wine were masked, wearing
costumes that ran from the hairy pelts of wood-woses to
robes and crowns of gilded leather that glittered with glass
jewels.

One slender man in a black doublet and hose was
disguised with a mask of leather tooled into bat-wings above
a short dark beard with a single silver tuft in it; his blue
eyes glittered unnervingly through the ribbed black leather.
Though Gottfried had not yet taken a sip of wine, his head
was beginning to swirl with the strangeness about him; it
almost felt as though the winds lashing against the hall's
broad windows were blowing inside as well.

"What do you mean, 'the last of my baggage-train'?"
Landgraf Friedrich was roaring at one of the servants.
"Christ's cods, can't any of my folk keep track of where they
are from prime to tierce without me to tell them what to
do? I clearly said I only wanted…well, send them up to my
rooms, then."

Everyone else was seated before Landgraf Gerhardt and his wife appeared at last. The Landgraf was dressed and masked all in black; as he came closer, Gottfried saw the horns arching above his crowned head like a huge halo of night blocking out the brightness of the candles. Pearled ribs and breastbone gleamed from the bodice of Ortlieb's dress, but her mask was that of an owl, tufted feathers spreading down above her white breasts and golden eyes gleaming wide and round from the mask's eyeholes.

From the minstrels' balcony, a bell rang, and suddenly there was silence in the room.

"My dear friends," Ortlieb cried, her deep voice echoing through the great hall. "This is the eve of All Souls': eat, drink, and be merry, for death will come to us all. But before the feast begins, I have news that will bring you both sorrow and gladness. This is my farewell feast, for a time: for after these years of marriage, at last there is a child in my womb, some four months along. A gift of such preciousness must be cared for, and the work of rule is strenuous, so tomorrow, I will be on my way to the Convent of the Holy Cross, where the good sisters will tend me until our child is born."

The guests were on their feet at once, loudly toasting the Landgräfin and her husband. Gottfried sipped at his wine, quietly relieved in his heart: the news of Ortlieb's pregnancy explained much of her strangeness, for everyone knew that women were prone to odd fancies while they were carrying children. And if she had just ascertained that she was with child, it was no wonder that her thoughts had been running to that subject, even to the point of speaking indecently to a guest. No wonder, as well, that she had needed another to play the part of Death in her Danse Macabre, for such a thing could not be good for an infant in the womb.

Ortlieb and Gerhardt sat down; their guests did likewise, and the first course was carried in to a mellow flourish of trumpets from the gallery above. This was a wild sow with a swollen belly, arranged standing so that she seemed to have been caught eating an apple; the carver, dressed in a physician's somber robes with a plain black mask upon his face, stepped up to open his huge black bag and display a variety of medical implements with a few carving knives upon them.

Slicing open the sow's belly, he drew forth several suckling piglets, all of them gilded with a glitter that spoke of a little real gold mixed with the saffron and egg-yolks that glazed their crisp skins. Their meat was as succulent as its presentation promised, so tender that it was almost falling from the little bones, but Gottfried ate only very carefully, knowing that there would be many courses to follow.

After the sow, the servers brought in a flock of swans, re-dressed in their feathers and adorned with golden crowns and chains around their necks. To Gottfried's amazement, when a taper was lifted to the bill of the head of the flock, a blue flame roared out, and burned brightly for a little while as the swans were paraded around the hall.

The following courses were less fantastic, but equally delicious: rabbits in gravy, lightly coated with sugar; a flock of small roasted and gilded birds, clinging to the branches of a golden tree from which gold apples hung; roe-deer that, like the sow, had been arranged standing in a lifelike manner, their heads raised as though they had just caught the scent of the hunter, but which fell apart into tender pieces of jellied meat as soon as the carver-physician cut through their hides; a subtlety shaped like a hedgehog with spikes of almond-slivers, which proved to be stuffed with chopped meat and spices...

The musicians played throughout the feast, and between courses, a troupe of jugglers ran into the middle of the hall to entertain. Gottfried knew that he should have been more delighted and amazed, for there was little chance that he would ever see such a spectacle again; but delicious as the food was, he found that his stomach was tight, as if he were expecting a battle in truth: it was not only care and good manners that kept him from eating much from each dish, or from drinking too deeply of the rich wine in his gilded goblet.

At last the final sweet was brought in, carried like a bier by four black-clad pall-bearers as a slow, mournful dirge floated down from the minstrels' gallery. The pall-bearers whipped off the black cloth covering it to reveal a subtlety that made even Gottfried, blurred as his vision of it was, catch his breath. The Schloss kitchens had made a very realistic skeleton, lying in a tattered shroud with its fingerbones clasped over its ribcage, the bones gleaming greenish-white against the black on which it was laid.

It did not ease Gottfried's mind to see how the sugar bones crumbled and the pastry shroud flaked away when the carver began his operation on it; though the sugar was flavoured with mint and a hint of anise, and the pastry was very delicate and sweet, he could not manage more than a few bites before he dipped his fingers in the fresh washing-bowl and wiped them on his napkin for the last time that evening.

Eventually the remains of the feast were cleared away. Ordinarily, it would have been time for the servants to take most of the tables away so that the dancing could begin - but instead, the masked figures began moving about, snuffing candles one by one until the light in the hall was no more than half of what it had been. Reminded of his resolve, Gottfried reached to the floor to set his helm on his head, and motioned to Arnmut to do the same.

The tune the minstrels struck up now was a dance-tune, gay and sprightly; but to Gottfried's sensitive ears, even through his helm, it sounded as if something were wrong with it, as though their instruments had gone slightly off-key through long playing. He could hear his own heart beating an ungainly counterpart to the drum above; though the hall was warm from candles and fires and bodies, even uncomfortably hot to him in his padded armour, it seemed to him as if a fine chill mist were seeping in from somewhere, and even with the sweat running down his spine, Gottfried shivered.

Gottfried did not see the figure appear in the middle of the floor between the tables, where the jugglers had performed before; it was simply there, wild-haired and ragged, feet lifting and bones clicking erratically to the steps of the dance. Despite the mist that made light-haloes of the remaining candles, Gottfried could see it clearly, more clearly than he should have been able to at that distance: a long-dead corpse, the darkened flesh peeling away to show the bones of its face - the maggots squirming in the tatters of meat that hung on either side where its abdomen had burst, and its winding sheet scattering gravemold.

A gold coronet glittered among the flying gray strands of its hair, half-sunk in what was left of its rotting scalp; a scythe swung in one bony hand. Shocked and sickened, Gottfried recognised where he had seen that jerky movement before: men in the latter stages of the Death would sometimes rise and dance so, twitching in those half-intoxicated, half-agonized throes.

Why was no one crying out in fear or revulsion? Gottfried wondered, daring for just a moment to glance about at the faces of his fellow-diners. What did they see - what was he seeing?

The corpse spoke, its voice shivering through the soles of Gottfried's boots, as though it were rising from the earth of a churchyard.

"I am Death: all before me fail,
None is so strong as to prevail.
From babe to greyhead, I take all,
And each must hearken to my call.
Slip into sleep, or wildly rave,
You each must follow to the grave.
No merchant's wealth, and no knight's sword,
No crown of kings, nor wise man's word,
Can stay my hand: here see your doom,
For even now you rush towards tomb."

A second figure joined the first: a young nobleman, dressed in a fashionable doublet with purple silk-lined sleeves hanging down in long dags. Gottfried watched, horrified, as his nimble dancing feet began to jerk and twitch like those of Death, his face, delicate beneath his sequined black mask, to swell and darken and slough as he spoke, his high bright voice deepening and slurring as though his throat were rotting from within.

"Dressed in silks and velvets fine,
I hunted, hawked, and drank French wine,
Though I am born of noble kin,
Death summons, and I must attend."

The icy mist was thick in the hall now, so that Gottfried could hardly see the faces of those beside him; and yet it brought him no mercy: it did not blur the two rotting shapes that danced in the middle of the hall, nor the third that joined them, a plump tonsured man in the long black robes of a Benedictine abbot - but at least the robes hid most of what was happening beneath them, though Gottfried could see the flesh of his body bloating until the black fabric was stretched taut, then sinking in again as the gases of decomposition burst through his abdomen with a muffled sound.

"Well I fed, despite my Rule,
Now Death proves me to be a fool,
For there was one thing I forgot:
The fattest flesh is first to rot."

All that is mortal dies, Gottfried reminded himself. But the soul is immortal; and beyond Death, by Christ's mercy, is the Kingdom of Heaven. He touched his crucifix: though he could not see its brightness, he could feel the smoothness of the imperishable gold beneath. There is no need to fear Death, if one trusts in God.

The next to enter Death's dance was a young woman with a babe in her arms - and now Gottfried almost did cry out in surprise, for there was something about the woman's long fair hair and slender body that reminded him terrifyingly of the Gräfin Margerite. She did not change as she danced, but her child's flesh darkened, infant plumpness flowing into green maggot-ridden liquescence.

"Not mother's milk nor mother's love,
Defiance over Death can prove.
I would have held him from all harms:
Death took him in my very arms."

Someone was weeping now, a soft feminine snuffling - the Margräfin? Gottfried could not tell: he could see nothing but Death and his dancers, and the gray shapes drawing closer to them through the mists, the grime-faced peasant in his black wool tunic and loose breeches shuffling out in a clumsy parody of the dance that the nobleman had tripped so nimbly.

"I lived and worked and ploughed the soil,
And earned my bread by honest toil,
I trusted in my lord and priest,
When Death called, that helped not the least."

To Gottfried's horror, he found that he was standing now, drawing closer to the ring where nobleman and abbot, mother and peasant, danced convulsively behind the figure of Death. He could hear footsteps behind him, and something brushed swift and leathery past his head, its wings ringing softly from his helm. His limbs were trembling faintly - in rhythm to the music, he realized; and when he tore his gaze away from the circle of dancers, he could see faces shaping themselves from the fog.

His father, gray-haired and pale; Herr Christoph, bleeding darkly from a great wound in his skull; Graf Heinrich, his bearded face slack and a trail of drool dribbling down from one corner of his mouth...All die. I will die someday as well: may Christ have mercy on my soul, and be with me in the hour of my death. But behind the ghostly images, Gottfried could see other things, dark twisted shapes cavorting in the mists - or writhing in torment: he could not tell which.

A faint stink of sulphur caught in the back of his throat like burning bile; a whisper of agonized laughter echoed behind the music, and something winged and clawed hovered over the heads of the dancers like a black carrion-bird. Christ forgive me for all my sins: how can Hell show itself so on Earth? But He is with me yet, even here; and though I must go with Death, like all men, I shall go with a firm faith and a strong heart, for I know that Heaven waits beyond the grave.

As he moved slowly towards the dance of Death, Gottfried could still hear the jingling of armour behind him. He was not going alone, he realized, even as he felt the pressure of the terrible song rising against the roof of his mouth: Arnmut was following him, his faithful Knappe to the last, even on this unholy path through Hell to Death...Arnmut!

With the last of his strength, Gottfried reached back, his mailed gauntlet closing on his squire's wrist. He flung himself headlong away - away from Death and his dancers, away through the half-seen shapes in the mist and the things that wailed above - dragging Arnmut with him, even as the words that he would not say rang in his ears.

"The sword and lance I lived to wield,
And by strength ever won the field,
My skill at arms yet could not stand
Against the sword in Death's cold hand."

Then they were through the door, safe in the candlelight of the triangular antechamber to the Great Hall. The music and singing still sounded faintly behind them, but they were no more than noise now. Gottfried tore off his helmet, and the velvet mask with it, dragging in deep breaths of clean air.

Arnmut also took off his helmet and mask, staring at his knight in bewilderment. His blue eyes were misted, a faint gray fog over the black pupils like the pale bloom on a dark grape. "Herr Gottfried, what is wrong?" he asked. "What happened?"

"What did you see?" Gottfried whispered.

The Knappe opened his mouth as if to answer, then closed it again. "I...Christ help me, I am not sure. It seemed...There was the figure of Death, and folk from different walks of life dancing with him...It seems as though there was something else, but I cannot remember: it is like a dream fading with morning already."

"Thank Christ for that," Gottfried said grimly. He remembered everything he had seen: he did not think he would ever forget it.

"What did you see, Herr Gottfried? Forgive me, my knight, but you look as though you are about to swoon - let me help you up to our room, and get you some wine."

Gottfried was about to refuse his squire's arm, but when he took a step, he found his knees beginning to buckle beneath him. Arnmut caught him swiftly, the young man's solid strength holding him up; only Gottfried's pride kept him from collapsing altogether into the Knappe's arms.

They were almost to the antechamber's other door - the one that led through the servants' hall to the tower stair - when it swung open and a tall, broad-shouldered figure in a raven-winged mask stepped through.

"Ritter Gottfried," a rough voice said. "I must speak with you."

Bernhardt had not known what to expect when Father Etienne came quietly back in from the great hall and told him to go to the upper antechamber at once. He certainly had not thought that he would see Ritter Gottfried shaking in his Knappe's embrace like a boy after his first battle, the young knight's skeletal face whiter than the piece of sweat-smirched velvet in his trembling hand. What happened in there? Bernhardt thought. What did Ortlieb do to him?

Arnmut let go of his knight and Gottfried straightened, his hand going to the hilt of his sword as he looked up at the taller man. "Bertram!"

Bernhardt put a finger to his lips. "I am not your foe, though you have been hunting me," he said quietly. "And I will explain everything to you, if you will come with me to a safer place - I give you my word that no harm will come to you." He knew that if Gottfried wanted to take him now, he could.

The knight and his Knappe were both armed and armoured, while Bernhardt was disguised as a castle servitor, his armour and sword still in the baggage that he had brought in with the Bear's Paw men; and whatever had shocked Gottfried to near-collapse, he seemed to be recovering from it quickly - he would, Bernhardt thought, be able to fight.

"Who are you to give your word?" Gottfried asked. "A common man-at-arms?" His gray eyes stared intensely into Bernhardt's, but Bernhardt did not quail before his gaze.

"You know better than that; else you would not have mistrusted me from the beginning. Now I swear by the Cross that I am of noble birth, and that you and I share an enemy, whether you know it yet or not."

Gottfried's cold eyes flickered away for a second - towards the door of the main hall. "I would be a fool to let you lead me away so without some proof of what you say. We are alone here, and I think shall be while...what is happening in there goes on: tell me what you must, or yield yourself as my prisoner."

"Father Etienne warned me not to enter the great hall after the last dishes were carried out," Bernhardt mused. "What is happening within?"

The young knight crossed himself, but did not speak, and Bernhardt pursued as he would press a retreating opponent in a fight. "Whatever it was that you fled, do you think that it comes from the powers of Heaven?"

Gottfried crossed himself again. "I think," he whispered, so softly that Bernhardt could barely hear it, "that Landgräfin Ortlieb has called up the powers of Hell."

"And," said Father Etienne's dry baritone from the door behind Bernhardt, "you are to be congratulated on your escape, Ritter Gottfried. Ortlieb was a fool to try to bring you into her dance: even knowing nothing of what she had conjured, you might have broken her spell."

"Who are you?" Gottfried demanded, looking at the priest. Like the rest of them, Father Etienne had adopted a disguise for the evening, and there was nothing priestly about it. He wore the tight black doublet and hose of a courtier, with his face hidden by a bat-winged leather mask; slim and agile as his body was, nothing betrayed his age save for the silver tuft that showed in his short beard beneath the mask's edge. Still, his air of authority was unmistakable as he spoke.

"I am Canon Etienne de Dion. And I can, and will, answer the questions you have - but it must be done quickly, and not here, for other folk might come upon us at any moment. Your chamber is at the top of the tower, I believe; that should be safe enough. Bernhardt, as you were: I do not believe that Ortlieb will leave the hall until her entertainment is done."

At such a feast as this, there was no time for the servants to sit and eat their own meal: those who had not been set to attending the guests' rooms were all occupied in carrying food in and out of the hall, clearing away or setting down dishes and bringing wine up from the cellars. The kitchens seemed like a mass of screaming chaos to Margerite; the long servants' hall was hardly better, its tables heaped with dirty plates and the remains of the many elaborate courses from which, as they passed, the castle folk would hastily snatch a piece or two to stay their hunger.

Though Wolfram might have been better off in the sewing room, or even the servants' quarters, Margerite had begged a crib from Irmingard so that she could put him in a corner of the servants' hall: since her dream, she had been even less willing than before to part from him for a second. If she could have, she would have carried Wolfram everywhere she went; but, her face concealed by the mask of a demure yellow cat, she had to do her part in serving food and clearing the tables.

At least Father Etienne, Bernhardt, and the men of the Bear's Paw had managed to make their way in through the gates: Bernhardt and the priest had joined the servitors almost unnoticed, while the Bear's Paw men, Etienne had whispered to her in a quick aside, were waiting outside. As was the way at such events, the drinking grew heavier as the evening wore on. Several times, Margerite had to run down to the cellars to bring up pitchers of the best wine for the high table, or to help other servants heave barrels up the stairs; and as soon as the last dishes had been cleared away, she was sent down to the cellars again.

A tiny part of her was almost disappointed that she would not get to see the performance for which she had been sewing costumes for the last weeks - but she was far more relieved, for she could feel the thick power gathering about her like the clouds of a thunderstorm. Even the stone flags of the cellar felt unsteady beneath her feet, as if something were heaving beneath them, gathering its strength to break free; and the faces of the other servants shone pale in the gloom, their talk all in hushed whispers.

Above, however, no one seemed to notice the trembling darkness in the air; they talked and laughed, Liutbirg shouting at her kitchen staff as if nothing out of the ordinary were happening. Some bore full pitchers of wine into the hall and empty ones out, and the snatches of music that came through the doors in their seconds of opening sent jangling shivers down Margerite's spine.

"Down for more wine, and be quick about it!" the cellarer shouted at Margerite and the three other women who had just heaved a full barrel into the place of an empty one. "God's teeth, I don't think I've ever seen a company drink like this one."

Even through the aching of her muscles and the burning of her lungs as she and her fellow-servants carried the next barrel up, though, Margerite's uneasiness was growing within her, swelling like rotten food in her belly until she was afraid that she would spew up from nervousness. This time, the cellarer was looking elsewhere when they put the barrel down, and Margerite hurried through the kitchens to make sure that Wolfram was still well.

Yes: he was sleeping quietly, a little bundle of blankets in the shadowed crib. As much to reassure herself against her own shivering uneasiness as anything, Margerite reached down to touch him - and her hand met only blankets, rolled up into a bundle with nothing warm and solid beneath them.

"Wolfram!" she whispered, hands tearing at the blankets as if he might be hiding beneath them. Her son was gone. If he had somehow managed to squirm out, if a slat had given way and let him fall to the floor - no: the wooden frame of the crib was solid: the child could not have gotten out on his own. Nevertheless, she dashed about the hall, dodging between the other hurrying servants to frantically search every heap of reeds; but Wolfram was not there.

"Margerite. Margerite, what is wrong?" Bernhardt asked, his strong hands grasping her shoulders. Shaking in his grip, she could not speak, only pointed mutely to the empty crib.

Bernhardt looked down at the pathetic tangle of blankets where Margerite had scrabbled. The raven-wing mask she had stolen for him hid the upper half of his face, so that only his hazel eyes gleamed through. His beard, grown out to its natural brown now, had been cropped close, and between that and the mask, she might almost have been looking at a stranger: she could not tell what the grim set of his mouth might mean. Ruprecht's child, the fair-haired image of the man he had slain...What did Bernhardt feel for Wolfram? Margerite had never dared to ask.

"Come, quickly," Bernhardt said.

Margerite followed him to the tower stairs. Bernhardt was almost running, slowing his pace only slightly so that Margerite's shorter legs could keep up with him. They were not half a story up when Margerite saw the light of the candles in the wall-sconces gleaming from two armoured backs, and the slim dark shadow of Father Etienne in front of them.

The three men turned; Margerite's heart missed a beat as Gottfried's icy gray eyes stared straight into hers.

"Frowe Gräfin! What are you doing here?" the knight asked her severely; and then, as if to himself, "I thought I had seen your cat in the woods."

Margerite ignored him, speaking directly to Etienne. "Father, Wolfram was taken from his crib while I was down in the cellars. Maria help us, I fear..."

The eyeholes of Father Etienne's batwing mask went dark a moment, and his lips moved silently - in prayer?"Go on to Ritter Gottfried's chamber," Etienne ordered. "I will join you in a few moments." The priest brushed downward past Margerite, taking the stairs three at a time.

Gottfried was still staring at Margerite. Hastily she said, "Herr Ritter, I will tell you everything when we have time. For now, my son is in danger: will you help me?"

The knight bowed to her, his chainmail ringing softly beneath the plates of his armour. "I will, Frowe Gräfin."

Father Etienne caught up with them as they reached the top of the tower. The priest was barely breathing hard, but Margerite could hear the stress cracking in his voice as he said, "The Danse Macabre is still going on, but I was wrong: Ortlieb has left the hall. Now, by all that is holy, we must find her sanctum at once, if Wolfram is to be saved."

"Father," Gottfried said, "will you not tell me at least a little more of what is happening, if I am to help you?" He opened the door, leading them into his chamber.

"Put quickly enough: Landgräfin Ortlieb is a black sorceress, aided by the powers of the Devil in summoning demons and spirits, and creating illusions - as you saw this night. She has stolen Gräfin Margerite's son - perhaps to sacrifice him to her Master. " Or perhaps, Margerite thought, to seal him to Lucifer by means of such a rite as Graf Günther was unable to perform - but better not to tell Gottfried that.

The eyes and mouth of Gottfried's Knappe opened wide in astonishment, but Gottfried listened quietly; though his narrow face might have gone a little paler, his thin lips were firmly set, and he nodded once as though Father Etienne's words only confirmed something he already knew.

"Ortlieb has the eyes of an owl," the knight whispered, which would have made no sense to Margerite if she had not seen the other woman's winged shape. "As I said: I am with you. Where shall we find her?"

"Somewhere in this castle or nearby, Ortlieb must have a place where she works her magic: all magicians of her Order do. But it is well-hidden, and I fear that we must...work quickly, and use dangerous means to find it."

Gottfried frowned, as though thinking on something. Starved from the privations of his long journey, with his dark hair tied back in a simple tail, he hardly looked any older than his squire; his deep baritone voice trembled uncertainly as he said, "Hidden, or guarded?"

Father Etienne's clear blue eyes gleamed sharply through the holes of his leather mask. "Why do you ask?" he said.

"The two guards at the end of the corridor on the fourth floor, just where it turns the corner towards the stairs - they are always there, and it always seems to be the same two men at every time of the day or night. I have never seen their faces, because even here within the castle, they wear full helms."

"But there is nothing there!" Margerite protested. "Only storerooms for linens and such..." Her voice trailed off. She had passed through that corridor hundreds of times, running up and down the stairs to fetch things for Isabella, and never paid any attention to what might lie behind that door, since it had nothing to do with her own duties.

"Herr Ritter," Father Etienne said, "we will have much to speak of later. But all of you, come swiftly, now."

The five of them hurried down to the fourth floor. The freezing rain hammered against the blackened windows, but all the candles on the walls blazed with light - and still Margerite saw nothing but the familiar storeroom door at the end of the corridor. Bernhardt was staring at Gottfried as if the knight had gone mad, but Etienne's mouth was tight beneath his mask.

"Do you still see the guards, Ritter Gottfried?" the priest asked softly.

"Do you not, Father?" Gottfried asked in turn, his voice quavering.

Margerite stared as hard as she could, half-closing her eyes so that the light of the candles caught rainbowed haloes from her lashes. It almost seemed to her that she could see two shadows looming there, but they were only shapeless blurs; she could not have sworn that they were anything more than a trick of the flickering lights. She would have given anything - the blood from her veins, the heart beating in her breast - to hear Wolfram's cry from beyond the plain door, but there was no sound save the breathing of her companions.

"Ritter Gottfried, if we are to pass here, I fear you must fight alone," Father Etienne said. "There is no time for me to do what I would need to do for the rest of us to see what you see. Herr Bernhardt, if you will, please go and fetch my sword - or Paul the Bear's, for I think plain steel will not bite on these guardians."

Gottfried drew his sword, holding it two-handed with the candlelight gleaming along its length. "Father, I have spent many nights in prayer with this blade upon my journey, and it has received the blessings of many holy men. By Christ's will, it shall not fail me now; and from what you say, we have no time to wait." The knight set his helmet upon his head, tightening the chin-strap. Then, suddenly, he was moving, his blade a bright blur through the air.

Margerite clasped her hands tightly together, her teeth set in her lower lip as she watched Gottfried whirl and slash at - ah, Maria, if only she could see his foes, could tell how hard-pressed the young knight was! She remembered that Christoph had spoken of Gottfried's prowess and speed: she had never seen a man move faster, but it seemed to her that even though Gottfried seemed to be blocking and striking against empty air, she could tell that he was fighting against two. Behind her, Arnmut was murmuring something softly, though she could not make out the words.

"Christ help him!" Bernhardt muttered through clenched teeth. "Father, is there nothing we can do to aid?"

"Pray!" Etienne snapped tightly.

Then a keening shriek rose in Margerite's head, higher and higher until she thought her skull would burst. She clapped her hands to her ears, but it did not help: the sound was inside, not outside. She was ready to cry out herself when it cut off abruptly.

"That was one," Etienne murmured. "If he can hold out..."

Bright blood spurted out from beneath the curved plates covering Gottfried's right shoulder, and Margerite saw Bernhardt wince. "That will slow him," Bernhardt whispered. But Gottfried did not seem even to feel the wound. Had he not been fighting in such deadly earnest, his sword blurring up and whistling through the air, Margerite would have thought of a child striking at an imaginary foe with a willow-wand, driving him back and back - pretending to stagger, as though an imaginary blow had caught him on the side of the helm, and then lunging up with his full strength to pierce an invisible heart...

A second shriek rose inside Margerite's skull, the echo of that unheard cry dying away like a wind whispering over an empty plain. Gottfried straightened, sheathing his sword. "They are gone," he stated. He did not seem to notice the rivulet of blood running down his arm to drip from the pointed steel cup over his elbow, but his Knappe ran to him at once, unfastening the leather straps that held his shoulder-plates on.

"Herr Gottfried, you are wounded!" Arnmut cried. Gottfried lifted his helm off, looking down at his arm as if surprised. The phantom blade had sliced neatly between two curved strips of metal, cutting through his gambeson; white bone gleamed beneath the welling blood. The Knappe pressed his hands to the wound, but the blood was already spilling red through his fingers.

"It is not much. It does not hurt yet," Gottfried said distantly. "We must go on."

"Back, and let your Knappe tend you," Father Etienne ordered. "You have done your part." He crouched before the door, doing something to the lock - Margerite could not tell what, but after a few moments, it sprang open.

Behind was another corridor with two doors leading off it. Etienne took a candle from one of the wall-sconces and led the way in, his empty right hand upraised; it almost seemed to Margerite that, if she looked sideways at the priest, she could see a blue flame flickering about his fingers in the darkness. She took another candle and followed him.

The moment she stepped through the doorway, Margerite wondered how she could ever have failed to miss Ortlieb's sanctum. All the hairs on her body prickled up, her bowels twisting within her: the feeling of Ortlieb's power still rang through the place like the echo of a deep bronze bell, tainted and terrifying. She could almost smell it: sweet incense and musty herbs, and beneath it the stink of flesh beginning to go bad.

Etienne opened the first door. The walls were lined with shelves, and dark patches stained the wooden table - but there were no books or glassware on the shelves, and the table was bare. Another illusion? Margerite wondered.

"There is nothing here," Bernhardt whispered. She could hear his breath coming hard, as though it were he who had done battle with the guardians - or is still doing battle, Margerite thought.

"So," Father Etienne breathed. A door on the southern wall led to the next room: the priest walked over and opened it.

The smells were thicker in here, and Margerite found herself struggling for breath, her head pounding with every gasp from her lungs. But the candle-flames flickered from bare walls that might have been freshly whitewashed, and the new-painted wooden floor was bare: no circle, no triangle, no altar - nothing to show that Order magic had ever been worked here, save the overwhelming feeling of its power crushing against Margerite's bones.

"Nothing here, either," said Gottfried's voice from behind her. Margerite turned to look at the knight. His squire had bandaged his shoulder with a strip of surcoat, but the blood was still seeping darkly through it: he should be lying down, not following them into Ortlieb's sanctum. But if Gottfried could see nothing, then Ortlieb's secrets were not hidden by illusion, and that meant...

"But this must be the place," Margerite protested, as if to convince herself. "I can feel it!"

"As can I," Etienne spat. "This is her sanctum, or it was. And I think -" the priest's finely chiseled mouth twisted bitterly beneath his mask -"I think we have been outmaneuvered."

Wolfram! Margerite's heart cried out.

"What do you mean, Father?" Bernhardt asked.

"This place was not cleared in a day, nor for any light cause. Ortlieb must mean to come back to it, or she would not have left it guarded; but she means to work her magic elsewhere for a time."

"Then where is she?" Margerite demanded. "Where is my son?"

"Margerite," Father Etienne said gently. "We must find Wolfram as soon as we can - but I believe that he is in no danger this night."

Margerite thought of her dream, and the priest's words drove the breath from her like a sharp blow beneath the breastbone. Gertrude had been warning her, indeed: Ortlieb would, as she had said before her assembled guests, disappear for a time - and come back with a boy-child, an heir to Schloss Niederwald; if the child seemed unusually large and strong for his age, what was that but proof of his noble blood?

Gerhardt would not question his wife, and certainly none of Ortlieb's servants would dare. And, at seven, Wolfram would be sent to learn the duties of a page in an Order-ruled castle; and after that...who knew how deep the corruption of the Order went, or how many of the imperial Electors were in their control? The Kaiser's son Wenzel was already, though but a small child, said to be weak-minded, and men said that he was unlikely to be chosen to succeed his father when Karl IV died...O my son, Margerite thought, what are you to become?

"If she is in the Schloss, we can find her," Gottfried said. "And if she has left, she cannot have gone far yet, though she is sure to be guarded." The knight's gray eyes looked about at his companions, and Margerite could guess what he was thinking.

Two proven fighting men, one of whom was wounded; a squire, a priest, and a woman: what chance had they? Yet the set of his thin shoulders told Margerite that he was willing to try the attack nevertheless; and though she could not quite bring herself to like the stern young knight, she could not help but admire him.

"We have the means to deal with that," Bernhardt told him. "And yet, think: it is dark, and if she is gone, there is no way to tell which road she has taken."

"But I can guess," Margerite said. "Ortlieb's father left her a small castle, deep in the Thuringer Wald. Though she claimed to be retiring to a convent and, God help us, the Order has its own cloisters, I think that I know her now, and she would not go to a place where she is not mistress. And unless she is travelling with wagon and train now, she must have sent all her tools of magic on before her, for they would have been no light burden - but I think that she must have meant to strike swiftly and leave swiftly, ever since she recognised me." And when had that been? Margerite wondered. How long did Ortlieb know who I, and perforce Wolfram, are? A wave of hatred roiled in her belly, thinking of the Order Princess' secret amusement in seeing the Gräfin von Fürstensee sent to fetch and carry and serve at table in her castle; her fury seemed to echo from the walls, resonating back into her bones.

"Soft, Margerite," Father Etienne said. "This is no place for that: Ortlieb's work here is only hidden, not gone."

But Ritter Gottfried crossed himself, staring at Margerite with a gaze that almost made her tremble. "What are you, Gräfin?" he asked, his voice faint, as though he were becoming lightheaded.

"What do you see, Herr Ritter?" Father Etienne enquired.

"The eyes of a bird of prey - like Ortlieb's," Gottfried murmured. He swayed on his feet, and Arnmut moved in quickly to support him, slipping an arm about his armoured waist.

"Knappe," Father Etienne said, "take your knight upstairs, make sure his bleeding is stanched, and put him into his bed. The rest of us will go on from here."

Gottfried shook his head firmly. "No, Father. I gave my word to the Gräfin that I would help her, and I will see it through to the end. Shall we ride after them now?"

"It will take a little time to ready the Bear's Paw," Bernhardt said. "Only a few of them are horsed - Margerite, can you think of when her wagon might have left?"

"She will not want to be parted from her tools for long,"
Margerite mused slowly, thinking of her own longing for the
smooth wood of her wand beneath her hand, the brightness
of blessed water in her goblet..."It was four days ago that I
stopped seeing two of the castle's knights and Ortlieb's maid
Hedwig in the great hall: they must have gone with her wain
- and travelling with a babe on horseback is no easy thing. I
think she will try to catch up with wagon and guards, and be
slowed thereafter. I do not know where her castle is, but it is
supposed to be deep within the Thuringer Wald."

"Then we will be able to arrange an ambush," Bernhardt
stated. "If Ortlieb's tools of sorcery are with her, my case
against her will be proven and certain. And a wagon will not
travel swiftly in this weather, with the roads all turned to
mud. I know where Ortlieb's father dwelt: they must go at
least part of the way on the main path, and the Bear's Paw
can outmarch them. Yes, Herr Ritter," he added to Gottfried,
"we have hired the same Free Company that defended Burg
Falkenstein, but I trust you will not think the worse of us
for that: since I can no longer call on those who should by
right be my liegemen, I needed troops in whom I could trust
- and you will remember that the Companies are no longer
excommunicate."

"You have much to explain to me yet, but it will wait,"
Gottfried replied. "Arnmut, tighten this bandage and put my
shoulder-pieces back on, then go pack our belongings and
meet me down by the stables, where I shall have our horses
ready." He inclined his head to Bernhardt. "You seem to
be in command of the fighting forces here. For now, I shall
accept your orders - so long as you do not order me not to
aid the Gräfin."

"Very well. We, and those men of the Bear's Paw who are
within the Schloss now, will meet up with you at the outer
stables. Go with God, Herr Ritter."

"And you, Herr...Bertram, or whatever your true name
may be."

It was easier to get out of the castle than to come in: the guardsmen made little challenge to the loaded train, swinging the gates back to let them by. The storm had eased, only the occasional spatter of rain hissing in the riders' torches. As soon as they had passed from the guards' immediate sight, Paul nudged his horse up beside Bernhardt's.

"Tell us the plan now," he said. "What is happening?"

"Ortlieb has stolen Margerite's son away, and we must catch her on the road, before she reaches her castle."

"Christ, that's awful," Paul gasped. "Do we ride straight after her?"

"No." Quickly Bernhardt outlined his plans for an ambush along the road. "Gather the Company, and meet us at the White Cockerel: we shall ride there directly. Only - let Jochanan stay with us, for I know he has some skill in healing, and Ritter Gottfried has a wound that needs to be washed and stitched."

"How did that happen? Never mind, no time for that. At the White Cockerel, then!" Paul took a torch and rode away, shouting orders to the other Company men who had come with him.

At Bernhardt's command, they halted at Lothar's house. "Have you triumphed, or are you fleeing, Herr Bernhardt?" the gamekeeper asked anxiously.

"Neither yet," Bernhardt replied. "But some of our company must stop here for a time."

As soon as Margerite was off her horse, Kobolt leapt into her arms, licking her face and purring ecstatically. "Good cat, fine cat," she murmured to him, stroking his fur.

Now that her tom was back with her, Margerite could let herself realize how much she had missed his company: it was as though, having lost the use of one hand for several weeks, she had tried to hide the infirmity from herself until it was suddenly restored. And yet his warm weight in her arms reminded her all the more sharply of Wolfram's, and she hid her face in Kobolt's black fur for a moment to keep the tears from her eyes.

Gottfried was able to dismount and walk to the door without any aid from his Knappe, but when Arnmut began taking his armour off, Margerite saw that the knight's gambeson was soaked all down the side with blood.

"Pride and suicide," Father Etienne said sternly, "are both mortal sins, Ritter Gottfried! And stubbornness is only a virtue when applied properly. Now sit down before you fall down, and let Jochanan see to you."

"Yes, Father," Gottfried replied with surprising meekness. Jochanan hurried over to him, long fingers unwrapping the blood-sodden bandage and gently touching the edges of the wound, from which blood still welled sluggishly.

"At least it is a clean cut," Jochanan said. "It will not be difficult to sew up, though it may hurt." He bent over, rifling through his pack for a moment, then brought out a small metal flask. "Drink some of this before I start."

Remembering the harsh strength of Jochanan's distillations, Margerite was about to warn Gottfried to take care, but he was already drinking. The knight coughed and spluttered a little, but a little colour began to come back to his face when he had swallowed the draught.

"Hold still, now, for this assuredly will hurt," Jochanan advised. He tilted the flask, dribbling a little clear liquid from its mouth into Gottfried's wound. Gottfried shuddered slightly, but gave no other sign that he felt anything from it.

"What has happened?" Eva asked, entering the room. Bernhardt explained briefly while Jochanan tended to Gottfried and Lothar fetched in food and ale for them.

As he carefully stitched up the knight's injury, Jochanan murmured softly over it - words that sounded almost familiar to Margerite. After a few moments, Margerite realized that she recognised some of the holy Names that she herself had learned in her study of magic, though they sounded richer and more melodious in Jochanan's voice - and likely better-pronounced, she admitted to herself. Father Etienne watched carefully, but did not interfere; though Margerite half-expected Gottfried to make some protest, or at least remark, he sat without moving as the linen thread pulled the gaping lips of his wound tightly together.

"You should not use this arm much for at least a week," Jochanan told Gottfried.

"But we are riding on tonight!" Gottfried protested.

Bernhardt shook his head. "No, Jochanan, Father Etienne, and I - and your Knappe, if you can spare him - are riding on tonight. Someone must stay behind to guard Margerite and Eva while the rest of us attack Ortlieb and her train, and I have seen that you can be trusted."

"I thank you for that," Gottfried said. "And I can honourably accept the charge of keeping the women safe here."

"What do you mean by that?" Margerite asked indignantly, Kobolt leaping from her lap as she sprang up. "Wolfram is my son; do you think I will sit idly by while he is in danger? And you cannot intend to face Ortlieb and her apprentices by yourself, Bernhardt!"

"Father Etienne will be with me," Bernhardt replied. "I am sure that he will be able to...defend me against her arts." He did not sound certain, though, and his hazel eyes did not meet Margerite's as he spoke.

"And besides," Margerite pressed, "Wolfram will need a woman to look after him, for you can hardly mean to leave him in the hands of whatever nurse Ortlieb has found. Even if you can buy goat's milk along the way and figure out how to get it into him - do you know how to change a baby's wet cloths, Bernhardt? Do you, Father Etienne?"

Even Etienne looked aside at that, delicate fingers playing nervously at the hem of his black velvet doublet.

"Frowe, I had five younger brothers and sisters," Jochanan said. "I know how to change a baby."

Margerite glared at the Bear's Paw lieutenant, and he fell silent, a sheepish look on his swarthy face.

"Wolfram is my son," Margerite repeated. "I will ride with you."

"And I," Eva added. "I have not spent these last weeks scrubbing pots and cleaning stoves only to be left behind now. If nothing else, I can help Margerite with the baby."

"Frowe Gräfin, Frowe Eva," Gottfried said formally. "It is not fitting that women should risk their lives by coming to a battlefield. And if any harm were to come to either of you, how should I explain it to Graf Heinrich and Herr Christoph?"

Margerite's glance flashed about the room, meeting the eyes of the others in turn. Of course Gottfried knew nothing of what had happened in Burg Fürstensee: how could he?

"As we said before, we have much to talk about, Ritter Gottfried," Father Etienne told him. "But as for who shall ride out - Bernhardt, I believe Margerite has the right of it. She shall not come near to the blade-play, just as I shall not. But just as you do, I shall need someone to guard my back, and I believe there will be no keeping Ritter Gottfried out of the fight. Though he would be better off lying in bed," the priest added pointedly. "This is not a Crusade, Ritter Gottfried, for you to win holy absolution by death in battle."

"Is it not a Crusade, Father?" Gottfried asked.

"I certainly hope not," Jochanan muttered, but Gottfried did not seem to hear him.

"It is at least a holy cause - and I do not mean to die in this fight, unless it be Christ's will to take me now," the knight went on.

Bernhardt made a noise that might almost have been a grunt of disgust at a young man's foolishness: though his hair and beard were neatly trimmed and, if not dressed as a Landgraf, he was at least decently clad in the dark doublet and hose he had worn for his disguise as a servitor, Margerite thought that it would be some time yet before he had lost all traces of the hard-bitten mercenary and guard Hauptmann.

"So we are all to go? Margerite, I mislike this greatly - but if Father Etienne wishes you to be there, then I can hardly gainsay him. We shall stay the night here and ride at dawn: even with the Bear's Paw marching hard, they will not be at the White Cockerel before us. Ritter Gottfried, there will be no shame in it if you have the sense to stay here and heal, for such would be my orders to you; but at least you can go to bed now."

"Not until you have explained all that you promised to me," Gottfried insisted stubbornly.

Bernhardt and Margerite looked at each other, but it was Father Etienne who spoke. "You saw... what you saw, Ritter Gottfried; and should you have doubted your eyes because no other shared your vision, you bear the proof on your body." Briefly the priest told Gottfried of Bernhardt's quest to regain his place, then of the events in Burg Fürstensee which had forced Margerite, Eva, and Georg to flee. For the first time, Margerite saw the lines of pain tightening on the young knight's pale face: Gottfried closed his eyes and clenched his fists, as if something were tearing dreadfully at him within.

"Christ help me, that I was not there to aid," he murmured.

"You are not the only one with regrets, Herr Ritter," Father Etienne said, his voice sharp. "We shall deal with Nikolaus in time, but this is the more urgent matter now."

"It is," Gottfried agreed. "Yet if I had known..."

"Only God knows all," Etienne reminded him gently, "and you left Burg Fürstensee at the orders of your liege lord, with no reason to think that anything might be amiss within. Eat a little more meat, if you can, for you have lost much blood this night, and you will need the strength if you insist on riding tomorrow."

They rode out at dawn beneath a gray sky, a raw wind tossing the bare branches of the trees above their heads and scouring their faces with cold. Margerite soon found her thighs aching, for the pace Bernhardt set pushed the horses as swiftly as he dared: cantering most of the way, though they had to pay for that haste with short breaks when they dismounted to let their steeds rest, since there would be little chance of gaining others along the way, if those they rode now failed from exhaustion.

Gottfried's rest - and, Margerite suspected, whatever healing charm or spell Jochanan had murmured over his wound - had done the thin knight good, for he had no trouble keeping pace with the rest of them, and the colour had come back to his narrow face. Despite Bernhardt's long confinement, he gave no sign that his months away from a horse's back had softened him; it was only Margerite and Eva who seemed to be suffering from the hard riding, for Margerite's buttocks and inner thighs felt like veal pounded tender with a mallet by midday, and her saddle's high cantle was rubbing a blister up her tailbone, while she could see Eva gritting her teeth at every surge of the horse beneath her.

Still, when they halted for the horses to rest, neither of the women said a word. The glance Eva traded with Margerite, her blue eyes cold as sparks from steel, said all that needed saying: they had struggled for the right to pursue Ortlieb, and they would not complain of the rigors of the track where Bernhardt or Gottfried might hear them now.

Kobolt and Kriemhilt watched their mistresses from the saddles of the grazing horses, golden and green eyes almost insolently amused: even during the hardest riding, the cats had managed to drape themselves over either cantle or pommel without seeming to notice the swift rising and falling of the horses' backs beneath them. Well enough for you, Herr Tomcat, Margerite thought to Kobolt: you do not have to control the beast as well as sit on its back. Kobolt slitted his eyes and gave a soft chirping purr, almost as if he had heard her speak.

They were close to the edge of the Thuringer Wald, the sun low behind the clouds, when they heard the hoofbeats pounding behind their own. Bernhardt and Gottfried whirled their horses, swords half-drawn; Margerite readied herself to put heels to her tired horse's sides and plunge out of their way. Then she saw the rider's red hair bright beneath his iron-bound leather cap, and slowed her horse to a walk instead, even as Bernhardt sheathed his weapon.

"Well-met, Georg!" he called. "What news from the Bear's Paw?"

"Herr Bernhardt, they march as you ordered," the Knappe answered. He was pale beneath his freckles, wide dark rings like bruises under his blue eyes, but he grinned at Bernhardt as he urged his horse up beside them. "I have been riding all night and all day with Hauptmann Paul's messages. Had you been a little swifter, you might already have caught up with the Bear himself on the road: his men are well used to making quick marches at need, he says, and should he be at the White Cockerel before you are, he says that it will be your duty to buy the beer."

"Does he, now?" Bernhardt murmured. He glanced about at his companions, a small smile on his lips. For a moment, beneath the harsh lines that scored his face, Margerite thought she could see a spark of youthful pride kindling - the young nobleman that he had been would certainly have taken up the dare, spurring his horse on until he overtook the Bear's Paw's leader - but the glimmer in his hazel eyes steadied as he measured the other riders and their heavy-breathing steeds.

"Well, no one, not even Paul, will be drinking too deep this night, for there is hard going ahead of us tomorow morning. I see the Bear's Paw managed a remount for you. Do you think you will be able to ride ahead of us and see to it that chambers are readied for the ladies and Father Etienne - and for Herr Gottfried, who was wounded last night?"

"Of course, Herr Bernhardt!" Georg replied enthusiastically. "The Gräfin and Frowe Eva will be staying at the inn?"

"They ride with us," Bernhardt said. He held up a hand to silence Georg before the youth could protest. "It is not your place to question the matter, Knappe. Hasten on, now."

Georg touched the roan gelding's flanks with his heels, breaking from a walk to a fast trot, speeding into a canter and then a full gallop. Soon he was out of sight. Bernhardt urged his own weary horse on, and the rest of them followed suit. Although Margerite's gray gelding had a smooth canter, its trot was punishingly rough: she gritted her teeth, clasping the horse's sides with trembling thighs. She could not help looking at the road ahead of them, as she had for most of the ride, trying to see if there was any trace of wagon tracks; but rain and travellers had churned the earth into sticky mud: no secrets were left to be read there.

It struck her that Bernhardt was putting a great deal of trust in her, to deploy all his forces according to her guess about Ortlieb's actions: what if she proved wrong? Would he think the less of her thereafter? Perhaps not: any commander could err - and it was Margerite, after all, who had the most at stake now. It warmed Margerite, too, to think that Bernhardt valued her thoughts so highly: it had been one thing for him to follow her orders at Burg Falkenstein, where she was Gräfin and he only the Hauptmann of the guard, but now that they were in the lands of his lordship, the final commands were his; and he had still chosen to let her guide him.

They arrived at the White Cockerel only a little after sunset. Georg was there to meet them, helping Arnmut with their horses. Inside, the inn was filled with men in rough jerkins of leather and iron plates, long unshaven and, from their smell, long unbathed - the very picture, Margerite had to admit, of a ruffianly Free Company. She recognised some of them from Burg Falkenstein, though many of the men she had seen there were gone, whether dead or departed for better lives elsewhere there was no telling.

They all bore the marks of a night and day of hard going, pale beneath their grime and beards, the pouches beneath their eyes dark and wrinkled, as though they had just come from the battlefield instead of marching towards it. But those who recognised her lifted their mugs of ale, some shouting, "To the Gräfin Margerite! Hail the Gräfin!" After her long weeks as a servant, the salutes brought the tears to Margerite's eyes; she barely noticed the deep-bruised aching of her thighs as Bernhardt led them all through the throng to the table where Paul the Bear sat.

The Bear sprang to his feet at once as the men with him moved away to make room for the new arrivals. "Greetings, Frowe Gräfin!" he cried out. "By Christ, it's good to see you again." Paul had not finished speaking before Kobolt sprang from the ground to his broad chest with a loud purr, digging hooked claws into his leather armour and sniffing hopefully at his short sandy-red beard. The mercenary stroked the cat, disengaging his claws and putting him down on the table, where Kobolt at once stuck his muzzle into Paul's tarred leather ale-jack and began to lap. "I see your cat hasn't changed a bit," he laughed.

"How stands it with the Bear's Paw?" Bernhardt asked, cutting Paul off. The Bear's round face sobered at once.

"Most of the Company is gathered here now, and the rest aren't far behind. But you were right about the Landgräfin, sure enough. The innkeeper said he'd had a wagon with a black-haired woman who had two knights and a score of men-at-arms to guard her stopping here the night before last."

"And what of Ortlieb herself?" Bernhardt questioned. "Has any sign of her been seen? I do not think she would have slept in the woods."

"You may underestimate her hardiness of will," Father Etienne said dryly. "She will have been riding fast, for she is likely to feel herself vulnerable until she is reunited with her tools of power; I would not be surprised if she does not rest until she has caught up with her wain."

Or if, Margerite thought, she would not stop in a place that reminds her too clearly of the village where the poor knight's daughter grew up.

Bernhardt's brow furrowed, an inward look in his hazel eyes. "If the wagon is moving at such a slow pace," he mused, "we should be able to catch up with it by tomorrow evening, Christ willing, and set our ambush as I had hoped."

He gestured to his companions to sit, waiting until Margerite, Eva, and Father Etienne were settled before seating himself on the bench across from Paul. Jochanan slid in beside his commander. Only Ritter Gottfried remained standing, staring suspiciously about himself, like a cat bristling up the fur along his spine. At least here, Margerite thought, there should be nothing strange for him to see - was there? If one of Ortlieb's apprentices had passed through...

"Who is that man?" Paul whispered loudly to Bernhardt. "And why is he staring at me?"

"Ritter Gottfried," Bernhardt said. "Allow me to present Hauptmann Paul of the Bear's Paw Company, our ally and my friend." He had not raised his voice, but his tone was sharp, bringing Gottfried to attention. The knight did not reach out to clasp Paul's forearm in greeting, but he nodded to acknowledge him. "Sit down, Ritter Gottfried, for we have plans to make."

Stiffly and mistrustfully, Gottfried settled himself on the bench beside Bernhardt. The bones of the young knight's face stood out harshly in the smoky light of the inn's flickering torches; Margerite hoped that his wound had not started to bleed again, but she could think of no way to ask. But Kobolt left off his lapping at Paul's beer, walking across the table without even bothering to investigate the half-gnawed beef ribs on the earthenware plates, and sniffed at Gottfried's shoulder with a worried chirp, rubbing his black head against the overlapping steel plates. Gottfried sat very still, staring intently at the cat.

"Are you holding well, Ritter Gottfried?" Jochanan asked, his voice worried. He leaned forward across the table as though he would examine his patient again right there.

"As well as I need to," Gottfried answered. "Your healing skills...are remarkable."

The innkeeper's plump wife bustled about clearing away the dirty plates and setting fresh mugs of beer in front of all of them. As if by common consent, they did not speak again until she was gone.

"Two knights and a score of men-at-arms: we should be able to overcome them easily," Paul said.

Bernhardt shook his head. "I do not think that Ortlieb left alone. She recognised Margerite, and she knew that I am here - no, for blessed Maria's sake, do not ask how. Even if she does not know that she is pursued, she is both wily and careful: she will not have ridden without a strong guard of her own. I think we may expect at least twice that force, if not more. We will still outnumber them, but if Ortlieb has brought more knights with her, our advantage may not be so great as we think."

And if she has more spirits like the ones who guarded her chamber? Margerite thought, remembering the sudden spurt of blood from beneath Gottfried's armour as he swung his sword against empty air. They would go through our men like blasts from Jochanan's cannon.

A similar thought must have been in Bernhardt's mind, for he asked,"Jochanan, what state are your guns in?"

"Five of the eight handguns are fit to shoot," the gunner replied. "I doubt we can use the cannon, for they can move no faster than the cart that draws them."

"Even those five will give us a good edge over Ortlieb's troops," Bernhardt said.

Father Etienne frowned. "In an ordinary fight, yes. But... Jochanan, I must speak to you alone a moment." The priest rose, and Jochanan followed him, dark brows drawn in apprehension.

"What is that about, Margerite?" Bernhardt asked her softly.

"I think," Margerite said, the words thick as bitter syrup on her tongue, "that Father Etienne fears what will happen if Ortlieb is able to assail the guns herself, and is questioning Jochanan about his alchemy now."

Paul shook his head in disbelief. "Do you never fight with ordinary humans anymore, Bertram? Sorcerors and witches: are you going to hire us on for a battle with Wodan's Host next, or just go straight to laying siege to Satan's castle in Hell?"

"You should not speak so of such things!" Gottfried told him sternly.

Paul's broad cheeks reddened, and he leaned across the table. "Who in Hell's name are you to tell me how to talk?" he asked.

Ritter Gottfried half-stood, his hand moving towards his sword-hilt, but Margerite caught his wrist. Though her hand circled the thin bone, fingers overlapping thumb on his arm, she could feel the strength of the wiry muscles beneath; he could have shaken her off easily, but he froze, staring at her. "Herr Ritter, Paul meant no harm, and the two of you have no cause to quarrel - especially not while my son is in danger."

"That is so," Gottfried murmured, a light flush blooming on his sharp cheekbones. Margerite let go of him, and he sat back down.

"Sorry, Herr Ritter," Paul said. "I didn't mean to offend you; I was only joking."

Gottfried nodded sharply in acknowledgement. Then the conversation stopped again, for the innkeeper and his wife were bringing around fresh trenchers of bread and beef ribs in savoury sauce. Arnmut and Georg were right behind them, taking their places at the table - Arnmut sat beside his knight, while Georg seated himself next to Eva with an almost unseemly look of delight on his homely face.

Father Etienne and Jochanan returned shortly after that. The gunner's swarthy face looked uneasy, the whites of his eyes bright in the torchlight. "Uh...we only have three guns we can use," he said to Bernhardt. "And not the longest of them, at that - though it's really not the length that matters, it's the width."

"Spoken like a circumcised man," Paul guffawed. Eva and Georg began to giggle; Bernhardt made a strangled grunt; Arnmut, as if mindful of his knight's modesty, seemed to muffle a coughing fit.

Margerite felt her own cheeks warming, but she darted a worried glance at Gottfried: he would know, as well as anyone, that it was unlawful for a Jew to bear arms, and as for marching in a mercenary company that did battle against Christians..! The young knight stared at Jochanan a moment, gray eyes cold. Then his left hand moved across his body to touch his wounded shoulder, and Margerite breathed easily again: for all his iron virtue, Gottfried would not turn against the man who had healed him. But Mother Maria help us, we are a strange band of allies, she thought.

"Three, then," Bernhardt said. "Even that will be a help, though your men must be very careful not to fire too near to the wain, as what we seek is likely to be in it - and the child will probably be riding there as well," he added. "We cannot risk harming the one we come to rescue."

Margerite was not sure whether his words relieved or disturbed her: it might be only a trick of her exhaustion after the day's long ride, but Bernhardt's voice sounded strangely bloodless as he spoke of Wolfram, as if no worry or love pulsed in his heart. But that was unfair: he could not do more than he was doing for her son's sake, and she could not go on constantly trying to measure his feelings for her son in every word he spoke, like a village woman guessing at the weight of a sack of carrots by sight.

"Now, if they are still on the road, which they must be, unless they have moved much faster than I think they can..." Bernhardt went on. He dipped a finger in his mug of beer, sketching a rough map on the wooden table-top with a trail of froth.

Gottfried, cutting neat small mouthfuls of meat from his beef-ribs and wiping the sauce surreptitiously from his fingers on his thick bread trencher, looked slightly appalled, but Paul and Jochanan leaned closer, and Margerite wondered how often Bernhardt had sketched out plans for an attack in just this manner. As the men talked, she saw the gleam of the beads at his neck, torchlight pooling in the clear crystal between the dark glints of garnet and amethyst, and a sudden wash of warmth rose within her, knowing that Bernhardt was still wearing her necklace.

She had come to love him as the Hauptmann of her guard; seeing him as the Free Company mercenary he had been, she loved him still. And as Landgraf, if we win our battle tomorrow, and the one that must come after that? Margerite thought. But there was no doubt in her heart: whether Bernhardt spoke roughly or courteously, he was still the rock against which she could lean for safety, the sword and shield that would defend her against any threat - at least, those against which sword and shield can prevail, she thought.

Father Etienne sat listening silently to the discussion of their strategy, only dropping in a brief comment now and again. The priest's quietness bothered Margerite, for she knew he must be thinking on what dangers they would face besides Ortlieb's armed guard. But she had to trust that he would tell her what she needed to know.

Margerite touched the little scar above her breast where Ortlieb had wounded her in bird-form: if she had listened to Father Etienne, she would not bear that mark now. The White Cockerel had only two guest-chambers: Margerite and Eva took one, while Father Etienne, Gottfried, and Arnmut shared the other. Margerite had just begun to get undressed by the light of the room's single candle when she heard a soft knock at the door.

"Who is it?" Margerite called out, her heart beating wildly. If Bernhardt had come to her now, on the eve of a battle in which they both might fall - how could she turn him away?

"It is I," Father Etienne's dry baritone replied, muffled by the door. "And Ritter Gottfried with me. We must speak."

Eva hastily buttoned up the back of Margerite's dress before going to let the men in. She walked carefully, as though trying not to wince with each step.

Both women's muscles had stiffened badly since dismounting at the inn, and Margerite could feel the ache of Eva's movements in her own legs: it was no comfort to be aware that she would doubtless hurt worse the next day, and she would have given a purse of silver for the salve Gerhild had made for her ride from Burg Falkenstein to Burg Fürstensee.

Father Etienne and Ritter Gottfried both carried tapers, the warm light flickering over their faces. The priest had a wooden box under one arm - his own magical tools? A fresh bandage wrapped Gottfried's shoulder, but if he had bled during the day's ride, it did not show on his deep red doublet.

"It will be no surprise to you," Etienne said without preamble, "that you will be in as much danger as those who fight - perhaps greater, depending on how well Ortlieb has prepared herself, for those who deal with the realm of spirit are most vulnerable to it as well. Therefore, I mean to do my best to shield you against her powers and those of any beings who may accompany her. Will you consent to this?"

"Of course, Father," Margerite said, and Eva also murmured her assent.

"Ritter Gottfried?"

"The blessing of a priest is always greatly welcome, Father," the knight replied. He drew his blade, kneeling before Father Etienne with the sword's point touching the floor and his hands clasped about the cross-hilt.

"Stay there, and make no sound," Etienne instructed him. "Do not be too startled by anything you see, for I give you my word that I call upon no powers but those of Heaven."

Gottfried bowed his head as Father Etienne spoke to him, though he could feel his muscles tightening as if with fear, in counterpoint to the constant throbbing of his wounded shoulder. He waited silently as Eva knelt beside him.

"Margerite, take your wand and cup, for you shall join with me in this," Father Etienne said. "And repeat each prayer after me: they are prayers that you must know."

Although he had early schooled himself to quietness, Gottfried could not help starting when Margerite opened a small chest and took out a goblet and a slim pale rod bound with glittering rings of different metals, for it seemed that when she lifted the rod, it blazed to life like a torch, casting a bright light through the room. The white brightness reflected back from the golden eyes of the Gräfin's black cat - and now, with no shadows to hide it, Gottfried could see that it was fully the size of a mastiff, and knew that it was no natural beast.

Though he did not move from his place, he gripped the cross-piece of his sword the more tightly: cross and blade, he knew that it would defend him so long as he had the strength to hold it. The priest was gathering his own implements from the wooden chest he had carried in: censer and incense, a wand very like Margerite's, a small steel dagger, a box of glittering white salt, a leaden flask, a tinderbox, and a candle of yellow beeswax.

Silently Etienne blew out all the candles in the room; but his wand burned as brightly as Margerite's, so that Gottfried could see everything more clearly than his blurred eyes allowed even in the fullest daylight - the rolled corners of the black canon's hat above the priest's serene face, the firm set of Margerite's delicate jaw...and the glitter of the falcon's wide-pupiled eyes beneath the arch of her ash-blond brows. This is sorcery, the knight thought, shaken. To what did I pledge myself, when I agreed to help the Gräfin recover her son?

Father Etienne knelt in front of them, his long black robe trailing on the floor, and Gottfried heard the sound of flint and steel striking. The priest's soft French accent was stronger in Latin; Gottfried's own command of that tongue might have been better, but he understood the prayer well enough for it to soothe his thundering heart.

"I exorcise thee, O Creature of Fire, by Him through Whom all things have been made, so that every kind of Phantasm may retire from thee and be unable to harm or deceive in any way, through the Invocation of the Most High Creator of all. Amen. " Margerite's voice, high and almost as pure as a boy's, intoned the words after Etienne; and the candle flared to life, its flame golden beneath the whiteness of the two wands' brightness as Father Etienne lit the charcoal in his censer. "Bless, O Lord All Powerful, and All Merciful, this Creature of Fire..."

Gottfried bit back a gasp as he looked at the flame. Creature of Fire, Father Etienne had called it: and it seemed to him that the leaping tongue of fire had taken on a human shape, a small figure of fiery beauty reaching up and outward. The sweet scent of incense touched his nostrils, bluish smoke streaming from the holes in the gilded censer as Etienne swung its chain about himself, striding in a circle around the others.

"I exorcise thee, O Creature of Air, by Him Who hath created thee, Who moved upon the waters before the beginning of time. Let all malignity and hindrance be cast forth from thee, and drive forth all the deceits of the Enemy, all the impurities and uncleanness of the Spirits of the World of Phantasm, so they may harm me not, through the virtue of God Almighty Who liveth and reigneth unto the Ages of Ages..." And, as Margerite's high voice echoed the prayer, Gottfried saw the fragrant smoke outlining the living form that swirled about them, driving forth the shapeless vapours that he had not even noticed until that moment.

Though his heart was beginning to beat wildly again, it was with excitement rather than fear. He had been wrong to think of what was happening as sorcery: rather, it was the height of holiness, that by God's grace made His presence manifest against the Enemy. Gottfried watched in awe as Father Etienne and Margerite repeated their blessings with water poured from Etienne's leaden pilgrim-flask into Margerite's shining goblet, then with the glittering salt. Then Father Etienne faced eastward, clasping the gold crucifix on his breast. He spoke several words: though Gottfried did not even recognise the language, it seemed to him that he could see white fire leaping from the priest's mouth.

"Before me, Raphael," Father Etienne intoned, echoed by Margerite. Gottfried's breath seemed to stop in his chest, for now he saw what seemed to be the rainbow glimmer of great wings sweeping down in front of him. He wanted to weep for joy and longing; only the priest's injunction to silence kept him still.

"Behind me, Gabriel..." Gottfried did not dare turn his head, but he thought that he felt a cool breeze on the back of his neck, like wind breathing over deep waters. "On my right hand, Michael..." From the corner of his eye, Gottfried saw a warm flare of fire. "On my left hand, Uriel..." Wings of shadow there, darker than the depths of the earth - and behind them, the gleam of two huge cats' eyes, golden and green.

"In the holy Names of God YOD HE VAU HE, ADONAI, EHIEH, AGLA. Lord, bless Thy servants, and protect us from all evil, and from the deceptions of Thy foe. Set upon us the whole armour of God, that we may be able to stand against the wiles of the Devil. For we wrestle not against flesh and blood, but against Principalities, against Powers, against the rulers of the darkness of this world, against spiritual wickedness in high places. Wherefore let us take onto us the whole armour of God, that we may be able to withstand all in the evil day, and having done all, to stand. Let us stand, therefore, having our loins girt about with truth -"

Father Etienne touched each of them with his shining rod as he spoke, and Gottfried saw the ghost-glimmering hanging about their loins like gilded tassets. "And having on the breastplate of righteousness -"

Again the priest tapped himself and each of his companions in turn.

"And our feet shod with the preparation of the gospel of peace; above all, taking the shield of faith, wherewith we shall be able to quench all the fiery darts of the wicked. And let us take the helmet of salvation -" Father Etienne made his rounds once more, touching his wand to their heads, then stopped before Gottfried, laying the rod's gleaming tip on the pommel of his sword.

"And the sword of the Spirit, which is the word of God, praying always with all prayer and supplication in the Spirit, and watching thereunto with all perseverance and supplication for all saints. Be warded against all ill, shielded from our enemies and all foes of the Kingdom of Heaven, fortresses unassailable and impervious, defended by the powers of the angelic hosts, and the strength of the Lord God ADONAI. Amen."

Dazzled by the brightness in his eyes, Gottfried hardly noticed the words Father Etienne spoke thereafter, nor the blessing he murmured as he quenched his candle. Even when the priest and Margerite had both put away their wands, leaving the room dark, with only the sweet scent of incense lingering in the air, the knight stayed kneeling with his sword's cross-hilt between his hands, as if he were holding his vigil once more.

"Rise, Ritter Gottfried," Father Etienne said gently. Someone had lit a candle, but its light flickered tiny after what Gottfried had just seen. The priest's warm hand closed over Gottfried's grip on the sword, raising him upward, and Gottfried was startled to feel wetness on his own face, as though his tears had flowed unnoticed. He sheathed his blade, still too awed to speak.

"We will have much to talk of later," Father Etienne murmured to him. "Now you should go to bed, for despite Jochanan's efforts, you are still far from healed."

"Father..." Gottfried's voice choked in his throat, as though he were speaking for the first time after a year-long vow of silence. He coughed, swallowed, and spoke again. "Father, I would make Confession to you this night."

Father Etienne lit his taper from the candle in Eva's hands, leading Gottfried back to the chamber where Arnmut was waiting.

"I would have a few moments alone with Father Etienne, and then it will be your turn," Gottfried said to his Knappe.

"Of course, Herr Gottfried," Arnmut answered warmly. "I shall wait outside."

The warm candlelight gilded the silver wings in the priest's thick dark hair and the tuft of silver on his chin, bringing out the ascetic beauty of his aristocratic features. Gottfried knelt before him, letting Father Etienne take his hands between his own, the warm human touch reassuring after the stark power of the rite Gottfried had just witnessed. "Father," he whispered, "forgive me, for I have sinned..."

The Bear's Paw marched out at dawn, those who were horsed riding beside them. The pace was slower today, for which Margerite was grateful: her legs had stiffened in her sleep so that it was all she could do to mount her horse with Bernhardt's assistance, and the first time her gelding broke into a trot, she had to bite back a cry as the horse's movement hammered into her sore thighs. Georg carried a pole with a red banner wrapped tightly about it - the Bear's Paw's? No, for that was a black paw-print on a white field, and one of the marchers was carrying it.

Bernhardt leaned over to the Knappe. "Give the word to Paul," he said. "This day, I wish the Company to set aside their usual battle-cry. Instead of 'Glück!', let them shout, 'Bernhardt von Niederwald!' for I wish our foes to know who has come upon them. I have been hidden too long, and I would triumph or fall under my own name." He sat straight in his saddle as he spoke.

Though much of his armour was piecework, hastily scrounged together from different members of the Bear's Paw, his borrowed breastplate rusty save for the shiny marks where large dents had been clumsily hammered out of it and one knee-cup shaped differently from the other, his face was stern and noble beneath his battered bascinet, and the heavy spear by his stirrup stood aloft with the knightly pride of a lance.

"That is well done, Herr Bernhardt!" Georg exclaimed, turning his horse to ride down the column of marchers. Margerite felt a warm glow in her own heart as she watched Bernhardt: if he was no glittering vision of martial glory such as Ruprecht, armed for battle, had been, he was a truer knight.

Although Margerite knew that it would be hours before they came within sight of Ortlieb's wain, and they would long since have left the main trackway to circle through the forest to their ambush-point, she could not help staring down the forest road until it vanished into shadow beneath the woven canopy of dripping black branches overhead. Somewhere ahead there is my Wolfram, she reminded herself, gritting her teeth as the riders broke into a painful trot again.

My son - and, as Christ is my witness, that woman shall not have him. Her body tightened at the thought, and her horse leapt forward between her legs until she had to rein it back, as though it were as eager as she to come to grips with Ortlieb. The rain grew harder through the day, pelting cold through the bare branches of oak and ash.

Margerite's hooded cloak shed the worst of it, but the wind was getting stronger, every gust flaying her face with hard icy drops so that sometimes she had to squint to see ahead of her. The company had stopped briefly at midday for a meal of bread and cheese and thin, sour watered wine; Margerite almost wished she had not eaten, for her stomach was knotting tight around the hard ball of food.

I am not afraid, she told herself. But before, when she had descended to Ruprecht's sanctum, when she had confronted the demon within Christoph, she had not had much time to think about what she was doing: now, riding knowingly towards battle, she could not keep her hands from shaking on the horse's reins, nor, however hard she swallowed, could she moisten her dry mouth.

How do men bear it? she wondered. The ride towards the battlefield, pitching their tents and waiting for the hosts to be arrayed, waiting for the order to charge - do they grow used to it after a few fights? Or does Bernhardt, or Gottfried, still feel as I do now? here was no answer, for no man would answer such a question; there was not even a way for Margerite to ask.

Sunset was still a few hours away when Bernhardt rode out a little ahead of the company, gesturing to show that here was where they would leave the road. The going was slower now, tangling tree-roots and rotting logs breaking the marchers' stride, while those who rode had to steer their horses carefully, leaning down to dodge the branches that clutched at their cloaks and slapped, stinging as wire, across their faces. Bernhardt rode at the fore; he had taken his spear from its place, and now held it carefully level to keep it from tangling in the trees.

Beside him, Georg was having more trouble managing the banner, its pole wobbling in his hands as he raised and dipped it between the bare tree-limbs. The horses' hooves squelched in the wet leaf-mould, and Margerite had to watch carefully, lest her gelding's foot come down in a badger-hole or plunge into a treacherous mass of fungus-grown wood. Wolfram, my darling, I'm coming.

The spot Bernhardt had chosen for his ambush was well-set: a high ridge of rock-crowned earth ran along the left side of the road, and a small hill rose just beyond it to the right. At Bernhardt's command, the men of the Bear's Paw spread out, concealing themselves as best they could. "They will be wary here," Margerite overheard Bernhardt saying to Paul, "for this is a favourite haunt of brigands. But I could think of no better place to take them."

"Good enough for me," Paul grunted.

Jochanan and the other two gunners were set behind the hill: they would fire first, trying to take down the knights riding at the head of the train. "But you shall go back farther into the woods," Bernhardt said to Father Etienne and the women. "I am loath to have you so near to the fighting, but at least you shall not come within sight until battle is fully joined - for if you can see, you may also be seen."

"As must be," Father Etienne said reluctantly. "For the first moments of the battle, then, you must rely on Ritter Gottfried. Ride close beside him, and mark well what he does, or as well as you can in combat, for neither illusion nor invisibility will delude him, and he is proof against phantasms."

"I shall keep that in mind, Father," Bernhardt replied. He rode away, speaking to Georg for a moment. The boy nodded vigorously, untying the banner he carried. A sharp gust of rain-laden wind caught the fabric, snapping it out.

Recognising the golden stag's head, helm and mantling, with the silver fish leaping below, Margerite caught her breath: Bernhardt would ride into battle beneath the banner of his lost inheritance, the arms of the Landgraf von Niederwald. She could not see Bernhardt's face, only the rain-brightened back of his bascinet; but his head was tilted back, gazing up at the banner. Softly Margerite whispered his family motto:"Unconquered", adding silently, Mother Maria, grant that it be so.

Bernhardt turned his horse, riding back towards Margerite. He had hooked the bascinet's chain-mail across the lower part of his face, hiding his short brown beard; but his familiar hazel eyes gazed down at her for what seemed like a long time. She wanted to lean over to embrace him, to feel his body beneath the dented breastplate and hole-riddled chainmail he had borrowed - to feel his lips near hers, even separated by the cold veil of iron links that covered half his face. We could both die this evening, Margerite thought.

"Be careful, Bernhardt," she whispered. "May Christ grant you victory this day, and Mother Maria bring you through safe - for the sake of the sorrow it would bring me if any ill befell you." For a moment, she did not know if Bernhardt had heard her beneath his helm; but then his eyes closed, as if wincing in pain - or filled by joy.

"I can only say the same," he replied. "Be very careful, Margerite, for you have risked too much for me already."

Bernhardt's mailed hand tugged at his horse's rein, and Margerite had to hold herself back from reaching out to grasp at him, to keep him close to her for one moment longer: such an effort would only shame them both. Father Etienne and Eva were waiting for her, and reluctantly, she kneed her horse about, following the other two deeper into the woods.

The three of them halted when they were out of sight of the road, able to see nothing but the dark gnarled treetrunks and brown bushes melting into shadows. "And now?" Margerite said softly to Father Etienne.

The priest looked down at her, his blue eyes shadowed by the overhanging point of his wet black hood. "Now, we wait."

"Will you know when they are coming?" Eva whispered.

Father Etienne shook his head, a few raindrops dripping from his short dark beard. "Ortlieb has warded herself well: I can no more sense her than she can detect us. The success of this ambush is down to Bernhardt's wisdom now, not mine."

They fell silent, sitting on their horses and pulling their cloaks tight against the rain and the icy wind that tossed the bare branches over their heads. Kobolt had crawled under Margerite's cloak to keep dry, sitting nestled against her back through most of the ride; now the cat rose, his claws hooking into her thigh as he crawled around her to stick his head out briefly. He gave a short miaow of disgust as a spatter of rain beaded on his gleaming black fur, then settled himself in Margerite's lap.

The nervousness fluttering in Margerite's bowels slowly faded to a dull ache as they waited. Though her ears strained for the sound of gunshots, she heard nothing - nothing save the wind rushing through the trees like a great river, the creak of branches rubbing together, and the heavy pattering of rain upon the sodden masses of brown leaves that covered the forest floor.

Father Etienne sat serenely, his blue eyes gazing into remote distance; Eva quietly stroked the cat in her own lap, her pretty face as still as the priest's; but of course, though it had been an Order convent that took her after her parents' deaths, she would have learned the skill of waiting in silence. But Margerite had never been trained to contemplation: even in a noblewoman's leisure, there was always something to be done, and matters that had to be attended to. Like a falcon tethered to her perch, she shifted her weight from side to side on the horse's back, trying to ease the numb ache of her buttocks - to do anything that would draw her mind from the horsefly thoughts tormenting it.

What if we were wrong? she asked herself. What if the wain does not come this way, or if Ortlieb is not with it - what if we moved too slowly, after all, and she has already passed us up? How long will we wait here before abandoning the ambush? At least Margerite's own task was an easy one, for now: if the wain had not appeared by nightfall, it would be Bernhardt, who knew the wood and had long since learned to calculate the speed of marchers and wagons in war, who would have to make the decision about waiting there another day or riding on in hopes of catching Ortlieb further down the road. For he is the commander here, as he should be - and I thank Christ that it is he, and not I!

A clump of Steinpilsen, thick white stems hooded in brown, grew among the gnarled roots of the tree in front of Margerite: she forced herself to look at them, to hold her mind from turning on itself. The oldest of the mushrooms were ragged with insect-bites, their brown caps stippled with black rot, but the younger ones, not yet fully-blown, were perfect, hoods gleaming like polished wood in the rain. Sliced in cream sauce, Margerite thought. With roast saddle of roe-deer...

But even the thought of food roiled her tight stomach, so that she had to look away from the mushrooms, staring instead at the tree above them, the cracked and mossy bark sodden black, the jagged stump where something had broken a thick branch away - some time ago, for the wood had long since darkened and moss grown over the wound. How long had it been? Had as much as an hour passed? Margerite looked up at the sky, wishing that she could see the sun; but there was nothing beyond the black branches save heavy grayness, ragged ridges of darkness scudding swiftly below the rippling blanket of clouds above.

The icy rain streamed over her face, dribbling uncomfortably down her throat to soak into the folds of cloak covering her bosom. Her breasts ached miserably, full to leaking, and she did not dare ask Father Etienne to turn his back while she pressed the milk from them - and besides, Wolfram might be hungry; frightened as he would surely be by the sounds of gunfire and battle, she did not want to offer him an empty breast. O, my little one...

But what if Ortlieb were ahead of them in this strange chess-game even now? Her wain had passed by the White Cockerel; what if she had sent it only as a decoy, knowing that Margerite would pursue her lost son? If the Order Princess were not with the wagon, she could be anywhere, wrapping Wolfram in spells like tainted swaddling cloths to hide him, to bind him to herself and her Master...

Thoughts of weakness will make you weak: thus it was written in the Black Book. They would not fail: Ortlieb's apprentice Hedwig was with the wain, and she would know her mistress' plans...if she could be made to tell. The thought chilled Margerite deep within: she had heard stories of torture, of eyes burned out and skin peeled slowly away, but to turn her own hand to such a frightful task - even to save Wolfram? Mother Maria, please grant that I do not have to make such a choice!

How long had it been? The sky seemed darker, the shadows deeper in the wood around them, but the rain was falling harder as well: was it truly nearing sunset, or was it only that the storm was strengthening, the wind whipping the heavy raindrops faster through the tossing branches? Will the weather slow them? Margerite wondered, and then, again, What if Bernhardt was wrong? What if they passed here before we did? If Ortlieb had not stayed with her wagon, but ridden ahead to get Wolfram safely into her castle...A siege, with barely more than fourscore men and the Landgraf's army to come behind us to her aid? She glanced at Father Etienne again, as if he might speak some word to soothe her doubts, but the priest's ascetic face was still perfectly composed, his pale lips moving slightly as if in prayer.

Suddenly a deep blast shattered through the storm, as though lightning had struck just beside them. Margerite's horse shied, almost throwing her from its back; as she desperately tried to gain control of it again, Kobolt's claws dug hard enough into her leg to bring a small cry from her lips. Eva's horse tossed its head, fighting the reins. Only Father Etienne's great black steed stood rock-steady, until the priest touched his heels to its sides, moving it forward.

"Come!" the priest called to the two women. "The battle has begun."

Margerite's gelding needed no urging to run; her only difficulty was in keeping it to the straight path forward when it would turn to the side. Branches blurred past, lashing her face like bitter whips, and Kobolt's caterwauling yowl rang in her ears; but above the cat's scream, she could hear the cry of"Bernhardt von Niederwald!" ahead.

The ridge that had concealed the Bear's Paw men rose before her, and Margerite had to haul on her horse's reins, pulling it back sharply before it plunged around and into the middle of the battle. She could smell the sulphurous reek of Jochanan's gunpowder through the rain, and hear the desperate, half-human screaming of a wounded horse.

Father Etienne's hood had fallen back, the wind whipping his thick dark hair about wildly. He gestured Margerite to follow him, guiding his black stallion up onto the ridge, and she rode after him. Below, the battle was joined in earnest, swirling about two wains - one open, its contents covered against the rain with thick woolen blankets, the other protected and hidden by a high cloth canopy.

Georg clung to Bernhardt's red and gold banner with one hand, swinging his sword with the other - chiefly to ward off his foes' blades, for he could not carry shield and standard at the same time. Bernhardt fought with deadly efficiency, seldom landing a blow that did not bite through the joints between metal plates. Gottfried moved with the same unbelievable speed and grace that he had shown in Schloss Niederwald, and if his wounded shoulder gave him any pain now, he did not show it.

On foot, the men of the Bear's Paw swarmed about their enemies: they had the advantage of numbers, but even those Niederwald men who fought on foot as simple guardsmen were well-trained and disciplined, holding shield by shield and closing their ranks tighter every time one of their comrades slipped bloody into the mud, and there was no surety that Bernhardt's forces would have the victory.

Eva wrestled her horse up onto the ridge beside Father Etienne and Margerite, breathing hard. The rain-whipped air seemed to be thickening, writhing against them like the coils of a great snake; almost unconsciously, Margerite lifted her hand, as if to protect herself from something.

"What is it?" Eva panted.

Father Etienne did not answer; he was staring into the distance again, as if he had fallen into a trance. Then he shook his head violently, rain flying from his wet hair.

"To the wagon, quickly," he ordered. "We must stop Ortlieb now, before she can finish what she is doing." He urged his horse on, and Margerite followed him, the coiled nervousness in her body suddenly kindled into a driving blaze.

This is madness! something in her mind shrieked. To
ride through a battle, unarmed and unarmoured...even if
I could fight, I could not...This close, the clashing of metal
on metal and the men's shouting was deafening, loud as the
gun-blasts. Etienne's black stallion reared, striking out with
its hooves at the guardsman in front of it. One hoof caught
him on the helm like a blow from a smith's hammer and he
dropped as two of his fellows dodged away from the horse's
deadly blows, clearing the way for the three riders to plunge
in. In those seconds the death bought him, Father Etienne
leapt from his stallion and vaulted up into the canopied
wagon, crawling under the fabric hangings that covered its
sides; with a loud yowl, Kobolt jumped from his precarious
perch on Margerite's saddle to follow him.

Hampered by her skirts, Margerite desperately clambered
from her mount, trying to keep the horse's body between
herself and the fighting, but her arms were not quite strong
enough for her to pull herself up. Clawing at the boards,
she suddenly felt a powerful shove from beneath lifting
her, and scrambled in, Eva close behind her. Beneath the
wagon's dark canopy, Ortlieb stood upon a thick tapestry, its
whiteness embroidered with the familiar Light-Bearer circle;
within the ring, her two maidens sat to either side of her.

The Order Princess wore a plain gown of thick black silk,
cinched with a girdle whose buckle was a golden lion's
head - it might have been a simple travelling habit, save that
Margerite knew it as ritual garb. The air was thicker in here,
pressing against Margerite's lungs until every breath was
a struggle - but Wolfram lay against Hedwig's velvet-clad
breasts, his bright eyes looking at his mother. With a cry,
Margerite lunged forward towards him.

"You cannot pass," Ortlieb told her, her deep voice
resonating strangely through the shadowed wagon. "You can
only die here." She lifted her wand, pointing it straight at
Margerite, and Margerite felt the darkness of Ortlieb's touch
tingling through her veins like a draught of poison.

She steeled herself, breathing deeply to force the prickling sensation and sudden weakness from her limbs. Loins girt about with truth...and having on the breastplate of righteousness...the shield of faith...and the helmet of salvation. Kobolt's warm fur brushed against her leg, and it seemed to her that she could feel the strength flowing into her from the cat.

"Give me my son," Margerite said. Her own voice sounded ragged and weak in her ears, like the high voice of a child.

"Your son? He belongs to me now." The boards of the wagon shuddered beneath Margerite's feet. Ortlieb threw her head back, long shining hair cascading over her black silken shoulders, and laughed. "And he is not the only one. What need have I of my spirits, when Bernhardt has left the fight to come to me?"

Without thought, Margerite turned her head - to see that Bernhardt had just heaved himself into the wagon as well, bloody sword still in his hand. "Margerite!" he cried out, his voice shaking with relief and anger. "I thought..."

Then he stopped dead, staring at Ortlieb. Even half-masked by chainmail, Margerite could see the stunned look on his face, as though he had just taken a heavy blow on the helm. Bernhardt's hazel eyes flickered from Ortlieb to Margerite and back again - Ortlieb polished and beautiful, her brown hair glinting gold and red around her palely bright face; Margerite wrapped in her sodden black cloak, like any peasant woman caught in the rain.

"No," Bernhardt whispered, the words catching in his throat like a river-current tugging futilely at a snagged boat. "No, I will not..."

"You will," Ortlieb said. She smiled at him, her lips perfectly soft as pink rose-petals, and lifted her wand again. "I am not done with you, nor you with me, Bernhardt von Niederwald."

Slowly, reluctantly, Bernhardt took a step towards her. Desperation rising in her heart, Margerite's glance darted towards Father Etienne. The priest's broad brow was furrowed, as if in concentration, and he was staring steadily at Bernhardt - but doing nothing; and Margerite heard the words as clearly as if he had spoken them. Bernhardt must win free of Ortlieb by himself, or he will never be free of her.

But if Ortlieb could call to him, so could Margerite. She spoke softly, but clearly - no power of enchantment behind her words, for this was not a battle to keep Bernhardt's soul for herself, but to free him. "Bernhardt," she said, "the Marienbrunnen still flows clean."

Bernhardt looked at her, lifting his hand as if to cross himself - or to touch the falcon-pendant Margerite had given him, hidden beneath breastplate and mail and gambeson.

"Come to me, Bernhardt," Ortlieb murmured, her voice a soft wind around them. "Remember how you swore your love to me, to be my knight and my beloved so long as blood flowed in your body? You were never a man to dishonour your oaths."

Bernhardt moved another step towards the edge of Ortlieb's circle. Just below his left cheekbone, a single strand of muscle had begun to twitch and jerk, as if it had given way beneath the terrible strain rending him.

"Bernhardt, I love you!" Margerite cried out. "Mother Maria have mercy on us both, I love you!"

Ortlieb's wand was still pointing at Bernhardt, and the sword trembled in his hand as he looked from Margerite to Ortlieb, from Ortlieb to Margerite. The streaks of blood on his blade had thickened to shiny red enamel against the mirror-bright steel: they blurred as the sword sliced through the darkening air - chopping downward into the tapestry at Bernhardt's feet, cutting through white cloth and black embroidery. With a powerful wrench of his shoulders, Bernhardt pulled his sword free of the boards beneath, striding forward with its point aimed at Ortlieb's breast.

The Order Princess did not move, nor did the faint smile leave her lips. "You cannot harm me," she said calmly, "for your soul would die with me. Even now, Bernhardt, do you not feel your longing for me? Can you set your sword to breasts you have kissed; can you plunge cold steel into a heart you have felt beating beneath your own, as you held me and murmured your words of love into my ears? True knight, pledged to defend the weak, can you really slay a woman?"

Slowly the point of Bernhardt's sword lowered, the bloodied steel following what might almost have been the line of a caress down Ortlieb's body. "No," he whispered, so softly that Margerite could barely hear him. "I cannot."

Ortlieb took a step towards Bernhardt, her green-flecked eyes fixed on his. She reached up, unhooking the chain-mail from his bascinet, and Margerite saw that his lips were trembling. "You see," Ortlieb said. There was no note of triumph in her low voice; only the softness of a woman speaking to her lover. "You are still mine."

She laid her left hand upon Bernhardt's breastplate, over his heart, then frowned, reaching up behind his neck in a lover's caress, her fingers fumbling beneath the edge of his chain-mail coif - searching for the clasp to the necklace Margerite had given him. Bernhardt's arm moved swiftly, grabbing her wrist and pulling it down.

"No," he said. "You shall not touch that."

"Shall I not?" Ortlieb said. She did not try to break free of his hold; instead she moved closer as though to press herself against him. The gold ring near the tip of her wand gleamed as she slowly raised it towards his forehead, and in an instant, Margerite knew what she meant to do: if Ortlieb touched Bernhardt thus once, he would be bound unbreakably to her, all his brave resistance rendered futile.

Margerite lunged forward, slamming the other woman away from Bernhardt with all her strength. Ortlieb went over backwards beneath her, crying out sharply. The wand flew from her hand in a glittering arc as they struck the wagon's floor together.

Ortlieb plunged clawed fingers at Margerite's eyes, and Margerite was barely able to grab her hands. The Order Princess' body heaved beneath Margerite's, struggling to roll her over even as she twisted one hand free. Ortlieb missed Margerite's eye, but her nails raked stingingly down Margerite's cheek; and Margerite felt all the wounds of their battle in bird-shape opening, the blood pouring out from the pain in her breast and the sharp, nauseating agony of her wrenched shoulder.

"I wounded you, too," Margerite gasped. Ortlieb's hand flailed at her face again, and she could see the long bloody streak down the other woman's arm. Margerite struck at Ortlieb, a clumsy blow that bounced off her cheekbone. The Order Princess was terrifyingly strong, but Margerite's fury drove her harder: the humiliation of her weeks as a servant and the blow Ortlieb had struck her without reason sharpening the bone-deep anger at the woman who had thought to rob her of both son and beloved.

Ortlieb's cheeks and eyes were bright with the heat of the struggle, shining brown hair flying disarrayed about her head and her lips drawn back in a fierce smile. "He was mine first," Ortlieb panted. "Never yours!"

Margerite hit her in the mouth, as if to batter her into silence; Ortlieb's nails dug into the soft flesh at the side of Margerite's neck, tearing downward. Then a sharper streak of pain ripped along Margerite's ribs, and she saw the red glint of the knife in Ortlieb's other hand. Heedless of Ortlieb's blows, Margerite desperately grabbed at the knife-fist with both hands, struggling to tear the weapon free.

Ortlieb's legs pushed powerfully against the wooden floor, rolling them over; now she was on top, and though Margerite still held her dagger-hand in a death-grip, her fingers were closing on Margerite's throat, pressing hard against the windpipe so that Margerite choked, a dizzy blackness rising over her. With her last strength, Margerite wrenched the knife free, stabbing up at Ortlieb's heart.

The point bit, tearing through black silk and flesh, then skidding over Ortlieb's breastbone. Ortlieb shrieked, her grip on Margerite's throat loosening as she grabbed at the dagger in her turn; but Margerite was too fast for her, drawing the blade quickly between Ortlieb's fingers in a spray of blood.

Then, as if a distant voice whispered in her ear, Merlin's words - that she had scorned so at the time - came back to her: Never go for the heart...go for the throat if you can, or the belly...Slice deep and far enough, and you're sure to cut something vital...Arching her back, with all her strength, Margerite drove the knife straight up into Ortlieb's white throat, sawing it wildly from side to side.

A gout of warm blood burst out, drenching Margerite's face and filling her eyes with hot redness; still clutching the knife, she tried to blink her sight clear, but Ortlieb's hands were already closing on her throat again, even as the Order Princess' body began to slump forward on top of her. Red and black swirled before Margerite's eyes; she clung tight to the dagger-hilt, but her shaking arms collapsed beneath Ortlieb's weight, and it was growing harder and harder to drag each breath into her lungs.

Then the choking heaviness was suddenly gone from her, and Father Etienne's face loomed close in her sight, blurred by blood and framed in ragged edges of blackness that rose and passed before Margerite's eyes like clouds in the wind. She felt strong hands prying the knife from her fingers, heard Bernhardt's voice crying out anxiously,"Margerite! Father, is she..."

"She lives, and Ortlieb is dead," Father Etienne said.

Bernhardt's arms were around her shoulders, helping her to sit up. Shakily, breath rasping through her bruised throat, Margerite wiped the blood from her eyes with her sleeve and looked about her. Hedwig and Oda were both bound and gagged, glaring angrily; Eva's golden hair was disheveled and there was a red mark under her left eye that would likely bruise, but she held Wolfram in her arms, grinning triumphantly.

Ortlieb...Ortlieb lay sprawled beside her, and her head had rolled back so that Margerite could see the fearful wound in her neck, jagged tatters of bloodied flesh hanging over the white ring of her severed windpipe, and Kriemhilt creeping closer as if she meant to lap at the spreading pool of blood soaking into the boards. Margerite coughed, gagging back the acid sear of bile, but did not look away from what she had done. The knife that had killed Ortlieb was beside the body, and Margerite realized that it was her own eating-dagger, which the other woman must have snatched from her belt in the fight.

"Thank you," Bernhardt whispered in her ear. "Thank you for saving me."

"As you saved me, before," Margerite murmured back to him. It hurt to speak, but she clung tightly to him to hold herself up. Something was wrong, though she did not know what...something missing...Kobolt stood up with his forepaws on her shoulders, eagerly licking the blood from her face, and she realized that the sounds of battle had ceased outside: there was nothing but the low talk of men, the moans of the wounded, and the loud pattering of rain against the wagon's canopy.

The heavy fabric moved: someone else was coming in. Bernhardt gently disengaged himself from Margerite, raising his sword and moving into a crouch of readiness. In the shadowed darkness, Margerite saw only the gleam of a polished bascinet marred by a few spatters of blood; then the newcomer stood, and she recognised Ritter Gottfried.

"Herr Bernhardt, Frowe Gräfin, we have the victory," he said. Gray eyes huge in the gloom, Gottfried looked about the wagon, his stare stopping on Ortlieb's body. He raised a hand, crossing himself; he seemed about to speak again, but his knees buckled beneath him, his sword falling from his grasp. Father Etienne stepped forward quickly, catching him before he could pitch face-first onto the floor and easing him down more gently. In a moment, Gottfried's eyes fluttered open again.

"What do you see?" Father Etienne asked him.

The knight gestured for the priest to lean closer, murmuring into his ear. Father Etienne straightened, hastening over to Ortlieb's body and kneeling beside it as he drew two phials from his belt-pouch. Margerite heard the murmured words of the Last Rites; but she could feel the prickling in the air, as though lightning were about to strike, and when Etienne dipped his finger in holy oil and brought it near Ortlieb's forehead, he suddenly jerked his hand back with a muffled hiss of pain, as though he had been burned.

"Lend me your sword, if you will, Herr Gottfried," Father Etienne said. "My own is too light for this work."

Gottfried nodded. Father Etienne picked up the knight's fallen blade, taking careful aim, and brought it down hard, the blade thunking solid through bone and into the wood beneath. Ortlieb's head rolled free.

It seemed to Margerite then that she felt a blistering rush of fire that burned without giving warmth, as though a tongue of flame had licked past her. Something soft brushed past her head, like the whisper of an owl's wing across her cheek; she heard a falling shriek, and could not say whether it was a cry of despair - or triumph.

Kobolt's raspy tongue was swiftly becoming painful on her skin. Margerite pushed the cat away, leaning against one of the canopy-posts as she got to her feet. She gingerly touched the knife-scrape along her ribs: it was still bleeding a little, but the bone had stopped the point from going deep.

"Margerite, are you wounded?" Bernhardt asked worriedly, his mailed arm carefully encircling her.

"Not badly," Margerite croaked. All of her muscles were beginning to ache; her face and neck still stung bitterly where Ortlieb's nails had dug in, and she thought it would hurt to speak or swallow for a good while yet. She knew that she should be delighted at their victory, and yet she could feel no more than a dull exhausted relief.

Then Wolfram, who had kept quiet throughout the fight, began to squall, balling up his fists and screaming red-faced. Margerite took him from Eva's arms at once, paying no heed to the pain the movement cost her, and held him tightly to herself. "My son, my son," she murmured to him. Wolfram cried harder, clutching at her right breast.

"Father, Bernhardt, Herr Gottfried - turn your heads for a few minutes, if you will, or go outside. My child is hungry, and I must feed him."

"I have work to do outside," Father Etienne replied calmly, and Bernhardt followed him out. Gottfried tried to rise, but slumped back, waving Eva away when she crouched down to see to him. "I can wait for someone with healing skills; there are many worse wounded than I outside," he said faintly. He closed his eyes, and Margerite could hear his breathing growing more ragged.

"Eva, fetch Jochanan in here at once, if he is able to come," she commanded, then turned her back and unfastened her bodice. Wolfram's lips tugged hard, almost painfully, against her nipple, and Margerite felt her tears of relief beginning to fall at last, carving wet tracks through the drying mask of blood on her face.

They made camp on the road that night, for many of the wounded were not fit to march. There were the bodies of the dead to think of, as well. Ortlieb's guards had defended her to the last, refusing to surrender when quarter was offered them, and their resistance had taken a harsh toll on the Bear's Paw: the dead outnumbered the living by nearly twice. Georg offered to ride back to the Free Company's campsite so that those men who had remained with their wains could bring them up, but Bernhardt shook his head.

"They should be coming up the road already," he said. "I expected that they would be needed; we will likely see them tomorrow morning." Of course, Margerite thought: Bernhardt would know the cost of battle, even in victory. She hugged Wolfram to herself, warm beneath her damp cloak. Someday he would have to learn that cost as well, as squire, or knight, or Graf...but not yet, thank Mother Maria, not yet.

"But you have done very well," Bernhardt added. "The standardbearer is always in the worst danger: it was brave of you to take that task, and called for both skill and luck to see you through with so little hurt." The side of Georg's face was bandaged - Margerite had sewn the wound herself, and knew that he would bear a scar from cheekbone to jaw all his life - and another bandage wrapped his leg, but the Knappe stood steadily, drawing himself up in pride at Bernhardt's next words. "When I next see Herr Christoph, I shall tell him that you have proven yourself fit to hold the vigil of knighthood."

"Thank you, Herr Bernhardt!" Georg answered joyously; if his grin pulled against the stitches in his face, he did not seem to notice.

Despite the rain, the men of the Bear's Paw had managed to get several large fires going, bundling the wounded up close beside them. Margerite and Bernhardt walked among the blazes, Bernhardt giving the injured his praises, and Margerite croaking her gratitude. Though many of the mercenaries stared curiously at the marks on Margerite's face, none of them asked her anything.

Arnmut had brought Gottfried out of the wagon, and the knight lay swathed in blankets beside the largest fire with his Knappe carefully feeding him pieces of cheese and dried meat.

"How fares it with you, Ritter Gottfried?" Bernhardt asked.

"Well enough," Gottfried answered, gray eyes glittering from his thin face like polished stones. "My wound came open again, and Jochanan says that I have lost a great deal of blood - but I did not even have to pay a physician to draw it, so I am the better off." Until Bernhardt laughed, Margerite did not realize that the somber knight had tried to make a joke.

"And you, Arnmut?" said Bernhardt.

Gottfried's squire smiled sweetly up at Bernhardt, the firelight glinting from the little specks of gold hair coming in along his jaw. He lifted his left hand: it was swollen and purple, and the last two fingers had been splinted. "This was the worst I received, from a spear-shaft that missed its aim and came down behind my shield, and it should heal to full usefulness quickly enough. Other than that, I got no more than a few small cuts and bruises."

"And Christ be thanked for it!" Gottfried added, his low baritone suddenly intense. "There was more than once when I feared I might lose you, but you acquitted yourself well, and defended me bravely when my strength began to fail."

"You were ever in the worse danger, Herr Gottfried," Arnmut replied. "No, do not try to rise: the healer says that you must rest. I wish you would go back into the wagon where it is dry."

"I shall not willingly go back in there," Gottfried said firmly. Margerite was about to argue with him, for she knew how quickly a deep wound could catch fever on cold wet ground. But though Father Etienne had wrapped Ortlieb's body and head carefully in a makeshift shroud of her own black silken robes turned inside out, Margerite knew that she would not consent to sleep where the Order Princess had died - and she, thanks be to Mother Maria's mercy, was not cursed with Gottfried's sight.

At least Gottfried had been unconscious when Father Etienne and Bernhardt had taken Ortlieb's keys and opened one of the locked chests: what they had seen had made Bernhardt swear like the mercenary he had been, dropping the lid and backing away fast; while Etienne, his face pale as marble, made the sign of the Cross over the box and locked it again. She shivered, holding Wolfram more closely to her. Arnmut would see to it that his knight kept warm: Margerite did not have to worry about the two of them now.

Father Etienne, too, was walking among the wounded. Now and again he would kneel by a man's side, bending down to hear a whispered Confession; and twice Margerite saw him anointing foreheads with holy oil and murmuring the words of the Last Rites.

Unwilling to disturb the priest at his work, Margerite and Bernhardt walked over to the fire where Paul and Jochanan sat with a few of the Bear's Paw men. A bloody bandage was tied rakishly around Paul's head, but he seemed in good spirits, tilting Jochanan's flask and knocking back a good gulp of the gunner's fiery distillate.

"I think we earned our pay this evening," Paul said, lifting the metal bottle up to Bernhardt.

"That you did," Bernhardt agreed gravely, tilting it back and taking a small sip before he passed it to Margerite. "I had hoped that the guardsmen, at least, would surrender rather than fighting to the last."

"I have never seen guards battle so furiously when offered quarter in a lost battle," Jochanan offered, his voice soft. "They seemed - much like men bewitched."

Bernhardt gave him a grim nod. Margerite had meant only to tilt the flask enough to wet her lips, but she found herself taking a solid swallow. The aqua vitae burned viciously going down her bruised throat, though it left a soothing warmth behind. She handed it down to the gunner.

"What about you, Gräfin Margerite?" Paul asked. "How did you get so battered?"

Margerite did not know how to answer him - how to speak in cold blood of what she had done in desperation and fury. It was Bernhardt who spoke for her, looking straight at the mercenary Hauptmann.

"Fighting for me," he said. "And for her son."

Hearing Bernhardt's words, Margerite felt as though an iron band had sprung loose from her heart. If Bernhardt did not yet love Wolfram, at least he accepted him...at least he understood what her child was to her.

The Bear took the metal bottle from Jochanan, lifting it towards Margerite. "Here's to a brave woman, then!" he said, taking a hearty gulp. At once Kobolt was upon him, sniffing hopefully at his red-gold beard in case any drops of the aqua vitae might still linger there. Paul pushed the black tom away, laughing. "Before God, Gräfin, if you weren't a noblewoman, I'd recruit you and your cat for the Bear's Paw - no offense meant, Bertram," he added at Bernhardt's sudden scowl. "Herr Bernhardt, I suppose I should say? Why didn't you ever tell us before, you black-arsed scoundrel?"

For a moment, looking at Bernhardt's face in the leaping firelight, Margerite could see all his years of pain graven deep upon him - in the set of his jaw beneath the short-cropped brown beard, in the brightness that could have been a glassing of tears over his hazel eyes; half-robbed of colour by the darkness, the brown hair that had grown over his scalp beneath the black dye could have been the gray of age or cruel shock. Then he shrugged, smiling ruefully.

"A man in the Companies has no history, Paul. You should know that by now."

Paul and Jochanan both laughed again, and Paul passed the aqua vitae to Bernhardt. "Well, it's worked out well enough, anyway, though I'll have to start recruiting again - and it won't be easy work, with every free soldier who can still swing a sword gone to France or Spain. What about that Knappe of yours, young Georg? How would he like to join the Bear's Paw?"

"Probably all too well," Bernhardt admitted. "But he is not my Knappe, he is Christoph's, and I think a very different future awaits him." He drank and again, as though she were a fellow soldier, handed the flask on to Margerite.

"What are you planning to do now?" Jochanan asked. "You have the Landgräfin; are you planning to treat with the Landgraf?"

"I do not think he will treat with me," Bernhardt replied. "And the Landgräfin is dead, of her own doing, for she tried to slay Margerite, and Margerite repaid her justly."

The two mercenaries looked up at Margerite, Paul giving a low whistle. "Well done, Gräfin!" he congratulated her. Margerite nodded in acknowledgement, though her stomach tightened in revulsion. And yet Ortlieb was a truly evil woman, as deserving of death as any has ever been. A man would be proud of killing his foe in single combat; why do I feel so ashamed?

"Well-done, indeed," Jochanan agreed, taking his flask from Margerite's hand. "But will that not make it more difficult for you to do - whatever it is you mean to do next?"

"It will not," Father Etienne said dryly, appearing out of the darkness beside them. "For what we discovered in Ortlieb's wagon has made all of this a matter for the Church - and for the Inquisition."

Even in the firelight, Margerite could see Jochanan's swarthy skin paling, and he murmured something beneath his breath - something that sounded very like Hebrew to her, though she did not recognise the words. Father Etienne looked down at him, a look of compassion softening his high-boned face. "You will have nothing to fear from them, Jochanan. I shall make sure of that - my word on it."

Jochanan looked down, flushing, then tilted his flask to his lips. Perhaps, as you say, a man in the Companies has no history, Margerite thought. But I think none of you can escape his past altogether. She did not know what might have driven the Jew into the Bear's Paw, but she thought she might be able to guess.

"When the rest of your wagons get here," Father Etienne went on,"we shall go to the Bishop of Niederwald, to put the evidence in his care and see to the proper burial of the dead. After that..." He paused. "An Inquisitorial trial can often be a lengthy process, and there is also a question of secular law in the matter, as regards Herr Bernhardt's status: even if Landgraf Gerhardt is implicated in his wife's doing, as I believe he must be to some degree, I think the final decision concerning the rule of Niederwald will be referred to the Kaiser."

Paul shook his head in amazement, his bandage slipping to the side to show the roughly stitched tear in his scalp. "Who would have thought that we could be mixed up in such things?" he asked the air. "Never mind: tonight we're alive and our foes are dead, and tomorrow is another fight." He took the flask from Jochanan, lifting it. "To the Bear's Paw Company - Glück!"

Chapter Ten

By dawn, the storm had swept past, leaving a clear glaze of ice over the dark branches and a thick white crust over the bloodied mud of the road. Several of the wounded had died in the night, a fine white fur of frost marking the blankets of the dead, but Ritter Gottfried was still alive; Margerite saw him trying to sit up, and his fair-haired squire gently pressing him back and urging him to rest. She had to walk off into the wood to relieve herself and feed Wolfram in private, her shoes crunching loudly through the frosted grass as Kobolt rustled beside her, pouncing playfully at every stray leaf that stirred in the freezing wind.

Every step was painful, awakening Margerite's bruises and strained muscles and pulling at the long scab over her ribs, and each breath felt like a draught from an ice-covered pool in her throat, chilling her lungs. And yet, as Paul had said last night, she was alive and her foe was dead - and, Mother Maria help her, it was good to be alive! Though it even hurt to smile, Margerite found that she was smiling, gazing up through the bare trees at the cold blue brightness of the sky.

"O, my little one," Margerite said to Wolfram as she undid her bodice and held him to her breast, rewrapping her cloak to keep him warm as he fed. Speaking hurt as much as moving, and she knew that if she could see her neck in a mirror, it would be dark with bruises, but she did not care, it was so good to have her son in her arms again. "How did they care for you, with no wet-nurse? Did they give you nasty goat's milk? It's all right now, for you are back with me, and no one shall ever take you away again."

The ice on the trees gleamed like polished adamant in the new sunlight, but the only mushrooms Margerite saw had gone black with the frost: when they thawed, they would melt away into foul slime and be quickly gone, until more sprang up next autumn. Above her head, Margerite heard a raven's croaking, deep and resonant. She looked up, and the huge black bird looked down at her, its dark eye glittering.

"You will win no carrion from this battle, gallows-bird," she said to the raven. "Those who fell in the fight were Christian men, and shall be buried in hallowed ground." Save for Ortlieb - and I hope that her body is sentenced to burning, and her ashes scattered far and wide.

The raven cawed again, almost scornfully, and launched itself from the branch where it perched. It circled over Margerite, mounting higher, and she watched it until it was nothing but a black speck against the heaven's blueness. Wolfram had let go of her nipple; when Margerite looked down, she saw that his little golden head was tilted back, his blue eyes gazing raptly upwards.

"You shall be a fine falconer someday," Margerite told him. "You shall have falcons of your own, peregrines and gyrfalcons; perhaps you shall even fly an eagle, as your father did." She joggled Wolfram in her arms until he belched, then let out a sharp wail, as if at the indignity of being treated so. "Hush, my son, hush. You are safe now, and all shall be well for us hereafter."

As she came back towards camp, Margerite saw Eva carrying a full chamberpot into the woods. As Margerite had suspected, the blow Eva had gotten in subduing Ortlieb's servants had blossomed into a spectacular black eye overnight; she did not want to think how she herself looked. But Eva greeted her cheerily, dumping the mess out under a bush and kicking up leaves over it. "I have tended to Hedwig and Oda, as you see, so you need not worry about them," she said. "It were best if we put them in the other wagon, though. Oda had almost gotten her hands free when I heard her moving and woke up, and I would hate to think what mischief she could have worked with whatever is in Ortlieb's chests."

Margerite shuddered at the thought, for both of Ortlieb's women wore the onyx rings of proven demon-summoners. And a woman desperate enough might not be too concerned with the safeties of circle and triangle...

"It is well that you are looking after them," she agreed. "It would not be seemly for any of the men here to do so."

Eva giggled. "Except perhaps for Father Etienne or Ritter Gottfried, who are above any temptations - and I do not think either of them would stoop to providing and emptying a chamberpot for our prisoners." Then her voice became more serious. "Margerite, what will happen to Hedwig and Oda when we have brought them to the Bishop?"

"They will be held and questioned, I suppose," Margerite said. Then it dawned on her what her words meant - what they must mean, in such circumstances as these. "They are likely to be tortured, and then executed, probably burnt to death," she added reluctantly. "That is, if the Order does not find means of its own to silence them first, before they can betray it under questioning."

Eva was quiet for a little while as they walked back, following the brown footprints they had left in the frost. In the distance, a small bird lifted its high chirp, and another answered it. "If matters were only a little different, it could be either of us going to the question."

"I know that," Margerite said. "Yet - I also know that Father Etienne will give them a chance to confess, and to repent, before it is too late. If they are able to turn away from the Order, even now..." She did not finish her sentence. Even in death, Ortlieb had resisted Father Etienne's last grace, and Margerite knew that the Order of Light-Bearers bound its members in a code of honour as stringent as that of any knight. She suspected that Hedwig and Oda would go silent to the stake, even as martyrs to their Lord; and even though she was sure they had aided Ortlieb in deeds that made their executions more than deserved, she could not help feeling the sorrow of their wasted lives.

"Mother Maria grant that it be so," Eva murmured.

The Bear's Paw wagons did not reach them until almost noontime. At Paul's barked commands, the men who were whole helped their wounded brethren into the wains, piling the corpses on another wagon. Ritter Gottfried insisted, over the protests of his Knappe, that he was well enough to sit a horse and that it would be shameful for a knight to be carried in a cart.

Even Father Etienne could not dissuade him, but finally agreed that, since they would be going no faster than the wagons could travel, Gottfried might be allowed to ride. Margerite, however, did not scorn the meager comfort of the Bear's Paw wains: even though it meant sitting beside Hedwig and Oda, who glared at her over their gags in impotent rage, it was better than trying to ride a horse and carry Wolfram in her battered state.

With the wagons, it took three days to reach the Bishop's palace. By then, except for those few cases where redness and discharge warned that fever was still a danger, all of the surviving wounded seemed likely to recover and live, though several men had been moved from the wagons of the injured to the one that bore the heap of corpses.

By God's mercy, the weather held freezing, so that only a slight taint of rot hung in the air around the dead-wagon. A troop of soldiers rode out to meet them before the palace gate, led by a graybearded man in the white-crossed black surcoat of the Teutonic Knights, whose right leg was stretched out stiffly in front of his saddle. The Bishop's guards were all neatly turned out, their armour and helms gleaming mirror-blue under the clear sky, in stark contrast to the ragged men of the Bear's Paw.

Father Etienne rode forward, gesturing to Bernhardt to follow him. Although he had had no more chance to wash than the rest of them, Etienne's robes were neat, the rolled corners of his canon's hat settled precisely on his head.

"Greetings, Brother Sigvrit," Father Etienne said. "I have returned, as you see, and with me is Herr Bernhardt von Niederwald. We will require lodgings for ourselves, a knight and his Knappe, two noble ladies, and some forty men-at-arms, of whom perhaps fifteen are too badly wounded to walk - and burial arrangements for more than threescore. There are also two prisoners who need to be kept secure."

"Christ help us, Father, what have you been doing?" the old Teutonic Knight asked, looking past Etienne at the mercenaries and the wagon piled high with corpses. "I will see to everything for you at once, if your men will agree to give over their weapons before they enter - for Christ's peace holds in this place," Brother Sigvrit added, a faint tinge of disappointment in his voice. He turned about and rode back to the gates, shouting, "Open up! These are friends and guests who have come."

The men of the Bear's Paw grumbled a great deal at having to surrender their weapons to the gate-guard, but when they saw that even Father Etienne was unbuckling the slender sword at his waist, they submitted willingly enough, if not happily. Margerite expected more of an argument out of Gottfried, but the knight gave over his blade without a word, his gray stare fixed raptly on Brother Sigvrit.

"Come with me, Father, and your noble guests as well. We'll let my lads take care of your soldiers for the time being - aye, and the bodies too: the dead are usually patient, I've found. As for the prisoners, we'll handle them easily enough."

"It would be best if they came with us," Father Etienne replied.

The Teutonic Knight beckoned to four of his men, who rode forward beside him. "Tell me where they are, and we'll take them for you."

Etienne gestured to the wagon in which Margerite sat. Looking at Hedwig and Oda, the old warrior blinked. "Those women are from the Landgräfin's court, aren't they?"

"Yes. Watch them very carefully, for we have evidence of their involvement in black sorcery - and murder."

Brother Sigvrit's soldiers dismounted, efficiently picking up the two bound women and slinging them in front of the two foremost saddles. Hedwig only grunted softly as she was thrown over the horse's neck, but Oda made small mewing sounds behind her gag, squirming until the guard slapped her lightly across the face. "None of that now, else you'll fall off," he said gruffly.

Margerite had never seen a Bishop's palace before, but, even with winter coming on fast, so that the close-mown turf of the lawns was stained with brown and the great oak trees lining the laneways bare, she was impressed with how well the grounds were laid out and tended. Far to the left, where the wall ended, she saw the shimmering brightness of a small lake - doubtless well-stocked with carp, bream, and perch to supply meals for the days of abstinence. Several ponds, their surfaces glittering with new ice, dotted the grounds, with carven stone benches beside them where the Bishop and his folk could sit for contemplation or pleasant conversation.

In the middle of one of the lawns, a few white doves fluttered and cooed around a beautiful dovecote, which had been built in the shape of a miniature Burg with crenellations and a ridge-tiled roof. Even riding through, though Ortlieb's wagon still rolled behind her and the guards rode ahead with Hedwig and Ortlieb, filled Margerite with a sense of peace such as she had seldom felt of late; she could only imagine how lovely the Bishop's gardens must be in summer, when the grass was green and the trees in full leaf.

After they had stabled their horses, Brother Sigvrit ordered his guardsmen to take the prisoners away to secure chambers. Limping on his crutch, he led the rest of them into the palace, through a hallway lined with stained-glass windows that shone like jewels in the bright cold November light. He stopped before one of the doors, knocking loudly and calling out, "Ho, Father Kunibert! Here is urgent business for the Bishop."

"Enter," a scratchy voice replied. A small bald man with gold-rimmed spectacles sat behind a huge carven oak desk, looking up at them curiously as they entered. "Father Etienne, be welcome here again," he said. "Who are your companions, and what is your urgent business?"

"Father Kunibert, these are Margerite, Gräfin von Fürstensee, with her son Graf Wolfram von Falkenstein, Frowe Eva von Bärenberg, Ritter Gottfried von Schlangenbad and his Knappe Arnmut von Eisenstein, Knappe Georg von Schwarzenfels - and Herr Bernhardt von Niederwald."

The little priest drew in his breath at the last name, pale eyes widening behind his spectacles, but Etienne continued without pause. "We must see the Bishop and Father Thomas immediately, for we have a most serious matter to set before them, which will allow no delay. And it were better if you went to summon them yourself, for you will be able to make our urgency clear to the Bishop."

Father Kunibert pushed his spectacles back on his nose, staring up at Father Etienne for a few moments, as if trying to decide whether or not to argue with the canon's demands. Etienne stared cooly back at him, his aristocratic features calm and implacable, and shortly Father Kunibert rose. "The Bishop is at his meditations in his private chapel, but if you insist on disturbing him now, you may come with me."

The Bishop's private chapel was small, but glowed everywhere with the coloured light through the stained-glass windows and the brightness of beeswax candles. The Bishop himself knelt before the altar, raven-black head bowed and purple silken vestments flowing around him like the water of a river at twilight. Though he must have heard their footsteps, he did not stir until Father Kunibert hurried up to kneel beside him, murmuring in his ear. Then he rose slowly and turned towards them, his ruddy face set in stern lines.

"Father Etienne," he said. "I trust that you have sufficient reason for intruding on my meditations like this."

Etienne went forward, kneeling gracefully before the Bishop to press his lips to the episcopal amethyst ring. "Your Grace, I believe you will think so. We have brought to you the body of Ortlieb, Landgräfin von Niederwald, together with proof of her practice of evil sorceries and two maidens who assisted her in her dark works."

The Bishop's mouth dropped open, his black eyebrows flying up; he almost snatched his hand back from Etienne. "The body! Christ help us all, Father Etienne, what have you done?"

"Gräfin Margerite was forced to slay the Landgräfin in self-defense," Father Etienne replied calmly. "When you - and Father Thomas - see what else we have brought, you will understand why. I believe this is a matter which requires a full Inquisitorial investigation."

"I shall be the judge of that," the Bishop said. "Father Kunibert, fetch Father Thomas at once. As for you, Father Etienne, I sincerely hope that you have not overstepped your bounds this time. As you know, I have never held with this modern hysteria concerning sorcery: the Devil may delude some poor souls into believing such things, but he holds no true power in this world."

"That is, perhaps, a matter for those more learned than we to discuss," Etienne answered, his voice still very calm. "Perhaps you may find the crimes which Landgräfin Ortlieb committed in, if you will, her delusion, to be more to the point now: and we have what I believe to be full proof of those."

"I shall be fascinated to see it. Now, who are these folk you have brought with you?" The Bishop's bright blue gaze moved over them, and Margerite wished deeply that she had had time to bathe and been able to dress in a manner more fitting to her station, instead of coming before him bedraggled as a peasant woman with her babe in her arms. At least - Heaven be thanked for small mercies as well as great - Kobolt had wandered off somewhere; she would not just yet have to apologize to the Bishop because her tomcat had sprayed in his chapel.

Etienne introduced them again, and in turn they each touched lips to the Bishop's ring. Etienne left Bernhardt for last; hearing his name, the Bishop's eyebrows went up, and he scrutinized Bernhardt's face very carefully. "It has been a long time since I saw you," he said. "But yes, you do indeed have the look of Herr Bernhardt von Niederwald. Why have you come back now?"

"To prove my innocence, and make my claim for my inheritance," Bernhardt said steadily. "I state now, before Christ and before all of you, that I am not guilty of the murder of which I was accused, but that the death and the accusation were concocted by Ortlieb and my brother in order to bring me down; and that will I gladly prove with my body against any champion, or by any ordeal to which I may be put."

"There will be time to deal with that when we are through with this matter, Herr Bernhardt," the Bishop said. "If you are indeed innocent, you may be sure that Heaven will aid you in proving your case - ah, Father Thomas. Your promptness is exemplary."

"Thank you, your Grace," said the new priest, limping up to them. Father Thomas was an inch or two shorter than Margerite; at first, because of his painful walk and the gray dusting his brown curls, she thought that he was an old man, but when he drew closer, she could see that, in spite of the faint lines of pain on his thin face, he could hardly be any older than Father Etienne. "Father Etienne, what have you found?" He coughed softly, a dry racking noise that Margerite could almost feel in her own chest.

Etienne looked sadly down at the other priest. "I fear I have found your missing children."

"Are they..?" Father Thomas whispered.

"We can do no more for them now," Etienne replied, "save blessing their bones and burying them as Christians in consecrated ground, where their remains will suffer no more sacrilege."

Father Thomas crossed himself, murmuring a prayer beneath his breath.

"Your Grace, if you would come with us now?" Father Etienne said. "And Father Thomas, Brother Sigvrit, Gräfin Margerite, and Ritter Gottfried. The rest of you may stay here: what I have to show is not something that should be seen by anyone who is not prepared for it." He met Bernhardt's gaze steadfastly. "That includes you, Herr Bernhardt. As I said before, this is a matter for the Church."

"And what of Gräfin Margerite and Ritter Gottfried?" Father Thomas asked hesitantly. "Should they..?"

"They are both prepared as lay assistants in exorcism," said Father Etienne. "Should it wonder you that I have laid such a burden on a noblewoman, you will remember that it is not seemly, except in dire emergencies, for a man to deal alone with a woman possessed, and that the Devil spares those of high estate no more than those of low. Brother Sigvrit, would you do me the courtesy of seeing Ritter Gottfried's sword, and my own, returned to us before we begin?"

"As you wish, Father," agreed the old Teutonic Knight. "I didn't mean you when I told Herr Bernhardt's men to disarm, anyway. I just didn't want such a lot of what, begging your forgiveness, Father, looked like such a load of ruffians running around with swords and spears inside the Bishop's grounds."

"Understandable," Etienne agreed, smiling slightly. "But they would never have given up their weapons willingly if I had come in armed."

"What is this, Father Etienne?" asked the Bishop sharply. "What manner of men have you brought into my palace?"

"Good men, and true, who fought with my name as their battle-cry," Bernhardt answered for the priest. "They will give you no trouble: they desire only Christian burial for their fallen comrades and foes, and perhaps there are some among them who will wish to make Confession."

By the time they got to Ortlieb's wagon, one of Brother Sigvrit's men was already waiting there with the requested swords. Ritter Gottfried stood more easily with his blade at his side. In spite of his insistence on riding, he had recovered from his wound with amazing speed.

"Now, your Grace," Father Etienne said. "Steel yourself, for you will see much here to dismay you."

Enclosed by its canopies, the inside of Ortlieb's wagon stank badly of rot: even with the freezing weather, her corpse had decayed more badly than the rest, and the black silken shroud that covered it was damp with leaking fluids. The Bishop lifted a scented handkerchief to his nose, but Father Thomas made no such gesture: his brown eyes were wide and dark, but a strange composure had come over his hollow-cheeked face, a veil of quiet sorrow over a steely sureness.

"Brother Sigvrit," Father Etienne said. "Will you do me the courtesy of examining the Landgräfin's body, so that you may testify to the manner of her death?"

Gottfried helped the old Teutonic Knight to lower himself to the wagon's floor. Leaning on his young companion, his right leg stretched out behind him, Brother Sigvrit pulled back the black silk from Ortlieb's corpse. The wave of corruption that rose from it was enough to make Margerite gag, but the old man hardly seemed to notice the smell.

"Throat cut by someone who wasn't very strong and didn't know how to use a dagger, but really wanted to kill her, and did," Brother Sigvrit said roughly. "But her head was cut off afterwards by a man using a good heavy sword."

"How can you tell?" the Bishop asked, leaning closer with his handkerchief pressed to his nose. The Teutonic Knight pointed to the tattered flesh of Ortlieb's neck. Swollen and green-marbled as her skin was, the cruel marks of Margerite's attack were still clear.

"See how the knife was sawed back and forth in the wound? No one who knew what he was doing would cut a throat like that. I'd wager she was on top when it happened, too: the knife went in almost straight up from below. But one clean cut severed the bone beneath."

"I will take your word for that," the Bishop said. The florid colour had faded from his broad cheeks; he looked ill, and Margerite could hardly blame him. "Father Etienne, what should we do with her body?"

"As you will see, we can hardly bury her in holy ground. My recommendation is that she be burnt, but that cannot be done until sentence has been passed by the Inquisition. For now, the best thing is to put her outside the churchyard walls."

The Bishop straightened up, breathing deeply through his handkerchief. "Cover her up again, Brother Sigvrit, and call for guards to take her away. If there is worse to be seen here, at least we do not need to breathe air that is thick with the smell of a rotting corpse."

Even after Ortlieb's body had been removed, her stench lingered in the air, but at least it was fainter. Father Etienne pointed to the embroidered piece of cloth that had been Ortlieb's circle. "She was standing in this when we came upon her. Gräfin Margerite, Ritter Gottfried, if you would hold it up so the Bishop can see it?"

Margerite took one corner and Gottfried the other. The thick fabric felt slimy beneath her fingers, as though tiny worms moved within it; she might have dropped it if Gottfried had not been watching. But the hatchet-faced knight was staring at her, as if to see if she would quail - or perhaps to keep from looking at Ortlieb's tapestry circle; there was no way to tell.

"You are correct about this being a matter for the Inquisition," the Bishop conceded. "I know nothing of such things, nor do I care to. Put it to the side there."

Margerite and Gottfried gratefully set the tapestry aside. Father Etienne took a ring of iron keys from his belt-pouch and unlocked the first chest. "I believe that these are the heads of your missing children, Father Thomas," he said quietly.

Margerite did not want to look, but she did. The boys' heads had been salted, perhaps, or smoked: the grayish-white flesh still clung to cheeks and jawbones, but the eyeballs had dried in their sockets. Only the close-cropped hair on the heads still kept the look of life: one sun-bleached blond, two dark brown. Margerite heard Gottfried swallowing hard beside her, and from the corner of her eye she saw him crossing himself.

Sadly Father Thomas leaned closer to the chest, scrutinizing the three ravaged half-faces for a time. "I believe that they are," he said. "Christ have mercy on their souls."

"Christ have mercy," Ritter Gottfried echoed hollowly. Again, Margerite wondered what he saw.

"Frowe Gräfin," the Bishop said. "You may leave now. Such things are not suited for a woman of gentle birth to see."

Father Etienne shook his head. "You may well see worse if you persist in your path, Margerite," he murmured, so softly that Margerite was not entirely sure he had spoken aloud at all. But she remembered searching through the ruins of Ruprecht's sanctum for the charred remains of Klingschor and Kundry. If she could do that, she could stand up to this.

"I slew her to save my son from this," Margerite choked. "I will stay."

"Your son?" the Bishop asked. "What reason did you have to think that he was in danger?"

"Because she stole him from his cradle," Margerite answered.

"I shall hear the whole tale when we are done with this," the Bishop told her. "But it seems to me that you acted well and rightly, as a veritable Judith. Father Thomas, Brother Sigvrit, Father Etienne, you may continue. I believe that I have seen all that I need to." With, perhaps, a little more haste than was seemly, he climbed down out of the wagon.

"Bishop Otto is a good man," Father Etienne mused. "And a wise one, perhaps, to realize when he is dealing with matters beyond his compass. I do not think we will have to wait too long for him to summon the Inquisition."

"Is your assistant well?" asked Father Thomas diffidently. Margerite was about to reply with indignation when she realized that he was not looking at her, but at Gottfried, who still stared transfixed at the three heads.

"Thomas," said Father Etienne, his dry voice very flat, as though he were fighting back an exclamation of horror, "you have been an exorcist almost as long as I. Can you not tell when a soul is not free?"

Father Thomas looked at the contents of the chest again and crossed himself. "She could not have - dear Christ, that is not possible!"

"I fear that it is," Etienne replied. "You are needed here as more than a witness, Father. Let us pray that these are the only spirits here." He moved to close the box, but Ritter Gottfried put out a thin hand to stop him.

"Let them see, Father," the knight said distantly. "They have been long in the dark, and should not be denied the sight of the Cross." He touched the gold crucifix hanging upon his breastplate.

Etienne opened chest after chest, displaying all of Ortlieb's paraphenalia. Some of the items were familiar to Margerite: candles of different colours, with the sigils of the planetary spirits inscribed upon them; a forked mandrake root in its own silk pouch; a mirror in the form of a shield with a single band of inscriptions around its edge, engraved with pentagrams in the corners and the name"Lilit" in the middle; a slender sword graven with signs along its length; incenses, oils, and herbs, neatly labelled with planetary symbols or names, and other things that Margerite recognised from her readings in the Black Book.

Others were stranger: a number of bones and animal skulls, including a long bone that had been painted along its length with words in an unknown language -"Human thighbone," Brother Sigvrit said briefly - a collection of dried hearts ranging from no larger than Margerite's thumbnail to the size of her two clenched fists together; several wax images, some plain, others inscribed, and one which had been wrapped in a piece of black silk and pierced through with needles.

The two largest boxes held an assortment of glassware carefully bedded in straw, which Margerite guessed Ortlieb must have used for alchemical experiments, and phials of liquids and powders, labelled in the same neat hand as that which had marked the other materials. There were a number of books as well, chiefly concerned with the raising of demons and spirits, but also some astrological and alchemical texts - but no trace of anything like the Black Book.

Father Etienne was bending down to open the last chest, a small plain wooden box, when Gottfried shouted, "Father, beware!" and drew his sword, stabbing forward. Father Thomas spun around, holding up the cross that hung about his neck; Father Etienne's narrow blade flickered out even as Brother Sigvrit unsheathed his own blade, bracing himself on his crutch. Margerite leapt out of the way, blinking hard. It seemed to her that she could see - something, a shadow in the dimness, striking out with half-seen claws.

"Begone from here, creature of Hell," Father Thomas said clearly. "There is nothing here for you, and you cannot prevail against the power of our Lord Jesus Christ."

Ritter Gottfried and Father Etienne struck at the same moment, their blades ringing against each other as their swords crossed in the middle of the wagon. A blue spark flew from the clashing steel edges; for a second, it seemed to Margerite that she saw it flaring up to brilliance, and then the shadow was gone.

Father Etienne sheathed his sword, nodding to the other two men. "That was well-seen, Ritter Gottfried. I had hoped that all Ortlieb's creatures would flee after her death - but I doubted it."

"Christ help us," Brother Sigvrit rasped, reluctantly returning his own blade to its sheath. "I've never seen anything like that, not in all my years with the Teutonic Order - and how in God's name we're going to tell the Bishop about it, I'm sure I don't know. But maybe the lady should go now, in case there's any more trouble?"

"I will stay," Margerite insisted. Father Thomas was unarmed, and more frail of body than she, and he had not hesitated in confronting Ortlieb's demon: how could she be less brave?

Etienne bent again to open the last box. Looking into it, he moved to hide the contents from Margerite behind his black clerical robe - then, as if belatedly remembering who she was, stepped back again. At first she did not recognise what she was looking at, dried and withered as the pieces of meat were: she only saw the glitter of the small pins through them. Then her hand went to her mouth to muffle her gasp: Ortlieb had kept other parts than the heads and hearts of her victims.

"She did these things of her own will, without being possessed?" Father Thomas asked quietly.

"That is so," Father Etienne confirmed.

"Then, Gräfin," the small exorcist said to Margerite, "you did very well to slay her. Praise be to God, who gave you the strength for that deed."

"Praise be to Him, indeed!" Brother Sigvrit added harshly. "If your son has inherited your spirit, he will be a fit candidate for the Teutonic Order when he is grown."

Margerite blinked back tears. For a moment, it seemed to her that she saw with a strange double vision: on the one side, the golden-haired youth with the ruby Order ring on his hand; on the other, the same youth kneeling in prayer, his fair beauty brought out by the stark black surcoat with its white cross. But what I want for Wolfram, she thought, is for him to rule in happiness over his own lands, his soul at peace with God - is there no path for him, save for Hell or renunciation of the world?

"Is that all?" Ritter Gottfried asked.

"I believe so," Father Etienne replied. "Unless Ortlieb sent some of her materials on beforehand, as she may have done - but there is more than enough here to convict her of sorcery and murder, and to bring her husband before an Inquisitorial investigation."

"Then, for Christ's sake, will you not do what you can for these poor children?" Gottfried gestured towards the box that held the three heads.

Etienne took his phials of holy oil and holy water from his belt-pouch. He and Father Thomas knelt before the grisly half-skulls, praying together. Gently Father Etienne anointed each of the wrinkled grayish foreheads with the oil, giving them the Last Rites.

"Ritter Gottfried," he said. "Grant them mercy - but do not destroy the skulls, for they will be needed as evidence."

Gottfried's sword trembled in his hand as he lifted it. He touched the point to each of the heads in turn, and with each, it seemed to Margerite that she could feel the air lightening until it was almost clean - as clean as it could be in the place where Ortlieb's blood had soaked into the wooden floor, with her unholy relics still gathered about.

Brother Sigvrit shook his head. "I guess we don't need to tell the Bishop about this, either?" he said.

"Tell him whatever you think is fitting," Father Etienne answered. "But I believe our job here is done. As for myself, I hope the Bishop's hospitality has extended to readying baths for his guests, for we have been travelling long, and this was unclean work."

The chamber which had been readied for Margerite and Eva was as luxurious as Margerite's own rooms at Burg Fürstensee, its enameled stove giving off a gentle heat and steam still rising from a wooden tub of water, and somewhere a cradle had been found for Wolfram. Eva had already washed and dressed herself, and sat combing her long golden hair and playing with the two cats. A familiar odour told Margerite that Kobolt had already marked the room, but the smell was nearly lost beneath the sweetness of strewing-herbs and incense.

Eva opened her mouth as though to ask a question, but Margerite held her hand up to stop her. "Do not ask me what we found in Ortlieb's wain, please," she said. "It is more than enough that those who were there know."

"O, I had nothing like that in mind," replied Eva artlessly. "I was only going to say that Wolfram seems a bit fretful, although he is not wet and should not yet be hungry."

Margerite went over to peer into the cradle. Wolfram was not wailing, but he tossed about anxiously, making unhappy little sounds. Margerite picked him up and cuddled him, patting his back in case his trouble was nothing more than gas in his belly - Mother Maria be thanked, he did not seem feverish. When she put the babe down again, however, he immediately began to wail.

"Wolfram," Margerite said gently to her son, "I cannot hold you all day, for surely the Bishop will wish to speak with me soon. I must wash and change my clothes, and the bathwater is getting no warmer." She bent to pick up Kobolt, setting the black cat into the cradle. "See, here is your dear cat. Will you not let him comfort you?"

Wolfram stopped crying at once, his eyes bright as a bird's as he reached out to grab the black plume of Kobolt's tail. As if he were playing with a kitten, Kobolt batted soft-pawed at Wolfram's little hands, twitching his tail away and back for the baby to snatch at.

The bathwater smelled sweetly of lavender, overlaid with the clean scent of hyssop. Before she stepped into the wooden tub, Margerite held her hands palm-downward over it, murmuring Father Etienne's prayer for the cleansing of waters. "Let there be a firmament in the midst of the waters... I exorcise thee, creature of water, that thou mayest become unto men a mirror of the living God in His works, a fount of life and ablution of sins." As she sank gratefully into the bath, she could feel the warm water loosening the grime from her body - but more: it seemed that it was seeping deep within her, washing away the uncleanness, gritty as dried blood, that she had felt since slaying Ortlieb. She stayed submerged in the tub until the water cooled, until a knock at the door summoned Eva and a man's voice said, "The Bishop would speak with you as soon as you are ready."

Even now, though she knew the Bishop's palace was as safe as any place on Earth, Margerite did not want to leave Wolfram unattended there. The Bishop might think her eccentric for bringing her baby with her, she thought as Eva helped her to hastily dress and braid her hair back - but it was not he who had almost lost his child, to a fate which, perhaps, might have been worse in the end than the freedom that the two exorcists and Ritter Gottfried had granted to Ortlieb's pitiful victims. If only, Margerite thought, I could be sure that saving Wolfram from her has saved him entirely from what I saw in my dream!

The Bishop was not waiting in an audience hall, as Margerite expected, but in a more private chamber, hung with beautifully worked tapestries: the Marriage at Cana, the Sermon on the Mount, and the Crucifixion. She and Eva were the last ones there; the rest of their small group had already gathered, standing before Bishop Otto in his great carven seat.

"Now we will begin," the Bishop said. "Gräfin Margerite, why did you and Frowe Eva come to Burg Fürstensee?"

On the long ride to the Bishop's palace, Father Etienne had drilled all of them carefully in their stories: there would be no deceit, but they could not relate everything that had happened without suspicion. Thus Margerite answered, "My husband, Graf Heinrich, was sorely stricken, and the physician could do nothing for him. Frowe Eva, Knappe Georg, and I were traveling towards Fulda on foot in the manner of poor folk, renouncing our pride -" she thought ruefully of how they had been accused of whoring; if they had not chosen that penance, God had set them to it nevertheless -"when we chanced to meet Father Etienne, whom we knew well, for he had been sent by the Bishop of Augsburg to negotiate a truce between Graf Heinrich and my first husband, Graf Ruprecht von Falkenstein. We continued north with him, and he said that taking the part of servants for a time would be a fitting penance for our sins, and a lesson in humility."

"A harsh penance for nobly-born women," Bishop Otto commented, "but that is hardly for me to judge. Ritter Gottfried?"

"I was pursuing a fugitive at the command of Graf Heinrich," Gottfried told him. "The trail led me to Schloss Niederwald. By God's grace, I was there in time to offer my help to the Gräfin as soon as I heard that her son had been stolen away."

Bishop Otto settled back in his seat, a smile touching his lips. "And now, as I guess, for the most important question. Father Etienne, what is your part in all of this? I do not think it was pure chance that you chose Schloss Niederwald for your penitents to serve in, nor that you simply happened to pass through here on your way from Hamburg."

The slender priest smiled back at the Bishop. "As you know, your Grace, my duties for the Church include many things besides a knowledge of canon law, or even the performance of exorcisms. Sometimes they involve investigations of rumours of sorcery and heresy, and it was so in this case: it was my duty to look into the rumours I had heard about Landgräfin Ortlieb, to see if there was any truth behind them, or if they were merely the maundering of folk jealous of a simple Ritter's daughter who had managed to become the Landgräfin von Niederwald. You understand that I could not speak directly of this, lest in the effort to determine whether there was any truth behind the gossip I should create three times the amount of malicious talk."

"And in the course of this...investigation, you managed to not only prove the case beyond any doubt, but also to bring forth Herr Bernhardt after his long exile and save Gräfin Margerite's son from..." The Bishop crossed himself, his gold pectoral flashing with the movement. "I never doubted that your reputation was well-founded, Father Etienne, but now I begin to see why you are given such extraordinary freedom of action."

Etienne bowed slightly. "Thank you, your Grace. Since the matter is in your hands now, may I ask what you mean to do?"

"I shall inform my superiors at once. In a matter of this gravity...I think that Cardinal von Rotenstein may even be willing to travel here from Avignon. At any rate, it will be he who writes the summons to Landgraf Gerhardt. I have even now begun the process to request the Inquisitorial investigation, as you suggested.

The Kaiser will also need to be informed, but that may take some time, as I understand he is now on the way to Budapest in order to come to an arrangement with King Ludwig in regards to dissolving Ludwig's niece's current engagement and betrothing her to his own son Wenzel. As for all of you..." Bishop Otto surveyed the little group before him for some time, chin resting on his fist as though he were contemplating a chessboard. "The Inquisition may move swiftly, or it may move slowly: they are not likely to be too hasty with such a case. When I receive their reply, in any case, they should tell me whether they wish you to remain here or return to your homes or duties until they are ready to summon you."

Georg met Margerite's gaze a moment, and in his worried expression and bright eyes she could read, as clearly as if he had spoken, the question, But what about Christoph? Ritter Gottfried shuffled uncomfortably, and Margerite guessed that he might be thinking the same thing, while Eva's pretty face was pale and stricken.

"If your consciences are clear, as they seem to be," Bishop Otto said comfortingly, "you have nothing to fear from the questions of the Inquisitors. And I trust you will not find my hospitality lacking while you are my guests. Indeed, it is growing late; and although our evening meals here are usually light, I have ordered that something more substantial be prepared for you, for I can see that you have been travelling long and hard."

To her regret, Margerite realized that she must leave Wolfram in her chamber, for she could hardly dine with the Bishop while holding a babe in her arms. "Guard him well," she whispered to Kobolt. The black tom gave a chirruping purr, leaping to the edge of the cradle and butting his furry head against Margerite's hand, as though to reassure her that no one would take Wolfram while he was there to watch the child.

Although the dishes served at the Bishop's table were not as showy as those Ortlieb had demanded, Margerite recognised several of them from the kitchens of Schloss Niederwald: capon stuffed with minced pork and spices, coated in saffron-gold batter; hare in a rich green sauce; and pastries containing delicious confections of meat or cheese. Lothar had not been boasting when he spoke of the Bishop's cook training under Liutbirg: the perfect succulence of the meat, the smoothness of the sauces, balanced exquisitely between sharp and mild, hot and cool, brought back the Schloss Niederwald kitchen back to Margerite with each bite.

She wondered who it was that scrubbed the Bishop's pots - young monks, perhaps, or poor women such as she had pretended to be? - and if the Bishop had the least idea of the huge amount of work that went into bringing each dish to be laid before him. It was good to be sitting at the high table and sipping the fine red wine, with bowls for washing the stains of sauce from her hands and the Bishop's cultivated conversation to listen to; but her memories of being a servant would linger long after the callouses from the weeks of constant sewing had faded from her fingers.

"Your Grace," said Gottfried in one of the rare pauses when no one was speaking, "I would ask a boon of you."

"And what would that be, Herr Ritter?" the Bishop enquired cordially.

"My Knappe Arnmut has borne himself as a man through this long journey, and proved himself worthy in pitched battle, defending me well when I began to grow weak from my wound. Though he is yet young, I believe him to be ready to take on the honours and duties of knighthood, and I would ask that, in a day or two when he is fully recovered from the rigours of travel, you permit him to hold his vigil in your cathedral."

The look of stunned joy on Arnmut's face, Margerite thought, was well worth any number of trials to see. The Bishop smiled benevolently at the knight and his squire. "I shall gladly let him hold vigil there, and shall say the celebratory Mass myself - unless you would prefer to have it done by Father Etienne, with whom you have shared some of your dangers."

Gottfried looked at his Knappe. "Well, Arnmut? It is your knighting; you may choose who shall bless it."

Blue eyes wide, Arnmut looked from Bishop Otto to Father Etienne, then back again. "Herr Gottfried, I do not know...Whom would you think best?"

"His Grace the Bishop is higher in station, and it would be a great honour to have him presiding over your vows," Gottfried responded slowly. "But...for myself, out of friendship, I should choose the good Father by whose help we won through."

"Then so shall I," replied Arnmut at once. "Your Grace, I thank you greatly for the offer, but..."

"I understand," Bishop Otto said kindly. "Father Etienne is a worthy priest and a good man, whose blessings are well to be sought."

Through their exchange, Georg had kept smiling bravely, but Margerite could see the muscles cording with tension in the redhead's wiry forearms as he sliced bits of meat from the hare's leg on his plate, and the twitch of his cheek against the black stitches holding the half-healed wound on his face together.

She could well guess what he was thinking: he, too, had proven himself well, and Bernhardt had named him worthy of the accolade of knighthood; but Bernhardt was too courteous to knight another man's Knappe, at least while there was hope that Christoph might be restored to himself. Did a worm of jealousy gnaw in Georg's heart, or was he merely tormented by the thought of Christoph's state and the uncertainty of his own place, as a runaway squire whose knight's body was still in the grip of a demon?

Margerite ached to reach out and comfort the youth, as she comforted Wolfram when he cried; but Georg was too old for such things, and it would be the worse for him if he knew that she was aware of what he was trying so staunchly to hide. When they had finished the last sweet - apples and raisins minced fine, cooked together with honey and spices - the Bishop dabbed his lips clean with a napkin and said, "Now, Father Etienne, I shall speak with the two women you brought, to see if they have anything to say which should be added to my report. You may come with me, if you wish."

"Thank you, your Grace," Father Etienne replied. "Perhaps, though, it were as well if the Gräfin Margerite were willing to accompany us for this, so that if they have any ill to say of her, she can answer it directly."

Bishop Otto looked at Margerite as if considering her, one black eyebrow slightly raised. "Well, Gräfin?"

"As you wish, your Grace."

If the room where Hedwig and Oda were secured was not a luxurious guest-chamber, it was at least far better than the stable in which Margerite and her companions had been confined: the two women had decent beds and bedding, fresh reeds strewing the stone floor, and a candle in a large iron wall-sconce. Their legs had been unbound and the gags taken from their mouths; their hands were tied loosely before them, allowing them some freedom of movement. Margerite noticed that their Order rings had disappeared, and wondered at that: did one of the Light-Bearers lurk even within the Bishop's palace, or had Father Etienne, for some reason of his own, hidden the rings away?

Although they were still dressed in the same grubby brocades of silk and velvet that they had worn through the journey, Hedwig and Oda had at least been allowed to wash their faces and comb their hair as best they could with their hands tied. If they were no longer the exquisitely clad and coiffed visions of beauty that had attended Ortlieb, at least they did not look like brutalized prisoners.

"Oda von Schwarzenstein and Hedwig von Rabenwald," the Bishop said, his voice resonant in the small chamber. "Are you aware of why you are here?"

The two women, fair and black-haired, exchanged a glance. It was Hedwig who sullenly answered him, "Through murder and unlawful force of arms. We have done nothing to deserve being captured and imprisoned so."

"Were you ladies-in-waiting to Landgräfin Ortlieb?"

"We served the Landgräfin, yes."

"For how long?"

"Five years," said Hedwig, even as Oda answered, "Three years."

"Were you aware of her sorcerous practices?"

Hedwig and Oda looked at each other again; then their eyes flickered to Father Etienne, still and slim as the black shadow of a sword beside the Bishop.

"You have no grounds to hold and question us so!" Hedwig said furiously, her blue eyes glinting with rage. "We are women of noble birth, who chanced to be with the Landgräfin when she was murdered, nothing more."

Oda lowered her face into her bound hands, her golden hair falling about them as her shoulders shook with weeping. "The Landgräfin was with child," she snuffled. "She only wanted to retire in peace while she carried - she and Landgraf Gerhardt had tried so hard..."

"And was this," Father Etienne pursued mercilessly, "why she abducted the child of a maidservant and fled in the dead of night, going towards the castle she had inherited from her father rather than the Convent of the Holy Cross, as she had announced to her noble guests that she would?"

"I do not know all the Landgräfin's thoughts," Oda wept. "I only went with her, as she ordered me to - I do not know why she took the child."

"She may have wanted a companion for her own child," Hedwig added. "What better could befall a serving-woman's babe?"

"Enough of this!" the Bishop thundered. "Do you mean to tell me that you had no idea what was in the chests in your wagon, or of what abominations your mistress practiced? If you do not answer me now," he added sternly, "you will surely find yourselves answering the queries of the Inquisition."

"You have no right to do this," Hedwig repeated steadfastly, staring straight at the Bishop. "It is not we whose hands are stained with the blood of murder. Rather, you should imprison the woman who stands beside you until she can be turned over to the Landgraf's justice."

"This is Church land, and the Landgraf has no power here!" Bishop Otto told her, his voice echoing with anger. "As for murder, the Landgräfin was guilty of at least three; the only question left is to determine what part you played in her crimes."

"None," said Hedwig at once. She tossed her long black hair back over her shoulder, still staring defiantly at the Bishop.

"None," Oda sniffled, wiping the shining tears from her face.

"I do not believe you. You served with her - five years in one case, three in the other; sleeping in her chambers, no doubt, and ministering to her needs. Now this grace I shall grant you: if you confess, you will be allowed to live - a penitent's life of bread and water in a well-guarded convent, to be sure, but life nonetheless. But if you both remain obdurate, you will pass swiftly from my hands into less merciful ones, and find your souls being purified by fire at the last." Bishop Otto turned on his heel and stalked out in a swirl of purple vestments. Margerite followed, her hands shaking and a chill dew of sweat on her forehead, and Father Etienne brought up the rear.

One of the two guardsmen outside locked the door, the iron keys on his ring clashing together with a harsh ringing sound.

"They may be more amenable to reasonable persuasion tomorrow, when they have had time to think on their situation," Father Etienne said mildly. "I shall speak to them then."

"That would be well-done," the Bishop agreed. He, too, was sweating, the little beads shiny against his florid skin. "I have never had to deal with such a thing. I know that they are both lying, for the Landgräfin could not have committed her murders alone - a woman could never have overcome three well-grown lads in turn - but, Christ be thanked, it is not in the end my duty to draw the truth out of them."

"No, it is not, your Grace. But it is to your credit that you tried. And while they live, they are not wholly lost."

"A noble and Christian thought, Etienne. I shall pray that it be so. Good night to both of you."

"Father," Margerite said when the Bishop was gone, "will you let me come to your chamber? I would make Confession now - and I have a question to ask you."

"Your question first," Father Etienne said as soon as they were both seated in his room. In the candlelight, his silver-winged dark hair still damp from his bath, he looked older than his years. Margerite could see the fine lines of tiredness around his clear blue eyes, and though his silver-tufted beard hid the marks of strain at the corners of his mouth, there was something in his look that made her sure they were there.

"Why did you hide all traces of the Order of Light-Bearers from the Bishop? Would revealing them not make it easier to do battle against them?"

Father Etienne closed his eyes, his shoulders sagging as though his black clerical robes were an unendurable burden. "You are not the first to ask that question, Margerite," he said, his voice rough as if with exhaustion. "I asked it too, once, when I was only a few years older than you are now."

"And the answer?"

"Perhaps you should enquire of Jochanan - Jochanan the Jew. You are too young to remember...Rather, let me make my point closer to home. If all good folk knew of the Order of Light-Bearers, what do you think they would make of a poor knight's daughter who managed to wed first one, then a second Graf, neither of whom lived a full year after marrying her; who is knowledgeable in matters of herb-lore and astrology; and who is always accompanied by a large black cat - one with, I have noted, a tendency to spray on Church property?" he added dryly.

"Heinrich is not dead yet, as far as we know," Margerite protested, then stopped.

"Anyone who might be jealous of you could point you out as a member of the Order, even if you had never heard of them. Even I thought that you were one of them at first."

And so did Bernhardt, Margerite thought.

"It will be bad enough to see what befalls Hedwig and Oda if they do not swiftly repent; and they aided Ortlieb in crimes of which Ruprecht, for all that was evil in him, could hardly have conceived. Consider, then, if the full might of the Inquisition were bent against the innocent, with ignorance read as obduracy - or if ordinary folk had reason to think that any great success by one of their own was gained through the Order of Light-Bearers. And the Order's branches stretch high: not king nor queen, perhaps not even the Pope himself, would be altogether safe from accusation, if the true extent of their power was known."

Margerite thought on it, and shuddered.

"Therefore I took the Black Book from Ortlieb's wain, and the rings from herself and her handmaidens. For in this, if nothing else, the Order's desires run in tandem with ours: that their existence must remain a secret." Father Etienne's voice was very intense as he spoke the last words, and he leaned close to Margerite, his eyes glowing with the clear brightness of sapphires in the candlelight. "It may be easiest to say, 'God will know His own', and let loose slaughter; but we are guided by an older tenet: 'First, do no harm'. "

"I understand," Margerite said quietly. "But if Hedwig and Oda speak..."

"Even if put to the worst of torments, they cannot speak of the Order: their tongues have long been bound to secrecy, by the oath which you never swore. To tell you the truth," Father Etienne went on sadly, "I will be surprised if they live long enough to be questioned."

"Are there Light-Bearers even here?" Margerite asked, her heart suddenly racing. Wolfram - I left him in his cradle; is he still there?

"Not to the best of my knowledge. But they have ways of reaching their fellows, even without the rings to link them - and I do not believe that Hedwig and Oda would allow me to ward them."

"Then their deaths, too, will be on my head?"

"They are not yet dead," Etienne told her gently. "There is no sense in repenting of something that has yet to happen. But turn the question around, and ask yourself if you would willingly let them walk free, after what you have seen?"

"No," Margerite admitted. "I would not. Not if I had to fasten shackles upon them, or even pull the gallows-rope myself."

For even now, the ghastly image of the three heads in their box was with her. One of the boys had been as fair-haired as Wolfram - his mother must have suckled him and sung to him, called him her darling and stroked his golden head, just as she did with her own son. And the terror of knowing her child missing, if she still lived, without hope or recourse to find him; and the sorrow that was waiting for her when the news reached her...

No: Hedwig and Oda must have played a part in those three deaths, and perhaps others, and Margerite was not sure that a lifetime of penance, even in true penitence, could make up for their deeds. Remembering Christ's forgiveness and Maria's mercy, and knowing something of the temptations that had led the other women along their path, she could pray for their souls and try to hope that they might, given the chance, repent and take Bishop Otto's offer of a holy life - but she could not loose them upon the world: she would have slain them herself first.

"I shall leave you to think on that for the night, then, and you may make your Confession to me in the morning, after you have decided what exactly it is that you have to confess." Father Etienne rose, striding over to open the door. "Good night, Margerite."

"Good night, Father."

Margerite thought that she would not be able to sleep that night, but the soft warmth of the bed, after three nights of rocky ground and hard frost, swept her into darkness before she knew it. It was dark when she awoke to the sounds of the wind howling outside and sleet hammering against the window, and the sound of a hunting horn fading from her dreams.

She lay frozen in her bed, trying to remember where she was. At first she thought she was still in Burg Falkenstein, listening in dread for the phantom horn on the wind and the distant barking of hounds through the storm. But no: that had been a long time ago. She was here, in the palace of the Bishop of Niederwald, and safe: no night-terrors, no unholy spirits, could pass onto this hallowed ground.

Yet something was wrong, some sound...Eva snored quietly on her own bed; beneath the groaning of the wind, Margerite could hear the soft rhythmic sound of Kobolt's purr. Wolfram was making his little noises of happiness - but they seemed strangely muffled, almost as if he were chewing on something. Leaping from her bed, Margerite lit a taper from the embers in the stove and hurried to her son's cradle. Kobolt was sitting on its edge, his tail draped over the baby and his eyes glimmering wide in the candlelight. But a dark stain of blood spread over Wolfram's face and throat; something was grasped in one of his little fists, and his jaws were moving as though he were choking on something.

Terrified, Margerite reached into her baby's mouth, hooking out what she found with two fingers. What she saw made her gag, nearly retching: Wolfram had been chewing on the head of a mouse, its gray fur matted and wet from his mouth, and he was clutching its little furry body in his left hand. The blood on him had all come from the small animal - had he torn it apart? Furiously she pried the remains of the mouse away from him, flinging them across the room in disgust.

She lifted Wolfram up almost without thought, not bothering to put on anything but a cloak over her simple linen night-dress before she ran down the corridor to Father Etienne's room, hammering furiously on the priest's door. It was only a few moments before Etienne came to let her in, the taper in his hand casting its brightness over his white smock.

"What is the matter?" he asked, gesturing him in.

Almost sobbing, clinging so tightly to Wolfram that he began to cry as well. Margerite told him what she had found. "Father, does he need to be exorcised? If Ortlieb did anything to him...Mother Maria, the dream I had about him..."

"Calm yourself, Margerite," Father Etienne told her. "Sit down." He poured a small glass of aqua vitae for each of them, pushing hers across the table to her. "Drink a little of that, and then tell me from the beginning."

Father Etienne's aqua vitae was very smooth, burning rich and spicy on Margerite's tongue. As its warmth seeped into her, she could feel her shivering limbs beginning to relax. Quietly she told the priest about how Gertrude had seemed to visit her in the night, and the images she had seen. "Is this something that must come to pass, Father?" Margerite asked, her voice trembling like a little girl's. "Is Wolfram doomed to evil, no matter what I do?"

Father Etienne stood, taking the crying child from Margerite's arms and lifting him up with the careful awkwardness of a man who seldom had much to do with babies. He gazed intensely at Wolfram; after a moment, Wolfram stopped wailing, looking back at Father Etienne in bright-eyed fascination.

"If a child's closest companion is a cat, especially one such as Kobolt, he is likely to behave like a kitten," Father Etienne said. "There is no demon's work in that, though you will have to teach them both that a human baby does not eat mice. But as for Wolfram being doomed to evil? All men are sons of Adam; Christ died to redeem us all; and each of us is born with free will. You may nurture him well and teach him what is right, but in the end, it will come down to his own choice - the same choice that everyone must make. Comfort yourself with that, if you may: you have as much, or as little, sway over the fate of his soul as any human being has over another. Even had Wolfram been in the hands of the Order from birth, he would still have had a chance to choose salvation; and even were he raised in a holy cloister, the chance of damnation would still have found its way to him. Remember that, now and when he is older, and it will save you from much sorrow."

"I thank you, Father," Margerite said, the tears still falling from her eyes.

Father Etienne gave Wolfram back to her, making the sign of the Cross. "God be with both of you," he said formally. To Margerite's relief, her son did nothing save follow the priest's movement expectantly with his eyes.

Margerite carried Wolfram back to her chamber, changing his blood-stained dress and then, because the fullness of her breasts warned her that he would be growing hungry soon, holding him to suckle. "Little Wolfram, my precious, my sweetling," she murmured, cuddling her baby's warmth against her and rocking slowly back and forth.

When Margerite awoke, the light of the sky through her windows was almost blindingly bright, with only a few dead leaves plastered to the glass to prove that the storm of the night before had not been a dream. Wolfram slept peacefully in his cradle, with Kobolt curled by his head and Kriemhilt's gold-shot black tail draped over his feet.

Eva was gone, but the stove had been freshly stocked, giving off a steady heat, and on the table was a tray with pitchers of wine and water, a small loaf of bread and a silvered plate that, from the faint smell lingering in the air, might have held smoked herrings before the cats' tongues had licked it clean. Still, a cup of watered wine and a slice of bread were enough to start the day with, Margerite reflected as she took the eating-knife Bernhardt had lent her and cut a piece from the loaf.

After she had woken Wolfram for his morning feeding, Margerite spent some time in washing her face, combing and rebraiding her hair, and dressing herself. Regarding herself in the small mirror that someone had thoughtfully left in the room, she saw that the marks of Ortlieb's nails were almost gone from her face, and the bruises on her throat had faded from virulent purple-black to mottled green and yellow. But her cheeks were thinner than she remembered, almost sunken, and the shadows of her interrupted sleep darkened the hollows of her eyesockets, the blue of her eyes pooling like clear water in their depths.

Looking at her own face as if it were the face of a stranger, Margerite realized that there was something in her steady gaze, in the ravaged serenity of her expression, that was familiar: she had seen the same look on the face of Father Etienne at times, and on Father Thomas, and Etienne's friend the Abbot. Perhaps the sort of battle in which they were engaged left its marks on the flesh as surely as warring with sword and lance: while Light-Bearers might still be able to deceive her, Margerite thought now that she would be able to recognise her allies on sight.

And Ritter Gottfried is truly one, she thought. For all that he seemed to know nothing of magic or the Order, the struggles of the young knight's soul had seared their light across his face like a scar. Suddenly discomfited by the quiet-eyed stranger staring out of the mirror, Margerite put it down hastily. It was strange, having nothing that needed doing. If she were a guest at another castle, there would have been amusements planned, hunting or hawking or watching tourney-fights during the day, with dancing in the evenings; but of course the Bishop would hardly have time to entertain his guests thus.

And yet, after the turmoil of the last days and the bone-draining work of a servant before - unconsciously Margerite rubbed her fingers together, the thick needle-callouses rasping softly - perhaps this peace was what she needed, as a wounded knight would lie abed for a week or two before taking up his sword again. Wrapping Wolfram in a warm blanket, she picked him up and stepped out into the cold of the hallway, pausing a moment to marvel at the beauty of the stained-glass windows.

There, in deep blue and milky white, was St. Catherine, holding the wheel of her martyrdom; there, in bright and dark shades of green, stood St. Hubert, patron of hunters, with his stag. Margerite paused a moment before that one, its light falling over herself and Wolfram as though they stood in the cool greenness of a summer wood. Ruprecht, she wondered, will I ever be free of your memory?

Farther along was St. Michael, glorious in his armour of gold; the flames running along his sword flared brightly in the sunlight above the baleful blue-black glow of the dragon that lay slain at his feet. Beside him was St. Walburga, crowned and sceptered, dressed in purple like an Empress, with rich golden oil flowing from the phial she held, and three ears of ripe wheat at her feet.

As Margerite neared the end of the corridor, a door opened and Bernhardt stepped out. He was clad simply, but well: dark blue hose clung to his muscular legs; he wore a sombre doublet of black velvet that was a little tight over the width of his broad shoulders, and a heavy black cloak trimmed with gray fur - the Bishop, Margerite thought, must have decided to supply him with clothing more nearly suited to his station than what he had brought.

His unruly hair had been freshly washed, the new brown growth pale above the damp black waves curling against his neck, and his beard was closely trimmed. The beads of Margerite's necklace still gleamed above the collar of his doublet, and there was a gold seal ring that Margerite had never seen before on his right forefinger. Margerite looked up to meet his serious hazel gaze.

"I was hoping that I would find you," Bernhardt said. "Will you walk in the Bishop's gardens with me?"

"Gladly." Margerite smiled at him, shifting Wolfram to her left arm and holding her right hand out so that Bernhardt could take it to escort her - as a nobleman should with a lady, no more; and yet the touch of his rough warm fingers against hers sent a shiver through her body. O, we must be careful, she thought. I am still married to Heinrich, and we cannot allow the Bishop to guess at any hint of what has passed between Bernhardt and I. Only those thoughts kept her from moving closer to Bernhardt, as she wished to do - close enough to feel the warmth of his body through their thick clothing, close enough that if he bent down, his soft lips could touch hers, her cheek rub against the strong line of his bearded jaw...

Bernhardt led her out of the palace, along one of the neatly paved paths through the lines of bare oak trees and past the dovecote. The white doves cooed and swirled above them, their bright wings almost silvery against the shining blue bowl of the sky. Without speaking, Margerite and Bernhardt followed the turn of the pathway to where a smaller paved track forked off, walking along it to where elaborately carved stone benches stood beside an ice-shimmering pond.

The leaves and petals had fallen from the low rosebushes that grew between the benches, but the rosehips were still bright red, like drops of blood caught on the thorny black branches. A thin layer of frost furred the stone seats, their cold numbing even through Margerite's thick cloak as the two of them sat down, a decorous distance apart. Still, Bernhardt did not let go of Margerite's hand, nor could she have pulled it away from him.

"Margerite," Bernhardt said, his hazel eyes looking deeply into hers. "I owe you my life, and my soul."

"That is not so," Margerite replied. "Or rather - say that I have repaid the debt I owed to you." A pang went through her as she spoke those words, for a repaid debt meant quits: did this, then, mean that their time together must come to an end?"And you broke Ortlieb's hold on your soul yourself, before I ever touched her."

Bernhardt shook his head, his damp hair falling back from his strong-boned face. "I do not think I could have done it without you - without knowing," he added softly, "true love to set against her falseness. And even there at the end..."

"There is no shame in it, that a true knight could not slay a woman, though she were the next thing to a demon. We agreed on it some time ago, that each of us should fight the battles for which we are most suited: this one was mine."

Bernhardt blinked, the deep brown-green of his eyes shining clear as coloured glass. "That is so. And yet that was not what I wanted to say...Forgive me, for my courtier's skills have grown rusty in their years without use. And I have a grievous thing to confess to you, as well. Though I have prayed for Graf Heinrich's recovery, I fear that I have not been able to pray with a whole heart.

I know that Graf Heinrich was a good man, and seemed to be treating you kindly, so that, for all it tore at my soul, I did not fear to leave you in his care. And yet..." Bernhardt paused and swallowed, then the words came out of him in a rending rush, like a river breaking its banks.

"I know that even if Gerhardt is proven guilty of complicity in Ortlieb's works, the Kaiser may yet decide that I am not fit to hold my lands in fealty to him: it would take only a few words about my past in the Free Companies to turn him against me, if any who knew chose to speak. And I know that, being yet married, you cannot contract any betrothal; but though it may be wrong to speak of such things while Graf Heinrich may still be living, nevertheless I must, lest my heart break my ribs asunder in its bursting. Margerite..."

Bernhardt's grasp on her hand was almost painful now, his gaze searing in its intensity, as though he would ravish her through his eyes. "I love you, and if it so comes to pass that you are freed from your wedding vows to Graf Heinrich, whether tomorrow or twenty years from now, I would marry you, and raise your son as my own...who might have been," he added in a whisper. "I know I am a fool to speak so, when I can promise you nothing - not even my life, for I know not what challenge will be brought for me to prove my innocence."

Greatly surprised at her own daring, Margerite withdrew her hand from Bernhardt's, lifting it to lay a finger upon his lips. At once Bernhardt fell silent, staring at her with a wild look in his eyes - despair or hope, she could not tell.

"Bernhardt," she breathed. "I love you more than any man, and I would be wedded to you, though while Heinrich lives, I must stand by the oath I swore to him. But if such time come as I am free of that vow - and, Christ have mercy on Heinrich, I fear that it will be sooner rather than later - I will marry you, whatever place you may or may not hold."

Bernhardt's lips trembled into a smile, and Margerite could see the tears welling up in his eyes, even as her own dripped onto Wolfram's head, the droplets darkening the fairness of his hair where they fell. Slowly Bernhardt drew the gold signet ring from his forefinger, the fine lines of his family crest glittering in the sunlight.

"Though we can make no pledge binding in law, and there is none but God and Wolfram to witness - I would have you take this ring, to wear over your heart, if you will, until you can bear it openly."

The ring's gold was still warm from Bernhardt's hand as Margerite slipped it onto her own finger. Looking into Bernhardt's eyes, she could feel his joy welling up like a warm spring, her own heart matching it with a tide too strong to let her speak, almost too strong to bear. His ring was far too large for her slender finger: she slipped it off, holding it clasped tightly in her hand, and pressed it against her heart. Though they could not kiss, there in the open garden where anyone might see them, Margerite and Bernhardt sat gazing at each other for a long time, the white doves fluttering and cooing above their heads.

to be continued in Book Three

Stephan & Melodi Grundy

Historical Notes

This book takes place in Germany of 1365, four years after the return of the Black Death. The Landgraf's realm (and the bishopric) of Niederwald are, like those of Fürstensee and Falkenstein, fictional, though Bernhardt's neighbors, the Markgraf of Meissen in Saxony and Landgraf Friedrich of Thuringia, are both historical. In this period, the Holy Roman Empire was highly fragmented, so that any number of smaller counties like the above could easily have existed without obvious historical impact.

The Order of Lightbearers is likewise fictional, though well-suited to the background of the fourteenth century, which was both a time of great heresies and the beginning of the Renaissance. The Order is chiefly based on a combination of ideas of the time concerning heretical beliefs and conspiracies, such as those expressed in the trials of the Templars in the early part of the century, and conspiracies of a later date, such as the Bavarian Illuminati. Had a proto-Illuminati existed in the fourteenth century, they might have been very like our Order of Lightbearers.

The magic practiced by the characters in this book is also based on late mediaeval/early Renaissance beliefs (and practices). The Satanism of the Order of Light-Bearers is more appropriate to the imagination of this period than to reality. Its origins lie in the trials of the Templars, the heretical theology of the Cathars, and similar sources. The actual rituals originate from books of dubious provenance (in particular the"Greater Key of Solomon" and the"Goetia"), altered in some cases to the view of the Light-Bearers, who hold to the Gnostic concept of honouring Lucifer as the source of intelligence.

Father Etienne and Margerite represent the traditional practice of late mediaeval magic, in which demons are ruled and banished by the strength of God and the angels; the rituals of the Light-Bearers are improvisations on this theme and should not be tried at home! Many rituals, charms, and descriptions which appear or are mentioned in this book come directly from the Münchener Handschrift der Schwarzen Magie, a work of the fifteenth century, which is in the Bayerischen Staatsbibliothek and has been published in English, with useful commentary, by Richard Kiekhefer, as Forbidden Rites: A Necromancer's Manual of the Fifteenth Century (Sutton: Gloucestershire, 1997).

The artistic feasts and delicacies which we describe in this book correspond relatively accurately to the height of fourteenth-century cooking. Mediaeval cooks in noble households had a particular affection for meals meant to briefly deceive (the goose in a peacock's skin and the fish made out of almond paste are typical examples) or amaze their audience. The animals presented as if in life and the fire-breathing swan (a candle with two wicks would be wrapped in cotton wool soaked with camphor and oil and put in the beak) are both authentic.

Colour also played an important role for mediaeval cooks, and towards this end occasionally rather unhealthy food colourings (such as powdered lapis lazuli for a strong blue) were used. When one considers, how difficult the preparation of such elaborate meals without temperature-controlled ovens was, and that timing and testing of temperature was dependent solely on the instinct of the cook, it is hardly surprising that the cooks of noble households were highly prized and allowed a good bit of personal leeway. Those who would like to know more about the fascinating world of mediaeval cookery might enjoy looking up Terence Scully's The Art of Cookery in the Middle Ages (Woodbridge, 1995).

Mediaeval medicine was an art that largely depended on the doctrine of humours (blood/sanguine; phlegm/phlegmatic; yellow gall/choleric; black gall/melancholic). Physicians' therapies were derived from this doctrine and were largely intended to regulate an unhealthy imbalance among the humours of the bodily fluids and restore the ideal balance.

The classification of foodstuffs according to their degrees of warmth and moistness and the prescription of diet based on this system was also an important element of the healing art, and complemented the concept of sickness as an unbalance of the humours, which could be diagnosed (and hence altered by the correct prescriptions and cured) by observation of the patient and the nature of the illness.

The Dance Macabre was documented in writing for the first time in 1376 in a poem of Jean le Fèvre from Anjou, but was certainly known previously; art showing Death's dance became popular from the time of the Plague's first appearance in Europe (1348-49) onwards. Ortlieb's presentation is meant to be on the very cutting edge of fashion (apart from its spiritual intent). Its general character corresponds to the written and artistic sources: Death seeks his dancing partners from every walk of life.

The usual intention of such depictions, such as the wall-painting in the Church of the Innocents in Paris, was to show that men should be brought, by contemplation of their fleshly mortality, to do good works and attend Mass in order to redeem their immortal souls. Pilgrimages were popular in the Middle Ages as an opportunity for penance and spiritual improvement. They also served respectable and well-off folk as an excuse for an enjoyable vacation, as Chaucer shows in his contemporary Canterbury Tales – an enchanting portrayal of such a group of English tourists. Where there is regular tourism, there will be regular tourist traps. Thus, the figure of Merlin, the travelling peddler of relics and nostrums on the pilgrim roads (who also owes a little to Chaucer's Pardoner).

Flight of The Falcon

Father Etienne's "unusual means" to rescue Margerite
and her companions may appear to be the least believable
element of this book, but it is based on a real historical
occurrence of the fourteenth century. The prisoners were
brought before the altar of the church, and the priest
gave a sermon about their misdeeds. At the high point of
the sermon there was a flash of lightning, and when the
congregation had recovered from their shock, there was
nothing left of the evil-doers but charcoaled bones. That in
the historical instance, as in our book, gunpowder was used
to cover an escape, is our best interpretation of the account.

The measurement of time in the Middle Ages was based
on the hours of the Church: Matins (between midnight and 2
AM), Lauds (dawn), Prime (around 6 AM), Terce (around 9
AM), Sext (midday), Nones (around 3 PM), Vespers (around
5 PM), and Compline (between 6 and 8 PM). The specific
times were naturally dependent on the time of year. The
fourteenth century already had proper clockworks, but these
were primarily found in large cities, in the form of the tower
clocks still visible in many German cities today.

This book takes place in Germany of 1365, four years after
the return of the Black Death. The Landgraf's realm (and
the bishopric) of Niederwald are, like those of Fürstensee
and Falkenstein, fictional, though Bernhardt's neighbors,
the Markgraf of Meissen in Saxony and Landgraf Friedrich
of Thuringia, are both historical. In this period, the Holy
Roman Empire was highly fragmented, so that any number
of smaller counties like the above could easily have existed
without obvious historical impact.

The Order of Lightbearers is likewise fictional, though
well-suited to the background of the fourteenth century,
which was both a time of great heresies and the beginning
of the Renaissance. The Order is chiefly based on a
combination of ideas of the time concerning heretical beliefs
and conspiracies, such as those expressed in the trials of the
Templars in the early part of the century, and conspiracies
of a later date, such as the Bavarian Illuminati. Had a proto-
Illuminati existed in the fourteenth century, they might have
been very like our Order of Lightbearers.

The magic practiced by the characters in this book is also based on late mediaeval/early Renaissance beliefs (and practices). The Satanism of the Order of Light-Bearers is more appropriate to the imagination of this period than to reality. Its origins lie in the trials of the Templars, the heretical theology of the Cathars, and similar sources. The actual rituals originate from books of dubious provenance (in particular the"Greater Key of Solomon" and the"Goetia"), altered in some cases to the view of the Light-Bearers, who hold to the Gnostic concept of honouring Lucifer as the source of intelligence.

Father Etienne and Margerite represent the traditional practice of late mediaeval magic, in which demons are ruled and banished by the strength of God and the angels; the rituals of the Light-Bearers are improvisations on this theme and should not be tried at home! Many rituals, charms, and descriptions which appear or are mentioned in this book come directly from the Münchener Handschrift der Schwarzen Magie, a work of the fifteenth century, which is in the Bayerischen Staatsbibliothek and has been published in English, with useful commentary, by Richard Kiekhefer, as Forbidden Rites: A Necromancer's Manual of the Fifteenth Century (Sutton: Gloucestershire, 1997).

The artistic feasts and delicacies which we describe in this book correspond relatively accurately to the height of fourteenth-century cooking. Mediaeval cooks in noble households had a particular affection for meals meant to briefly deceive (the goose in a peacock's skin and the fish made out of almond paste are typical examples) or amaze their audience. The animals presented as if in life and the fire-breathing swan (a candle with two wicks would be wrapped in cotton wool soaked with camphor and oil and put in the beak) are both authentic.

Colour also played an important role for mediaeval cooks, and towards this end occasionally rather unhealthy food colourings (such as powdered lapis lazuli for a strong blue) were used. When one considers, how difficult the preparation of such elaborate meals without temperature-controlled ovens was, and that timing and testing of temperature was dependent solely on the instinct of the cook, it is hardly surprising that the cooks of noble households were highly prized and allowed a good bit of personal leeway. Those who would like to know more about the fascinating world of mediaeval cookery might enjoy looking up Terence Scully's The Art of Cookery in the Middle Ages (Woodbridge, 1995).

Mediaeval medicine was an art that largely depended on the doctrine of humours (blood/sanguine; phlegm/phlegmatic; yellow gall/choleric; black gall/melancholic). Physicians' therapies were derived from this doctrine and were largely intended to regulate an unhealthy imbalance among the humours of the bodily fluids and restore the ideal balance. The classification of foodstuffs according to their degrees of warmth and moistness and the prescription of diet based on this system was also an important element of the healing art, and complemented the concept of sickness as an unbalance of the humours, which could be diagnosed (and hence altered by the correct prescriptions and cured) by observation of the patient and the nature of the illness.

The Dance Macabre was documented in writing for the first time in 1376 in a poem of Jean le Fèvre from Anjou, but was certainly known previously; art showing Death's dance became popular from the time of the Plague's first appearance in Europe (1348-49) onwards. Ortlieb's presentation is meant to be on the very cutting edge of fashion (apart from its spiritual intent). Its general character corresponds to the written and artistic sources: Death seeks his dancing partners from every walk of life. The usual intention of such depictions, such as the wall-painting in the Church of the Innocents in Paris, was to show that men should be brought, by contemplation of their fleshly mortality, to do good works and attend Mass in order to redeem their immortal souls.

Pilgrimages were popular in the Middle Ages as an opportunity for penance and spiritual improvement. They also served respectable and well-off folk as an excuse for an enjoyable vacation, as Chaucer shows in his contemporary Canterbury Tales – an enchanting portrayal of such a group of English tourists. Where there is regular tourism, there will be regular tourist traps. Thus, the figure of Merlin, the travelling peddler of relics and nostrums on the pilgrim roads (who also owes a little to Chaucer's Pardoner).

Father Etienne's "unusual means" to rescue Margerite and her companions may appear to be the least believable element of this book, but it is based on a real historical occurrence of the fourteenth century. The prisoners were brought before the altar of the church, and the priest gave a sermon about their misdeeds. At the high point of the sermon there was a flash of lightning, and when the congregation had recovered from their shock, there was nothing left of the evil-doers but charcoaled bones. That in the historical instance, as in our book, gunpowder was used to cover an escape, is our best interpretation of the account.

The measurement of time in the Middle Ages was based on the hours of the Church: Matins (between midnight and 2 AM), Lauds (dawn), Prime (around 6 AM), Terce (around 9 AM), Sext (midday), Nones (around 3 PM), Vespers (around 5 PM), and Compline (between 6 and 8 PM). The specific times were naturally dependent on the time of year. The fourteenth century already had proper clockworks, but these were primarily found in large cities, in the form of the tower clocks still visible in many German cities today.

Glossary

aventail - a throat-protector of chain-mail worn with a bascinet.

bascinet - an open-faced helmet with a conical top, sometimes worn under a greathelm.

Frowe - Lady. The masculine equivalent, fro, had probably been lost before the conversion of the Germanic peoples; hence the modern Frau and Herr (the latter from the Old High German herro, implying age and wisdom). Herr is used here roughly as "lord".

fustian - a type of relatively inexpensive fabric, usually wool, with a raised nap, similar to velveteen.

Graf - specifically, "Count", but in practise, a Graf could be anything from a local lord with three knights to the prince of a very large area. Ruprecht and Heinrich are on the lower end of the title's implications.

Gräfin - the feminine equivalent to Graf.

greathelm - the typical knight's helmet of the Middle Ages, covering head and neck. It offered better protection than the open-faced bascinet, but also restricted the vision, head-movement, and breathing of the wearer. Modern re-enactors have been known to refer to helmets of this type as "sweat-buckets", and for good reason.

Landgraf/gräfin - a title similar to Graf, but suggesting a realm of very significant size.

Knappe - squire. Young men of noble birth would be
squired to a knight, and would expect to be knighted
either on the battlefield after a significant deed, or in the
general course of proper service.

Ritter - knight. "Ritter Gottfried" would be equivalent to
the English "Sir Gottfried".

Óðinn - the Old Norse name of the god also known as
Wodan or Wotan in Germany. He is the Germanic god
who is most often associated with magic, particularly the
magic of runes and incantations.

panache - a crest of feathers, most popular in eastern
Europe at this time.

rondel - a flat circle.

Verjuice - a sharp flavouring made from unripe grapes
or sometimes crabapples, used in much the same way as
lemon juice is commonly used nowadays.

Melodi Lammond-Grundy grew up in California and went to college at the University of Southern Mississippi. She spent some years in Colorado, then moved to San Francisco, where she was, for a time, a member of the well-known household and writers' community. She has been in the pagan/heathen community since the 1990s and has degrees in both history and anthropology.

In her spiritual life, she has studied spae-craft, a form of trance-based native Germanic divination. A spákona is the diviner, not the art of divination. which she learned from Diana Paxson.

She still practices divination and psychic readings to this day, lending herself to speak about current events. Her writing skills were first shown in several online publications, followed by co-authoring the Falcon Dream Trilogy. Melodi was one of the first authors to come on-board at Three Little Sisters, and we are pleased to be able to present both her non-fiction work and her upcoming Atlantis novel.

From his humble beginnings, Stephan Grundy/Kveldulf Gundarsson would make his mark on the world by writing on the rarest and obscure myths breathing new life into them, for a new generation of readers. His fictional works written under Stephan Grundy focused on mythology and history and were met with international success. Along with his fictional works, under the pen name Kveldulf Gundarsson he stamped his mark on Germanic Paganism (also known as heathenry) and Germanic Culture.

He is an Elder in the organization The Troth where he has dedicated a majority of his life influencing major changes in the organization, including the development of anti-racist and anti-sexist ideals. He has fought for equality in transgendered communities, as well as fighting for the acceptance of Loki. Gundarsson has shaped heathenry through his numerous academic and fictional works as well as his extensive articles, thesis papers, and his creation and sustainment of the lore program within The Troth. His hobbies included wood-working, jewelry making, and gardening as well as historical re-enactment. He is currently attending medical school in Ireland supported by his loving wife Melodi where they maintain a local hof called The Tribe of Thor

The Three Little Sisters

The Three Little Sisters is an indie publisher that puts authors first. We specalize in the strange and unusual. From titles about pagan and heathen spirituality to traditional fiction and non-fiction we bring books to life.

https://the3littlesisters.com